Agatha Christie is known throughout the world as the Queen of Crime. Her books have sold over a billion copies in English with another billion in foreign languages. She is the most widely published author of all time and in any language, outsold only by the Bible and Shakespeare. She is the author of 80 crime novels and short story collections, 20 plays, and six novels written under the name of Mary Westmacott.

Agatha Christie's first novel, *The Mysterious Affair at Styles*, was written towards the end of the First World War, in which she served as a VAD. In it she created Hercule Poirot, the little Belgian detective who was destined to become the most popular detective in crime fiction since Sherlock Holmes. It was eventually published by The Bodley Head in 1920.

In 1926, after averaging a book a year, Agatha Christie wrote her masterpiece. *The Murder of Roger Ackroyd* was the first of her books to be published by Collins and marked the beginning of an author-publisher relationship which lasted for 50 years and well over 70 books. *The Murder of Roger Ackroyd* was also the first of Agatha Christie's books to be dramatized – under the name *Alibi* – and to have a successful run in London's West End. *The Mousetrap*, her most famous play of all, opened in 1952 and is the longest-running play in history.

Agatha Christie was made a Dame in 1971. She died in 1976, since when a number of books have been published posthumously: the bestselling novel *Sleeping Murder* appeared later that year, followed by her autobiography and the short story collections *Miss Marple's Final Cases*, *Problem at Pollensa Bay* and *While the Light Lasts*. In 1998 *Black Coffee* was the first of her plays to be novelized by another author, Charles Osborne.

THE AGATHA CHRISTIE COLLECTION

The Man in the Brown Suit
The Secret of Chimneys
The Seven Dials Mystery
The Mysterious Mr Quin
The Sittaford Mystery
The Hound of Death
The Listerdale Mystery
Why Didn't They Ask Evans?
Parker Pyne Investigates
Murder is Easy
And Then There Were None
Towards Zero
Death Comes as the End
Sparkling Cyanide
Crooked House
They Came to Baghdad
Destination Unknown
Ordeal by Innocence
The Pale Horse
Endless Night
Passenger to Frankfurt
Problem at Pollensa Bay
While the Light Lasts

Poirot
The Mysterious Affair at Styles
The Murder on the Links
Poirot Investigates
The Murder of Roger Ackroyd
The Big Four
The Mystery of the Blue Train
Peril at End House
Lord Edgware Dies
Murder on the Orient Express
Three-Act Tragedy
Death in the Clouds
The ABC Murders
Murder in Mesopotamia
Cards on the Table
Murder in the Mews
Dumb Witness
Death on the Nile
Appointment With Death
Hercule Poirot's Christmas
Sad Cypress
One, Two, Buckle My Shoe
Evil Under the Sun
Five Little Pigs
The Hollow
The Labours of Hercules
Taken at the Flood
Mrs McGinty's Dead
After the Funeral
Hickory Dickory Dock
Dead Man's Folly
Cat Among the Pigeons
The Adventure of the Christmas Pudding
The Clocks
Third Girl
Hallowe'en Party
Elephants Can Remember
Poirot's Early Cases
Curtain: Poirot's Last Case

Marple
The Murder at the Vicarage
The Thirteen Problems
The Body in the Library
The Moving Finger
A Murder is Announced
They Do It With Mirrors
A Pocket Full of Rye
4.50 from Paddington
The Mirror Crack'd from Side to Side
A Caribbean Mystery
At Bertram's Hotel
Nemesis
Sleeping Murder
Miss Marple's Final Cases

Tommy & Tuppence
The Secret Adversary
Partners in Crime
N or M?
By the Pricking of My Thumbs
Postern of Fate

Published as Mary Westmacott
Giant's Bread
Unfinished Portrait
Absent in the Spring
The Rose and the Yew Tree
A Daughter's a Daughter
The Burden

Memoirs
An Autobiography
Come, Tell Me How You Live

Play Collections
The Mousetrap and Selected Plays
Witness for the Prosecution
and Selected Plays

Play Adaptations by Charles Osborne
Black Coffee (Poirot)
Spider's Web
The Unexpected Guest

Agatha Christie

1920s OMNIBUS

•

THE SECRET ADVERSARY

•

THE MAN IN THE BROWN SUIT

•

THE SECRET OF CHIMNEYS

•

THE SEVEN DIALS MYSTERY

•

HarperCollins*Publishers*
77–85 Fulham Palace Road,
Hammersmith, London W6 8JB
www.harpercollins.co.uk

This edition first published 2006
1

ISBN-13 978-0-00-720862-3
ISBN-10 0-00-720862-6

Typeset in Plantin Light and Gill Sans by
Palimpsest Book Production Limited,
Polmont, Stirlingshire

Printed and bound in Great Britain by
Clays Ltd, St Ives plc

CONTENTS

THE SECRET ADVERSARY

To all those who lead monotonous lives in the hope that they may experience at second-hand the delights and dangers of adventure.

Agatha Christie

PROLOGUE

It was 2 p.m. on the afternoon of May 7th, 1915. The *Lusitania* had been struck by two torpedoes in succession and was sinking rapidly, while the boats were being launched with all possible speed. The women and children were being lined up awaiting their turn. Some still clung desperately to husbands and fathers; others clutched their children closely to their breasts. One girl stood alone, slightly apart from the rest. She was quite young, not more than eighteen. She did not seem afraid, and her grave steadfast eyes looked straight ahead.

'I beg your pardon.'

A man's voice beside her made her start and turn. She had noticed the speaker more than once amongst the first-class passengers. There had been a hint of mystery about him which had appealed to her imagination. He spoke to no one. If anyone spoke to him he was quick to rebuff the overture. Also he had a nervous way of looking over his shoulder with a swift, suspicious glance.

She noticed now that he was greatly agitated. There were beads of perspiration on his brow. He was evidently in a state of overmastering fear. And yet he did not strike her as the kind of man who would be afraid to meet death!

'Yes?' Her grave eyes met his inquiringly.

He stood looking at her with a kind of desperate irresolution.

'It must be!' he muttered to himself. 'Yes – it is the only way.' Then aloud he said abruptly: 'You are an American?'

'Yes.'

'A patriotic one?'

The girl flushed.

'I guess you've no right to ask such a thing! Of course I am!'

'Don't be offended. You wouldn't be if you knew how much there was at stake. But I've got to trust someone – and it must be a woman.'

'Why?'

'Because of "women and children first".' He looked round and lowered his voice. 'I'm carrying papers – vitally important papers. They may make all the difference to the Allies in the war. You understand? These papers have *got* to be saved! They've more chance with you than with me. Will you take them?'

The girl held out her hand.

'Wait – I must warn you. There may be a risk – if I've been followed. I don't think I have, but one never knows. If so, there will be danger. Have you the nerve to go through with it?'

The girl smiled.

'I'll go through with it all right. And I'm real proud to be chosen! What am I to do with them afterwards?'

'Watch the newspapers! I'll advertise in the personal column of *The Times*, beginning "Shipmate". At the end of three days if there's nothing – well, you'll know I'm down and out. Then take the packet to the American Embassy, and deliver it into the Ambassador's own hands. Is that clear?'

'Quite clear.'

'Then be ready – I'm going to say goodbye.' He took her hand in his. 'Goodbye. Good luck to you,' he said in a louder tone.

Her hand closed on the oilskin packet that had lain in his palm.

The *Lusitania* settled with a more decided list to starboard. In answer to a quick command, the girl went forward to take her place in the boat.

CHAPTER 1

THE YOUNG ADVENTURERS, LTD.

'Tommy, old thing!'

'Tuppence, old bean!'

The two young people greeted each other affectionately, and momentarily blocked the Dover Street Tube exit in doing so. The adjective 'old' was misleading. Their united ages would certainly not have totalled forty-five.

'Not seen you for simply centuries,' continued the young man. 'Where are you off to? Come and chew a bun with me. We're getting a bit unpopular here – blocking the gangway as it were. Let's get out of it.'

The girl assenting, they started walking down Dover Street towards Piccadilly.

'Now then,' said Tommy, 'where shall we go?'

The very faint anxiety which underlay his tone did not escape the astute ears of Miss Prudence Cowley, known to her intimate friends for some mysterious reason as 'Tuppence.' She pounced at once.

'Tommy, you're stony!'

'Not a bit of it,' declared Tommy unconvincingly. 'Rolling in cash.'

'You always were a shocking liar,' said Tuppence severely, 'though you did once persuade Sister Greenbank that the doctor had ordered you beer as a tonic, but forgotten to write it on the chart. Do you remember?'

Tommy chuckled.

'I should think I did! Wasn't the old cat in a rage when she found out? Not that she was a bad sort really, old Mother Greenbank! Good old hospital – demobbed like everything else, I suppose?'

Tuppence sighed.

'Yes. You too?'

Tommy nodded.

'Two months ago.'

'Gratuity?' hinted Tuppence.

'Spent.'

'Oh, Tommy!'

'No, old thing, not in riotous dissipation. No such luck! The cost of living – ordinary plain, or garden living nowadays is, I assure you, if you do not know –'

'My dear child,' interrupted Tuppence, 'there is nothing I do *not* know about the cost of living. Here we are at Lyons', and we will each of us pay for our own. That's that!' And Tuppence led the way upstairs.

The place was full, and they wandered about looking for a table, catching odds and ends of conversation as they did so.

'And – do you know, she sat down and *cried* when I told her she couldn't have the flat after all.' 'It was simply a *bargain*, my dear! Just like the one Mabel Lewis brought from Paris –'

'Funny scraps one does overhear,' murmured Tommy. 'I passed two Johnnies in the street today talking about someone called Jane Finn. Did you ever hear such a name?'

But at that moment two elderly ladies rose and collected parcels, and Tuppence deftly ensconced herself in one of the vacant seats.

Tommy ordered tea and buns. Tuppence ordered tea and buttered toast.

'And mind the tea comes in separate teapots,' she added severely.

Tommy sat down opposite her. His bared head revealed a shock of exquisitely slicked-back red hair. His face was pleasantly ugly – nondescript, yet unmistakably the face of a gentleman and a sportsman. His brown suit was well cut, but perilously near the end of its tether.

They were an essentially modern-looking couple as they sat there. Tuppence had no claim to beauty, but there was character and charm in the elfin lines of her little face, with its determined chin and large, wide-apart grey eyes that looked mistily out from under straight, black brows. She wore a small bright green toque over her black bobbed hair, and her extremely short and rather shabby skirt revealed a pair of uncommonly dainty ankles. Her appearance presented a valiant attempt at smartness.

The tea came at last, and Tuppence, rousing herself from a fit of meditation, poured it out.

'Now then,' said Tommy, taking a large bite of bun, 'lets's get up-to-date. Remember, I haven't seen you since that time in hospital in 1916.'

'Very well.' Tuppence helped herself liberally to buttered toast. 'Abridged biography of Miss Prudence Cowley, fifth daughter of Archdeacon Cowley of Little Missendell, Suffolk. Miss Cowley left the delights (and drudgeries) of her home life early in the war and came up to London, where she entered an officers' hospital. First month: Washed up six hundred and forty-eight plates every day. Second month: Promoted to drying aforesaid plates. Third month: Promoted to peeling potatoes. Fourth month: Promoted to cutting bread and butter. Fifth month: Promoted one floor up to duties of wardmaid with mop and pail. Sixth month: Promoted to waiting at table. Seventh month: Pleasing appearance and nice manners so striking that am promoted to waiting on the Sisters! Eighth month: Slight check in career. Sister Bond ate Sister Westhaven's egg! Grand row! Wardmaid clearly to blame! Inattention in such important matters cannot be too highly censured. Mop and pail again! How are the mighty fallen! Ninth month: Promoted to sweeping out wards, where I found a friend of my childhood in Lieutenant Thomas Beresford (bow, Tommy!), whom I had not seen for five long years. The meeting was affecting! Tenth month: Reproved by matron for visiting the pictures in company with one of the patients, namely: the aforementioned Lieutenant Thomas Beresford. Eleventh and twelfth months: Parlourmaid duties resumed with entire success. At the end of the year left hospital in a blaze of glory. After that, the talented Miss Cowley drove successively a trade delivery van, a motor-lorry and a general. The last was the pleasantest. He was quite a young general!'

'What blighter was that?' inquired Tommy. 'Perfectly sickening the way those brass hats drove from the War Office to the Savoy, and from the Savoy to the War Office!'

'I've forgotten his name now,' confessed Tuppence. 'To resume, that was in a way the apex of my career. I next entered a Government office. We had several very enjoyable tea parties. I had intended to become a land girl, a post-woman, and a bus conductress by way of rounding off my career – but the Armistice intervened! I clung to the office with the true limpet touch for many long months, but, alas, I was combed out at last. Since then I've been looking for a job. Now then – your turn.'

'There's not so much promotion in mine,' said Tommy regretfully, 'and a great deal less variety. I went out to France again, as you know. Then they sent me to Mesopotamia, and I got wounded for the second time, and went into hospital out there. Then I got stuck in Egypt till the Armistice happened, kicked my heels there some time longer, and, as I told you, finally got demobbed. And, for ten long, weary months I've been job hunting! There aren't any jobs! And, if there were, they wouldn't give 'em to me. What good am I? What do I know about business? Nothing.'

Tuppence nodded gloomily.

'What about the colonies?' she suggested.

Tommy shook his head.

'I shouldn't like the colonies – and I'm perfectly certain they wouldn't like me!'

'Rich relations?'

Again Tommy shook his head.

'Oh, Tommy, not even a great-aunt?'

'I've got an old uncle who's more or less rolling, but he's no good.'

'Why not?'

'Wanted to adopt me once. I refused.'

'I think I remember hearing about it,' said Tuppence slowly. 'You refused because of your mother –'

Tommy flushed.

'Yes, it would have been a bit rough on the mater. As you know, I was all she had. Old boy hated her – wanted to get me away from her. Just a bit of spite.'

'Your mother's dead, isn't she?' said Tuppence gently.

Tommy nodded.

Tuppence's large grey eyes looked misty.

'You're a good sort, Tommy. I always knew it.'

'Rot!' said Tommy hastily. 'Well, that's my position. I'm just about desperate.'

'So am I! I've hung out as long as I could. I've touted round. I've answered advertisements. I've tried every mortal blessed thing. I've screwed and saved and pinched! But it's no good. I shall have to go home!'

'Don't you want to?'

'Of course I don't want to! What's the good of being sentimental? Father's a dear – I'm awfully fond of him – but you've no idea how I worry him! He has that delightful early Victorian view that short skirts and smoking are immoral. You can imagine what a thorn in the flesh I am to him! He just heaved a sigh of relief when the war took me off. You see, there are seven of us at home. It's awful! All housework and mothers' meetings! I have always been the changeling. I don't want to go back, but – oh, Tommy, what else is there to do?'

Tommy shook his head sadly. There was a silence, and then Tuppence burst out:

'Money, money, money! I think about money morning, noon and night! I dare say it's mercenary of me, but there it is!'

'Same here,' agreed Tommy with feeling.

'I've thought over every imaginable way of getting it, too,' continued Tuppence. 'There are only three! To be left it, to marry it, or to make it. First is ruled out. I haven't got any rich elderly relatives. Any relatives I have are in homes for decayed gentlewomen! I always help old ladies over crossings, and pick up parcels for old gentlemen, in case they should turn out to be eccentric millionaires. But not one of them has ever asked me my name – and quite a lot never said "Thank you."'

There was a pause.

'Of course,' resumed Tuppence, 'marriage is my best chance. I made up my mind to marry money when I was quite young. Any thinking girl would! I'm not sentimental, you know.' She paused. 'Come now, you can't say I'm sentimental,' she added sharply.

'Certainly not,' agreed Tommy hastily. 'No one would ever think of sentiment in connection with you.'

'That's not very polite,' replied Tuppence. 'But I dare say you mean it all right. Well, there it is! I'm ready and willing – but I never meet any rich men! All the boys I know are about as hard up as I am.'

'What about the general?' inquired Tommy.

'I fancy he keeps a bicycle shop in time of peace,' explained Tuppence. 'No, there it is! Now *you* could marry a rich girl.'

'I'm like you. I don't know any.'

'That doesn't matter. You can always get to know one. Now, if I see a man in a fur coat come out of the Ritz I can't rush up to him and say: "Look here, you're rich. I'd like to know you."'

'Do you suggest that I should do that to a similarly garbed female?'

'Don't be silly. You tread on her foot, or pick up her handkerchief, or something like that. If she thinks you want to know her she's flattered, and will manage it for you somehow.'

'You overrate my manly charms,' murmured Tommy.

'On the other hand,' proceeded Tuppence, 'my millionaire would probably run for his life! No – marriage is fraught with difficulties. Remains – to *make* money!'

'We've tried that, and failed,' Tommy reminded her.

'We've tried all the orthodox ways, yes. But suppose we try the unorthodox. Tommy, let's be adventurers!'

'Certainly,' replied Tommy cheerfully. 'How do we begin?'

'That's the difficulty. If we could make ourselves known, people might hire us to commit crimes for them.'

'Delightful,' commented Tommy. 'Especially coming from a clergyman's daughter!'

'The moral guilt,' Tuppence pointed out, 'would be theirs – not mine. You must admit that there's a difference between stealing a diamond necklace for yourself and being hired to steal it?'

'There wouldn't be the least difference if you were caught!'

'Perhaps not. But I shouldn't be caught. I'm so clever.'

'Modesty always was your besetting sin,' remarked Tommy.

'Don't rag. Look here, Tommy, shall we really? Shall we form a business partnership?'

'Form a company for the stealing of diamond necklaces?'

'That was only an illustration. Let's have a – what do you call it in book-keeping?'

'Don't know. Never did any.'

'I have – but I always got mixed up, and used to put credit entries on the debit side, and vice versa – so they fired me out. Oh, I know – a joint venture! It struck me as such a romantic phrase to come across in the middle of musty old figures. It's got an Elizabethan flavour about it – makes one think of galleons and doubloons. A joint venture!'

'Trading under the name of the Young Adventurers, Ltd.? Is that your idea, Tuppence?'

'It's all very well to laugh, but I feel there might be something in it.'

'How do you propose to get in touch with your would-be employers?'

'Advertisement,' replied Tuppence promptly. 'Have you got a bit of paper and a pencil? Men usually seem to have. Just like we have hairpins and powder-puffs.'

Tommy handed over a rather shabby green notebook, and Tuppence began writing busily.

'Shall we begin: "Young officer, twice wounded in the war –"'

'Certainly not.'

'Oh, very well, my dear boy. But I can assure you that that sort of thing might touch the heart of an elderly spinster, and she might adopt you, and then there would be no need for you to be a young adventurer at all.'

'I don't want to be adopted.'

'I forgot you had a prejudice against it. I was only ragging you! The papers are full up to the brim with that type of thing. Now listen – how's this? "Two young adventurers for hire. Willing to do anything, go anywhere. Pay must be good." (We might as well make that clear from the start.) Then we might add: "No reasonable offer refused" – like flats and furniture.'

'I should think any offer we get in answer to that would be a pretty *un*reasonable one!'

'Tommy! You're a genius! That's ever so much more chic. "No unreasonable offer refused – if pay is good." How's that?'

'I shouldn't mention pay again. It looks rather eager.'

'It couldn't look as eager as I feel! But perhaps you are right. Now I'll read it straight through. "Two young adventures for hire. Willing to do anything, go anywhere. Pay must be good. No unreasonable offer refused." How would that strike you if you read it?'

'It would strike me as either being a hoax, or else written by a lunatic.'

'It's not half so insane as a thing I read this morning beginning "Petunia" and signed "Best Boy".' She tore out the leaf and handed it to Tommy. 'There you are. *The Times*, I think. Reply to Box so-and-so. I expect it will be about five shillings. Here's half a crown for my share.'

Tommy was holding the paper thoughtfully. His face burned a deeper red.

'Shall we really try it?' he said at last. 'Shall we, Tuppence? Just for the fun of the thing?'

'Tommy, you're a sport! I knew you would be! Let's drink to success.' She poured some cold dregs of tea into the two cups.

'Here's to our joint venture, and may it prosper!'

'The Young Adventurers, Ltd.!' responded Tomm

They put down the cups and laughed rath

Tuppence rose.

'I must return to my palatial suite at th

'Perhaps it is time I strolled round to the Ritz,' agreed Tommy with a grin. 'Where shall we meet? And when?'

'Twelve o'clock tomorrow. Piccadilly Tube station. Will that suit you?'

'My time is my own,' replied Mr Beresford magnificently.

'So long, then.'

'Goodbye, old thing.'

The two young people went off in opposite directions. Tuppence's hostel was situated in what was charitably called Southern Belgravia. For reasons of economy she did not take a bus.

She was half-way across St James's Park, when a man's voice behind her made her start.

'Excuse me,' it said. 'But may I speak to you for a moment?'

CHAPTER 2

MR WHITTINGTON'S OFFER

Tuppence turned sharply, but the words hovering on the tip of her tongue remained unspoken for the man's appearance and manner did not bear out her first and most natural assumption. She hesitated. As if he read her thoughts, the man said quickly:

'I can assure you I mean no disrespect.'

Tuppence believed him. Although she disliked and distrusted him instinctively, she was inclined to acquit him of the particular motive which she had at first attributed to him. She looked him up and down. He was a big man, clean shaven, with a heavy jowl. His eyes were small and cunning, and shifted their glance under her direct gaze.

'Well, what is it?' she asked.

The man smiled.

'I happened to overhear part of your conversation with the young gentleman in Lyons'.'

'Well – what of it?'

'Nothing – except that I think I may be of some use to you.'

Another inference forced itself into Tuppence's mind.

'You followed me here?'

'I took that liberty.'

… in what way do you think you could be of use to me?'

The man took a card from his pocket and handed it to her with a bow.

Tuppence took it and scrutinized it carefully. It bore the inscription 'Mr Edward Whittington'. Below the name were the words 'Esthonia Glassware Co.', and the address of a city office. Mr Whittington spoke again:

'If you will call upon me tomorrow morning at eleven o'clock, I will lay the details of my proposition before you.'

'At eleven o'clock?' said Tuppence doubtfully.

'At eleven o'clock.'

Tuppence made up her mind.

'Very well. I'll be there.'

'Thank you. Good evening.'

He raised his hat with a flourish, and walked away. Tuppence remained for some minutes gazing after him. Then she gave a curious movement of her shoulders, rather as a terrier shakes himself.

'The adventures have begun,' she murmured to herself. 'What does he want me to do, I wonder? There's something about you, Mr Whittington, that I don't like at all. But, on the other hand, I'm not the least bit afraid of you. And as I've said before, and shall doubtless say again, little Tuppence can look after herself, thank you!'

And with a short, sharp nod of her head she walked briskly onward. As a result of further meditations, however, she turned aside from the direct route and entered a post office. There she pondered for some moments, a telegraph form in her hand. The thought of a possible five shillings spent unnecessarily spurred her to action, and she decided to risk the waste of ninepence.

Disdaining the spiky pen and thick, black treacle which a beneficent Government had provided, Tuppence drew out Tommy's pencil which she had retained and wrote rapidly: 'Don't put in advertisement. Will explain tomorrow.' She addressed it to Tommy at his club, from which in one short month he would have to resign, unless a kindly fortune permitted him to renew his subscription.

'It may catch him,' she murmured. 'Anyway it's worth trying.'

After handing it over the counter she set out briskly for home, stopping at a baker's to buy three-pennyworth of new buns.

Later, in her tiny cubicle at the top of the house she munched buns and reflected on the future. What was the Esthonia Glassware Co., and what earthly need could it have for her services? A pleasurable thrill of excitement made Tuppence tingle. At any rate, the country vicarage had retreated into the background again. The morrow held possibilities.

It was a long time before Tuppence went to sleep that night, and, when at length she did, she dreamed that Mr Whittington had set her to washing up a pile of Esthonia Glassware, which bore an unaccountable resemblance to hospital plates!

It wanted some five minutes to eleven when Tuppence reached the block of buildings in which the offices of the Esthonia Glassware Co. were situated. To arrive before the time would look over-eager. So Tuppence decided to walk to the end of the street and back again. She did so. On the stroke of eleven she plunged into the recesses of the building. The Esthonia Glassware Co. was on the top floor. There was a lift, but Tuppence chose to walk up.

Slightly out of breath, she came to a halt outside the ground glass door with the legend painted across it: 'Esthonia Glassware Co.'

Tuppence knocked. In response to a voice from within, she turned the handle and walked into a small, rather dirty office.

A middle-aged clerk got down from a high stool at a desk near the window and came towards her inquiringly.

'I have an appointment with Mr Whittington,' said Tuppence.

'Will you come this way, please.' He crossed to a partition door with 'Private' on it, knocked, then opened the door and stood aside to let her pass in.

Mr Whittington was seated behind a large desk covered with papers. Tuppence felt her previous judgment confirmed. There was something wrong about Mr Whittington. The combination of his sleek prosperity and his shifty eye was not attractive.

He looked up and nodded.

'So you've turned up all right? That's good. Sit down, will you?'

Tuppence sat down on the chair facing him. She looked particularly small and demure this morning. She sat there meekly with downcast eyes whilst Mr Whittington sorted and rustled amongst his papers. Finally he pushed them away, and leaned over the desk.

'Now, my dear young lady, let us come to business.' His large face broadened into a smile. 'You want work? Well, I have work to offer you. What should you say now to £100 down, and all expenses paid?' Mr Whittington leaned back in his chair, and thrust his thumbs into the arm-holes of his waistcoat.

Tuppence eyed him warily.

'And the nature of the work?' she demanded.

'Nominal – purely nominal. A pleasant trip, that is all.'

'Where to?'

Mr Whittington smiled again.

'Paris.'

'Oh!' said Tuppence thoughtfully. To herself she said: 'Of course, if father heard that he would have a fit! But somehow I don't see Mr Whittington in the role of the gay deceiver.'

'Yes,' continued Whittington. 'What could be more delightful? To put the clock back a few years – a very few, I am sure – and re-enter one of those charming *pensionnats de jeunes filles* with which Paris abounds –'

Tuppence interrupted him.

'A *pensionnat*?'

'Exactly. Madame Colombier's in the Avenue de Neuilly.'

Tuppence knew the name well. Nothing could have been more select. She had had several American friends there. She was more than ever puzzled.

'You want me to go to Madame Colombier's? For how long?'

'That depends. Possibly three months.'

'And that is all? There are no other conditions?'

'None whatever. You would, of course, go in the character of my ward, and you would hold no communication with your friends. I should have to request absolute secrecy for the time being. By the way, you are English, are you not?'

'Yes.'

'Yet you speak with a slight American accent?'

'My great pal in hospital was a little American girl. I dare say I picked it up from her. I can soon get out of it again.'

'On the contrary, it might be simpler for you to pass as an American. Details about your past life in England might be more difficult to sustain. Yes, I think that would be decidedly better. Then –'

'One moment, Mr Whittington! You seem to be taking my consent for granted.'

Whittington looked surprised.

'Surely you are not thinking of refusing? I can assure you that Madame Colombier's is a most high-class and orthodox establishment. And the terms are most liberal.'

'Exactly,' said Tuppence. 'That's just it. The terms are almost too liberal, Mr Whittington. I cannot see any way in which I can be worth that amount of money to you.'

'No?' said Whittington softly. 'Well, I will tell you. I could doubtless obtain someone else for very much less. What I am willing to pay for is a young lady with sufficient intelligence and presence of mind to sustain her part well, and also one who will have sufficient discretion not to ask too many questions.'

Tuppence smiled a little. She felt that Whittington had scored.

'There's another thing. So far there has been no mention of Mr Beresford. Where does he come in.'

'Mr Beresford?'

'My partner,' said Tuppence with dignity. 'You saw us together yesterday.'

'Ah, yes. But I'm afraid we shan't require his services.'

'Then it's off!' Tuppence rose. 'It's both or neither. Sorry – but that's how it is. Good morning, Mr Whittington.'

'Wait a minute. Let us see if something can't be managed. Sit down again, Miss –' He paused interrogatively.

Tuppence's conscience gave her a passing twinge as she remembered the archdeacon. She seized hurriedly on the first name that came into her head.

'Jane Finn,' she said hastily; and then paused open-mouthed at the effect of those two simple words.

All the geniality had faded out of Whittington's face. It was purple with rage, and the veins stood out on the forehead. And behind it all there lurked a sort of incredulous dismay. He leaned forward and hissed savagely:

'So that's your little game, is it?'

Tuppence, though utterly taken aback, nevertheless kept her head. She had not the faintest comprehension of his meaning, but she was naturally quick-witted, and felt it imperative to 'keep her end up' as she phrased it.

Whittington went on:

'Been playing with me, have you, all the time, like a cat and mouse? Knew all the time what I wanted you for, but kept up the comedy. Is that it, eh?' He was cooling down. The red colour was ebbing out of his face. He eyed her keenly. 'Who's been blabbing? Rita?'

Tuppence shook her head. She was doubtful as to how long she could sustain this illusion, but she realized the importance of not dragging an unknown Rita into it.

'No,' she replied with perfect truth. 'Rita knows nothing about me.'

His eyes still bored into her like gimlets.

'How much do you know?' he shot out.

'Very little indeed,' answered Tuppence, and was pleased to note that Whittington's uneasiness was augmented instead of allayed. To have boasted that she knew a lot might have raised doubts in his mind.

'Anyway,' snarled Whittington, 'you knew enough to come in here and plump out that name.'

'It might be my own name,' Tuppence pointed out.

'It's likely, isn't it, that there would be two girls with a name like that?'

'Or I might just have hit upon it by chance,' continued Tuppence, intoxicated with the success of truthfulness.

Mr Whittington brought his fist down upon the desk with a bang.

'Quit fooling! How much do you know? And how much do you want?'

The last five words took Tuppence's fancy mightily, especially after a meagre breakfast and a supper of buns the night before. Her present part was of the adventuress rather than the adventurous order, but she did not deny its possibilities. She sat up and smiled with the air of one who has the situation thoroughly well in hand.

'My dear Mr Whittington,' she said, 'let us by all means lay our cards upon the table. And pray do not be so angry. You heard me say yesterday that I proposed to live by my wits. It seems to me that I have now proved I have some wits to live by! I admit I have knowledge of a certain name, but perhaps my knowledge ends there.'

'Yes – and perhaps it doesn't,' snarled Whittington.

'You insist on misjudging me,' said Tuppence, and sighed gently.

'As I said once before,' said Whittington angrily, 'quit fooling, and come to the point. You can't play the innocent with me. You know a great deal more than you're willing to admit.'

Tuppence paused a moment to admire her own ingenuity, and then said softly:

'I shouldn't like to contradict you, Mr Whittington.'

'So we come to the usual question – how much?'

Tuppence was in a dilemma. So far she had fooled Whittington with complete success, but to mention a palpably impossible sum might awaken his suspicions. An idea flashed across her brain.

'Suppose we say a little something down, and a fuller discussion of the matter later?'

Whittington gave her an ugly glance.

'Blackmail, eh?'

Tuppence smiled sweetly.

'Oh no! Shall we say payment of services in advance?'

Whittington grunted.

'You see,' explained Tuppence sweetly, 'I'm not so very fond of money!'

'You're about the limit, that's what you are,' growled Whittington, with a sort of unwilling admiration. 'You took me in all right. Thought you were quite a meek little kid with just enough brains for my purpose.'

'Life,' moralized Tuppence, 'is full of surprises.'

'All the same,' continued Whittington, 'someone's been talking. You say it isn't Rita. Was it –? Oh, come in.'

The clerk followed his discreet knock into the room, and laid a paper at his master's elbow.

'Telephone message just come for you, sir.'

Whittington snatched it up and read it. A frown gathered on his brow.

'That'll do, Brown. You can go.'

The clerk withdrew, closing the door behind him. Whittington turned to Tuppence.

'Come tomorrow at the same time. I'm busy now. Here's fifty to go on with.'

He rapidly sorted out some notes, and pushed them across the table to Tuppence, then stood up, obviously impatient for her to go.

The girl counted the notes in a business-like manner, secured them in her handbag, and rose.

'Good morning, Mr Whittington,' she said politely. 'At least *au revoir*, I should say.'

'Exactly. *Au revoir*!' Whittington looked almost genial again, a reversion that aroused in Tuppence a faint misgiving. '*Au revoir*, my clever and charming young lady.'

Tuppence sped lightly down the stairs. A wild elation possessed her. A neighbouring clock showed the time to be five minutes to twelve.

'Let's give Tommy a surprise!' murmured Tuppence, and hailed a taxi.

The cab drew up outside the Tube station. Tommy was just within the entrance. His eyes opened to their fullest extent as he hurried forward to assist Tuppence to alight. She smiled at him affectionately, and remarked in a slightly affected voice:

'Pay the thing, will you, old bean? I've got nothing smaller than a five-pound note!'

CHAPTER 3

A SETBACK

The moment was not quite so triumphant as it ought to have been. To begin with, the resources of Tommy's pockets were somewhat limited. In the end the fare was managed, the lady recollecting a plebeian twopence, and the driver, still holding the varied assortment of coins in his hand, was prevailed upon to move on, which he did after one last hoarse demand as to what the gentleman thought he was giving him?

'I think you've given him too much, Tommy,' said Tuppence innocently. 'I fancy he wants to give some of it back.'

It was possibly this remark which induced the driver to move away.

'Well,' said Mr Beresford, at length able to relieve his feelings, 'what the – dickens, did you want to take a taxi for?'

'I was afraid I might be late and keep you waiting,' said Tuppence gently.

'Afraid – you – might – be – late! Oh, Lord, I give it up!' said Mr Beresford.

'And really and truly,' continued Tuppence, opening her eyes very wide, 'I haven't got anything smaller than a five-pound note.'

'You did that part of it very well, old bean, but all the same the fellow wasn't taken in – not for a moment!'

'No,' said Tuppence thoughtfully, 'he didn't believe it. That's the curious part about speaking the truth. No one does believe it. I found that out this morning. Now let's go to lunch. How about the Savoy?'

Tommy grinned.

'How about the Ritz?'

'On second thoughts, I prefer the Piccadilly. It's nearer. We shan't have to take another taxi. Come along.'

'Is this a new brand of humour? Or is your brain really unhinged?' inquired Tommy.

'Your last supposition is the correct one. I have come into money, and the shock has been too much for me! For that particular form of mental trouble an eminent physician recommends unlimited *hors d'oeuvre*, lobster *à l'américaine*, chicken Newberg, and *pêche Melba*! Let's go and get them!'

'Tuppence, old girl, what has really come over you?'

'Oh, unbelieving one!' Tuppence wrenched open her bag. 'Look here, and here, and here!'

'My dear girl, don't wave pound notes aloft like that!'

'They're not pound notes. They're five times better, and this one's ten times better!'

Tommy groaned.

'I must have been drinking unawares! Am I dreaming, Tuppence, or do I really behold a large quantity of five-pound notes being waved about in a dangerous fashion?'

'Even so, O King! *Now*, will you come and have lunch?'

'I'll come anywhere. But what have you been doing? Holding up a bank?'

'All in good time. What an awful place Piccadilly Circus is. There's a huge bus bearing down on us. It would be too terrible if they killed the five-pound notes!'

'Grill room?' inquired Tommy, as they reached the opposite pavement in safety.

'The other's more expensive,' demurred Tuppence.

'That's mere wicked wanton extravagance. Come on below.'

'Are you sure I can get all the things I want there?'

'That extremely unwholesome menu you were outlining just now? Of course you can – or as much as is good for you, anyway.'

'And now tell me,' said Tommy, unable to restrain his pent-up curiosity any longer, as they sat in state surrounded by the many *hors d'oeuvre* of Tuppence's dreams.

Miss Cowley told him.

'And the curious part of it is,' she ended, 'that I really did invent the name of Jane Finn! I didn't want to give my own because of poor father – in case I should get mixed up in anything shady.'

'Perhaps that's so,' said Tommy slowly. 'But you didn't invent it.'

'What?'

'No. *I* told it to you. Don't you remember, I said yesterday I'd overheard two people talking about a female called Jane Finn? That's what brought the name into your mind so pat.'

'So you did. I remember now. How extraordinary –' Tuppence tailed off into silence. Suddenly she roused herself. 'Tommy!'

'Yes?'

'What were they like, the two men you passed?'

Tommy frowned in an effort at remembrance.

'One was a big fat sort of chap. Clean shaven. I think – and dark.'

'That's him,' cried Tuppence, in an ungrammatical squeal. 'That's Whittington! What was the other man like?'

'I can't remember. I didn't notice him particularly. It was really the outlandish name that caught my attention.'

'And people say that coincidences don't happen!' Tuppence tackled her *pêche Melba* happily.

But Tommy had become serious.

'Look here, Tuppence, old girl, what is this going to lead to?'

'More money,' replied his companion.

'I know that. You've only got one idea in your head. What I mean is, what about the next step? How are you going to keep the game up?'

'Oh!' Tuppence laid down her spoon. 'You're right, Tommy, it is a bit of a poser.'

'After all, you know, you can't bluff him for ever. You're sure to slip up sooner or later. And, anyway, I'm not at all sure that it isn't actionable – blackmail, you know.'

'Nonsense. Blackmail is saying you'll tell unless you are given money. Now, there's nothing I could tell, because I don't really know anything.'

'H'm,' said Tommy doubtfully. 'Well, anyway, what *are* we going to do? Whittington was in a hurry to get rid of you this morning, but next time he'll want to know something more before he parts with his money. He'll want to know how much you know, and where you got your information from, and a lot of other things that you can't cope with. What are you going to do about it?'

Tuppence frowned severely.

'We must think. Order some Turkish coffee, Tommy. Stimulating to the brain. Oh, dear, what a lot I have eaten!'

'You have made rather a hog of yourself! So have I for that matter, but I flatter myself that my choice of dishes was more judicious than yours. Two coffees.' (This was to the waiter.) 'One Turkish, one French.'

Tuppence sipped her coffee with a deeply reflective air, and snubbed Tommy when he spoke to her.

'Be quiet. I'm thinking.'

'Shades of Pelmanism!' said Tommy, and relapsed into silence.

'There!' said Tuppence at last. 'I've got a plan. Obviously what we've got to do is find out more about it all.'

Tommy applauded.

'Don't jeer. We can only find out through Whittington. We must discover where he lives, what he does – sleuth him, in fact! Now I can't do it, because he knows me, but he only saw you for a minute or two in Lyons'. He's not likely to recognize you. After all, one young man is much like another.'

'I repudiate that remark utterly. I'm sure my pleasing features and distinguished appearance would single me out from any crowd.'

'My plan is this,' Tuppence went on calmly. 'I'll go alone tomorrow. I'll put him off again like I did today. It doesn't matter if I don't get any more money at once. Fifty pounds ought to last us a few days.'

'Or even longer!'

'You'll hang about outside. When I come out I shan't speak to you in case he's watching. But I'll take up my stand somewhere near, and when he comes out of the building I'll drop a handkerchief or something, and off you go!'

'Off I go where?'

'Follow him, of course, silly! What do you think of the idea?'

'Sort of thing one reads about in books. I somehow feel that in real life one will feel a bit of an ass standing in the street for hours with nothing to do. People will wonder what I'm up to.'

'Not in the city. Everyone's in such a hurry. Probably no one will even notice you at all.'

'That's the second time you've made that sort of remark. Never mind, I forgive you. Anyway, it will be rather a lark. What are you doing this afternoon?'

'Well,' said Tuppence meditatively. 'I *had* thought of hats! Or perhaps silk stockings! Or perhaps –'

'Hold hard,' admonished Tommy. 'There's a limit to fifty pounds! But let's do dinner and a show tonight at all events.'

'Rather.'

The day passed pleasantly. The evening even more so. Two of the five-pound notes were now irretrievably dead.

They met by arrangement the following morning, and proceeded citywards. Tommy remained on the opposite side of the road while Tuppence plunged into the building.

Tommy strolled slowly down to the end of the street, then back again. Just as he came abreast of the buildings, Tuppence darted across the road.

'Tommy!'

'Yes. What's up?'

'The place is shut. I can't make anyone hear.'

'That's odd.'

'Isn't it? Come up with me, and let's try again.'

Tommy followed her. As they passed the third floor landing a young clerk came out of an office. He hesitated a moment, then addressed himself to Tuppence.

'Were you wanting the Esthonia Glassware?'

'Yes, please.'

'It's closed down. Since yesterday afternoon. Company being wound up, they say. Not that I've ever heard of it myself. But anyway the office is to let.'

'Th – thank you,' faltered Tuppence. 'I suppose you don't know Mr Whittington's address?'

'Afraid I don't. They left rather suddenly.'

'Thank you very much,' said Tommy. 'Come on, Tuppence.'

They descended to the street again where they gazed at one another blankly.

'That's torn it,' said Tommy at length.

'And I never suspected it,' wailed Tuppence.

'Cheer up, old thing, it can't be helped.'

'Can't it, though!' Tuppence's little chin shot out defiantly. 'Do you think this is the end? If so, you're wrong. It's just the beginning!'

'The beginning of what?'

'Of our adventure! Tommy, don't you see, if they are scared enough to run away like this, it shows that there must be a lot in this Jane Finn business! Well, we'll get to the bottom of it. We'll run them down! We'll be sleuths in earnest!'

'Yes, but there's no one left to sleuth.'

'No, that's why we'll have to start all over again. Lend me that bit of pencil. Thanks. Wait a minute – don't interrupt. There!' Tuppence handed back the pencil, and surveyed the piece of paper on which she had written with a satisfied eye.

'What's that?'

'Advertisement.'

'You're not going to put that thing in after all?'

'No, it's a different one.' She handed him the slip of paper.

Tommy read the words on it aloud:

'WANTED, any information respecting Jane Finn. Apply Y. A.'

CHAPTER 4

WHO IS JANE FINN?

The next day passed slowly. It was necessary to curtail expenditure. Carefully husbanded, forty pounds will last a long time. Luckily the weather was fine, and 'walking is cheap,' dictated Tuppence. An outlying picture-house provided them with recreation for the evening.

The day of disillusionment had been a Wednesday. On Thursday the advertisement had duly appeared. On Friday letters might be expected to arrive at Tommy's rooms.

He had been bound by an honourable promise not to open any such letters if they did arrive, but to repair to the National Gallery, where his colleague would meet him at ten o'clock.

Tuppence was first at the rendezvous. She ensconced herself on a red velvet seat, and gazed at the Turners with unseeing eyes until she saw the familiar figure enter the room.

'Well?'

'Well,' returned Mr Beresford provokingly. 'Which is your favourite picture?'

'Don't be a wretch. Aren't there *any* answers?'

Tommy shook his head with a deep and somewhat overacted melancholy.

'I didn't want to disappoint you, old thing, by telling you right off. It's too bad. Good money wasted.' He sighed. 'Still, there it is. The advertisement has appeared, and – there are only two answers!'

'Tommy, you devil!' almost screamed Tuppence. 'Give them to me. How could you be so mean!'

'Your luggage, Tuppence, your luggage! They're very particular at the National Gallery. Government show, you know. And do remember, as I have pointed out to you before, that as a clergyman's daughter –'

'I ought to be on the stage!' finished Tuppence with a snap.

'That is not what I intended to say. But if you are sure that you have enjoyed to the full the reaction of joy after despair with which I have kindly provided you free of charge, let us get down to our mail, as the saying goes.'

Tuppence snatched the two precious envelopes from him unceremoniously, and scrutinized them carefully.

'Thick paper, this one. It looks rich. We'll keep it to the last and open the other first.'

'Right you are. One, two, three, go!'

Tuppence's little thumb ripped open the envelope, and she extracted the contents.

Dear Sir,

Referring to your advertisement in this morning's paper, I may be able to be of some use to you. Perhaps you could call and see me at the above address at eleven o'clock tomorrow morning.

Yours truly,

A. Carter

'27 Carshalton Terrace,' said Tuppence, referring to the address. 'That's Gloucester Road way. Plenty of time to get there if we Tube.'

'The following,' said Tommy, 'is the plan of campaign. It is my turn to assume the offensive. Ushered into the presence of Mr Carter, he and I wish each other good morning as is customary. He then says: "Please take a seat, Mr – er?" To which I reply promptly and significantly: "Edward Whittington!" whereupon Mr Carter turns purple in the face and gasps out: "How much?" Pocketing the usual fee of fifty pounds, I rejoin you in the road outside, and we proceed to the next address and repeat the performance.'

'Don't be absurd, Tommy. Now for the other letter. Oh, this is from the Ritz!'

'A hundred pounds instead of fifty!'

'I'll read it:

'Dear Sir,

'Re your advertisement, I should be glad if you would call round somewhere about lunch-time.

'Yours truly,

'Julius P. Hersheimmer.'

'Ha!' said Tommy. 'Do I smell a Boche? Or only an American

millionaire of unfortunate ancestry? At all events we'll call at lunch-time. It's a good time – frequently leads to free food for two.'

Tuppence nodded assent.

'Now for Carter. We'll have to hurry.'

Carshalton Terrace proved to be an unimpeachable row of what Tuppence called 'ladylike-looking houses'. They rang the bell at No. 27, and a neat maid answered the door. She looked so respectable that Tuppence's heart sank. Upon Tommy's request for Mr Carter, she showed them into a small study on the ground floor, where she left them. Hardly a minute elapsed, however, before the door opened, and a tall man with a lean hawklike face and a tired manner entered the room.

'Mr Y.A.?' he said, and smiled. His smile was distinctly attractive. 'Do sit down, both of you.'

They obeyed. He himself took a chair opposite to Tuppence and smiled at her encouragingly. There was something in the quality of his smile that made the girl's usual readiness desert her.

As he did not seem inclined to open the conversation, Tuppence was forced to begin.

'We wanted to know – that is, would you be so kind as to tell us anything you know about Jane Finn?'

'Jane Finn? Ah!' Mr Carter appeared to reflect. 'Well, the question is, what do you know about her?'

Tuppence drew herself up.

'I don't see that that's got anything to do with it.'

'No? But it has, you know, really it has.' He smiled again in his tired way, and continued reflectively. 'So that brings us down to it again. What do *you* know about Jane Finn?'

'Come now,' he continued, as Tuppence remained silent. 'You must know *something* to have advertised as you did?' He leaned forward a little, his weary voice held a hint of persuasiveness. 'Suppose you tell me . . .'

There was something very magnetic about Mr Carter's personality. Tuppence seemed to shake herself free of it with an effort, as she said:

'We couldn't do that, could we, Tommy?'

But to her surprise, her companion did not back her up. His

eyes were fixed on Mr Carter, and his tone when he spoke held an unusual note of deference.

'I dare say the little we know won't be any good to you, sir. But such as it is, you're welcome to it.'

'Tommy!' cried out Tuppence in surprise.

Mr Carter slewed round in his chair. His eyes asked a question.

Tommy nodded.

'Yes, sir, I recognized you at once. Saw you in France when I was with the Intelligence. As soon as you came into the room, I knew –'

Mr Carter held up his hand.

'No names, please. I'm known as Mr Carter here. It's my cousin's house, by the way. She's willing to lend it to me sometimes when it's a case of working on strictly unofficial lines. Well, now,' – he looked from one to the other – 'who's going to tell me the story?'

'Fire ahead, Tuppence,' directed Tommy. 'It's your yarn.'

'Yes, little lady, out with it.'

And obediently Tuppence did out with it, telling the whole story from the forming of the Young Adventurers, Ltd., downwards.

Mr Carter listened in silence with a resumption of his tired manner. Now and then he passed his hand across his lips as though to hide a smile. When she had finished he nodded gravely.

'Not much. But suggestive. Quite suggestive. If you'll excuse me saying so, you're a curious young couple. I don't know – you might succeed where others have failed . . . I believe in luck, you know – always have . . .'

He paused a moment and then went on.

'Well, how about it? You're out for adventure. How would you like to work for me? All quite unofficial, you know. Expenses paid, and a moderate screw?'

Tuppence gazed at him, her lips parted, her eyes growing wider and wider. 'What should we have to do?' she breathed.

Mr Carter smiled.

'Just go on with what you're doing now. *Find Jane Finn.*'

'Yes, but – who is Jane Finn?'

Mr Carter nodded gravely.

'Yes, you're entitled to know that, I think.'

He leaned back in his chair, crossed his legs, brought the tips of his fingers together, and began in a low monotone:

'Secret diplomacy (which, by the way, is nearly always bad policy!) does not concern you. It will be sufficient to say that in the early days of 1915 a certain document came into being. It was the draft of a secret agreement – treaty – call it what you like. It was drawn up ready for signature by the various representatives, and drawn up in America – at that time a neutral country. It was dispatched to England by a special messenger selected for that purpose, a young fellow called Danvers. It was hoped that the whole affair had been kept so secret that nothing would have leaked out. That kind of hope is usually disappointed. Somebody always talks!

'Danvers sailed for England on the *Lusitania*. He carried the precious papers in an oilskin packet which he wore next his skin. It was on that particular voyage that the *Lusitania* was torpedoed and sunk. Danvers was among the list of those missing. Eventually his body was washed ashore, and identified beyond any possible doubt. But the oilskin packet was missing!

'The question was, had it been taken from him, or had he himself passed it on into another's keeping? There were a few incidents that strengthened the possibility of the latter theory. After the torpedo struck the ship, in the few moments during the launching of the boats, Danvers was seen speaking to a young American girl. No one actually saw him pass anything to her, but he might have done so. It seems to me quite likely that he entrusted the papers to this girl, believing that she, as a woman, had a greater chance of bringing them safely to shore.

'But if so, where was the girl, and what had she done with the papers? By later advice from America it seemed likely that Danvers had been closely shadowed on the way over. Was this girl in league with his enemies? Or had she, in her turn, been shadowed and either tricked or forced into handing over the precious packet?

'We set to work to trace her out. It proved unexpectedly difficult. Her name was Jane Finn, and it duly appeared among the list of the survivors, but the girl herself seemed to have vanished completely. Inquiries into her antecedents did little to help us. She was an orphan, and had been what we should call over here a pupil-teacher in a small school out West. Her passport had been made out for Paris, where she was going to join the staff of a hospital. She had offered her services voluntarily, and after some correspondence they had been accepted. Having seen her name in the list of the saved from the *Lusitania*, the staff of the hospital were naturally very surprised at her not arriving to take up her billet, and at not hearing from her in any way.

'Well, every effort was made to trace the young lady – but all in vain. We tracked her across Ireland, but nothing could be heard of her after she set foot in England. No use was made of the draft treaty – as might very easily have been done – and we therefore came to the conclusion that Danvers had, after all, destroyed it. The war entered on another phase, the diplomatic aspect changed accordingly, and the treaty was never redrafted. Rumours as to its existence were emphatically denied. The disappearance of Jane Finn was forgotten and the whole affair was lost in oblivion.'

Mr Carter paused, and Tuppence broke in impatiently:

'But why has it all cropped up again? The war's over.'

A hint of alertness came into Mr Carter's manner.

'Because it seemed that the papers were not destroyed after all, and that they might be resurrected today with a new and deadly significance.'

Tuppence stared. Mr Carter nodded.

'Yes, five years ago, that draft treaty was a weapon in our hands; today it is a weapon against us. It was a gigantic blunder. If its terms were made public, it would mean disaster . . . It might possibly bring about another war – not with Germany this time! That is an extreme possibility, and I do not believe in its likelihood myself, but that document undoubtedly implicates a number of our statesmen whom we cannot afford to have discredited in any way at the present moment. As a party cry for Labour it would be irresistible, and a Labour Government at this juncture would, in my opinion, be a grave disability for British trade, but that is a mere nothing to the *real* danger.'

He paused, and then said quietly:

'You may perhaps have heard or read that there is Bolshevist influence at work behind the present labour unrest?'

Tuppence nodded.

'That is the truth, Bolshevist gold is pouring into this country for the specific purpose of procuring a Revolution. And there is a certain man, a man whose real name is unknown to us, who is working in the dark for his own ends. The Bolshevists are behind the labour unrest – but this man is *behind the Bolshevists*. Who is he? We do not know. He is always spoken of by the unassuming title of "Mr Brown". But one thing is certain, he is the master criminal of this age. He controls a marvellous organization. Most of the peace propaganda during the war was originated and financed by him. His spies are everywhere.'

'A naturalized German?' asked Tommy.

'On the contrary, I have every reason to believe he is an Englishman. He was pro-German, as he would have been pro-Boer. What he seeks to attain we do not know – probably supreme power for himself, of a kind unique in history. We have no clue as to his real personality. It is reported that even his own followers are ignorant of it. Where we have come across his tracks, he has always played a secondary part. Somebody else assumes the chief role. But afterwards we always find that there had been some nonentity, a servant or a clerk, who had remained in the background unnoticed, and that the elusive Mr Brown has escaped us once more.'

'Oh!' Tuppence jumped. 'I wonder –'

'Yes?'

'I remember in Mr Whittington's office. The clerk – he called him Brown. You don't think –'

Carter nodded thoughtfully.

'Very likely. A curious point is that the name is usually mentioned. An idiosyncracy of genius. Can you describe him at all?'

'I really didn't notice. He was quite ordinary – just like anyone else.'

Mr Carter sighed in his tired manner.

'That is the invariable description of Mr Brown! Brought a telephone message to the man Whittington, did he? Notice a telephone in the outer office?'

Tuppence thought.

'No, I don't think I did.'

'Exactly. That "message" was Mr Brown's way of giving an order to his subordinate. He overheard the whole conversation of course. Was it after that that Whittington handed you over the money, and told you to come the following day?'

Tuppence nodded.

'Yes, undoubtedly the hand of Mr Brown!' Mr Carter paused. 'Well, there it is, you see what you are pitting yourself against? Possibly the finest criminal brain of the age. I don't quite like it, you know. You're such young things, both of you. I shouldn't like anything to happen to you.'

'It won't,' Tuppence assured him positively.

'I'll look after her, sir,' said Tommy.

'And *I'll* look after you,' retorted Tuppence, resenting the manly assertion.

'Well, then, look after each other,' said Mr Carter, smiling. 'Now let's get back to business. There's something mysterious about this draft treaty that we haven't fathomed yet. We've been threatened with it – in plain and unmistakable terms. The Revolutionary elements as good as declared that it's in their hands, and that they intend to produce it at a given moment. On the other hand, they are clearly at fault about many of its provisions. The Government consider it as mere bluff on their part, and, rightly or wrongly, have stuck to the policy of absolute denial. I'm not so sure. There have been hints, indiscreet allusions, that seem to indicate that the menace is a real one. The position is much as though they had got hold of an incriminating document, but couldn't read it because it was in cipher – but we know that the draft treaty wasn't in cipher – couldn't be in the nature of things – so that won't wash. But there's *something*. Of course, Jane Finn may be dead for all we know – but I don't think so. The curious thing is that *they're trying to get information about the girl from us*.'

'What?'

'Yes. One or two little things have cropped up. And your story, little lady, confirms my idea. They know we're looking for Jane Finn. Well, they'll produce a Jane Finn of their own – say at a *pensionnat* in Paris.' Tuppence gasped, and Mr Carter smiled. 'No one knows in the least what she looks like, so that's all right. She's primed with a trumped-up tale, and her real business is to get as much information as possible out of us. See the idea?'

'Then you think' – Tuppence paused to grasp the supposition fully – 'that it *was* as Jane Finn that they wanted me to go to Paris?'

Mr Carter smiled more wearily than ever.

'I believe in coincidences, you know,' he said.

CHAPTER 5

MR JULIUS P. HERSHEIMMER

'Well,' said Tuppence, recovering herself, 'it really seems as though it were meant to be.'

Carter nodded.

'I know what you mean. I'm superstitious myself. Luck, and all that sort of thing. Fate seems to have chosen you out to be mixed up in this.'

Tommy indulged in a chuckle.

'My word! I don't wonder Whittington got the wind up when Tuppence plumped out that name! I should have myself. But look here, sir, we're taking up an awful lot of your time. Have you any tips to give us before we clear out?'

'I think not. My experts, working in stereotyped ways, have failed. You will bring imagination and an open mind to the task. Don't be discouraged if that too does not succeed. For one thing there is a likelihood of the pace being forced.'

Tuppence frowned uncomprehendingly.

'When you had that interview with Whittington, they had time before them. I have information that the big *coup* was planned for early in the new year. But the Government is contemplating legislative action which will deal effectually with the strike menace. They'll get wind of it soon, if they haven't already, and it's possible that they may bring things to a head. I hope it will myself. The less time they have to mature their plans the better. I'm just warning you that you haven't much time before you, and that you needn't be cast down if you fail. It's not an easy proposition anyway. That's all.'

Tuppence rose.

'I think we ought to be business-like. What exactly can we count upon you for, Mr Carter?'

Mr Carter's lips twitched slightly, but he replied succinctly:

'Funds within reason, detailed information on any point, and no *official recognition*. I mean that if you get yourselves into trouble with the police, I can't officially help you out of it. You're on your own.'

Tuppence nodded sagely.

'I quite understand that. I'll write out a list of the things I want to know when I've had time to think. Now – about money –'

'Yes, Miss Tuppence. Do you want to say how much?'

'Not exactly. We've got plenty to go on with for the present, but when we want more –'

'It will be waiting for you.'

'Yes, but – I'm sure I don't want to be rude about the Government if you've got anything to do with it, but you know one really has the devil of a time getting anything out of it! And if we have to fill up a blue form and send it in, and then, after three months, they send us a green one, and so on – well, that won't be much use, will it?'

Mr Carter laughed outright.

'Don't worry, Miss Tuppence. You will send a personal demand to me here, and the money, in notes, shall be sent by return of post. As to salary, shall we say at the rate of three hundred a year? And an equal sum for Mr Beresford, of course.'

Tuppence beamed upon him.

'How lovely. You are kind. I do love money! I'll keep beautiful accounts of our expenses – all debit and credit, and the balance on the right side, and a red line drawn sideways with the totals the same at the bottom. I really know how to do it when I think.'

'I'm sure you do. Well, goodbye, and good luck to you both.'

He shook hands with them and in another minute they were descending the steps of 27 Carshalton Terrace with their heads in a whirl.

'Tommy! Tell me at once, who is "Mr Carter"?'

Tommy murmured a name in her ear.

'Oh!' said Tuppence, impressed.

'And I can tell you, old bean, he's rr!'

'Oh!' said Tuppence again. Then she added reflectively: 'I like him, don't you? He looks so awfully tired and bored, and yet you feel that underneath he's just like steel, all keen and flashing. Oh!' She gave a skip. 'Pinch me, Tommy, do pinch me. I can't believe it's real!'

Mr Beresford obliged.

'Ow! That's enough! Yes, we're not dreaming. We've got a job!'

'And what a job! The joint venture has really begun.'

'It's more respectable than I thought it would be,' said Tuppence thoughtfully.

'Luckily I haven't got your craving for crime! What time is it? Let's have lunch – oh!'

The same thought sprang to the minds of each. Tommy voiced it first.

'Julius P. Hersheimmer!'

'We never told Mr Carter about hearing from him.'

'Well, there wasn't much to tell – not till we've seen him. Come on, we'd better take a taxi.'

'Now who's being extravagant?'

'All expenses paid, remember. Hop in.'

'At any rate, we shall make a better effect arriving this way,' said Tuppence, leaning back luxuriously. 'I'm sure blackmailers never arrive in buses!'

'We've ceased being blackmailers,' Tommy pointed out.

'I'm not sure I have,' said Tuppence darkly.

On inquiring for Mr Hersheimmer, they were at once taken up to his suite. An impatient voice cried 'Come in' in answer to the page-boy's knock, and the lad stood aside to let them pass in.

Mr Julius P. Hersheimmer was a great deal younger than either Tommy or Tuppence had pictured him. The girl put him down as thirty-five. He was of middle height, and squarely built to match his jaw. His face was pugnacious but pleasant. No one could have mistaken him for anything but an American, though he spoke with very little accent.

'Get my note?' Sit down and tell me right away all you know about my cousin.'

'Your cousin?'

'Sure thing. Jane Finn.'

'Is she your cousin?'

'My father and her mother were brother and sister,' explained Mr Hersheimmer meticulously.

'Oh!' cried Tuppence. 'Then you know where she is?'

'No!' Mr Hersheimmer brought down his fist with a bang on the table. 'I'm darned if I do! Don't you?'

'We advertised to receive information, not to give it,' said Tuppence severely.

'I guess I know that. I can read. But I thought maybe it was her back history you were after, and that you'd know where she was now?'

'Well, we wouldn't mind hearing her back history,' said Tuppence guardedly.

But Mr Hersheimmer seemed to grow suddenly suspicious.

'See here,' he declared. 'This isn't Sicily! No demanding ransom or threatening to crop her ears if I refuse. These are the British Isles, so quit the funny business, or I'll just sing out for that beautiful big British policeman I see out there in Piccadilly.'

Tommy hastened to explain.

'We haven't kidnapped your cousin. On the contrary, we're trying to find her. We're employed to do so.'

Mr Hersheimmer leant back in his chair.

'Put me wise,' he said succinctly.

Tommy fell in with this demand in so far as he gave him a guarded version of the disappearance of Jane Finn, and of the possibility of her having been mixed up unawares in 'some political show'. He alluded to Tuppence and himself as 'private inquiry agents' commissioned to find her, and added that they would therefore be glad of any details Mr Hersheimmer could give them.

That gentleman nodded approval.

'I guess that's my right. I was just a mite hasty. But London gets my goat! I only know little old New York. Just trot your questions and I'll answer.'

For the moment this paralysed the Young Adventurers, but Tuppence, recovering herself, plunged boldly into the breach with a reminiscence culled from detective fiction.

'When did you last see the dece – your cousin, I mean?'

'Never seen her,' responded Mr Hersheimmer.

'What?' demanded Tommy astonished.

Hersheimmer turned to him.

'No, sir. As I said before, my father and her mother were brother and sister, just as you might be' – Tommy did not correct this view of their relationship – 'but they didn't always get on together. And when my aunt made up her mind to marry

Amos Finn, who was a poor school teacher out West, my father was just mad! Said if he made his pile, as he seemed in a fair way to do, she'd never see a cent of it. Well, the upshot was that Aunt Jane went out West and we never heard from her again.

'The old man *did* pile it up. He went into oil, and he went into steel, and he played a bit with railroads, and I can tell you he made Wall Street sit up!' He paused. 'Then he died – last fall – and I got the dollars. Well, would you believe it, my conscience got busy! Kept knocking me up and saying: What about your Aunt Jane, way out West? It worried me some. You see, I figured it out that Amos Finn would never make good. He wasn't the sort. End of it was, I hired a man to hunt her down. Result, she was dead, and Amos Finn was dead, but they'd left a daughter – Jane – who'd been torpedoed in the *Lusitania* on her way to Paris. She was saved all right, but they didn't seem able to hear of her over this side. I guessed they weren't hustling any, so I thought I'd come along over, and speed things up. I phoned Scotland Yard and the Admiralty first thing. The Admiralty rather choked me off, but Scotland Yard were very civil – said they would make inquiries, even sent a man round this morning to get her photograph. I'm off to Paris tomorrow, just to see what the Prefecture is doing. I guess if I go to and fro hustling them, they ought to get busy!'

The energy of Mr Hersheimmer was tremendous. They bowed before it.

'But say now,' he ended, 'you're not after her for anything? Contempt of court, or something British? A proud-spirited young American girl might find your rules and regulations in wartime rather irksome, and get up against it. If that's the case, and there's such a thing as graft in this country, I'll buy her off.'

Tuppence reassured him.

'That's good. Then we can work together. What about some lunch? Shall we have it up here, or go down to the restaurant?'

Tuppence expressed a preference for the latter, and Julius bowed to her decision.

Oysters had just given place to sole Colbert when a card was brought to Hersheimmer.

'Inspector Japp, C.I.D. Scotland Yard again. Another man this time. What does he expect I can tell him that I didn't tell the first chap? I hope they haven't lost that photograph. That Western photographer's place was burned down and all his negatives destroyed – this is the only copy in existence. I got it from the principal of the college there.'

An unformulated dread swept over Tuppence.

'You – you don't know the name of the man who came this morning?'

'Yes, I do. No, I don't. Half a second. It was on his card. Oh, I know! Inspector Brown. Quiet unassuming sort of chap.'

CHAPTER 6

A PLAN OF CAMPAIGN

A veil might with profit be drawn over the events of the next half-hour. Suffice it to say that no such person as 'Inspector Brown' was known to Scotland Yard. The photograph of Jane Finn, which would have been of the utmost value to the police in tracing her, was lost beyond recovery. Once again 'Mr Brown' had triumphed.

The immediate result of this set-back was to effect a *rapprochement* between Julius Hersheimmer and the Young Adventurers. All barriers went down with a crash, and Tommy and Tuppence felt they had known the young American all their lives. They abandoned the discreet reticence of 'private inquiry agents', and revealed to him the whole history of the joint venture, whereat the young man declared himself 'tickled to death'.

He turned to Tuppence at the close of the narration.

'I've always had a kind of idea that English girls were just a mite moss-grown. Old-fashioned and sweet, you know, but scared to move round without a footman or a maiden aunt. I guess I'm a bit behind the times!'

The upshot of these confidential relations was that Tommy and Tuppence took up their abode forthwith at the Ritz, in order, as Tuppence put it, to keep in touch with Jane Finn's only living relation. 'And put like that,' she added confidentially to Tommy, 'nobody could boggle at the expense!'

Nobody did, which was the great thing.

'And now,' said the young lady on the morning after their installation, 'to work!'

Mr Beresford put down the *Daily Mail*, which he was reading, and applauded with somewhat unnecessary vigour. He was politely requested by his colleague not to be an ass.

'Dash it all, Tommy, we've got to *do* something for our money.'

Tommy sighed.

'Yes, I fear even the dear old Government will not support us at the Ritz in idleness for ever.'

'Therefore, as I said before, we must *do* something.'

'Well,' said Tommy, picking up the *Daily Mail* again, '*do* it. I shan't stop you.'

'You see,' continued Tuppence. 'I've been thinking –'

She was interrupted by a fresh bout of applause.

'It's all very well for you to sit there being funny, Tommy. It would do you no harm to do a little brain work too.'

'My union, Tuppence, my union! It does not permit me to work before 11 a.m.'

'Tommy, do you want something thrown at you? It is absolutely essential that we should without delay map out a plan of campaign.'

'Hear, hear!'

'Well, let's do it.'

Tommy laid his paper finally aside. 'There's something of the simplicity of the truly great mind about you, Tuppence. Fire ahead. I'm listening.'

'To begin with,' said Tuppence, 'what have we to go upon?'

'Absolutely nothing,' said Tommy cheerily.

'Wrong!' Tuppence wagged an energetic finger. 'We have two distinct clues.'

'What are they?'

'First clue, we know one of the gang.'

'Whittington?'

'Yes. I'd recognize him anywhere.'

'Hum,' said Tommy doubtfully. 'I don't call that much of a clue. You don't know where to look for him, and it's about a thousand to one against your running against him by accident.'

'I'm not so sure about that,' replied Tuppence thoughtfully. 'I've often noticed that once coincidences start happening they go on happening in the most extraordinary way. I dare say it's some natural law that we haven't found out. Still, as you say, we can't rely on that. But there *are* places in London where simply everyone is bound to turn up sooner or later. Piccadilly Circus, for instance. One of my ideas was to take up my stand there every day with a tray of flags.'

'What about meals?' inquired the practical Tommy.

'How like a man! What does mere food matter?'

'That's all very well. You've just had a thundering good breakfast. No one's got a better appetite than you have, Tuppence, and by tea-time you'd be eating the flags, pins and all. But, honestly, I don't think much of the idea. Whittington mayn't be in London at all.'

'That's true. Anyway, I think clue No. 2 is more promising.'

'Let's hear it.'

'It's nothing much. Only a Christian name – Rita. Whittington mentioned it that day.'

'Are you proposing a third advertisement: Wanted, female crook, answering to the name of Rita?'

'I am not. I propose to reason in a logical manner. That man, Danvers, was shadowed on the way over, wasn't he? And it's more likely to have been a woman than a man –'

'I don't see that at all.'

'I am absolutely certain that it would be a woman, and a good-looking one,' replied Tuppence calmly.

'On these technical points I bow to your decision,' murmured Mr Beresford.

'Now, obviously, this woman, whoever she was, was saved.'

'How do you make that out?'

'If she wasn't, how would they have known Jane Finn had got the papers?'

'Correct. Proceed, O Sherlock!'

'Now there's just a chance, I admit it's only a chance, that this woman may have been "Rita".'

'And if so?'

'If so, we've got to hunt through the survivors of the *Lusitania* till we find her.'

'Then the first thing is to get a list of the survivors.'

'I've got it. I wrote a long list of things I wanted to know, and sent it to Mr Carter. I got his reply this morning, and among other things it encloses the official statement of those saved from the *Lusitania*. How's that for clever little Tuppence?'

'Full marks for industry, zero for modesty. But the great point is, is there a "Rita" on the list?'

'That's just what I don't know,' confessed Tuppence.

'Don't know?'

'Yes, look here.' Together they bent over the list. 'You see, very few Christian names are given. They're nearly all Mrs or Miss.'

Tommy nodded.

'That complicates matters,' he murmured thoughtfully.

Tuppence gave her characteristic 'terrier' shake.

'Well, we've just got to get down to it, that's all. We'll start with the London area. Just note down the addresses of any of the females who live in London or roundabout, while I put on my hat.'

Five minutes later the young couple emerged into Piccadilly, and a few seconds later a taxi was bearing them to The Laurels, Glendower Road, N.7., the residence of Mrs Edgar Keith, whose name figured first in a list of seven reposing in Tommy's pocket-book.

The Laurels was a dilapidated house, standing back from the road with a few grimy bushes to support the fiction of a front garden. Tommy paid off the taxi, and accompanied Tuppence to the front door bell. As she was about to ring it, he arrested her hand.

'What are you going to say?'

'What am I going to say? Why, I shall say – Oh dear, I don't know. It's very awkward.'

'I thought as much,' said Tommy with satisfaction. 'How like a woman! No foresight! Now just stand aside, and see how easily the mere male deals with the situation.' He pressed the bell. Tuppence withdrew to a suitable spot.

A slatternly-looking servant, with an extremely dirty face and a pair of eyes that did not match, answered the door.

Tommy had produced a notebook and pencil.

'Good morning,' he said briskly and cheerfully. 'From the Hampstead Borough Council. The New Voting Register. Mrs Edgar Keith lives here, does she not?'

'Yaas,' said the servant.

'Christian name?' asked Tommy, his pencil poised.

'Missus's? Eleanor Jane.'

'Eleanor,' spelt Tommy. 'Any sons or daughters over twenty-one?'

'Naow.'

'Thank you.' Tommy closed the notebook with a brisk snap. 'Good morning.'

The servant volunteered her first remark:

'I thought perhaps as you'd come about the gas,' she observed cryptically, and shut the door.

Tommy rejoined his accomplice.

'You see, Tuppence,' he observed. 'Child's play to the masculine mind.'

'I don't mind admitting that for once you've scored handsomely. I should never have thought of that.'

'Good wheeze, wasn't it? And we can repeat it *ad lib.*'

Lunch-time found the young couple attacking steak and chips in an obscure hostelry with avidity. They had collected a Gladys Mary and a Marjorie, been baffled by one change of address, and had been forced to listen to a long lecture on universal suffrage from a vivacious American lady whose Christian name had proved to be Sadie.

'Ah!' said Tommy, imbibing a long draught of beer. 'I feel better. Where's the next draw?'

The notebook lay on the table between them. Tuppence picked it up.

'Mrs Vandemeyer,' she read, '20 South Audley Mansions. Miss Wheeler, 43 Clapington Road, Battersea. She's a lady's maid, as far as I remember, so probably won't be there, and, anyway, she's not likely.'

'Then the Mayfair lady is clearly indicated as the first port of call.'

'Tommy, I'm getting discouraged.'

'Buck up, old bean. We always knew it was an outside chance. And, anyway, we're only starting. If we draw a blank in London, there's a fine tour of England, Ireland and Scotland before us.'

'True,' said Tuppence, her flagging spirits reviving. 'And all expenses paid! But, oh, Tommy, I do like things to happen quickly. So far, adventure has succeeded adventure, but this morning has been dull as dull.'

'You must stifle this longing for vulgar sensation, Tuppence. Remember that if Mr Brown is all he is reported to be, it's a wonder that he has not ere now done us to death. That's a good sentence, quite a literary flavour about it.'

'You're really more conceited than I am – with less excuse! Ahem! But it certainly is queer that Mr Brown has not yet wreaked vengeance upon us. (You see, I can do it too.) We pass on our way unscathed.'

'Perhaps he doesn't think us worth bothering about,' suggested the young man simply.

Tuppence received the remark with great disfavour.

'How horrid you are, Tommy. Just as though we didn't count.'

'Sorry, Tuppence. What I meant was that we work like moles in the dark, and that he has no suspicion of our nefarious schemes. Ha ha!'

'Ha ha!' echoed Tuppence approvingly, as she rose.

South Audley Mansions was an imposing-looking block of flats just off Park Lane. No. 20 was on the second floor.

Tommy had by this time the glibness born of practice. He rattled off the formula to the elderly woman, looking more like a housekeeper than a servant, who opened the door to him.

'Christian name?'

'Margaret.'

Tommy spelt it, but the other interrupted him.

'No, *g u e*.'

'Oh, Marguerite; French way, I see.' He paused, then plunged boldly. 'We had her down as Rita Vandermeyer, but I suppose that's correct?'

'She's mostly called that, sir, but Marguerite's her name.'

'Thank you. That's all. Good morning.'

Hardly able to contain his excitement, Tommy hurried down the stairs. Tuppence was waiting at the angle of the turn.

'You heard?'

'Yes. Oh, *Tommy*!'

Tommy squeezed her arm sympathetically.

'I know, old thing. I feel the same.'

'It's – it's so lovely to think of things – and then for them really to happen!' cried Tuppence enthusiastically.

Her hand was still in Tommy's. They had reached the entrance hall. There were footsteps on the stairs above them, and voices.

Suddenly, to Tommy's complete surprise, Tuppence dragged him into the little space by the side of the lift where the shadow was deepest.

'What the –'

'Hush!'

Two men came down the stairs and passed out through the entrance. Tuppence's hand closed tighter on Tommy's arm.

'Quick – follow them. I daren't. He might recognize me. I don't know who the other man is, but the bigger of the two was Whittington.'

CHAPTER 7

THE HOUSE IN SOHO

Whittington and his companion were walking at a good pace. Tommy started in pursuit at once, and was in time to see them turn the corner of the street. His vigorous strides soon enabled him to gain upon them, and by the time he, in his turn, reached the corner the distance between them was sensibly lessened. The small Mayfair streets were comparatively deserted, and he judged it wise to content himself with keeping them in sight.

The sport was a new one to him. Though familiar with the technicalities from a course of novel reading, he had never before attempted to 'follow' anyone, and it appeared to him at once that, in actual practice, the proceeding was fraught with difficulties. Supposing, for instance, that they should suddenly hail a taxi? In books, you simply leapt into another, promised the driver a sovereign – or its modern equivalent – and there you were. In actual fact, Tommy foresaw that it was extremely likely there would be no second taxi. Therefore he would have to run. What happened in actual fact to a young man who ran incessantly and persistently through the London streets? In a main road he might hope to create the illusion that he was merely running for a bus. But in these obscure aristocratic byways he could not but feel that an officious policeman might stop him to explain matters.

At this juncture in his thoughts a taxi with flag erect turned the corner of the street ahead. Tommy held his breath. Would they hail it?

He drew a sigh of relief as they allowed it to pass unchallenged. Their course was a zigzag one designed to bring them as quickly as possible to Oxford Street. When at length they turned into it, proceeding in an easterly direction, Tommy slightly increased his pace. Little by little he gained upon them. On the crowded pavement there was little chance of his attracting their notice, and he was anxious if possible to catch a word or two of their conversation. In this he was completely foiled: they spoke low and the din of the traffic drowned their voices effectually.

Just before the Bond Street Tube station they crossed the road, Tommy, unperceived, faithfully at their heels, and entered the big Lyons'. There they went up to the first floor, and sat at a small table in the window. It was late, and the place was thinning out. Tommy took a seat at the table next to them sitting directly behind Whittington in case of recognition. On the other hand, he had a full view of the second man and studied him attentively. He was fair, with a weak, unpleasant face, and Tommy put him down as being either a Russian or a Pole. He was probably about fifty years of age, his shoulders cringed a little as he talked, and his eyes, small and crafty, shifted unceasingly.

Having already lunched heartily, Tommy contented himself with ordering a Welsh rarebit and a cup of coffee. Whittington ordered a substantial lunch for himself and his companion; then, as the waitress withdrew, he moved his chair a little closer to the table and began to talk earnestly in a low voice. The other man joined in. Listen as he would, Tommy could only catch a word here and there; but the gist of it seemed to be some directions or orders which the big man was impressing on his companion, and with which the latter seemed from time to time to disagree. Whittington addressed the other as Boris.

Tommy caught the word 'Ireland' several times, also 'propaganda', but of Jane Finn there was no mention. Suddenly, in a lull in the clatter of the room, he got one phrase entire. Whittington was speaking. 'Ah, but you don't know Flossie.

She's a marvel. An archbishop would swear she was his own mother. She gets the voice right every time, and that's really the principal thing.'

Tommy did not hear Boris's reply, but in response to it Whittington said something that sounded like: 'of course – only in an emergency . . .'

Then he lost the thread again. But presently the phrases became distinct again, whether because the other two had insensibly raised their voices, or because Tommy's ears were getting more attuned, he could not tell. But two words certainly had a most stimulating effect upon the listener. They were uttered by Boris and they were: 'Mr Brown.'

Whittington seemed to remonstrate with him, but he merely laughed.

'Why not, my friend? It is a name most respectable – most common. Did he not choose it for that reason? Ah, I should like to meet him – Mr Brown.'

There was a steely ring in Whittington's voice as he replied:

'Who knows? You may have met him already.'

'Bah!' retorted the other. 'That is children's talk – a fable for the police. Do you know what I say to myself sometimes? That he is a fable invented by the Inner Ring, a bogy to frighten us with. It might be so.'

'And it might not.'

'I wonder . . . or is it indeed true that he is with us and amongst us, unknown to all but a chosen few? If so, he keeps his secret well. And the idea is a good one, yes. We never know. We look at each other – *one of us is Mr Brown* – which? He commands – but also he serves. Among us – in the midst of us. And no one knows which he is . . .'

With an effort the Russian shook off the vagary of his fancy. He looked at his watch.

'Yes,' said Whittington. 'We might as well go.'

He called the waitress and asked for his bill. Tommy did likewise, and a few moments later was following the two men down the stairs.

Outside, Whittington hailed a taxi, and directed the driver to Waterloo.

Taxis were plentiful here, and before Whittington's had driven off another was drawing up to the curb in obedience to Tommy's peremptory hand.

'Follow that other taxi,' directed the young man. 'Don't lose it.'

The elderly chauffeur showed no interest. He merely grunted and jerked down his flag. The drive was uneventful. Tommy's taxi came to rest at the departure platform just after Whittington's. Tommy was behind him at the booking-office. He took a first-class single to Bournemouth, Tommy did the same. As he emerged, Boris remarked, glancing up at the clock: 'You are early. You have nearly half an hour.'

Boris's words had aroused a new train of thought in Tommy's mind. Clearly Whittington was making the journey alone, while the other remained in London. Therefore he was left with a choice as to which he would follow. Obviously, he could not follow both of them unless – Like Boris, he glanced up at the clock, and then to the announcement board of the trains. The Bournemouth train left at 3.30. It was now ten past. Whittington and Boris were walking up and down by the bookstall. He gave one doubtful look at them, then hurried into an adjacent telephone box. He dared not waste time in trying to get hold of Tuppence. In all probability she was still in the neighbourhood of South Audley Mansions. But there remained another ally. He rang up the Ritz and asked for Julius Hersheimmer. There was a click and a buzz. Oh, if only the young American was in his room! There was another click, and then 'Hello' in unmistakable accents came over the wire.

'That you, Hersheimmer? Beresford speaking. I'm at Waterloo. I've followed Whittington and another man here. No time to explain. Whittington's off to Bournemouth by the 3.30. Can you get here by then?'

The reply was reassuring.

'Sure. I'll hustle.'

The telephone rang off. Tommy put back the receiver with a sigh of relief. His opinion of Julius's power of hustling was high. He felt instinctively that the American would arrive in time.

Whittington and Boris were still where he had left them. If Boris remained to see his friend off, all was well. Then Tommy fingered his pocket thoughtfully. In spite of the *carte blanche* assured to him, he had not yet acquired the habit of going about with any considerable sum of money on him. The taking of the first-class ticket to Bournemouth had left him with only a few shillings in his pocket. It was to be hoped that Julius would arrive better provided.

In the meantime, the minutes were creeping by: 3.15, 3.20, 3.25, 3.27. Supposing Julius did not get there in time. 3.29. . . . Doors were banging. Tommy felt cold waves of despair pass over him. Then a hand fell on his shoulder.

'Here I am, son. Your British traffic beats description! Put me wise to the crooks right away.'

'That's Whittington – there, getting in now, that big dark man. The other is the foreign chap he's talking to.'

'I'm on to them. Which of the two is my bird?'

Tommy had thought out this question.

'Got any money with you?'

Julius shook his head, and Tommy's face fell.

'I guess I haven't more than three or four hundred dollars with me at the moment,' explained the American.

Tommy gave a faint whoop of relief.

'Oh, Lord, you millionaires! You don't talk the same language! Climb aboard the lugger. Here's your ticket. Whittington's your man.'

'Me for Whittington!' said Julius darkly. The train was just starting as he swung himself aboard. 'So long, Tommy.' The train slid out of the station.

Tommy drew a deep breath. The man Boris was coming along the platform towards him. Tommy allowed him to pass and then took up the chase once more.

From Waterloo Boris took the Tube as far as Piccadilly Circus. Then he walked up Shaftesbury Avenue, finally turning off into the maze of mean streets round Soho. Tommy followed him at a judicious distance.

They reached at length a small, dilapidated square. The houses there had a sinister air in the midst of their dirt and decay. Boris looked round, and Tommy drew back into the shelter of a friendly porch. The place was almost deserted. It was a cul-de-sac, and consequently no traffic passed that way. The stealthy way the other had looked round stimulated Tommy's imagination. From the shelter of the doorway he watched him go up the steps of a particularly evil-looking house and rap sharply, with a peculiar rhythm, on the door. It was opened promptly, he said a word or two to the doorkeeper, then passed inside. The door was shut to again.

It was at this juncture that Tommy lost his head. What he ought to have done, what any sane man would have done, was to remain patiently where he was and wait for his man to come out again. What he did do was entirely foreign to the sober common sense which was, as a rule, his leading characteristic. Something, as he expressed it, seemed to snap in his brain. Without a moment's pause for reflection he, too, went up the steps, and reproduced as far as he was able the peculiar knock.

The door swung open with the same promptness as before. A villainous-faced man with close-cropped hair stood in the doorway.

'Well?' he grunted.

It was at that moment that the full realization of his folly began to come home to Tommy. But he dared not hesitate. He seized at the first words that came into his mind.

'Mr Brown?' he said.

To his surprise the man stood aside.

'Upstairs,' he said, jerking his thumb over his shoulder, 'second door on your left.'

CHAPTER 8

THE ADVENTURES OF TOMMY

Taken aback though he was by the man's words, Tommy did not hesitate. If audacity had successfully carried him so far, it was to be hoped it would carry him yet farther. He quietly passed into the house and mounted the ramshackle staircase. Everything in the house was filthy beyond words. The grimy paper, of a pattern now indistinguishable, hung in loose festoons from the wall. In every angle was a grey mass of cobweb.

Tommy proceeded leisurely. By the time he reached the bend of the staircase, he had heard the man below disappear into a back room. Clearly no suspicion attached to him as yet. To come to the house and ask for 'Mr Brown' appeared indeed to be a reasonable and natural proceeding.

At the top of the stairs Tommy halted to consider his next move. In front of him ran a narrow passage, with doors opening on either side of it. From the one nearest him on the left came a low murmur of voices. It was this room which he had been directed to enter. But what held his glance fascinated was a small recess immediately on his right, half concealed by a torn velvet curtain. It was directly opposite the left-hand door and, owing to its angle, it also commanded a good view of the upper part of the staircase. As a hiding-place for one or, at a pinch, two men, it was ideal, being about two feet deep and three feet wide. It attracted Tommy mightily. He thought things over in his usual slow and steady way, deciding that the mention of 'Mr Brown' was not a request for an individual, but in all probability a password used by the gang. His lucky use of it had gained him admission. So far he had aroused no suspicion. But he must decide quickly on his next step.

Suppose he were boldly to enter the room on the left of the passage. Would the mere fact of his having been admitted to the house be sufficient? Perhaps a further password would be required, or, at any rate, some proof of identity. The doorkeeper clearly did not know all the members of the gang by sight, but it might be different upstairs. On the whole it seemed to him that luck had served him very well so far, but that there was such a thing as trusting it too far. To enter that room was a colossal risk. He could not hope to sustain his part indefinitely; sooner or later he was almost bound to betray himself, and then he would have thrown away a vital chance in mere foolhardiness.

A repetition of the signal sounded on the door below, and Tommy, his mind made up, slipped quickly into the recess, and cautiously drew the curtain farther across so that it shielded him completely from sight. There were several rents and slits in the ancient material which afforded him a good view. He would watch events, and any time he chose could, after all, join the assembly, modelling his behaviour on that of the new arrival.

The man who came up the staircase with a furtive, soft-footed tread was quite unknown to Tommy. He was obviously of the very dregs of society. The low, beetling brows and the criminal jaw, the bestiality of the whole countenance were new to the young man, though he was of a type that Scotland Yard would have recognized at a glance.

The man passed the recess, breathing heavily as he went. He stopped at the door opposite, and gave a repetition of the signal knock. A voice inside called out something, and the man opened the door and passed in, affording Tommy a momentary glimpse of the room inside. He thought there must be about four or five people seated round a long table that took up most of the space, but his attention was caught and held by a tall man with close-cropped hair and a short, pointed, naval-looking beard, who sat at the head of the table with papers in front of him. As the newcomer entered he glanced up, and with a correct but curiously precise enunciation, which attracted Tommy's notice, he asked: 'Your number, comrade?'

'Fourteen, guv'nor,' replied the other hoarsely.

'Correct.'

The door shut again.

'If that isn't a Hun, I'm a Dutchman!' said Tommy to himself. 'And running the show darned systematically, too – as they always do. Lucky I didn't roll in. I'd have given the wrong number, and there would have been the deuce to pay. No, this is the place for me. Hullo, here's another knock.'

This visitor proved to be of an entirely different type to the last. Tommy recognized in him an Irish Sinn Feiner. Certainly Mr Brown's organization was a far-reaching concern. The common criminal, the well-bred Irish gentleman, the pale Russian, and the efficient German master of the ceremonies! Truly a strange and sinister gathering! Who was this man who held in his fingers these curiously variegated links of an unknown chain?

In this case, the procedure was exactly the same. The signal knock, the demand for a number, and the reply 'Correct.'

Two knocks followed in quick succession on the door below. The first man was quite unknown to Tommy, who put him down as a city clerk. A quiet, intelligent-looking man, rather shabbily dressed. The second was of the working classes, and his face was vaguely familiar to the young man.

Three minutes later came another, a man of commanding appearance, exquisitely dressed, and evidently well born. His face, again, was not unknown to the watcher, though he could not for the moment put a name to it.

After his arrival there was a long wait. In fact, Tommy concluded that the gathering was now complete, and was just cautiously creeping out from his hiding-place, when another knock sent him scuttling back to cover.

This last-comer came up the stairs so quietly that he was almost abreast of Tommy before the young man had realized his presence.

He was a small man, very pale, with a gentle, almost womanish air. The angle of the cheek-bones hinted at his Slavonic ancestry, otherwise there was nothing to indicate his nationality. As he passed the recess, he turned his head slowly. The strange light eyes seemed to burn through the curtain; Tommy could hardly believe that the man did not know he was there and in spite of himself he shivered. He was no more fanciful than the majority of young Englishmen, but he could not rid himself of the impression that some unusually potent force emanated from the man. The creature reminded him of a venomous snake.

A moment later his impression was proved correct. The newcomer knocked on the door as all had done, but his reception was very different. The bearded man rose to his feet, and all the others followed suit. The German came forward and shook hands. His heels clicked together.

'We are honoured,' he said. 'We are greatly honoured. I much feared that it would be impossible.'

The other answered in a low voice that had a kind of hiss in it:

'There were difficulties. It will not be possible again, I fear. But one meeting is essential – to define my policy. I can do nothing without – Mr Brown. He is here?'

The change in the German's air was audible as he replied with slight hesitation:

'We have received a message. It is impossible for him to be present in person.' He stopped, giving a curious impression of having left the sentence unfinished.

A very slow smile overspread the face of the other. He looked round at a circle of uneasy faces.

'Ah! I understand. I have read of his methods. He works in the dark and trusts no one. But, all the same, it is possible that he is among us now . . .' He looked round him again, and again that expression of fear swept over the group. Each man seemed to be eyeing his neighbour doubtfully.

The Russian tapped his cheek.

'So be it. Let us proceed.'

The German seemed to pull himself together. He indicated the place he had been occupying at the head of the table. The Russian demurred, but the other insisted.

'It is the only possible place,' he said, 'for – Number One. Perhaps Number Fourteen will shut the door!'

In another moment Tommy was once more confronting bare wooden panels, and the voices within had sunk once more to a mere undistinguishable murmur. Tommy became restive. The conversation he had overheard had stimulated his curiosity. He felt that, by hook or by crook, he must hear more.

There was no sound from below, and it did not seem likely that the doorkeeper would come upstairs. After listening intently for a minute or two, he put his head round the curtain. The passage was deserted. Tommy bent down and removed his shoes, then, leaving them behind the curtain, he walked gingerly out on his stockinged feet, and kneeling down by the closed door he laid his ear cautiously to the crack. To his intense annoyance he could distinguish little more; just a chance word here and there if a voice was raised, which merely served to whet his curiosity still further.

He eyed the handle of the door tentatively. Could he turn it by degrees so gently and imperceptibly that those in the room would notice nothing? He decided that with great care it could be done. Very slowly, a fraction of an inch at a time, he moved it round, holding his breath in his excessive care. A little more – a little more still – would it never be finished? Ah! at last it would turn no farther.

He stayed so for a minute or two, then drew a deep breath, and pressed it ever so slightly inward. The door did not budge. Tommy was annoyed. If he had to use too much force, it would almost certainly creak. He waited until the voices rose a little, then he tried again. Still nothing happened. He increased the pressure. Had the beastly thing stuck? Finally, in desperation, he pushed with all his might. But the door remained firm, and at last the truth dawned upon him. It was locked or bolted on the inside.

For a moment or two Tommy's indignation got the better of him.

'Well, I'm damned!' he said. 'What a dirty trick!'

As his indignation cooled, he prepared to face the situation. Clearly the first thing to be done was to restore the handle to its original position. If he let it go suddenly, the men inside would be almost certain to notice it, so with the same infinite pains he reversed his former tactics. All went well, and with a sigh of relief the young man rose to his feet. There was a certain bulldog tenacity about Tommy that made him slow to admit defeat. Checkmated for the moment, he was far from abandoning the conflict. He still intended to hear what was going on in the locked room. As one plan had failed, he must hunt about for another.

He looked round him. A little farther along the passage on the left was a second door. He slipped silently along to it. He listened for a moment or two, then tried the handle. It yielded, and he slipped inside.

The room, which was untenanted, was furnished as a bedroom. Like everything else in the house, the furniture was falling to pieces, and the dirt was, if anything, more abundant.

But what interested Tommy was the thing he had hoped to find, a communicating door between the two rooms, up on the left by the window. Carefully closing the door into the passage behind him, he stepped across to the other and examined it closely. The bolt was shot across it. It was very rusty, and had clearly not been used for some time. By gently wriggling it to and fro, Tommy managed to draw it back without making too much noise. Then he repeated his former manœuvres with the handle – this time with complete success. The door swung open – a crack, a mere fraction, but enough for Tommy to hear what went on. There was a velvet *portière* on the inside of this door which prevented him from seeing, but he was able to recognize the voices with a reasonable amount of accuracy.

The Sinn Feiner was speaking. His rich Irish voice was unmistakable:

'That's all very well. But more money is essential. No money – no results!'

Another voice which Tommy rather thought was that of Boris replied:

'Will you guarantee that there *are* results?'

'In a month from now – sooner or later as you wish – I will guarantee you such a reign of terror in Ireland as shall shake the British Empire to its foundations.'

There was a pause, and then came the soft, sibilant accents of Number One:

'Good! You shall have the money. Boris, you will see to that.'

Boris asked a question:

'Via the Irish Americans, and Mr Potter as usual?'

'I guess that'll be all right!' said a new voice, with a transatlantic intonation, 'though I'd like to point out, here and now, that things are getting a mite difficult. There's not the sympathy there was, and a growing disposition to let the Irish settle their own affairs without interference from America.'

Tommy felt that Boris had shrugged his shoulders as he answered:

'Does that matter, since the money only nominally comes from the States?'

'The chief difficulty is the landing of the ammunition,' said the Sinn Feiner. 'The money is conveyed in easily enough – thanks to our colleague here.'

Another voice, which Tommy fancied was that of the tall, commanding-looking man whose face had seemed familiar to him, said:

'Think of the feelings of Belfast if they could hear you!'

'That is settled, then,' said the sibilant tones. 'Now, in the matter of the loan to an English newspaper, you have arranged the details satisfactorily, Boris?'

'I think so.'

'That is good. An official denial from Moscow will be forthcoming if necessary.'

There was a pause, and then the clear voice of the German broke the silence:

'I am directed by – Mr Brown, to place the summaries of the reports from the different unions before you. That of the miners is most satisfactory. We must hold back the railways. There may be trouble with the A.S.E.'

For a long time there was a silence, broken only by the rustle of papers and an occasional word of explanation from the German.

Then Tommy heard the light tap-tap of fingers drumming on the table.

'And – the date, my friend?' said Number One.

'The 29th.'

The Russian seemed to consider.

'That is rather soon.'

'I know. But it was settled by the principal Labour leaders, and we cannot seem to interfere too much. They must believe it to be entirely their own show.'

The Russian laughed softly, as though amused.

'Yes, yes,' he said. 'That is true. They must have no inkling that we are using them for our own ends. They are honest men – and that is their value to us. It is curious – but you cannot make a revolution without honest men. The instinct of the populace is infallible.' He paused, and then repeated, as though the phrase pleased him: 'Every revolution has had its honest men. They are soon disposed of afterwards.'

There was a sinister note in his voice.

The German resumed:

'Clymes must go. He is too far-seeing. Number Fourteen will see to that.'

There was a hoarse murmur.

'That's all right, guv'nor.' And then after a moment or two: 'Suppose I'm nabbed.'

'You will have the best legal talent to defend you,' replied the German quietly. 'But in any case you will wear gloves fitted with the finger-prints of a notorious housebreaker. You have little to fear.'

'Oh, I ain't afraid, guv'nor. All for the good of the cause. The streets is going to run with blood, so they say.' He spoke with a grim relish. 'Dreams of it, sometimes, I does. And diamonds and pearls rolling about in the gutter for anyone to pick up!'

Tommy heard a chair shifted. Then Number One spoke:

'Then all is arranged. We are assured of success?'

'I – I think so.' But the German spoke with less than his usual confidence.

Number One's voice held suddenly a dangerous quality:

'What has gone wrong?'

'Nothing; but –'

'But what?'

'The labour leaders. Without them, as you say, we can do nothing. If they do not declare a general strike on the 29th –'

'Why should they not?'

'As you've said, they're honest. And, in spite of everything we've done to discredit the Government in their eyes, I'm not sure that they haven't got a sneaking faith and belief in it.'

'But –'

'I know. They abuse it unceasingly. But, on the whole, public opinion swings to the side of the Government. They will not go against it.'

Again the Russian's fingers drummed on the table.

'To the point, my friend. I was given to understand that there was a certain document in existence which assured success.'

'That is so. If that document were placed before the leaders, the result would be immediate. They would publish it broadcast throughout England, and declare for the revolution without a moment's hesitation. The Government would be broken finally and completely.'

'Then what more do you want?'

'The document itself,' said the German bluntly.

'Ah! It is not in your possession? But you know where it is?'

'No.'

'Does anyone know where it is?'

'One person – perhaps. And we are not sure of that even.'

'Who is this person?'

'A girl.'

Tommy held his breath.

'A girl?' The Russian's voice rose contemptuously. 'And you have not made her speak? In Russia we have ways of making a girl talk.'

'This case is different,' said the German sullenly.

'How – different?' He paused a moment, then went on: 'Where is the girl now?'

'The girl?'

'Yes.'

'She is –'

But Tommy heard no more. A crashing blow descended on his head, and all was darkness.

CHAPTER 9

TUPPENCE ENTERS DOMESTIC SERVICE

When Tommy set forth on the trail of the two men, it took all Tuppence's self-command to refrain from accompanying him. However, she contained herself as best she might, consoled by the reflection that her reasoning had been justified by events. The two men had undoubtedly come from the second-floor flat, and that one slender thread of the name 'Rita' had set the Young Adventurers once more upon the track of the abductors of Jane Finn.

The question was what to do next? Tuppence hated letting the grass grow under her feet. Tommy was amply employed, and debarred from joining him in the chase, the girl felt at a loose end. She retraced her steps to the entrance hall of the mansions. It was now tenanted by a small lift-boy, who was polishing brass fittings, and whistling the latest air with a good deal of vigour and a reasonable amount of accuracy.

He glanced round at Tuppence's entry. There was a certain amount of the *gamin* element in the girl, at all events she invariably got on well with small boys. A sympathetic bond seemed instantly to be formed. She reflected that an ally in the enemy's camp, so to speak, was not to be despised.

'Well, William,' she remarked cheerfully, in the best approved hospital-early-morning style, 'getting a good shine up?'

The boy grinned responsively.

'Albert, miss,' he corrected.

'Albert be it,' said Tuppence. She glanced mysteriously round the hall. The effect was purposely a broad one in case Albert should miss it. She leaned towards the boy and dropped her voice: 'I want a word with you, Albert.'

Albert ceased operations on the fittings and opened his mouth slightly.

'Look! Do you know what this is?' With dramatic gesture she flung back the left side of her coat and exposed a small enamelled badge. It was extremely unlikely that Albert would have any knowledge of it – indeed, it would have been fatal for Tuppence's plans, since the badge in question was the device of a local training corps originated by the archdeacon in the early days of the war. Its presence in Tuppence's coat was due to the fact that she had used it for pinning in some flowers a day or two before. But Tuppence had sharp eyes, and had noted the corner of a threepenny detective novel protruding from Albert's pocket, and the immediate enlargement of his eyes told her that her tactics were good, and that the fish would rise to the bait.

'American Detective Force!' she hissed.

Albert fell for it.

'Lord!' he murmured ecstatically.

Tuppence nodded at him with the air of one who has established a thorough understanding.

'Know who I'm after?' she inquired genially.

Albert, still round-eyed, demanded breathlessly:

'One of the flats?'

Tuppence nodded and jerked a thumb up the stairs.

'No. 20. Calls herself Vandemeyer. Vandemeyer! Ha! ha!'

Albert's hand stole to his pocket.

'A crook?' he queried eagerly.

'A crook? I should say so. Ready Rita they call her in the States.'

'Ready Rita,' repeated Albert deliriously. 'Oh, ain't it just like the pictures!'

It was. Tuppence was a great frequenter of the cinema.

'Annie always said as how she was a bad lot,' continued the boy.

'Who's Annie?' inquired Tuppence idly.

''Ouse-parlourmaid. She's leaving today. Many's the time Annie's said to me: "Mark my words, Albert, I wouldn't wonder if the police was to come after her one of these days." Just like that. But she's a stunner to look at, ain't she?'

'She's some peach,' allowed Tuppence carefully. 'Finds it useful in her lay-out, you bet. Has she been wearing any of the emeralds, by the way?'

'Emeralds? Them's the green stones, isn't they?'

Tuppence nodded.

'That's what we're after her for. You know old man Rysdale?'

Albert shook his head.

'Peter B. Rysdale, the oil king?'

'It seems sort of familiar to me.'

'The sparklers belonged to him. Finest collection of emeralds in the world. Worth a million dollars!'

'Lumme!' came ecstatically from Albert. 'It sounds more like the pictures every minute.'

Tuppence smiled, gratified at the success of her efforts.

'We haven't exactly proved it yet. But we're after her. And' – she produced a long drawn-out wink – 'I guess she won't get away with the goods this time.'

Albert uttered another ejaculation indicative of delight.

'Mind you, sonny, not a word of this,' said Tuppence suddenly. 'I guess I oughtn't to have put you wise, but in the States we know a real smart lad when we see one.'

'I'll not breathe a word,' protested Albert eagerly. 'Ain't there anything I could do? A bit of shadowing, maybe, or suchlike?'

Tuppence affected to consider, then shook her head.

'Not at the moment, but I'll bear you in mind, son. What's this about the girl you say is leaving?'

'Annie? Regular turn up, they 'ad. As Annie said, servants is someone nowadays, and to be treated accordingly, and, what with her passing the word round, she won't find it so easy to get another.'

'Won't she?' said Tuppence thoughtfully. 'I wonder –'

An idea was dawning in her brain. She thought a minute or two, then tapped Albert on the shoulder.

'See here, son, my brain's got busy. How would it be if you mentioned that you'd got a young cousin, or a friend of yours had, that might suit the place. You get me?'

'I'm there,' said Albert instantly. 'You leave it to me, miss, and I'll fix the whole thing up in two ticks.'

'Some lad!' commented Tuppence, with a nod of approval. 'You might say that the young woman could come right away. You let me know, and if it's O.K. I'll be round tomorrow at eleven o'clock.'

'Where am I to let you know to?'

'Ritz,' replied Tuppence laconically. 'Name of Cowley.'

Albert eyed her enviously.

'It must be a good job, this tec business.'

'It sure is,' drawled Tuppence, 'especially when old man Rysdale backs the bill. But don't fret, son. If this goes well, you shall come in on the ground floor.'

With which promise she took leave of her new ally, and walked briskly away from South Audley Mansions, well pleased with her morning's work.

But there was no time to be lost. She went straight back to the Ritz and wrote a few brief words to Mr Carter. Having dispatched this, and Tommy not having yet returned – which did not surprise her – she started off on a shopping expedition which, with an interval for tea and assorted creamy cakes, occupied her until well after six o'clock, and she returned to the hotel jaded, but satisfied with her purchases. Starting with a cheap clothing store, and passing through one or two second-hand establishments, she had finished the day at a well-known hairdresser's. Now, in the seclusion of her bedroom, she unwrapped that final purchase. Five minutes later she smiled contentedly at her reflection in the glass. With an actress's pencil she had slightly altered the line of her eyebrows, and that, taken in conjunction with the new luxuriant growth of fair hair above, so changed her appearance that she felt confident that even if she came face to face with Whittington he would not recognize her. She would wear elevators in her shoes, and the cap and apron would be an even more valuable disguise. From hospital experience she knew only too well that a nurse out of uniform is frequently unrecognized by her patients.

'Yes,' said Tuppence aloud, nodding at the pert reflection in the glass, 'you'll do.' She then resumed her normal appearance.

Dinner was a solitary meal. Tuppence was rather surprised at Tommy's non-return. Julius, too, was absent – but that to the girl's mind was more easily explained. His 'hustling' activities were not confined to London, and his abrupt appearances and disappearances were fully accepted by the Young Adventurers as part of the day's work. It was quite on the cards that Julius P. Hersheimmer had left for Constantinople at a moment's notice if he fancied that a clue to his cousin's disappearance was to be found there. The energetic young man had succeeded in making the lives of several Scotland Yard men unbearable to them, and the telephone girls at the Admiralty had learned to know and dread the familiar 'Hullo!' He had spent three hours in Paris hustling the Prefecture, and had returned from there imbued with the idea, possibly inspired by a weary French official, that the true clue to the mystery was to be found in Ireland.

'I dare say he's dashed off there now,' thought Tuppence. 'All very well, but this is very dull for *me*! Here I am bursting with news, and absolutely no one to tell it to! Tommy might have wired, or something. I wonder where he is. Anyway, he can't have "lost the trail" as they say. That reminds me –' And Miss Cowley broke off in her meditations, and summoned a small boy.

Ten minutes later the lady was ensconced comfortably on her bed, smoking cigarettes and deep in the perusal of *Barnaby Williams, the Boy Detective*, which, with other threepenny works of lurid fiction, she had sent out to purchase. She felt, and rightly, that before the strain of attempting further intercourse with Albert, it would be as well to fortify herself with a good supply of local colour.

The morning brought a note from Mr Carter:

Dear Miss Tuppence

You have made a splendid start, and I congratulate you. I feel, though, that I should like to point out to you once more the risks you are running, especially if you pursue the course you indicate. Those people are absolutely desperate and incapable of either mercy or pity. I feel that you probably underestimate the danger, and therefore warn you again that I can promise you no protection. You have given us valuable information, and if you choose to withdraw now no one could blame you. At any rate, think the matter over well before you decide.

If, in spite of my warnings, you make up your mind to go through with it, you will find everything arranged. You have lived for two years with Miss Dufferin, the Parsonage, Llanelly, and Mrs Vandemeyer can apply to her for a reference.

May I be permitted a word or two of advice? Stick as near to the truth as possible – it minimizes the danger of 'slips'. I suggest that you should represent yourself to be what you are, a former V.A.D., who has chosen domestic service as a profession. There are many such at the present time. That explains away any incongruities of voice or manner which otherwise might awaken suspicion.

Whichever way you decide, good luck to you.

Your sincere friend,

Mr Carter

Tuppence's spirits rose mercurially. Mr Carter's warnings passed unheeded. The young lady had far too much confidence in herself to pay any heed to them.

With some reluctance she abandoned the interesting part she had sketched out for herself. Although she had no doubts of her own powers to sustain a role indefinitely, she had too much common sense not to recognize the force of Mr Carter's arguments.

There was still no word or message from Tommy, but the morning post brought a somewhat dirty postcard with the words: 'It's O.K.' scrawled upon it.

At 10.30 Tuppence surveyed with pride a slightly battered tin trunk containing her new possessions. It was artistically corded. It was with a slight blush that she rang the bell and ordered it to be placed in a taxi. She drove to Paddington, and left the box in the cloak-room. She then repaired with a handbag to the fastnesses of the ladies' waiting-room. Ten minutes later a metamorphosed Tuppence walked demurely out of the station and entered a bus.

It was a few minutes past eleven when Tuppence again entered the hall of South Audley Mansions. Albert was on the look-out, attending to his duties in a somewhat desultory fashion. He did not immediately recognize Tuppence. When he did, his admiration was unbounded.

'Blest if I'd have known you! That rig-out's top-hole.'

'Glad you like it, Albert,' replied Tuppence modestly. 'By the way, am I your cousin, or am I not?'

'Your voice too,' cried the delighted boy. 'It's as English as anything! No, I said as a friend of mine knew a young gal. Annie wasn't best pleased. She stopped on till today – to oblige, *she* said, but really it's so as to put you against the place.'

'Nice girl,' said Tuppence.

Albert suspected no irony.

'She's style about her, and keeps her silver a treat – but, my word, ain't she got a temper. Are you going up now, miss? Step inside the lift. No. 20 did you say?' And he winked.

Tuppence quelled him with a stern glance, and stepped inside.

As she rang the bell of No. 20 she was conscious of Albert's eyes descending beneath the level of the floor.

A smart young woman opened the door.

'I've come about the place,' said Tuppence.

'It's a rotten place,' said the young woman without hesitation. 'Regular old cat – always interfering. Accused me of tampering with her letters. Me! The flap was half undone anyway. There's never anything in the waste-paper basket – she burns everything. She's a wrong 'un, that's what she is. Swell clothes but no class. Cook knows something about her – but she won't tell – scared to death of her. And suspicious! She's on to you in a minute if you as much as speak to a fellow. I can tell you –'

'But what more Annie could tell, Tuppence was never destined to learn, for at that moment a clear voice with a peculiarly steely ring to it called:

'Annie!'

The smart young woman jumped as if she had been shot.

'Yes, ma'am?'

'Who are you talking to?'

'It's a young woman about the situation, ma'am.'

'Show her in then. At once.'

'Yes, ma'am.'

Tuppence was ushered into a room on the right of the long passage. A woman was standing by the fire-place. She was no longer in her first youth, and the beauty she undeniably possessed was hardened and coarsened. In her youth she must have been dazzling. Her pale gold hair, owing a slight assistance to art, was coiled low on her neck, her eyes, of a piercing electric blue, seemed to possess a faculty of boring into the very soul of the person she was looking at. Her exquisite figure was enhanced by a wonderful gown of indigo charmeuse. And yet, despite her swaying grace, and the almost ethereal beauty of her face, you felt instinctively the presence of something hard and menacing, a kind of metallic strength that found expression in the tones of her voice and in that gimlet-like quality of her eyes.

For the first time Tuppence felt afraid. She had not feared Whittington, but this woman was different. As if fascinated, she watched the long cruel line of the red curving mouth, and again she felt that sensation of panic pass over her. Her usual self-confidence deserted her. Vaguely she felt that deceiving this woman would be very different to deceiving Whittington. Mr Carter's warning recurred to her mind. Here, indeed, she might expect no mercy.

Fighting down that instinct of panic which urged her to turn tail and run without further delay, Tuppence returned the lady's gaze firmly and respectfully.

As though that first scrutiny had been satisfactory, Mrs Vandemeyer motioned to a chair.

'You can sit down. How did you hear I wanted a house-parlourmaid?'

'Through a friend who knows the lift-boy here. He thought the place might suit me.'

Again that basilisk glance seemed to pierce her through.

'You speak like an educated girl?'

Glibly enough, Tuppence ran through her imaginary career on the lines suggested by Mr Carter. It seemed to her, as she did so, that the tension of Mrs Vandemeyer's attitude relaxed.

'I see,' she remarked at length. 'Is there anyone I can write to for a reference?'

'I lived last with a Miss Dufferin, The Parsonage, Llanelly. I was with her two years.'

'And then you thought you would get more money by coming to London, I suppose? Well, it doesn't matter to me. I will give you £50-£60 – whatever you want. You can come at once?'

'Yes, ma'am. Today, if you like. My box is at Paddington.'

'Go and fetch it by taxi, then. It's an easy place. I am out a good deal. By the way, what's your name?'

'Prudence Cooper, ma'am.'

'Very well, Prudence. Go away and fetch your box. I shall be out to lunch. The cook will show you where everything is.'

'Thank you, ma'am.'

Tuppence withdrew. The smart Annie was not in evidence. In the hall below a magnificent hall porter had relegated Albert to the background. Tuppence did not even glance at him as she passed meekly out.

The adventure had begun, but she felt less elated than she had done earlier in the morning. It crossed her mind that if the unknown Jane Finn had fallen into the hands of Mrs Vandemeyer, it was likely to have gone hard with her.

CHAPTER 10

ENTER SIR JAMES PEEL EDGERTON

Tuppence betrayed no awkwardness in her new duties. The daughters of the archdeacon were well grounded in household tasks. They were also experts in training a 'raw girl', the inevitable result being that the raw girl, once trained, departed somewhere where her newly-acquired knowledge commanded a more substantial remuneration than the archdeacon's meagre purse allowed.

Tuppence had therefore very little fear of proving inefficient. Mrs Vandemeyer's cook puzzled her. She evidently went in deadly terror of her mistress. The girl thought it probable that the other woman had some hold over her. For the rest, she cooked like a *chef*, as Tuppence had an opportunity of judging that evening. Mrs Vandemeyer was expecting a guest to dinner, and Tuppence accordingly laid the beautifully polished table for two. She was a little exercised in her own mind as to this visitor. It was highly possible that it might prove to be Whittington. Although she felt fairly confident that he would not recognize her, yet she would have been better pleased had the guest proved to be a total stranger. However, there was nothing for it but to hope for the best.

At a few minutes past eight the front door bell rang, and Tuppence went to answer it with some inward trepidation. She was relieved to see that the visitor was the second of the two men whom Tommy had taken upon himself to follow.

He gave his name as Count Stepanov. Tuppence announced him, and Mrs Vandemeyer rose from her seat on a low divan with a quick murmur of pleasure.

'It is delightful to see you, Boris Ivanovitch,' she said.

'And you, madame!' He bowed low over her hand.

Tuppence returned to the kitchen.

'Count Stepanov, or some such,' she remarked, and affecting a frank and unvarnished curiosity: 'Who's he?'

'A Russian gentleman, I believe.'

'Come here much?'

'Once in a while. What d'you want to know for?'

'Fancied he might be sweet on the missus, that's all,' explained the girl, adding with an appearance of sulkiness: 'How you do take one up!'

'I'm not quite easy in my mind about the *soufflé*,' explained the other.

'You know something,' thought Tuppence to herself, but aloud she only said: 'Going to dish up now? Right-o.'

Whilst waiting at table, Tuppence listened closely to all that was said. She remembered that this was one of the men Tommy was shadowing when she had last seen him. Already, although she would hardly admit it, she was becoming uneasy about her partner. Where was he? Why had no word of any kind come from him? She had arranged before leaving the Ritz to have all letters or messages sent on at once by special messenger to a small stationer's shop near at hand where Albert was to call in frequently. True, it was only yesterday morning that she had parted from Tommy, and she told herself that any anxiety on his behalf would be absurd. Still, it was strange he had sent no word of any kind.

But, listen as she might, the conversation presented no clue. Boris and Mrs Vandemeyer talked on purely indifferent subjects: plays they had seen, new dances, and the latest society gossip. After dinner they repaired to the small boudoir where Mrs Vandemeyer, stretched on the divan, looked more wickedly beautiful than ever. Tuppence brought in the coffee and liqueurs and unwillingly retired. As she did so, she heard Boris say:

'New, isn't she?'

'She came in today. The other was a fiend. This girl seems all right. She waits well.'

Tuppence lingered a moment longer by the door which she had carefully neglected to close, and heard him say:

'Quite safe, I suppose?'

'Really, Boris, you are absurdly suspicious. I believe she's the cousin of the hall porter, or something of the kind. And nobody even dreams that I have any connection with our – mutual friend, Mr Brown.'

'For Heaven's sake, be careful, Rita. That door isn't shut.'

'Well, shut it then,' laughed the woman.

Tuppence removed herself speedily.

She dared not absent herself longer from the back premises, but she cleared away and washed up with a breathless speed acquired in hospital. Then she slipped quietly back to the boudoir door. The cook, more leisurely, was still busy in the kitchen and, if she missed the other, would only suppose her to be turning down the beds.

Alas! The conversation inside was being carried on in too low a tone to permit of her hearing anything of it. She dared not reopen the door, however gently. Mrs Vandemeyer was sitting almost facing it, and Tuppence respected her mistress's lynx-eyed powers of observation.

Nevertheless, she felt she would give a good deal to overhear what was going on. Possibly, if anything unforeseen had happened, she might get news of Tommy. For some moments she reflected desperately, then her face brightened. She went quickly along the passage to Mrs Vandemeyer's bedroom, which had long French windows leading on to a balcony that ran the length of the flat. Slipping quickly through the window, Tuppence crept noiselessly along till she reached the boudoir window. As she had thought it stood a little ajar, and the voices within were plainly audible.

Tuppence listened attentively, but there was no mention of anything that could be twisted to apply to Tommy. Mrs Vandemeyer and the Russian seemed to be at variance over some matter, and finally the latter exclaimed bitterly:

'With your persistent recklessness, you will end by ruining us!'

'Bah!' laughed the woman. 'Notoriety of the right kind is the best way of disarming suspicion. You will realize that one of these days – perhaps sooner than you think!'

'In the meantime, you are going about everywhere with Peel Edgerton. Not only is he, perhaps, the most celebrated K.C. in England, but his special hobby is criminology! It is madness!'

'I know that his eloquence has saved untold men from the gallows,' said Mrs Vandemeyer calmly. 'What of it? I may need his assistance in that line myself some day. If so, how fortunate to have such a friend at court – or perhaps it would be more to the point to say *in* court.'

Boris got up and began striding up and down. He was very excited.

'You are a clever woman, Rita; but you are also a fool! Be guided by me, and give up Peel Edgerton.'

Mrs Vandemeyer shook her head gently.

'I think not.'

'You refuse?' There was an ugly ring in the Russian's voice.

'I do.'

'Then, by Heaven,' snarled the Russian, 'we will see –'

But Mrs Vandemeyer also rose to her feet, her eyes flashing.

'You forget, Boris,' she said. 'I am accountable to no one. I take my orders only from – Mr Brown.'

The other threw up his hands in despair.

'You are impossible,' he muttered. 'Impossible! Already it may be too late. They say Peel Edgerton can *smell* a criminal! How do we know what is at the bottom of his sudden interest in you? Perhaps even now his suspicions are aroused. He guesses –'

Mrs Vandemeyer eyed him scornfully.

'Reassure yourself, my dear Boris. He suspects nothing. With less than your usual chivalry, you seem to forget that I am commonly accounted a beautiful woman. I assure you that is all that interests Peel Edgerton.'

Boris shook his head doubtfully.

'He has studied crime as no other man in this kingdom has studied it. Do you fancy that you can deceive him?'

Mrs Vandemeyer's eyes narrowed.

'If he is all that you say – it would amuse me to try!'

'Good heavens, Rita –'

'Besides,' added Mrs Vandemeyer, 'he is extremely rich. I am not one who despises money. The "sinews of war" you know, Boris!'

'Money – money! That is always the danger with you, Rita. I believe you would sell your soul for money. I believe –' He paused, then in a low, sinister voice he said slowly: 'Sometimes I believe that you would sell – *us*!'

Mrs Vandemeyer smiled and shrugged her shoulders.

'The price, at any rate, would have to be enormous,' she said lightly. 'It would be beyond the power of anyone but a millionaire to pay.'

'Ah!' snarled the Russian. 'You see, I was right.'

'My dear Boris, can you not take a joke?'

'Was it a joke?'

'Of course.'

'Then all I can say is that your ideas of humour are peculiar, my dear Rita.'

Mrs Vandemeyer smiled.

'Let us not quarrel, Boris. Touch the bell. We will have some drinks.'

Tuppence beat a hasty retreat. She paused a moment to survey herself in Mrs Vandemeyer's long glass, and be sure that nothing was amiss with her appearance. Then she answered the bell demurely.

The conversation that she had overheard, although interesting in that it proved beyond doubt the complicity of both Rita and Boris, threw very little light on the present preoccupations. The name of Jane Finn had not even been mentioned.

The following morning a few brief words with Albert informed her that nothing was waiting for her at the stationer's. It seemed incredible that Tommy, if all was well with him, should not send any word to her. A cold hand seemed to close round her heart ... Supposing ... She choked her fears down bravely. It was no good worrying. But she leapt at a chance offered her by Mrs Vandemeyer.

'What day do you usually go out, Prudence?'

'Friday's my usual day, ma'am.'

Mrs Vandemeyer lifted her eyebrows.

'And today is Friday! But I suppose you hardly wish to go out today, as you only came yesterday.'

'I was thinking of asking you if I might, ma'am.'

Mrs Vandemeyer looked at her a minute longer, and then smiled.

'I wish Count Stepanov could hear you. He made a suggestion about you last night.' Her smile broadened, cat-like. 'Your request is very – typical. I am satisfied. You do not understand all this – but you can go out today. It makes no difference to me, as I shall not be dining at home.'

'Thank you, ma'am.'

Tuppence felt a sensation of relief once she was out of the other's presence. Once again she admitted to herself that she was afraid, horribly afraid, of the beautiful woman with the cruel eyes.

In the midst of a final desultory polishing of her silver, Tuppence was disturbed by the ringing of the front door bell, and went to answer it. This time the visitor was neither Whittington nor Boris, but a man of striking appearance.

Just a shade over average height, he nevertheless conveyed the impression of a big man. His face, clean-shaven and exquisitely mobile, was stamped with an expression of power and force far beyond the ordinary. Magnetism seemed to radiate from him.

Tuppence was undecided for the moment whether to put him down as an actor or a lawyer, but her doubts were soon solved as he gave her his name: Sir James Peel Edgerton.

She looked at him with renewed interest. This, then, was the famous K.C. whose name was familiar all over England. She had heard it said that he might one day be Prime Minister. He was known to have refused office in the interests of his profession, preferring to remain a simple Member for a Scottish constituency.

Tuppence went back to her pantry thoughtfully. The great man had impressed her. She understood Boris's agitation. Peel Edgerton would not be an easy man to deceive.

In about a quarter of an hour the bell rang, and Tuppence repaired to the hall to show the visitor out. He had given her a piercing glance before. Now, as she handed him his hat and stick, she was conscious of his eyes raking her through. As she opened the door and stood aside to let him pass out, he stopped in the doorway.

'Not been doing this long, eh?'

Tuppence raised her eyes, astonished. She read in his glance kindliness, and something else more difficult to fathom.

He nodded as though she had answered.

'V.A.D. and hard up, I suppose?'

'Did Mrs Vandemeyer tell you that?' asked Tuppence suspiciously.

'No, child. The look of you told me. Good place here?'

'Very good, thank you, sir.'

'Ah, but there are plenty of good places nowadays. And a change does no harm sometimes.'

'Do you mean –?' began Tuppence.

But Sir James was already on the topmost stair. He looked back with his kindly, shrewd glance.

'Just a hint,' he said. 'That's all.'

Tuppence went back to the pantry more thoughtful than ever.

CHAPTER 11

JULIUS TELLS A STORY

Dressed appropriately, Tuppence duly sallied forth for her 'afternoon out'. Albert was in temporary abeyance, but Tuppence went herself to the stationer's to make quite sure that nothing had come for her. Satisfied on this point, she made her way to the Ritz. On inquiry she learnt that Tommy had not yet returned. It was the answer she had expected, but it was another nail in the coffin of her hopes. She resolved to appeal to Mr Carter, telling him when and where Tommy had started on his quest, and asking him to do something to trace him. The prospect of his aid revived her mercurial spirits, and she next inquired for Julius Hersheimmer. The reply she got was to the effect that he had returned about half an hour ago, but had gone out immediately.

Tuppence's spirits revived still more. It would be something to see Julius. Perhaps he could devise some plan for finding out what had become of Tommy. She wrote her note to Mr Carter in Julius's sitting-room, and was just addressing the envelope when the door burst open.

'What the hell –' began Julius, but checked himself abruptly. 'I beg your pardon, Miss Tuppence. Those fools down at the office would have it that Beresford wasn't here any longer – hadn't been here since Wednesday. Is that so?'

Tuppence nodded.

'You don't know where he is?' she asked faintly.

'I? How should I know? I haven't had one darned word from him, though I wired him yesterday morning.'

'I expect your wire's at the office unopened.'

'But where is he?'

'I don't know. I hoped you might.'

'I tell you I haven't had one darned word from him since we parted at the depot on Wednesday.'

'What depot?'

'Waterloo. Your London and South Western road.'

'Waterloo?' frowned Tuppence.

'Why, yes. Didn't he tell you?'

'I haven't seen him either,' replied Tuppence impatiently. 'Go on about Waterloo. What were you doing there?'

'He gave me a call. Over the phone. Told me to get a move on, and hustle. Said he was trailing two crooks.'

'Oh!' said Tuppence, her eyes opening. 'I see. Go on.'

'I hurried along right away. Beresford was there. He pointed out the crooks. The big one was mine, the guy you bluffed. Tommy shoved a ticket into my hand and told me to get aboard the cars. He was going to sleuth the other crook.' Julius paused. 'I thought for sure you'd know all this.'

'Julius,' said Tuppence firmly, 'stop walking up and down. It makes me giddy. Sit down in that arm-chair, and tell me the whole story with as few fancy turns of speech as possible.'

Mr Hersheimmer obeyed.

'Sure,' he said. 'Where shall I begin?'

'Where you left off. At Waterloo.'

'Well,' began Julius, 'I got into one of your dear old-fashioned first-class British compartments. The train was just off. First thing I knew a guard came along and informed me mightily politely that I wasn't in a smoking-carriage. I handed him out half a dollar, and that settled that. I did a bit of prospecting along the corridor to the next coach. Whittington was there right enough. When I saw the skunk, with his big sleek fat face, and thought of poor little Jane in his clutches, I felt real mad that I hadn't got a gun with me. I'd have tickled him up some.

'We got to Bournemouth all right. Whittington took a cab and gave the name of an hotel. I did likewise, and we drove up within three minutes of each other. He hired a room, and I hired one too. So far it was all plain sailing. He hadn't the remotest notion that anyone was on to him. Well, he just sat around in the hotel lounge, reading the papers and so on, till it was time for dinner. He didn't hurry any over that either.

'I began to think that there was nothing doing, that he'd just come on the trip for his health, but I remembered that he hadn't changed for dinner, though it was by way of being a slap-up hotel, so it seemed likely enough that he'd be going out on his real business afterwards.

'Sure enough, about nine o'clock, so he did. Took a car across the town – mighty pretty place by the way, I guess I'll take Jane there for a spell when I find her – and then paid it off and struck out along those pine-woods on the top of the cliff. I was there too, you understand. We walked, maybe, for half an hour. There's a lot of villas all the way along, but by degrees they seemed to get more and more thinned out, and in the end we got to one that seemed the last of the bunch. Big house it was, with a lot of piny grounds around it.

'It was a pretty black night, and the carriage drive up to the house was dark as pitch. I could hear him ahead, though I couldn't see him. I had to walk carefully in case he might get on to it that he was being followed. I turned a curve and I was just in time to see him ring the bell and get admitted to the house. I just stopped where I was. It was beginning to rain, and I was soon pretty near soaked through. Also, it was almighty cold.

'Whittington didn't come out again, and by and by I got kind of restive, and began to mooch around. All the ground-floor windows were shuttered tight, but upstairs, on the first floor (it was a two-storied house) I noticed a window with a light burning and the curtains not drawn.

'Now, just opposite to that window, there was a tree growing. It was about thirty foot away from the house, maybe, and I sort of got it into my head that, if I climbed up that tree, I'd very likely be able to see into that room. Of course, I knew there was no reason why Whittington should be in that room rather than in any other – less reason, in fact, for the betting would be on his being in one of the reception-rooms downstairs. But I guess I'd got the hump from standing so long in the rain, and anything seemed better than going on doing nothing. So I started up.

'It wasn't so easy, by a long chalk! The rain had made the boughs mighty slippery, and it was all I could do to keep a foothold, but bit by bit I managed it, until at last there I was level with the window.

'But then I was disappointed. I was too far to the left. I could only see sideways into the room. A bit of curtain, and a yard of wall-paper was all I could command. Well, that wasn't any manner of good to me, but just as I was going to give it up, and climb down ignominiously, someone inside moved and threw his shadow on my little bit of wall – and, by gum, it was Whittington!

'After that, my blood was up. I'd just *got* to get a look into that room. It was up to me to figure out how. I noticed that there was a long branch running out from the tree in the right direction. If I could only swarm about half-way along it, the proposition would be solved. But it was mighty uncertain whether it would bear my weight. I decided I'd just got to risk that, and I started. Very cautiously, inch by inch, I crawled along. The bough creaked and swayed in a nasty fashion, and it didn't do to think of the drop below, but at last I got safely to where I wanted to be.

'The room was medium-sized, furnished in a kind of bare hygienic way. There was a table with a lamp on it in the middle of the room, and sitting at that table, facing towards me, was Whittington right enough. He was talking to a woman dressed as a hospital nurse. She was sitting with her back to me, so I couldn't see her face. Although the blinds were up, the window itself was shut, so I couldn't catch a word of what they said. Whittington seemed to be doing all the talking, and the nurse just listened. Now and then she nodded, and sometimes she'd shake her head, as though she were answering questions. He seemed very emphatic – once or twice he beat with his fist on the table. The rain had stopped now, and the sky was clearing in that sudden way it does.

'Presently, he seemed to get to the end of what he was saying. He got up, and so did she. He looked towards the window and asked something – I guess it was whether it was raining. Anyway, she came right across and looked out. Just then the moon came out from behind the clouds. I was scared the woman would catch sight of me, for I was full in the moonlight. I tried to move back a bit. The jerk I gave was too much for that rotten old branch. With an almighty crash, down it came, and Julius P. Hersheimmer with it!'

'Oh, Julius,' breathed Tuppence, 'how exciting! Go on.'

'Well, luckily for me, I pitched down into a good soft bed of earth – but it put me out of action for the time, sure enough. The next thing I knew, I was lying in bed with a hospital nurse (not Whittington's one) on one side of me, and a little black-bearded man with gold glasses, and medical man written all over him, on the other. He rubbed his hands together, and raised his eyebrows as I stared at him. "Ah!" he said. "So our young friend is coming round again. Capital. Capital."

'I did the usual stunt. Said: "What's happened?" And "Where am I?" But I knew the answer to the last well enough. There's no moss growing on my brain. "I think that'll do for the present, sister," said the little man, and the nurse left the room in a sort of brisk well-trained way. But I caught her handing me out a look of deep curiosity as she passed through the door.

'That look of hers gave me an idea. "Now then, doc," I said, and tried to sit up in bed, but my right foot gave me a nasty twinge as I did so. "A slight sprain," explained the doctor. "Nothing serious. You'll be about again in a couple of days."

'I noticed you walked lame,' interpolated Tuppence.

Julius nodded, and continued:

'"How did it happen?" I asked again. He replied dryly. "You fell, with a considerable portion of one of my trees, into one of my newly-planted flower-beds."

'I liked the man. He seemed to have a sense of humour. I felt sure that he, at least, was plumb straight. "Sure, doc," I said, "I'm sorry about the tree, and I guess the new bulbs will be on me. But perhaps you'd like to know what I was doing in your garden?" "I think the facts do call for an explanation," he replied. "Well, to begin with, I wasn't after the spoons."

'He smiled. "My first theory. But I soon altered my mind. By the way, you are an American, are you not?" I told him my name. "And you?" "I am Dr Hall, and this, as you doubtless know, is my private nursing home."

'I didn't know, but wasn't going to put him wise. I was just thankful for the information. I liked the man, and I felt he was straight, but I wasn't going to give him the whole story. For one thing he probably wouldn't have believed it.

'I made up my mind in a flash. "Why, doctor," I said, "I guess I feel an almighty fool, but I owe it to you to let you know that it wasn't the Bill Sikes business I was up to." Then I went on and mumbled out something about a girl. I trotted out the stern guardian business, and a nervous breakdown, and finally explained that I had fancied I recognized her among the patients at the home, hence my nocturnal adventures.

'I guess it was just the kind of story he was expecting. "Quite a romance," he said genially, when I'd finished. "Now, doc," I went on, "will you be frank with me? Have you here now, or have you had here at any time, a young girl called Jane Finn?" He repeated the name thoughtfully. "Jane Finn?" he said. "No."

'I was chagrined, and I guess I showed it. "You are sure?" "Quite sure, Mr Hersheimmer. It is an uncommon name, and I should not have been likely to forget it."

'Well, that was flat. It laid me out for a space. I'd kind of hoped my search was at an end. "That's that," I said at last. "Now, there's another matter. When I was hugging that darned branch I thought I recognized an old friend of mine talking to one of your nurses." I purposely didn't mention any name because, of course, Whittington might be calling himself something quite different down here, but the doctor answered at once. "Mr Whittington, perhaps?" "That's the fellow," I replied. "What's he doing down here? Don't tell me *his* nerves are out of order?"

'Dr Hall laughed. "No. He came down to see one of my nurses, Nurse Edith, who is a niece of his." "Why, fancy that!" I exclaimed, "Is he still here?" "No, he went back to town almost immediately." "What a pity!" I ejaculated. "But perhaps I could speak to his niece – Nurse Edith, did you say her name was?"

'But the doctor shook his head. "I'm afraid that, too, is impossible. Nurse Edith left with a patient tonight also." "I seem to be real unlucky," I remarked. "Have you Mr Whittington's address in town? I guess I'd like to look him up when I get back." "I don't know his address. I can write to Nurse Edith for it if you like." I thanked him. "Don't say who it is wants it. I'd like to give him a little surprise."

'That was about all I could do for the moment. Of course, if the girl was really Whittington's niece, she might be too cute to fall into the trap, but it was worth trying. Next thing I did was to write out a wire to Beresford saying where I was, and that I was laid up with a sprained foot, and telling him to come down if he wasn't busy. I had to be guarded in what I said. However, I didn't hear from him, and my foot soon got all right. It was only ricked, not really sprained, so today I said goodbye to the little doctor chap, asked him to send me word if he heard from Nurse Edith, and came right away back to town. Say, Miss Tuppence, you're looking mighty pale?'

'It's Tommy,' said Tuppence. 'What can have happened to him?'

'Buck up, I guess he's all right really. Why shouldn't he be? See here, it was a foreign-looking guy he went off after. Maybe they've gone abroad – to Poland, or something like that?'

Tuppence shook her head.

'He couldn't without passports and things. Besides I've seen that man, Boris Something, since. He dined with Mrs Vandemeyer last night.'

'Mrs Who?'

'I forgot. Of course you don't know all that.'

'I'm listening,' said Julius, and gave vent to his favourite expression. 'Put me wise.'

Tuppence thereupon related the events of the last two days. Julius's astonishment and admiration were unbounded.

'Bully for you! Fancy you a menial. It just tickles me to death!' Then he added seriously: 'But say now, I don't like it, Miss Tuppence, I sure don't. You're just as plucky as they make 'em, but I wish you'd keep right out of this. These crooks we're up against would as soon croak a girl as a man any day.'

'Do you think I'm afraid?' said Tuppence indignantly, valiantly repressing memories of the steely glitter in Mrs Vandemeyer's eyes.

'I said before you were darned plucky. But that doesn't alter facts.'

'Oh, bother *me*!' said Tuppence impatiently. 'Let's think about what can have happened to Tommy. I've written to Mr Carter about it,' she added, and told him the gist of her letter.

Julius nodded gravely.

'I guess that's good as far as it goes. But it's for us to get busy and do something.'

'What can we do?' asked Tuppence, her spirits rising.

'I guess we'd better get on the track of Boris. You say he's been to your place. Is he likely to come again?'

'He might. I really don't know.'

'I see. Well, I guess I'd better buy a car, a slap-up one, dress as a chauffeur and hang about outside. Then if Boris comes, you could make some kind of signal, and I'd trail him. How's that?'

'Splendid, but he mightn't come for weeks.'

'We'll have to chance that. I'm glad you like the plan.' He rose.

'Where are you going?'

'To buy the car, of course,' replied Julius, surprised. 'What make do you like? I guess you'll do some riding in it before we've finished.'

'Oh,' said Tuppence faintly. 'I *like* Rolls-Royces, but –'

'Sure,' agreed Julius. 'What you say goes. I'll get one.'

'But you can't at once,' cried Tuppence. 'People wait ages sometimes.'

'Little Julius doesn't,' affirmed Mr Hersheimmer. 'Don't you worry any. I'll be round in the car in half an hour.'

Tuppence got up.

'You're awfully good, Julius. But I can't help feeling that it's rather a forlorn hope. I'm really pinning my faith to Mr Carter.'

'Then I shouldn't.'

'Why?'

'Just an idea of mine.'

'Oh, but he must do something. There's no one else. By the way, I forgot to tell you of a queer thing that happened this morning.'

And she narrated her encounter with Sir James Peel Edgerton. Julius was interested.

'What did the guy mean, do you think?' he asked.

'I don't quite know,' said Tuppence meditatively. 'But I think that, in an ambiguous, legal, without prejudicish lawyer's way, he was trying to warn me.'

'Why should he?'

'I don't know,' confessed Tuppence. 'But he looked kind, and simply awfully clever. I wouldn't mind going to him and telling him everything.'

Somewhat to her surprise, Julius negatived the idea sharply.

'See here,' he said, 'we don't want any lawyers mixed up in this. That guy couldn't help us any.'

'Well, I believe he could,' reiterated Tuppence obstinately.

'Don't you think it. So long. I'll be back in half an hour.'

Thirty-five minutes had elapsed when Julius returned. He took Tuppence by the arm, and walked her to the window.

'There she is.'

'Oh!' said Tuppence with a note of reverence in her voice, as she gazed down at the enormous car.

'She's some pace-maker, I can tell you,' said Julius complacently.

'How did you get it?' gasped Tuppence.

'She was just being sent home to some bigwig.'

'Well?'

'I went round to his house,' said Julius. 'I said that I reckoned a car like that was worth every penny of twenty thousand dollars. Then I told him that it was worth just about fifty thousand dollars to me if he'd get out.'

'Well?' said Tuppence, intoxicated.

'Well,' returned Julius, 'he got out, that's all.'

CHAPTER 12

A FRIEND IN NEED

Friday and Saturday passed uneventfully. Tuppence had received a brief answer to her appeal from Mr Carter. In it he pointed out that the Young Adventurers had undertaken the work at their own risk, and had been fully warned of the dangers. If anything had happened to Tommy he regretted it deeply, but he could do nothing.

This was cold comfort. Somehow, without Tommy, all the savour went out of the adventure, and, for the first time, Tuppence felt doubtful of success. While they had been together she had never questioned it for a minute. Although she was accustomed to take the lead, and to pride herself on her quick-wittedness, in reality she had relied upon Tommy more than she realized at the time. There was something so eminently sober and clear-headed about him, his common sense and soundness of vision were so unvarying, that without him Tuppence felt much like a rudderless ship. It was curious that Julius, who was undoubtedly much cleverer than Tommy, did not give her the same feeling of support. She had accused Tommy of being a pessimist, and it is certain that he always saw the disadvantages and difficulties which she herself was optimistically given to overlooking, but nevertheless she had really relied a good deal on his judgment. He might be slow, but he was very sure.

It seemed to the girl that, for the first time, she realized the sinister character of the mission they had undertaken so light-heartedly. It had begun like a page of romance. Now, shorn of its glamour, it seemed to be turning to grim reality. Tommy – that was all that mattered. Many times in the day Tuppence blinked the tears out of her eyes resolutely. 'Little fool,' she would apostrophize herself, 'don't snivel. Of course you're fond of him. You've known him all your life. But there's no need to be sentimental about it.'

In the meantime, nothing more was seen of Boris. He did not come to the flat, and Julius and the car waited in vain. Tuppence gave herself over to new meditations. Whilst admitting the truth of Julius's objections, she had nevertheless not entirely relinquished the idea of appealing to Sir James Peel Edgerton. Indeed, she had gone so far as to look up his address in the *Red Book*. Had he meant to warn her that day? If so, why? Surely she was at least entitled to demand an explanation. He had looked at her so kindly. Perhaps he might tell them something concerning Mrs Vandemeyer which might lead to a clue to Tommy's whereabouts.

Anyway, Tuppence decided, with her usual shake of the shoulders, it was worth trying, and try it she would. Sunday was her afternoon out. She would meet Julius, persuade him to her point of view, and they would beard the lion in his den.

When the day arrived Julius needed a considerable amount of persuading, but Tuppence held firm. 'It can do no harm,' was what she always came back to. In the end Julius gave in, and they proceeded in the car to Carlton House Terrace.

The door was opened by an irreproachable butler. Tuppence felt a little nervous. After all, perhaps it *was* colossal cheek on her part. She had decided not to ask if Sir James was 'at home', but to adopt a more personal attitude.

'Will you ask Sir James if I can see him for a few minutes? I have an important message for him.'

The butler retired, returning a moment or two later.

'Sir James will see you. Will you step this way?'

He ushered them into a room at the back of the house, furnished as a library. The collection of books was a magnificent one, and Tuppence noticed that all one wall was devoted to works on crime and criminology. There were several deep-padded leather arm-chairs, and an old-fashioned open hearth. In the window was a big roll-top desk strewn with papers at which the master of the house was sitting.

He rose as they entered.

'You have a message for me? Ah' – he recognized Tuppence with a smile – 'it's you, is it? Brought a message from Mrs Vandemeyer, I suppose?'

'Not exactly,' said Tuppence. 'In fact, I'm afraid I only said that to be quite sure of getting in. Oh, by the way, this is Mr Hersheimmer, Sir James Peel Edgerton.'

'Pleased to meet you,' said the American, shooting out a hand.

'Won't you both sit down?' asked Sir James. He drew forward two chairs.

'Sir James,' said Tuppence, plunging boldly, 'I dare say you will think it is most awful cheek of me coming here like this. Because, of course, it's nothing whatever to do with you, and then you're a very important person, and of course Tommy and I are very unimportant.' She paused for breath.

'Tommy?' queried Sir James, looking across at the American.

'No, that's Julius,' explained Tuppence. 'I'm rather nervous, and that makes me tell it badly. What I really want to know is what you meant by what you said to me the other day? Did you mean to warn me against Mrs Vandemeyer? You did, didn't you?'

'My dear young lady, as far as I recollect I only mentioned that there were equally good situations to be obtained elsewhere.'

'Yes, I know. But it was a hint, wasn't it?'

'Well, perhaps it was,' admitted Sir James gravely.

'Well, I want to know more. I want to know just *why* you gave me a hint.'

Sir James smiled at her earnestness.

'Suppose the lady brings a libel action against me for defamation of character?'

'Of course,' said Tuppence. 'I know lawyers are always dreadfully careful. But can't we say "without prejudice" first, and then say just what we want to?'

'Well,' said Sir James, still smiling, 'without prejudice, then, if I had a young sister forced to earn her living, I should not like to see her in Mrs Vandemeyer's service. I felt it incumbent on me just to give you a hint. It is no place for a young and inexperienced girl. That is all I can tell you.'

'I see,' said Tuppence thoughtfully. 'Thank you very much. But I'm not *really* inexperienced, you know. I knew perfectly that she was a bad lot when I went there – as a matter of fact that's *why* I went –' She broke off, seeing some bewilderment on the lawyer's face, and went on: 'I think perhaps I'd better tell you the whole story, Sir James. I've a sort of feeling that you'd know in a minute if I didn't tell the truth, and so you might as well know all about it from the beginning. What do you think, Julius?'

'As you're bent on it, I'd go right ahead with the facts,' replied the American, who had so far sat in silence.

'Yes, tell me all about it,' said Sir James. 'I want to know who Tommy is.'

Thus encouraged Tuppence plunged into her tale, and the lawyer listened with close attention.

'Very interesting,' he said, when she finished. 'A great deal of what you tell me, child, is already known to me. I've had certain theories of my own about this Jane Finn. You've done extraordinarily well so far, but it's rather too bad of – what do you know him as? – Mr Carter to pitchfork you two young things into an affair of this kind. By the way, where did Mr Hersheimmer come in originally? You didn't make that clear?'

Julius answered for himself.

'I'm Jane's first cousin,' he explained, returning the lawyer's keen gaze.

'Ah!'

'Oh, Sir James,' broke out Tuppence, 'what do you think has become of Tommy?'

'H'm.' The lawyer rose, and paced slowly up and down. 'When you arrived, young lady, I was just packing up my traps. Going to Scotland by the night train for a few days' fishing. But there are different kinds of fishing. I've a good mind to stay, and see if we can't get on the track of that young chap.'

'Oh!' Tuppence clasped her hands ecstatically.

'All the same, as I said before, it's too bad of – of Carter to set you two babies on a job like this. Now, don't get offended, Miss – er –'

'Cowley. Prudence Cowley. But my friends call me Tuppence.'

'Well, Miss Tuppence, then, as I'm certainly going to be a friend. Don't be offended because I think you're young. Youth is a failing only too easily outgrown. Now, about this young Tommy of yours –'

'Yes.' Tuppence clasped her hands.

'Frankly, things look bad for him. He's been butting in somewhere where he wasn't wanted. Not a doubt of it. But don't give up hope.'

'And you really will help us? There, Julius! He didn't want me to come,' she added by way of explanation.

'H'm,' said the lawyer, favouring Julius with another keen glance. 'And why was that?'

'I reckoned it would be no good worrying you with a petty little business like this.'

'I see.' He paused a moment. 'This petty little business, as you call it, bears directly on a very big business, bigger perhaps than either you or Miss Tuppence know. If this boy is alive, he may have very valuable information to give us. Therefore, we must find him.'

'Yes, but how?' cried Tuppence. 'I've tried to think of everything.'

Sir James smiled.

'And yet there's one person quite near at hand who in all probability knows where he is, or at all events where he is likely to be.'

'Who is that?' asked Tuppence, puzzled.

'Mrs Vandemeyer.'

'Yes, but she'd never tell us.'

'Ah, that is where I come in. I think it quite likely that I shall be able to make Mrs Vandemeyer tell me what I want to know.'

'How?' demanded Tuppence, opening her eyes very wide.

'Oh, just by asking her questions,' replied Sir James easily. 'That's the way we do it, you know.'

He tapped with his fingers on the table, and Tuppence felt again the intense power that radiated from the man.

'And if she won't tell?' asked Julius suddenly.

'I think she will. I have one or two powerful levers. Still, in that unlikely event, there is always the possibility of bribery.'

'Sure. And that's where I come in!' cried Julius, bringing his fist down on the table with a bang. 'You can count on me, if necessary, for one million dollars. Yes, sir, one million dollars!'

Sir James sat down and subjected Julius to a long scrutiny.

'Mr Hersheimmer,' he said at last, 'that is a very large sum.'

'I guess it'll have to be. These aren't the kind of folk to offer sixpence to.'

'At the present rate of exchange it amounts to considerably over two hundred and fifty thousand pounds.'

'That's so. Maybe you think I'm talking through my hat, but I can deliver the goods all right, with enough over to spare for your fee.'

Sir James flushed slightly.

'There is no question of a fee, Mr Hersheimmer. I am not a private detective.'

'Sorry. I guess I was just a mite hasty, but I've been feeling bad about this money question. I wanted to offer a big reward for news of Jane some days ago, but your crusted institution of Scotland Yard advised me against it. Said it was undesirable.'

'They were probably right,' said Sir James dryly.

'But it's all O.K. about Julius,' put in Tuppence. 'He's not pulling your leg. He's got simply pots of money.'

'The old man piled it up in style,' explained Julius. 'Now, let's get down to it. What's your idea?'

Sir James considered for a moment or two.

'There is no time to be lost. The sooner we strike the better.' He turned to Tuppence. 'Is Mrs Vandemeyer dining out tonight, do you know?'

'Yes, I think so, but she will not be out late. Otherwise, she would have taken the latchkey.'

'Good. I will call upon her about ten o'clock. What time are you supposed to return?'

'About nine-thirty or ten, but I could go back earlier.'

'You must not do that on any account. It might arouse suspicion if you did not stay out till the usual time. Be back by nine-thirty.

I will arrive at ten. Mr Hersheimmer will wait below in a taxi perhaps.'

'He's got a new Rolls-Royce car,' said Tuppence with vicarious pride.

'Even better. If I succeed in obtaining the address from her, we can go there at once, taking Mrs Vandemeyer with us if necessary. You understand?'

'Yes.' Tuppence rose to her feet with a skip of delight. 'Oh, I feel so much better!'

'Don't build on it too much, Miss Tuppence. Go easy.'

Julius turned to the lawyer.

'Say, then, I'll call for you in the car round about nine-thirty. Is that right?'

'Perhaps that will be the best plan. It would be unnecessary to have two cars waiting about. Now, Miss Tuppence, my advice to you is to go and have a good dinner, a *really* good one, mind. And don't think ahead more than you can help.'

He shook hands with them both, and a moment later they were outside.

'Isn't he a duck?' inquired Tuppence ecstatically, as she skipped down the steps. 'Oh, Julius, isn't he just a duck?'

'Well, I allow he seems to be the goods all right. And I was wrong about it being useless to go to him. Say, shall we go right away back to the Ritz?'

'I must walk a bit, I think. I feel so excited. Drop me in the Park, will you? Unless you'd like to come too?'

Julius shook his head.

'I want to get some petrol,' he explained. 'And send off a cable or two.'

'All right. I'll meet you at the Ritz at seven. We'll have to dine upstairs. I can't show myself in these glad rags.'

'Sure. I'll get Felix to help me choose the menu. He's some head waiter, that. So long.'

Tuppence walked briskly along towards the Serpentine, first glancing at her watch. It was nearly six o'clock. She remembered that she had had no tea, but felt too excited to be conscious of hunger. She walked as far as Kensington Gardens and then slowly retraced her steps, feeling infinitely better for the fresh air and exercise. It was not so easy to follow Sir James's advice and put the possible events of the evening out of her head. As she drew nearer and nearer to Hyde Park Corner, the temptation to return to South Audley Mansions was almost irresistible.

At any rate, she decided, it would do no harm just to go and *look* at the building. Perhaps, then, she could resign herself to waiting patiently for ten o'clock.

South Audley Mansions looked exactly the same as usual. What Tuppence had expected she hardly knew, but the sight of its red-brick solidity slightly assuaged the growing and entirely unreasonable uneasiness that possessed her. She was just turning away when she heard a piercing whistle, and the faithful Albert came running from the building to join her.

Tuppence frowned. It was no part of the programme to have attention called to her presence in the neighbourhood, but Albert was purple with suppressed excitement.

'I say, miss, she's a-going!'

'Who's going?' demanded Tuppence sharply.

'The crook. Ready Rita. Mrs Vandemeyer. She's a-packing up, and she's just sent down word for me to get her a taxi.'

'What?' Tuppence clutched his arm.

'It's the truth, miss. I thought maybe as you didn't know about it.'

'Albert,' cried Tuppence, 'you're a brick. If it hadn't been for you we'd have lost her.'

Albert flushed with pleasure at this tribute.

'There's no time to lose,' said Tuppence, crossing the road. 'I've got to stop her. At all costs I must keep her here until –' She broke off. 'Albert, there's a telephone here, isn't there?'

The boy shook his head.

'The flats mostly have their own, miss. But there's a box just round the corner.'

'Go to it then, at once, and ring up the Ritz Hotel. Ask for Mr Hersheimmer, and when you get him tell him to get Sir James and come at once, as Mrs Vandemeyer is trying to hook it. If you can't get him, ring up Sir James Peel Edgerton, you'll find his number in the book, and tell him what's happening. You won't forget the names, will you?'

Albert repeated them glibly. 'You trust to me, miss, it'll be all right. But what about you? Aren't you afraid to trust yourself with her?'

'No, no, that's all right. *But go and telephone.* Be quick.'

Drawing a long breath, Tuppence entered the Mansions and ran up to the door of No. 20. How she was to detain Mrs Vandemeyer until the two men arrived, she did not know, but somehow or other it had to be done, and she must accomplish the task single-handed. What had occasioned this precipitate departure? Did Mrs Vandemeyer suspect her?

Speculations were idle. Tuppence pressed the bell firmly. She might learn something from the cook.

Nothing happened and, after waiting some minutes, Tuppence pressed the bell again, keeping her finger on the button for some little while. At last she heard footsteps inside, and a moment later Mrs Vandemeyer herself opened the door. She lifted her eyebrows at the sight of the girl.

'You?'

'I had a touch of toothache, ma'am,' said Tuppence glibly. 'So thought it better to come home and have a quiet evening.'

Mrs Vandemeyer said nothing, but she drew back and let Tuppence pass into the hall.

'How unfortunate for you,' she said coldly. 'You had better go to bed.'

'Oh, I shall be all right in the kitchen, ma'am. Cook will –'

'Cook is out,' said Mrs Vandemeyer, in a rather disagreeable tone. 'I sent her out. So you see you had better go to bed.'

Suddenly Tuppence felt afraid. There was a ring in Mrs Vandemeyer's voice that she did not like at all. Also, the other woman was slowly edging her up the passage. Tuppence turned at bay.

'I don't want –'

Then, in a flash, a rim of cold steel touched her temple, and Mrs Vandemeyer's voice rose cold and menacing:

'You damned little fool! Do you think I don't know? No, don't answer. If you struggle or cry out, I'll shoot you like a dog.'

The rim of steel pressed a little harder against the girl's temple.

'Now then, march,' went on Mrs Vandemeyer. 'This way – into my room. In a minute, when I've done with you, you'll go to bed as I told you to. And you'll sleep – oh yes, my little spy, you'll sleep all right!'

There was a sort of hideous geniality in the last words which Tuppence did not at all like. For the moment there was nothing to be done, and she walked obediently into Mrs Vandemeyer's bedroom. The pistol never left her forehead. The room was in a state of wild disorder, clothes were flung about right and left, a suitcase and a hat box, half-packed, stood in the middle of the floor.

Tuppence pulled herself together with an effort. Her voice shook a little, but she spoke out bravely.

'Come now,' she said, 'this is nonsense. You can't shoot me. Why, everyone in the building would hear the report.'

'I'd risk that,' said Mrs Vandemeyer cheerfully. 'But, as long as you don't sing out for help, you're all right – and I don't think you will. You're a clever girl. You deceived *me* all right. I hadn't a suspicion of you! So I've no doubt that you understand perfectly well that this is where I'm on top and you're underneath. Now then – sit on the bed. Put your hands above your head, and if you value your life don't move them.'

Tuppence obeyed passively. Her good sense told her that there was nothing else to do but accept the situation. If she shrieked for help there was very little chance of anyone hearing her, whereas there was probably quite a good chance of Mrs Vandemeyer's shooting her. In the meantime, every minute of delay gained was valuable.

Mrs Vandemeyer laid down the revolver on the edge of the wash-stand within reach of her hand, and, still eyeing Tuppence like a lynx in case the girl should attempt to move, she took a little stoppered bottle from its place on the marble and poured some of its contents into a glass which she filled up with water.

'What's that?' asked Tuppence sharply.

'Something to make you sleep soundly.'

Tuppence paled a little.

'Are you going to poison me?' she asked in a whisper.

'Perhaps,' said Mrs Vandemeyer, smiling agreeably.

'Then I shan't drink it,' said Tuppence firmly. 'I'd much rather be shot. At any rate that would make a row, and someone might hear it. But I won't be killed off quietly like a lamb.'

Mrs Vandemeyer stamped her foot.

'Don't be a little fool! Do you really think I want a hue and cry for murder out after me? If you've any sense at all, you'll realize that poisoning you wouldn't suit my book at all. It's a sleeping-draught, that's all. You'll wake up tomorrow morning none the worse. I simply don't want the bother of tying you up and gagging you. That's the alternative – and you won't like it, I can tell you! I can be very rough if I choose. So drink this down like a good girl, and you'll be none the worse for it.'

In her heart of hearts Tuppence believed her. The arguments she had adduced rang true. It was a simple and effective method of getting her out of the way for the time being. Nevertheless, the girl did not take kindly to the idea of being tamely put to sleep without as much as one bid for freedom. She felt that once Mrs Vandemeyer gave them the slip, the last hope of finding Tommy would be gone.

Tuppence was quick in her mental processes. All these reflections passed through her mind in a flash, and she saw where a chance, a very problematic chance, lay, and she determined to risk all in one supreme effort.

Accordingly, she lurched suddenly off the bed and fell on her knees before Mrs Vandemeyer, clutching her skirts frantically.

'I don't believe it,' she moaned. 'It's poison – I know it's poison. Oh, don't make me drink it' – her voice rose to a shriek – 'don't make me drink it!'

Mrs Vandemeyer, glass in hand, looked down with a curling lip at this sudden collapse.

'Get up, you little idiot! Don't go on drivelling there. How you ever had the nerve to play your part as you did I can't think.' She stamped her foot. 'Get up, I say.'

But Tuppence continued to cling and sob, interjecting her sobs with incoherent appeals for mercy. Every minute gained was to the good. Moreover, as she grovelled, she moved imperceptibly nearer to her objective.

Mrs Vandemeyer gave a sharp impatient exclamation, and jerked the girl to her knees.

'Drink it at once!' Imperiously she pressed the glass to the girl's lips.

Tuppence gave one last despairing moan.

'You swear it won't hurt me?' she temporized.

'Of course it won't hurt you. Don't be a fool.'

'Will you swear it?'

'Yes, yes,' said the other impatiently. 'I swear it.'

Tuppence raised a trembling left hand to the glass.

'Very well.' Her mouth opened meekly.

Mrs Vandemeyer gave a sigh of relief, off her guard for the moment. Then, quick as a flash, Tuppence jerked the glass upward as hard as she could. The fluid in it splashed into Mrs Vandemeyer's face, and during her momentary gasp, Tuppence's right hand shot out and grasped the revolver where it lay on the edge of the wash-stand. The next moment she had sprung back a pace, and the revolver pointed straight at Mrs Vandemeyer's heart, with no unsteadiness in the hand that held it.

In the moment of victory, Tuppence betrayed a somewhat unsportsman-like triumph.

'Now who's on top and who's underneath?' she crowed.

The other's face was convulsed with rage. For a minute Tuppence thought she was going to spring upon her, which would have placed the girl in an unpleasant dilemma, since she meant to draw the line at actually letting off the revolver. However, with an effort, Mrs Vandemeyer controlled herself, and at last a slow, evil smile crept over her face.

'Not a fool then, after all! You did that well, girl. But you shall pay for it – oh, yes, you shall pay for it! I have a long memory!'

'I'm surprised you should have been gulled so easily,' said Tuppence scornfully. 'Did you really think I was the kind of girl to roll about on the floor and whine for mercy?'

'You may do – some day!' said the other significantly.

The cold malignity of her manner sent an unpleasant chill down Tuppence's spine, but she was not going to give in to it.

'Supposing we sit down,' she said pleasantly. 'Our present attitude is a little melodramatic. No – not on the bed. Draw a chair up to the table, that's right. Now I'll sit opposite you with the revolver in front of me – just in case of accidents. Splendid. Now, let's talk.'

'What about?' said Mrs Vandemeyer sullenly.

Tuppence eyed her thoughtfully for a minute. She was remembering several things. Boris's words, 'I believe you would sell – *us*!'

and her answer, 'The price would have to be enormous,' given lightly, it was true, yet might not there be a substratum of truth in it? Long ago, had not Whittington asked: 'Who's been blabbing? Rita?' Would Rita Vandemeyer prove to be the weak spot in the armour of Mr Brown?

Keeping her eyes fixed steadily on the other's face, Tuppence replied quietly:

'Money –'

Mrs Vandemeyer started. Clearly, the reply was unexpected.

'What do you mean?'

'I'll tell you. You said just now that you had a long memory. A long memory isn't half as useful as a long purse! I dare say it relieves your feelings a good deal to plan out all sorts of dreadful things to do to me, but is that *practical*? Revenge is very unsatisfactory. Everyone always says so. But money' – Tuppence warmed to her pet creed – 'well, there's nothing unsatisfactory about money, is there?'

'Do you think,' said Mrs Vandemeyer scornfully, 'that I am the kind of woman to sell my friends?'

'Yes,' said Tuppence promptly, 'if the price was big enough.'

'A paltry hundred pounds or so!'

'No,' said Tuppence. 'I should suggest – a hundred thousand!'

Her economical spirit did not permit her to mention the whole million dollars suggested by Julius.

A flush crept over Mrs Vandemeyer's face.

'What did you say?' she asked, her fingers playing nervously with a brooch on her breast. In that moment Tuppence knew that the fish was hooked, and for the first time she felt a horror of her own money-loving spirit. It gave her a dreadful sense of kinship to the woman fronting her.

'A hundred thousand pounds,' repeated Tuppence.

The light died out of Mrs Vandemeyer's eyes. She leaned back in her chair.

'Bah!' she said. 'You haven't got it.'

'No,' admitted Tuppence, 'I haven't – but I know someone who has.'

'Who?'

'A friend of mine.'

'Must be a millionaire,' remarked Mrs Vandemeyer unbelievingly.

'As a matter of fact he is. He's an American. He'll pay you that without a murmur. You can take it from me that it's a perfectly genuine proposition.'

Mrs Vandemeyer sat up again.

'I'm inclined to believe you,' she said slowly.

There was silence between them for some time, then Mrs Vandemeyer looked up.

'What does he want to know, this friend of yours?'

Tuppence want through a momentary struggle, but it was Julius's money, and his interests must come first.

'He wants to know where Jane Finn is,' she said boldly.

Mrs Vandemeyer showed no surprise.

'I'm not sure where she is at the present moment,' she replied.

'But you could find out?'

'Oh, yes,' returned Mrs Vandemeyer carelessly. 'There would be no difficulty about that.'

'Then' – Tuppence's voice shook a little – 'there's a boy, a friend of mine. I'm afraid something's happened to him, through your pal, Boris.'

'What's his name?'

'Tommy Beresford.'

'Never heard of him. But I'll ask Boris. He'll tell me anything he knows.'

'Thank you.' Tuppence felt a terrific rise in her spirits. It impelled her to more audacious efforts. 'There's one thing more.'

'Well?'

Tuppence leaned forward and lowered her voice.

'*Who is Mr Brown?*'

Her quick eyes saw the sudden paling of the beautiful face. With an effort Mrs Vandemeyer pulled herself together and tried to resume her former manner. But the attempt was a mere parody.

She shrugged her shoulders.

'You can't have learnt much about us if you don't know that *nobody knows who Mr Brown is . . .*'

'You do,' said Tuppence quietly.

Again the colour deserted the other's face.

'What makes you think that?'

'I don't know,' said the girl truthfully. 'But I'm sure.'

Mrs Vandemeyer stared in front of her for a long time.

'Yes,' she said hoarsely, at last, '*I* know. I was beautiful, you see – very beautiful –'

'You are still,' said Tuppence with admiration.

Mrs Vandemeyer shook her head. There was a strange gleam in her electric-blue eyes.

'Not beautiful enough,' she said in a soft, dangerous voice. 'Not – beautiful – enough! And sometimes, lately, I've been afraid . . . It's dangerous to know too much!' She leaned forward across the table. 'Swear that my name shan't be brought into it – that no one shall ever know.'

'I swear it. And, once he's caught, you'll be out of danger.'

A terrified look swept across Mrs Vandemeyer's face.

'Shall I? Shall I ever be?' She clutched Tuppence's arm. 'You're sure about the money?'

'Quite sure.'

'When shall I have it? There must be no delay.'

'This friend of mine will be here presently. He may have to send cables, or something like that. But there won't be any delay – he's a terrific hustler.'

A resolute look settled on Mrs Vandemeyer's face.

'I'll do it. It's a great sum of money, and besides' – she gave a curious smile – 'it is not – wise to throw over a woman like me!'

For a moment or two, she remained smiling, and lightly tapping her fingers on the table. Suddenly she started, and her face blanched.

'What was that?'

'I heard nothing.'

Mrs Vandemeyer gazed round her fearfully.

'If there should be someone listening –'

'Nonsense. Who could there be?'

'Even the walls might have ears,' whispered the other. 'I tell you I'm frightened. You don't know him!'

'Think of the hundred thousand pounds,' said Tuppence soothingly.

Mrs Vandemeyer passed her tongue over her dried lips.

'You don't know him,' she reiterated hoarsely. 'He's – ah!'

With a shriek of terror she sprang to her feet. Her outstretched hand pointed over Tuppence's head. Then she swayed to the ground in a dead faint.

Tuppence looked round to see what had startled her.

In the doorway were Sir James Peel Edgerton and Julius Hersheimmer.

CHAPTER 13

THE VIGIL

Sir James brushed past Julius and hurriedly bent over the fallen woman.

'Heart,' he said sharply. 'Seeing us so suddenly must have given her a shock. Brandy – and quickly, or she'll slip through our fingers.'

Julius hurried to the wash-stand.

'Not here,' said Tuppence over her shoulder. 'In the tantalus in the dining-room. Second door down the passage.'

Between them Sir James and Tuppence lifted Mrs Vandemeyer and carried her to the bed. There they dashed water on her face, but with no result. The lawyer fingered her pulse.

'Touch and go,' he muttered. 'I wish that young fellow would hurry up with the brandy.'

At that moment Julius re-entered the room, carrying a glass half full of the spirit which he handed to Sir James. While Tuppence lifted her head the lawyer tried to force a little of the spirit between her closed lips. Finally the woman opened her eyes feebly. Tuppence held the glass to her lips.

'Drink this.'

Mrs Vandemeyer complied. The brandy brought the colour back to her white cheeks, and revived her in a marvellous fashion. She tried to sit up – then fell back with a groan, her hand to her side.

'It's my heart,' she whispered. 'I mustn't talk.'

She lay back with closed eyes.

Sir James kept his finger on her wrist a minute longer, then withdrew it with a nod.

'She'll do now.'

All three moved away, and stood together talking in low voices.

One and all were conscious of a certain feeling of anticlimax. Clearly any scheme for cross-questioning the lady was out of the question for the moment. For the time being they were baffled, and could do nothing.

Tuppence related how Mrs Vandemeyer had declared herself willing to disclose the identity of Mr Brown, and how she had consented to discover and reveal to them the whereabouts of Jane Finn. Julius was congratulatory.

'That's all right, Miss Tuppence. Splendid! I guess that hundred thousand pounds will look just as good in the morning to the lady as it did overnight. There's nothing to worry over. She won't speak without the cash anyway, you bet!'

There was certainly a good deal of common sense in this, and Tuppence felt a little comforted.

'What you say is true,' said Sir James meditatively. 'I must confess, however, that I cannot help wishing we had not interrupted at the minute we did. Still, it cannot be helped, it is only a matter of waiting until the morning.'

He looked across at the inert figure on the bed. Mrs Vandemeyer lay perfectly passive with closed eyes. He shook his head.

'Well,' said Tuppence, with an attempt at cheerfulness, 'we must wait until the morning, that's all. But I don't think we ought to leave the flat.'

'What about leaving that bright boy of yours on guard?'

'Albert? And suppose she came round again and hooked it. Albert couldn't stop her.'

'I guess she won't want to make tracks away from the dollars.'

'She might. She seemed very frightened of "Mr Brown".'

'What? Real plumb scared of him?'

'Yes. She looked round and said even walls had ears.'

'Maybe she meant a dictaphone,' said Julius with interest.

'Miss Tuppence is right,' said Sir James quietly. 'We must not leave the flat – if only for Mrs Vandemeyer's sake.'

Julius stared at him.

'You think he'd get after her? Between now and tomorrow morning. How could he know, even?'

'You forget your own suggestion of a dictaphone,' said Sir James dryly. 'We have a very formidable adversary. I believe, if we exercise all due care, that there is a very good chance of his being delivered into our hands. But we must neglect no precaution. We have an important witness, but she must be safeguarded. I would suggest that Miss Tuppence should go to bed, and that you and I, Mr Hersheimmer, should share the vigil.'

Tuppence was about to protest, but happening to glance at the bed she saw Mrs Vandemeyer, her eyes half-open, with such an expression of mingled fear and malevolence on her face that it quite froze the words on her lips.

For a moment she wondered whether the faint and the heart attack had been a gigantic sham, but remembering the deadly pallor she could hardly credit the supposition. As she looked the expression disappeared as by magic, and Mrs Vandemeyer lay inert and motionless as before. For a moment the girl fancied she must have dreamt it. But she determined nevertheless to be on the alert.

'Well,' said Julius, 'I guess we'd better make a move out of here anyway.'

The others fell in with his suggestion. Sir James again felt Mrs Vandemeyer's pulse.

'Perfectly satisfactory,' he said in a low voice to Tuppence. 'She'll be absolutely all right after a night's rest.'

The girl hesitated a moment by the bed. The intensity of the expression she had surprised had impressed her powerfully. Mrs Vandemeyer lifted her eyelids. She seemed to be struggling to speak. Tuppence bent over her.

'Don't – leave –' she seemed unable to proceed, murmuring something that sounded like 'sleepy'. Then she tried again.

Tuppence bent lower still. It was only a breath.

'Mr – Brown –' The voice stopped.

But the half-closed eyes seemed still to send an agonized message.

Moved by a sudden impulse, the girl said quickly:

'I shan't leave the flat. I shall sit up all night.'

A flash of relief showed before the lids descended once more. Apparently Mrs Vandemeyer slept. But her words had awakened a new uneasiness in Tuppence. What had she meant by that low murmur. 'Mr Brown?' Tuppence caught herself nervously looking over her shoulder. The big wardrobe loomed up in a sinister fashion before her eyes. Plenty of room for a man to hide in that . . . Half-ashamed of herself Tuppence pulled it open and looked inside. No one – of course! She stooped down and looked under the bed. There was no other possible hiding-place.

Tuppence gave her familiar shake of the shoulders. It was absurd, this giving way to nerves! Slowly she went out of the room. Julius and Sir James were talking in a low voice. Sir James turned to her.

'Lock the door on the outside, please, Miss Tuppence, and take out the key. There must be no chance of anyone entering that room.'

The gravity of his manner impressed them, and Tuppence felt less ashamed of her attack of 'nerves'.

'Say,' remarked Julius suddenly, 'there's Tuppence's bright boy. I guess I'd better go down and ease his young mind. That's some lad, Tuppence.'

'How did you get in, by the way?' asked Tuppence suddenly. 'I forgot to ask.'

'Well, Albert got me on the phone all right. I ran round for Sir James here, and we came right on. The boy was on the look out for us, and was just a mite worried about what might have happened to you. He'd been listening outside the door of the flat, but couldn't hear anything. Anyhow he suggested sending us up in the coal lift instead of ringing the bell. And sure enough we landed in the scullery and came right along to find you. Albert's still below, and must be hopping mad by this time.' With which Julius departed abruptly.

'Now then, Miss Tuppence,' said Sir James, 'you know this place better than I do. Where do you suggest we should take up our quarters?'

Tuppence considered for a moment or two.

'I think Mrs Vandemeyer's boudoir would be the most comfortable,' she said at last, and led the way there.

Sir James looked round approvingly.

'This will do very well, and now, my dear young lady, do go to bed and get some sleep.'

Tuppence shook her head resolutely.

'I couldn't, thank you, Sir James. I should dream of Mr Brown all night!'

'But you'll be so tired, child.'

'No, I shan't. I'd rather stay up – really.'

The lawyer gave in.

Julius reappeared some minutes later, having reassured Albert and rewarded him lavishly for his services. Having in his turn failed to persuade Tuppence to go to bed, he said decisively:

'At any rate, you've got to have something to eat right away. Where's the larder?'

Tuppence directed him, and he returned in a few minutes with a cold pie and three plates.

After a hearty meal, the girl felt inclined to pooh-pooh her fancies of half an hour before. The power of the money bribe could not fail.

'And now, Miss Tuppence,' said Sir James, 'we want to hear your adventures.'

'That's so,' agreed Julius.

Tuppence narrated her adventures with some complacence. Julius occasionally interjected an admiring 'Bully'. Sir James said nothing until she had finished, when his quiet 'Well done, Miss Tuppence,' made her flush with pleasure.

'There's one thing I don't get clearly,' said Julius. 'What put her up to clearing out?'

'I don't know,' confessed Tuppence.

Sir James stroked his chin thoughtfully.

'The room was in great disorder. That looks as though her flight was unpremeditated. Almost as though she got a sudden warning to go from someone.'

'Mr Brown, I suppose,' said Julius scoffingly.

The lawyer looked at him deliberately for a minute or two.

'Why not?' he said. 'Remember, you yourself have once been worsted by him.'

Julius flushed with vexation.

'I feel just mad when I think of how I handed out Jane's photograph to him like a lamb. Gee, if I ever lay hands on it again, I'll freeze on to it – like hell!'

'That contingency is likely to be a remote one,' said the other dryly.

'I guess you're right,' said Julius frankly. 'And, in any case, it's the original I'm out after. Where do you think she can be, Sir James?'

The lawyer shook his head.

'Impossible to say. But I've a very good idea where she *has* been.'

'You have? Where?'

Sir James smiled.

'At the scene of your nocturnal adventures, the Bournemouth nursing home.'

'There? Impossible. I asked.'

'No, my dear sir, you asked if anyone of the name of Jane Finn had been there. Now, if the girl had been placed there it would almost certainly be under an assumed name.'

'Bully for you,' cried Julius. 'I never thought of that!'

'It was fairly obvious,' said the other.

'Perhaps the doctor's in it too,' suggested Tuppence.

Julius shook his head.

'I don't think so. I took to him at once. No, I'm pretty sure Dr Hall's all right.'

'Hall, did you say?' asked Sir James. 'That is curious – really very curious.'

'Why?' demanded Tuppence.

'Because I happened to meet him this morning. I've known him slightly on and off for some years, and this morning I ran across him in the street. Staying at the Metropole, he told me.' He turned to Julius. 'Didn't he tell you he was coming up to town?'

Julius shook his head.

'Curious,' mused Sir James. 'You did not mention his name this afternoon, or I would have suggested your going to him for further information with my card as introduction.'

'I guess I'm a mutt,' said Julius with unusual humility. 'I ought to have thought of the false name stunt.'

'How could you think of anything after falling out of that tree?' cried Tuppence. 'I'm sure anyone else would have been killed right off.'

'Well, I guess it doesn't matter now, anyway,' said Julius. 'We've got Mrs Vandemeyer on a string, and that's all we need.'

'Yes,' said Tuppence, but there was a lack of assurance in her voice.

A silence settled down over the party. Little by little the magic of the night began to gain hold on them. There were sudden creaks in the furniture, imperceptible rustlings in the curtains. Suddenly Tuppence sprang up with a cry.

'I can't help it. I know Mr Brown's somewhere in the flat! I can *feel* him.'

'Sure, Tuppence, how could he be? This door's open into the hall. No one could have come in by the front door without our seeing and hearing him.'

'I can't help it. I *feel* he's here!'

She looked appealingly at Sir James, who replied gravely:

'With due deference to your feelings, Miss Tuppence (and mine as well for that matter), I do not see how it is humanly possible for anyone to be in the flat without our knowledge.'

The girl was a little comforted by his words.

'Sitting up at night is always rather jumpy,' she confessed.

'Yes,' said Sir James. 'We are in the condition of people holding a séance. Perhaps if a medium were present we might get some marvellous results.'

'Do you believe in spiritualism?' asked Tuppence, opening her eyes wide.

The lawyer shrugged his shoulders.

'There is some truth in it, without a doubt. But most of the testimony would not pass muster in the witness-box.'

The hours drew on. With the first faint glimmerings of dawn, Sir James drew aside the curtains. They beheld, what few Londoners see, the slow rising of the sun over the sleeping city. Somehow, with the coming of the light, the dreads and fancies of the past night seemed absurd. Tuppence's spirits revived to the normal.

'Hooray!' she said. 'It's going to be a gorgeous day. And we shall find Tommy. And Jane Finn. And everything will be lovely. I shall ask Mr Carter if I can't be made a Dame!'

At seven o'clock Tuppence volunteered to go and make some tea. She returned with a tray, containing the teapot and four cups.

'Who's the other cup for?' inquired Julius.

'The prisoner, of course. I suppose we might call her that?'

'Taking her tea seems a kind of anticlimax to last night,' said Julius thoughtfully.

'Yes, it does,' admitted Tuppence. 'But, anyway, here goes. Perhaps you'd both come, too, in case she springs on me, or anything. You see, we don't know what mood she'll wake up in.'

Sir James and Julius accompanied her to the door.

'Where's the key? Oh, of course, I've got it myself.'

She put it in the lock, and turned it, then paused.

'Supposing, after all, she's escaped?' she murmured in a whisper.

'Plumb impossible,' replied Julius reassuringly.

But Sir James said nothing.

Tuppence drew a long breath and entered. She heaved a sigh of relief as she saw that Mrs Vandemeyer was lying on the bed.

'Good morning,' she remarked cheerfully. 'I've brought you some tea.'

Mrs Vandemeyer did not reply. Tuppence put down the cup on the table by the bed and went across to draw up the blinds. When she turned, Mrs Vandemeyer still lay without a movement. With a sudden fear clutching at her heart, Tuppence ran to the bed. The hand she lifted was cold as ice . . . Mrs Vandemeyer would never speak now . . .

Her cry brought the others. A very few minutes sufficed. Mrs Vandemeyer was dead – must have been dead some hours. She had evidently died in her sleep.

'If that isn't the cruellest luck,' cried Julius in despair.

The lawyer was calmer, but there was a curious gleam in his eyes.

'If it is luck,' he replied.

'You don't think – but, say, that's plumb impossible – no one could have got in.'

'No,' admitted the lawyer. 'I don't see how they could. And yet – she is on the point of betraying Mr Brown, and – she dies. Is it only chance?'

'But how –'

'Yes, *how*! That is what we must find out.' He stood there silently, gently stroking his chin. 'We must find out,' he said quietly, and Tuppence felt that if she was Mr Brown she would not like the tone of those simple words.

Julius's glance went to the window.

'The window's open,' he remarked. 'Do you think –'

Tuppence shook her head.

'The balcony only goes along as far as the boudoir. We were there.'

'He might have slipped out –' suggested Julius.

But Sir James interrupted him.

'Mr Brown's methods are not so crude. In the meantime we must send for a doctor, but before we do so is there anything in this room that might be of value to us?'

Hastily, the three searched. A charred mass in the grate indicated that Mrs Vandemeyer had been burning papers on the eve of her flight. Nothing of importance remained, though they searched the other rooms as well.

'There's that,' said Tuppence suddenly, pointing to a small, old-fashioned safe let into the wall. 'It's for jewellery, I believe, but there might be something else in it.'

The key was in the lock, and Julius swung open the door, and searched inside. He was some time over the task.

'Well,' said Tuppence impatiently.

There was a pause before Julius answered, then he withdrew his head and shut the door.

'Nothing,' he said.

In five minutes a brisk young doctor arrived, hastily summoned. He was deferential to Sir James, whom he recognized.

'Heart failure, or possibly an overdose of some sleeping-draught. He sniffed. 'Rather an odour of chloral in the air.'

Tuppence remembered the glass she had upset. A new thought drove her to the wash-stand. She found the little bottle from which Mrs Vandemeyer had poured a few drops.

It had been three parts full. Now – *it was empty*.

CHAPTER 14

A CONSULTATION

Nothing was more surprising and bewildering to Tuppence than the ease and simplicity with which everything was arranged, owing to Sir James's skilful handling. The doctor accepted quite readily the theory that Mrs Vandemeyer had accidentally taken an overdose of chloral. He doubted whether an inquest would be necessary. If so, he would let Sir James know. He understood that Mrs Vandemeyer was on the eve of departure for abroad, and that the servants had already left? Sir James and his young friends had been paying a call upon her, when she was suddenly stricken down and they had spent the night in the flat, not liking to leave her alone. Did they know of any relatives? They did not, but Sir James referred him to Mrs Vandemeyer's solicitor.

Shortly afterwards a nurse arrived to take charge, and the others left the ill-omened building.

'And what now?' asked Julius, with a gesture of despair. 'I guess we're down and out for good.'

Sir James stroked his chin thoughtfully.

'No,' he said quietly. 'There is still the chance that Dr Hall may be able to tell us something.'

'Gee! I'd forgotten him.'

'The chance is slight, but it must not be neglected. I think I told you that he is staying at the Metropole. I should suggest that we call upon him there as soon as possible. Shall we say after a bath and breakfast?'

It was arranged that Tuppence and Julius should return to the Ritz, and call for Sir James in the car. The programme was faithfully carried out, and a little after eleven they drew up before the Metropole. They asked for Dr Hall, and a page-boy went in search of him. In a few minutes the little doctor came hurrying towards them.

'Can you spare us a few minutes, Dr Hall?' said Sir James pleasantly. 'Let me introduce you to Miss Cowley. Mr Hersheimmer, I think, you already know.'

A quizzical gleam came into the doctor's eye as he shook hands with Julius.

'Ah, yes, my young friend of the tree episode! Ankle all right, eh?'

'I guess it's cured owing to your skilful treatment, doc.'

'And the heart trouble? Ha! ha!'

'Still searching,' said Julius briefly.

'To come to the point, can we have a word with you in private?' asked Sir James.

'Certainly. I think there is a room here where we shall be quite undisturbed.'

He led the way, and the others followed him. They sat down, and the doctor looked inquiringly at Sir James.

'Dr Hall, I am very anxious to find a certain young lady for the purpose of obtaining a statement from her. I have reason to believe that she has been at one time or another in your establishment at Bournemouth. I hope I am transgressing no professional etiquette in questioning you on the subject?'

'I suppose it is a matter of testimony?'

Sir James hesitated a moment, then he replied:

'Yes.'

'I shall be pleased to give you any information in my power. What is the young lady's name? Mr Hersheimmer asked me, I remember –' He half turned to Julius.

'The name,' said Sir James bluntly, 'is really immaterial. She would be almost certainly sent to you under an assumed one. But I should like to know if you are acquainted with a Mrs Vandemeyer?'

'Mrs Vandemeyer, of 20 South Audley Mansions? I know her slightly.'

'You are not aware of what has happened?'

'What do you mean?'

'You do not know that Mrs Vandemeyer is dead?'

'Dear, dear, I had no idea of it! When did it happen?'

'She took an overdose of chloral last night.'

'Purposely?'

'Accidentally, it is believed. I should not like to say myself. Anyway, she was found dead this morning.'

'Very sad. A singularly handsome woman. I presume she was a friend of yours, since you are acquainted with all these details?'

'I am acquainted with the details because – well, it was I who found her dead.'

'Indeed,' said the doctor, starting.

'Yes,' said Sir James, and stroked his chin reflectively.

'This is very sad news, but you will excuse me if I say that I do not see how it bears on the subject of your inquiry?'

'It bears on it in this way, is it not a fact that Mrs Vandemeyer committed a young relative of hers to your charge?'

Julius leaned forward eagerly.

'That is the case,' said the doctor quietly.

'Under the name of –?'

'Janet Vandemeyer. I understood her to be a niece of Mrs Vandemeyer's.'

'And she came to you?'

'As far as I can remember in June or July of 1915.'

'Was she a mental case?'

'She is perfectly sane, if that is what you mean. I understood from Mrs Vandemeyer that the girl had been with her on the *Lusitania* when that ill-fated ship was sunk, and had suffered a severe shock in consequence.'

'We're on the right track, I think?' Sir James looked round.

'As I said before, I'm a mutt!' returned Julius.

The doctor looked at them all curiously.

'You spoke of wanting a statement from her,' he said. 'Supposing she is not able to give one?'

'What? You have just said that she is perfectly sane.'

'So she is. Nevertheless, if you want a statement from her concerning any events prior to May 7th, 1915, she will not be able to give it to you.'

They looked at the little man, stupefied. He nodded cheerfully.

'It's a pity,' he said. 'A great pity, especially as I gather, Sir James, that the matter is important. But there it is, she can tell you nothing.'

'But why, man? Darn it all, why?'

The little man shifted his benevolent glance to the excited young American.

'Because Janet Vandemeyer is suffering from a complete loss of memory!'

'*What?*'

'Quite so. An interesting case, a *very* interesting case. Not so uncommon, really, as you would think. There are several very well known parallels. It's the first case of the kind that I've had under my own personal observation, and I must admit that I've found it of absorbing interest.' There was something rather ghoulish in the little man's satisfaction.

'And she remembers nothing,' said Sir James slowly.

'Nothing prior to May 7th, 1915. After that date her memory is as good as yours or mine.'

'Then the first thing she remembers?'

'Is landing with the survivors. Everything before that is a blank. She did not know her own name, or where she had come from, or where she was. She couldn't even speak her own tongue.'

'But surely all this is most unusual?' put in Julius.

'No, my dear sir. Quite normal under the circumstances. Severe shock to the nervous system. Loss of memory proceeds nearly always on the same lines. I suggested a specialist, of course. There's a very good man in Paris – makes a study of these cases – but Mrs Vandemeyer opposed the idea of publicity that might result from such a course.'

'I can imagine she would,' said Sir James grimly.

'I fell in with her views. There *is* a certain notoriety given to these cases. And the girl was very young – nineteen, I believe. It seemed a pity that her infirmity should be talked about – might damage her prospects. Besides, there is no special treatment to pursue in such cases. It is really a matter of waiting.'

'Waiting?'

'Yes, sooner or later, the memory will return – as suddenly as it went. But in all probability the girl will have entirely forgotten the intervening period, and will take up life where she left off – at the sinking of the *Lusitania*.'

'And when do you expect this to happen?'

The doctor shrugged his shoulders.

'Ah, that I cannot say. Sometimes it is a matter of months, sometimes it has been known to be as long as twenty years! Sometimes another shock does the trick. One restores what the other took away.'

'Another shock, eh?' said Julius thoughtfully.

'Exactly. There was a case in Colorado –' The little man's voice trailed on, voluble, mildly enthusiastic.

Julius did not seem to be listening. He had relapsed into his own thoughts and was frowning. Suddenly he came out of his brown study, and hit the table such a resounding bang with his fist that everyone jumped, the doctor most of all.

'I've got it! I guess, doc, I'd like your medical opinion on the plan I'm about to outline. Say Jane was to cross the herring pond again, and the same thing was to happen. The submarine, the sinking ship, everyone to take to the boats – and so on. Wouldn't that do the trick? Wouldn't it give a mighty big bump to her subconscious self, or whatever the jargon is, and start it functioning again right away?'

'A very interesting speculation, Mr Hersheimmer. In my own opinion, it would be successful. It is unfortunate that there is no chance of the conditions repeating themselves as you suggest.'

'Not by nature, perhaps, doc. But I'm talking about art.'

'Art?'

'Why, yes. What's the difficulty? Hire the liner –'

'A liner!' murmured Dr Hall faintly.

'Hire some passengers, hire a submarine – that's the only difficulty, I guess. Governments are apt to be a bit hidebound over their engines of war. They won't sell to the first comer. Still, I guess that can be got over. Ever heard of the word 'graft', sir? Well, graft gets there every time! I reckon that we shan't really need to fire a torpedo. If everyone hustles round and screams loud enough that the ship is sinking, it ought to be enough for an innocent young girl like Jane. By the time she's got a life-belt on her, and is being hustled into a boat, with a well-drilled lot of artistes doing the hysterical stunt on deck, why – she ought to be right back again where she was in May, 1915. How's that for the bare outline?'

Dr Hall looked at Julius. Everything that he was for the moment incapable of saying was eloquent in that look.

'No,' said Julius, in answer to it, 'I'm not crazy. The thing's perfectly possible. It's done every day in the States for the movies. Haven't you seen trains in collision on the screen? What's the difference between buying up a train and buying up a liner? Get the properties and you can go right ahead!'

Dr Hall found his voice.

'But the expense, my dear sir.' His voice rose. 'The expense! It will be *colossal*!'

'Money doesn't worry me any,' explained Julius simply.

Dr Hall turned an appealing face to Sir James, who smiled slightly.

'Mr Hersheimmer is very well off – very well off indeed.'

The doctor's glance came back to Julius with a new and subtle quality in it. This was no longer an eccentric young fellow with a habit of falling off trees. The doctor's eyes held the deference accorded to a really rich man.

'Very remarkable plan. Very remarkable,' he murmured. 'The movies – of course! Your American word for the cinema. Very interesting. I fear we are perhaps a little behind the times over here in our methods. And you really mean to carry out this remarkable plan of yours?'

'You bet your bottom dollar I do.'

The doctor believed him – which was a tribute to his nationality. If an Englishman had suggested such a thing, he would have had grave doubts as to his sanity.

'I cannot guarantee a cure,' he pointed out. 'Perhaps I ought to make that quite clear.'

'Sure, that's all right,' said Julius. 'You just trot out Jane, and leave the rest to me.'

'Jane?'

'Miss Janet Vandemeyer, then. Can we get on the long distance to your place right away, and ask them to send her up; or shall I run down and fetch her in my car?'

The doctor stared.

'I beg your pardon, Mr Hersheimmer. I thought you understood.'

'Understood what?'

'That Miss Vandemeyer is no longer under my care.'

CHAPTER 15

TUPPENCE RECEIVES A PROPOSAL

Julius sprang up.

'What?'

'I thought you were aware of that.'

'When did she leave?'

'Let me see. Today is Monday, is it not? It must have been last Wednesday – why, surely – yes, it was the same evening that you – er – fell out of my tree.'

'That evening? Before, or after?'

'Let me see – oh yes, afterwards. A very urgent message arrived from Mrs Vandemeyer. The young lady and the nurse who was in charge of her left by the night train.'

Julius sank back again into his chair.

'Nurse Edith – left with a patient – I remember,' he muttered. 'My God, to have been so near!'

Dr Hall looked bewildered.

'I don't understand. Is the young lady not with her aunt, after all?'

Tuppence shook her head. She was about to speak when a warning glance from Sir James made her hold her tongue. The lawyer rose.

'I'm much obliged to you, Hall. We're very grateful for all you've told us. I'm afraid we're now in the position of having to track Miss Vandemeyer anew. What about the nurse who accompanied her; I suppose you don't know where she is?'

The doctor shook his head.

'We've not heard from her, as it happens. I understood she was to remain with Miss Vandemeyer for a while. But what can have happened? Surely the girl has not been kidnapped?'

'That remains to be seen,' said Sir James gravely.

The other hesitated.

'You do not think I ought to go to the police?'

'No, no. In all probability the young lady is with other relations.'

The doctor was not completely satisfied, but he saw that Sir James was determined to say no more, and realized that to try to extract more information from the famous K.C. would be mere waste of labour. Accordingly, he wished them goodbye, and they left the hotel. For a few minutes they stood by the car talking.

'How maddening,' cried Tuppence. 'To think that Julius must have been actually under the same roof with her for a few hours.'

'I was a darned idiot,' muttered Julius gloomily.

'You couldn't know,' Tuppence consoled him. 'Could he?' She appealed to Sir James.

'I should advise you not to worry,' said the latter kindly. 'No use crying over spilt milk, you know.'

'The great thing is what to do next,' added Tuppence the practical.

Sir James shrugged his shoulders.

'You might advertise for the nurse who accompanied the girl. That is the only course I can suggest, and I must confess I do not hope for much result. Otherwise there is nothing to be done.'

'Nothing?' said Tuppence blankly. 'And – Tommy?'

'We must hope for the best,' said Sir James. 'Oh yes, we must go on hoping.'

But over her downcast head his eyes met Julius's, and almost imperceptibly he shook his head. Julius understood. The lawyer considered the case hopeless. The young American's face grew grave. Sir James took Tuppence's hand.

'You must let me know if anything further comes to light. Letters will always be forwarded.'

Tuppence stared at him blankly.

'You are going away?'

'I told you. Don't you remember? To Scotland.'

'Yes, but I thought –' The girl hesitated.

Sir James shrugged his shoulders.

'My dear young lady, I can do nothing more, I fear. Our clues have all ended in thin air. You can take my word for it that there is nothing more to be done. If anything should arise, I shall be glad to advise you in any way I can.'

His words gave Tuppence an extraordinary desolate feeling.

'I suppose you're right,' she said. 'Anyway, thank you very much for trying to help us. Goodbye.'

Julius was bending over the car. A momentary pity came into Sir James's keen eyes, as he gazed into the girl's downcast face.

'Don't be too disconsolate, Miss Tuppence,' he said in a low voice. 'Remember, holiday-time isn't always all play-time. One sometimes manages to put in some work as well.'

Something in his tone made Tuppence glance up sharply. He shook his head with a smile.

'No, I shan't say any more. Great mistake to say too much. Remember that. Never tell all you know – not even to the person you know best. Understand? Goodbye.'

He strode away. Tuppence stared after him. She was beginning to understand Sir James's methods. Once before he had thrown her a hint in the same careless fashion. Was this a hint? What exactly lay behind those last brief words? Did he mean that, after all, he had not abandoned the case: that secretly, he would be working on it still while –

Her meditations were interrupted by Julius, who adjured her to 'get right in'.

'You're looking kind of thoughtful,' he remarked as they started off. 'Did the old guy say anything more?'

Tuppence opened her mouth impulsively, and then shut it again. Sir James's words sounded in her ears: 'Never tell all you know – not even to the person you know best.' And like a flash there came into her mind another memory. Julius before the safe in the flat, her own question and the pause before his reply, 'Nothing.' Was there really nothing? Or had he found something he wished to keep to himself? If he could make a reservation, so could she.

'Nothing particular,' she replied.

She felt rather than saw Julius throw a sideways glance at her.

'Say, shall we go for a spin in the park?'

'If you like.'

For a while they ran on under the trees in silence. It was a beautiful day. The keen rush through the air brought a new exhilaration to Tuppence.

'Say, Miss Tuppence, do you think I'm ever going to find Jane?'

Julius spoke in a discouraged voice. The mood was so alien to him that Tuppence turned and stared at him in surprise. He nodded.

'That's so. I'm getting down and out over the business. Sir James today hadn't got any hope at all, I could see that, I don't like him – we don't gee together somehow – but he's pretty cute, and I guess he wouldn't quit if there was any chance of success – now, would he?'

Tuppence felt rather uncomfortable, but clinging to her belief that Julius also had withheld something from her, she remained firm.

'He suggested advertising for the nurse,' she reminded him.

'Yes, with a "forlorn hope" flavour to his voice! No – I'm about fed up. I've half a mind to go back to the States right away.'

'Oh no!' cried Tuppence. 'We've got to find Tommy.'

'I sure forgot Beresford,' said Julius contritely. 'That's so. We must find him. But after – well, I've been day-dreaming ever since I started on this trip – and these dreams are rotten poor business. I'm quit of them. Say, Miss Tuppence, there's something I'd like to ask you.'

'Yes.'

'You and Beresford. What about it?'

'I don't understand you,' replied Tuppence with dignity, adding rather inconsequently: 'And, anyway, you're wrong!'

'Not got a sort of kindly feeling for one another?'

'Certainly not,' said Tuppence with warmth. 'Tommy and I are friends – nothing more.'

'I guess every pair of lovers has said that some time or another,' observed Julius.

'Nonsense!' snapped Tuppence. 'Do I look the sort of girl that's always falling in love with every man she meets?'

'You do not. You look the sort of girl that's mighty often getting fallen in love with!'

'Oh!' said Tuppence, rather taken aback. 'That's a compliment, I suppose?'

'Sure. Now let's get down to this. Supposing we never find Beresford and – and –'

'All right – say it! I can face facts. Supposing he's – dead! Well?'

'And all this business fiddles out. What are you going to do?'

'I don't know,' said Tuppence forlornly.

'You'll be darned lonesome, you poor kid.'

'I shall be all right,' snapped Tuppence with her usual resentment of any kind of pity.

'What about marriage?' inquired Julius. 'Got any views on the subject?'

'I intend to marry, of course,' replied Tuppence. 'That is, if' – she paused, knew a momentary longing to draw back, and then stuck to her guns bravely – 'I can find some one rich enough to make it worth my while. That's frank, isn't it? I dare say you despise me for it.'

'I never despise business instinct,' said Julius. 'What particular figure have you in mind?'

'Figure?' asked Tuppence, puzzled. 'Do you mean tall or short?'

'No. Sum – income.'

'Oh, I – haven't quite worked that out.'

'What about me?'

'*You?*'

'Sure thing.'

'Oh, I couldn't!'

'Why not?'

'I tell you I couldn't.'

'Again, why not?'

'It would seem so unfair.'

'I don't see anything unfair about it. I call your bluff, that's all. I admire you immensely, Miss Tuppence, more than any girl I've ever met. You're so darned plucky. I'd just love to give you a real, rattling good time. Say the word, and we'll run round right away to some high-class jeweller, and fix up the ring business.'

'I can't,' gasped Tuppence.

'Because of Beresford?'

'No, no, *no*!'

'Well then?'

Tuppence merely continued to shake her head violently.

'You can't reasonably expect more dollars than I've got.'

'Oh, it isn't that,' gasped Tuppence with an almost hysterical laugh. 'But thanking you very much, and all that, I think I'd better say no.'

'I'd be obliged if you'd do me the favour to think it over until tomorrow.'

'It's no use.'

'Still, I guess we'll leave it like that.'

'Very well,' said Tuppence meekly.

Neither of them spoke again until they reached the Ritz.

Tuppence went upstairs to her room. She felt morally battered to the ground after her conflict with Julius's vigorous personality. Sitting down in front of the glass, she stared at her own reflection for some minutes.

'Fool,' murmured Tuppence at length, making a grimace. 'Little fool. Everything you want – everything you've ever hoped for, and you go and bleat out "no" like an idiotic little sheep. It's your one chance. Why don't you take it? Grab it? Snatch at it? What more do you want?'

As if in answer to her own question, her eyes fell on a small snapshot of Tommy that stood on her dressing-table in a shabby frame. For a moment she struggled for self-control, and then abandoning all pretence, she held it to her lips and burst into a fit of sobbing.

'Oh, Tommy, Tommy,' she cried, 'I do love you so – and I may never see you again . . .'

At the end of five minutes Tuppence sat up, blew her nose, and pushed back her hair.

'That's that,' she observed sternly. 'Let's look facts in the face. I seem to have fallen in love – with an idiot of a boy who probably doesn't care two straws about me.' Here she paused. 'Anyway,' she resumed, as though arguing with an unseen opponent, 'I don't *know* that he does. He'd never have dared to say so. I've always jumped on sentiment – and here I am being more sentimental than anybody. What idiots girls are! I've always thought so. I suppose I shall sleep with his photograph under my pillow, and dream about him all night. It's dreadful to feel you've been false to your principles.'

Tuppence shook her head sadly, as she reviewed her backsliding.

'I don't know what to say to Julius, I'm sure. Oh, what a fool I feel! I'll have to say *something* – he's so American and thorough, he'll insist upon having a reason. I wonder if he did find anything in that safe –'

Tuppence's meditations went off on another track. She reviewed the events of last night carefully and persistently. Somehow, they seemed bound up with Sir James's enigmatical words . . .

Suddenly she gave a great start – the colour faded out of her face. Her eyes, fascinated, gazed in front of her, the pupils dilated.

'Impossible,' she murmured. 'Impossible! I must be going mad even to think of such a thing . . .'

Monstrous – yet it explained everything . . .

After a moment's reflection she sat down and wrote a note, weighing each word as she did so. Finally she nodded her head as though satisfied, and slipped it into an envelope which she addressed to Julius. She went down the passage to his sitting-room and knocked at the door. As she had expected, the room was empty. She left the note on the table.

A small page-boy was waiting outside her own door when she returned to it.

'Telegram for you, miss.'

Tuppence took it from the salver, and tore it open carelessly. Then she gave a cry. The telegram was from Tommy!

CHAPTER 16

FURTHER ADVENTURES OF TOMMY

From a darkness punctuated with throbbing stabs of fire, Tommy dragged his senses slowly back to life. When he at last opened his eyes, he was conscious of nothing but an excruciating pain through his temples. He was vaguely aware of unfamiliar surroundings. Where was he? What had happened? He blinked feebly. This was not his bedroom at the Ritz. And what the devil was the matter with his head?

'Damn!' said Tommy, and tried to sit up. He had remembered. He was in that sinister house in Soho. He uttered a groan and fell back. Through his almost-closed eyelids he reconnoitred carefully.

'He is coming to,' remarked a voice very near Tommy's ear. He recognized it at once for that of the bearded and efficient German, and lay artistically inert. He felt that it would be a pity to come round too soon; and until the pain in his head became a little less acute, he felt quite incapable of collecting his wits. Painfully he tried to puzzle out what had happened. Obviously somebody must have crept up behind him as he listened and struck him down with a blow on the head. They knew him now for a spy, and would in all probability give him short shrift. Undoubtedly he was in a tight place. Nobody knew where he was, therefore he need expect no outside assistance, and must depend solely on his own wits.

'Well, here goes,' murmured Tommy to himself, and repeated his former remark.

'Damn!' he observed, and this time succeeded in sitting up.

In a minute the German stepped forward and placed a glass to his lips, with the brief command 'Drink.' Tommy obeyed. The potency of the draught made him choke, but it cleared his brain in a marvellous manner.

He was lying on a couch in the room in which the meeting had been held. On one side of him was the German, on the other the villainous-faced doorkeeper who had let him in. The others were grouped together at a little distance away. But Tommy missed one face. The man known as Number One was no longer of the company.

'Feel better?' asked the German, as he removed the empty glass.

'Yes, thanks,' returned Tommy cheerfully.

'Ah, my young friend, it is lucky for you your skull is so thick. The good Conrad struck hard.' He indicated the evil-faced doorkeeper by a nod.

The man grinned.

Tommy twisted his head round with an effort.

'Oh,' he said, 'so you're Conrad, are you? It strikes me the thickness of my skull was lucky for you too. When I look at you I feel it's almost a pity I've enabled you to cheat the hangman.'

The man snarled, and the bearded man said quietly:

'He would have run no risk of that.'

'Just as you like,' replied Tommy. 'I know it's the fashion to run down the police. I rather believe in them myself.'

His manner was nonchalant to the last degree. Tommy Beresford was one of those young Englishmen not distinguished by any special intellectual ability, but who are emphatically at their best in what is known as a 'tight place'. Their natural diffidence and caution falls from them then like a glove. Tommy realized perfectly that in his own wits lay the only chance of escape, and behind his casual manner he was racking his brains furiously.

The cold accents of the German took up the conversation:

'Have you anything to say before you are put to death as a spy?'

'Simply lots of things,' replied Tommy with the same urbanity as before.

'Do you deny that you were listening at that door?'

'I do not. I must really apologize – but your conversation was so interesting that it overcame my scruples.'

'How did you get in?'

'Dear old Conrad here.' Tommy smiled deprecatingly at him. 'I hesitate to suggest pensioning off a faithful servant, but you really ought to have a better watchdog.'

Conrad snarled impotently, and said sullenly, as the man with the beard swung round upon him:

'He gave the word. How was I to know?'

'Yes,' Tommy chimed in. 'How was he to know? Don't blame the poor fellow. His hasty action has given me the pleasure of seeing you all face to face.'

He fancied that his words caused some discomposure among the group, but the watchful German stilled it with a wave of his hand.

'Dead men tell no tales,' he said evenly.

'Ah,' said Tommy, 'but I'm not dead yet!'

'You soon will be, my young friend,' said the German.

An assenting murmur came from the others.

Tommy's heart beat faster, but his casual pleasantness did not waver.

'I think not,' he said firmly. 'I should have a great objection to dying.'

He had got them puzzled, he saw that by the look on his captor's face.

'Can you give us any reason why we should not put you to death?' asked the German.

'Several,' replied Tommy. 'Look here, you've been asking me a lot of questions. Let me ask you one for a change. Why didn't you kill me off at once before I regained consciousness?'

The German hesitated, and Tommy seized his advantage.

'Because you didn't know how much I knew – and where I obtained that knowledge. If you kill me now, you never will know.'

But here the emotions of Boris became too much for him. He stepped forward waving his arms.

'You hell-hound of a spy,' he screamed. 'We will give you short shrift. Kill him! Kill him!'

There was a roar of applause.

'You hear?' said the German, his eyes on Tommy. 'What have you got to say to that?'

'Say?' Tommy shrugged his shoulders. 'Pack of fools. Let them ask themselves a few questions. How did I get into this place? Remember what dear old Conrad said – *with your own password*, wasn't it? How did I get hold of that? You don't suppose I came up those steps haphazard and said the first thing that came into my head?'

Tommy was pleased with the concluding words of this speech. His only regret was that Tuppence was not present to appreciate its full flavour.

'That is true,' said the working man suddenly. 'Comrades, we have been betrayed!'

An ugly murmur arose. Tommy smiled at them encouragingly.

'That's better. How can you hope to make a success of any job if you don't use your brains?'

'You will tell us who has betrayed us,' said the German. 'But that shall not save you – oh, no! You shall tell us all that you know. Boris, here, knows pretty ways of making people speak!'

'Bah!' said Tommy scornfully, fighting down a singularly unpleasant feeling in the pit of his stomach. 'You will neither torture me nor kill me.'

'And why not?' asked Boris.

'Because you'd kill the goose that lays the golden eggs,' replied Tommy quietly.

There was a momentary pause. It seemed as though Tommy's persistent assurance was at last conquering. They were no longer completely sure of themselves. The man in the shabby clothes stared at Tommy searchingly.

'He's bluffing you, Boris,' he said quietly.

Tommy hated him. Had the man seen through him?

The German, with an effort, turned roughly to Tommy.

'What do you mean?'

'What do you think I mean?' parried Tommy, searching desperately in his own mind.

Suddenly Boris stepped forward, and shook his fist in Tommy's face.

'Speak, you swine of an Englishman – speak!'

'Don't get so excited, my good fellow,' said Tommy calmly. 'That's the worst of you foreigners. You can't keep calm. Now, I ask you, do I look as though I thought there were the least chance of your killing me?'

He looked confidently round, and was glad they could not hear the persistent beating of his heart which gave the lie to his words.

'No,' admitted Boris at last sullenly, 'you do not.'

'Thank God, he's not a mind reader,' thought Tommy. Aloud he pursued his advantage:

'And why am I so confident? Because I know something that puts me in a position to propose a bargain.'

'A bargain?' The bearded man took him up sharply.

'Yes – a bargain. My life and liberty against –' He paused.

'Against what?'

The group pressed forward. You could have heard a pin drop.

Slowly Tommy spoke.

'The papers that Danvers brought over from America in the *Lusitania*.'

The effect of his words was electrical. Everyone was on his feet. The German waved them back. He leaned over Tommy, his face purple with excitement.

'*Himmel*! You have got them, then?'

With magnificent calm Tommy shook his head.

'You know where they are?' persisted the German.

Again Tommy shook his head. 'Not in the least.'

'Then – then –' angry and baffled, the words failed him.

Tommy looked round. He saw anger and bewilderment on every face, but his calm assurance had done its work – no one doubted but that something lay behind his words.

'I don't know where the papers are – but I believe that I can find them. I have a theory –'

'Pah!'

Tommy raised his hand, and silenced the clamours of disgust.

'I call it a theory – but I'm pretty sure of my facts – facts that are known to no one but myself. In any case what do you lose? If I can produce the papers – you give me my life and liberty in exchange. Is it a bargain?'

'And if we refuse?' said the German quietly.

Tommy lay back on the couch.

'The 29th,' he said thoughtfully, 'is less than a fortnight ahead –'

For a moment the German hesitated. Then he made a sign to Conrad.

'Take him into the other room.'

For five minutes Tommy sat on the bed in the dingy room next door. His heart was beating violently. He had risked all on this throw. How would they decide? And all the while that this agonized questioning went on within him, he talked flippantly to Conrad, enraging the cross-grained doorkeeper to the point of homicidal mania.

At last the door opened, and the German called imperiously to Conrad to return.

'Let's hope the judge hasn't put his black cap on,' remarked Tommy frivolously. 'That's right, Conrad, march me in. The prisoner is at the bar, gentlemen.'

The German was seated once more behind the table. He motioned to Tommy to sit down opposite to him.

'We accept,' he said harshly, 'on terms. The papers must be delivered to us before you go free.'

'Idiot!' said Tommy amiably. 'How do you think I can look for them if you keep me tied by the leg here?'

'What do you expect, then?'

'I must have liberty to go about the business in my own way.'

The German laughed.

'Do you think we are little children to let you walk out of here leaving us a pretty story full of promises?'

'No,' said Tommy thoughtfully. 'Though infinitely simpler for me, I did not really think you would agree to that plan. Very well, we must arrange a compromise. How would it be if you attached little Conrad here to my person. He's a faithful fellow, and very ready with the fist.'

'We prefer,' said the German coldly, 'that you should remain here. One of our number will carry out your instructions minutely. If the operations are complicated, he will return to you with a report and you can instruct him further.'

'You're tying my hands,' complained Tommy. 'It's a very delicate affair, and the other fellow will muff it up as likely as not, and then where shall I be? I don't believe one of you has got an ounce of tact.'

The German rapped the table.

'Those are our terms. Otherwise, death!'

Tommy leaned back wearily.

'I like your style. Curt, but attractive. So be it, then. But one thing is essential, I must see the girl.'

'What girl?'

'Jane Finn, of course.'

The other looked at him curiously for some minutes, then he said slowly, and as though choosing his words with care:

'Do you not know that she can tell you nothing?'

Tommy's heart beat a little faster. Would he succeed in coming face to face with the girl he was seeking?

'I shall not ask her to tell me anything,' he said quietly. 'Not in so many words, that is.'

'Then why see her?'

Tommy paused.

'To watch her face when I ask her one question,' he replied at last.

Again there was a look in the German's eyes that Tommy did not quite understand.

'She will not be able to answer your question.'

'That does not matter. I shall have seen her face when I ask it.'

'And you think that will tell you anything?' He gave a short disagreeable laugh. More than ever, Tommy felt that there was a factor somewhere that he did not understand. The German looked at him searchingly. 'I wonder whether, after all, you know as much as we think?' he said softly.

Tommy felt his ascendancy less sure than a moment before. His hold had slipped a little. But he was puzzled. What had he said wrong? He spoke out on the impulse of the moment.

'There may be things that you know which I do not. I have not pretended to be aware of all the details of your show. But equally I've got something up my sleeve that *you* don't know about. And that's where I mean to score. Danvers was a damned clever fellow –' He broke off as if he had said too much.

But the German's face had lightened a little.

'Danvers,' he murmured. I see –' He paused a minute, then waved to Conrad. 'Take him away. Upstairs – you know.'

'Wait a minute,' said Tommy. 'What about the girl?'

'That may perhaps be arranged.'

'It must be.'

'We will see about it. Only one person can decide that.'

'Who?' asked Tommy. But he knew the answer.

'Mr Brown –'

'Shall I see him?'

'Perhaps.'

'Come,' said Conrad harshly.

Tommy rose obediently. Outside the door his gaoler motioned to him to mount the stairs. He himself followed close behind. On the floor above Conrad opened a door and Tommy passed into a small room. Conrad lit a hissing gas burner and went out. Tommy heard the sound of the key being turned in the lock.

He set to work to examine his prison. It was a smaller room than the one downstairs, and there was something peculiarly airless about the atmosphere of it. Then he realized that there was no window. He walked round it. The walls were filthily dirty, as everywhere else. Four pictures hung crookedly on the wall representing scenes from *Faust*, Marguerite with her box of jewels, the church scene, Siebel and his flowers, and Faust and Mephistopheles. The latter brought Tommy's mind back to Mr Brown again. In this sealed and closed chamber, with its close-fitting heavy door, he felt cut off from the world, and the sinister power of the arch-criminal seemed more real. Shout as he would, no one could ever hear him. The place was a living tomb . . .

With an effort Tommy pulled himself together. He sank on to the bed and gave himself up to reflection. His head ached badly; also, he was hungry. The silence of the place was dispiriting.

'Anyway,' said Tommy, trying to cheer himself, 'I shall see the chief – the mysterious Mr Brown, and with a bit of luck in bluffing I shall see the mysterious Jane Finn also. After that –'

After that Tommy was forced to admit the prospect looked dreary.

CHAPTER 17

ANNETTE

The troubles of the future, however, soon faded before the troubles of the present. And of these, the most immediate and pressing was that of hunger. Tommy had a healthy and vigorous appetite. The steak and chips partaken of for lunch seemed now to belong to another decade. He regretfully recognized the fact that he would not make a success of a hunger strike.

He prowled aimlessly about his prison. Once or twice he discarded dignity, and pounded on the door. But nobody answered the summons.

'Hang it all!' said Tommy indignantly. 'They can't mean to starve me to death.' A new-born fear passed through his mind that this might, perhaps, be one of those 'pretty ways' of making a prisoner speak, which had been attributed to Boris. But on reflection he dismissed the idea.

'It's that sour-faced brute Conrad,' he decided. 'That's a fellow I shall enjoy getting even with one of these days. This is just a bit of spite on his part. I'm certain of it.'

Further meditations induced in him the feeling that it would be extremely pleasant to bring something down with a whack on Conrad's egg-shaped head. Tommy stroked his own head tenderly, and gave himself up to the pleasures of imagination. Finally a bright idea flashed across his brain. Why not convert imagination into reality! Conrad was undoubtedly the tenant of the house. The others, with the possible exception of the bearded German, merely used it as a rendezvous. Therefore, why not wait in ambush for Conrad behind the door, and when he entered bring down a chair, or one of the decrepit pictures, smartly on to his head. One would, of course, be careful not to hit too hard. And then – and then, simply walk out! If he met anyone on the way down, well – Tommy brightened at the thought of an encounter with his fists. Such an affair was infinitely more in his line than the verbal encounter of this afternoon. Intoxicated by his plan, Tommy gently unhooked the picture of the Devil and Faust, and settled himself in position. His hopes were high. The plan seemed to him simple but excellent.

Time went on, but Conrad did not appear. Night and day were the same in this prison room, but Tommy's wrist-watch, which enjoyed a certain degree of accuracy, informed him that it was nine o'clock in the evening. Tommy reflected gloomily that if supper did not arrive soon it would be a question of waiting for breakfast. At ten o'clock hope deserted him, and he flung himself on the bed to seek consolation in sleep. In five minutes his woes were forgotten.

The sound of the key turning in the lock awoke him from his slumbers. Not belonging to the type of hero who is famous for awaking in full possession of his faculties, Tommy merely blinked at the ceiling and wondered vaguely where he was. Then he remembered, and looked at his watch. It was eight o'clock.

'It's either early morning tea or breakfast,' deduced the young man, 'and pray God it's the latter!'

The door swung open. Too late, Tommy remembered his scheme of obliterating the unprepossessing Conrad. A moment later he was glad that he had, for it was not Conrad who entered, but a girl. She carried a tray which she set down on the table.

In the feeble light of the gas burner Tommy blinked at her. He decided at once that she was one of the most beautiful girls he had ever seen. Her hair was a full rich brown, with sudden glints of gold in it as though there were imprisoned sunbeams struggling in its depths. There was a wild-rose quality about her face. Her eyes, set wide apart, were hazel, a golden hazel that again recalled a memory of sunbeams.

A delirious thought shot through Tommy's mind.

'Are you Jane Finn?' he asked breathlessly.

The girl shook her head wonderingly.

'My name is Annette, monsieur.'

She spoke in a soft, broken English.

'Oh!' said Tommy, rather taken aback. '*Française*?' he hazarded.

'*Oui, monsieur. Monsieur parle français*?'

'Not for any length of time,' said Tommy. 'What's that? Breakfast?'

The girl nodded. Tommy dropped off the bed and came and inspected the contents of the tray. It consisted of a loaf, some margarine, and a jug of coffee.

'The living is not equal to the Ritz,' he observed with a sigh. 'But for what we are at last about to receive the Lord has made me truly thankful. Amen.'

He drew up a chair, and the girl turned away to the door.

'Wait a sec,' cried Tommy. 'There are lots of things I want to ask you, Annette. What are you doing in this house? Don't tell me you're Conrad's niece, or daughter, or anything, because I can't believe it.'

'I do the *service*, monsieur. I am not related to anybody.'

'I see,' said Tommy. 'You know what I asked you just now. Have you ever heard that name?'

'I have heard people speak of Jane Finn, I think.'

'You don't know where she is?'

Annette shook her head.

'She's not in this house, for instance?'

'Oh no, monsieur. I must go now – they will be waiting for me.'

She hurried out. They key turned in the lock.

'I wonder who "they" are,' mused Tommy, as he continued to make inroads on the loaf. 'With a bit of luck, that girl might help me to get out of here. She doesn't look like one of the gang.'

At one o'clock Annette reappeared with another tray, but this time Conrad accompanied her.

'Good morning,' said Tommy amiably. 'You have *not* used Pear's soap, I see.'

Conrad growled threateningly.

'No light repartee, have you, old bean? There, there, we can't always have brains as well as beauty. What have we for lunch? Stew? How did I know? Elementary, my dear Watson – the smell of onions is unmistakable.'

'Talk away,' grunted the man. 'It's little enough time you'll have to talk in, maybe.'

The remark was unpleasant in its suggestion, but Tommy ignored it. He sat down at the table.

'Retire, varlet,' he said, with a wave of his hand. 'Prate not to thy betters.'

That evening Tommy sat on the bed, and cogitated deeply. Would Conrad again accompany the girl? If he did not, should he risk trying to make an ally of her? He decided that he must leave no stone unturned. His position was desperate.

At eight o'clock the familiar sound of the key turning made him spring to his feet. The girl was alone.

'Shut the door,' he commanded. 'I want to speak to you.'

She obeyed.

'Look here, Annette, I want you to help me get out of this.'

She shook her head.

'Impossible. There are three of them on the floor below.'

'Oh!' Tommy was secretly grateful for the information. 'But you would help me if you could?'

'No, monsieur.'

'Why not?'

The girl hesitated.

'I think – they are my own people. You have spied upon them. They are quite right to keep you here.'

'They're a bad lot, Annette. If you'll help me, I'll take you away from the lot of them. And you'd probably get a good whack of money.'

But the girl merely shook her head.

'I dare not, monsieur. I am afraid of them.'

She turned away.

'Wouldn't you do anything to help another girl?' cried Tommy. 'She's about your age too. Won't you save her from their clutches?'

'You mean Jane Finn?'

'Yes.'

'It is her you came here to look for? Yes?'

'That's it.'

The girl looked at him, then passed her hand across her forehead.

'Jane Finn. Always I hear that name. It is familiar.'

Tommy came forward eagerly.

'You must know *something* about her?'

But the girl turned away abruptly.

'I know nothing – only the name.' She walked towards the door. Suddenly she uttered a cry. Tommy stared. She had caught sight of the picture he had laid against the wall the night before. For a moment he caught a look of terror in her eyes. As inexplicably it changed to relief. Then abruptly, she went out of the room. Tommy could make nothing of it. Did she fancy that he had meant to attack her with it? Surely not. He rehung the picture on the wall thoughtfully.

Three more days went by in dreary inaction. Tommy felt the strain telling on his nerves. He saw no one but Conrad and Annette, and the girl had become dumb. She spoke only in monosyllables. A kind of dark suspicion smouldered in her eyes. Tommy felt that if this solitary confinement went on much longer he would go mad. He gathered from Conrad that they were waiting for orders from 'Mr Brown'. Perhaps, thought Tommy, he was abroad or away, and they were obliged to wait for his return.

But the evening of the third day brought a rude awakening.

It was barely seven o'clock when he heard the tramp of footsteps outside in the passage. In another minute the door was flung open. Conrad entered. With him was the evil-looking Number Fourteen. Tommy's heart sank at the sight of them.

'Evenin', gov'nor,' said the man with a leer. 'Got those ropes, mate?'

The silent Conrad produced a length of fine cord. The next minute Number Fourteen's hands, horribly dexterous, were winding the cord round his limbs, while Conrad held him down.

'What the devil –?' began Tommy.

But the slow, speechless grin of the silent Conrad froze the words on his lips.

Number Fourteen proceeded deftly with his task. In another minute Tommy was a mere helpless bundle. Then at last Conrad spoke:

'Thought you'd bluffed us, did you? With what you knew, and what you didn't know. Bargained with us! And all the time it was bluff! Bluff! You know less than a kitten. But your number's up all right, you b— swine.'

Tommy lay silent. There was nothing to say. He had failed. Somehow or other the omnipotent Mr Brown had seen through his pretensions. Suddenly a thought occurred to him.

'A very good speech, Conrad,' he said approvingly. 'But wherefore the bonds and fetters? Why not let this kind gentleman here cut my throat without delay?'

'Garn,' said Number Fourteen unexpectedly. 'Think we're as green as to do you in here, and have the police nosing round? Not 'alf! We've ordered the carriage for your lordship tomorrow mornin', but in the meantime we're not taking any chances, see!'

'Nothing,' said Tommy, 'could be plainer than your words – unless it was your face.'

'Stow it,' said Number Fourteen.

'With pleasure,' replied Tommy. 'You're making a sad mistake – but yours will be the loss.'

'You don't kid us that way again,' said Number Fourteen. 'Talking as though you were still at the blooming Ritz, aren't you?'

Tommy made no reply. He was engaged in wondering how Mr Brown had discovered his identity. He decided that Tuppence, in the throes of anxiety, had gone to the police, and that his disappearance having been made public the gang had not been slow to put two and two together.

The two men departed and the door slammed. Tommy was left to his meditations. They were not pleasant ones. Already his limbs felt cramped and stiff. He was utterly helpless, and he could see no hope anywhere.

About an hour had passed when he heard the key softly turned, and the door opened. It was Annette. Tommy's heart beat a little faster. He had forgotten the girl. Was it possible that she had come to his help?

Suddenly he heard Conrad's voice:

'Come out of it, Annette. He doesn't want any supper tonight.'

'*Oui, oui, je sais bien.* But I must take the other tray. We need the things on it.'

'Well, hurry up,' growled Conrad.

Without looking at Tommy the girl went over to the table, and picked up the tray. She raised a hand and turned out the light.

'Curse you,' – Conrad had come to the door – 'why did you do that?'

'I always turn it out. You should have told me. Shall I relight it, Monsieur Conrad?'

'No, come on out of it.'

'*Le beau petit monsieur*,' cried Annette, pausing by the bed in the darkness. 'You have tied him up well, *hein*? He is liked a trussed chicken!' The frank amusement in her tone jarred on the boy but at that moment to his amazement, he felt her hand running lightly over his bonds, and something small and cold was pressed into the palm of his hand.

'Come on, Annette.'

'*Mais me voilà.*'

The door shut. Tommy heard Conrad say:

'Lock it and give me the key.'

The footsteps died away. Tommy lay petrified with amazement. The object Annette had thrust into his hand was a small penknife, the blade open. From the way she had studiously avoided looking at him, and her action with the light, he came to the conclusion that the room was overlooked. There must be a peep-hole somewhere in the walls. Remembering how guarded she had always been in her manner, he saw that he had probably been under observation all the time. Had he said anything to give himself away? Hardly. He had revealed a wish to escape and a desire to find Jane Finn, but nothing that could have given a clue to his own identity. True, his question to Annette had proved that he was personally unacquainted with Jane Finn, but he had never pretended otherwise. The question now was, did Annette really know more? Were her denials intended primarily for the listeners? On that point he could come to no conclusion.

But there was a more vital question that drove out all others. Could he, bound as he was, manage to cut his bonds? He essayed cautiously to rub the open blade up and down on the cord that bound his two wrists together. It was an awkward business and drew a smothered 'Ow' of pain from him as the knife cut into his wrist. But slowly and doggedly he went on sawing to and fro. He cut the flesh badly, but at last he felt the cord slacken. With his hands free, the rest was easy. Five minutes later he stood upright with some difficulty owing to the cramp in his limbs. His first care was to bind up his bleeding wrist. Then he sat on the edge of the bed to think. Conrad had taken the key of the door, so he could expect little more assistance from Annette. The only outlet from the room was the door, consequently he would perforce have to wait until the two men returned to fetch him. But when they did . . . Tommy smiled! Moving with infinite caution in the dark room, he found and unhooked the famous picture. He felt an economical pleasure that his first plan would not be wasted. There was now nothing to do but to wait. He waited.

The night passed slowly. Tommy lived through an eternity of hours, but at last he heard footsteps. He stood upright, drew a deep breath, and clutched the picture firmly.

The door opened. A faint light streamed in from outside. Conrad went straight towards the gas to light it. Tommy deeply regretted that it was he who had entered first. It would have been pleasant to get even with Conrad. Number Fourteen followed. As he stepped across the threshold, Tommy brought the picture down with terrific force on his head. Number Fourteen went down amidst a stupendous crash of broken glass. In a minute Tommy had slipped out and pulled to the door. The key was in the lock. He turned it and withdrew it just as Conrad hurled himself against the door from the inside with a volley of curses.

For a moment Tommy hesitated. There was the sound of someone stirring on the floor below. Then the German's voice came up the stairs.

'*Gott im Himmel*! Conrad, what is it?'

Tommy felt a small hand thrust into his. Beside him stood Annette. She pointed up a rickety ladder that apparently led to some attics.

'Quick – up here!' She dragged him after her up the ladder. In another moment they were standing in a dusty garret littered with lumber. Tommy looked round.

'This won't do. It's a regular trap. There's no way out.'

'Hush! Wait.' The girl put her finger to her lips. She crept to the top of the ladder and listened.

The banging and beating on the door was terrific. The German and another were trying to force the door in. Annette explained in a whisper:

'They will think you are still inside. They cannot hear what Conrad says. The door is too thick.'

'I thought you could hear what went on in the room?'

'There is a peep-hole into the next room. It was clever of you to guess. But they will not think of that – they are only anxious to get in.'

'Yes – but look here –'

'Leave it to me.' She bent down. To his amazement, Tommy saw that she was fastening the end of a long piece of string to the handle of a big cracked jug. She arranged it carefully, then turned to Tommy.

'Have you the key of the door?'

'Yes.'

'Give it to me.'

He handed it to her.

'I am going down. Do you think you can go half-way, and

then swing yourself down *behind* the ladder, so that they will not see you?'

Tommy nodded.

'There's a big cupboard in the shadow of the landing. Stand behind it. Take the end of this string in your hand. When I've let the others out – *pull*!'

Before he had time to ask her anything more, she had flitted lightly down the ladder and was in the midst of the group with a loud cry:

'*Mon Dieu! Mon Dieu! Qu'est-ce qu'il y a*?'

The German turned on her with an oath.

'Get out of this. Go to your room!'

Very cautiously Tommy swung himself down the back of the ladder. So long as they did not turn round, all was well. He crouched behind the cupboard. They were still between him and the stairs.

'Ah!' Annette appeared to stumble over something. She stooped. '*Mon Dieu, voilà la clef*!'

The German snatched it from her. He unlocked the door. Conrad stumbled out, swearing.

'Where is he? Have you got him?'

'We have seen no one,' said the German sharply. His face paled. 'Who do you mean?'

Conrad gave vent to another oath.

'He's got away.'

'Impossible. He would have passed us.'

At that moment, with an ecstatic smile Tommy pulled the string. A crash of crockery came from the attic above. In a trice the men were pushing each other up the rickety ladder and had disappeared into the darkness above.

Quick as a flash Tommy leapt from his hiding-place and dashed down the stairs, pulling the girl with him. There was no one in the hall. He fumbled over the bolts and chain. At last they yielded, the door swung open. He turned. Annette had disappeared.

Tommy stood spell-bound. Had she run upstairs again? What madness possessed her! He fumed with impatience, but he stood his ground. He would not go without her.

And suddenly there was an outcry overhead, an exclamation from the German, and then Annette's voice, clear and high:

'*Ma foi*, he has escaped! And quickly! Who would have thought it?'

Tommy still stood rooted to the ground. Was that a command to him to go? He fancied it was.

And then, louder still, the words floated down to him:

'This is a terrible house. I want to go back to Marguerite. To Marguerite. *To Marguerite*!'

Tommy had run back to the stairs. She wanted him to go and leave her? But why? At all costs he must try to get her away with him. Then his heart sank. Conrad was leaping down the stairs uttering a savage cry at the sight of him. After him came the others.

Tommy stopped Conrad's rush with a straight blow with his fist. It caught the other on the point of the jaw and he fell like a log. The second man tripped over his body and fell. From higher up the staircase there was a flash, and a bullet grazed Tommy's ear. He realized that it would be good for his health to get out of this house as soon as possible. As regards Annette he could do nothing. He had got even with Conrad, which was one satisfaction. The blow had been a good one.

He leapt for the door, slamming it behind him. The square was deserted. In front of the house was a baker's van. Evidently he was to have been taken out of London in that, and his body found many miles from the house in Soho. The driver jumped to the pavement and tried to bar Tommy's way. Again Tommy's fist shot out, and the driver sprawled on the pavement.

Tommy took to his heels and ran – none too soon. The front door opened and a hail of bullets followed him. Fortunately none of them hit him. He turned the corner of the square.

'There's one thing,' he thought to himself, 'they can't go on shooting. They'll have the police after them if they do. I wonder they dared to there.'

He heard the footsteps of his pursuers behind him, and redoubled his own pace. Once he got out of these by-ways he would be safe. There would be a policeman about somewhere – not that he really wanted to invoke the aid of the police if he could possibly do without it. It meant explanation, and general awkwardness. In another moment he had reason to bless his luck. He stumbled over a prostrate figure, which started up with a yell of alarm and dashed off down the street. Tommy drew back into a doorway. In a minute he had the pleasure of seeing his two pursuers, of whom the German was one, industriously tracking down the red herring!

Tommy sat down quietly on the doorstep and allowed a few moments to elapse while he recovered his breath. Then he strolled gently in the opposite direction. He glanced at his watch. It was a little after half-past five. It was rapidly growing light. At the next corner he passed a policeman. The policeman cast a suspicious eye on him. Tommy felt slightly offended. Then, passing his hand over his face, he laughed. He had not shaved or washed for three days! What a guy he must look.

He betook himself without more ado to a Turkish Bath establishment which he knew to be open all night. He emerged into the busy daylight feeling himself once more, and able to make plans.

First of all, he must have a square meal. He had eaten nothing since midday yesterday. He turned into an A.B.C. shop and ordered eggs and bacon and coffee. Whilst he ate, he read a morning paper propped up in front of him. Suddenly he stiffened. There was a long article on Kramenin, who was described as the 'man behind Bolshevism' in Russia, and who had just arrived in London – some thought as an unofficial envoy. His career was sketched lightly, and it was firmly asserted that he, and not the figurehead leaders, had been the author of the Russian Revolution.

In the centre of the page was his portrait.

'So that's who Number One is,' said Tommy with his mouth full of eggs and bacon. 'Not a doubt about it. I must push on.'

He paid for his breakfast, and betook himself to Whitehall. There he sent up his name, and the message that it was urgent. A few minutes later he was in the presence of the man who did not here go by the name of 'Mr Carter'. There was a frown on his face.

'Look here, you've no business to come asking for me in this way. I thought that was distinctly understood?'

'It was, sir. But I judged it important to lose no time.'

And as briefly and succinctly as possible he detailed the experiences of the last few days.

Half-way through, Mr Carter interrupted him to give a few

cryptic orders through the telephone. All traces of displeasure had now left his face. He nodded energetically when Tommy had finished.

'Quite right. Every moment's of value. Fear we shall be too late anyway. They wouldn't wait. Would clear out at once. Still, they may have left something behind them that will be a clue. You say you've recognized Number One to be Kramenin? That's important. We want something against him badly to prevent the Cabinet falling on his neck too freely. What about the others? You say two faces were familiar to you? One's a Labour man, you think? Just look through these photos, and see if you can spot him.'

A minute later, Tommy held one up. Mr Carter exhibited some surprise.

'Ah, Westway! Shouldn't have thought it. Poses as being moderate. As for the other fellow, I think I can give a good guess.' He handed another photograph to Tommy, and smiled at the other's exclamation. 'I'm right, then. Who is he? Irishman. Prominent Unionist M.P. All a blind, of course. We've suspected it – but couldn't get any proof. Yes, you've done very well, young man. The 29th, you say, is the date. That gives us very little time – very little time indeed.'

'But –' Tommy hesitated.

Mr Carter read his thoughts.

'We can deal with the General Strike menace, I think. It's a toss-up – but we've got a sporting chance! But if that draft treaty turns up – we're done. England will be plunged in anarchy. Ah, what's that? The car? Come on, Beresford, we'll go and have a look at this house of yours.'

Two constables were on duty in front of the house in Soho. An inspector reported to Mr Carter in a low voice. The latter turned to Tommy.

'The birds have flown – as we thought. We might as well go over it.'

Going over the deserted house seemed to Tommy to partake of the character of a dream. Everything was just as it had been. The prison room with the crooked pictures, the broken jug in the attic, the meeting room with its long table. But nowhere was there a trace of papers. Everything of that kind had either been destroyed or taken away. And there was no sign of Annette.

'What you tell me about the girl puzzled me,' said Mr Carter. 'You believe that she deliberately went back?'

'It would seem so, sir. She ran upstairs while I was getting the door open.'

'H'm, she must belong to the gang, then; but, being a woman, didn't feel like standing by to see a personable young man killed. But evidently she's in with them, or she wouldn't have gone back.'

'I can't believe she's really one of them, sir. She – seemed so different –'

'Good-looking, I suppose?' said Mr Carter with a smile that made Tommy flush to the roots of his hair.

He admitted Annette's beauty rather shame-facedly.

'By the way,' observed Mr Carter, 'have you shown yourself to Miss Tuppence yet? She's been bombarding me with letters about you.'

'Tuppence? I was afraid she might get a bit rattled. Did she go to the police?'

Mr Carter shook his head.

'Then I wonder how they twigged me.'

Mr Carter looked inquiringly at him, and Tommy explained. The other nodded thoughtfully.

'True, that's rather a curious point. Unless the mention of the Ritz was an accidental remark?'

'It might have been, sir. But they must have found out about me suddenly in some way.'

'Well,' said Mr Carter, looking round him, 'there's nothing more to be done here. What about some lunch with me?'

'Thanks awfully, sir. But I think I'd better get back and rout out Tuppence.'

'Of course. Give her my kind regards and tell her not to believe you're killed too readily next time.'

Tommy grinned.

'I take a lot of killing, sir.'

'So I perceive,' said Mr Carter dryly. 'Well, goodbye. Remember you're a marked man now, and take reasonable care of yourself.'

'Thank you, sir.'

Hailing a taxi briskly Tommy stepped in, and was swiftly borne to the Ritz, dwelling the while on the pleasurable anticipation of startling Tuppence.

'Wonder what she's been up to. Dogging "Rita" most likely. By the way, I suppose that's who Annette meant by Marguerite. I didn't get it at the time.' The thought saddened him a little, for it seemed to prove that Mrs Vandemeyer and the girl were on intimate terms.

The taxi drew up at the Ritz. Tommy burst into its sacred portals eagerly, but his enthusiasm received a check. He was informed that Miss Cowley had gone out a quarter of an hour ago.

CHAPTER 18

THE TELEGRAM

Baffled for the moment, Tommy strolled into the restaurant, and ordered a meal of surpassing excellence. His four days' imprisonment had taught him anew to value good food.

He was in the middle of conveying a particularly choice morsel of *sole à la Jeannette* to his mouth, when he caught sight of Julius entering the room. Tommy waved a menu cheerfully, and succeeded in attracting the other's attention. At the sight of Tommy, Julius's eyes seemed as though they would pop out of his head. He strode across, and pump-handled Tommy's hand with what seemed to the latter quite unnecessary vigour.

'Holy snakes!' he ejaculated. 'Is it really you?'

'Of course it is. Why shouldn't it be?'

'Why shouldn't it be? Say, man, don't you know you've been given up for dead? I guess we'd have had a solemn requiem for you in another few days.'

'Who thought I was dead?' demanded Tommy.

'Tuppence.'

'She remembered the proverb about the good dying young, I suppose. There must be a certain amount of original sin in me to have survived. Where is Tuppence, by the way?'

'Isn't she here?'

'No, the fellows at the office said she'd just gone out.'

'Gone shopping, I guess. I dropped her here in the car about an hour ago. But, say, can't you shed that British calm of yours, and get down to it? What on God's earth have you been doing all this time?'

'If you're feeding here,' replied Tommy, 'order now. It's going to be a long story.'

Julius drew up a chair to the opposite side of the table, summoned a hovering waiter, and dictated his wishes. Then he turned to Tommy.

'Fire ahead. I guess you've had some few adventures.'

'One or two,' replied Tommy modestly, and plunged into his recital.

Julius listened spell-bound. Half the dishes that were placed before him he forgot to eat. At the end he heaved a long sigh.

'Bully for you. Reads like a dime novel!'

'And now for the home front,' said Tommy, stretching out his hand for a peach.

'W – ell,' drawled Julius, 'I don't mind admitting we've had some adventures too.'

He, in his turn, assumed the role of narrator. Beginning with his unsuccessful reconnoitring at Bournemouth, he passed on to his return to London, the buying of the car, the growing anxieties of Tuppence, the call upon Sir James, and the sensational occurrences of the previous night.

'But who killed her?' asked Tommy. 'I don't quite understand.'

'The doctor kidded himself she took it herself,' replied Julius dryly.

'And Sir James? What did he think?'

'Being a legal luminary, he is likewise a human oyster,' replied Julius. 'I should say he "reserved judgment".' He went on to detail the events of the morning.

'Lost her memory, eh?' said Tommy with interest. 'By Jove, that explains why they looked at me so queerly when I spoke of questioning her. Bit of a slip on my part, that! But it wasn't the sort of thing a fellow would be likely to guess.'

'They didn't give you any sort of hint as to where Jane was?'

Tommy shook his head regretfully.

'Not a word. I'm a bit of an ass, as you know. I ought to have got more out of them somehow.'

'I guess you're lucky to be here at all. That bluff of yours was the goods all right. How you ever came to think of it all so pat beats me to a frazzle!'

'I was in such a funk I had to think of something,' said Tommy simply.

There was a moment's pause, and then Tommy reverted to Mrs Vandemeyer's death.

'There's no doubt it was chloral?'

'I believe not. At least they call it heart failure induced by an overdose, or some such claptrap. It's all right. We don't want to be worried with an inquest. But I guess Tuppence and I and even the highbrow Sir James have all got the same idea.'

'Mr Brown?' hazarded Tommy.

'Sure thing.'

Tommy nodded.

'All the same,' he said thoughtfully, 'Mr Brown hasn't got wings. I don't see how he got in and out.'

'How about some high-class thought transference stunt? Some magnetic influence that irresistibly impelled Mrs Vandemeyer to commit suicide?'

Tommy looked at him with respect.

'Good, Julius. Distinctly good. Especially the phraseology. But it leaves me cold. I yearn for a real Mr Brown of flesh and blood. I think the gifted young detectives must get to work, study the entrances and exits, and tap the bumps on their foreheads until the solution of the mystery dawns on them. Let's go round to the scene of the crime. I wish we could get hold of Tuppence. The Ritz would enjoy the spectacle of the glad reunion.'

Inquiry at the office revealed the fact that Tuppence had not yet returned.

'All the same, I guess I'll have a look round upstairs,' said Julius. 'She might be in my sitting-room.' He disappeared.

Suddenly a diminutive boy spoke at Tommy's elbow:

'The young lady – she's gone away by train, I think, sir,' he murmured shyly.

'What?' Tommy wheeled round upon him.

The small boy became pinker than before.

'The taxi, sir. I heard her tell the driver Charing Cross and to look sharp.'

Tommy stared at him, his eyes opening wide in surprise. Emboldened, the small boy proceeded. 'So I thought, having asked for an A.B.C. and a Bradshaw.'

Tommy interrupted him:

'When did she ask for an A.B.C. and a Bradshaw?'

'When I took her the telegram, sir.'

'A telegram?'

'Yes, sir.'

'When was that?'

'About half-past twelve, sir.'

'Tell me exactly what happened.'

The small boy drew a long breath.

'I took up a telegram to No. 891 – the lady was there. She opened it and gave a gasp, and then she said, very jolly like: "Bring me up a Bradshaw, and an A.B.C., and look sharp, Henry." My name isn't Henry, but –'

'Never mind your name,' said Tommy impatiently. 'Go on.'

'Yes, sir. I brought them, and she told me to wait, and looked up something. And then she looks up at the clock, and "Hurry up," she says. "Tell them to get me a taxi," and she begins a-shoving on of her hat in front of the glass, and she was down in two ticks, almost as quick as I was, and I seed her going down the steps and into the taxi, and I heard her call out what I told you.'

The small boy stopped and replenished his lungs. Tommy continued to stare at him. At that moment Julius rejoined him. He held an open letter in his hand.

'I say, Hersheimmer,' – Tommy turned to him – 'Tuppence has gone off sleuthing on her own.'

'Shucks!'

'Yes, she has. She went off in a taxi to Charing Cross in the deuce of a hurry after getting a telegram.' His eye fell on the letter in Julius's hand. 'Oh; she left a note for you. That's all right. Where's she off to?'

Almost unconsciously, he held out his hand for the letter, but Julius folded it up and placed it in his pocket. He seemed a trifle embarrassed.

'I guess this is nothing to do with it. It's about something else – something I asked her that she was to let me know about.'

'Oh!' Tommy looked puzzled, and seemed waiting for more.

'See here,' said Julius suddenly, 'I'd better put you wise. I asked Miss Tuppence to marry me this morning.'

'Oh!' said Tommy mechanically. He felt dazed. Julius's words were totally unexpected. For the moment they benumbed his brain.

'I'd like to tell you,' continued Julius, 'that before I suggested anything of the kind to Miss Tuppence, I made it clear that I didn't want to butt in in any way between her and you –'

Tommy roused himself.

'That's all right,' he said quickly. 'Tuppence and I have been pals for years. Nothing more.' He lit a cigarette with a hand that shook ever so little. 'That's quite all right. Tuppence always said that she was looking out for –'

He stopped abruptly, his face crimsoning, but Julius was in no way discomposed.

'Oh, I guess it'll be the dollars that'll do the trick. Miss Tuppence put me wise to that right away. There's no humbug about her. We ought to gee along together very well.'

Tommy looked at him curiously for a minute, as though he were about to speak, then changed his mind and said nothing. Tuppence and Julius! Well, why not? Had she not lamented the fact that she knew no rich men? Had she not openly avowed her intention of marrying for money if she ever had the chance? Her meeting with the young American millionaire had given her the chance – and it was unlikely she would be slow to avail herself of it. She was out for money. She had always said so. Why blame her because she had been true to her creed?

Nevertheless, Tommy did blame her. He was filled with a passionate and utterly illogical resentment. It was all very well to *say* things like that – but a *real* girl would never marry for money. Tuppence was utterly cold-blooded and selfish, and he would be delighted if he never saw her again! And it was a rotten world!

Julius's voice broke in on these meditations.

'Yes, we ought to gee along together very well. I've heard that a girl always refuses you once – a sort of convention.'

Tommy caught his arm.

'Refuses? Did you say *refuses*?'

'Sure thing. Didn't I tell you that? She just rapped out a "no" without any kind of reason to it. The eternal feminine, the Huns call it, I've heard. But she'll come round right enough. Likely enough, I hustled her some –'

But Tommy interrupted regardless of decorum.

'What did she say in that note?' he demanded fiercely.

The obliging Julius handed it to him.

'There's no earthly clue in it as to where she's gone,' he assured Tommy. 'But you might as well see for yourself if you don't believe me.'

The note, in Tuppence's well-known schoolboy writing, ran as follows:

Dear Julius,

It's always better to have things in black and white. I don't feel I can be bothered to think of marriage until Tommy is found. Let's leave it till then.

Yours affectionately,

Tuppence.

Tommy handed it back, his eyes shining. His feelings had undergone a sharp reaction. He now felt that Tuppence was all that was noble and disinterested. Had she not refused Julius without hesitation? True, the note betokened signs of weakening, but he could excuse that. It read almost like a bribe to Julius to spur him on in his efforts to find Tommy, but he supposed she had not really meant it that way. Darling Tuppence, there was not a girl in the world to touch her! When he saw her – His thoughts were brought up with a sudden jerk.

'As you say,' he remarked, pulling himself together, 'there's not a hint here as to what she's up to. Hi – Henry!'

The small boy came obediently. Tommy produced five shillings.

'One thing more. Do you remember what the young lady did with the telegram?'

Henry gasped and spoke.

'She crumpled it up into a ball and threw it into the grate, and made a sort of noise like "Whoop!" sir.'

'Very graphic, Henry,' said Tommy. 'Here's your five shillings. Come on, Julius. We must find that telegram.'

They hurried upstairs. Tuppence had left the key in her door. The room was as she had left it. In the fire-place was a crumpled ball of orange and white. Tommy disentangled it and smoothed out the telegram.

Come at once, Moat House, Ebury, Yorkshire, great developments – Tommy.

They looked at each other in stupefaction. Julius spoke first:

'*You* didn't send it?'

'Of course not. What does it mean?'

'I guess it means the worst,' said Julius quietly. 'They've got her.'

'*What*?'

'Sure thing! They signed your name, and she fell into the trap like a lamb.'

'My God! What shall we do?'

'Get busy, and go after her! Right now! There's no time to waste. It's almighty luck that she didn't take the wire with her. If she had we'd probably never have traced her. But we've got to hustle. Where's that Bradshaw?'

The energy of Julius was infectious. Left to himself, Tommy would probably have sat down to think things out for a good half-hour before he decided on a plan of action. But with Julius Hersheimmer about, hustling was inevitable.

After a few muttered imprecations he handed the Bradshaw to Tommy as being more conversant with its mysteries. Tommy abandoned it in favour of an A.B.C.

'Here we are. Ebury, Yorks. From King's Cross. Or St Pancras. (Boy must have made a mistake. It was King's Cross, not *Charing* Cross) 12.50, that's the train she went by; 2.10, that's gone; 3.20 is the next – and a damned slow train, too.'

'What about the car?'

Tommy shook his head.

'Send it up if you like, but we'd better stick to the train. The great thing is to keep calm.'

Julius groaned.

'That's so. But it gets my goat to think of that innocent young girl in danger!'

Tommy nodded abstractedly. He was thinking. In a moment or two, he said:

'I say, Julius, what do they want her for, anyway?'

'Eh? I don't get you?'

'What I mean is that I don't think it's their game to do her any harm,' explained Tommy, puckering his brow with the strain of his mental processes. 'She's a hostage, that's what she is. She's in no immediate danger, because if we tumble on to anything, she'd be damned useful to them. As long as they've got her, they've got the whip hand of us. See?'

'Sure thing,' said Julius thoughtfully. 'That's so.'

'Besides,' added Tommy, as an afterthought, 'I've great faith in Tuppence.'

The journey was wearisome, with many stops, and crowded carriages. They had to change twice, once at Doncaster, once at a small junction. Ebury was a deserted station with a solitary porter, to whom Tommy addressed himself:

'Can you tell me the way to the Moat House?'

'The Moat House? It's a tidy step from here. The big house near the sea, you mean?'

Tommy assented brazenly. After listening to the porter's meticulous but perplexing directions, they prepared to leave the station. It was beginning to rain, and they turned up the collars of their coats as they trudged through the slush of the road. Suddenly Tommy halted.

'Wait a moment.' He ran back to the station and tackled the porter anew.

'Look here, do you remember a young lady who arrived by an earlier train, the 12.10 from London? She'd probably ask you the way to the Moat House.'

He described Tuppence as well as he could, but the porter shook his head. Several people had arrived by the train in question. He could not call to mind one young lady in particular. But he was quite certain that no one had asked him the way to the Moat House.

Tommy rejoined Julius, and explained. Depression was settling down on him like a leaden weight. He felt convinced that their quest was going to be unsuccessful. The enemy had over three hours' start. Three hours was more than enough for Mr Brown.

He would not ignore the possibility of the telegram having been found.

The way seemed endless. Once they took the wrong turning and went nearly half a mile out of their direction. It was past seven o'clock when a small boy told them that 't' Moat House' was just past the next corner.

A rusty iron gate swinging dismally on its hinges! An overgrown drive thick with leaves. There was something about the place that struck a chill to both their hearts. They went up the deserted drive. The leaves deadened their footsteps. The daylight was almost gone. It was like walking in a world of ghosts. Overhead the branches flapped and creaked with a mournful note. Occasionally a sodden leaf drifted silently down, startling them with its cold touch on their cheeks.

A turn of the drive brought them in sight of the house. That, too, seemed empty and deserted. The shutters were closed, the steps up to the door overgrown with moss. Was it indeed to this desolate spot that Tuppence had been decoyed? It seemed hard to believe that a human footstep had passed this way for months.

Julius jerked the rusty bell handle. A jangling peal rang discordantly, echoing through the emptiness within. No one came. They rang again and again – but there was no sign of life. Then they walked completely round the house. Everywhere silence, and shuttered windows. If they could believe the evidence of their eyes the place was empty.

'Nothing doing,' said Julius.

They retraced their steps slowly to the gate.

'There must be a village handy,' continued the young American. 'We'd better make inquiries there. They'll know something about the place, and whether there's been anyone there lately.'

'Yes, that's not a bad idea.'

Proceeding up the road they soon came to a little hamlet. On the outskirts of it, they met a workman swinging his bag of tools, and Tommy stopped him with a question.

'The Moat House? It's empty. Been empty for years. Mrs Sweeney's got the key if you want to go over it – next to the post office.'

Tommy thanked him. They soon found the post office, which was also a sweet and general fancy shop, and knocked at the door of the cottage next to it. A clean, wholesome-looking woman opened it. She readily produced the key of the Moat House.

'Though I doubt if it's the kind of place to suit you, sir. In a terrible state of repair. Ceilings leaking and all. 'Twould need a lot of money spent on it.'

'Thanks,' said Tommy cheerily. 'I dare say it'll be a wash-out, but houses are scarce nowadays.'

'That they are,' declared the woman heartily. 'My daughter and son-in-law have been looking for a decent cottage for I don't know how long. It's all the war. Upset things terribly, it has. But excuse me, sir, it'll be too dark for you to see much of the house. Hadn't you better wait until tomorrow?'

'That's all right. We'll have a look round this evening, anyway. We'd have been here before only we lost our way. What's the best place to stay at for the night round here?'

Mrs Sweeney looked doubtful.

'There's the Yorkshire Arms, but it's not much of a place for gentlemen like you.'

'Oh, it will do very well. Thanks. By the way, you've not had a young lady here asking for this key today?'

The woman shook her head.

'No one's been over the place for a long time.'

'Thanks very much.'

They retraced their steps to the Moat House. As the front door swung back on its hinges, protesting loudly, Julius struck a match and examined the floor carefully. Then he shook his head.

'I'd swear no one's passed this way. Look at the dust. Thick. Not a sign of a footmark.'

They wandered round the deserted house. Everywhere the same tale. Thick layers of dust apparently undisturbed.

'This gets me,' said Julius. 'I don't believe Tuppence was ever in this house.'

'She must have been.'

Julius shook his head without replying.

'We'll go over it again tomorrow,' said Tommy. 'Perhaps we'll see more in the daylight.'

On the morrow they took up the search once more, and were reluctantly forced to the conclusion that the house had not been invaded for some considerable time. They might have left the village altogether but for a fortunate discovery of Tommy's. As they were retracing their steps to the gate, he gave a sudden cry, and stooping, picked something up from among the leaves, and held it out to Julius. It was a small gold brooch.

'That's Tuppence's!'

'Are you sure?'

'Absolutely. I've often seen her wear it.'

Julius drew a deep breath.

'I guess that settles it. She came as far as here, anyway. We'll make that pub our headquarters, and raise hell round here until we find her. Somebody *must* have seen her.'

Forthwith the campaign began. Tommy and Julius worked separately and together, but the result was the same. Nobody answering to Tuppence's description had been seen in the vicinity. They were baffled – but not discouraged. Finally they altered their tactics. Tuppence had certainly not remained long in the neighbourhood of the Moat House. That pointed to her having been overcome and carried away in a car. They renewed inquiries. Had anyone seen a car standing somewhere near the Moat House that day? Again they met with no success.

Julius wired to town for his own car, and they scoured the neighbourhood daily with unflagging zeal. A grey limousine on which they had set high hopes was traced to Harrogate, and turned out to be the property of a highly respectable maiden lady!

Each day saw them set out on a new quest. Julius was like a hound on the leash. He followed up the slenderest clue. Every car that had passed through the village on the fateful day was tracked down. He forced his way into country properties and submitted the owners of the cars to searching cross-examination. His apologies were as thorough as his methods, and seldom failed in disarming the indignation of his victims; but, as day succeeded day, they were no nearer to discovering Tuppence's whereabouts. So well had the abduction been planned that the girl seemed literally to have vanished into thin air.

And another preoccupation was weighing on Tommy's mind.

'Do you know how long we've been here?' he asked one morning as they sat facing each other at breakfast. 'A week! We're no nearer to finding Tuppence, *and next Sunday is the 29th*!'

'Shucks!' said Julius thoughtfully. 'I'd almost forgotten about the 29th. I've been thinking of nothing but Tuppence.'

'So have I. At least, I hadn't forgotten about the 29th, but it didn't seem to matter a damn in comparison to finding Tuppence. But today's the 23rd, and time's getting short. If we're ever going to get hold of her at all, we must do it before the 29th – her life won't be worth an hour's purchase afterwards. The hostage game will be played out by then. I'm beginning to feel that we've made a big mistake in the way we've set about this. We've wasted time and we're no forrader.'

'I'm with you there. We've been a couple of mutts, who've bitten off a bigger bit than they can chew. I'm going to quit fooling right away!'

'What do you mean?'

'I'll tell you. I'm going to do what we ought to have done a week ago. I'm going right back to London to put the case in the hands of your British police. We fancied ourselves as sleuths. Sleuths! It was a piece of damn-fool foolishness! I'm through! I've had enough of it. Scotland Yard for me!'

'You're right,' said Tommy slowly. 'I wish to God we'd gone there right away.'

'Better late than never. We've been like a couple of babes playing "Here we go round the Mulberry Bush". Now I'm going right along to Scotland Yard to ask them to take me by the hand and show me the way I should go. I guess the professional always scores over the amateur in the end. Are you coming along with me?'

Tommy shook his head.

'What's the good? One of us is enough. I might as well stay here and nose round a bit longer. Something *might* turn up. One never knows.'

'Sure thing. Well, so long. I'll be back in a couple of shakes with a few inspectors along. I shall tell them to pick out their brightest and best.'

But the course of events was not to follow the plan Julius had laid down. Later in the day Tommy received a wire:

Join me Manchester Midland Hotel. Important news
– Julius.

At 7.30 that night Tommy alighted from a slow cross-country train. Julius was on the platform.

'Thought you'd come by this train if you weren't out when my wire arrived.'

Tommy grasped him by the arm.

'What is it? Is Tuppence found?'

Julius shook his head.

'No. But I found this waiting in London. Just arrived.'

He handed the telegraph form to the other. Tommy's eyes opened as he read:

Jane Finn found. Come Manchester Midland Hotel immediately – PEEL EDGERTON.

Julius took the form back and folded it up.

'Queer,' he said thoughtfully. 'I thought that lawyer chap had quit!'

CHAPTER 19

JANE FINN

'My train got in half an hour ago,' explained Julius, as he led the way out of the station. 'I reckoned you'd come by this before I left London, and wired accordingly to Sir James. He's booked rooms for us, and will be round to dine at eight.'

'What made you think he'd ceased to take any interest in the case?' asked Tommy curiously.

'What he said,' replied Julius dryly. 'The old bird's as close as an oyster! Like all the darned lot of them, he wasn't going to commit himself till he was sure he could deliver the goods.'

'I wonder,' said Tommy thoughtfully.

Julius turned on him.

'You wonder what?'

'Whether that was his real reason.'

'Sure. You bet your life it was.'

Tommy shook his head unconvinced.

Sir James arrived punctually at eight o'clock, and Julius introduced Tommy. Sir James shook hands with him warmly.

'I am delighted to make your acquaintance, Mr Beresford. I have heard so much about you from Miss Tuppence' – he smiled involuntarily – 'that it really seems as though I already know you quite well.'

'Thank you, sir,' said Tommy with his cheerful grin. He scanned the great lawyer eagerly. Like Tuppence, he felt the magnetism of the other's personality. He was reminded of Mr Carter. The two men, totally unlike so far as physical resemblance went, produced a similar effect. Beneath the weary manner of the one and the professional reserve of the other lay the same quality of mind, keen-edged like a rapier.

In the meantime he was conscious of Sir James's close scrutiny. When the lawyer dropped his eyes the young man had the feeling that the other had read him through and through like an open book. He could not but wonder what the final judgment was, but there was little chance of learning that. Sir James took in everything, but gave out only what he chose. A proof of that occurred almost at once.

Immediately the first greetings were over Julius broke out into a flood of eager questions. How had Sir James managed to track the girl? Why had he not let them know that he was still working on the case? And so on.

Sir James stroked his chin and smiled. At last he said:

'Just so, just so. Well, she's found. And that's the great thing, isn't it? Eh! Come now, that's the great thing?'

'Sure it is. But just how did you strike her trail? Miss Tuppence and I thought you'd quit for good and all.'

'Ah!' The lawyer shot a lightning glance at him, then resumed operations on his chin. 'You thought that, did you? Did you really? H'm, dear me.'

'But I guess I can take it we were wrong?' pursued Julius.

'Well, I don't know that I should go so far as to say that. But it's certainly fortunate for all parties that we've managed to find the young lady.'

'But where is she?' demanded Julius, his thoughts flying off on another tack. 'I thought you'd be sure to bring her along?'

'That would hardly be possible,' said Sir James gravely.

'Why?'

'Because the young lady was knocked down in a street accident, and has sustained slight injuries to the head. She was taken to the infirmary, and on recovering consciousness gave her name as Jane Finn. When – ah! – I heard that, I arranged for her to be removed to the house of a doctor – a friend of mine, and wired at once for you. She relapsed into unconsciousness and has not spoken since.'

'She's not seriously hurt?'

'Oh, a bruise and a cut or two; really, from a medical point of view, absurdly slight injuries to have produced such a condition. Her state is probably to be attributed to the mental shock consequent on recovering her memory.'

'It's come back?' cried Julius excitedly.

Sir James tapped the table rather impatiently.

'Undoubtedly, Mr Hersheimmer, since she was able to give her real name. I thought you had appreciated that point.'

'And you just happened to be on the spot?' said Tommy. 'Seems quite like a fairy tale.'

But Sir James was far too wary to be drawn.

'Coincidences are curious things,' he said dryly.

Nevertheless, Tommy was now certain of what he had before only suspected. Sir James's presence in Manchester was not accidental. Far from abandoning the case, as Julius supposed, he had by some means of his own successfully run the missing girl to earth. The only thing that puzzled Tommy was the reason for all this secrecy? He concluded that it was a foible of the legal mind.

Julius was speaking.

'After dinner,' he announced, 'I shall go right away and see Jane.'

'That will be impossible, I fear,' said Sir James. 'It is very unlikely they would allow her to see visitors at this time of night. I should suggest tomorrow morning about ten o'clock.'

Julius flushed. There was something in Sir James which always stirred him to antagonism. It was a conflict of two masterful personalities.

'All the same, I reckon I'll go round there tonight and see if I can't ginger them up to break through their silly rules.'

'It will be quite useless, Mr Hersheimmer.'

The words came out like the crack of a pistol, and Tommy looked up with a start. Julius was nervous and excited. The hand with which he raised his glass to his lips shook slightly, but his eyes held Sir James's defiantly. For a moment the hostility between the two seemed likely to burst into flame, but in the end Julius lowered his eyes, defeated.

'For the moment, I reckon you're the boss.'

'Thank you,' said the other. 'We will say ten o'clock then?' With consummate ease of manner he turned to Tommy. 'I must confess, Mr Beresford, that it was something of a surprise to me to see you here this evening. The last I heard of you was that your friends were in grave anxiety on your behalf. Nothing had been heard of you for some days, and Miss Tuppence was inclined to think you had got into difficulties.'

'I had, sir!' Tommy grinned reminiscently. 'I was never in a tighter place in my life.'

Helped out by questions from Sir James, he gave an abbreviated account of his adventures. The lawyer looked at him with renewed interest as he brought the tale to a close.

'You got yourself out of a tight place very well,' he said gravely. 'I congratulate you. You displayed a great deal of ingenuity and carried your part through well.'

Tommy blushed, his face assuming a prawn-like hue at the praise.

'I couldn't have got away but for the girl, sir.'

'No.' Sir James smiled a little. 'It was lucky for you she happened to – er – take a fancy to you.' Tommy appeared about to protest, but Sir James went on. 'There's no doubt about her being one of the gang, I suppose?'

'I'm afraid not, sir. I thought perhaps they were keeping her there by force, but the way she acted didn't fit in with that. You see, she went back to them when she could have got away.'

Sir James nodded thoughtfully.

'What did she say? Something about wanting to be taken to Marguerite?'

'Yes, sir. I suppose she meant Mrs Vandemeyer.

'She always signed herself Rita Vandemeyer. All her friends spoke of her as Rita. Still, I suppose the girl must have been in the habit of calling her by her full name. And, at the moment she was crying out to her, Mrs Vandemeyer was either dead or dying! Curious! There are one or two points that strike me as being obscure – their sudden change of attitude towards yourself, for instance. By the way, the house was raided, of course?'

'Yes, sir, but they'd cleared out.'

'Naturally,' said Sir James dryly.

'And not a clue left behind.'

'I wonder –' The lawyer tapped the table thoughtfully.

Something in his voice made Tommy look up. Would this man's eyes have seen something where theirs had been blind? He spoke impulsively:

'I wish you'd been there, sir, to go over the house!'

'I wish I had,' said Sir James quietly. He sat for a moment in silence. Then he looked up. 'And since then? What have you been doing?'

For a moment, Tommy stared at him. Then it dawned on him that of course the lawyer did not know.

'I forgot that you didn't know about Tuppence,' he said slowly. The sickening anxiety, forgotten for a while in the excitement of knowing Jane Finn found at last, swept over him again.

The lawyer laid down his knife and fork sharply.

'Has anything happened to Miss Tuppence?' His voice was keen-edged.

'She's disappeared,' said Julius.

'When?'

'A week ago.'

'How?'

Sir James's questions fairly shot out. Between them Tommy and Julius gave the history of the last week and their futile search.

Sir James went at once to the root of the matter.

'A wire signed with your name? They knew enough of you both for that. They weren't sure of how much you had learnt in that house. Their kidnapping of Miss Tuppence is the counter-move to your escape. If necessary they could seal your lips with what might happen to her.'

Tommy nodded.

'That's just what I thought, sir.'

Sir James looked at him keenly. '*You* had worked that out, had you? Not bad – not at all bad. The curious thing is that they certainly did not know anything about you when they first held you prisoner. You are sure that you did not in any way disclose your identity?'

Tommy shook his head.

'That's so,' said Julius with a nod. 'Therefore I reckon someone put them wise – and not earlier than Sunday afternoon.'

'Yes, but who?'

'That almighty omniscient Mr Brown, of course!'

There was a faint note of derision in the American's voice which made Sir James look up sharply.

'You don't believe in Mr Brown, Mr Hersheimmer?'

'No, sir, I do not,' returned the young American with emphasis. 'Not as such, that is to say. I reckon it out that he's a figurehead – just a bogy name to frighten the children with. The real head of this business is that Russian chap Kramenin. I guess he's quite capable of running revolutions in three countries at once if he chose! The man Whittington is probably the head of the English branch.'

'I disagree with you,' said Sir James shortly. 'Mr Brown exists.' He turned to Tommy. 'Did you happen to notice where that wire was handed in?'

'No, sir, I'm afraid I didn't.'

'H'm. Got it with you?'

'It's upstairs, sir, in my kit.'

'I'd like to have a look at it sometime. No hurry. You've wasted a week,' – Tommy hung his head – 'a day or so more is immaterial. We'll deal with Miss Jane Finn first. Afterwards, we'll set to work to rescue Miss Tuppence from bondage. I don't think she's in any immediate danger. That is, so long as they don't know that we've got Jane Finn, and that her memory has returned. We must keep that dark at all costs. You understand?'

The other two assented, and, after making arrangements for meeting on the morrow, the great lawyer took his leave.

At ten o'clock, the two young men were at the appointed spot. Sir James had joined them on the doorstep. He alone appeared unexcited. He introduced them to the doctor.

'Mr Hersheimmer – Mr Beresford – Dr Roylance. How's the patient?'

'Going on well. Evidently no idea of the flight of time. Asked this morning how many had been saved from the *Lusitania*. Was it in the papers yet? That, of course, was only what was to be expected. She seems to have something on her mind, though.'

'I think we can relieve her anxiety. May we go up?'

'Certainly.'

Tommy's heart beat sensibly faster as they followed the doctor upstairs. Jane Finn at last! The long-sought, the mysterious, the elusive Jane Finn! How wildly improbable success had seemed! And here in this house, her memory almost miraculously restored, lay the girl who held the future of England in her hands. A half groan broke from Tommy's lips. If only Tuppence could have been at his side to share in the triumphant conclusion of their joint venture! Then he put the thought of Tuppence resolutely aside. His confidence in Sir James was growing. There was a man who would unerringly ferret out Tuppence's whereabouts. In the meantime, Jane Finn! And suddenly a dread clutched at his heart. It seemed too easy . . . Suppose they should find her dead . . . stricken down by the hand of Mr Brown?

In another minute he was laughing at these melodramatic fancies. The doctor held open the door of a room and they passed in. On the white bed, bandages round her head, lay the girl. Somehow the whole scene seemed unreal. It was so exactly what one expected that it gave the effect of being beautifully staged.

The girl looked from one to the other of them with large wondering eyes. Sir James spoke first.

'Miss Finn,' he said, 'this is your cousin, Mr Julius P. Hersheimmer.'

A faint flush flitted over the girl's face, as Julius stepped forward and took her hand.

'How do, Cousin Jane?' he said lightly.

But Tommy caught the tremor in his voice.

'Are you really Uncle Hiram's son?' she asked wonderingly.

Her voice, with the slight warmth of the Western accent, had an almost thrilling quality. It seemed vaguely familiar to Tommy, but he thrust the impression aside as impossible.

'Sure thing.'

'We used to read about Uncle Hiram in the newspapers,' continued the girl, in her soft tones. 'But I never thought I'd meet you one day. Mother figured it out that Uncle Hiram would never get over being mad with her.'

'The old man was like that,' admitted Julius. 'But I guess the new generation's sort of different. Got no use for the family feud business. First thing I thought about, soon as the war was over, was to come along and hunt you up.'

A shadow passed over the girl's face.

'They've been telling me things – dreadful things – that my memory went, and that there are years I shall never know about – years lost out of my life.'

'You didn't realize that yourself?'

The girl's eyes opened wide.

'Why, no. It seems to me as though it were no time since we were being hustled into those boats. I can see it all now!' She closed her eyes with a shudder.

Julius looked across at Sir James, who nodded.

'Don't worry any. It isn't worth it. Now, see here, Jane, there's something we want to know about. There was a man aboard that boat with some mighty important papers on him, and the big guns in this country have got a notion that he passed on the goods to you. Is that so?'

The girl hesitated, her glance shifting to the other two. Julius understood.

'Mr Beresford is commissioned by the British Government to get those papers back. Sir James Peel Edgerton is an English Member of Parliament, and might be a big gun in the Cabinet if he liked. It's owing to him that we've ferreted you out at last. So you can go right ahead and tell us the whole story. Did Danvers give you the papers?'

'Yes. He said they'd have a better chance with me, because they would have the women and children first.'

'Just as we thought,' said Sir James.

'He said they were very important – that they might make all the difference to the Allies. But, if it's all so long ago, and the war's over, what does it matter now?'

'I guess history repeats itself, Jane. First there was a great hue and cry over those papers, then it all died down, and now the whole caboodle's started all over again – for rather different reasons. Then you can hand them over to us right away?'

'But I can't.'

'What?'

'I haven't got them.'

'You – haven't – got them?' Julius punctuated the words with little pauses

'No – I hid them.'

'You *hid* them?'

'Yes. I got uneasy. People seemed to be watching me. It scared me – badly.' She put her hand to her head. 'It's almost the last thing I remember before waking up in the hospital . . .'

'Go on,' said Sir James, in his quiet penetrating tones. 'What do you remember?'

She turned to him obediently.

'It was at Holyhead. I came that way – I don't remember why . . .'

'That doesn't matter. Go on.'

'In the confusion on the quay I slipped away. Nobody saw me. I took a car. Told the man to drive me out of the town. I watched when we got on the open road. No other car was following us. I saw a path at the side of the road. I told the man to wait.'

She paused, then went on. 'The path led to the cliff, and down to the sea between big yellow gorse bushes – they were like golden flames. I looked round. There wasn't a soul in sight. But just level with my head there was a hole in the rock. It was quite small – I could only just get my hand in, but it went a long way back. I took the oilskin packet from round my neck and shoved it right in as far as I could. Then I tore off a bit of gorse – My! but it did prick – and plugged the hole with it so that you'd never guess there was a crevice of any kind there. Then I marked the place carefully in my own mind, so that I'd find it again. There was a queer boulder in the path just there – for all the world like a dog sitting up begging. Then I went back to the road. The car was waiting, and I drove back. I just caught the train. I was a bit ashamed of myself for fancying things maybe, but, by and by, I saw the man opposite me wink at a woman who was sitting next to me, and I felt scared again, and was glad the papers were safe. I went out in the corridor to get a little air. I thought I'd slip into another carriage. But the woman called me back, said I'd dropped something, and when I stooped to look, something seemed to hit me – here.' She placed her hand to the back of her head. 'I don't remember anything more until I woke up in the hospital.'

There was a pause.

'Thank you, Miss Finn.' It was Sir James who spoke. 'I hope we have not tired you?'

'Oh, that's all right. My head aches a little, but otherwise I feel fine.'

Julius stepped forward and took her hand again.

'So long, Cousin Jane. I'm going to get busy after those papers, but I'll be back in two shakes of a dog's tail, and I'll tote you up to London and give you the time of your young life before we go back to the States! I mean it – so hurry up and get well.'

CHAPTER 20

TOO LATE

In the street they held an informal council of war. Sir James had drawn a watch from his pocket.

'The boat train to Holyhead stops at Chester at 12.14. If you start at once I think you can catch the connection.'

Tommy looked up, puzzled.

'Is there any need to hurry, sir? Today is only the 24th.'

'I guess it's always well to get up early in the morning,' said Julius, before the lawyer had time to reply. 'We'll make tracks for the depot right away.'

A little frown had settled on Sir James's brow.

'I wish I could come with you. I am due to speak at a meeting at two o'clock. It is unfortunate.'

The reluctance in his tone was very evident. It was clear, on the other hand, that Julius was easily disposed to put up with the loss of the other's company.

'I guess there's nothing complicated about this deal,' he remarked. 'Just a game of hide-and-seek, that's all.'

'I hope so,' said Sir James.

'Sure thing. What else could it be?'

'You are still young, Mr Hersheimmer. At my age you will probably have learnt one lesson: "Never underestimate your adversary."'

The gravity of his tone impressed Tommy, but had little effect upon Julius.

'You think Mr Brown might come along and take a hand! If he does, I'm ready for him.' He slapped his pocket. 'I carry a gun. Little Willie here travels round with me everywhere.' He produced a murderous-looking automatic, and tapped it affectionately before returning it to its home. 'But he won't be needed on this trip. There's nobody to put Mr Brown wise.'

The lawyer shrugged his shoulders.

'There was nobody to put Mr Brown wise to the fact that Mrs Vandemeyer meant to betray him. Nevertheless, *Mrs Vandemeyer died without speaking*.'

Julius was silenced for once, and Sir James added on a lighter note:

'I only want to put you on your guard. Goodbye, and good luck. Take no unnecessary risks once the papers are in your hands. If there is any reason to believe that you have been shadowed, destroy them at once. Good luck to you. The game is in your hands now.' He shook hands with them both.

Ten minutes later the two men were seated in a first-class carriage *en route* for Chester.

For a long time neither of them spoke. When at length Julius broke the silence, it was with a totally unexpected remark.

'Say,' he observed thoughtfully, 'did you ever make a darn fool of yourself over a girl's face?'

Tommy, after a moment's astonishment, searched his mind.

'Can't say I have,' he replied at last. 'Not that I can recollect, anyhow. Why?'

'Because for the last two months I've been making a sentimental idiot of myself over Jane! First moment I clapped eyes on her photograph my heart did all the usual stunts you read about in novels. I guess I'm ashamed to admit it, but I came over here determined to find her and fix it all up, and take her back as Mrs Julius P. Hersheimmer!'

'Oh!' said Tommy, amazed.

Julius uncrossed his legs brusquely and continued:

'Just shows what an almighty fool a man can make of himself! One look at the girl in the flesh, and I was cured!'

Feeling more tongue-tied than ever, Tommy ejaculated 'Oh!' again.

'No disparagement to Jane, mind you,' continued the other.

'She's a real nice girl, and some fellow will fall in love with her right away.'

'I thought her a very good-looking girl,' said Tommy, finding his tongue.

'Sure she is. But she's not like her photo one bit. At least I suppose she is in a way – must be – because I recognized her right off. If I'd seen her in a crowd I'd have said "There's a girl whose face I know" right away without hesitation. But there was something about that photo' – Julius shook his head, and heaved a sigh – 'I guess romance is a mighty queer thing!'

'It must be,' said Tommy coldly, 'if you can come over here in love with one girl, and propose to another within a fortnight.'

Julius had the grace to look discomposed.

'Well, you see, I'd got sort of tired feeling that I'd never find Jane – and that it was all plumb foolishness anyway. And then – oh well, the French, for instance, are much more sensible in the way they look at things. They keep romance and marriage apart –'

Tommy flushed.

'Well, I'm damned! If that's –'

Julius hastened to interrupt.

'Say now, don't be hasty. I don't mean what you mean. I take it Americans have a higher opinion of morality than you have even. What I meant was that the French set about marriage in a business-like way – find two people who are suited to one another, look after the money affairs, and see the whole thing practically, and in a business-like spirit.'

'If you ask me,' said Tommy, 'we're all too damned business-like nowadays. We're always saying, "Will it pay?" The men are bad enough, and the girls are worse!'

'Cool down, son. Don't get so heated.'

'I feel heated,' said Tommy.

Julius looked at him and judged it wise to say no more.

However, Tommy had plenty of time to cool down before they reached Holyhead, and the cheerful grin had returned to his countenance as they alighted at their destination.

After consultation and with the aid of a road map, they were fairly well agreed as to direction, so were able to hire a taxi without more ado and drive out on the road leading to Treaddur Bay. They instructed the man to go slowly, and watched narrowly so as not to miss the path. They came to it not long after leaving the town, and Tommy stopped the car promptly, asked in a casual tone whether the path led down to the sea, and hearing it did paid off the man in handsome style.

A moment later the taxi was slowly chugging back to Holyhead. Tommy and Julius watched it out of sight, and then turned to the narrow path.

'It's the right one, I suppose?' asked Tommy doubtfully. 'There must be simply heaps along here.'

'Sure it is. Look at the gorse. Remember what Jane said?'

Tommy looked at the swelling hedges of golden blossom which bordered the path on either side, and was convinced.

They went down in single file, Julius leading. Twice Tommy turned his head uneasily. Julius looked back.

'What is it?'

'I don't know. I've got the wind up somehow. Keep fancying there's someone following us.'

'Can't be,' said Julius positively. 'We'd see him.'

Tommy had to admit that this was true. Nevertheless, his sense of uneasiness deepened. In spite of himself he believed in the omniscience of the enemy.

'I rather wish that fellow would come along,' said Julius. He patted his pocket. 'Little William here is just aching for exercise!'

'Do you always carry it – him – with you?' inquired Tommy with burning curiosity.

'Most always. I guess you never know what might turn up.'

Tommy kept a respectful silence. He was impressed by Little William. It seemed to remove the menace of Mr Brown farther away.

The path was now running along the side of the cliff, parallel to the sea. Suddenly Julius came to such an abrupt halt that Tommy cannoned into him.

'What's up?' he inquired.

'Look there. If that doesn't beat the band!'

Tommy looked. Standing out and half obstructing the path was a huge boulder which certainly bore a fanciful resemblance to a 'begging' terrier.

'Well,' said Tommy, refusing to share Julius's emotion, 'it's what we expected to see, isn't it?'

Julius looked at him sadly and shook his head.

'British phlegm! Sure we expected it – but it kind of rattles me, all the same, to see it sitting there just where we expected to find it!'

Tommy, whose calm was, perhaps, more assumed than natural, moved his feet impatiently.

'Push on. What about the hole?'

They scanned the cliff-side narrowly. Tommy heard himself saying idiotically:

'The gorse won't be there after all these years.'

And Julius replied solemnly:

'I guess you're right.'

Tommy suddenly pointed with a shaking hand.

'What about that crevice there?'

Julius replied in an awestricken voice:

'That's it – for sure.'

They looked at each other.

'When I was in France,' said Tommy reminiscently, 'whenever my batman failed to call me, he always said that he had come over queer. I never believed it. But whether he felt it or not, there *is* such a sensation. I've got it now! Badly!'

He looked at the rock with a kind of agonized passion.

'Damn it!' he cried. 'It's impossible! Five years! Think of it! Birds'-nesting boys, picnic parties, thousands of people passing! It can't be there! It's a hundred to one against its being there! It's against all reason!'

Indeed, he felt it to be impossible – more, perhaps, because he could not believe in his own success where so many others had failed. The thing was too easy, therefore it could not be. The hole would be empty.

Julius looked at him with a widening smile.

'I guess you're rattled now all right,' he drawled with some enjoyment. 'Well, here goes!' He thrust his hand into the crevice, and made a slight grimace. 'It's a tight fit. Jane's hand must be a few sizes smaller than mine. I don't feel anything – no – say, what's this? Gee whiz!' And with a flourish he waved aloft a small discoloured packet. 'It's the goods all right. Sewn up in oilskin. Hold it while I get my penknife.'

The unbelievable had happened. Tommy held the precious packet tenderly between his hands. They had succeeded!

'It's queer,' he murmured idly, 'you'd think the stitches would have rotted. They look just as good as new.'

They cut them carefully and ripped away the oilskin. Inside was a small folded sheet of paper. With trembling fingers they unfolded it. The sheet was blank! They stared at each other, puzzled.

'A dummy!' hazarded Julius. 'Was Danvers just a decoy?'

Tommy shook his head. That solution did not satisfy him. Suddenly his face cleared.

'I've got it! *Invisible ink!*'

'You think so?'

'Worth trying anyhow. Heat usually does the trick. Get some sticks. We'll make a fire.'

In a few minutes the little fire of twigs and leaves was blazing merrily. Tommy held the sheet of paper near the glow. The paper curled a little with the heat. Nothing more.

Suddenly Julius grasped his arm, and pointed to where characters were appearing in a faint brown colour.

'Gee whiz! You've got it! Say, that idea of yours was great. It never occurred to me.'

Tommy held the paper in position some minutes longer until he judged the heat had done its work. Then he withdrew it. A moment later he uttered a cry.

Across the sheet in neat brown printing ran the words:

WITH THE COMPLIMENTS OF MR BROWN.

CHAPTER 21

TOMMY MAKES A DISCOVERY

For a moment or two they stood staring at each other stupidly, dazed with the shock. Somehow, inexplicably, Mr Brown had forestalled them. Tommy accepted defeat quietly. Not so Julius.

'How in tarnation did he get ahead of us? That's what beats me!' he ended up.

Tommy shook his head, and said dully:

'It accounts for the stitches being new. We might have guessed . . .'

'Never mind the darned stitches. How did he get ahead of us? We hustled all we knew. It's downright impossible for anyone to get here quicker than we did. And, anyway, how did he know? Do you reckon there was a dictaphone in Jane's room? I guess there must have been.'

But Tommy's common sense pointed out objections.

'No one could have known beforehand that she was going to be in that house – much less that particular room.'

'That's so,' admitted Julius. 'Then one of the nurses was a crook and listened at the door. How's that?'

'I don't see that it matters anyway,' said Tommy wearily. 'He may have found out some months ago, and removed the papers, then – No, by Jove, that won't wash! They'd have been published at once.'

'Sure thing they would! No, someone's got ahead of us today by an hour or so. But how they did it gets my goat.'

'I wish that chap Peel Edgerton had been with us,' said Tommy thoughtfully.

'Why?' Julius stared. 'The mischief was done when we came.'

'Yes –' Tommy hesitated. He could not explain his own feeling – the illogical idea that the K.C.'s presence would somehow have averted the catastrophe. He reverted to his former point of view. 'It's no good arguing about how it was done. The game's up. We've failed. There's only one thing for me to do.'

'What's that?'

'Get back to London as soon as possible. Mr Carter must be warned. It's only a matter of hours now before the blow falls. But, at any rate, he ought to know the worst.'

The duty was an unpleasant one, but Tommy had no intention of shirking it. He must report his failure to Mr Carter. After that his work was done. He took the midnight mail to London. Julius elected to stay the night at Holyhead.

Half an hour after arrival, haggard and pale, Tommy stood before his chief.

'I've come to report, sir. I've failed – failed badly.'

Mr Carter eyed him sharply.

'You mean that the treaty –'

'Is in the hands of Mr Brown, sir.'

'Ah!' said Mr Carter quietly. The expression on his face did not change, but Tommy caught the flicker of despair in his eyes. It convinced him as nothing else had done that the outlook was hopeless.

'Well,' said Mr Carter after a minute or two, 'we mustn't sag at the knees, I suppose. I'm glad to know definitely. We must do what we can.'

Through Tommy's mind flashed the assurance: 'It's hopeless, and he knows it's hopeless!'

The other looked up at him.

'Don't take it to heart, lad,' he said kindly. 'You did your best. You were up against one of the biggest brains of the century. And you came very near success. Remember that.'

'Thank you, sir. It's awfully decent of you.'

'I blame myself. I have been blaming myself ever since I heard this other news.'

Something in his tone attracted Tommy's attention. A new fear gripped at his heart.

'Is there – something more, sir?'

'I'm afraid so,' said Mr Carter gravely. He stretched out his hand to a sheet on the table.

'Tuppence –?' faltered Tommy.

'Read for yourself.'

The typewritten words danced before his eyes. The description of a green toque, a coat with a handkerchief in the pocket marked P.L.C. He looked an agonized question at Mr Carter. The latter replied to it:

'Washed up on the Yorkshire coast – near Ebury. I'm afraid – it looks very much like foul play.'

'My God!' gasped Tommy. '*Tuppence!* Those devils – I'll never rest till I've got even with them! I'll hunt them down! I'll –'

The pity on Mr Carter's face stopped him.

'I know what you feel like, my poor boy. But it's no good. You'll waste your strength uselessly. It may sound harsh, but my advice to you is: Cut your losses. Time's merciful. You'll forget.'

'Forget Tuppence? Never!'

Mr Carter shook his head.

'So you think now. Well, it won't bear thinking of – that brave little girl! I'm sorry about the whole business – confoundedly sorry.'

Tommy came to himself with a start.

'I'm taking up your time, sir,' he said with an effort. 'There's no need for you to blame yourself. I dare say we were a couple of young fools to take on such a job. You warned us all right. But I wish to God *I*'d been the one to get it in the neck. Goodbye, sir.'

Back at the Ritz, Tommy packed up his few belongings mechanically, his thoughts far away. He was still bewildered by the introduction of tragedy into his cheerful commonplace existence. What fun they had had together, he and Tuppence! And now – oh, he couldn't believe it – it couldn't be true! *Tuppence – dead!* Little Tuppence, brimming over with life! It was a dream, a horrible dream. Nothing more.

They brought him a note, a few kind words of sympathy from Peel Edgerton, who had read the news in the paper. (There had been a large headline: EX-V.A.D. FEARED DROWNED.) The letter ended with the offer of a post on a ranch in the Argentine, where Sir James had considerable interests.

'Kind old beggar,' muttered Tommy, as he flung it aside.

The door opened, and Julius burst in with his usual violence. He held an open newspaper in his hand.

'Say, what's all this? They seem to have got some fool idea about Tuppence.'

'It's true,' said Tommy quietly.

'You mean they've done her in?'

Tommy nodded.

'I suppose when they got the treaty she – wasn't any good to them any longer, and they were afraid to let her go.'

'Well, I'm darned!' said Julius. 'Little Tuppence. She sure was the pluckiest little girl –'

But suddenly something seemed to crack in Tommy's brain. He rose to his feet.

'Oh, get out! You don't really care, damn you! You asked her to marry you in your rotten cold-blooded way, but I *loved* her. I'd have given the soul out of my body to save her from harm. I'd have stood by without a word and let her marry you, because you could have given her the sort of time she ought to have had, and I was only a poor devil without a penny to bless himself with. But it wouldn't have been because I didn't care!'

'See here,' began Julius temperately.

'Oh, go to the devil! I can't stand your coming here and talking about "little Tuppence". Go and look after your cousin. Tuppence is my girl! I've always loved her, from the time we played together as kids. We grew up and it was just the same. I shall never forget when I was in hospital, and she came in in that ridiculous cap and apron! It was like a miracle to see the girl I loved turn up in a nurse's kit –'

But Julius interrupted him.

'A nurse's kit! Gee whiz! I must be going to Coney Hatch! I could swear I've seen Jane in a nurse's cap too. And that's plumb impossible! No, by gum, I've got it! It was her I saw talking to Whittington at that nursing home in Bournemouth. She wasn't a patient there! She was a nurse!'

'I dare say,' said Tommy angrily, 'she's probably been in with them from the start. I shouldn't wonder if she stole those papers from Danvers to begin with.'

'I'm darned if she did!' shouted Julius. 'She's my cousin, and as patriotic a girl as ever stepped.'

'I don't care a damn who she is, but get out of here!' retorted Tommy, also at the top of his voice.

The young men were on the point of coming to blows. But suddenly, with an almost magical abruptness, Julius's anger abated.

'All right, son,' he said quietly, 'I'm going. I don't blame you any for what you've been saying. It's mighty lucky you did say it. I've been the most almighty blithering darned idiot that it's possible to imagine. Calm down,' – Tommy had made an impatient gesture – 'I'm going right away now – going to the London and North Western Railway depot, if you want to know.'

'I don't care a damn where you're going,' growled Tommy.

As the door closed behind Julius, he returned to his suitcase.

'That's the lot,' he murmured, and rang the bell.

'Take my luggage down.'

'Yes, sir. Going away, sir?'

'I'm going to the devil,' said Tommy, regardless of the menial's feelings.

That functionary, however, merely replied respectfully:

'Yes, sir. Shall I call a taxi?'

Tommy nodded.

Where was he going? He hadn't the faintest idea. Beyond a fixed determination to get even with Mr Brown he had no plans. He had re-read Sir James's letter, and shook his head. Tuppence must be avenged. Still, it was kind of the old fellow.

'Better answer it, I suppose.' He went across to the writing-table. With the usual perversity of bedroom stationery, there were innumerable envelopes and no paper. He rang. No one came. Tommy fumed at the delay. Then he remembered that there was a good supply in Julius's sitting-room. The American had announced his immediate departure. There would be no fear of running up against him. Besides, he wouldn't mind if he did. He was beginning to be rather ashamed of the things he had said. Old Julius had taken them jolly well. He'd apologize if he found him there.

But the room was deserted. Tommy walked across to the writing-table, and opened the middle drawer. A photograph, carelessly thrust in face upwards, caught his eye. For a moment he stood rooted to the ground. Then he took it out, shut the drawer, walked slowly over to an arm-chair, and sat down still staring at the photograph in his hand.

What on earth was a photograph of the French girl Annette doing in Julius Hersheimmer's writing-table?

CHAPTER 22

IN DOWNING STREET

The Prime Minister tapped the desk in front of him with nervous fingers. His face was worn and harassed. He took up his conversation with Mr Carter at the point it had broken off.

'I don't understand,' he said. 'Do you really mean that things are not so desperate after all?'

'So this lad seems to think.'

'Let's have a look at his letter again.'

Mr Carter handed it over. It was written in a sprawling boyish hand.

Dear Mr Carter,

Something's turned up that has given me a jar. Of course I may be simply making an awful ass of myself, but I don't think so. If my conclusions are right, that girl at Manchester was just a plant. The whole thing was prearranged, sham packet and all, with the object of making us think the game was up – therefore I fancy that we must have been pretty hot on the scent.

I think I know who the real Jane Finn is, and I've even got an idea where the papers are. That last's only a guess, of course, but I've a sort of feeling it'll turn out right. Anyhow, I enclose it in a sealed envelope for what it's worth. I'm going to ask you not to open it until the very last moment, midnight on the 28th, in fact. You'll understand why in a minute. You see, I've figured it out that those things of Tuppence's are a plant too, and she's no more drowned than I am. The way I reason is this: as a last chance they'll let Jane Finn escape in the hope that she's been shamming this memory stunt, and that once she thinks she's free she'll go right away to the cache. Of course it's an awful risk for them to take, because she knows all about them – but they're pretty desperate to get hold of that treaty. But if they know that the papers have been recovered by us, *neither of those two girls' lives will be worth an hour's purchase. I must try and get hold of Tuppence before Jane escapes.*

I want a repeat of that telegram that was sent to Tuppence at the Ritz. Sir James Peel Edgerton said you would be able to manage that for me. He's frightfully clever.

One last thing – please have that house in Soho watched day and night.

Yours, etc.,

Thomas Beresford.

The Prime Minister looked up.

'The enclosure?'

Mr Carter smiled dryly.

'In the vaults of the Bank. I am taking no chances.'

'You don't think' – the Prime Minister hesitated a minute – 'that it would be better to open it now? Surely we ought to secure the document, that is, provided the young man's guess turns out to be correct, at once. We can keep the fact of having done so quite secret.'

'Can we? I'm not so sure. There are spies all round us. Once it's known I wouldn't give that' – he snapped his fingers – 'for the life of those two girls. No, the boy trusted me, and I shan't let him down.'

'Well, well, we must leave it at that, then. What's he like, this lad?'

'Outwardly, he's an ordinary, clean-limbed, rather block-headed young Englishman. Slow in his mental processes. On the other hand, it's quite impossible to lead him astray through his imagination. He hasn't got any – so he's difficult to deceive. He worries things out slowly, and once he's got hold of anything he doesn't let go. The little lady's quite different. More intuition and less common sense. They make a pretty pair working together. Pace and stamina.'

'He seems confident,' mused the Prime Minister.

'Yes, and that's what gives me hope. He's the kind of diffident youth who would have to be *very* sure before he ventured an opinion at all.'

A half smile came to the other's lips.

'And it is this – boy who will defeat the master criminal of our time?'

'This – boy, as you say! But I sometimes fancy I see a shadow behind.'

'You mean?'

'Peel Edgerton.'

'Peel Edgerton?' said the Prime Minister in astonishment.

'Yes. I see his hand in *this*.' He struck the open letter. 'He's there – working in the dark, silently, unobtrusively. I've always felt that if anyone was to run Mr Brown to earth, Peel Edgerton would be the man. I tell you he's on the case now, but doesn't want it known. By the way, I got rather an odd request from him the other day.'

'Yes?'

'He sent me a cutting from some American paper. It referred to a man's body found near the docks in New York about three weeks ago. He asked me to collect any information on the subject I could.'

'Well?'

Carter shrugged his shoulders.

'I couldn't get much. Young fellow about thirty-five – poorly dressed – face very badly disfigured. He was never identified.'

'And you fancy that the two matters are connected in some way?'

'Somehow I do. I may be wrong, of course.'

There was a pause, then Mr Carter continued:

'I asked him to come round here. Not that we'll get anything out of him he doesn't want to tell. His legal instincts are too strong. But there's no doubt he can throw light on one or two obscure points in young Beresford's letter. Ah, here he is!'

The two men rose to greet the newcomer. A half-whimsical thought flashed across the Premier's mind. 'My successor, perhaps!'

'We've had a letter from young Beresford,' said Mr Carter, coming to the point at once. 'You've seen him, I suppose?'

'You suppose wrong,' said the lawyer.

'Oh!' Mr Carter was a little nonplussed.

Sir James smiled, and stroked his chin.

'He rang me up,' he volunteered.

'Would you have any objection to telling us exactly what passed between you?'

'Not at all. He thanked me for a certain letter which I had written to him – as a matter of fact, I had offered him a job. Then he reminded me of something I had said to him at Manchester respecting that bogus telegram which lured Miss Cowley away. I asked him if anything untoward had occurred. He said it had – that in a drawer in Mr Hersheimmer's room he had discovered a photograph.' The lawyer paused, then continued: 'I asked him if the photograph bore the name and address of a Californian photographer. He replied: "You're on to it, sir. It had." Then he went on to tell me something I *didn't* know. The original of that photograph was the French girl, Annette, who saved his life.'

'What?'

'Exactly. I asked the young man with some curiosity what he had done with the photograph. He replied that he had put it back where he found it.' The lawyer paused again. 'That was good, you know – distinctly good. He can use his brains, that young fellow. I congratulated him. The discovery was a providential one. Of course, from the moment that the girl in Manchester was proved to be a plant everything was altered. Young Beresford saw that for himself without my having to tell it him. But he felt he couldn't trust his judgment on the subject of Miss Cowley. Did I think she was alive? I told him, duly weighing the evidence, that there was a very decided chance in favour of it. That brought us back to the telegram.'

'Yes?'

'I advised him to apply to you for a copy of the original wire. It had occurred to me as probable that, after Miss Cowley flung it on the floor, certain words might have been erased and altered with the express intention of setting searchers on a false trail.'

Carter nodded. He took a sheet from his pocket, and read aloud:

> *Come at once, Astley Priors, Gatehouse, Kent. Great developments – Tommy.*

'Very simple,' said Sir James, 'and very ingenious. Just a few words to alter, and the thing was done. And the one important clue they overlooked.'

'What was that?'

'The page-boy's statement that Miss Cowley drove to Charing Cross. They were so sure of themselves that they took it for granted he had made a mistake.'

'Then young Beresford is now?'

'At Gatehouse, Kent, unless I am much mistaken.'

Mr Carter looked at him curiously.

'I rather wonder you're not there too, Peel Edgerton?'

'Ah, I'm busy on a case.'

'I thought you were on your holiday?'

'Oh, I've not been briefed. Perhaps it would be more correct to say I'm preparing a case. Any more facts about that American chap for me?'

'I'm afraid not. Is it important to find out who he was?'

'Oh, I know who he was,' said Sir James easily. 'I can't prove it yet – but I know.'

The other two asked no questions. They had an instinct that it would be mere waste of breath.

'But what I don't understand,' said the Prime Minister suddenly, 'is how that photograph came to be in Mr Hersheimmer's drawer?'

'Perhaps it never left it,' suggested the lawyer gently.

'But the bogus inspector? Inspector Brown?'

'Ah!' said Sir James thoughtfully. He rose to his feet, 'I mustn't keep you. Go on with the affairs of the nation. I must get back to – my case.'

Two days later Julius Hersheimmer returned from Manchester. A note from Tommy lay on his table:

Dear Hersheimmer,

Sorry I lost my temper. In case I don't see you again, goodbye. I've been offered a job in the Argentine, and might as well take it.

Yours,

Tommy Beresford.

A peculiar smile lingered for a moment on Julius's face. He threw the letter into the waste-paper basket.

'The darned fool!' he murmured.

CHAPTER 23

A RACE AGAINST TIME

After ringing up Sir James, Tommy's next procedure was to make a call at South Audley Mansions. He found Albert discharging his professional duties, and introduced himself without more ado as a friend of Tuppence's. Albert unbent immediately.

'Things has been very quiet here lately,' he said wistfully. 'Hope the young lady's keeping well, sir?'

'That's just the point, Albert. She's disappeared.'

'You don't mean as the crooks have got her?'

'They have.'

'In the Underworld?'

'No, dash it all, in this world!'

'It's a h'expression, sir,' explained Albert. 'At the pictures the crooks always have a restoorant in the Underworld. But do you think as they've done her in, sir?'

'I hope not. By the way, have you by any chance an aunt, a cousin, grandmother, or any other suitable female relation who might be represented as being likely to kick the bucket?'

A delighted grin spread slowly over Albert's countenance.

'I'm on, sir. My poor aunt what lives in the country has been mortal bad for a long time, and she's asking for me with her dying breath.'

Tommy nodded approval.

'Can you report this in the proper quarter and meet me at Charing Cross in an hour's time?'

'I'll be there, sir. You can count on me.'

As Tommy had judged, the faithful Albert proved an invaluable ally. The two took up their quarters at the inn in Gatehouse. To Albert fell the task of collecting information. There was no difficulty about it.

Astley Priors was the property of a Dr Adams. The doctor no longer practised, had retired, the landlord believed, but he took a few private patients – here the good fellow tapped his forehead knowingly – 'Balmy ones! You understand!' The doctor was a popular figure in the village, subscribed freely to all the local sports – 'a very pleasant affable gentleman'. Been there long? Oh, a matter of ten years or so – might be longer. Scientific gentleman, he was. Professors and people often came down from town to see him. Anyway, it was a gay house, always visitors.

In the face of all this volubility, Tommy felt doubts. Was it possible that this genial, well-known figure could be in reality a dangerous criminal? His life seemed so open and above-board. No hint of sinister doings. Suppose it was all a gigantic mistake? Tommy felt a cold chill at the thought.

Then he remembered the private patients – 'barmy ones'. He inquired carefully if there was a young lady amongst them, describing Tuppence. But nothing much seemed to be known about the patients – they were seldom seen outside the grounds. A guarded description of Annette also failed to provoke recognition.

Astley Priors was a pleasant red-brick edifice, surrounded by well-wooded grounds which effectually shielded the house from observation from the road.

On the first evening Tommy, accompanied by Albert, explored

the grounds. Owing to Albert's insistence they dragged themselves along painfully on their stomachs, thereby producing a great deal more noise than if they had stood upright. In any case, these precautions were totally unnecessary. The grounds, like those of any other private house after nightfall, seemed untenanted. Tommy had imagined a possible fierce watchdog. Albert's fancy ran to a puma, or a tame cobra. But they reached a shrubbery near the house quite unmolested.

The blinds of the dining-room window were up. There was a large company assembled round the table. The port was passing from hand to hand. It seemed a normal, pleasant company. Through the open window scraps of conversation floated out disjointedly on the night air. It was a heated discussion on county cricket!

Again Tommy felt that cold chill of uncertainty. It seemed impossible to believe that these people were other than they seemed. Had he been fooled once more? The fair-bearded, spectacled gentleman who sat at the head of the table looked singularly honest and normal.

Tommy slept badly that night. The following morning the indefatigable Albert, having cemented an alliance with the greengrocer's boy, took the latter's place and ingratiated himself with the cook at Malthouse. He returned with the information that she was undoubtedly 'one of the crooks', but Tommy mistrusted the vividness of his imagination. Questioned, he could adduce nothing in support of his statement except his own opinion that she wasn't the usual kind. You could see that at a glance.

The substitution being repeated (much to the pecuniary advantage of the real greengrocer's boy) on the following day, Albert brought back the first piece of hopeful news. There *was* a French young lady staying in the house. Tommy put his doubts aside. Here was confirmation of his theory. But time pressed. Today was the 27th. The 29th was the much-talked-of 'Labour Day', about which all sorts of rumours were running riot. Newspapers were getting agitated. Sensational hints of a Labour *coup d'état* were freely reported. The Government said nothing. It knew and was prepared. There were rumours of dissension among the Labour leaders. They were not of one mind. The more far-seeing among them realized that what they proposed might well be a death-blow to the England that at heart they loved. They shrank from the starvation and misery a general strike would entail, and were willing to meet the Government half-way. But behind them were subtle, insistent forces at work, urging the memories of old wrongs, deprecating the weakness of half-and-half measures, fomenting misunderstandings.

Tommy felt that, thanks to Mr Carter, he understood the position fairly accurately. With the fatal document in the hands of Mr Brown, public opinion would swing to the side of the Labour extremists and revolutionists. Failing that, the battle was an even chance. The Government with a loyal army and police force behind them might win – but at a cost of great suffering. But Tommy nourished another and a preposterous dream. With Mr Brown unmasked and captured he believed, rightly or wrongly, that the whole organization would crumble ignominiously and instantaneously. The strange permeating influence of the unseen chief held it together. Without him, Tommy believed an instant panic would set in; and, the honest men left to themselves, an eleventh-hour reconciliation would be possible.

'This is a one-man show,' said Tommy to himself. 'The thing to do is to get hold of the man.'

It was partly in furtherance of this ambitious design that he had requested Mr Carter not to open the sealed envelope. The draft treaty was Tommy's bait. Every now and then he was aghast at his own presumption. How dared he think that he had discovered what so many wiser and cleverer men had overlooked? Nevertheless, he stuck tenaciously to his idea.

That evening he and Albert once more penetrated the grounds of Astley Priors. Tommy's ambition was somehow or other to gain admission to the house itself. As they approached cautiously, Tommy gave a sudden gasp.

On the second-floor window someone standing between the window and the light in the room threw a silhouette on the blind. It was one Tommy would have recognized anywhere! Tuppence was in that house!

He clutched Albert by the shoulder.

'Stay here! When I begin to sing, watch that window.'

He retreated hastily to a position on the main drive, and began in a deep roar, coupled with an unsteady gait, the following ditty:

I am a soldier
A jolly British soldier;
You can see that I'm a soldier by my feet . . .

It had been a favourite on the gramophone in Tuppence's hospital days. He did not doubt but that she would recognize it and draw her own conclusions. Tommy had not a note of music in his voice, but his lungs were excellent. The noise he produced was terrific.

Presently an unimpeachable butler, accompanied by an equally unimpeachable footman, issued from the front door. The butler remonstrated with him. Tommy continued to sing, addressing the butler affectionately as 'dear old whiskers'. The footman took him by one arm, the butler by the other. They ran him down the drive, and neatly out of the gate. The butler threatened him with the police if he intruded again. It was beautifully done – soberly and with perfect decorum. Anyone would have sworn that the butler was a real butler, the footman a real footman – only, as it happened, the butler was Whittington!

Tommy retired to the inn and waited for Albert's return. At last that worthy made his appearance.

'Well?' cried Tommy eagerly.

'It's all right. While they was a-running of you out the window opened, and something was chucked out.' He handed a scrap of paper to Tommy. 'It was wrapped round a letter-weight.'

On the paper were scrawled three words: 'Tomorrow – same time.'

'Good egg!' cried Tommy. 'We're getting going.'

'I wrote a message on a piece of paper, wrapped it round a stone, and chucked it through the window,' continued Albert breathlessly.

Tommy groaned.

'Your zeal will be the undoing of us, Albert. What did you say?'

'Said we was a-staying at the inn. If she could get away, to come there and croak like a frog.'

'She'll know that's you,' said Tommy with a sigh of relief. 'Your imagination runs away with you, you know, Albert. Why, you wouldn't recognize a frog croaking if you heard it.'

Albert looked rather crestfallen.

'Cheer up,' said Tommy. 'No harm done. That butler's an old friend of mine – I bet he knew who I was, though he didn't let on. It's not their game to show suspicion. That's why we've found it fairly plain sailing. They don't want to discourage me altogether. On the other hand, they don't want to make it too easy. I'm a pawn in their game, Albert, that's what I am. You see, if the spider lets the fly walk out too easily, the fly might suspect it was a put-up job. Hence the usefulness of that promising youth, Mr T. Beresford, who's blundered in just at the right moment for them. But later, Mr T. Beresford had better look out!'

Tommy retired for the night in a state of some elation. He had elaborated a careful plan for the following evening. He felt sure that the inhabitants of Astley Priors would not interfere with him up to a certain point. It was after that that Tommy proposed to give them a surprise.

About twelve o'clock, however, his calm was rudely shaken. He was told that someone was demanding him in the bar. The applicant proved to be a rude-looking carter well coated with mud.

'Well, my good fellow, what is it?' asked Tommy.

'Might this be for you, sir?' The carter held out a very dirty folded note, on the outside of which was written: 'Take this to the gentleman at the inn near Astley Priors. He will give you ten shillings.'

The handwriting was Tuppence's. Tommy appreciated her quick-wittedness in realizing that he might be staying at the inn under an assumed name. He snatched at it.

'That's all right.'

The man withheld it.

'What about my ten shillings?'

Tommy hastily produced a ten-shilling note, and the man relinquished his find. Tommy unfastened it.

Dear Tommy,

I knew it was you last night. Don't go this evening. They'll be lying in wait for you. They're taking us away this morning. I heard something about Wales – Holyhead, I think. I'll drop this on the road if I get a chance. Annette told me how you'd escaped. Buck up.

Yours,

Twopence.

Tommy raised a shout for Albert before he had even finished perusing this characteristic epistle.

'Pack my bag! We're off!'

'Yes, sir.' The boots of Albert could be heard racing upstairs.

Holyhead? Did that mean that, after all – Tommy was puzzled. He read on slowly.

The boots of Albert continued to be active on the floor above.

Suddenly a second shout came from below.

'Albert! I'm a damned fool! Unpack that bag!'

'Yes, sir.'

Tommy smoothed out the note thoughtfully.

'Yes, a damned fool,' he said softly. 'But so's someone else! And at last I know who it is!'

CHAPTER 24

JULIUS TAKES A HAND

In his suite at Claridge's, Kramenin reclined on a couch and dictated to his secretary in sibilant Russian.

Presently the telephone at the secretary's elbow purred, and he took up the receiver, spoke for a minute or two, then turned to his employer.

'Someone below is asking for you.'

'Who is it?'

'He gives the name of Mr Julius P. Hersheimmer.'

'Hersheimmer,' repeated Kramenin thoughtfully. 'I have heard that name before.'

'His father was one of the steel kings of America,' explained the secretary, whose business it was to know everything. 'This young man must be a millionaire several times over.'

The other's eyes narrowed appreciatively.

'You had better go down and see him, Ivan. Find out what he wants.'

The secretary obeyed, closing the door noiselessly behind him. In a few minutes he returned.

'He declines to state his business – says it is entirely private and personal, and that he must see you.'

'A millionaire several times over,' murmured Kramenin. 'Bring him up, my dear Ivan.'

The secretary left the room once more, and returned escorting Julius.

'Monsieur Kramenin?' said the latter abruptly.

The Russian, studying him attentively with his pale venomous eyes, bowed.

'Pleased to meet you,' said the American. 'I've got some very important business I'd like to talk over with you, if I can see you alone.' He looked pointedly at the other.

'My secretary, Monsieur Grieber, from whom I have no secrets.'

'That may be so – but I have,' said Julius dryly. 'So I'd be obliged if you'd tell him to scoot.'

'Ivan,' said the Russian softly, 'perhaps you would not mind retiring into the next room –'

'The next room won't do,' interrupted Julius. 'I know these ducal suites – and I want this one plumb empty except for you and me. Send him round to a store to buy a penn'orth of peanuts.'

Though not particularly enjoying the American's free and easy manner of speech, Kramenin was devoured by curiosity.

'Will your business take long to state?'

'Might be an all-night job if you caught on.'

'Very good. Ivan, I shall not require you again this evening. Go to the theatre – take a night off.'

'Thank you, your excellency.'

The secretary bowed and departed.

Julius stood at the door watching his retreat. Finally, with a satisfied sigh, he closed it, and came back to his position in the centre of the room.

'Now, Mr Hersheimmer, perhaps you will be so kind as to come to the point?'

'I guess that won't take a minute,' drawled Julius. Then, with an abrupt change of manner: 'Hands up – or I shoot!'

For a moment Kramenin stared blindly into the big automatic, then, with almost comical haste, he flung up his hands above his head. In that instant Julius had taken his measure. The man he had to deal with was an abject physical coward – the rest would be easy.

'This is an outrage,' cried the Russian in a high hysterical voice. 'An outrage! Do you mean to kill me?'

'Not if you keep your voice down. Don't go edging sideways towards that bell. That's better.'

'What do you want? Do nothing rashly. Remember my life is of the utmost value to my country. I may have been maligned –'

'I reckon,' said Julius, 'that the man who let daylight into you would be doing humanity a good turn. But you needn't worry any. I'm not proposing to kill you this trip – that is, if you're reasonable.'

The Russian quailed before the stern menace in the other's eyes. He passed his tongue over his dry lips.

'What do you want? Money?'

'No. I want Jane Finn.'

'Jane Finn? I – never heard of her!'

'You're a darned liar! You know perfectly who I mean.'

'I tell you I've never heard of the girl.'

'And I tell you,' retorted Julius, 'that Little Willie here is just hopping mad to go off!'

The Russian wilted visibly.

'You wouldn't dare –'

'Oh, yes I would, son!'

Kramenin must have recognized something in the voice that carried conviction, for he said sullenly:

'Well? Granted I do know who you mean – what of it?'

'You will tell me now – right here – where she is to be found.'

Kramenin shook his head.

'I daren't.'

'Why not?'

'I daren't. You ask an impossibility.'

'Afraid, eh? Of whom? Mr Brown? Ah, that tickles you up! There is such a person, then? I doubted it. And the mere mention of him scares you stiff!'

'I have seen him,' said the Russian slowly. 'Spoken to him face to face. I did not know it until afterwards. He was one of the crowd. I should not know him again. Who is he really? I do not know. But I know this – he is a man to fear.'

'He'll never know,' said Julius.

'He knows everything – and his vengeance is swift. Even I – Kramenin! – would not be exempt!'

'Then you won't do as I ask you?'

'You ask an impossibility.'

'Sure that's a pity for you,' said Julius cheerfully. 'But the world in general will benefit.' He raised the revolver.

'Stop,' shrieked the Russian. 'You cannot mean to shoot me?'

'Of course I do. I've always heard you Revolutionists held life cheap, but it seems there's a difference when it's your own life in question. I gave you just one chance of saving your dirty skin, and that you wouldn't take!'

'They would kill me!'

'Well,' said Julius pleasantly, 'it's up to you. But I'll just say this. Little Willie here is a dead cert, and if I was you I'd take a sporting chance with Mr Brown!'

'You will hang if you shoot me,' muttered the Russian irresolutely.

'No, stranger, that's where you're wrong. You forget the dollars. A big crowd of solicitors will get busy, and they'll get some high-brow doctors on the job, and the end of it all will be that they'll say my brain was unhinged. I shall spend a few months in a quiet sanatorium, my mental health will improve, the doctors will declare me sane again, and all will end happily for little Julius. I guess I can bear a few months' retirement in order to rid the world of you, but don't you kid yourself I'll hang for it!'

The Russian believed him. Corrupt himself, he believed implicitly in the power of money. He had read of American murder trials running much on the lines indicated by Julius. He had bought and sold justice himself. This virile young American with the significant drawling voice had the whip hand of him.

'I'm going to count five,' continued Julius, 'and I guess, if you let me get past four, you needn't worry any about Mr Brown. Maybe he'll send some flowers to the funeral, but *you* won't smell them! Are you ready? I'll begin. One – two – three – four –'

The Russian interrupted with a shriek:

'Do not shoot. I will do all you wish.'

Julius lowered the revolver.

'I thought you'd hear sense. Where is the girl?'

'At Gatehouse, in Kent. Astley Priors, the place is called.'

'Is she a prisoner there?'

'She's not allowed to leave the house – though it's safe enough really. The little fool has lost her memory, curse her!'

'That's been annoying for you and your friends, I reckon. What about the other girl, the one you decoyed away over a week ago?'

'She's there too,' said the Russian sullenly.

'That's good,' said Julius. 'Isn't it all panning out beautifully? And a lovely night for the run!'

'What run?' demanded Kramenin, with a stare.

'Down to Gatehouse, sure. I hope you're fond of motoring?'

'What do you mean? I refuse to go.'

'Now don't get mad. You must see I'm not such a kid as to leave you here. You'd ring up your friends on that telephone first thing! Ah!' He observed the fall on the other's face. 'You see, you'd got it all fixed. No, sir, you're coming along with me. This your bedroom next door here? Walk right in. Little Willie and I will come behind. Put on a thick coat, that's right. Fur lined? And you a Socialist! Now we're ready. We walk downstairs and out through the hall to where my car's waiting. And don't you forget I've got you covered every inch of the way. I can shoot just as well through my coat pocket. One word, or a glance even, at one of those liveried menials, and there'll sure be a strange face in the Sulphur and Brimstone Works!'

Together they descended the stairs, and passed out to the waiting car. The Russian was shaking with rage. The hotel servants surrounded them. A cry hovered on his lips, but at the last minute his nerve failed him. The American was a man of his word.

When they reached the car, Julius breathed a sigh of relief, the danger-zone was passed. Fear had successfully hypnotized the man by his side.

'Get in,' he ordered. Then as he caught the other's side-long glance, 'No, the chauffeur won't help you any. Naval man. Was on a submarine in Russia when the Revolution broke out. A brother of his was murdered by your people. George!'

'Yes, sir?' The chauffeur turned his head.

'This gentleman is a Russian Bolshevik. We don't want to shoot him, but it may be necessary. You understand?'

'Perfectly, sir.'

'I want to go to Gatehouse in Kent. Know the road at all?'

'Yes, sir, it will be about an hour and a half's run.'

'Make it an hour. I'm in a hurry.'

'I'll do my best, sir.' The car shot forward through the traffic.

Julius ensconced himself comfortably by the side of his victim. He kept his hand in the pocket of his coat, but his manner was urbane to the last degree.

'There was a man I shot once in Arizona –' he began cheerfully.

At the end of the hour's run the unfortunate Kramenin was more dead than alive. In succession to the anecdote of the Arizona man, there had been a tough from 'Frisco, and an episode in the Rockies. Julius's narrative style, if not strictly accurate, was picturesque!

Slowing down, the chauffeur called over his shoulder that they were just coming into Gatehouse. Julius bade the Russian direct them. His plan was to drive straight up to the house. There Kramenin was to ask for the two girls. Julius explained to him that Little Willie would not be tolerant of failure. Kramenin, by this time, was as putty in the other's hand. The terrific pace they had come had still further unmanned him. He had given himself up for dead at every corner.

The car swept up the drive, and stopped before the porch. The chauffeur looked round for orders.

'Turn the car first, George. Then ring the bell, and get back to your place. Keep the engine going, and be ready to scoot like hell when I give the word.'

'Very good, sir.'

The front door was opened by the butler. Kramenin felt the muzzle of the revolver pressed against his ribs.

'Now,' hissed Julius. 'And be careful.'

The Russian beckoned. His lips were white, and his voice was not very steady:

'It is I – Kramenin! Bring down the girl at once! There is no time to lose!'

Whittington had come down the steps. He uttered an exclamation of astonishment at seeing the other.

'You! What's up? Surely you know the plan –'

Kramenin interrupted him, using the words that have created many unnecessary panics:

'We have been betrayed! Plans must be abandoned. We must save our own skins. The girl! And at once! It's our only chance.'

Whittington hesitated, but for hardly a moment.

'You have orders – from *him?*'

'Naturally! Should I be here otherwise? Hurry! There is no time to be lost. The other little fool had better come too.'

Whittington turned and ran back into the house. The agonizing minutes went by. Then – two figures hastily huddled in cloaks appeared on the steps and were hustled into the car. The smaller of the two was inclined to resist and Whittington shoved her in unceremoniously. Julius leaned forward, and in doing so the light from the open door lit up his face. Another man on the steps behind Whittington gave a startled exclamation. Concealment was at an end.

'Get a move on, George,' shouted Julius.

The chauffeur slipped in his clutch, and with a bound the car started.

The man on the steps uttered an oath. His hand went to his pocket. There was a flash and a report. The bullet just missed the taller girl by an inch.

'Get down, Jane,' cried Julius. 'Flat on the bottom of the car.' He thrust her sharply forward, then standing up, he took careful aim and fired.

'Have you hit him?' cried Tuppence eagerly.

'Sure,' replied Julius. 'He isn't killed, though. Skunks like that take a lot of killing. Are you all right, Tuppence?'

'Of course I am. Where's Tommy? And who's this?' She indicated the shivering Kramenin.

'Tommy's making tracks for the Argentine. I guess he thought you'd turned up your toes. Steady through the gate, George! That's right. It'll take 'em at least five minutes to get busy after us. They'll use the telephone, I guess, so look out for snares ahead – and don't take the direct route. Who's this, did you say, Tuppence? Let me present Monsieur Kramenin. I persuaded him to come on the trip for his health.'

The Russian remained mute, still livid with terror.

'But what made them let us go?' demanded Tuppence suspiciously.

'I reckon Monsieur Kramenin here asked them so prettily they just couldn't refuse!'

This was too much for the Russian. He burst out vehemently:

'Curse you – curse you! They know now that I betrayed them. My life won't be safe for an hour in this country.'

'That's so,' assented Julius. 'I'd advise you to make tracks for Russia right away.'

'Let me go, then,' cried the other. 'I have done what you asked. Why do you still keep me with you?'

'Not for the pleasure of your company. I guess you can get right off now if you want to. I thought you'd rather I tooled you back to London.'

'You may never reach London,' snarled the other. 'Let me go here and now.'

'Sure thing. Pull up, George. The gentleman's not making the return trip. If I ever come to Russia, Monsieur Kramenin, I shall expect a rousing welcome and –'

But before Julius had finished his speech, and before the car had finally halted, the Russian had swung himself out and disappeared into the night.

'Just a mite impatient to leave us,' commented Julius, as the car gathered way again. 'And no idea of saying goodbye politely to the ladies. Say, Jane, you can get up on the seat now.'

For the first time the girl spoke.

'How did you "persuade" him?' she asked.

Julius tapped his revolver.

'Little Willie here takes the credit!'

'Splendid!' cried the girl. The colour surged into her face, her eyes looked admiringly at Julius.

'Annette and I didn't know what was going to happen to us,' said Tuppence. 'Old Whittington hurried us off. We thought it was lambs to the slaughter.'

'Annette,' said Julius. 'Is that what you call her?'

His mind seemed to be trying to adjust itself to a new idea.

'It's her name,' said Tuppence, opening her eyes very wide.

'Shucks!' retorted Julius. 'She may think it's her name, because her memory's gone, poor kid. But it's the one real and original Jane Finn we've got here.'

'What –?' cried Tuppence.

But she was interrupted. With an angry spurt, a bullet embedded itself in the upholstery of the car just behind her head.

'Down with you,' cried Julius. 'It's an ambush. These guys have got busy pretty quickly. Push her a bit, George.'

The car fairly leapt forward. Three more shots rang out, but went happily wide. Julius, upright, leant over the back of the car.

'Nothing to shoot at,' he announced gloomily. 'But I guess there'll be another little picnic soon. Ah!'

He raised his hand to his cheek.

'You are hurt?' said Annette quickly.

'Only a scratch.'

The girl sprang to her feet.

'Let me out! Let me out, I say! Stop the car. It is me they're after. I'm the one they want. You shall not lose your lives because of me. Let me go.' She was fumbling with the fastenings of the door.

Julius took her by both arms, and looked at her. She had spoken with no trace of foreign accent.

'Sit down, kid,' he said gently. 'I guess there's nothing wrong with your memory. Been fooling them all the time, eh?'

The girl looked at him, nodded, and then suddenly burst into tears. Julius patted her on the shoulder.

'There, there – just you sit tight. We're not going to let you quit.'

Through her sobs the girl said indistinctly:

'You're from home. I can tell by your voice. It makes me home-sick.'

'Sure I'm from home. I'm your cousin – Julius Hersheimmer. I came over to Europe on purpose to find you – and a pretty dance you've led me.'

The car slackened speed. George spoke over his shoulder:

'Cross-roads here, sir. I'm not sure of the way.'

The car slowed down till it hardly moved. As it did so a figure climbed suddenly over the back, and plunged head first into the midst of them.

'Sorry,' said Tommy, extricating himself.

A mass of confused exclamations greeted him. He replied to them severally:

'Was in the bushes by the drive. Hung on behind. Couldn't let you know before at the pace you were going. It was all I could do to hang on. Now then, you girls, get out!'

'Get out?'

'Yes. There's a station just up that road. Train due in three minutes. You'll catch it if you hurry.'

'What the devil are you driving at?' demanded Julius. 'Do you think you can fool them by leaving the car?'

'You and I aren't going to leave the car. Only the girls.'

'You're crazed, Beresford. Stark staring mad! You can't let those girls go off alone. It'll be the end of it if you do.'

Tommy turned to Tuppence.

'Get out at once, Tuppence. Take her with you, and do just as I say. No one will do you any harm. You're safe. Take the train to London. Go straight to Sir James Peel Edgerton. Mr Carter lives out of town, but you'll be safe with him.'

'Darn you!' cried Julius. 'You're mad. Jane, you stay where you are.'

With a sudden swift movement, Tommy snatched the revolver from Julius's hand, and levelled it at him.

'Now will you believe I'm in earnest? Get out, both of you, and do as I say – or I'll shoot!'

Tuppence sprang out, dragging the unwilling Jane after her.

'Come on, it's all right. If Tommy's sure – he's sure. Be quick. We'll miss the train.'

They started running.

Julius's pent-up rage burst forth.

'What the hell –'

Tommy interrupted him.

'Dry up! I want a few words with you, Mr Julius Hersheimmer.'

CHAPTER 25

JANE'S STORY

Her arm through Jane's, dragging her along, Tuppence reached the station. Her quick ears caught the sound of the approaching train.

'Hurry up,' she panted, 'or we'll miss it.'

They arrived on the platform just as the train came to a standstill. Tuppence opened the door of an empty first-class compartment, and the two girls sank down breathless on the padded seats.

A man looked in, then passed on to the next carriage. Jane started nervously. Her eyes dilated with terror. She looked questioningly at Tuppence.

'Is he one of them, do you think?' she breathed.

Tuppence shook her head.

'No, no. It's all right.' She took Jane's hand in hers. 'Tommy wouldn't have told us to do this unless he was sure we'd be all right.'

'But he doesn't know them as I do!' The girl shivered. 'You can't understand. Five years! Five long years! Sometimes I thought I should go mad.'

'Never mind. It's all over.'

'Is it?'

The train was moving now, speeding through the night at a gradually increasing rate. Suddenly Jane Finn started up.

'What was that? I thought I saw a face – looking in through the window.'

'No, there's nothing. See.' Tuppence went to the window, and lifting the strap let the pane down.

'You're sure?'

'Quite sure.'

The other seemed to feel some excuse was necessary:

'I guess I'm acting like a frightened rabbit, but I can't help it. If they caught me now they'd –' Her eyes opened wide and staring.

'*Don't*!' implored Tuppence. 'Lie back, and *don't think*. You can be quite sure that Tommy wouldn't have said it was safe if it wasn't.'

'My cousin didn't think so. He didn't want us to do this.'

'No,' said Tuppence, rather embarrassed.

'What are you thinking of?' said Jane sharply.

'Why?'

'Your voice was so – queer!'

'I *was* thinking of something,' confessed Tuppence. 'But I don't want to tell you – not now. I may be wrong, but I don't think so. It's just an idea that came into my head a long time ago. Tommy's got it too – I'm almost sure he has. But don't *you* worry – there'll be time enough for that later. And it mayn't be so at all! Do what I tell you – lie back and don't think of anything.'

'I'll try.' The long lashes drooped over the hazel eyes.

Tuppence, for her part, sat bolt upright – much in the attitude of a watchful terrier on guard. In spite of herself she was nervous. Her eyes flashed continually from one window to the other. She noted the exact position of the communication cord. What it was that she feared, she would have been hard put to it to say. But in her own mind she was far from feeling the confidence displayed in her words. Not that she disbelieved in Tommy, but occasionally she was shaken with doubts as to whether anyone so simple and honest as he was could ever be a match for the fiendish subtlety of the arch-criminal.

If they once reached Sir James Peel Edgerton in safety, all would be well. But would they reach him? Would not the silent forces of Mr Brown already be assembling against them? Even that last picture of Tommy, revolver in hand, failed to comfort her. By now he might be overpowered, borne down by sheer force of numbers . . . Tuppence mapped out her plan of campaign.

As the train at length drew slowly into Charing Cross, Jane Finn sat up with a start.

'Have we arrived? I never thought we should!'

'Oh, I thought we'd get to London all right. If there's going to be any fun, now is when it will begin. Quick, get out. We'll nip into a taxi.'

In another minute they were passing the barrier, had paid the necessary fares, and were stepping into a taxi.

'King's Cross,' directed Tuppence. Then she gave a jump. A man looked in at the window, just as they started. She was almost certain it was the same man who had got into the carriage next to them. She had a horrible feeling of being slowly hemmed in on every side.

'You see,' she explained to Jane, 'if they think we're going to Sir James, this will put them off the scent. Now they'll imagine we're going to Mr Carter. His country place is north of London somewhere.'

Crossing Holborn there was a block, and the taxi was held up. This was what Tuppence had been waiting for.

'Quick,' she whispered. 'Open the right-hand door!'

The two girls stepped out into the traffic. Two minutes later they were seated in another taxi and were retracing their steps, this time direct to Carlton House Terrace.

'There,' said Tuppence, with great satisfaction, 'this ought to do them. I can't help thinking that I'm really rather clever! How that other taxi man will swear! But I took his number, and I'll send him a postal order tomorrow, so that he won't lose by it if he happens to be genuine. What's this thing swerving – Oh!'

There was a grinding noise and a bump. Another taxi had collided with them.

In a flash Tuppence was out on the pavement. A policeman was approaching. Before he arrived Tuppence had handed the driver five shillings, and she and Jane had merged themselves in the crowd.

'It's only a step or two now,' said Tuppence breathlessly. The accident had taken place in Trafalgar Square.

'Do you think the collision was an accident, or done deliberately?'

'I don't know. It might have been either.'

Hand-in-hand, the two girls hurried along.

'It may be my fancy,' said Tuppence suddenly, 'but I feel as though there was someone behind us.'

'Hurry!' murmured the other. 'Oh, hurry!'

They were now at the corner of Carlton House Terrace, and their spirits lightened. Suddenly a large and apparently intoxicated man barred their way.

'Good evening, ladies,' he hiccupped. 'Whither away so fast?'

'Let us pass, please,' said Tuppence imperiously.

'Just a word with your pretty friend here.' He stretched out an unsteady hand, and clutched Jane by the shoulder. Tuppence heard other footsteps behind. She did not pause to ascertain whether they were friends or foes. Lowering her head, she repeated a manœuvre of childish days, and butted their aggressor full in the capacious middle. The success of these unsportsmanlike tactics was immediate. The man sat down abruptly on the pavement. Tuppence and Jane took to their heels. The house they sought was some way down. Other footsteps echoed behind them. Their breath was coming in choking gasps as they reached Sir James's door. Tuppence seized the bell and Jane the knocker.

The man who had stopped them reached the foot of the steps. For a moment he hesitated, and as he did so the door opened.

They fell into the hall together. Sir James came forward from the library door.

'Hullo! What's this?'

He stepped forward and put his arm round Jane as she swayed uncertainly. He half carried her into the library, and laid her on the leather couch. From a tantalus on the table he poured out a few drops of brandy, and forced her to drink them. With a sigh she sat up, her eyes still wild and frightened.

'It's all right. Don't be afraid, my child. You're quite safe.'

Her breath came more normally, and the colour was returning to her cheeks. Sir James looked at Tuppence quizzically.

'So you're not dead, Miss Tuppence, any more than that Tommy boy of yours was!'

'The Young Adventurers take a lot of killing,' boasted Tuppence.

'So it seems,' said Sir James dryly. 'Am I right in thinking that the joint venture has ended in success, and that this' – he turned to the girl on the couch – 'is Miss Jane Finn?'

Jane sat up.

'Yes,' she said quietly, 'I am Jane Finn. I have a lot to tell you.'

'When you are stronger –'

'No – now!' Her voice rose a little. 'I shall feel safer when I have told everything.'

'As you please,' said the lawyer.

He sat down in one of the big arm-chairs facing the couch. In a low voice Jane began her story.

'I came over on the *Lusitania* to take up a post in Paris. I was fearfully keen about the war, and just dying to help somehow or other. I had been studying French, and my teacher said they were wanting help in a hospital in Paris, so I wrote and offered my services, and they were accepted. I hadn't got any folk of my own, so it made it easy to arrange things.

'When the *Lusitania* was torpedoed, a man came up to me. I'd noticed him more than once – and I'd figured it out in my own mind that he was afraid of somebody or something. He asked me if I was a patriotic American, and told me he was carrying papers which were just life or death to the Allies. He asked me to take charge of them. I was to watch for an advertisement in

The Times. If it didn't appear, I was to take them to the American Ambassador.

'Most of what followed seems like a nightmare still. I see it in my dreams sometimes . . . I'll hurry over that part. Mr Danvers had told me to watch out. He might have been shadowed from New York, but he didn't think so. At first I had no suspicions, but on the boat to Holyhead I began to get uneasy. There was one woman who had been very keen to look after me, and chum up with me generally – a Mrs Vandemeyer. At first I'd been only grateful to her for being so kind to me; but all the time I felt there was something about her I didn't like, and on the Irish boat I saw her talking to some queer-looking men, and from the way they looked I saw that they were talking about me. I remembered that she'd been quite near me on the *Lusitania* when Mr Danvers gave me the packet, and before that she'd tried to talk to him once or twice. I began to get scared, but I didn't quite see what to do.

'I had a wild idea of stopping at Holyhead, and not going on to London that day, but I soon saw that would be plumb foolishness. The only thing was to act as though I'd noticed nothing, and hope for the best. I couldn't see how they could get me if I was on my guard. One thing I'd done already as a precaution – ripped open the oilskin packet and substituted blank paper, and then sewn it up again. So, if anyone did manage to rob me of it, it wouldn't matter.

'What to do with the real thing worried me no end. Finally I opened it out flat – there were only two sheets – and laid it between two of the advertisement pages of a magazine. I stuck the two pages together round the edge with some gum off an envelope. I carried the magazine carelessly stuffed into the pocket of my ulster.

'At Holyhead I tried to get into a carriage with people that looked all right, but in a queer way there seemed always to be a crowd round me shoving and pushing me just the way I didn't want to go. There was something uncanny and frightening about it. In the end I found myself in a carriage with Mrs Vandemeyer after all. I went out into the corridor, but all the other carriages were full, so I had to go back and sit down. I consoled myself with the thought that there were other people in the carriage – there was quite a nice-looking man and his wife sitting just opposite. So

I felt almost happy about it until just outside London. I had leaned back and closed my eyes. I guess they thought I was asleep, but my eyes weren't quite shut, and suddenly I saw the nice-looking man get something out of his bag and hand it to Mrs Vandemeyer, and as he did so he *winked* . . .

'I can't tell you how that wink sort of froze me through and through. My only thought was to get out in the corridor as quick as ever I could. I got up, trying to look natural and easy. Perhaps they saw something – I don't know – but suddenly Mrs Vandemeyer said "Now", and flung something over my nose and mouth as I tried to scream. At the same moment I felt a terrific blow on the back of my head . . .'

She shuddered. Sir James murmured something sympathetically. In a minute she resumed:

'I don't know how long it was before I came back to consciousness. I felt very ill and sick. I was lying on a dirty bed. There was a screen round it, but I could hear two people talking in the room. Mrs Vandemeyer was one of them. I tried to listen, but at first I couldn't take much in. When at last I did begin to grasp what was going on – I was just terrified! I wonder I didn't scream right out there and then.

'They hadn't found the papers. They'd got the oilskin packet with the blanks, and they were just mad! They didn't know whether *I*'d changed the papers, or whether Danvers had been carrying a dummy message, while the real one was sent another way. They spoke of' – she closed her eyes – 'torturing me to find out!'

'I'd never known what fear – really sickening fear – was before! Once they came to look at me. I shut my eyes and pretended to be still unconscious, but I was afraid they'd hear the beating of my heart. However, they went away again. I began thinking madly. What could I do? I knew I wouldn't be able to stand up against torture very long.

'Suddenly something put the thought of loss of memory into my head. The subject had always interested me, and I'd read an awful lot about it. I had the whole thing at my finger-tips. If only I could succeed in carrying the bluff through, it might save me. I said a prayer, and drew a long breath. Then I opened my eyes and started babbling in *French*!

'Mrs Vandemeyer came round the screen at once. Her face was so wicked I nearly died, but I smiled up at her doubtfully, and asked her in French where I was.

'It puzzled her, I could see. She called the man she had been talking to. He stood by the screen with his face in shadow. He spoke to me in French. His voice was very ordinary and quiet but somehow, I don't know why, he scared me, but I went on playing my part. I asked again where I was, and then went on that there was something I *must* remember – *must* remember – *only* for the moment it was all gone. I worked myself up to be more and more distressed. He asked me my name. I said I didn't know – that I couldn't remember anything at all.

'Suddenly he caught my wrist, and began twisting it. The pain was awful. I screamed. He went on. I screamed and screamed, but I managed to shriek out things in French. I don't know how long I could have gone on, but luckily I fainted. The last thing I heard was his voice saying: "That's not bluff! Anyway, a kid of her age wouldn't know enough.' I guess he forgot American girls are older for their age than English ones, and take more interest in scientific subjects.

'When I came to, Mrs Vandemeyer was sweet as honey to me. She'd had her orders, I guess. She spoke to me in French – told me I'd had a shock and been very ill. I should be better soon. I pretended to be rather dazed – murmured something about the "doctor" having hurt my wrist. She looked relieved when I said that.

'By and by she went out of the room altogether. I was suspicious still, and lay quite quiet for some time. In the end, however, I got up and walked round the room, examining it. I thought that even if anyone *was* watching me from somewhere, it would seem natural enough under the circumstances. It was a squalid, dirty place. There were no windows, which seemed queer. I guessed the door would be locked, but I didn't try it. There were some battered old pictures on the walls, representing scenes from *Faust*.'

Jane's two listeners gave a simultaneous 'Ah!' The girl nodded.

'Yes – it was the place in Soho where Mr Beresford was imprisoned. Of course at the time I didn't even know if I was in London. One thing was worrying me dreadfully, but my heart gave a great throb of relief when I saw my ulster lying carelessly over the back of a chair. *And the magazine was still rolled up in the pocket!*

'If only I could be certain that I was not being overlooked! I looked carefully round the walls. There didn't seem to be a peep-hole of any kind – nevertheless I felt kind of sure there must be. All of a sudden I sat down on the edge of the table, and put my face in my hands, sobbing out a "*Mon Dieu*! *Mon Dieu*!" I've got very sharp ears. I distinctly heard the rustle of a dress, and a slight creak. That was enough for me. I was being watched!

'I lay down on the bed again, and by and by Mrs Vandemeyer brought me some supper. She was still sweet as they make them. I guess she'd been told to win my confidence. Presently she produced the oilskin packet, and asked me if I recognized it, watching me like a lynx all the time.

'I took it and turned it over in a puzzled sort of way. Then I shook my head. I said that I felt I *ought* to remember something about it, that it was just as though it was all coming back, and then, before I could get hold of it, it went again. Then she told me that I was her niece, and that I was to call her "Aunt Rita". I did obediently, and she told me not to worry – my memory would soon come back.

'That was an awful night. I'd made my plan whilst I was waiting for her. The papers were safe so far, but I couldn't take the risk of leaving them there any longer. They might throw that magazine away any minute. I lay awake waiting until I judged it must be about two o'clock in the morning. Then I got up as softly as I could, and felt in the dark along the left-hand wall. Very gently, I unhooked one of the pictures from its nail – Marguerite with her casket of jewels. I crept over to my coat and took out the magazine, and an odd envelope or two that I had shoved in. Then I went to the wash-stand, and damped the brown paper at the back of the picture all round. Presently I was able to pull it away. I had already torn out the two stuck-together pages from the magazine, and now I slipped them with their precious enclosure between the picture and its brown paper backing. A little gum from the envelopes helped me to stick the latter up again. No one would dream the picture had ever been tampered with. I rehung it on the wall, put the magazine back in my coat pocket, and crept back to bed. I was pleased with my hiding-place. They'd never think of pulling to pieces one of their own pictures. I hoped that they'd come to the conclusion that Danvers had been carrying a dummy all along, and that, in the end, they'd let me go.

'As a matter of fact, I guess that's what they did think at first and, in a way, it was dangerous for me. I learnt afterwards that they nearly did away with me then and there – there was never much chance of their "letting me go" – but the first man, who was the boss, preferred to keep me alive on the chance of my having hidden them, and being able to tell where if I recovered my memory. They watched me constantly for weeks. Sometimes they'd ask me questions by the hour – I guess there was nothing they didn't know about the third degree! – but somehow I managed to hold my own. The strain of it was awful, though . . .

'They took me back to Ireland, and over every step of the journey again, in case I'd hidden it somewhere *en route*. Mrs Vandemeyer and another woman never left me for a moment. They spoke of me as a young relative of Mrs Vandemeyer's whose mind was affected by the shock of the *Lusitania*. There was no one I could appeal to for help without giving myself away to *them*, and if I risked it and failed – and Mrs Vandemeyer looked so rich, and so beautifully dressed, that I felt convinced they'd take her word against mine, and think it was part of my mental trouble to think myself "persecuted" – I felt that the horrors in store for me would be too awful once they knew I'd been only shamming.'

Sir James nodded comprehendingly.

'Mrs Vandemeyer was a woman of great personality. With that and her social position she would have had little difficulty in imposing her point of view in preference to yours. Your sensational accusations against her would not easily have found credence.'

'That's what I thought. It ended in my being sent to a sanatorium at Bournemouth. I couldn't make up my mind at first whether it was a sham affair or genuine. A hospital nurse had charge of me. I was a special patient. She seemed so nice and normal that at last I determined to confide in her. A merciful providence just saved me in time from falling into the trap. My door happened to be ajar, and I heard her talking to someone in the passage. *She was one of them!* They still fancied it might be a bluff on my part, and she was put in charge of me to make sure! After that, my nerve went completely. I dared trust nobody.

'I think I almost hypnotized myself. After a while, I almost forgot that I was really Jane Finn. I was so bent on playing the part of Janet Vandemeyer that my nerves began to play tricks. I became really ill – for months I sank into a sort of stupor. I felt sure I should die soon, and that nothing really mattered. A sane person shut up in a lunatic asylum often ends by becoming insane, they say. I guess I was like that. Playing my part had become second nature to me. I wasn't even unhappy in the end – just apathetic. Nothing seemed to matter. And the years went on.

'And then suddenly things seemed to change. Mrs Vandemeyer came down from London. She and the doctor asked me questions, experimented with various treatments. There was some talk of sending me to a specialist in Paris. In the end, they did not dare risk it. I overheard something that seemed to show that other people – friends – were looking for me. I learnt later that the nurse who had looked after me went to Paris, and consulted a specialist, representing herself to be me. He put her through some searching tests, and exposed her loss of memory to be fraudulent; but she had taken a note of his methods and reproduced them on me. I dare say I couldn't have deceived the specialist for a minute – a man who has made a lifelong study of a thing is unique – but I managed once again to hold my own with them. The fact that I'd not thought of myself as Jane Finn for so long made it easier.

'One night I was whisked off to London at a moment's notice. They took me back to the house in Soho. Once I got away from the sanatorium I felt different – as though something in me that had been buried for a long time was waking up again.

'They sent me in to wait on Mr Beresford. (Of course I didn't know his name then.) I was suspicious – I thought it was another trap. But he looked so honest, I could hardly believe it. However I was careful in all I said, for I knew we could be overheard. There's a small hole, high up in the wall.

'But on the Sunday afternoon a message was brought to the house. They were all very disturbed. Without their knowing, I listened. Word had come that he was to be killed. I needn't tell the next part, because you know it. I thought I'd have time to rush up and get the papers from their hiding-place, but I was caught. So I screamed out that he was escaping, and I said I wanted to go back to Marguerite. I shouted the name three times very loud. I knew the others would think I meant Mrs Vandemeyer, but I hoped it might make Mr Beresford think of the picture. He'd unhooked one the first day – that's what made me hesitate to trust him.'

She paused.

'Then the papers,' said Sir James slowly, 'are still at the back of the picture in that room.'

'Yes.' The girl had sunk back on the sofa exhausted with the strain of the long story.

Sir James rose to his feet. He looked at his watch.

'Come,' he said, 'we must go at once.'

'Tonight? queried Tuppence, surprised.

'Tomorrow may be too late,' said Sir James gravely. 'Besides, by going tonight we have the chance of capturing that great man and super-criminal – Mr Brown!'

There was dead silence, and Sir James continued:

'You have been followed here – not a doubt of it. When we leave the house we shall be followed again, but not molested *for it is Mr Brown's plan that we are to lead him*. But the Soho house is under police supervision night and day. There are several men watching it. When we enter that house, Mr Brown will not draw back – he will risk all, on the chance of obtaining the spark to fire his mine. And he fancies the risk not great – since he will enter in the guise of a friend!'

Tuppence flushed, then opened her mouth impulsively.

'But there's something you don't know – that we haven't told you.' Her eyes dwelt on Jane in perplexity.

'What is that?' asked the other sharply. 'No hesitations, Miss Tuppence. We need to be sure of our going.'

But Tuppence, for once, seemed tongue-tied.

'It's so difficult – you see, if I'm wrong – oh, it would be dreadful.' She made a grimace at the unconscious Jane. 'Never forgive me,' she observed cryptically.

'You want me to help you out, eh?'

'Yes, please. *You* know who Mr Brown is, don't you?'

'Yes,' said Sir James gravely. 'At last I do.'

'At last?' queried Tuppence doubtfully. 'Oh, but I thought –' She paused.

'You thought correctly, Miss Tuppence. I have been morally certain of his identity for some time – ever since the night of Mrs Vandemeyer's mysterious death.'

'Ah!' breathed Tuppence.

'For there we are up against the logic of facts. There are only two solutions. Either the chloral was administered by her own hand, which theory I reject utterly, or else –'

'Yes?'

'Or else it was administered in the brandy you gave her. Only three people touched that brandy – you, Miss Tuppence, I myself, and one other – Mr Julius Hersheimmer!'

Jane Finn stirred and sat up, regarding the speaker with wide astonished eyes.

'At first, the thing seemed utterly impossible. Mr Hersheimmer, as the son of a prominent millionaire, was a well-known figure in America. It seemed utterly impossible that he and Mr Brown could be one and the same. But you cannot escape from the logic of facts. Since the thing was so – it must be accepted. Remember Mrs Vandemeyer's sudden and inexplicable agitation. Another proof, if proof was needed.

'I took an early opportunity of giving you a hint. From some words of Mr Hersheimmer's at Manchester, I gathered that you had understood and acted on that hint. Then I set to work to prove the impossible possible. Mr Beresford rang me up and told me, what I had already suspected, that the photograph of Miss Jane Finn had never really been out of Mr Hersheimmer's possession –'

But the girl interrupted. Springing to her feet, she cried out angrily:

'What do you mean? What are you trying to suggest? That Mr Brown is *Julius*? Julius – my own cousin!'

'No, Miss Finn,' said Sir James unexpectedly. 'Not your cousin. The man who calls himself Julius Hersheimmer is no relation to you whatsoever.'

CHAPTER 26

MR BROWN

Sir James's words came like a bombshell. Both girls looked equally puzzled. The lawyer went across to his desk, and returned with a small newspaper cutting, which he handed to Jane. Tuppence read it over her shoulder. Mr Carter would have recognized it. It referred to the mysterious man found dead in New York.

'As I was saying to Miss Tuppence,' resumed the lawyer, 'I set to work to prove the impossible possible. The great stumbling-block was the undeniable fact that Julius Hersheimmer was not an assumed name. When I came across this paragraph my problem was solved. Julius Hersheimmer set out to discover what had become of his cousin. He went out West, where he obtained news of her and her photograph to aid him in his search. On the eve of his departure from New York he was set upon and murdered. His body was dressed in shabby clothes, and the face disfigured to prevent identification. Mr Brown took his place. He sailed immediately for England. None of the real Hersheimmer's friends or intimates saw him before he sailed – though indeed it would hardly have mattered if they had, the impersonation was so perfect. Since then he had been hand in glove with those sworn to hunt him down. Every secret of theirs had been known to him. Only once did he come near disaster. Mrs Vandemeyer knew his secret. It was no part of his plan that that huge bribe should ever be offered to her. But for Miss Tuppence's fortunate change of plan, she would have been far away from the flat when we arrived there. Exposure stared him in the face. He took a desperate step, trusting in his assumed character to avert suspicion. He nearly succeeded – but not quite.'

'I can't believe it,' murmured Jane. 'He seemed so splendid.'

'The real Julius Hersheimmer *was* a splendid fellow! And Mr Brown is a consummate actor. But ask Miss Tuppence if she also has not had her suspicions.'

Jane turned mutely to Tuppence. The latter nodded.

'I didn't want to say it, Jane – I knew it would hurt you. And, after all, I couldn't be sure. I still don't understand why, if he's Mr Brown, he rescued us.'

'Was it Julius Hersheimmer who helped you to escape?'

Tuppence recounted to Sir James the exciting events of the evening, ending up: 'But I can't see *why*!'

'Can't you? I can. So can young Beresford, by his actions. As a last hope Jane Finn was to be allowed to escape – and the escape must be managed so that she harbours no suspicions of its being a put-up job. They're not averse to young Beresford's being in the neighbourhood, and, if necessary, communicating with you. They'll take care to get him out of the way at the right minute. Then Julius Hersheimmer dashes up and rescues you in true melodramatic style. Bullets fly – but don't hit anybody. What would have happened next? You would have driven straight to the house in Soho and secured the document which Miss Finn would probably have entrusted to her cousin's keeping. Or, if he conducted the search, he would have pretended to find the hiding-place already rifled. He would have had a dozen ways of dealing with the situation, but the result would have been the same. And I rather fancy some accident would have happened to both of you. You see, you know rather an inconvenient amount. That's a rough outline. I admit I was caught napping; but somebody else wasn't.'

'Tommy,' said Tuppence softly.

'Yes. Evidently when the right moment came to get rid of him – he was too sharp for them. All the same, I'm not too easy in my mind about him.'

'Why?'

'Because Julius Hersheimmer is Mr Brown,' said Sir James dryly. 'And it takes more than one man and a revolver to hold up Mr Brown . . .'

Tuppence paled a little.

'What can we do?'

'Nothing until we've been to the house in Soho. If Beresford has still got the upper hand, there's nothing to fear. If otherwise, our enemy will come to find us, and he will not find us unprepared!' From a drawer in the desk, he took a Service revolver, and placed it in his coat pocket.

'Now we're ready. I know better than even to suggest going without you, Miss Tuppence –'

'I should think so indeed!'

'But I do suggest that Miss Finn should remain here. She will be perfectly safe, and I am afraid she is absolutely worn out with all she has been through.'

But to Tuppence's surprise Jane shook her head.

'No. I guess I'm going too. Those papers were my trust. I must go through with this business to the end. I'm heaps better now anyway.'

Sir James's car was ordered round. During the short drive Tuppence's heart beat tumultuously. In spite of momentary qualms of uneasiness respecting Tommy, she could not but feel exultation. They were going to win!

The car drew up at the corner of the square and they got out. Sir James went up to a plain-clothes man who was on duty with several others, and spoke to him. Then he rejoined the girls.

'No one has gone into the house so far. It is being watched at the back as well, so they are quite sure of that. Anyone who attempts to enter after we have done so will be arrested immediately. Shall we go in?'

A policeman produced a key. They all knew Sir James well. They had also had orders respecting Tuppence. Only the third member of the party was unknown to them. The three entered the house, pulling the door to behind them. Slowly they mounted the rickety stairs. At the top was the ragged curtain hiding the recess where Tommy had hidden that day. Tuppence had heard the story from Jane in her character of 'Annette'. She looked at the tattered velvet with interest. Even now she could almost swear it moved – as though *someone* was behind it. So strong was the illusion that she almost fancied she could make out the outline of a form . . . Supposing Mr Brown – Julius – was there waiting . . .

Impossible of course! Yet she almost went back to put the curtain aside and make sure . . .

Now they were entering the prison room. No place for anyone to hide here, thought Tuppence, with a sigh of relief, then chided herself indignantly. She must not give way to this foolish fancying – this curious insistent feeling that *Mr Brown was in the house* . . . Hark! what was that? A stealthy footstep on the stairs? There *was* someone in the house! Absurd! She was becoming hysterical.

Jane had gone straight to the picture of Marguerite. She unhooked it with a steady hand. The dust lay thick upon it, and festoons of cobwebs lay between it and the wall. Sir James handed her a pocket-knife, and she stripped away the brown paper from the back . . . The advertisement page of a magazine fell out. Jane picked it up. Holding apart the frayed inner edges she extracted two thin sheets covered with writing!

No dummy this time! The real thing!

'We've got it,' said Tuppence. 'At last . . .'

The moment was almost breathless in its emotion. Forgotten the faint creakings, the imagined noises of a minute ago. None of them had eyes for anything but what Jane held in her hand.

Sir James took it, and scrutinized it attentively.

'Yes,' he said quietly, 'this is the ill-fated draft treaty!'

'We've succeeded,' said Tuppence. There was awe and an almost wondering unbelief in her voice.

Sir James echoed her words as he folded the paper carefully and put it away in his pocket-book, then he looked curiously round the dingy room.

'It was here that your young friend was confined for so long, was it not?' he said. 'A truly sinister room. You notice the absence of windows, and the thickness of the close-fitting door. Whatever took place here would never be heard by the outside world.'

Tuppence shivered. His words woke a vague alarm in her. What if there *was* someone concealed in the house? Someone who might bar that door on them, and leave them to die like rats in a trap? Then she realized the absurdity of her thought. The house was surrounded by police who, if they failed to reappear, would not hesitate to break in and make a thorough search. She smiled at her own foolishness – then looked up with a start to find Sir James watching her. He gave her an emphatic little nod.

'Quite right, Miss Tuppence. You scent danger. So do I. So does Miss Finn.'

'Yes,' admitted Jane. 'It's absurd – but I can't help it.'

Sir James nodded again.

'You feel – as we all feel – *the presence of Mr Brown*. Yes' – as

Tuppence made a movement – 'not a doubt of it – *Mr Brown is here . . .*'

'In this house?'

'In this room . . . You don't understand? *I am Mr Brown . . .*'

Stupefied, unbelieving, they stared at him. The very lines of his face had changed. It was a different man who stood before them. He smiled a slow, cruel smile.

'Neither of you will leave this room alive! You said just now we had succeeded. *I* have succeeded! The draft treaty is mine.' His smile grew wider as he looked at Tuppence. 'Shall I tell you how it will be? Sooner or later the police will break in, and they will find three victims of Mr Brown – three, not two, you understand, but fortunately the third will not be dead, only wounded, and will be able to describe the attack with a wealth of detail! The treaty? It is in the hands of Mr Brown. So no one will think of searching the pockets of Sir James Peel Edgerton!'

He turned to Jane.

'You outwitted me. I make my acknowledgments. But you will not do it again.'

There was a faint sound behind him, but intoxicated with success he did not turn his head.

He slipped his hand into his pocket.

'Checkmate to the Young Adventurers,' he said, and slowly raised the big automatic.

But, even as he did so, he felt himself seized from behind in a grip of iron. The revolver was wrenched from his hand, and the voice of Julius Hersheimmer said drawlingly:

'I guess you're caught red-handed with the goods upon you.'

The blood rushed to the K.C.'s face, but his self-control was marvellous, as he looked from one to the other of his two captors. He looked longest at Tommy.

'You,' he said beneath his breath. '*You!* I might have known.'

Seeing that he was disposed to offer no resistance, their grip slackened. Quick as a flash his left hand, the hand which bore the big signet ring, was raised to his lips . . .

'"*Ave Cæsar! te morituri salutant,*"' he said, still looking at Tommy.

Then his face changed, and with a long, convulsive shudder he fell forward in a crumpled heap, whilst an odour of bitter almonds filled the air.

CHAPTER 27

A SUPPER PARTY AT THE SAVOY

The supper party given by Mr Julius Hersheimmer to a few friends on the evening of the 30th will long be remembered in catering circles. It took place in a private room, and Mr Hersheimmer's orders were brief and forcible. He gave *carte blanche* – and when a millionaire gives *carte blanche* he usually gets it!

Every delicacy out of season was duly provided. Waiters carried bottles of ancient and royal vintage with loving care. The floral decorations defied the seasons, and fruits of the earth as far apart as May and November found themselves miraculously side by side. The list of guests was small and select. The American Ambassador, Mr Carter, who had taken the liberty, he said, of bringing an old friend, Sir William Beresford, with him, Archdeacon Cowley, Dr Hall, those two youthful adventurers, Miss Prudence Cowley and Mr Thomas Beresford, and last, but not least, as guest of honour, Miss Jane Finn.

Julius had spared no pains to make Jane's appearance a success. A mysterious knock had brought Tuppence to the door of the apartment she was sharing with the American girl. It was Julius. In his hand he held a cheque.

'Say, Tuppence,' he began, 'will you do me a good turn? Take this, and get Jane regularly togged up for this evening. You're all coming to supper with me at the Savoy. See? Spare no expense. You get me?'

'Sure thing,' mimicked Tuppence. 'We shall enjoy ourselves! It will be a pleasure dressing Jane. She's the loveliest thing I've ever seen.'

'That's so,' agreed Mr Hersheimmer fervently.

His fervour brought a momentary twinkle to Tuppence's eye.

'By the way, Julius,' she remarked demurely, 'I – haven't given you my answer yet.'

'Answer?' said Julius. His face paled.

'You know – when you asked me to – marry you,' faltered Tuppence, her eyes downcast in the true manner of the early Victorian heroine, 'and wouldn't take no for an answer. I've thought it well over –'

'Yes?' said Julius. The perspiration stood on his forehead.

Tuppence relented suddenly.

'You great idiot!' she said. 'What on earth induced you to do it? I could see at the time you didn't care a twopenny dip for me!'

'Not at all. I had – and still have – the highest sentiments of esteem and respect – and admiration for you –'

'H'm!' said Tuppence. 'Those are the kind of sentiments that very soon go to the wall when the other sentiment comes along! Don't they, old thing?'

'I don't know what you mean,' said Julius stiffly, but a large and burning blush overspread his countenance.

'Shucks!' retorted Tuppence. She laughed and closed the door, reopening it to add with dignity: 'Morally, I shall always consider I have been jilted!'

'What was it?' asked Jane as Tuppence rejoined her.

'Julius.'

'What did he want?'

'Really, I think, he wanted to see you, but I wasn't going to let him. Not until tonight, when you're going to burst upon everyone like King Solomon in his glory! Come on! *We're going to shop!*'

To most people the 29th, the much-heralded 'Labour Day', had passed much as any other day. Speeches were made in the Park and Trafalgar Square. Straggling processions, singing *The Red Flag*, wandered through the streets in a more or less aimless manner. Newspapers which had hinted at a general strike, and the inauguration of a reign of terror, were forced to hide their diminished heads. The bolder and more astute among them sought to prove that peace had been effected by following their counsels. In the Sunday papers a brief notice of the sudden death of Sir James Peel Edgerton, the famous K.C., had appeared. Monday's paper dealt appreciatively with the dead man's career. The exact manner of his sudden death was never made public.

Tommy had been right in his forecast of the situation. It had been a one-man show. Deprived of their chief, the organization fell to pieces. Kramenin had made a precipitate return to Russia, leaving England early on Sunday morning. The gang had fled from Astley Priors in a panic, leaving behind, in their haste, various damaging documents which compromised them hopelessly. With these proofs of conspiracy in their hands, aided further by a small brown diary, taken from the pocket of the dead man, which had contained a full and damning résumé of the whole plot, the Government had called an eleventh-hour conference. The Labour leaders were forced to recognize that they had been used as a cat's paw. Certain concessions were made by the Government, and were eagerly accepted. It was to be Peace, not War!

But the Cabinet knew by how narrow a margin they had escaped utter disaster. And burnt in on Mr Carter's brain was the strange scene which had taken place in the house in Soho the night before.

He had entered the squalid room to find that great man, the friend of a lifetime, dead – betrayed out of his own mouth. From the dead man's pocket-book he had retrieved the ill-omened draft treaty, and then and there, in the presence of the other three, it had been reduced to ashes . . . England was saved!

And now, on the evening of the 30th, in a private room at the Savoy, Mr Julius P. Hersheimmer was receiving his guests.

Mr Carter was the first to arrive. With him was a choleric-looking old gentleman, at sight of whom Tommy flushed up to the roots of his hair. He came forward.

'Ha!' said the old gentleman surveying him apoplectically. 'So you're my nephew, are you? Not much to look at – but you've done good work, it seems. Your mother must have brought you up well after all. Shall we let bygones be bygones, eh? You're my heir, you know; and in future I propose to make you an allowance – and you can look upon Chalmers Park as your home.'

'Thank you, sir, it's awfully decent of you.'

'Where's this young lady I've been hearing such a lot about?'

Tommy introduced Tuppence.

'Ha!' said Sir William, eyeing her. 'Girls aren't what they used to be in my young days.'

'Yes, they are,' said Tuppence. 'Their clothes are different, perhaps, but they themselves are just the same.'

'Well, perhaps you're right. Minxes then – minxes now!'

'That's it,' said Tuppence. 'I'm a frightful minx myself.'

'I believe you,' said the old gentleman, chuckling, and pinched her ear in high good-humour. Most young women were terrified of the 'old bear', as they termed him. Tuppence's pertness delighted the old misogynist.

Then came the timid archdeacon, a little bewildered by the company in which he found himself, glad that his daughter was considered to have distinguished herself, but unable to help glancing at her from time to time with nervous apprehension. But Tuppence behaved admirably. She forbore to cross her legs, set a guard upon her tongue, and steadfastly refused to smoke.

Dr Hall came next, and he was followed by the American Ambassador.

'We might as well sit down,' said Julius, when he had introduced all his guests to each other. 'Tuppence, will you –'

He indicated the place of honour with a wave of his hand.

But Tuppence shook her head.

'No – that's Jane's place! When one thinks of how she's held out all these years, she ought to be made the queen of the feast tonight.'

Julius flung her a grateful glance, and Jane came forward shyly to the allotted seat. Beautiful as she had seemed before, it was as nothing to the loveliness that now went fully adorned. Tuppence had performed her part faithfully. The model gown supplied by a famous dressmaker had been entitled 'A tiger lily'. It was all golds and reds and browns, and out of it rose the pure column of the girl's white throat, and the bronze masses of hair that crowned her lovely head. There was admiration in every eye, as she took her seat.

Soon the supper party was in full swing, and with one accord Tommy was called upon for a full and complete explanation.

'You've been too darned close about the whole business,' Julius accused him. 'You let on to me that you were off to the Argentine – though I guess you had your reasons for that. The idea of both you and Tuppence casting me for the part of Mr Brown just tickles me to death!'

'The idea was not original to them,' said Mr Carter gravely. 'It was suggested, and the poison very carefully instilled, by a past-master in the art. The paragraph in the New York paper suggested the plan to him, and by means of it he wove a web that nearly enmeshed you fatally.'

'I never liked him,' said Julius. 'I felt from the first that there was something wrong about him, and I always suspected that it was he who silenced Mrs Vandemeyer so appositely. But it wasn't till I heard that the order for Tommy's execution came right on the heels of our interview with him that Sunday that I began to tumble to the fact that he was the big bug himself.'

'I never suspected it at all,' lamented Tuppence. 'I've always thought I was so much cleverer than Tommy – but he's undoubtedly scored over me handsomely.'

Julius agreed.

'Tommy's been the goods this trip! And, instead of sitting there as dumb as a fish, let him banish his blushes, and tell us all about it.'

'Hear! hear!'

'There's nothing to tell,' said Tommy, acutely uncomfortable. 'I was an awful mug – right up to the time I found that photograph of Annette, and realized that she was Jane Finn. Then I remembered how persistently she had shouted out that word "Marguerite" – and I thought of the pictures, and – well, that's that. Then of course I went over the whole thing to see where I'd made an ass of myself.'

'Go on,' said Mr Carter, as Tommy showed signs of taking refuge in silence once more.

'That business about Mrs Vandemeyer had worried me when Julius told me about it. On the face of it, it seemed that he or Sir James must have done the trick. But I didn't know which. Finding that photograph in the drawer, after that story of how it had been got from him by Inspector Brown, made me suspect Julius. Then I remembered that it was Sir James who had discovered the false Jane Finn. In the end, I couldn't make up my mind – and just decided to take no chances either way. I left a note for Julius, in case he was Mr Brown, saying I was off to the Argentine, and I dropped Sir James's letter with the offer of the job by the desk so that he would see it was a genuine stunt. Then I wrote my letter to Mr Carter and rang up Sir James. Taking him into my confidence would be the best thing either way, so I told him everything except where I believed the papers to be hidden. The way he helped me to get on the track of Tuppence and Annette almost disarmed me, but not quite. I kept my mind open between the two of them. And then I got a bogus note from Tuppence – and then I knew!'

'But how?'

Tommy took the note in question from his pocket and passed it round the table.

'It's her handwriting all right, but I knew it wasn't from her because of the signature. She'd never spell her name "Twopence," but anyone who'd never seen it written might quite easily do so. Julius *had* seen it – he showed me a note of hers to him once – but *Sir James hadn't*! After that everything was plain sailing. I sent off Albert post-haste to Mr Carter. I pretended to go away, but doubled back again. When Julius came bursting up in his car, I felt it wasn't part of Mr Brown's plan – and that there would probably be trouble. Unless Sir James was actually caught in the act, so to speak, I knew Mr Carter would never believe it of him on my bare word –'

'I didn't,' interposed Mr Carter ruefully.

'That's why I sent the girls off to Sir James. I was sure they'd fetch up at the house in Soho sooner or later. I threatened Julius with the revolver, because I wanted Tuppence to repeat that to Sir James, so that he wouldn't worry about us. The moment the girls were out of sight I told Julius to drive like hell for London, and as we went along I told him the whole story. We got to the Soho house in plenty of time and met Mr Carter outside. After arranging things with him we went in and hid behind the curtain in the recess. The policemen had orders to say, if they were asked, that no one had gone into the house. That's all.'

And Tommy came to an abrupt halt.

There was silence for a moment.

'By the way,' said Julius suddenly, 'you're all wrong about that photograph of Jane. It *was* taken from me, but I found it again.'

'Where?' cried Tuppence.

'In that little safe on the wall in Mrs Vandermeyer's bedroom.'

'I knew you found something,' said Tuppence reproachfully. 'To tell you the truth, that's what started me off suspecting you. Why didn't you say?'

'I guess I was a mite suspicious too. It had been got away from me once, and I determined I wouldn't let on I'd got it until a photographer had made a dozen copies of it!'

'We all kept back something or other,' said Tuppence thoughtfully. 'I suppose secret service work makes you like that!'

In the pause that ensued, Mr Carter took from his pocket a small shabby brown book.

'Beresford has just said that I would not have believed Sir James Peel Edgerton to be guilty unless, so to speak, he was caught in the act. That is so. Indeed, not until I read the entries in this little book could I bring myself fully to credit the amazing truth. This book will pass into the possession of Scotland Yard, but it will never be publicly exhibited. Sir James's long association with the law would make it undesirable. But to you, who know the truth, I propose to read certain passages which will throw some light on the extraordinary mentality of this great man.'

He opened the book, and turned the thin pages.

'. . . It is madness to keep this book. I know that. It is documentary evidence against me. But I have never shrunk from taking risks. And I feel an urgent need for self-expression . . . The book will only be taken from my dead body . . .

'. . . From an early age I realized that I had exceptional abilities. Only a fool underestimates his capabilities. My brain power was greatly above the average. I know that I was born to succeed. My appearance was the only thing against me. I was quiet and insignificant – utterly nondescript . . .

'. . . When I was a boy I heard a famous murder trial. I was deeply impressed by the power and eloquence of the counsel for the defence. For the first time I entertained the idea of taking my talents to that particular market . . . Then I studied the criminal in the dock . . . The man was a fool – he had been incredibly, unbelievably stupid. Even the eloquence of his counsel was hardly likely to save him . . . I felt an immeasurable contempt for him . . . Then it occurred to me that the criminal standard was a low one. It was the wastrels, the failures, the general riff-raff of civilization who drifted into crime . . . Strange that men of brains had never realized its extraordinary opportunities . . . I played with the idea . . . What a magnificent field – what unlimited possibilities! It made my brain reel . . .

'. . . I read standard works on crime and criminals. They all confirmed my opinion. Degeneracy, disease – never the deliberate embracing of a career by a far-seeing man. Then I considered. Supposing my utmost ambitions were realized – that I was called to the bar, and rose to the height of my profession? That I entered politics – say, even, that I became Prime Minister of England? What then? Was that power? Hampered at every turn by my colleagues, fettered by the democratic system of which I should be the mere figurehead! No – the power I dreamed of was absolute! An autocrat! A dictator! And such power could only be obtained by working outside the law. To play on the weaknesses of human nature, then on the weaknesses of nations – to get together and control a vast organization, and finally to overthrow the existing order, and rule! The thought intoxicated me . . .

'. . . I saw that I must lead two lives. A man like myself is bound to attract notice. I must have a successful career which would mask my true activities . . . Also I must cultivate a personality. I modelled myself upon famous K.C.s. I reproduced their mannerisms, their magnetism. If I had chosen to be an actor, I should have been the greatest actor living! No disguises – no grease paint – no false beards! Personality! I put it on like a glove! When I shed it, I was myself, quiet, unobtrusive, a man like every other man. I called myself Mr Brown. There are hundreds of men called Brown – there are hundreds of men looking just like me . . .

'. . . I succeeded in my false career. I was bound to succeed. I shall succeed in the other. A man like me cannot fail . . .

'. . . I have been reading a life of Napoleon. He and I have much in common . . .

'. . . I make a practice of defending criminals. A man should look after his own people . . .

'. . . Once or twice I have felt afraid. The first time was in Italy. There was a dinner given. Professor D—, the great alienist, was present. The talk fell on insanity. He said, "A great many men are mad, and no one knows it. They do not know it themselves." I do not understand why he looked at me when he said that. His glance was strange . . . I did not like it . . .

'. . . The war has disturbed me . . . I thought it would further my plans. The Germans are so efficient. Their spy system, too, was excellent. The streets are full of these boys in khaki. All empty-headed young fools . . . Yet I do not know . . . They won the war . . . It disturbs me . . .

'. . . My plans are going well . . . A girl butted in – I do not think she really knew anything . . . But we must give up the Esthonia . . . No risks now . . .

'. . . All goes well. The loss of memory is vexing. It cannot be a fake. No girl could deceive ME! . . .

'. . . The 29th . . . That is very soon . . .' Mr Carter paused.

'I will not read the details of the *coup* that was planned. But there are just two small entries that refer to the three of you. In the light of what happened they are interesting.

'. . . By inducing the girl to come to me of her own accord, I have succeeded in disarming her. But she has intuitive flashes that might be dangerous . . . She must be got out of the way . . . I can do nothing with the American. He suspects and dislikes me. But he cannot know. I fancy my armour is impregnable . . . Sometimes I fear I have underestimated the other boy. He is not clever, but it is hard to blind his eyes to facts . . .'

Mr Carter shut the book.

'A great man,' he said. 'Genius, or insanity, who can say?'

There was silence.

Then Mr Carter rose to his feet.

'I will give you a toast. The Joint Venture which has so amply justified itself by success!'

It was drunk with acclamation.

'There's something more we want to hear,' continued Mr Carter. He looked at the American Ambassador. 'I speak for you also, I know. We'll ask Miss Jane Finn to tell us the story that only Miss Tuppence has heard so far – but before we do so we'll drink her health. The health of one of the bravest of America's daughters, to whom is due the thanks and gratitude of two great countries!'

CHAPTER 28

AND AFTER

'That was a mighty good toast, Jane,' said Mr Hersheimmer, as he and his cousin were being driven back in the Rolls-Royce to the Ritz.

'The one to the joint venture?'

'No – the one to you. There isn't another girl in the world who could have carried it through as you did. You were just wonderful!'

Jane shook her head.

'I don't feel wonderful. At heart I'm just tired and lonesome – and longing for my own country.'

'That brings me to something I wanted to say. I heard the Ambassador telling you his wife hoped you would come to them at the Embassy right away. That's good enough, but I've got another plan. Jane – I want you to marry me! Don't get scared and say no at once. You can't love me right away, of course, that's impossible. But I've loved you from the very moment I set eyes on your photo – and now I've seen you I'm simply crazy about you! If you'll only marry me, I won't worry you any – you shall take your own time. Maybe you'll never come to love me, and if that's the case I'll manage to set you free. But I want the right to look after you, and take care of you.'

'That's what I want,' said the girl wistfully. 'Someone who'll be good to me. Oh, you don't know how lonesome I feel!'

'Sure thing I do. Then I guess that's all fixed up, and I'll see the archbishop about a special licence tomorrow morning.'

'Oh, Julius!'

'Well, I don't want to hustle you any, Jane, but there's no sense in waiting about. Don't be scared – I shan't expect you to love me all at once.'

But a small hand was slipped into his.

'I love you now, Julius,' said Jane Finn. 'I loved you that first moment in the car when the bullet grazed your cheek . . .'

Five minutes later Jane murmured softly:

'I don't know London very well, Julius, but is it such a very long way from the Savoy to the Ritz?'

'It depends how you go,' explained Julius unblushingly. 'We're going by way of Regent's Park!'

'Oh, Julius – what will the chauffeur think?'

'At the wages I pay him, he knows better than to do any independent thinking. Why, Jane, the only reason I had the supper at the Savoy was so that I could drive you home. I didn't see how I was ever going to get hold of you alone. You and Tuppence have been sticking together like Siamese twins. I guess another day of it would have driven me and Beresford stark staring mad!'

'Oh. Is he –?'

'Of course he is. Head over ears.'

'I thought so,' said Jane thoughtfully.

'Why?'

'From all the things Tuppence didn't say!'

'There you have me beat,' said Mr Hersheimmer.

But Jane only laughed.

In the meantime, the Young Adventurers were sitting bolt upright, very stiff and ill at ease, in a taxi which, with a singular lack of originality, was also returning to the Ritz via Regent's Park.

A terrible constraint seemed to have settled down between them. Without quite knowing what had happened, everything seemed changed. They were tongue-tied – paralysed. All the old *cameraderie* was gone.

Tuppence could think of nothing to say.

Tommy was equally afflicted.

They sat very straight and forbore to look at each other.

At last Tuppence made a desperate effort.

'Rather fun, wasn't it?'

'Rather.'

Another silence.

'I like Julius,' essayed Tuppence again.

Tommy was suddenly galvanized into life.

'You're not going to marry him, do you hear?' he said dictatorially. 'I forbid it.'

'Oh!' said Tuppence meekly.

'Absolutely, you understand.'

'He doesn't want to marry me – he really only asked me out of kindness.'

'That's not very likely,' scoffed Tommy.

'It's quite true. He's head over ears in love with Jane. I expect he's proposing to her now.'

'She'll do for him very nicely,' said Tommy condescendingly.

'Don't you think she's the most lovely creature you've ever seen?'

'Oh, I dare say.'

'But I suppose you prefer sterling worth,' said Tuppence demurely.

'I – oh, dash it all, Tuppence, you know!'

'I like your uncle, Tommy,' said Tuppence, hastily creating a diversion. 'By the way, what are you going to do, accept Mr Carter's offer of a Government job, or accept Julius's invitation and take a richly remunerated post in America on his ranch?'

'I shall stick to the old ship, I think, though it's awfully good of Hersheimmer. But I feel you'd be more at home in London.'

'I don't see where I come in.'

'I do,' said Tommy positively.

Tuppence stole a glance at him sideways.

'There's the money, too,' she observed thoughtfully.

'What money?'

'We're going to get a cheque each. Mr Carter told me so.'

'Did you ask how much?' inquired Tommy sarcastically.

'Yes,' said Tuppence triumphantly. 'But I shan't tell you.'

'Tuppence, you are the limit!'

'It has been fun, hasn't it, Tommy? I do hope we shall have lots more adventures.'

'You're insatiable, Tuppence. I've had quite enough adventures for the present.'

'Well, shopping is almost as good,' said Tuppence dreamily. 'Thinking of buying old furniture, and bright carpets, and futurist silk curtains, and a polished dining-table, and a divan with lots of cushions –'

'Hold hard,' said Tommy. 'What's all this for?'

'Possibly a house – but I think a flat.'

'Whose flat?'

'You think I mind saying it, but I don't in the least! *Ours*, so there!'

'You darling!' cried Tommy, his arms tightly round her. 'I

was determined to make you say it. I owe you something for the relentless way you've squashed me whenever I've tried to be sentimental.'

Tuppence raised her face to his. The taxi proceeded on its course round the north side of Regent's Park.

'You haven't really proposed now,' pointed out Tuppence. 'Not what our grandmothers would call a proposal. But after listening to a rotten one like Julius's, I'm inclined to let you off.'

'You won't be able to get out of marrying me, so don't you think it.'

'What fun it will be,' responded Tuppence. 'Marriage is called all sorts of things, a haven, a refuge, and a crowning glory, and a state of bondage, and lots more. But do you know what I think it is?'

'What?'

'A sport!'

'And a damned good sport too,' said Tommy.

THE MAN IN THE BROWN SUIT

To E.A.B
In memory of a journey, some lion stories
and a request that I should some day write
the 'Mystery of the Mill House'

PROLOGUE

Nadina, the Russian dancer who had taken Paris by storm, swayed to the sound of the applause, bowed and bowed again. Her narrow black eyes narrowed themselves still more, the long line of her scarlet mouth curved faintly upwards. Enthusiastic Frenchmen continued to beat the ground appreciatively as the curtain fell with a swish, hiding the reds and blues and magentas of the bizarre *décor*. In a swirl of blue and orange draperies the dancer left the stage. A bearded gentleman received her enthusiastically in his arms. It was the manager.

'Magnificent, *petite*, magnificent,' he cried. 'Tonight you have surpassed yourself.' He kissed her gallantly on both cheeks in a somewhat matter-of-fact manner.

Madame Nadina accepted the tribute with the ease of long habit and passed on to her dressing-room, where bouquets were heaped carelessly everywhere, marvellous garments of futuristic design hung on pegs, and the air was hot and sweet with the scent of the massed blossoms and with the more sophisticated perfumes and essences. Jeanne, the dresser, ministered to her mistress, talking incessantly and pouring out a stream of fulsome compliments.

A knock at the door interrupted the flow, Jeanne went to answer it, and returned with a card in her hand.

'Madame will receive?'

'Let me see.'

The dancer stretched out a languid hand, but at the sight of the name on the card, 'Count Sergius Paulovitch', a sudden flicker of interest came into her eyes.

'I will see him. The maize *peignoir*, Jeanne, and quickly. And when the Count comes you may go.'

'*Bien, Madame.*'

Jeanne brought the *peignoir*, an exquisite wisp of corn-coloured chiffon and ermine. Nadina slipped into it, and sat smiling to herself, whilst one long white hand beat a slow tattoo on the glass of the dressing-table.

The Count was prompt to avail himself of the privilege accorded to him – a man of medium height, very slim, very elegant, very pale, extraordinarily weary. In feature, little to take hold of, a man difficult to recognize again if one left his mannerisms out of account. He bowed over the dancer's hand with exaggerated courtliness.

'Madame, this is a pleasure indeed.'

So much Jeanne heard before she went out, closing the door behind her. Alone with her visitor, a subtle change came over Nadina's smile.

'Compatriots though we are, we will not speak Russian, I think,' she observed.

'Since we neither of us know a word of the language, it might be as well,' agreed her guest.

By common consent, they dropped into English, and nobody, now that the Count's mannerisms had dropped from him, could doubt that it was his native language. He had, indeed, started life as a quick-change music-hall artiste in London.

'You had great success tonight,' he remarked. 'I congratulate you.'

'All the same,' said the woman, 'I am disturbed. My position is not what it was. The suspicions aroused during the war have never died down. I am continually watched and spied upon.'

'But no charge of espionage was ever brought against you?'

'Our chief lays his plans too carefully for that.'

'Long life to the "Colonel",' said the Count, smiling. 'Amazing news, is it not, that he means to retire? To retire! Just like a doctor, or a butcher, or a plumber –'

'Or any other business man,' finished Nadina. 'It should not surprise us. That is what the "Colonel" has always been – an excellent man of business. He has organized crime as another man might organize a boot factory. Without committing himself, he has planned and directed a series of stupendous *coups*, embracing every branch of what we might call his "profession". Jewel robberies, forgery, espionage (the latter very profitable in war-time), sabotage, discreet assassination, there is hardly anything he has not touched. Wisest of all, he knows when to stop. The game begins to be dangerous? – he retires gracefully – with an enormous fortune!'

'H'm!' said the Count doubtfully. 'It is rather – upsetting for all of us. We are at a loose end, as it were.'

'But we are being paid off – on a most generous scale!'

Something, some undercurrent of mockery in her tone, made the man look at her sharply. She was smiling to herself, and the quality of her smile aroused his curiosity. But he proceeded diplomatically:

'Yes, the "Colonel" has always been a great paymaster. I attribute much of his success to that – and to his invariable plan of providing a suitable scapegoat. A great brain, undoubtedly a great brain! And an apostle of the maxim, "If you want a thing done safely, do not do it yourself!" Here are we, every one of us incriminated up to the hilt and absolutely in his power, and not one of us has anything on him.'

He paused, almost as though he were expecting her to disagree with him, but she remained silent, smiling to herself as before.

'Not one of us,' he mused. 'Still, you know, he is superstitious, the old man. Years ago, I believe, he went to one of these fortune-telling people. She prophesied a lifetime of success, but declared that his downfall would be brought about through a woman.'

He had interested her now. She looked up eagerly.

'That is strange, very strange! Through a woman, you say?'

He smiled and shrugged his shoulders.

'Doubtless, now that he has – retired, he will marry. Some young society beauty, who will disperse his millions faster than he acquired them.'

Nadina shook her head.

'No, no, that is not the way of it. Listen, my friend, tomorrow I go to London.'

'But your contract here?'

'I shall be away only one night. And I go incognito, like Royalty. No one will ever know that I have left France. And why do you think that I go?'

'Hardly for pleasure at this time of the year. January, a detestable foggy month! It must be for profit, eh?'

'Exactly.' She rose and stood in front of him, every graceful line of her arrogant with pride. 'You said just now that none of us had anything on the chief. You were wrong. I have. I, a woman, have had the wit and, yes, the courage – for it needs courage – to double-cross him. You remember the De Beer diamonds?'

'Yes, I remember. At Kimberley, just before the war broke out? I had nothing to do with it, and I never heard the details, the case was hushed up for some reason, was it not? A fine haul, too.'

'A hundred thousand pounds' worth of stones. Two of us worked it – under the "Colonel's" orders, of course. And it was then that I saw my chance. You see, the plan was to substitute some of the De Beer diamonds for some sample diamonds brought from South America by two young prospectors who happened to be in Kimberley at the time. Suspicion was then bound to fall on them.'

'Very clever,' interpolated the Count approvingly.

'The "Colonel" is always clever. Well, I did my part – but I also did one thing which the "Colonel" had not foreseen. I kept back some of the South American stones – one or two are unique and could easily be proved never to have passed through De Beers' hands. With these diamonds in my possession, I have the whip hand of my esteemed chief. Once the two young men are cleared, his part in the matter is bound to be suspected. I have said nothing all these years, I have been content to know that I had this weapon in reverse, but now matters are different. I want my price – and it will be big, I might almost say a staggering price.'

'Extraordinary,' said the Count. 'And doubtless you carry these diamonds about with you everywhere?'

His eyes roamed gently around the disordered room.

Nadina laughed softly.

'You need suppose nothing of the sort. I am not a fool. The diamonds are in a safe place where no one will dream of looking for them.'

'I never thought you a fool, my dear lady, but may I venture to suggest that you are somewhat foolhardy? The "Colonel" is not the type of man to take kindly to being blackmailed, you know.'

'I am not afraid of him,' she laughed. 'There is only one man I have ever feared – and he is dead.'

The man looked at her curiously.

'Let us hope that he will not come to life again, then,' he remarked lightly.

'What do you mean?' cried the dancer sharply.

The Count looked slightly surprised.

'I only meant that resurrection would be awkward for you,' he explained. 'A foolish joke.'

She gave a sigh of relief.

'Oh, no, he is dead all right. Killed in the war. He was a man who once – loved me.'

'In South Africa?' asked the Count negligently.

'Yes, since you ask it, in South Africa.'

'That is your native country, is it not?'

She nodded. Her visitor rose and reached for his hat.

'Well,' he remarked, 'you know your own business best, but, if I were you, I should fear the "Colonel" far more than any disillusioned lover. He is a man whom it is particularly easy to – underestimate.'

She laughed scornfully.

'As if I did not know him after all these years!'

'I wonder if you do?' he said softly. 'I very much wonder if you do.'

'Oh, I am not a fool! And I am not alone in this. The South African mail-boat docks at Southampton tomorrow, and on board her is a man who has come specially from Africa at my request and who has carried out certain orders of mine. The "Colonel" will have not one of us to deal with, but two.'

'Is that wise?'

'It is necessary.'

'You are sure of this man?'

A rather peculiar smile played over the dancer's face.

'I am quite sure of him. He is inefficient, but perfectly trustworthy.' She paused, and then added in an indifferent tone of voice: 'As a matter of fact, he happens to be my husband.'

CHAPTER I

Everybody has been at me, right and left, to write this story, from the great (represented by Lord Nasby) to the small (represented by our late maid-of-all-work, Emily, whom I saw when I was last in England. 'Lor, miss, what a beyewtiful book you might make out of it all – just like the pictures!').

I'll admit that I've certain qualifications for the task. I was mixed up in the affair from the very beginning, I was in the thick of it all through, and I was triumphantly 'in at the death'. Very fortunately, too, the gaps that I cannot supply from my own knowledge are amply covered by Sir Eustace Pedler's diary, of which he has kindly begged me to make use.

So here goes. Anne Beddingfeld starts to narrate her adventures.

I'd always longed for adventures. You see, my life had such a dreadful sameness. My father, Professor Beddingfeld, was one of England's greatest living authorities on Primitive Man. He really was a genius – everyone admits that. His mind dwelt in Palaeolithic times, and the inconvenience of life for him was that his body inhabited the modern world. Papa did not care for modern man – even Neolithic Man he despised as a mere herder of cattle, and he did not rise to enthusiasm until he reached the Mousterian period.

Unfortunately one cannot entirely dispense with modern men. One is forced to have some kind of truck with butchers and bakers and milkmen and greengrocers. Therefore, Papa being immersed in the past, Mama having died when I was a baby, it fell to me to undertake the practical side of living. Frankly, I hate Palaeolithic Man, be he Aurignacian, Mousterian, Chellian, or anything else, and though I typed and revised most of Papa's *Neanderthal Man and his Ancestors*, Neanderthal Men themselves fill me with loathing, and I always reflect what a fortunate circumstance it was that they became extinct in remote ages.

I do not know whether Papa guessed my feelings on the subject, probably not, and in any case he would not have been interested. The opinion of other people never interested him in the slightest degree. I think it was really a sign of his greatness. In the same way, he lived quite detached from the necessities of daily life. He ate what was put before him in an exemplary fashion, but seemed mildly pained when the question of paying for it arose. We never seemed to have any money. His celebrity was not of the kind that brought in a cash return. Although he was a fellow of almost every important society and had rows of letters after his name, the general public scarcely knew of his existence, and his long learned books, though adding signally to the sum-total of human knowledge, had no attraction for the masses. Only on one occasion did he leap into the public gaze. He had read a paper before some society on the subject of the young of the chimpanzee. The young of the human race show some anthropoid features, whereas the young of the chimpanzee approach more nearly to the human than the adult chimpanzee does. That seems to show that whereas our ancestors were more Simian than we are, the chimpanzee's were of a higher type than the present species – in other words, the chimpanzee is a degenerate. That enterprising newspaper, the *Daily Budget*, being hard up for something spicy, immediately brought itself out with large headlines. '*We* are not descended from monkeys, but are monkeys descended from *us*? Eminent Professor says chimpanzees are decadent humans.' Shortly afterwards, a reporter called to see Papa, and endeavoured to induce him to write a series of popular articles on the theory. I have seldom seen Papa so angry. He turned the reporter out of the house with scant ceremony, much to my secret sorrow, as we were particularly short of money at the moment. In fact, for a moment I meditated running after the young man and informing him that my father had changed his mind and would send the articles in question. I could easily have written them myself, and the probabilities were that Papa would never have learnt of the transaction, not being a reader of the *Daily Budget*. However, I rejected this course as being too risky, so I merely put on my best hat and went sadly down the village to interview our justly irate grocer.

The reporter from the *Daily Budget* was the only young man who ever came to our house. There were times when I envied Emily, our little servant, who 'walked out' whenever occasion offered with a large sailor to whom she was affianced. In between times, to 'keep her hand in', as she expressed it, she walked out with the greengrocer's young man, and the chemist's assistant. I reflected sadly that I had no one to 'keep my hand in' with. All Papa's friends were aged professors – usually with long beards. It is true that Professor Peterson once clasped me affectionately and said I had a 'neat little waist' and then tried to kiss me. The phrase alone dated him hopelessly. No self-respecting female has had a 'neat little waist' since I was in my cradle.

I yearned for adventure, for love, for romance, and I seemed condemned to an existence of drab utility. The village possessed a lending library, full of tattered works of fiction, and I enjoyed perils and love-making at second hand, and went to sleep dreaming of stern silent Rhodesians, and of strong men who always 'felled their opponent with a single blow'. There was no one in the village who even looked as though they could 'fell' an opponent, with a single blow or several.

There was the cinema too, with a weekly episode of *The Perils of Pamela.* Pamela was a magnificent young woman. Nothing daunted her. She fell out of aeroplanes, adventured in submarines, climbed skyscrapers and crept about in the Underworld without turning a hair. She was not really clever, the Master Criminal of the Underworld caught her each time, but as he seemed loath to knock her on the head in a simple way, and always doomed her to death in a sewer-gas-chamber or by some new and marvellous means, the hero was always able to rescue her at the beginning of the following week's episode. I used to come out with my head in a delirious whirl – and then I would get home and find a notice from the Gas Company threatening to cut us off if the outstanding account was not paid!

And yet, though I did not suspect it, every moment was bringing adventure nearer to me.

It is possible that there are many people in the world who have never heard of the finding of an antique skull at the Broken Hill Mine in Northern Rhodesia. I came down one morning to find Papa excited to the point of apoplexy. He poured out the whole story to me.

'You understand, Anne? There are undoubtedly certain resemblances to the Java skull, but superficial – superficial only. No, here we have what I have always maintained – the ancestral form of the Neanderthal race. You grant that the Gibraltar skull is the most primitive of the Neanderthal skulls found? Why? The cradle of the race was in Africa. They passed to Europe –'

'Not marmalade on kippers, Papa,' I said hastily, arresting my parent's absent-minded hand. 'Yes, you were saying?'

'They passed to Europe on –'

Here he broke down with a bad fit of choking, the result of an immoderate mouthful of kipper bones.

'But we must start at once,' he declared, as he rose to his feet at the conclusion of the meal. 'There is no time to be lost. We must be on the spot – there are doubtless incalculable finds to be found in the neighbourhood. I shall be interested to note whether the implements are typical of the Mousterian period – there will be the remains of the primitive ox, I should say, but not those of the woolly rhinoceros. Yes, a little army will be starting soon. We must get ahead of them. You will write to Cook's today, Anne?'

'What about money, Papa?' I hinted delicately.

He turned a reproachful eye upon me.

'Your point of view always depresses me, my child. We must not be sordid. No, no, in the cause of science one must not be sordid.'

'I feel Cook's might be sordid, Papa.'

Papa looked pained.

'My dear Anne, you will pay them in ready money.'

'I haven't got any ready money.'

Papa looked thoroughly exasperated.

'My child, I really cannot be bothered with these vulgar money details. The bank – I had something from the Manager yesterday, saying I had twenty-seven pounds.'

'That's your overdraft, I fancy.'

'Ah, I have it! Write to my publishers.'

I acquiesced doubtfully, Papa's books bringing in more glory than money. I liked the idea of going to Rhodesia immensely. 'Stern, silent men,' I murmured to myself in an ecstasy. Then something in my parent's appearance struck me as unusual.

'You have odd boots on, Papa,' I said. 'Take off the brown one and put on the other black one. And don't forget your muffler. It's a very cold day.'

In a few minutes Papa stalked off, correctly booted and well mufflered.

He returned late that evening, and, to my dismay, I saw his muffler and overcoat were missing.

'Dear me, Anne, you are quite right. I took them off to go into the cavern. One gets so dirty there.'

I nodded feelingly, remembering an occasion when Papa had returned literally plastered from head to foot with rich Pleistocene clay.

Our principal reason for settling in Little Hampsley had been the neighbourhood of Hampsley Cavern, a buried cave rich in deposits of the Aurignacian culture. We had a tiny museum in the village, and the curator and Papa spent most of their days messing about underground and bringing to light portions of woolly rhinoceros and cave bear.

Papa coughed badly all the evening, and the following morning I saw he had a temperature and sent for the doctor.

Poor Papa, he never had a chance. It was double pneumonia. He died four days later.

CHAPTER 2

Everyone was very kind to me. Dazed as I was, I appreciated that. I felt no overwhelming grief. Papa had never loved me. I knew that well enough. If he had, I might have loved him in return. No, there had not been love between us, but we had belonged together, and I had looked after him, and had secretly admired his learning and his uncompromising devotion to science. And it hurt me that Papa should have died just when the interest of life was at its height for him. I should have felt happier if I could have buried him in a cave, with paintings of reindeer and flint implements, but the force of public opinion constrained a neat tomb (with marble slab) in our hideous local churchyard. The vicar's consolations, though well meant, did not console me in the least.

It took some time to dawn upon me that the thing I had always longed for – freedom – was at last mine. I was an orphan, and practically penniless, but free. At the same time I realized the extraordinary kindness of all these good people. The vicar did his best to persuade me that his wife was in urgent need of a companion help. Our tiny local library suddenly made up its mind to have an assistant librarian. Finally, the doctor called upon me, and after making various ridiculous excuses for failing to send a proper bill, he hummed and hawed a good deal and suddenly suggested I should marry him.

I was very much astonished. The doctor was nearer forty than thirty and a round, tubby little man. He was not at all like the hero of *The Perils of Pamela*, and even less like the stern and silent Rhodesian. I reflected a minute and then asked why he wanted to marry me. That seemed to fluster him a good deal, and he murmured that a wife was a great help to a general practitioner. The position seemed even more unromantic than before, and yet something in me urged towards its acceptance. Safety, that was what I was being offered. Safety – and a Comfortable Home. Thinking it over now, I believe I did the little man an injustice. He was honestly in love with me, but a mistaken delicacy prevented him from pressing his suit on those lines. Anyway, my love of romance rebelled.

'It's extremely kind of you,' I said. 'But it's impossible. I could never marry a man unless I loved him madly.'

'You don't think –?'

'No, I don't,' I said firmly.

He sighed.

'But, my dear child, what do you propose to do?'

'Have adventures and see the world,' I replied, without the least hesitation.

'Miss Anne, you are very much a child still. You don't understand –'

'The practical difficulties? Yes, I do, doctor. I'm not a sentimental schoolgirl – I'm a hard-headed mercenary shrew! You'd know it if you married me!'

'I wish you would reconsider –'

'I can't.'

He sighed again.

'I have another proposal to make. An aunt of mine who lives in Wales is in want of a young lady to help her. How would that suit you?'

'No, doctor, I'm going to London. If things happen anywhere, they happen in London. I shall keep my eyes open and, you'll see, something will turn up! You'll hear of me next in China or Timbuctoo.'

My next visitor was Mr Flemming, Papa's London solicitor. He came down specially from town to see me. An ardent anthropologist himself, he was a great admirer of Papa's work. He was a tall, spare man with a thin face and grey hair. He rose to meet me as I entered the room and taking both my hands in his, patted them affectionately.

'My poor child,' he said. 'My poor, poor child.'

Without conscious hypocrisy, I found myself assuming the demeanour of a bereaved orphan. He hypnotized me into it. He was benignant, kind and fatherly – and without the least doubt he regarded me as a perfect fool of a girl left adrift to face an unkind world. From the first I felt that it was quite useless to try to convince him of the contrary. As things turned out, perhaps it was just as well I didn't.

'My dear child, do you think you can listen to me whilst I try to make a few things clear to you?'

'Oh, yes.'

'Your father, as you know, was a very great man. Posterity will appreciate him. But he was not a good man of business.'

I knew that quite as well, if not better, than Mr Flemming, but I restrained myself from saying so. He continued: 'I do not suppose you understand much of these matters. I will try to explain as clearly as I can.'

He explained at unnecessary length. The upshot seemed to be that I was left to face life with the sum of £87 17*s.* 4*d.* It seemed a strangely unsatisfying amount. I waited in some trepidation for what was coming next. I feared that Mr Flemming would be sure to have an aunt in Scotland who was in want of a bright young companion. Apparently, however, he hadn't.

'The question is,' he went on, 'the future. I understand you have no living relatives?'

'I'm alone in the world,' I said, and was struck anew by my likeness to a film heroine.

'You have friends?'

'Everyone has been very kind to me,' I said gratefully.

'Who would not be kind to one so young and charming?' said Mr Flemming gallantly. 'Well, well, my dear, we must see what can be done.' He hesitated a minute, and then said: 'Supposing – how would it be if you came to us for a time?'

I jumped at the chance. London! The place for things to happen.

'It's awfully kind of you,' I said. 'Might I really? Just while I'm looking around. I must start out to earn my living, you know?'

'Yes, yes, my dear child. I quite understand. We will look round for something – suitable.'

I felt instictively that Mr Flemming's ideas of 'something suitable' and mine were likely to be widely divergent, but it was certainly not the moment to air my views.

'That is settled then. Why not return with me today?'

'Oh, thank you, but will Mrs Flemming –'

'My wife will be delighted to welcome you.'

I wonder if husbands know as much about their wives as they think they do. If I had a husband, I should hate him to bring home orphans without consulting me first.

'We will send her a wire from the station,' continued the lawyer.

My few personal belongings were soon packed. I contemplated my hat sadly before putting it on. It had originally been what I call a 'Mary' hat, meaning by that the kind of hat a housemaid ought to wear on her day out – but doesn't! A limp thing of black straw with a suitably depressed brim. With the inspiration of genius, I had kicked it once, punched it twice, dented in the crown and affixed to it a thing like a cubist's dream of a jazz carrot. The result had been distinctly chic. The carrot I had already removed, of course, and now I proceeded to undo the rest of my handiwork. The 'Mary' hat resumed its former status with an additional battered appearance which made it even more depressing than formerly. I might as well look as much like the popular conception of an orphan as possible. I was just a shade nervous of Mrs Flemming's reception, but hoped my appearance might have a sufficiently disarming effect.

Mr Flemming was nervous too. I realized that as we went up the stairs of the tall house in a quiet Kensington square. Mrs Flemming greeted me pleasantly enough. She was a stout, placid woman of the 'good wife and mother' type. She took me up to a spotless chintz-hung bedroom, hoped I had everything I wanted, informed me that tea would be ready in about a quarter of an hour, and left me to my own devices.

I heard her voice slightly raised, as she entered the drawing-room below on the first floor.

'Well, Henry, why on earth –' I lost the rest, but the acerbity of the tone was evident. And a few minutes later another phrase floated up to me, in an even more acid voice: 'I agree with you! She is certainly *very* good-looking.'

It is really a very hard life. Men will not be nice to you if you are not good-looking, and women will not be nice to you if you are.

With a deep sigh I proceeded to do things with my hair. I have nice hair. It is black – a real black, not dark brown – and it grows well back from my forehead and down over the ears. With a ruthless hand I dragged it upwards. As ears, my ears are quite all right, but there is no doubt about it, ears are *démodé* nowadays. They are quite like the 'Queen of Spain's legs' in Professor Peterson's young day. When I had finished I looked almost unbelievably like the kind of orphan that walks out in a queue with a little bonnet and red cloak.

I noticed when I went down that Mrs Flemming's eyes rested on my exposed ears with quite a kindly glance. Mr Flemming seemed puzzled. I had no doubt that he was saying to himself, 'What *has* the child done to herself?'

On the whole the rest of the day passed off well. It was settled that I was to start at once to look for something to do.

When I went to bed, I stared earnestly at my face in the glass. Was I really good-looking? Honestly I couldn't say I thought so! I hadn't got a straight Grecian nose, or a rosebud mouth, or any of the things you ought to have. It is true that a curate once told me that my eyes were like 'imprisoned sunshine in a dark, dark wood' – but curates always know so many quotations, and fire them off at random. I'd much prefer to have Irish blue eyes than dark green ones with yellow flecks! Still, green is a good colour for adventuresses.

I wound a black garment tightly round me, leaving my arms and shoulders bare. Then I brushed back my hair and pulled it well down over my ears again. I put a lot of powder on my face, so that the skin seemed even whiter than usual. I fished about until I found some lip-salve, and I put oceans of it on my lips. Then I did under my eyes with burnt cork. Finally I draped a red ribbon over my bare shoulder, stuck a scarlet feather in my hair, and placed a cigarette in one corner of my mouth. The whole effect pleased me very much.

'Anna the Adventuress,' I said aloud, nodding at my reflection. 'Anna the Adventuress. Episode I, "The House in Kensington"!'

Girls are foolish things.

CHAPTER 3

In the succeeding weeks I was a good deal bored. Mrs Flemming and her friends seemed to me to be supremely uninteresting. They talked for hours of themselves and their children and of the difficulties of getting good milk for the children and of what they say to the dairy when the milk wasn't good. Then they would go on to the servants, and the difficulties of getting good servants and of what they had said to the woman at the registry office and of what the woman at the registry office had said to them. They never seemed to read the papers or to care about what went on in the world. They disliked travelling – everything was so different to England. The Riviera was all right, of course, because one met all one's friends there.

I listened and contained myself with difficulty. Most of these women were rich. The whole wide beautiful world was theirs to wander in and they deliberately stayed in dirty dull London and talked about milkmen and servants! I think now, looking back, that I was perhaps a shade intolerant. But they *were* stupid – stupid even at their chosen job: most of them kept the most extraordinarily inadequate and muddled housekeeping accounts.

My affairs did not progress very fast. The house and furniture had been sold, and the amount realized had just covered our debts. As yet, I had not been successful in finding a post. Not that I really wanted one! I had the firm conviction that, if I went about looking for adventure, adventure would meet me half-way. It is a theory of mine that one always gets what one wants.

My theory was about to be proved in practice.

It was early in January – the 8th, to be exact. I was returning from an unsuccessful interview with a lady who said she wanted a secretary-companion, but really seemed to require a strong charwoman who would work twelve hours a day for £25 a year. Having parted with mutual veiled impolitenesses, I walked down Edgware Road (the interview had taken place in a house in St John's Wood), and across Hyde Park to St George's Hospital. There I entered Hyde Park Corner Tube Station and took a ticket to Gloucester Road.

Once on the platform I walked to the extreme end of it. My inquiring mind wished to satisfy itself as to whether there really *were* points and an opening between the two tunnels just beyond the station in the direction of Down Street. I was foolishly pleased to find I was right. There were not many people on the platform, and at the extreme end there was only myself and one man. As I passed him, I sniffed dubiously. If there is one smell I cannot bear it is that of moth-balls! This man's heavy overcoat simply reeked of them. And yet most men begin to wear their winter overcoats before January, and consequently by this time the smell ought to have worn off. The man was beyond me, standing close to the edge of the tunnel. He seemed lost in thought, and I was able to stare at him without rudeness. He was a small thin man, very brown of face, with blue light eyes and a small dark beard.

'Just come from abroad,' I deduced. 'That's why his overcoat smells so. He's come from India. Not an officer, or he wouldn't have a beard. Perhaps a tea-planter.'

At this moment the man turned as though to retrace his steps along the platform. He glanced at me and then his eyes went on to something behind me, and his face changed. It was distorted by fear – almost panic. He took a step backwards as though involuntarily recoiling from some danger, forgetting that he was standing on the extreme edge of the platform, and went down and over. There was a vivid flash from the rails and a crackling sound. I shrieked. People came running up. Two station officials seemed to materialize from nowhere and took command.

I remained where I was, rooted to the spot by a sort of horrible fascination. Part of me was appalled at the sudden disaster, and another part of me was coolly and disapassionately interested in the methods employed for lifting the man off the live rail and back on to the platform.

'Let me pass, please. I am a medical man.'

A tall man with a brown beard pressed past me and bent over the motionless body.

As he examined it, a curious sense of unreality seemed to possess me. The thing wasn't real – couldn't be. Finally, the doctor stood upright and shook his head.

'Dead as a door-nail. Nothing to be done.'

We had all crowded nearer, and an aggrieved porter raised his voice. 'Now then, stand back there, will you? What's the sense in crowding round?'

A sudden nausea seized me, and I turned blindly and ran up the stairs again towards the lift. I felt that it was too horrible. I must get out into the open air. The doctor who had examined the body was just ahead of me. The lift was just about to go up, another having descended, and he broke into a run. As he did so, he dropped a piece of paper.

I stopped, picked it up, and ran after him. But the lift gates clanged in my face, and I was left holding the paper in my hand. By the time the second lift reached street level, there was no sign of my quarry. I hoped it was nothing important that he had lost, and for the first time I examined it. It was a plain half-sheet of notepaper with some figures and words scrawled upon it in pencil. This is a facsimile of it:

17·1 22 Kilmorden Castle

On the face of it, it certainly did not appear to be of any importance. Still, I hesitated to throw it away. As I stood there holding it, I involuntarily wrinkled my nose in displeasure. Moth-balls again! I held the paper gingerly to my nose. Yes, it smelt strongly of them. But, then –

I folded up the paper carefully and put it in my bag. I walked home slowly and did a good deal of thinking.

I explained to Mrs Flemming that I had witnessed a nasty accident in the Tube and that I was rather upset and would go to my room and lie down. The kind woman insisted on my having a cup of tea. After that I was left to my own devices, and I proceeded to carry out a plan I had formed coming home. I wanted to know what it was that had produced that curious feeling of unreality whilst I was watching the doctor examine the body. First I lay down on the floor in the attitude of the corpse, then I laid a bolster down in my stead, and proceeded to duplicate, so far as I could remember, every motion and gesture of the doctor. When I had finished I had got what I wanted. I sat back on my heels and frowned at the opposite walls.

There was a brief notice in the evening papers that a man had been killed in the Tube, and a doubt was expressed whether it was suicide or accident. That seemed to me to make my duty clear, and when Mr Flemming heard my story he quite agreed with me.

'Undoubtedly you will be wanted at the inquest. You say no one else was near enough to see what happened?'

'I had the feeling someone was coming up behind me, but I can't be sure – and, anyway, they wouldn't be as near as I was.'

The inquest was held. Mr Flemming made all the arrangements and took me there with him. He seemed to fear that it would be a great ordeal for me, and I had to conceal from him my complete composure.

The deceased had been identified as L. B. Carton. Nothing had been found in his pockets except a house-agent's order to view a house on the river near Marlow. It was in the name of L. B. Carton, Russell Hotel. The bureau clerk from the hotel indentified the man as having arrived the day before and booked a room under that name. He had registered as L. B. Carton, Kimberley, S. Africa. He had evidently come straight off the steamer.

I was the only person who had seen anything of the affair.

'You think it was an accident?' the coroner asked me.

'I am positive of it. Something alarmed him, and he stepped backwards blindly without thinking what he was doing.'

'But what could have alarmed him?'

'That I don't know. But there was something. He looked panic-stricken.'

A stolid juryman suggested that some men were terrified of cats. The man might have seen a cat. I didn't think his suggestion a very brilliant one, but it seemed to pass muster with the jury, who were obviously impatient to get home and only too pleased at being able to give a verdict of accident as opposed to suicide.

'It is extraordinary to me,' said the coroner, 'that the doctor who first examined the body has not come forward. His name and address should have been taken at the time. It was most irregular not to do so.'

I smiled to myself. I had my own theory in regard to the doctor. In pursuance of it, I determined to make a call upon Scotland Yard at an early date.

But the next morning brought a surprise. The Flemmings took in the *Daily Budget*, and the *Daily Budget* was having a day after its own heart.

EXTRAORDINARY SEQUEL
TO TUBE ACCIDENT

WOMAN FOUND STRANGLED
IN LONELY HOUSE

I read eagerly.

'A sensational discovery was made yesterday at the Mill House, Marlow. The Mill House, which is the property of Sir Eustace Pedler, M.P., is to be let unfurnished, and an order to view this property was found in the pocket of the man who was at first thought to have commited suicide by throwing himself on the live rail at Hyde Park Corner Tube Station. In an upper room of the Mill House the body of a beautiful young woman was discovered yesterday, strangled. She is thought to be a foreigner, but so far has not been identified. The police are reported to have a clue. Sir Eustace Pedler, the owner of the Mill House, is wintering on the Riviera.'

CHAPTER 4

Nobody came forward to identify the dead woman. The inquest elicited the following facts.

Shortly after one o'clock on January 8th, a well-dressed woman with a slight foreign accent had entered the offices of Messrs Butler and Park, house-agents, in Knightsbridge. She explained that she wanted to rent or purchase a house on the Thames within easy reach of London. The particulars of several were given to her, including those of the Mill House. She gave the name of Mrs de Castina and her address at the Ritz, but there proved to be no one of that name staying there, and the hotel people failed to identify the body.

Mrs James, the wife of Sir Eustace Pedler's gardener, who acted as caretaker to the Mill House and inhabited the small lodge opening on the main road, gave evidence. About three o'clock that afternoon, a lady came to see over the house. She produced an order from the house-agents, and, as was the usual custom, Mrs James gave her the keys to the house. It was situated at some distance from the lodge, and she was not in the habit of accompanying prospective tenants. A few minutes later a young man arrived. Mrs James described him as tall and broad-shouldered, with a bronzed face and light grey eyes. He was clean-shaven and was wearing a brown suit. He explained to Mrs James that he was a friend of the lady who had come to look over the house, but had stopped at the post office to send a telegram. She directed him to the house, and thought no more about the matter.

Five minutes later he reappeared, handed back the keys and explained that he feared the house would not suit them. Mrs James did not see the lady, but thought that she had gone on ahead. What she did notice was that the young man seemed very much upset about something. 'He looked like a man who'd seen a ghost. I thought he was taken ill.'

On the following day another lady and gentleman came to see the property and discovered the body lying on the floor in one of the upstairs rooms. Mrs James identified it as that of the lady who had come the day before. The house-agents also recognized it as that of 'Mrs de Castina'. The police surgeon gave it as his opinion that the woman had been dead about twenty-four hours. The *Daily Budget* had jumped to the conclusion that the man in the Tube had murdered the woman and afterwards committed suicide. However, as the Tube victim was dead at two o'clock and the woman was alive and well at three o'clock, the only logical conclusion to come to was that the two occurrences had nothing to do with each other, and that the order to view the house at

Marlow found in the dead man's pocket was merely one of those coincidences which so often occur in this life.

A verdict of 'Wilful Murder against some person or persons unknown' was returned, and the police (and the *Daily Budget*) were left to look for 'the man in the brown suit'. Since Mrs James was positive that there was no one in the house when the lady entered it, and that nobody except the young man in question entered it until the following afternoon, it seemed only logical to conclude that he was the murderer of the unfortunate Mrs de Castina. She had been strangled with a piece of stout black cord, and had evidently been caught unawares with no time to cry out. The black silk handbag which she carried contained a well-filled notecase and some loose change, a fine lace handkerchief, unmarked, and the return half of a first-class ticket to London. Nothing much there to go upon.

Such were the details published broadcast by the *Daily Budget*, and 'Find the Man in the Brown Suit' was their daily war-cry. On an average about five hundred people wrote daily to announce their success in the quest, and tall young men with well-tanned faces cursed the day when their tailors had persuaded them to a brown suit. The accident in the Tube, dismissed as a coincidence, faded out of the public mind.

Was it a coincidence? I was not so sure. No doubt I was prejudiced – the Tube incident was my own pet mystery – but there certainly seemed to me to be a connection of some kind between the two fatalities. In each there was a man with a tanned face – evidently an Englishman living abroad – and there were other things. It was the consideration of these other things that finally impelled me to what I considered a dashing step. I presented myself at Scotland Yard and demanded to see whoever was in charge of the Mill House case.

My request took some time to understand, as I had inadvertently selected the department for lost umbrellas, but eventually I was ushered into a small room and presented to Detective Inspector Meadows.

Inspector Meadows was a small man with a ginger head and what I considered a peculiarly irritating manner. A satellite, also in plain clothes, sat unobtrusively in a corner.

'Good morning,' I said nervously.

'Good morning. Will you take a seat? I understand you've something to tell me that you think may be of use to us.'

His tone seemed to indicate that such a thing was unlikely in the extreme. I felt my temper stirred.

'Of course you know about the man who was killed in the Tube? The man who had an order to view this same house at Marlow in his pocket.'

'Ah!' said the inspector. 'You are the Miss Beddingfeld who gave evidence at the inquest. Certainly the man had an order in his pocket. A lot of other people may have had too – only they didn't happen to be killed.'

I rallied my forces.

'You didn't think it odd that this man had no ticket in his pocket?'

'Easiest thing in the world to drop your ticket. Done it myself.'

'And no money.'

'He had some loose change in his trousers pocket.'

'But no notecase.'

'Some men don't carry a pocket-book or notecase of any kind.'

I tried another tack.

'You don't think it's odd that the doctor never came forward afterwards?'

'A busy medical man very often doesn't read the papers. He probably forgot all about the accident.'

'In fact, inspector, you are determined to find nothing odd,' I said sweetly.

'Well, I'm inclined to think you're a little too fond of the word, Miss Beddingfeld. Young ladies are romantic, I know – fond of mysteries and such-like. But as I'm a busy man –'

I took the hint and rose.

The man in the corner raised a meek voice.

'Perhaps if the young lady would tell us briefly what her ideas really are on the subject, inspector?'

The inspector fell in with the suggestion readily enough.

'Yes, come now, Miss Beddingfeld, don't be offended. You've asked questions and hinted things. Just straight out what it is you've got in your head.'

I wavered between injured dignity and the overwhelming desire to express my theories. Injured dignity went to the wall.

'You said at the inquest you were positive it wasn't suicide?'

'Yes, I'm quite certain of that. The man was frightened. What frightened him? It wasn't me. But someone might have been walking up the platform towards us – someone he recognized.'

'You didn't see anyone?'

'No,' I admitted. 'I didn't turn my head. Then, as soon as the body was recovered from the line, a man pushed forward to examine it, saying he was a doctor.'

'Nothing unusual in that,' said the inspector dryly.

'But he wasn't a doctor.'

'What?'

'He wasn't a doctor,' I repeated.

'How do you know that, Miss Beddingfeld?'

'It's difficult to say, exactly. I've worked in hospitals during the war, and I've seen doctors handle bodies. There's a sort of deft professional callousness that this man hadn't got. Besides, a doctor doesn't usually feel for the heart on the right side of the body.'

'He did that?'

'Yes, I didn't notice it specially at the time – except that I felt there was something wrong. But I worked it out when I got home, and then I saw why the whole thing had looked so unhandy to me at the time.'

'H'm,' said the inspector. He was reaching slowly for pen and paper.

'In running his hands over the upper part of the man's body he would have ample opportunity to take anything he wanted from the pockets.'

'Doesn't sound likely to me,' said the inspector. 'But – well, can you describe him at all?'

'He was tall and broad-shouldered, wore a dark overcoat and black boots, a bowler hat. He had a dark pointed beard and gold-rimmed eyeglasses.'

'Take away the overcoat, the beard and the eyeglasses, and there wouldn't be much to know him by,' grumbled the inspector. 'He could alter his appearance easily enough in five minutes if he wanted to – which he would do if he's the swell pickpocket you suggest.'

I had not intended to suggest anything of the kind. But from this moment I gave the inspector up as hopeless.

'Nothing more you can tell us about him?' he demanded, as I rose to depart.

'Yes,' I said. I seized my opportunity to fire a parting shot. 'His head was markedly brachycephalic. He will not find it so easy to alter that.'

I observed with pleasure that Inspector Meadows's pen wavered. It was clear that he did not know how to spell brachycephalic.

CHAPTER 5

In the first heat of indignation, I found my next step unexpectedly easy to tackle. I had had a half-formed plan in my head when I went to Scotland Yard. One to be carried out if my interview there was unsatisfactory (it had been profoundly unsatisfactory). That is, if I had the nerve to go through with it.

Things that one would shrink from attempting normally are easily tackled in a flush of anger. Without giving myself time to reflect, I walked straight to the house of Lord Nasby.

Lord Nasby was the millionaire owner of the *Daily Budget*. He owned other papers – several of them, but the *Daily Budget* was his special child. It was as the owner of the *Daily Budget* that he was known to every householder in the United Kingdom. Owing to the fact that an itinerary of the great man's daily proceedings had just been published, I knew exactly where to find him at this moment. It was his hour for dictating to his secretary in his own house.

I did not, of course, suppose that any young woman who chose to come and ask for him would be at once admitted to the august presence. But I had attended to that side of the matter. In the card-tray in the hall of the Flemmings' house, I had observed the card of the Marquis of Loamsley, England's most famous sporting peer. I had removed the card, cleaned it carefully with bread-crumbs, and pencilled upon it the words: 'Please give Miss Beddingfeld a few moments of your time.' Adventuresses must not be too scrupulous in their methods.

The thing worked. A powdered footman received the card and bore it away. Presently a pale secretary appeared. I fenced with him successfully. He retired in defeat. He again reappeared and begged me to follow him. I did so. I entered a large room, a frightened-looking shorthand-typist fled past me like a visitant from the spirit-world. Then the door shut and I was face to face with Lord Nasby.

A big man. Big head. Big face. Big moustache. Big stomach. I pulled myself together. I had not come here to comment on Lord Nasby's stomach. He was already roaring at me.

'Well, what is it? What does Loamsley want? You are his secretary? What's it all about?'

'To begin with,' I said with as great an appearance of coolness as I could manage, 'I don't know Lord Loamsley, and he certainly knows nothing about me. I took his card from the tray in the house of the people I'm staying with, and I wrote those words on it myself. It was important that I should see you.'

For a moment it appeared to be a toss up as to whether Lord Nasby had apoplexy or not. In the end he swallowed twice and got over it.

'I admire your coolness, young woman. Well, you see me! If you interest me, you will continue to see me for exactly two minutes longer.'

'That will be ample,' I replied. 'And I shall interest you. It's the Mill House Mystery.'

'If you've found "The Man in the Brown Suit", write to the editor,' he interrupted hastily.

'If you will interrupt, I shall be more than two minutes,' I said sternly. 'I haven't found "The Man in the Brown Suit", but I'm quite likely to do so.'

In as few words as possible I put the facts of the Tube accident and the conclusions I had drawn from them before him. When I had finished he said unexpectedly, 'What do you know of brachycephalic heads?'

I mentioned Papa.

'The Monkey man? Eh? Well, you seem to have a head of some kind upon your shoulders, young woman. But it's all pretty thin, you know. Not much to go upon. And no use to us – as it stands.'

'I'm perfectly aware of that.'

'What d'you want, then?'

'I want a job on your paper to investigate this matter.'

'Can't do that. We've got our own special man on it.'

'And I've got my own special knowledge.'

'What you've just told me, eh?'

'Oh, no, Lord Nasby. I've still got something up my sleeve.'

'Oh, you have, have you? You seem a bright sort of girl. Well, what is it?'

'When this so-called doctor got into the lift, he dropped a piece of paper. I picked it up. It smelt of moth-balls. So did the dead man. The doctor didn't. So I saw at once that the doctor must have taken it off the body. It had two words written on it and some figures.'

'Let's see it.'

Lord Nasby stretched out a careless hand.

'I think not,' I said, smiling. 'It's my find, you see.'

'I'm right. You *are* a bright girl. Quite right to hang on to it. No scruples about not handing it over to the police?'

'I went there to do so this morning. They persisted in regarding the whole thing as having nothing to do with the Marlow affair, so I thought that in the circumstances I was justified in retaining the paper. Besides, the inspector put my back up.'

'Short-sighted man. Well, my dear girl, here's all I can do for you. Go on working on this line of yours. If you get anything – anything that's publishable – send it along and you shall have your chance. There's always room for real talent on the *Daily Budget*. But you've got to make good first. See?'

I thanked him and apologized for my methods.

'Don't mention it. I rather like cheek – from a pretty girl. By the way, you said two minutes and you've been three, allowing for interruptions. For a woman, that's quite remarkable! Must be your scientific training.'

I was in the street again, breathing hard as though I had been running. I found Lord Nasby rather wearing as a new acquaintance.

CHAPTER 6

I went home with a feeling of exultation. My scheme had succeeded far better than I could possibly have hoped. Lord Nasby had been positively genial. It only now remained for me to 'make good', as he expressed it. Once locked in my own room, I took out my precious piece of paper and studied it attentively. Here was the clue to the mystery.

To begin with, what did the figures represent? There were five of them, and a dot after the first two. 'Seventeen – one hundred and twenty two,' I murmured.

That did not seem to lead to anything.

Next I added them up. That is often done in works of fiction and leads to surprising deductions.

'One and seven make eight and one is nine and two are eleven and two are thirteen!'

Thirteen! Fateful number! Was this a warning to me to leave the whole thing alone? Very possibly. Anyway, except as a warning, it seemed to be singularly useless. I declined to believe that any conspirator would take that way of writing thirteen in real life. If he meant thirteen, he would write thirteen. '13' – like that.

There was a space between the one and the two. I accordingly subtracted twenty-two from a hundred and seventy-one. The result was a hundred and fifty-nine. I did it again and made it a hundred and forty-nine. These arithmetical exercises were doubtless excellent practice, but as regarded the solution of the mystery, they seemed totally ineffectual. I left arithmetic alone, not attempting fancy division or multiplication, and went on to the words.

Kilmorden Castle. That was something definite. A place. Probably the cradle of an aristocratic family. (Missing heir? Claimant to title?) Or possibly a picturesque ruin. (Buried treasure?)

Yes, on the whole I inclined to the theory of buried treasure. Figures always go with buried treasure. One pace to the right, seven paces to the left, dig one foot, descend twenty-two steps. That sort of idea. I could work out that later. The thing was to get to Kilmorden Castle as quickly as possible.

I made a strategic sally from my room, and returned laden with books of reference. *Who's Who*, Whitaker, a Gazetteer, a History of Scotch Ancestral Homes, and Somebody or other's British Isles.

Time passed. I searched diligently, but with growing annoyance. Finally, I shut the last book with a bang. There appeared to be no such place as Kilmorden Castle.

Here was an unexpected check. There *must* be such a place. Why should anyone invent a name like that and write it down on a piece of paper? Absurd!

Another idea occurred to me. Possibly it was a castellated abomination in the suburbs with a high-sounding name invented by its owner. But if so, it was going to be extraordinarily hard to find. I sat back gloomily on my heels (I always sit on the floor to do anything really important) and wondered how on earth I was to set about it.

Was there any other line I could follow? I reflected earnestly and then sprang to my feet delightedly. Of course! I must visit the 'scene of the crime'. Always done by the best sleuths! And no matter how long afterwards it may be they always find something that the police have overlooked. My course was clear. I must go to Marlow.

But how was I to get into the house? I discarded several adventurous methods, and plumped for stern simplicity. The house had been to let – presumably was still to let. I would be a prospective tenant.

I also decided on attacking the local house-agents, as having fewer houses on their books.

Here, however, I reckoned without my host. A pleasant clerk produced particulars of about half a dozen desirable properties. It took me all my ingenuity to find objections to them. In the end I feared I had drawn a blank.

'And you've really nothing else?' I asked, gazing pathetically into the clerk's eyes. 'Something right on the river, and with a fair amount of garden and a small lodge.' I added, summing up the main points of the Mill House, as I had gathered them from the papers.

'Well, of course, there's Sir Eustace Pedler's place,' said the man doubtfully. 'The Mill House, you know.'

'Not – not where –' I faltered. (Really, faltering is getting to be my strong point.)

'That's it! Where the murder took place. But perhaps you wouldn't like –'

'Oh, I don't think I should mind,' I said with an appearance of rallying. I felt my *bona fides* was now quite established. 'And perhaps I might get it cheap – in the circumstances.'

A master touch that, I thought.

'Well, it's possible. There's no pretending that it will be easy to let now – servants and all that, you know. If you like the place after you've seen it, I should advise you to make an offer. Shall I write you out an order?'

'If you please.'

A quarter of an hour later I was at the lodge of the Mill House. In answer to my knock, the door flew open and a tall middle-aged woman literally bounced out.

'Nobody can go into the house, do you hear that? Fairly sick of you reporters, I am. Sir Eustace's orders are –'

'I understood the house was to let,' I said freezingly, holding out my order. 'Of course, if it's already taken –'

'Oh, I'm sure I beg your pardon, miss. I've been fairly pestered with these newspaper people. Not a minute's peace. No, the house isn't let – nor likely to be now.'

'Are the drains wrong?' I asked in an anxious whisper.

'Oh, Lord, miss, the *drains* is all right! But surely you've heard about that foreign lady as was done to death here?'

'I believe I did read something about it in the papers,' I said carelessly.

My indifference piqued the good woman. If I had betrayed any interest, she would probably have closed up like an oyster. As it was she positively bridled.

'I should say you did, miss! It's been in all the newspapers. The *Daily Budget*'s out still to catch the man who did it. It seems, according to them, as our police are no good at all. Well I hope they'll get him – although a nice-looking fellow he was and no mistake. A kind of soldierly look about him – ah, well, I dare say he'd been wounded in the war, and sometimes they go a bit queer aftwards; my sister's boy did. Perhaps she'd used him bad – they're a bad lot, those foreigners.

Though she was a fine-looking woman. Stood there where you're standing now.'

'Was she dark or fair?' I ventured. 'You can't tell from these newspaper portraits.'

'Dark hair, and a very white face – too white for nature, I thought – had her lips reddened something cruel. I don't like to see it – a little powder now and then is quite another thing.'

We were conversing like old friends now. I put another question.

'Did she seem nervous or upset at all?'

'Not a bit. She was smiling to herself, quiet like, as though she was amused at something. That's why you could have knocked me down with a feather when, the next afternoon, those people came running out calling for the police and saying there'd been murder done. I shall never get over it, and as for setting foot in that house after dark I wouldn't do it, not if it was ever so. Why, I wouldn't even stay here at the lodge, if Sir Eustace hadn't been down on his bended knees to me.'

'I thought Sir Eustace Pedler was at Cannes?'

'So he was, miss. He came back to England when he heard the news, and, as to the bended knees, that was a figure of speech, his secretary, Mr Pagett, having offered us double pay to stay on, and, as my John says, money is money nowadays.'

I concurred heartily with John's by no means original remarks.

'The young man now,' said Mrs James, reverting suddenly to a former point in the conversation. 'He *was* upset. His eyes, light eyes, they were, I noticed them particular, was all shining. Excited, *I* thought. But I never dreamt of anything being wrong. Not even when he came out again looking all queer.'

'How long was he in the house?'

'Oh, not long, a matter of five minutes maybe.'

'How tall was he, do you think? About six foot?'

'I should say so maybe.'

'He was clean-shaven, you say?'

'Yes, miss – not even one of these toothbrush moustaches.'

'Was his chin at all shiny?' I asked on a sudden impulse.

Mrs James stared at me with awe.

'Well, now you come to mention it, miss, it *was*. However did you know?'

'It's a curious thing, but murderers often have shiny chins,' I explained wildly.

Mrs James accepted the statement in all good faith.

'Really, now, miss. I never heard that before.'

'You didn't notice what kind of head he had, I suppose?'

'Just the ordinary kind, miss. I'll fetch you the keys, shall I?'

I accepted them, and went on my way to the Mill House. My reconstructions so far I considered good. All along I had realized that the differences between the man Mrs James had described and my Tube 'doctor' were those of non-essentials. An overcoat, a beard, gold-rimmed eye-glasses. The 'doctor' had appeared middle-aged, but I remembered that he had stooped over the body like a comparatively young man. There had been a suppleness which told of young joints.

The victim of the accident (the Moth-Ball man, as I called him to myself) and the foreign woman, Mrs de Castina, or whatever her real name was, had had an assignation to meet at the Mill House. That was how I pieced the thing together. Either because they feared they were being watched or for some other reason, they chose the rather ingenious method of both getting an order to view the same house. Thus their meeting there might have the appearance of pure chance.

That the Moth-Ball man had suddenly caught sight of the 'doctor', and that the meeting was totally unexpected and alarming to him, was another fact of which I was fairly sure. What had happened next? The 'doctor' had removed his disguise and followed the woman to Marlow. But it was possible that had he removed it rather hastily traces of spirit-gum might still linger on his chin. Hence my question to Mrs James.

Whilst occupied with my thoughts I had arrived at the low old-fashioned door of the Mill House. Unlocking it with the key, I passed inside. The hall was low and dark, the place smelt forlorn and mildewy. In spite of myself, I shivered. Did the woman who had come here 'smiling to herself' a few days ago feel no chill of premonition as she entered this house? I wondered. Did the smile fade from her lips, and did a nameless dread close round her heart? Or had she gone upstairs, smiling still, unconscious of the doom that was so soon to overtake her? My heart beat a little faster. Was the house really empty? Was doom waiting for me in it also? For the first time, I understood the meaning of the much-used word, 'atmosphere'. There was an atmosphere in this house, an atmosphere of cruelty, of menace, of evil.

CHAPTER 7

Shaking off the feelings that oppressed me, I went quickly upstairs. I had no difficulty in finding the room of the tragedy. On the day the body was discovered it had rained heavily, and large muddy boots had trampled the uncarpeted floor in every direction. I wondered if the murderer had left any footmarks the previous day. It was likely that the police would be reticent on the subject if he had, but on consideration I decided it was unlikely. The weather had been fine and dry.

There was nothing of interest about the room. It was almost square with two big bay windows, plain white walls and a bare floor, the boards being stained round the edges where the carpet had ceased. I searched it carefully, but there was not so much as a pin lying about. The gifted young detective did not seem likely to discover a neglected clue.

I had brought with me a pencil and notebook. There did not seem much to note, but I duly dotted down a brief sketch of the room to cover my disappointment at the failing of my quest. As I was in the act of returning the pencil to my bag, it slipped from my fingers and rolled along the floor.

The Mill House was really old, and the floors were very uneven. The pencil rolled steadily, with increasing momentum, until it came to rest under one of the windows. In the recess of each window there was a broad window-seat, underneath which there was a cupboard. My pencil was lying right against the cupboard door. The cupboard was shut, but it suddenly occurred to me that if it had been open my pencil would have rolled inside. I opened the door, and my pencil immediately rolled in and sheltered modestly in the farthest corner. I retrieved it, noting as I did so that owing to lack of light and the peculiar formation of the cupboard one could not see it, but had to feel for it. Apart from my pencil the cupboard was empty, but being thorough by nature I tried the one under the opposite window.

At first sight, it looked as though that also was empty, but I grubbed about perseveringly, and was rewarded by feeling my hand close on a hard paper cylinder which lay in a sort of trough, or depression, in the far corner of the cupboard. As soon as I had it in my hand, I knew what it was. A roll of Kodak films. Here was a find!

I realized, of course, that these films might very well be an old roll belonging to Sir Eustace Pedler which had rolled in here and had not been found when the cupboard was emptied. But I did not think so. The red paper was far too fresh-looking. It was just as dusty as it would have been had it lain there for two or three days – that is to say, since the murder. Had it been there for any length of time, it would have been thickly coated.

Who had dropped it? The woman or the man? I remembered that the contents of her handbag had appeared to be intact. If it had been jerked open in the struggle and the roll of films had fallen out, surely some of the loose money would have been scattered about also? No, it was not the woman who had dropped the films.

I sniffed suddenly and suspiciously. Was the smell of moth-balls becoming an obsession with me? I could swear that the roll of films smelt of it also. I held them under my nose. They had, as usual, a strong smell of their own, but apart from that I could clearly detect the odour I disliked so much. I soon found the cause. A minute thread of cloth had caught on a rough edge of the centre wood, and that shred was strongly impregnated with moth-balls. At some time or another the films had been carried in the overcoat pocket of the man who was killed in the Tube. Was it he who had dropped them here? Hardly. His movements were all accounted for.

No, it was the other man, the 'doctor'. He had taken the films when he had taken the paper. It was he who had dropped them here during his struggle with the woman.

I had got my clue! I would have the roll developed, and then I would have further developments to work upon.

Very elated, I left the house, returned the keys to Mrs James and made my way as quickly as possible to the station. On the way back to town, I took out my paper and studied it afresh. Suddenly the figures took on a new significance. Suppose they were a date? 17 1 22. The 17th of January, 1922. Surely that must be it! Idiot that I was not to have thought of it before. But in that case I *must* find out the whereabouts of Kilmorden Castle, for today was actually the 14th. Three days. Little enough – almost hopeless when one had no idea of where to look!

It was too late to hand in my roll today. I had to hurry home to Kensington so as not to be late for dinner. It occurred to me that there was an easy way of verifying whether some of my conclusions were correct. I asked Mr Flemming whether there had been a camera amongst the dead man's belongings. I knew that he had taken an interest in the case and was conversant with all the details.

To my surprise and annoyance he replied that there had been no camera. All Carton's effects had been gone over very carefully in the hopes of finding something that might throw light upon his state of mind. He was positive that there had been no photographic apparatus of any kind.

That was rather a set-back to my theory. If he had no camera, why should he be carrying a roll of films?

I set out early next morning to take my precious roll to be developed. I was so fussy that I went all the way to Regent Street to the big Kodak place. I handed it in and asked for a print of each film. The man finished stacking together a heap of films packed in yellow tin cylinders for the tropics, and picked up my roll.

He looked at me.

'You've made a mistake, I think,' he said, smiling.

'Oh, no,' I said. 'I'm sure I haven't.'

'You've given me the wrong roll. This is an *unexposed* one.'

I walked out with what dignity I could muster. I dare say it is good for one now and again to realize what an idiot one can be! But nobody relishes the process.

And then, just as I was passing one of the big shipping offices, I came to a sudden halt. In the window was a beautiful model of one of the company's boats, and it was labelled 'Kenilworth Castle'. A wild idea shot through my brain. I pushed the door open and went in. I went up to the counter and in a faltering voice (genuine this time!) I murmured:

'Kilmorden Castle?'

'On the 17th from Southampton. Cape Town? First or second class?'

'How much is it?'

'First class, eighty-seven pounds –'

I interrupted him. The coincidence was too much for me. Exactly the amount of my legacy! I would put all my eggs in one basket.

'First class,' I said.

I was now definitely committed to the adventure.

CHAPTER 8

(EXTRACTS FROM THE DIARY OF SIR EUSTACE PEDLER, M.P.)

It is an extraordinary thing that I never seem to get any peace. I am a man who likes a quiet life. I like my Club, my rubber of bridge, a well-cooked meal, a sound wine. I like England in the summer, and the Riviera in the winter. I have no desire to participate in sensational happenings. Sometimes, in front of a good fire, I do not object to reading about them in the newspaper. But that is as far as I am willing to go. My object in life is to be thoroughly comfortable. I have devoted a certain amount of thought, and a considerable amount of money, to further that end. But I cannot say that I always succeed. If things do not actually happen to me, they happen round me, and frequently, in spite of myself, I become involved. I hate being involved.

All this because Guy Pagett came into my bedroom this morning with a telegram in his hand and a face as long as a mute at a funeral.

Guy Pagett is my secretary, a zealous, painstaking, hard-working fellow, admirable in every respect. I know no one who annoys me more. For a long time I have been racking my brains as to how to get rid of him. But you cannot very well dismiss a secretary because he prefers work to play, likes getting up early in the morning, and has positively no vices. The only amusing thing about the fellow is his face. He has the face of a fourteenth-century poisoner – the sort of man the Borgias got to do their odd jobs for them.

I wouldn't mind so much if Pagett didn't make me work too.

My idea of work is something that should be undertaken lightly and airily – trifled with, in fact! I doubt if Guy Pagett has ever trifled with anything in his life. He takes everything seriously. That is what makes him so difficult to live with.

Last week I had the brilliant idea of sending him off to Florence. He talked about Florence and how much he wanted to go there.

'My dear fellow,' I cried, 'You shall go tomorrow. I will pay all your expenses.'

January isn't the usual time for going to Florence, but it would be all one to Pagett. I could imagine him going about, guidebook in hand, religiously doing all the picture galleries. And a week's freedom was cheap to me at the price.

It has been a delightful week. I have done everything I wanted to, and nothing that I did not want to do. But when I blinked my eyes open, and perceived Pagett standing between me and the light at the unearthly hour of 9 a.m. this morning, I realized that freedom was over.

'My dear fellow,' I said, 'has the funeral already taken place, or is it for later in the morning?'

Pagett does not appreciate dry humour. He merely stared.

'So you know, Sir Eustace?'

'Know what?' I said crossly. 'From the expression on your face I inferred that one of your near and dear relatives was to be interred this morning.'

Pagett ignored the sally as far as possible.

'I thought you couldn't know about this.' He tapped the telegram. 'I know you dislike being aroused early – but it is nine o'clock' – Pagett insists on regarding 9 a.m. as practically the middle of the day – 'and I thought that under the circumstances –' He tapped the telegram again.

'What is that thing?' I asked.

'It's a telegram from the police at Marlow. A woman has been murdered in your house.'

That aroused me in earnest.

'What colossal cheek,' I exclaimed. 'Why in my *house? Who murdered her?'*

'They don't say. I suppose we shall go back to England at once, Sir Eustace?'

'You need suppose nothing of the kind. Why should we go back?'

'The police –'

'What on earth have I to do with the police?'

'Well, it is your house.'

'That,' I said, 'appears to be more my misfortune than my fault.'

Guy Pagett shook his head gloomily.

'It will have a very unfortunate effect upon the constituency,' he remarked lugubriously.

I don't see why it should have – and yet I have a feeling that in such matters Pagett's instincts are always right. On the face of it, a Member of Parliament will be none the less efficient because a stray young woman comes and gets herself murdered in an empty house that belongs to him – but there is no accounting for the view the respectable British public takes of a matter.

'She's a foreigner too, and that makes it worse,' continued Pagett gloomily.

Again I believe he is right. If it is disreputable to have a woman murdered in your house, it becomes more disreputable if the woman is a foreigner. Another idea struck me.

'Good heavens,' I exclaimed, 'I hope this won't upset Caroline.'

Caroline is the lady who cooks for me. Incidentally she is the wife of my gardener. What kind of a wife she makes I do not know, but she is an excellent cook. James, on the other hand, is not a good gardener – but I support him in idleness and give him the lodge to live in solely on account of Caroline's cooking.

'I don't suppose she'll stay after this,' said Pagett.

'You always were a cheerful fellow,' I said.

I expect I shall have to go back to England. Pagett clearly intends that I shall. And there is Caroline to pacify.

Three days later.

It is incredible to me that anyone who can get away from England in winter does not do so! It is an abominable climate. All this trouble is very annoying. The house-agents say it will be next to impossible to let the Mill House after all the publicity. Caroline has been pacified – with double pay. We could have sent her a cable to that effect from Cannes. In fact, as I have said all along, there was no earthly purpose to serve by our coming over. I shall go back tomorrow.

One day later.

Several very suprising things have occurred. To begin with, I met Augustus Milray, the most perfect example of an old ass the present Government has produced. His manner oozed diplomatic secrecy as he drew me aside in the Club into a quiet corner. He talked a good deal. About South Africa and the industrial situation there. About the growing rumours of a strike on the Rand. Of the secret causes actuating that strike. I listened as patiently as I could. Finally, he dropped his voice to a whisper and explained that certain documents had come to light which ought to be placed in the hands of General Smuts.

'I've no doubt you're quite right,' I said, stifling a yawn.

'But how are we to get them to him? Our position in the matter is delicate – very delicate.'

'What's wrong with the post?' I said cheerfully. 'Put a twopenny stamp on and drop 'em in the nearest letter-box.'

He seemed quite shocked at the suggestion.

'My dear Pedler! The common post!'

It has always been a mystery to me why Governments employ King's Messengers and draw such attention to their confidential documents.

'If you don't like the post, send one of your own young fellows. He'll enjoy the trip.'

'Impossible,' said Milray, wagging his head in a senile fashion. 'There are reasons, my dear Pedler – I assure you there are reasons.'

'Well,' I said rising, 'all this is very interesting, but I must be off –'

'One minute, my dear Pedler, one minute, I beg of you. Now tell me, in confidence, is it not true that you intend visiting South Africa shortly yourself? You have large interests in Rhodesia, I know, and the question of Rhodesia joining in the Union is one in which you have a vital interest.'

'Well, I had thought of going out in about a month's time.'

'You couldn't possibly make it sooner? This month? This week, in fact?'

'I could,' I said, eyeing him with some interest. 'But I don't know that I particularly want to.'

'You would be doing the Government a great service – a very

great service. You would not find them – er – ungrateful.'

'Meaning, you want me to be the postman?'

'Exactly. Your position is an unofficial one, your journey is bona fide. *Everything would be eminently satisfactory.'*

'Well,' I said slowly, 'I don't mind if I do. The one thing I am anxious to do is to get out of England again as soon as possible.'

'You will find the climate of South Africa delightful – quite delightful.'

'My dear fellow, I know all about the climate. I was out there shortly before the war.'

'I am really much obliged to you, Pedler. I will send you round the package by messenger. To be placed in General Smuts's own hands, you understand? The Kilmorden Castle *sails on Saturday – quite a good boat.'*

I accompanied him a short way along Pall Mall, before we parted. He shook me warmly by the hand, and thanked me again effusively. I walked home reflecting on the curious by-ways of Governmental policy.

It was the following evening that Jarvis, my butler, informed me that a gentleman wished to see me on private business, but declined to give his name. I have always a lively apprehension of insurance touts, so told Jarvis to say I could not see him. Guy Pagett, unfortunately, when he might for once have been of real use, was laid up with a bilious attack. These earnest, hard-working young men with weak stomachs are always liable to bilious attacks.

Jarvis returned.

'The gentleman asked me to tell you, Sir Eustace, that he comes to you from Mr Milray.'

That altered the complexion of things. A few minutes later I was confronting my visitor in the library. He was a well-built young fellow with a deeply tanned face. A scar ran diagonally from the corner of his eye to the jaw, disfiguring what would otherwise have been a handsome though somewhat reckless countenance.

'Well,' I said, 'what's the matter?'

'Mr Milray sent me to you, Sir Eustace. I am to accompany you to South Africa as your secretary.'

'My dear fellow,' I said, 'I've got a secretary already. I don't want another.'

'I think you do, Sir Eustace. Where is your secretary now?'

'He's down with a bilious attack,' I explained.

'You are sure it's only a bilious attack?'

'Of course it is. He's subject to them.'

My visitor smiled.

'It may or may not be a bilious attack. Time will show. But I can tell you this, Sir Eustace, Mr Milray would not be surprised if an attempt were made to get your secretary out of the way. Oh, you need have no fear for yourself' – I suppose a momentary alarm had flickered across my face – 'you are not threatened. Your secretary out of the way, access to you would be easier. In any case, Mr Milray wishes me to accompany you. The passage-money will be our affair, of course, but you will take the necessary steps about the passport, as though you had decided that you needed the services of a second secretary.'

He seemed a determined young man. We stared at each other and he stared me down.

'Very well,' I said feebly.

'You will say nothing to anyone as to my accompanying you.'

'Very well,' I said again.

After all, perhaps it was better to have this fellow with me, but I had a premonition that I was getting into deep waters. Just when I thought I had attained peace!

I stopped my visitor as he was turning to depart.

'It might be just as well if I knew my new secretary's name,' I observed sarcastically.

He considered for a minute.

'Harry Rayburn seems quite a suitable name,' he observed.

It was a curious way of putting it.

'Very well,' I said for the third time.

CHAPTER 9

(ANNE'S NARRATIVE RESUMED)

It is most undignified for a heroine to be sea-sick. In books the more it rolls and tosses, the better she likes it. When everybody else is ill, she alone staggers along the deck, braving the elements and positively rejoicing in the storm. I regret to say that at the first roll the *Kilmorden* gave, I turned pale and hastened below.

A sympathetic stewardess received me. She suggested dry toast and ginger ale.

I remained groaning in my cabin for three days. Forgotten was my quest. I had no longer any interest in solving mysteries. I was a totally different Anne to the one who had rushed back to the South Kensington square so jubilantly from the shipping office.

I smiled now as I remember my abrupt entry into the drawing-room. Mrs Flemming was alone there. She turned her head as I entered.

'Is that you, Anne, my dear? There is something I want to talk over with you.'

'Yes?' I said, curbing my impatience.

'Miss Emery is leaving me.' Miss Emery was the governess. 'As you have not yet succeeded in finding anything, I wondered if you would care – it would be so nice if you remained with us altogether?'

I was touched. She didn't want me, I knew. It was sheer Christian charity that prompted the offer. I felt remorseful for my secret criticism of her. Getting up, I ran impulsively across the room and flung my arms round her neck.

'You're a dear,' I said. 'A dear, a dear, a dear! And thank you ever so much. But it's all right, I'm off to South Africa on Saturday.'

My abrupt onslaught had startled the good lady. She was not used to sudden demonstrations of affection. My words startled her still more.

'To South Africa? My dear Anne. We would have to look into anything of that kind very carefully.'

That was the last thing I wanted. I explained that I had already taken my passage, and that upon arrival I proposed to take up duties as a parlourmaid. It was the only thing I could think of on the spur of the moment. There was, I said, a great demand for parlourmaids in South Africa. I assured her that I was equal to taking care of myself, and in the end, with a sigh of relief at getting me off her hands, she accepted the project without further query. At parting, she slipped an envelope into my hand. Inside it I found five new crisp five-pound notes and the words: 'I hope you will not be offended and will accept this with my love.' She was a very good, kind woman. I could not have continued to live in the same house with her, but I did recognize her intrinsic worth.

So here I was, with twenty-five pounds in my pocket, facing the world and pursuing my adventure.

It was on the fourth day that the stewardess finally urged me up on deck. Under the impression that I should die quicker below, I had steadfastly refused to leave my bunk. She now tempted me with the advent of Madeira. Hope rose in my breast. I could leave the boat and go ashore and be a parlourmaid there. Anything for dry land.

Muffled in coats and rugs, and weak as a kitten on my legs, I was hauled up and deposited, an inert mass, on a deck-chair. I lay there with my eyes closed, hating life. The purser, a fair-haired young man, with a round boyish face, came and sat down beside me.

'Hullo! Feeling rather sorry for yourself, eh?'

'Yes,' I replied, hating him.

'Ah, you won't know yourself in another day or two. We've had a rather nasty dusting in the Bay, but there's smooth weather ahead. I'll be taking you on at quoits tomorrow.'

I did not reply.

'Think you'll never recover, eh? But I've seen people much worse than you, and two days later they were the life and soul of the ship. You'll be the same.'

I did not feel sufficiently pugnacious to tell him outright that he was a liar. I endeavoured to convey it by a glance. He chatted pleasantly for a few minutes more, then he mercifully departed. People passed and repassed, brisk couples 'exercising', curveting children, laughing young people. A few other pallid sufferers lay, like myself, in deck-chairs.

The air was pleasant, crisp, not too cold, and the sun was shining brightly. Insensibly, I felt a little cheered. I began to watch the people. One woman in particular attracted me. She was about thirty, of medium height and very fair with a round dimpled face and very blue eyes. Her clothes, though perfectly plain, had that indefinable air of 'cut' about them which spoke of Paris. Also, in a pleasant but self-possessed way, she seemed to own the ship!

Deck stewards ran to and fro obeying her commands. She had a special deck-chair, and an apparently inexhaustible supply of cushions. She changed her mind three times as to where she would like it placed. Throughout everything she remained attractive and charming. She appeared to be one of those rare people in the world who know what they want, see that they get it, and manage to do so without being offensive. I decided that if ever I recovered – but of course I shouldn't – it would amuse me to talk to her.

We reached Madeira about midday. I was still too inert to move, but I enjoyed the picturesque-looking merchants who came on board and spread their merchandise about the decks. There were flowers too. I buried my nose in an enormous bunch of sweet wet violets and felt distinctly better. In fact, I thought I might just possibly last out the end of the voyage. When my stewardess spoke of the attractions of a little chicken broth, I only protested feebly. When it came I enjoyed it.

My attractive woman had been ashore. She came back escorted by a tall, soldierly-looking man with dark hair and a bronzed face whom I had noticed striding up and down the deck earlier in the day. I put him down at once as one of the strong, silent men of Rhodesia. He was about forty, with a touch of greying hair at either temple, and was easily the best-looking man on board.

When the stewardess brought me up an extra rug, I asked her if she knew who my attractive woman was.

'That's a well-known society lady, the Hon. Mrs Clarence Blair. You must have read about her in the papers.'

I nodded, looking at her with renewed interest. Mrs Blair was very well known indeed as one of the smartest women of the day. I observed, with some amusement, that she was the centre of a good deal of attention. Several people essayed to scrape acquaintance with the pleasant informality that a boat allows. I admired the polite way that Mrs Blair snubbed them. She appeared to have adopted the strong, silent man as her special cavalier, and he seemed duly sensible of the privilege accorded him.

The following morning, to my surprise, after taking a few turns round the deck with her attentive companion, Mrs Blair came to a halt by my chair.

'Feeling better this morning?'

I thanked her, and said I felt slightly more like a human being.

'You did look ill yesterday. Colonel Race and I decided that we should have the excitement of a funeral at sea – but you've disappointed us.'

I laughed.

'Being up in the air has done me good.'

'Nothing like fresh air,' said Colonel Race, smiling.

'Being shut up in those stuffy cabins would kill anyone,' declared Mrs Blair, dropping into a seat by my side and dismissing her companion with a little nod. 'You've got an outside one, I hope?'

I shook my head.

'My dear girl! Why don't you change? There's plenty of room. A lot of people got off at Madeira, and the boat's very empty. Talk to the purser about it. He's a nice little boy – he changed me into a beautiful cabin because I didn't care for the one I'd got. You talk to him at lunch-time when you go down.'

I shuddered.

'I couldn't move.'

'Don't be silly. Come and take a walk now with me.'

She dimpled at me encouragingly. I felt very weak on my legs at first, but as we walked briskly up and down I began to feel a brighter and better being.

After a turn or two, Colonel Race joined us again.

'You can see the Grand Peak of Tenerife from the other side.'

'Can we? Can I get a photograph of it, do you think?'

'No – but that won't deter you from snapping off at it.'

Mrs Blair laughed.

'You are unkind. Some of my photographs are very good.'

'About three per cent effective, I should say.'

We all went round to the other side of the deck. There, glimmering white and snowy, enveloped in a delicate rose-coloured mist, rose the glistening pinnacle. I uttered an exclamation of delight. Mrs Blair ran for her camera.

Undeterred by Colonel Race's sardonic comments, she snapped vigorously:

'There, that's the end of the roll. Oh,' her tone changed to one of chagrin, 'I've had the thing at "bulb" all the time.'

'I always like to see a child with a new toy,' murmured the Colonel.

'How horrid you are – but I've got another roll.'

She produced it in triumph from the pocket of her sweater. A sudden roll of the boat upset her balance, and as she caught at the rail to steady herself the roll of films flashed over the side.

'Oh!' cried Mrs Blair, comically dismayed. She leaned over. 'Do you think they have gone overboard?'

'No, you may have been fortunate enough to brain an unlucky steward in the deck below.'

A small boy who had arrived unobserved a few paces to our rear blew a deafening blast on a bugle.

'Lunch,' declared Mrs Blair ecstatically. 'I've had nothing to eat since breakfast, except two cups of beef tea. Lunch, Miss Beddingfeld?'

'Well,' I said waveringly. 'Yes, I *do* feel rather hungry.'

'Splendid. You're sitting at the purser's table, I know. Tackle him about the cabin.'

I found my way down to the saloon, began to eat gingerly, and finished by consuming an enormous meal. My friend of yesterday congratulated me on my recovery. Everyone was changing cabins today, he told me, and he promised that my things should be moved to an outside one without delay.

There were only four at our table. Myself, a couple of elderly ladies, and a missionary who talked a lot about 'our poor black brothers'.

I looked round at the other tables. Mrs Blair was sitting at the Captain's table. Colonel Race next to her. On the other side of the Captain was a distinguished-looking, grey-haired man. A good many people I had already noticed on deck, but there was one man who had not previously appeared. Had he done so, he could hardly have escaped my notice. He was tall and dark, and had such a peculiarly sinister type of countenance that I was quite startled. I asked the purser, with some curiosity, who he was.

'That man? Oh, that's Sir Eustace Pedler's secretary. Been very sea-sick, poor chap, and not appeared before. Sir Eustace has got two secretaries with him, and the sea's been too much for both of them. The other fellow hasn't turned up yet. This man's name is Pagett.'

So Sir Eustace Pedler, the owner of the Mill House, was on board. Probably only a coincidence, and yet –

'That's Sir Eustace,' my informant continued, 'sitting next to the Captain. Pompous old ass.'

The more I studied the secretary's face, the less I liked it. Its even pallor, the secretive, heavy-lidded eyes, the curiously flattened head – it all gave a feeling of distaste, of apprehension.

Leaving the saloon at the same time as he did, I was close behind him as he went up on deck. He was speaking to Sir Eustace, and I overheard a fragment or two.

'I'll see about the cabin at once then, shall I? It's impossible to work in yours, with all your trunks.'

'My dear fellow,' Sir Eustace replied. 'My cabin is intended (*a*) for me to sleep in, and (*b*) to attempt to dress in. I never had any intentions of allowing you to sprawl about the place making an infernal clicking with that typewriter of yours.'

'That's just what I say, Sir Eustace, we must have somewhere to work –'

Here I parted company from them, and went below to see if my removal was in progress. I found my steward busy at the task.

'Very nice cabin, miss. On D deck. No. 13.'

'Oh, no!' I cried. '*Not* 13.'

Thirteen is the one thing I am superstitious about. It was a nice cabin too. I inspected it, wavered, but a foolish superstition prevailed. I appealed almost tearfully to the steward.

'Isn't there any other cabin I can have?'

The steward reflected.

'Well, there's 17, just along the starboard side. That was empty this morning, but I rather fancy it's been allotted to someone. Still, as the gentleman's things aren't in yet, and as gentlemen aren't anything like so superstitious as ladies, I dare say he wouldn't mind changing.'

I hailed the proposition gratefully, and the steward departed to obtain permission from the purser. He returned grinning.

'That's all right, miss. We can go along.'

He led the way to 17. It was not quite as large as No. 13, but I found it eminently satisfactory.

'I'll fetch your things right away, miss,' said the steward.

But at that moment the man with the sinister face (as I had nicknamed him) appeared in the doorway.

'Excuse me,' he said, 'but this cabin is reserved for the use of Sir Eustace Pedler.'

'That's all right, sir,' explained the steward. 'We're fitting up No. 13 instead.'

'No, it was No. 17 I was to have.'

'No. 13 is a better cabin, sir – larger.'

'I specially selected No. 17, and the purser said I could have it.'

'I'm sorry,' I said coldly. 'But No. 17 has been allotted to me.'

'I can't agree to that.'

The steward put in his oar.

'The other cabin's just the same, only better.'

'I want No. 17.'

'What's all this?' demanded a new voice. 'Steward, put my things in here. This is my cabin.'

It was my neighbour at lunch, the Rev. Edward Chichester.

'I beg your pardon,' I said. 'It's my cabin.'

'It is allotted to Sir Eustace Pedler,' said Mr Pagett.

We were all getting rather heated.

'I'm sorry to have to dispute the matter,' said Chichester with a meek smile which failed to mask his determination to get his own way. Meek men are always obstinate, I have noticed.

He edged himself sideways into the doorway.

'You're to have No. 28 on the port side,' said the steward. 'A very good cabin, sir.'

'I am afraid that I must insist. No. 17 was the cabin promised to me.'

We had come to an impasse. Each one of us was determined not to give way. Strictly speaking, I, at any rate, might have retired from the contest and eased matters by offering to accept Cabin 28. So long as I did not have 13 it was immaterial to me what other cabin I had. But my blood was up. I had not the least intention of being the first to give way. And I disliked Chichester. He had false teeth that clicked when he ate. Many men have been hated for less.

We all said the same things over again. The steward assured us, even more strongly, that both the other cabins were better cabins. None of us paid any attention to him.

Pagett began to lose his temper. Chichester kept his serenely.

With an effort I also kept mine. And still none of us would give way an inch.

A wink and a whispered word from the steward gave me my cue. I faded unobtrusively from the scene. I was lucky enough to encounter the purser almost immediately.

'Oh, please,' I said, 'you did say I could have cabin 17? And the others won't go away. Mr Chichester and Mr Pagett. You *will* let me have it, won't you?'

I always say that there are no people like sailors for being nice to women. My little purser came up to scratch splendidly. He strode to the scene, informed the disputants that No. 17 was my cabin, they could have Nos 13 and 28 respectively or stay where they were – whichever they chose.

I permitted my eyes to tell him what a hero he was and then installed myself in my new domain. The encounter had done me worlds of good. The sea was smooth, the weather growing daily warmer. Sea-sickness was a thing of the past!

I went up on deck and was initiated into the mysteries of deck-quoits. I entered my name for various sports. Tea was served on deck, and I ate heartily. After tea, I played shovel-board with some pleasant young men. They were extraordinarily nice to me. I felt that life was satisfactory and delightful.

The dressing bugle came as a surprise and I hurried to my new cabin. The stewardess was awaiting me with a troubled face.

'There's a terrible smell in your cabin, miss. What it is, I'm sure I can't think, but I doubt if you'll be able to sleep here. There's a deck cabin up on C deck. You might move into that – just for the night, anyway.'

The smell really was pretty bad – quite nauseating. I told the stewardess I would think over the question of moving whilst I dressed. I hurried over my toilet, sniffing distastefully as I did so.

What *was* the smell? Dead rat? No, worse than that – and quite different. Yet I knew it! It was something I had smelt before. Something – Ah! I had got it. Asafoetida! I had worked in a hospital dispensary during the war for a short time and had become acquainted with various nauseous drugs.

Asafoetida, that was it. But how –

I sank down on the sofa, suddenly realizing the thing. Somebody had put a pinch of asafoetida in my cabin. Why? So that

I should vacate it? Why were they so anxious to get me out? I thought of the scene this afternoon from a rather different point of view. What was it about Cabin 17 that made so many people anxious to get hold of it? The other two cabins were better cabins; why had both men insisted on sticking to 17?

Seventeen. How the number persisted! It was on the 17th I had sailed from Southampton. It was a 17 – I stopped with a sudden gasp. Quickly I unlocked my suitcase, and took my precious paper from its place of concealment in some rolled stockings.

17 1 22 – I had taken that for a date, the date of departure of the *Kilmorden Castle*. Supposing I was wrong. When I came to think of it, would anyone, writing down a date, think it necessary to put the year as well as the month? Supposing 17 meant *Cabin* 17? and 1? The time – one o'clock. Then 22 must be the date. I looked up at my little almanac.

Tomorrow was the 22nd!

CHAPTER 10

I was violently excited. I was sure that I had hit on the right trail at last. One thing was clear, I must not move out of the cabin. The asafoetida had got to be borne. I examined my facts again.

Tomorrow was the 22nd, and at 1 a.m. or 1 p.m. something would happen. I plumped for 1 a.m. It was now seven o'clock. In six hours I should know.

I don't know how I got through the evening. I retired to my cabin fairly early. I had told the stewardess that I had a cold in the head and didn't mind smells. She still seemed distressed, but I was firm.

The evening seemed interminable. I duly retired to bed, but in view of emergencies I swathed myself in a thick flannel dressing-gown, and encased my feet in slippers. Thus attired I felt that I could spring up and take an active part in anything that happened.

What did I expect to happen? I hardly knew. Vague fancies, most of them wildly improbable, flitted through my brain. But one thing I was firmly convinced of, at one o'clock *something* would happen.

At various times I heard fellow-passengers coming to bed. Fragments of conversation, laughing good-nights, floated in through the open transom. Then, silence. Most of the lights went out. There was still one in the passage outside, and there was therefore a certain amount of light in my cabin. I heard eight bells go. The hour that followed seemed the longest I had ever known. I consulted my watch surreptitiously to be sure I had not overshot the time.

If my deductions were wrong, if nothing happened at one o'clock, I should have made a fool of myself, and spent all the money I had in the world on a mare's nest. My heart beat painfully.

Two bells went overhead. One o'clock! And nothing. Wait – what was that? I heard the quick light patter of feet running – running along the passage.

Then with the suddenness of a bombshell my cabin door burst open and a man almost fell inside.

'Save me,' he said hoarsely. 'They're after me.'

It was not a moment for argument or explanation. I could hear footsteps outside. I had about forty seconds in which to act. I had sprung to my feet and was standing facing the stranger in the middle of the cabin.

A cabin does not abound in hiding-places for a six-foot man. With one arm I pulled out my cabin trunk. He slipped down behind it under the bunk. I raised the lid. At the same time, with the other hand I pulled down the washbasin. A deft movement and my hair was screwed into a tiny knot on the top of my head. From the point of view of appearance it was inartistic, from another standpoint it was supremely artistic. A lady, with her hair screwed into an unbecoming knob and in the act of removing a piece of soap from her trunk with which, apparently, to wash her neck, could hardly be suspected of harbouring a fugitive.

There was a knock at the door, and without waiting for me to say 'Come in' it was pushed open.

I don't know what I expected to see. I think I had vague ideas of Mr Pagett brandishing a revolver. Or my missionary friend with a sandbag, or some other lethal weapon. But I certainly did not expect to see a night stewardess, with an inquiring face and looking the essence of respectability.

'I beg your pardon, miss, I thought you called out.'

'No,' I said, 'I didn't.'

'I'm sorry for interrupting you.'

'That's all right,' I said. 'I couldn't sleep. I thought a wash would do me good.' It sounded rather as though it were a thing I never had as a general rule.

'I'm so sorry, miss,' said the stewardess again. 'But there's a gentleman about who's rather drunk and we are afraid he might get into one of the ladies' cabins and frighten them.'

'How dreadful!' I said, looking alarmed. 'He won't come in here, will he?'

'Oh, I don't think so, miss. Ring the bell if he does. Good night.'

'Good night.'

I opened the door and peeped down the corridor. Except for the retreating form of the stewardess, there was nobody in sight.

Drunk! So that was the explanation of it. My histrionic talents had been wasted. I pulled the cabin trunk out a little farther and said: 'Come out at once, please,' in an acid voice.

There was no answer. I peered under the bunk. My visitor lay immovable. He seemed to be asleep. I tugged at his shoulder. He did not move.

'Dead drunk,' I thought vexedly. 'What *am* I to do?'

Then I saw something that made me catch my breath, a small scarlet spot on the floor.

Using all my strength, I succeeded in dragging the man out into the middle of the cabin. The dead whiteness of his face showed that he had fainted. I found the cause of his fainting easily enough. He had been stabbed under the left shoulder-blade – a nasty deep wound. I got his coat off and set to work to attend to it.

At the sting of the cold water he stirred, then sat up.

'Keep still, please,' I said.

He was the kind of young man who recovers his faculties very quickly. He pulled himself to his feet and stood there swaying a little.

'Thank you; I don't need anything done for me.'

His manner was defiant, almost aggressive. Not a word of thanks – of even common gratitude!

'That is a nasty wound. You must let me dress it.'

'You will do nothing of the kind.'

He flung the words in my face as though I had been begging a favour of him. My temper, never placid, rose.

'I cannot congratulate you on your manners,' I said coldly.

'I can at least relieve you of my presence.' He started for the door, but reeled as he did so. With an abrupt movement I pushed him down upon the sofa.

'Don't be a fool,' I said unceremoniously. 'You don't want to go bleeding all over the ship, do you?'

He seemed to see the sense of that, for he sat quietly whilst I bandaged up the wound as best I could.

'There,' I said, bestowing a pat on my handiwork, 'that will have to do for the present. Are you better-tempered now and do you feel inclined to tell me what it's all about?'

'I'm sorry that I can't satisfy your very natural curiosity.'

'Why not?' I said, chagrined.

He smiled nastily.

'If you want a thing broadcast, tell a woman. Otherwise keep your mouth shut.'

'Don't you think I could keep a secret?'

'I don't think – I know.'

He rose to his feet.

'At any rate,' I said spitefully, 'I shall be able to do a little broadcasting about the events of this evening.'

'I've no doubt you will too,' he said indifferently.

'How dare you!' I cried angrily.

We were facing each other, glaring at each other with the ferocity of bitter enemies. For the first time, I took in the details of his appearance, the close-cropped dark head, the lean jaw, the scar on the brown cheek, the curious light grey eyes that looked into mine with a sort of reckless mockery hard to describe. There was something dangerous about him.

'You haven't thanked me yet for saving your life!' I said with false sweetness.

I hit him there. I saw him flinch distinctly. Intuitively I knew that he hated above all to be reminded that he owed his life to me. I didn't care. I wanted to hurt him. I had never wanted to hurt anyone so much.

'I wish to God you hadn't!' he said explosively. 'I'd be better dead and out of it.'

'I'm glad you acknowledge the debt. You can't get out of it. I saved your life and I'm waiting for you to say "Thank you".'

If looks could have killed, I think he would have liked to kill me then. He pushed roughly past me. At the door he turned back, and spoke over his shoulder.

'I shall not thank you – now or at any other time. But I acknowledge the debt. Some day I will pay it.'

He was gone, leaving me with clenched hands, and my heart beating like a mill race.

CHAPTER 11

There were no further excitements that night. I had breakfast in bed and got up late the next morning. Mrs Blair hailed me as I came on deck.

'Good morning, gipsy girl. Sit down here by me. You look as though you hadn't slept well.'

'Why do you call me that?' I asked, as I sat down obediently.

'Do you mind? It suits you somehow. I've called you that in my own mind from the beginning. It's the gipsy element in you that makes you so different from anyone else. I decided in my own mind that you and Colonel Race were the only two people on board who wouldn't bore me to death to talk to.'

'That's funny,' I said. 'I thought the same about you – only it's more understandable in your case. You're – you're such an exquisitely finished product.'

'Not badly put,' said Mrs Blair, nodding her head. 'Tell me about yourself, gipsy girl. Why are you going to South Africa?'

I told her something about Papa's life work.

'So you're Charles Beddingfeld's daughter? I thought you weren't a mere provincial miss! Are you going to Broken Hill to grub up more skulls?'

'I may,' I said cautiously. 'I've got other plans as well.'

'What a mysterious minx you are. But you do look tired this morning. Didn't you sleep well? I can't keep awake on board a boat. Ten hours' sleep for a fool, they say! I could do with twenty!'

She yawned, looking like a sleepy kitten. 'An idiot of a steward woke me up in the middle of the night to return me that roll of films I dropped yesterday. He did it in the most melodramatic manner, stuck his arm through the ventilator and dropped them neatly in the middle of my tummy. I thought it was a bomb for a moment!'

'Here's your Colonel,' I said, as the tall, soldierly figure of Colonel Race appeared on the deck.

'He's not my Colonel particularly. In fact he admires *you* very much, gipsy girl. So don't run away.'

'I want to tie something round my head. It will be more comfortable than a hat.'

I slipped quickly away. For some reason or other I was uncomfortable with Colonel Race. He was one of the few people who were capable of making me feel shy.

I went down to my cabin and began looking for something with which I could restrain my rebellious locks. Now I am a tidy person, I like my things always arranged in a certain way and I keep them so. I had no sooner opened my drawer than I realized that somebody had been disarranging my things. Everything had been turned over and scattered. I looked in the other drawers and the small hanging cupboard. They told the same tale. It was as though someone had been making a hurried and ineffectual search for something.

I sat down on the edge of the bunk with a grave face. Who had been searching my cabin and what had they been looking for? Was it the half-sheet of paper with scribbled figures and words? I shook my head, dissatisfied. Surely that was past history now. But what else could there be?

I wanted to think. The events of last night, though exciting, had not really done anything to elucidate matters. Who was the young man who had burst into my cabin so abruptly? I had not seen him on board previously, either on deck or in the saloon. Was he one of the ship's company or was he a passenger? Who had stabbed him? Why had they stabbed him? And why, in the name of goodness, should Cabin No. 17 figure so prominently? It was all a mystery, but there was no doubt that some very peculiar occurrences were taking place on the *Kilmorden Castle*.

I counted off on my fingers the people on whom it behoved me to keep watch.

Setting aside my visitor of the night before, but promising myself that I would discover him on board before another day had passed, I selected the following persons as worthy of my notice:

(1) Sir Eustace Pedler. He was the owner of the Mill House, and his presence on the *Kilmorden Castle* seemed something of a coincidence.

(2) Mr Pagett, the sinister-looking secretary, whose eagerness to obtain Cabin 17 had been so very marked. N.B. – Find out whether he had accompanied Sir Eustace to Cannes.

(3) The Rev. Edward Chichester. All I had against him was his obstinacy over Cabin 17, and that might be entirely due to his own peculiar temperament. Obstinacy can be an amazing thing.

But a little conversation with Mr Chichester would not come amiss, I decided. Hastily tying a handkerchief round my hair, I went up on deck again, full of purpose. I was in luck. My quarry was leaning against the rail, drinking beef tea. I went up to him.

'I hope you've forgiven me over Cabin 17,' I said, with my best smile.

'I consider it unchristian to bear a grudge,' said Mr Chichester coldly. 'But the purser had distinctly promised me that cabin.'

'Pursers are such busy men, aren't they?' I said vaguely. 'I suppose they're bound to forget sometimes.'

Mr Chichester did not reply.

'Is this your first visit to South Africa?' I inquired conversationally.

'To South Africa, yes. But I have worked for the last two years amongst the cannibal tribes in the interior of East Africa.'

'How thrilling! Have you had many narrow escapes?'

'Escapes?'

'Of being eaten, I mean?'

'You should not treat sacred subjects with levity, Miss Beddingfeld.'

'I didn't know that cannibalism was a sacred subject,' I retorted, stung.

As the words left my lips, another idea struck me. If Mr

Chichester had indeed spent the last two years in the interior of Africa, how was it that he was not more sun-burnt? His skin was as pink and white as a baby's. Surely there was something fishy there? Yet his manner and voice were so absolutely *it*. Too much so, perhaps. Was he – or was he not – just a little like a *stage* clergyman?

I cast my mind back to the curates I had known at Little Hampsley. Some of them I had liked, some of them I had not, but certainly none of them had been quite like Mr Chichester. They had been human – he was a glorified type.

I was debating all this when Sir Eustace Pedler passed down the deck. Just as he was abreast of Mr Chichester, he stooped and picked up a piece of paper which he handed to him, remarking, 'You've dropped something.'

He passed on without stopping, and so probably did not notice Mr Chichester's agitation. I did. Whatever it was he had dropped, its recovery agitated him considerably. He turned a sickly green, and crumpled up the sheet of paper into a ball. My suspicions were accentuated a hundredfold.

He caught my eye, and hurried into explanations.

'A – a – fragment of a sermon I was composing,' he said with a sickly smile.

'Indeed?' I rejoined politely.

A fragment of a sermon, indeed! No, Mr Chichester – too weak for words!

He soon left me with a muttered excuse. I wished, oh, how I wished, that I had been the one to pick up that paper and not Sir Eustace Pedler! One thing was clear, Mr Chichester could not be exempted from my list of suspects. I was inclined to put him top of the three.

After lunch, when I came up to the lounge for coffee, I noticed Sir Eustace and Pagett sitting with Mrs Blair and Colonel Race. Mrs Blair welcomed me with a smile, so I went over and joined them. They were talking about Italy.

'But it *is* misleading,' Mrs Blair insisted. '*Aqua calda* certainly *ought* to be cold water – not hot.'

'You're not a Latin scholar,' said Sir Eustace, smiling.

'Men are so superior about their Latin,' said Mrs Blair. 'But all the same I notice that when you ask them to translate inscriptions in old churches they can never do it! They hem and haw, and get out of it somehow.'

'Quite right,' said Colonel Race. 'I always do.'

'But I love the Italians,' continued Mrs Blair. 'They're so obliging – though even that has its embarrassing side. You ask them the way somewhere, and instead of saying "first to the right, second to the left" or something that one could follow, they pour out a flood of well-meaning directions, and when you look bewildered they take you kindly by the arm and walk all the way there with you.'

'Is that your experience in Florence, Pagett?' asked Sir Eustace, turning with a smile to his secretary.

For some reason the question seemed to disconcert Mr Pagett. He stammered and flushed.

'Oh, quite so, yes – er quite so.'

Then with a murmured excuse, he rose and left the table.

'I am beginning to suspect Guy Pagett of having committed some dark deed in Florence,' remarked Sir Eustace, gazing after his secretary's retreating figure. 'Whenever Florence or Italy is mentioned, he changes the subject or bolts precipitately.'

'Perhaps he murdered someone there,' said Mrs Blair hopefully. 'He looks – I hope I'm not hurting your feelings, Sir Eustace – but he does look as though he might murder someone.'

'Yes, pure Cinquecento! It amuses me sometimes – especially when one knows as well as I do how essentially law-abiding and respectable the poor fellow really is.'

'He's been with you some time, hasn't he, Sir Eustace?' asked Colonel Race.

'Six years,' said Sir Eustace with a deep sigh.

'He must be quite invaluable to you,' said Mrs Blair.

'Oh, invaluable! Yes, quite invaluable.' The poor man sounded even more depressed, as though the invaluableness of Mr Pagett was a secret grief to him. Then he added more briskly: 'But his face should really inspire you with confidence, my dear lady. No self-respecting murderer would ever consent to look like one. Crippen, now, I believe, was one of the pleasantest fellows imaginable.'

'He was caught on a liner, wasn't he?' murmured Mrs Blair.

There was a slight rattle behind us. I turned quickly. Mr Chichester had dropped his coffee-cup.

Our party soon broke up; Mrs Blair went below to sleep and I went out on deck. Colonel Race followed me.

'You're very elusive, Miss Beddingfeld. I looked for you everywhere last night at the dance.'

'I went to bed early,' I explained.

'Are you going to run away tonight too? Or are you going to dance with me?'

'I shall be very pleased to dance with you,' I murmured shyly. 'But Mrs Blair –'

'Our friend, Mrs Blair, doesn't care for dancing.'

'And do you?'

'I care for dancing with you.'

'Oh!' I said nervously.

I was a little afraid of Colonel Race. Nevertheless I was enjoying myself. This was better than discussing fossilized skulls with stuffy old professors! Colonel Race was really just my ideal of a stern, silent Rhodesian. Possibly I might marry him! I hadn't been asked, it is true, but, as the Boy Scouts say, Be Prepared! And all women, without in the least meaning it, consider every man they meet as a possible husband for themselves or their best friend.

I danced several times with him that evening. He danced well. When the dancing was over, and I was thinking of going to bed, he suggested a turn round the deck. We walked round three times and finally subsided into two deck-chairs. There was nobody else in sight. We made desultory conversation for some time.

'Do you know, Miss Beddingfeld, I think I once met your father? A very interesting man – on his own subject, and it's a subject that has a special fascination for me. In my humble way, I've done a bit in that line myself. Why, when I was in the Dordogne region –'

Our talk became technical. Colonel Race's boast was not an idle one. He knew a great deal. At the same time, he made one or two curious mistakes – slips of the tongue, I might almost have thought them. But he was quick to take his cue from me and to cover them up. Once he spoke of the Mousterian period as succeeding the Aurignacian – an absurd mistake for one who knew anything of the subject.

It was twelve o'clock when I went to my cabin. I was still puzzling over those queer discrepancies. Was it possible that he had 'got the whole subject up' for the occasion – that really he knew nothing of anthropology? I shook my head, vaguely dissatisfied with that solution.

Just as I was dropping off to sleep, I sat up with a sudden start as another idea flashed into my head. Had *he* been pumping *me*? Were those slight inaccuracies just tests – to see whether I really knew what I was talking about? In other words, he suspected me of not being genuinely Anne Beddingfeld.

Why?

CHAPTER 12

(EXTRACT FROM THE DIARY OF SIR EUSTACE PEDLER)

There is something to be said for life on board ship. It is peaceful. My grey hairs fortunately exempt me from the indignities of bobbing for apples, running up and down deck with potatoes and eggs, and the more painful sports of 'Brother Bill' and Bolster Bar. What amusement people can find in these painful proceedings has always been a mystery to me. But there are many fools in the world. One praises God for their existence and keeps out of their way.

Fortunately I am an excellent sailor. Pagett, poor fellow, is not. He began turning green as soon as we were out of the Solent. I presume my other so-called secretary is also sea-sick. At any rate he has not yet made an appearance. But perhaps it is not sea-sickness, but high diplomacy. The great thing is that I *have not been worried by him.*

On the whole, the people on board are a mangy lot. Only two decent Bridge players and one decent-looking woman – Mrs Clarence Blair. I've met her in town, of course. She is one of the only women I know who can lay claim to a sense of humour. I enjoy talking to her, and should enjoy it more if it were not for a long-legged taciturn ass who attached himself to her like a limpet. I cannot think that this Colonel Race really amuses her. He's good-looking in his way, but dull as ditch water. One of these strong, silent men that lady novelists and young girls always rave over.

Guy Pagett struggled up on deck after we left Madeira and began babbling in a hollow voice about work. What the devil does anyone want to work for on board ship? It is true that I promised my publishers my 'Reminiscences' early in the summer, but what of it? Who really reads reminiscences? Old ladies in the suburbs. And what do my reminiscences amount to? I've knocked against a certain number of so-called famous people in my lifetime. With the assistance of Pagett, I invented insipid anecdotes about them. And, the truth of the matter is, Pagett is too honest for the job. He won't let me invent anecdotes about the people I might have met but haven't.

I tried kindness with him.

'You look a perfect wreck still, my dear chap,' I said easily. 'What you need is a deck-chair in the sun. No – not another word. The work must wait.'

The next thing I knew he was worrying about an extra cabin. 'There's no room to work in your cabin, Sir Eustace. It's full of trunks.'

From his tone, you might have thought the trunks were black beetles, something that had no business to be there.

I explained to him that, though he might not be aware of the fact, it was usual to take a change of clothing with one when travelling. He gave the wan smile with which he always greets my attempts at humour, and then reverted to the business in hand.

'And we could hardly work in my little hole.'

I know Pagett's 'little holes' – he usually has the best cabin on the ship.

'I'm sorry the Captain didn't turn out for you this time,' I said sarcastically. 'Perhaps you'd like to dump some of your extra luggage in my cabin?'

Sarcasm is dangerous with a man like Pagett. He brightened up at once.

'Well, if I could get rid of the typewriter and the stationery trunk –'

The stationery trunk weighs several solid tons. It causes endless unpleasantness with the porters, and it is the aim of Pagett's life to foist it on me. It is a perpetual struggle between us. He seems to regard it as my special personal property. I, on the other hand, regard the charge of it as the only thing where a secretary is really useful.

'We'll get an extra cabin,' I said hastily.

The thing seemed simple enough, but Pagett is a person who loves to make mysteries. He came to me the next day with a face like a Renaissance conspirator.

'You know you told me to get Cabin 17 for an office?'

'Well, what of it? Has the stationery trunk jammed in the doorway?'

'The doorways are the same size in all the cabins,' replied Pagett seriously. 'But I tell you, Sir Eustace, there's something very queer about that cabin.'

Memories of reading The Upper Berth *floated through my mind.*

'If you mean that it's haunted,' I said, 'we're not going to sleep there, so I don't see that it matters. Ghosts don't affect typewriters.'

Pagett said that it wasn't a ghost and that, after all, he hadn't got Cabin 17. He told me a long, garbled story. Apparently, he and a Mr Chichester, and a girl called Beddingfeld, had almost come to blows over the cabin. Needless to say, the girl had won, and Pagett was apparently feeling sore over the matter.

'Both 13 and 28 are better cabins,' he reiterated. 'But they wouldn't look at them.'

'Well,' I said, stifling a yawn, 'for that matter, no more would you, my dear Pagett.'

He gave me a reproachful look.

'You told *me to get Cabin 17.'*

There is a touch of the 'boy upon the burning deck' about Pagett.

'My dear fellow,' I said testily, 'I mentioned No. 17 because I happened to observe that it was vacant. But I didn't mean you to make a stand to the death about it – 13 or 28 would have done us equally well.'

He looked hurt.

'There's something more, though,' he insisted. 'Miss Beddingfeld got the cabin, but this morning I saw Chichester coming out of it in a furtive sort of way.'

I looked at him severely.

'If you're trying to get up a nasty scandal about Chichester, who is a missionary – though a perfectly poisonous person – and that attractive child, Anne Beddingfeld, I don't believe a word of it,' I said coldly. 'Anne Beddingfeld is an extremely nice girl – with particularly good legs. I should say she had far and away the best legs on board.'

Pagett did not like my reference to Anne Beddingfeld's legs. He is the sort of man who never notices legs himself – or, if he does, would die sooner than say so. Also he thinks my appreciation of such things frivolous. I like annoying Pagett, so I continued maliciously:

'As you've made her acquaintance, you might ask her to dine at our table tomorrow night. It's the Fancy Dress dance. By the way, you'd better go down to the barber and select a fancy costume for me.'

'Surely you will not go in fancy dress?' said Pagett, in tones of horror.

I could see that it was quite incompatible with his idea of my dignity. He looked shocked and pained. I had really had no intention of donning fancy dress, but the complete discomfiture of Pagett was too tempting to be forborne.

'What do you mean?' I said. 'Of course I shall wear fancy dress. So will you.'

Pagett shuddered.

'So go down to the barber's and see about it,' I finished.

'I don't think he'll have any out sizes,' murmured Pagett, measuring my figure with his eye.

Without meaning it, Pagett can occasionally be extremely offensive.

'And order a table for six in the saloon,' I said. 'We'll have the Captain, the girl with the nice legs, Mrs Blair –'

'You won't get Mrs Blair, without Colonel Race,' Pagett interposed. 'He's asked her to dine with him, I know.'

Pagett always knows everything. I was justifiably annoyed.

'Who is Race?' I demanded, exasperated.

As I said before, Pagett always knows everything – or thinks he does. He looked mysterious again.

'They say he's a Secret Service chap, Sir Eustace. Rather a great gun too. But of course I don't know for certain.'

'Isn't that like the Government?' I exclaimed. 'Here's a man on board whose business it is to carry about secret documents, and they go giving them to a peaceful outsider, who only asks to be let alone.'

Pagett looked even more mysterious. He came a pace nearer and dropped his voice.

'If you ask me, the whole thing is very queer, Sir Eustace. Look at the illness of mine before we started –'

'My dear fellow,' I interrupted brutally, 'that was a bilious attack. You're always having bilious attacks.'

Pagett winced slightly.

'It wasn't the usual sort of bilious attack. This time –'

'For God's sake, don't go into details of your condition, Pagett. I don't want to hear them.'

'Very well, Sir Eustace. But my belief is that I was deliberately poisoned!'

'Ah!' I said. 'You've been talking to Rayburn.'

He did not deny it.

'At any rate, Sir Eustace, he thinks so – and he should be in a position to know.'

'By the way, where is the chap?' I asked. 'I've not set eyes on him since we came on board.'

'He gives out that he's ill, and stays in his cabin, Sir Eustace.' Pagett's voice dropped again. 'But that's camouflage, *I'm sure. So that he can watch better.'*

'Watch?'

'Over your safety, Sir Eustace. In case an attack should be made upon you.'

'You're such a cheerful fellow, Pagett,' I said. 'I trust that your imagination runs away with you. If I were you I should go to the dance as a death's head or an executioner. It will suit your mournful style of beauty.'

That shut him up for the time being. I went on deck. The Beddingfeld girl was deep in conversation with the missionary parson, Chichester. Women always flutter round parsons.

A man of my figure hates stooping, but I had the courtesy to pick up a bit of paper that was fluttering round the parson's feet.

I got no word of thanks for my pains. As a matter of fact I couldn't help seeing what was written on the sheet of paper. There was just one sentence.

'Don't try to play a lone hand or it will be the worse for you.'

That's a nice thing for a parson to have. Who is this fellow Chichester, I wonder? He looks *mild as milk. But looks are deceptive. I shall ask Pagett about him. Pagett always knows everything.*

I sank gracefully into my deck-chair by the side of Mrs Blair, thereby interrupting her tête-à-tête *with Race, and remarked that I didn't know what the clergy were coming to nowadays.*

Then I asked her to dine with me on the night of the Fancy Dress dance. Somehow or other Race managed to get included in the invitation.

After lunch the Beddingfeld girl came and sat with us for coffee. I was right about her legs. They are *the best on the ship. I shall certainly ask her to dinner as well.*

I would very much like to know what mischief Pagett was up to in Florence. Whenever Italy is mentioned, he goes to pieces. If I did not know how intensely respectable he is – I should suspect him of some disreputable amour . . .

I wonder now! Even the most respectable men – it would cheer me up enormously if it was so.

Pagett – with a guilty secret! Splendid!

CHAPTER 13

It has been a curious evening.

The only costume that fitted me in the barber's emporium was that of a Teddy Bear. I don't mind playing bears with some nice young girls on a winter's evening in England – but it's hardly an ideal costume for the equator. However, I created a good deal of merriment, and won first prize for 'brought on board' – an absurd term for a costume hired for the evening. Still, as nobody seemed to have the least idea whether they were made or brought, it didn't matter.

Mrs Blair refused to dress up. Apparently she is at one with Pagett on the matter. Colonel Race followed her example. Anne Beddingfeld had concocted a gipsy costume for herself, and looked extraordinarily well. Pagett said he had a headache and didn't appear. To replace him I asked a quaint little fellow called Reeves. He's a prominent member of the South African Labour Party. Horrible little man, but I want to keep in with him, as he gives me information that I need. I want to understand this Rand business from both sides.

Dancing was a hot affair. I danced twice with Anne Beddingfeld and she had to pretend she liked it. I danced once with Mrs Blair, who didn't trouble to pretend, and I victimized various other damsels whose appearance struck me favourably.

Then we went down to supper. I had ordered champagne; the steward suggested Clicquot 1911 as being the best they had on the boat and I fell in with his suggestion. I seemed to have hit on the one thing that would loosen Colonel Race's tongue. Far from being taciturn, the man became actually talkative. For a while this amused me, then it occurred to me that Colonel Race, and not myself, was becoming the life and soul of the party. He chaffed me at length about keeping a diary.

'It will reveal all your indiscretions one of these days, Pedler.'

'My dear Race,' I said, 'I venture to suggest that I am not quite the fool you think me. I may commit indiscretions, but I don't write them down in black and white. After my death, my executors will know my opinion of a great many people, but I doubt if they will find anything to add or detract from their opinion of me. *A diary is useful for recording the idiosyncrasies of other people – but not one's own.'*

'There is such a thing as unconscious self-revelation, though.'

'In the eyes of the psycho-analyst, all things are vile,' I replied sententiously.

'You must have had a very interesting life, Colonel Race?' said Miss Beddingfeld, gazing at him with wide, starry eyes.

That's how they do it, these girls! Othello charmed Desdemona by telling her stories, but, oh, didn't Desdemona charm Othello by the way she listened?

Anyway, the girl set Race off all right. He began to tell lion stories. A man who has shot lions in large quantities has an unfair advantage over other men. It seemed to me that it was time I, too, told a lion story. One of a more sprightly character.

'By the way,' I remarked, 'that reminds me of a rather exciting tale I heard. A friend of mine was out on a shooting trip somewhere in East Africa. One night he came out of his tent for some reason, and was startled by a low growl. He turned sharply and saw a lion crouching to spring. He had left his rifle in the tent. Quick as thought, he ducked, and the lion sprang right over his head. Annoyed at having missed him, the animal growled and prepared to spring again. Again he ducked, and again the lion sprang right over him. This happened a third time, but by now he was close to the entrance of his tent, and he darted in and seized his rifle. When he emerged, rifle in hand, the lion had disappeared. That puzzled him greatly. He crept round the back of the tent, where there was a little clearing. There, sure enough, was the lion, busily practising low jumps.'

This was received by a roar of applause. I drank some champagne.

'On another occasion,' I remarked, 'this friend of mine had a second curious experience. He was trekking across country, and being anxious to arrive at his destination before the heat of the day he ordered his boys to inspan whilst it was still dark. They had some trouble in doing so, as the mules were very restive, but at last they managed it, and a start was made. The mules raced along like the wind, and when daylight came they saw why. In the darkness, the boys had inspanned a lion as the near wheeler.'

This, too, was well received, a ripple of merriment going round the table, but I am not sure that the greatest tribute did not come from my friend the Labour Member, who remained pale and serious.

'My God!' he said anxiously. 'Who un'arnessed them?'

'I must go to Rhodesia,' said Mrs Blair. 'After what you have told us, Colonel Race, I simply must. It's a horrible journey though, five days in the train.'

'You must join me in my private car,' I said gallantly.

'Oh, Sir Eustace, how sweet of you! Do you really mean it?'

'Do I mean it!' I exclaimed reproachfully, and drank another glass of champagne.

'Just about another week, and we shall be in South Africa,' sighed Mrs Blair.

'Ah, South Africa,' I said sentimentally, and began to quote from a recent speech of mine at the Colonial Institute. 'What has South Africa to show the world? What indeed? Her fruit and her farms, her wool and her wattles, her herds and her hides, her gold mines and her diamonds –'

I was hurrying on, because I knew that as soon as I paused Reeves would butt in and inform me that the hides were worthless because the animals hung themselves up on barbed wire or something of that sort, would crab everything else, and end up with the hardships of the miners on the Rand. And I was not in the mood to be abused as a Capitalist. However, the interruption came from another source at the magic word diamonds.

'Diamonds!' said Mrs Blair ecstatically.

'Diamonds!' breathed Miss Beddingfeld.

They both addressed Colonel Race.

'I suppose you've been to Kimberley?'

I had been to Kimberley too, but I didn't manage to say so in time. Race was being inundated with questions. What were mines like? Was it true that the natives were kept shut up in compounds? And so on.

Race answered their questions and showed a good knowledge of his subject. He described the methods of housing the natives, the searches instituted, and the various precautions that De Beers took.

'Then it's practically impossible to steal any diamonds?' asked Mrs Blair with as keen an air of disappointment as though she had been journeying there for the express purpose.

'Nothing's impossible, Mrs Blair. Thefts do occur – like the case I told you of where the Kafir hid the stone in his wound.'

'Yes, but on a large scale?'

'Once, in recent years. Just before the war, in fact. You must remember the case, Pedler. You were in South Africa at the time?'

I nodded.

'Tell us,' cried Miss Beddingfeld. 'Oh, do tell us!'

Race smiled.

'Very well, you shall have the story. I suppose most of you have heard of Sir Laurence Eardsley, the great South African mining magnate? His mines were gold mines, but he comes into the story through his son. You may remember that just before the war rumours were afield of a new potential Kimberley hidden somewhere in the rocky floor of the British Guiana jungles. Two young explorers, so it was reported, had returned from that part of South America bringing with them a remarkable collection of rough diamonds, some of them of considerable size. Diamonds of small size had been found before in the neighbourhood of the Essequibo and Mazaruni rivers, but these two young men, John Eardsley and his friend Lucas, claimed to have discovered beds of great carbon deposits at the common head of two streams. The diamonds were of every colour, pink, blue, yellow, green, black, and the purest white. Eardsley and Lucas came to Kimberley, where they were to submit their gems to inspection. At the same time a sensational robbery was found to have taken place at De Beers. When sending diamonds to England they are made up into a packet. This remains in the big safe, of which the two keys are held by two different men whilst a third man knows the combination. They are handed to the Bank, and the Bank send them to England. Each package is worth, roughly, about £100,000.

'On this occasion the Bank were struck by something a little unusual about the sealing of the packet. It was opened, and found to contain knobs of sugar!

'Exactly how suspicion came to fasten on John Eardsley I do not know. It was remembered that he had been very wild at Cambridge and that his father had paid his debts more than once. Anyhow, it soon got about that this story of South American diamond fields was all a fantasy. John Eardsley was arrested. In his possession was found a portion of the De Beers diamonds.

'But the case never came to court. Sir Laurence Eardsley paid over a sum equal to the missing diamonds, and De Beers did not prosecute. Exactly how the robbery was committed has never been known. But the knowledge that his son was a thief broke the old man's heart. He had a stroke shortly afterwards. As for John, his Fate was in a way merciful. He enlisted, went to the war, fought there bravely, and was killed, thus wiping out the stain on his name. Sir Laurence himself had a third stroke and died about a month ago. He died intestate and his vast fortune passed to his next of kin, a man whom he hardly knew.'

The Colonel paused. A babel of ejaculations and questions broke out. Something seemed to attract Miss Beddingfeld's attention, and she turned in her chair. At the little gasp she gave, I, too, turned.

My new secretary, Rayburn, was standing in the doorway. Under his tan, his face had the pallor of one who has seen a ghost. Evidently Race's story had moved him profoundly.

Suddenly conscious of our scrutiny, he turned abruptly and disappeared.

'Do you know who that is?' asked Anne Beddingfeld abruptly.

'That's my other secretary,' I explained. 'Mr Rayburn. He's been seedy up to now.'

She toyed with the bread by her plate.

'Has he been your secretary long?'

'Not very long,' I said cautiously.

But caution is useless with a woman, the more you hold back, the more she presses forward. Anne Beddingfeld made no bones about it.

'How long?' she asked bluntly.

'Well – er – I engaged him just before I sailed. Old friend of mine recommended him.'

She said nothing more, but relapsed into a thoughtful silence. I turned to Race with the feeling that it was my turn to display an interest in his story.

'Who is Sir Laurence's next of kin, Race? Do you know?'

'I should do so,' he replied, with a smile. 'I am!'

CHAPTER 14

(ANNE'S NARRATIVE RESUMED)

It was on the night of the Fancy Dress dance that I decided that the time had come for me to confide in someone. So far I had played a lone hand and rather enjoyed it. Now suddenly everything was changed. I distrusted my own judgment and for the first time a feeling of loneliness and desolation crept over me.

I sat on the edge of my bunk, still in my gipsy dress, and considered the situation. I thought first of Colonel Race. He had seemed to like me. He would be kind, I was sure. And he was no fool. Yet, as I thought it over, I wavered. He was a man of commanding personality. He would take the whole matter out of my hands. And it was *my* mystery! There were other reasons, too, which I would hardly acknowledge to myself, but which made it inadvisable to confide in Colonel Race.

Then I thought of Mrs Blair. She, too, had been kind to me. I did not delude myself into the belief that that really meant anything. It was probably a mere whim of the moment. All the same, I had it in my power to interest her. She was a woman who had experienced most of the ordinary sensations in life. I proposed to supply her with an extraordinary one! And I liked her; liked her ease of manner, her lack of sentimentality, her freedom from any form of affectation.

My mind was made up. I decided to seek her out then and there. She would hardly be in bed yet.

Then I remembered that I did not know the number of her cabin. My friend, the night stewardess, would probably know.

I rang the bell. After some delay it was answered by a man. He gave me the information I wanted. Mrs Blair's cabin was No. 71. He apologized for the delay in answering the bell, but explained that he had all the cabins to attend to.

'Where is the stewardess, then?' I asked.

'They all go off duty at ten o'clock.'

'No – I mean the night stewardess.'

'No stewardess on at night, miss.'

'But – but a stewardess came the other night – about one o'clock.'

'You must have been dreaming, miss. There's no stewardess on duty after ten.'

He withdrew and I was left to digest this morsel of information. Who was the woman who had come to my cabin on the night of the 22nd? My face grew graver as I realized the cunning and audacity of my unknown antagonists. Then, pulling myself together, I left my own cabin and sought that of Mrs Blair. I knocked at the door.

'Who's that?' called her voice from within.

'Its me – Anne Beddingfeld.'

'Oh, come in, gipsy girl.'

I entered. A good deal of scattered clothing lay about, and Mrs Blair herself was draped in one of the loveliest kimonos I had ever seen. It was all orange and gold and black and made my mouth water to look at it.

'Mrs Blair,' I said abruptly, 'I want to tell you the story of my life – that is, if it isn't too late, and you won't be bored.'

'Not a bit. I always hate going to bed,' said Mrs Blair, her face crinkling into smiles in the delightful way it had. 'And I should love to hear the story of your life. You're a most unusual creature, gipsy girl. Nobody else would think of bursting in on me at 1 a.m. to tell me the story of their life. Especially after snubbing my natural curiosity for weeks as you have done! I'm not accustomed to being snubbed. It's been quite a pleasing novelty. Sit down on the sofa and unburden your soul.'

I told her the whole story. It took some time as I was conscientious over all the details. She gave a deep sigh when I had finished, but she did not say at all what I had expected her to say. Instead she looked at me, laughed a little and said:

'Do you know, Anne, you're a very unusual girl? Haven't you ever had qualms?'

'Qualms?' I asked, puzzled.

'Yes, qualms, qualms, qualms! Starting off alone with practically no money. What will you do when you find yourself in a strange country with all your money gone?'

'It's no good bothering about that until it comes. I've got plenty of money still. The twenty-five pounds that Mrs Flemming gave me is practically intact, and then I won the sweep yesterday. That's another fifteen pounds. Why, I've got *lots* of money. Forty pounds!'

'Lots of money! My God!' murmured Mrs Blair. 'I couldn't do it, Anne, and I've plenty of pluck in my own way. I couldn't start off gaily with a few pounds in my pocket and no idea as to what I was doing and where I was going.'

'But that's the fun of it,' I cried, thoroughly roused. 'It gives one such a splendid feeling of adventure.'

She looked at me, nodded once or twice, and then smiled.

'Lucky Anne! There aren't many people in the world who feel as you do.'

'Well,' I said impatiently, 'what do you think of it all, Mrs Blair?'

'I think it's the most thrilling thing I ever heard! Now, to begin with, you will stop calling me Mrs Blair. Suzanne will be ever so much better. Is that agreed?'

'I should love it, Suzanne.'

'Good girl. Now let's get down to business. You say that in Sir Eustace's secretary – not that long-faced Pagett, the other one – you recognized the man who was stabbed and came into your cabin for shelter?'

I nodded.

'That gives us two links connecting Sir Eustace with the tangle. The woman was murdered in *his* house, and it's *his* secretary who gets stabbed at the mystic hour of one o'clock. I don't suspect Sir Eustace himself, but it can't be all coincidence. There's a connection somewhere even if he himself is unaware of it.

'Then there's the queer business of the stewardess,' she continued thoughtfully. 'What was she like?'

'I hardly noticed her. I was so excited and strung up – and a stewardess seemed such an anticlimax. But – yes – I did think her face was familiar. Of course it would be if I'd seen her about the ship.'

'Her face seemed familiar to you,' said Suzanne. 'Sure she wasn't a man?'

'She was very tall,' I admitted.

'Hum. Hardly Sir Eustace, I should think, nor Mr Pagett – Wait!'

She caught up a scrap of paper and began drawing feverishly. She inspected the result with her head poised on one side.

'A very good likeness of the Rev. Edward Chichester. Now for the etceteras.' She passed the paper over to me. 'Is that your stewardess?'

'Why, yes,' I cried. 'Suzanne, how clever of you!'

She disdained the compliment with a light gesture.

'I've always had suspicions about that Chichester creature. Do you remember how he dropped his coffee-cup and turned a sickly green when we were discussing Crippen the other day?'

'And he tried to get Cabin 17!'

'Yes, it all fits in so far. But what does it all *mean*? What was really meant to happen at one o'clock in Cabin 17? It can't be the stabbing of the secretary. There would be no point in timing that for a special hour on a special day in a special place. No, it must have been some kind of appointment and he was on his way to keep it when they knifed him. But who was the appointment with? Certainly not with you. It might have been with Chichester. Or it might have been with Pagett.'

'That seems unlikely,' I objected; 'they can see each other any time.'

We both sat silent for a minute or two, then Suzanne started off on another tack.

'Could there have been anything hidden in the cabin?'

'That seems more probable,' I agreed. 'It would explain my things being ransacked the next morning. But there was nothing hidden there, I'm sure of it.'

'The young man couldn't have slipped something into a drawer the night before?'

I shook my head.

'I should have seen him.'

'Could it have been your precious bit of paper they were looking for?'

'It might have been, but it seems rather senseless. It was only a time and a date – and they were both past by then.'

Suzanne nodded.

'That's so, of course. No, it wasn't the paper. By the way, have you got it with you? I'd rather like to see it.'

I had brought the paper with me as Exhibit A, and I handed it over to her. She scrutinized it, frowning.

'There's a dot after the 17. Why isn't there a dot after the 1 too?'

'There's a space,' I pointed out.

'Yes, there's a space, but –'

Suddenly she rose and peered at the paper, holding it as close under the light as possible. There was a repressed excitement in her manner.

'Anne, that isn't a dot! That's a flaw in the paper! A flaw in the paper, you see? So you've got to ignore it, and just go by the spaces – the spaces!'

I had risen and was standing by her. I read out the figures as I now saw them.

'1 71 22.'

'You see,' said Suzanne. 'It's the same, but not quite. It's one o'clock still, and the 22nd – but it's Cabin 71! *My* cabin, Anne!'

We stood staring at each other, so pleased with our new discovery and so rapt with excitement that you might have thought we had solved the whole mystery. Then I fell to earth with a bump.

'But, Suzanne, nothing happened here at one o'clock on the 22nd?'

Her face fell also.

'No – it didn't.'

Another idea struck me.

'This isn't your own cabin, is it, Suzanne? I mean not the one you originally booked?'

'No, the purser changed me into it.'

'I wonder if it was booked before sailing for someone – someone who didn't turn up. I suppose we could find out.'

'We don't need to find out, gipsy girl,' cried Suzanne. 'I know! The purser was telling me about it. The cabin was booked in the name of Mrs Grey – but it seems that Mrs Grey was merely a pseudonym for the famous Madame Nadina. She's a celebrated Russian dancer, you know. She's never appeared in London, but Paris has been quite mad about her. She had a terrific success there all through the war. A thoroughly bad lot, I believe, but most attractive. The purser expressed his regrets that she wasn't on board in a most heartfelt fashion when he gave me her cabin, and then Colonel Race told me a lot about her. It seems there were very queer stories afloat in Paris. She was suspected of espionage, but they couldn't prove anything. I rather fancy Colonel Race was over there simply on that account. He's told me some very interesting things. There was a regular organized gang, not German in origin at all. In fact the head of it, a man always referred to as "the Colonel", was thought to be an Englishman, but they never got any clue to his identity. But there is no doubt that he controlled a considerable organization of international crooks. Robberies, espionage, assaults, he undertook them all – and usually provided an innocent scapegoat to pay the penalty. Diabolically clever, he must have been! This woman was supposed to be one of his agents, but they couldn't get hold of anything to go upon. Yes, Anne, we're on the right tack. Nadina is just the woman to be mixed up in this business. The appointment on the morning of the 22nd was with her in this cabin. But where is she? Why didn't she sail?'

A light flashed upon me.

'She meant to sail,' I said slowly.

'Then why didn't she?'

'*Because she was dead.* Suzanne, Nadina was the woman murdered at Marlow!'

My mind went back to the bare room in the empty house and there swept over me again the indefinable sensation of menace and evil. With it came the memory of the falling pencil and the discovery of the roll of films. A roll of films – that struck a more recent note. Where had I heard of a roll of films? And why did I connect that thought with Mrs Blair?

Suddenly I flew at her and almost shook her in my excitement.

'Your films! The ones that were passed to you through the ventilator? Wasn't that on the 22nd?'

'The ones I lost?'

'How do you know they were the same? Why would anyone

return them to you that way – in the middle of the night? It's a mad idea. No – they were a message, the films had been taken out of the yellow tin case, and something else put inside. Have you still got it?'

'I may have used it. No, here it is. I remember I tossed it into the rack at the side of the bunk.'

She held it out to me.

It was an ordinary round tin cylinder, such as films are packed in for the tropics. I took it with trembling hand, but even as I did so my heart leapt. It was noticeably heavier than it should have been.

With shaking fingers I peeled off the strip of adhesive plaster that kept it air-tight. I pulled off the lid, and a stream of dull glassy pebbles rolled on to the bed.

'Pebbles,' I said, keenly disappointed.

'Pebbles?' cried Suzanne.

The ring in her voice excited me.

'Pebbles? No, Anne, not pebbles! *Diamonds!*'

CHAPTER 15

Diamonds!

I stared, fascinated, at the glassy heap on the bunk. I picked up one which, but for the weight, might have been a fragment of broken bottle.

'Are you sure, Suzanne?'

'Oh, yes, my dear. I've seen rough diamonds too often to have any doubts. They're beauties too, Anne – and some of them are unique, I should say. There's a history behind these.'

'The history we heard tonight,' I cried.

'You mean –'

'Colonel Race's story. It can't be a coincidence. He told it for a purpose.'

'To see its effect, you mean?'

I nodded.

'Its effect on Sir Eustace?'

'Yes.'

But, even as I said it, a doubt assailed me. *Was* it Sir Eustace who had been subjected to a test, or had the story been told for *my* benefit? I remembered the impression I had received on that former night of having been deliberately 'pumped'. For some reason or other, Colonel Race was suspicious. But where did he come in? What possible connexion could he have with the affair?

'Who *is* Colonel Race?' I asked.

'That's rather a question,' said Suzanne. 'He's pretty well known as a big-game hunter, and, as you heard him say tonight, he was a distant cousin of Sir Laurence Eardsley. I've never actually met him until this trip. He journeys to and from Africa a good deal. There's a general idea that he does Secret Service work. I don't know whether it's true or not. He's certainly rather a mysterious creature.'

'I suppose he came into a lot of money as Sir Laurence Eardsley's heir?'

'My dear Anne, he must be *rolling*. You know, he'd be a splendid match for you.'

'I can't have a good go at him with you aboard the ship,' I said, laughing. 'Oh, these married women!'

'We do have a pull,' murmured Suzanne complacently. 'And everybody knows that I am absolutely devoted to Clarence – my husband, you know. It's so safe and pleasant to make love to a devoted wife.'

'It must be very nice for Clarence to be married to someone like you.'

'Well, I'm wearing to live with! Still, he can always escape to the Foreign Office, where he fixes his eyeglass in his eye, and goes to sleep in a big arm-chair. We might cable him to tell us all he knows about Race. I love sending cables. And they annoy Clarence so. He always says a letter would have done as well. I don't suppose he'd tell us anything though. He is so frightfully discreet. That's what makes him so hard to live with for long on end. But let us go on with our matchmaking. I'm sure Colonel Race is very attracted to you, Anne. Give him a couple of glances from those wicked eyes of yours, and the deed is done. Everyone gets engaged on board ship. There's nothing else to do.'

'I don't want to get married.'

'Don't you?' said Suzanne. 'Why not? I love being married – even to Clarence!'

I disdained her flippancy.

'What I want to know is,' I said with determination, 'what has Colonel Race got to do with this? He's in it somewhere.'

'You don't think it was mere chance, his telling that story?'

'No, I don't,' I said decidedly. 'He was watching us all narrowly. You remember, *some* of the diamonds were recovered, not all. Perhaps these are the missing ones – or perhaps –'

'Perhaps what?'

I did not answer directly.

'I should like to know,' I said, 'what became of the other young man. Not Eardsley but – what was his name? – Lucas!'

'We're getting some light on the thing, anyway. It's the diamonds all these people are after. It must have been to obtain possession of the diamonds that "The Man in the Brown Suit" killed Nadina.'

'He didn't kill her,' I said sharply.

'Of course he killed her. Who else could have done so?'

'I don't know. But I'm sure he didn't kill her.'

'He went into the house three minutes after her and came out as white as a sheet.'

'Because he found her dead.'

'But nobody else went in.'

'Then the murderer was in the house already, or else he got in some other way. There's no need for him to pass the lodge, he could have climbed over the wall.'

Suzanne glanced at me sharply.

'"The Man in the Brown Suit",' she mused. 'Who was he, I wonder? Anyway, he was identical with the "doctor" in the Tube. He would have had time to remove his make-up and follow the woman to Marlow. She and Carton were to have met there, they both had an order to view the same house, and if they took such elaborate precautions to make their meeting appear accidental they must have suspected they were being followed. All the same, Carton did *not* know that his shadower was "The Man in the Brown Suit". When he recognized him, the shock was so great that he lost his head completely and stepped back on to the line. That all seems pretty clear, don't you think so, Anne?'

I did not reply.

'Yes, that's how it was. He took the paper from the dead man, and in his hurry to get away he dropped it. Then he followed the woman to Marlow. What did he do when he left there, when he had killed her – or, according to you, found her dead? Where did he go?'

Still I said nothing.

'I wonder, now,' said Suzanne musingly. 'Is it possible that he induced Sir Eustace Pedler to bring him on board as his secretary? It would be a unique chance of getting safely out of England, and dodging the hue and cry. But how did he square Sir Eustace? It looks as though he had some hold over him.'

'Or over Pagett,' I suggested in spite of myself.

'You don't seem to like Pagett, Anne. Sir Eustace says he's a most capable and hard-working young man. And, really, he may be for all we know against him. Well, to continue my surmises, Rayburn is "The Man in the Brown Suit". He had read the paper he dropped. Therefore, misled by the dot as you were, he attempts to reach Cabin 17 at one o'clock on the 22nd, having previously tried to get possession of the cabin through Pagett. On the way there somebody knifes him –'

'Who?' I interpolated.

'Chichester. Yes, it all fits in. Cable to Lord Nasby that you have found "The Man in the Brown Suit", and your fortune's made, Anne!'

'There are several things you've overlooked.'

'What things? Rayburn's got a scar, I know – but a scar can be faked easily enough. He's the right height and build. What's the description of a head with which you pulverized them at Scotland Yard?'

I trembled. Suzanne was a well-educated, well-read woman, but I prayed that she might not be conversant with technical terms of anthropology.

'Dolichocephalic,' I said lightly.

Susanne looked doubtful.

'Was that it?'

'Yes. Long-headed, you know. A head whose width is less than 75 per cent of its length,' I explained fluently.

There was a pause. I was just beginning to breathe freely when Suzanne said suddenly:

'What's the opposite?'

'What do you mean – the opposite?'

'Well, there must be an opposite. What do you call heads whose breadth is more than 75 per cent of their length?'

'Brachycephalic,' I murmured unwillingly.

'That's it. I thought that was what you said.'

'Did I? It was a slip of the tongue. I meant dolichocephalic,' I said with all the assurance I could muster.

Suzanne looked at me searchingly. Then she laughed.

'You lie very well, gipsy girl. But it will save time and trouble now if you tell me all about it.'

'There is nothing to tell,' I said unwillingly.

'Isn't there?' said Suzanne gently.

'I suppose I shall have to tell you,' I said slowly. 'I'm not ashamed of it. You can't be ashamed of something that just – happens to you. That's what he did. He was detestable – rude and ungrateful – but that I think I understand. It's like a dog that's been chained up – or badly treated – it'll bite anybody. That's what he was like – bitter and snarling. I don't know why I care – but I do. I care horribly. Just seeing him has turned my whole life upside-down. I love him. I want him. I'll walk all over Africa barefoot till I find him, and I'll make him care for me. I'd die for him. I'd work for him, slave for him, steal for him, even beg or borrow for him! There – now you know!'

Suzanne looked at me for a long time.

'You're very un-English, gipsy girl,' she said at last. 'There's not a scrap of the sentimental about you. I've never met anyone who was at once so practical and so passionate. I shall never care for anyone like that – mercifully for me – and yet – and yet I envy you, gipsy girl. It's something to be able to care. Most people can't. But what a mercy for your little doctor man that you didn't marry him. He doesn't sound at all the sort of individual who would enjoy keeping high explosive in the house! So there's to be no cabling to Lord Nasby?'

I shook my head.

'And yet you believe him to be innocent?'

'I also believe that innocent people can be hanged.'

'H'm! yes. But, Anne dear, you can face facts, face them now. In spite of all you say, he may have murdered this woman.'

'No,' I said. 'He didn't.'

'That's sentiment.'

'No, it isn't. He might have killed her. He may even have followed her there with that idea in mind. But he wouldn't take a bit of black cord and strangle her with it. If he'd done it, he would have strangled her with his bare hands.'

Suzanne gave a little shiver. Her eyes narrowed appreciatively.

'H'm! Anne, I am beginning to see why you find this young man of yours so attractive!'

CHAPTER 16

I got an opportunity of tackling Colonel Race on the following morning. The auction of the sweep had just been concluded, and we walked up and down the deck together.

'How's the gipsy this morning? Longing for land and her caravan?'

I shook my head.

'Now that the sea is behaving so nicely, I feel I should like to stay on it for ever and ever.'

'What enthusiasm!'

'Well, isn't it lovely this morning?'

We leant together over the rail. It was a glassy calm. The sea looked as though it had been oiled. There were great patches of colour on it, blue, pale green, emerald, purple and deep orange, like a cubist picture. There was an occasional flash of silver that showed the flying fish. The air was moist and warm, almost sticky. Its breath was like a perfumed caress.

'That was a very interesting story you told us last night,' I said, breaking the silence.

'Which one?'

'The one about the diamonds.'

'I believe women are always interested in diamonds.'

'Of course we are. By the way, what became of the other young man? You said there were two of them.'

'Young Lucas? Well, of course, they couldn't prosecute one without the other, so he went scot-free too.'

'And what happened to him? – eventually, I mean. Does anyone know?'

Colonel Race was looking straight ahead of him out to sea. His face was as devoid of expression as a mask, but I had an idea that he did not like my questions. Nevertheless, he replied readily enough.

'He went to the war and acquitted himself bravely. He was reported missing and wounded – believed killed.'

That told me what I wanted to know. I asked no more. But more than ever I wondered how much Colonel Race knew. The part he was playing in all this puzzled me.

One other thing I did. That was to interview the night steward. With a little financial encouragement, I soon got him to talk.

'The lady wasn't frightened, was she, miss? It seemed a harmless sort of joke. A bet, or so I understood.'

I got it all out of him, little by little. On the voyage from Cape Town to England one of the passengers had handed him a roll of film with instructions that they were to be dropped on to the bunk in Cabin 71 at 1 a.m. on January 22nd on the outward journey. A lady would be occupying the cabin, and the affair was described as a bet. I gathered the steward had been liberally paid for his part in the transaction. The lady's name had not been mentioned. Of course, as Mrs Blair went straight into Cabin 71, interviewing the purser as soon as she got on board, it never occurred to the steward that she was not the lady in question. The name of the passenger who had arranged the transaction was Carton, and his description tallied exactly with that of the man killed on the Tube.

So one mystery, at all events, was cleared up, and the diamonds were obviously the key to the whole situation.

Those last days on the *Kilmorden* seemed to pass very quickly. As we drew nearer and nearer to Cape Town, I was forced to consider carefully my future plans. There were so many people I wanted to keep an eye on. Mr Chichester, Sir Eustace and his secretary, and – yes, Colonel Race! What was I to do about it? Naturally it was Chichester who had first claim on my attention. Indeed, I was on the point of reluctantly dismissing Sir Eustace and Mr Pagett from their position of suspicious characters when a chance conversation awakened fresh doubts in my mind.

I had forgotten Mr Pagett's incomprehensible emotion at the mention of Florence. On the last evening on board we were all sitting on deck and Sir Eustace addressed a perfectly innocent question to his secretary. I forget exactly what it was, something to do with railway delays in Italy, but at once I noticed that Mr Pagett was displaying the same uneasiness which had caught my attention before. When Sir Eustace claimed Mrs Blair for a dance, I quickly moved into the chair next to the secretary. I was determined to get to the bottom of the matter.

'I have always longed to go to Italy,' I said. 'And especially to Florence. Didn't you enjoy it very much there?'

'Indeed I did, Miss Beddingfeld. If you will excuse me, there is some correspondence of Sir Eustace's that –'

I took hold of him firmly by his coat sleeve.

'Oh, you mustn't run away!' I cried with the skittish accent of an elderly dowager. 'I'm sure Sir Eustace wouldn't like you to leave me alone with no one to talk to. You never seem to want to talk about Florence. Oh, Mr Pagett, I believe you have a guilty secret!'

I still had my hand on his arm, and I could feel the sudden start he gave.

'Not at all, Miss Beddingfeld, not at all,' he said earnestly. 'I should be only too delighted to tell you all about it, but there really are some cables –'

'Oh, Mr Pagett, what a thin pretence! I shall tell Sir Eustace –'

I got no further. He gave another jump. The man's nerves seemed in a shocking state.

'What is it you want to know?'

The resigned martyrdom of his tone made me smile inwardly.

'Oh, everything! The pictures, the olive trees –'

I paused, rather at a loss myself.

'I suppose you speak Italian?' I resumed.

'Not a word, unfortunately. But of course, with hall porters and – er – guides.'

'Exactly,' I hastened to reply. 'And which was your favourite picture?'

'Oh, er – the Madonna – er, Raphael, you know.'

'Dear old Florence,' I murmured sentimentally. So picturesque on the banks of the Arno. A beautiful river. And the Duomo, you remember the Duomo?'

'Of course, of course.'

'Another beautiful river, is it not?' I hazarded. 'Almost more beautiful than the Arno?'

'Decidedly so, I should say.'

Emboldened by the success of my little trap, I proceeded further. But there was little room for doubt. Mr Pagett delivered himself into my hands with every word he uttered. The man had never been in Florence in his life.

But if not in Florence, where had he been? In England? Actually in England at the time of the Mill House Mystery? I decided on a bold step.

'The curious thing is,' I said, 'that I fancied I had seen you before somewhere. But I must be mistaken – since you were in Florence at the time. And yet –'

I studied him frankly. There was a hunted look in his eyes. He passed his tongue over dry lips.

'Where – er – where –'

'Did I think I had seen you?' I finished for him. 'At Marlow. You know Marlow? Why, of course, how stupid of me, Sir Eustace has a house there!'

But with an incoherent muttered excuse, my victim rose and fled.

That night I invaded Suzanne's cabin, alight with excitement.

'You see, Suzanne,' I urged, as I finished my tale, 'he was in England, in Marlow, at the time of the murder. Are you so sure now that "The Man in the Brown Suit" is guilty?'

'I'm sure of one thing,' Suzanne said, twinkling, unexpectedly.

'What's that?'

'That "The Man in the Brown Suit" is better-looking than poor Mr Pagett. No, Anne, don't get cross. I was only teasing. Sit down here. Joking apart, I think you've made a very important discovery. Up till now, we've considered Pagett as having an alibi. Now we know he hasn't.'

'Exactly,' I said. 'We must keep an eye on him.'

'As well as everybody else,' she said ruefully. 'Well, that's one of the things I wanted to talk to you about. That – and finance.

No, don't stick your nose in the air. I know you are absurdly proud and independent, but you've got to listen to horse sense over this. We're partners – I wouldn't offer you a penny because I liked you, or because you're a friendless girl – what I want is a thrill, and I'm prepared to pay for it. We're going into this together regardless of expense. To begin with you'll come with me to the Mount Nelson Hotel at my expense, and we'll plan out our campaign.'

We argued the point. In the end I gave in. But I didn't like it. I wanted to do the thing on my own.

'That's settled,' said Suzanne at last, getting up and stretching herself with a big yawn. 'I'm exhausted with my own eloquence. Now then, let us discuss our victims. Mr Chichester is going on to Durban. Sir Eustace is going to the Mount Nelson Hotel in Cape Town and then up to Rhodesia. He's going to have a private car on the railway, and in a moment of expansion, after his fourth glass of champagne the other night, he offered me a place in it. I dare say he didn't really mean it, but, all the same, he can't very well back out if I hold him to it.'

'Good,' I approved. 'You keep an eye on Sir Eustace and Mr Pagett, and I take on Chichester. But what about Colonel Race?'

Suzanne looked at me queerly.

'Anne, you can't possibly suspect –'

'I do. I suspect everybody. I'm in the mood when one looks round for the most unlikely person.'

'Colonel Race is going to Rhodesia too,' said Suzanne thoughtfully. 'If we could arrange for Sir Eustace to invite him also –'

'You can manage it. You can manage anything.'

'I love butter,' purred Suzanne.

We parted on the understanding that Suzanne should employ her talents to her best advantage.

I felt too excited to go to bed immediately. It was my last night on board. Early tomorrow morning we should be in Table Bay.

I slipped up on deck. The breeze was fresh and cool. The boat was rolling a little in the choppy sea. The decks were dark and deserted. It was after midnight.

I leaned over the rail, watching the phosphorescent trail of foam. Ahead of us lay Africa, we were rushing towards it through the dark water. I felt alone in a wonderful world. Wrapped in a strange peace, I stood there, taking no heed of time, lost in a dream.

And suddenly I had a curious intimate premonition of danger. I had heard nothing, but I swung round instinctively. A shadowy form had crept up behind me. As I turned, it sprang. One hand gripped my throat, stifling any cry I might have uttered. I fought desperately, but I had no chance. I was half choking from the grip on my throat, but I bit and clung and scratched in the most approved feminine fashion. The man was handicapped by having to keep me from crying out. If he had succeeded in reaching me unawares it would have been easy enough for him to sling me overboard with a sudden heave. The sharks would have taken care of the rest.

Struggle as I would, I felt myself weakening. My assailant felt it too. He put out all his strength. And then, running on swift noiseless feet, another shadow joined in. With one blow of his fist, he sent my opponent crashing headlong to the deck. Released, I fell back against the rail, sick and trembling.

My rescuer turned to me with a quick movement.

'You're hurt!'

There was something savage in his tone – a menace against the person who had dared to hurt me. Even before he spoke I had recognized him. It was my man – the man with the scar.

But that one moment in which his attention had been diverted to me had been enough for the fallen enemy. Quick as a flash he had risen to his feet and taken to his heels down the deck. With an oath Rayburn sprang after him.

I always hate being out of things. I joined the chase – a bad third. Round the deck we went to the starboard side of the ship. There by the saloon door lay the man in a crumpled heap. Rayburn was bending over him.

'Did you hit him again?' I called breathlessly.

'There was no need,' he replied grimly. 'I found him collapsed by the door. Or else he couldn't get it open and is shamming. We'll soon see about that. And we'll see who he is too.'

With a beating heart I drew nearer. I had realized at once that my assailant was a bigger man than Chichester. Anyway, Chichester was a flabby creature who might use a knife at a pinch, but who would have little strength in his bare hands.

Rayburn struck a match. We both uttered an ejaculation. The man was Guy Pagett.

Rayburn appeared absolutely stupefied by the discovery.

'Pagett,' he muttered. 'My God, Pagett.'

I felt a slight sense of superiority.

'You seem surprised.'

'I am,' he said heavily. 'I never suspected –' He wheeled suddenly round on me. 'And you? You're not? You recognized him, I suppose, when he attacked you?'

'No, I didn't. All the same, I'm not so very surprised.'

He stared at me suspiciously.

'Where do you come in, I wonder? And how much do you know?'

I smiled.

'A good deal, Mr – er – Lucas!'

He caught my arm, the unconscious strength of his grip made me wince.

'Where did you get that name?' he asked hoarsely.

'Isn't it yours?' I demanded sweetly. 'Or do you prefer to be called "The Man in the Brown Suit"?'

That did stagger him. He released my arm and fell back a pace or two.

'Are you a girl, or a witch?' he breathed.

'I'm a friend,' I advanced a step towards him. 'I offered you my help once – I offer it again. Will you have it?'

The fierceness of his answer took me aback.

'No. I'll have no truck with you or with any woman. Do your damnedest.'

As before, my own temper began to rise.

'Perhaps,' I said, 'you don't realize how much in my power you are? A word from me to the Captain –'

'Say it,' he sneered. Then advancing with a quick step: 'And whilst we're realizing things, my dear girl, do you realize you're in *my* power this minute? I could take you by the throat like this.' With a swift gesture he suited the action to the word. I felt his two hands clasp my throat and press – ever so little. 'Like this – and squeeze the life out of you! And then – like our unconscious friend here, but with more success – fling your dead body to the sharks. What do you say to that?'

I said nothing. I laughed. And yet I knew that the danger was real. Just at that moment he hated me. But I knew that I loved the danger, loved the feeling of his hands on my throat. That I would not have exchanged that moment for any moment in my life.

With a short laugh he released me.

'What's your name?' he asked abruptly.

'Anne Beddingfeld.'

'Does nothing frighten you, Anne Beddingfeld?'

'Oh, yes,' I said, with an assumption of coolness I was far from feeling. 'Wasps, sarcastic women, very young men, cockroaches, and superior shop assistants.'

He gave the same short laugh as before. Then he stirred the unconscious form of Pagett with his feet.

'What shall we do with this junk? Throw it overboard?' he asked carelessly.

'If you like,' I answered with equal calm.

'I admire your whole-hearted, bloodthirsty instincts, Miss Beddingfeld. But we will leave him to recover at his leisure. He is not seriously hurt.'

'You shrink from a second murder, I see,' I said sweetly.

'A second murder?'

He looked genuinely puzzled.

'The woman at Marlow,' I reminded him, watching the effect of my words closely.

An ugly brooding expression settled down on his face. He seemed to have forgotten my presence.

'I might have killed her,' he said. 'Sometimes I believe that I meant to kill her . . .'

A wild rush of feeling, hatred of the dead woman, surged through me. *I* could have killed her that moment, had she stood before me . . . For he must have loved her once – he must – he must – to have felt like that!

I regained control of myself and spoke in my normal voice:

'We seem to have said all there is to be said – except good night.'

'Good night and goodbye, Miss Beddingfeld.'

'Au revoir, Mr Lucas.'

Again he flinched at the name. He came nearer.

'Why do you say that – *au revoir*, I mean?'

'Because I have a fancy that we shall meet again.'

'Not if I can help it!'

Emphatic as his tone was, it did not offend me. On the contrary, I hugged myself with secret satisfaction. I am not quite a fool.

'All the same,' I said gravely, 'I think we shall.'

'Why?'

I shook my head, unable to explain the feeling that had actuated my words.

'I never wish to see you again,' he said suddenly, and violently.

It was really a very rude thing to say, but I only laughed softly and slipped away into the darkness.

I heard him start after me, and then pause, and a word floated down the deck. I think it was 'witch'!

CHAPTER 17

(EXTRACT FROM THE DIARY OF SIR EUSTACE PEDLER)

Mount Nelson Hotel, Cape Town.

It is really the greatest relief to get off the Kilmorden. *The whole time that I was on board I was conscious of being surrounded by a network of intrigue. To put the lid on everything, Guy Pagett must needs engage in a drunken brawl the last night. It is all very well to explain it away, but that is what it actually amounts to. What else would you think if a man comes to you with a lump the size of an egg on the side of his head and an eye coloured all the tints of the rainbow?*

Of course Pagett would insist on trying to be mysterious about the whole thing. According to him, you would think his black eye was the direct result of his devotion to my interests. His story was extraordinarily vague and rambling and it was a long time before I could make head or tail of it.

To begin with, it appears he caught sight of a man behaving suspiciously. Those are Pagett's words. He has taken them straight from the pages of a German spy story. What he means by a man behaving suspiciously he doesn't know himself. I said so to him.

'He was slinking along in a very furtive manner, and it was the middle of the night, Sir Eustace.'

'Well, what were you doing yourself? Why weren't you in bed and asleep like a good Christian?' I demanded irritably.

'I had been coding those cables of yours, Sir Eustace, and typing the diary up to date.'

Trust Pagett to be always in the right and a martyr over it!

'Well?'

'I just thought I would have a look round before turning in, Sir Eustace. The man was coming down the passage from your cabin. I thought at once there was something wrong by the way he looked about him. He slunk up the stairs by the saloon. I followed him.'

'My dear Pagett,' I said, 'why shouldn't the poor chap go on deck without having his footsteps dogged? Lots of people even sleep on deck – very uncomfortable, I've always thought. The sailors wash you down with the rest of the deck at five in the morning.' I shuddered at the idea.

'Anyway,' I continued, 'if you went worrying some poor devil who was suffering from insomnia, I don't wonder he landed you one.'

Pagett looked patient.

'If you would hear me out, Sir Eustace. I was convinced the man had been prowling about near your cabin where he had no business to be. The only two cabins down that passage are yours and Colonel Race's.'

'Race,' I said, lighting a cigar carefully, 'can look after himself without your assistance, Pagett.' I added as an afterthought: 'So can I.'

Pagett came nearer and breathed heavily as he always does before imparting a secret.

'You see, Sir Eustace, I fancied – and now indeed I am sure – it was Rayburn.'

'Rayburn?'

'Yes, Sir Eustace.'

I shook my head.

'Rayburn has far too much sense to attempt to wake me up in the middle of the night.'

'Quite so, Sir Eustace. I think it was Colonel Race he went to see. A secret meeting – for orders!'

'Don't hiss at me, Pagett,' I said, drawing back a little, 'and do control your breathing. Your idea is absurd. Why should they want to have a secret meeting in the middle of the night? If they'd anything

to say to each other, they could hob-nob over beef-tea in a perfectly casual and natural manner.'

I could see that Pagett was not in the least convinced.

'Something *was going on last night, Sir Eustace,' he urged, 'or why should Rayburn assault me so brutally?'*

'You're quite sure it was Rayburn?'

Pagett appeared to be perfectly convinced of that. It was the only part of the story that he wasn't vague about.

'There's something very queer about all this,' he said. 'To begin with, where is Rayburn?'

It's perfectly true that we haven't seen the fellow since we came on shore. He did not come up to the hotel with us. I decline to believe that he is afraid of Pagett, however.

Altogether the whole thing is very annoying. One of my secretaries has vanished into the blue, and the other looks like a disreputable prize-fighter. I can't take him about with me in his present condition. I shall be the laughing-stock of Cape Town. I have an appointment later in the day to deliver old Milray's billet-doux, *but I shall not take Pagett with me. Confound the fellow and his prowling ways.*

Although I am decidedly out of temper. I had a poisonous breakfast with poisonous people. Dutch waitresses with thick ankles who took half an hour to bring me a bad bit of fish. And this farce of getting up at 5 a.m. on arrival at the port to see a blinking doctor and hold your hands above your head simply makes me tired.

Later.

A very serious thing has occurred. I went to my appointment with the Prime Minister, taking Milray's sealed letter. It didn't look as though it had been tampered with, but inside was a blank sheet of paper!

Now, I suppose, I'm in the devil of a mess. Why I ever let that bleating old fool Milray embroil me in the matter I can't think.

Pagett is a famous Job's comforter. He displays a certain gloomy satisfaction that maddens me. Also, he had taken advantage of my perturbation to saddle me with the stationery trunk. Unless he is careful, the next funeral he attends will be his own.

However in the end I had to listen to him.

'Supposing, Sir Eustace, that Rayburn had overheard a word or two of your conversation with Mr Milray in the street? Remember,

you had no written authority from Mr Milray. You accepted Rayburn on his own valuation.'

'You think Rayburn is a crook, then?' I said slowly.

Pagett did. How far his views were influenced by resentment over his black eye I don't know. He made out a pretty fair case against Rayburn. And the appearance of the latter told against him. My idea was to do nothing in the matter. A man who has permitted himself to be made a thorough fool of is not anxious to broadcast the fact.

But Pagett, his energy unimpaired by his recent misfortunes, was all for vigorous measures. He had his way, of course. He bustled out to the police station, sent innumerable cables, and brought a herd of English and Dutch officials to drink whiskies and sodas at my expense.

We got Milray's answer that evening. He knew nothing of my late secretary! There was only one spot of comfort to be extracted from the situation.

'At any rate,' I said to Pagett, 'you weren't poisoned. You had one of your ordinary bilious attacks.'

I saw him wince. It was my only score.

Later.

Pagett is in his element. His brain positively scintillates with bright ideas. He will have it now that Rayburn is none other than the famous 'Man in the Brown Suit'. I dare say he is right. He usually is. But all this is getting unpleasant. The sooner I get off to Rhodesia the better. I have explained to Pagett that he is not to accompany me.

'You see, my dear fellow,' I said, 'you must remain here on the spot. You might be required to identify Rayburn any minute. And, besides, I have my dignity as an English Member of Parliament to think of. I can't go about with a secretary who has apparently recently been indulging in a vulgar street-brawl.'

Pagett winced. He is such a respectable fellow that his appearance is pain and tribulation to him.

'But what will you do about your correspondence, and the notes for your speeches, Sir Eustace?'

'I shall manage,' I said airily.

'Your private car is to be attached to the eleven-o'clock train tomorrow, Wednesday, morning,' Pagett continued. 'I have made all arrangements. Is Mrs Blair taking a maid with her?'

'Mrs Blair?' I gasped.

'She tells me you offered her a place.'

So I did, now I come to think of it. On the night of the Fancy Dress ball. I even urged her to come. But I never thought she would. Delightful as she is, I do not know that I want Mrs Blair's society all the way to Rhodesia and back. Women require such a lot of attention. And they are confoundedly in the way sometimes.

'Have I asked anyone else?' I said nervously. One does these things in moments of expansion.

'Mrs Blair seemed to think you had asked Colonel Race as well.'

I groaned.

'I must have been very drunk if I asked Race. Very drunk indeed. Take my advice, Pagett, and let your black eye be a warning to you, don't go on the bust again.'

'As you know, I am a teetotaller, Sir Eustace.'

'Much wiser to take the pledge if you have a weakness that way. I haven't asked anyone else, have I, Pagett?'

'Not that I know of, Sir Eustace.'

I heaved a sigh of relief.

'There's Miss Beddingfeld,' I said thoughtfully. 'She wants to get to Rhodesia to dig up bones, I believe. I've a good mind to offer her a temporary job as a secretary. She can typewrite, I know, for she told me so.'

To my surprise, Pagett opposed the idea vehemently. He does not like Anne Beddingfeld. Ever since the night of the black eye, he has displayed uncontrollable emotion whenever she is mentioned. Pagett is full of mysteries nowadays.

Just to annoy him, I shall ask the girl. As I said before, she has extremely nice legs.

CHAPTER 18

(ANNE'S NARRATIVE RESUMED)

I don't suppose that as long as I live I shall forget my first sight of Table Mountain. I got up frightfully early and went out on deck. I went right up to the boat deck, which I believe is a heinous offence, but I decided to dare something in the cause of solitude. We were just steaming into Table Bay. There were fleecy white clouds hovering above Table Mountain, and nestling on the slopes below, right down to the sea, was the sleeping town, gilded and bewitched by the morning sunlight.

It made me catch my breath and have that curious hungry pain inside that seizes one sometimes when one comes across something that's extra beautiful. I'm not very good at expressing these things, but I knew well enough that I had found, if only for a fleeting moment, the thing that I had been looking for ever since I left Little Hampsley. Something new, something hitherto undreamed of, something that satisfied my aching hunger for romance.

Perfectly silently, or so it seemed to me, the *Kilmorden* glided nearer and nearer. It was still very like a dream. Like all dreamers, however, I could not let my dream alone. We poor humans are so anxious not to miss anything.

'This is South Africa,' I kept saying to myself industriously. 'South Africa, South Africa. You are seeing the world. This is the world. You are seeing it. Think of it, Anne Beddingfeld, you pudding-head. You're seeing the world.'

I had thought that I had the boat deck to myself, but now I observed another figure leaning over the rail, absorbed as I had been in the rapidly approaching city. Even before he turned his head I knew who it was. The scene of last night seemed unreal and melodramatic in the peaceful morning sunshine. What must he have thought of me? It made me hot to realize the things that I had said. And I hadn't meant them – or had I?

I turned my head resolutely away, and stared hard at Table Mountain. If Rayburn had come up here to be alone, I, at least, need not disturb him by advertising my presence.

But to my intense surprise I heard a light footfall on the deck behind me, and then his voice, pleasant and normal:

'Miss Beddingfeld.'

'Yes?'

I turned.

'I want to apologize to you. I behaved like a perfect boor last night.'

'It – it was a peculiar night,' I said hastily.

It was not a very lucid remark, but it was absolutely the only thing I could think of.

'Will you forgive me?'

I held out my hand without a word. He took it.

'There's something else I want to say.' His gravity deepened. 'Miss Beddingfeld, you may not know it, but you are mixed up in a rather dangerous business.'

'I gather as much,' I said.

'No, you don't. You can't possibly know. I want to warn you. Leave the whole thing alone. It can't concern you really. Don't let your curiosity lead you to tamper with other people's business. No, please don't get angry again. I'm not speaking of myself. You've no idea of what you might come up against – these men will stop at nothing. They are absolutely ruthless. Already you're in danger – look at last night. They fancy you know something. Your only chance is to persuade them that they're mistaken. But be careful, always be on the lookout for danger, and, look here, if at any time you should fall into their hands, don't try and be clever – tell the whole truth; it will be your only chance.'

'You make my flesh creep, Mr Rayburn,' I said, with some truth. 'Why do you take the trouble to warn me?'

He did not answer for some minutes, then he said in a low voice:

'It may be the last thing I can do for you. Once on shore I shall be all right – but I may not get on shore.'

'What?' I cried.

'You see, I'm afraid you're not the only person on board who knows that I am "The Man in the Brown Suit".'

'If you think that I told –' I said hotly.

He reassured me with a smile.

'I don't doubt you, Miss Beddingfeld. If I ever said I did, I lied. No, but there's one person on board who's known all along. He's only to speak – and my number's up. All the same, I'm taking a sporting chance that he won't speak.'

'Why?'

'Because he's a man who likes playing a lone hand. And when the police have got me I should be of no further use to him. Free, I might be! Well, an hour will show.'

He laughed rather mockingly, but I saw his face harden. If he had gambled with Fate, he was a good gambler. He could lose and smile.

'In any case,' he said lightly, 'I don't suppose we shall meet again.'

'No,' I said slowly. 'I suppose not.'

'So – goodbye.'

'Goodbye.'

He gripped my hand hard, just for a minute his curious light eyes seemed to burn into mine, then he turned abruptly and left me. I heard his footsteps ringing along the deck. They echoed and re-echoed. I felt that I should hear them always. Footsteps – going out of my life.

I can admit frankly that I did not enjoy the next two hours. Not till I stood on the wharf, having finished with most of the ridiculous formalities that bureaucracies require, did I breathe freely once more. No arrest had been made, and I realized that it was a heavenly day, and that I was extremely hungry. I joined Suzanne. In any case, I was staying the night with her at the hotel. The boat did not go on to Port Elizabeth and Durban until the following morning. We got into a taxi and drove to the Mount Nelson.

It was all heavenly. The sun, the air, the flowers! When I thought of Little Hampsley in January, the mud knee-deep, and the sure-to-be-falling rain, I hugged myself with delight. Suzanne was not nearly so enthusiastic. She has travelled a great deal of course. Besides, she is not the type that gets excited before breakfast. She snubbed me severely when I let out an enthusiastic yelp at the sight of a giant blue convolvulus.

By the way, I should like to make clear here and now that this story will not be a story of South Africa. I guarantee no genuine local colour – you know the sort of thing – half a dozen words in italics on every page. I admire it very much, but I can't do it. In South Sea Islands, of course, you make an immediate reference to *bêche-de-mer*. I don't know what *bêche-de-mer* is, I have never known, I probably never shall know. I've guessed once or twice and guessed wrong. In South Africa I know you at once begin to talk about a *stoep* – I do know what a *stoep* is – it's the thing round a house and you sit on it. In various other parts of the world you call it a veranda, a piazza, and a ha-ha. Then again, there are pawpaws. I had often read of pawpaws. I discovered at once what they were, because I had one plumped down in front of me for breakfast. I thought at first that it was a melon gone bad. The Dutch waitress enlightened me, and persuaded me to use lemon juice and sugar and try again. I was very pleased to meet a pawpaw. I had always vaguely associated it with a *hula-hula*, which, I believe, though I may be wrong, is a kind of straw skirt that Hawaiian girls dance in. No, I think I am wrong – that is a *lava-lava*.

At any rate, all these things are very cheering after England. I can't help thinking that it would brighten our cold island life if one could have a breakfast of *bacon-bacon*, and then go out clad in a *jumper-jumper* to pay the books.

Suzanne was a little tamer after breakfast. They had given me a room next to hers with a lovely view right out over Table Bay. I looked at the view whilst Suzanne hunted for some special face-cream. When she had found it and started an immediate application, she became capable of listening to me.

'Did you see Sir Eustace?' I asked. 'He was marching out of the breakfast-room as we went in. He'd had some bad fish or something and was just telling the head waiter what he thought about it, and he bounced a peach on the floor to show how hard it was – only it wasn't quite as hard as he thought and it squashed.'

Suzanne smiled.

'Sir Eustace doesn't like getting up early any more than I do. But, Anne, did you see Mr Pagett? I ran against him in the passage. He's got a black eye. What can he have been doing?'

'Only trying to push me overboard,' I replied nonchalantly.

It was a distinct score for me. Suzanne left her face half anointed and pressed for details. I gave them to her.

'It all gets more and more mysterious,' she cried. 'I thought I was going to have the soft job sticking to Sir Eustace, and that you would have all the fun with the Rev. Edward Chichester, but now I'm not so sure. I hope Pagett won't push me off the train some dark night.'

'I think you're still above suspicion, Suzanne. But, if the worst happens I'll wire to Clarence.'

'That reminds me – give me a cable form. Let me see now,

what shall I say? "Implicated in the most thrilling mystery please send me a thousand pounds at once Suzanne."'

I took the form from her, and pointed out that she could eliminate a 'the', an 'a', and possibly, if she didn't care about being polite, a 'please'. Suzanne, however, appears to be perfectly reckless in money matters. Instead of attending to my economical suggestions, she added three more words: 'enjoying myself hugely'.

Suzanne was engaged to lunch with friends of hers, who came to the hotel about eleven o'clock to fetch her. I was left to my own devices. I went down through the grounds of the hotel, crossed the tram-lines and followed a cool shady avenue right down till I came to the main street. I strolled about, seeing the sights, enjoying the sunlight and the black-faced sellers of flowers and fruits. I also discovered a place where they had the most delicious ice-cream sodas. Finally, I bought a sixpenny basket of peaches and retraced my steps to the hotel.

To my surprise and pleasure I found a note awaiting me. It was from the curator of the Museum. He had read of my arrival on the *Kilmorden*, in which I was described as the daughter of the late Professor Beddingfeld. He had known my father slightly and had had great admiration for him. He went on to say that his wife would be delighted if I would come out and have tea with them that afternoon at their villa at Muizenberg. He gave me instructions for getting there.

It was pleasant to think that poor Papa was still remembered and highly thought of. I foresaw that I would have to be personally escorted round the Museum before I left Cape Town, but I risked that. To most people it would have been a treat – but one can have too much of a good thing if one is brought up on it, morning, noon, and night.

I put on my best hat (one of Suzanne's cast-offs) and my least crumpled white linen and started off after lunch. I caught a fast train to Muizenberg and got there in about half an hour. It was a nice trip. We wound slowly round the base of Table Mountain, and some of the flowers were lovely. My geography being weak, I had never fully realized that Cape Town is on a peninsula, consequently I was rather surprised on getting out of the train to find myself facing the sea once more. There was some perfectly entrancing bathing going on. The people had short curved boards and came floating in on the waves. It was far too early to go to tea. I made for the bathing pavilion, and when they said would I have a surf board, I said 'Yes, please.' Surfing looks perfectly easy. *It isn't.* I say no more. I got very angry and fairly hurled my plank from me. Nevertheless, I determined to return on the first possible opportunity and have another go. I would not be beaten. Quite by mistake I then got a good run on my board, and came out delirious with happiness. Surfing is like that. You are either vigorously cursing or else you are idiotically pleased with yourself.

I found the Villa Medgee after some difficulty. It was right up on the side of the mountain, isolated from the other cottages and villas. I rang the bell, and a smiling Kafir boy answered it.

'Mrs Raffini?' I inquired.

He ushered me in, preceded me down the passage and flung open a door. Just as I was about to pass in, I hesitated. I felt a sudden misgiving. I stepped over the threshold and the door swung sharply behind me.

A man rose from his seat behind a table and came forward with outstretched hand.

'So glad we have persuaded you to visit us, Miss Beddingfeld,' he said.

He was a tall man, obviously a Dutchman, with a flaming orange beard. He did not look in the least like the curator of a museum. In fact, I realized in a flash that I had made a fool of myself.

I was in the hands of the enemy.

CHAPTER 19

It reminded me forcibly of Episode III in *The Perils of Pamela.* How often had I not sat in the sixpenny seats, eating a twopenny bar of milk chocolate, and yearning for similar things to happen to me! Well, they had happened with a vengeance. And somehow it was not nearly so amusing as I had imagined. It's all very well on the screen – you have the comfortable knowledge that there's bound to be an Episode IV. But in real life there was absolutely no guarantee that Anna the Adventuress might not terminate abruptly at the end of any Episode.

Yes, I was in a tight place. All the things that Rayburn had said that morning came back to me with unpleasant distinctness. Tell the truth, he had said. Well, I could always do that, but was it going to help me? To begin with, would my story be believed? Would they consider it likely or possible that I had started off on this mad escapade simply on the strength of a scrap of paper smelling of moth-balls? It sounded to me a wildly incredible tale. In that moment of cold sanity I cursed myself for a melodramatic idiot, and yearned for the peaceful boredom of Little Hampsley.

All this passed through my mind in less time than it takes to tell. My first instinctive movement was to step backwards and feel for the handle of the door. My captor merely grinned.

'Here you are and here you stay,' he remarked facetiously.

I did my best to put a bold face upon the matter.

'I was invited to come here by the curator of the Cape Town Museum. If I have made a mistake –'

'A mistake? Oh, yes, a big mistake!'

He laughed coarsely.

'What right have you to detain me? I shall inform the police –'

'Yap, yap, yap – like a little toy dog.' He laughed.

I sat down on a chair.

'I can only conclude that you are a dangerous lunatic,' I said coldly.

'Indeed?'

'I should like to point out to you that my friends are perfectly well aware where I have gone, and that if I have not returned by this evening, they will come in search of me. You understand?'

'So your friends know where you are, do they? Which of them?'

Thus challenged, I did a lightning calculation of chances. Should I mention Sir Eustace? He was a well-known man, and his name might carry weight. But if they were in touch with Pagett, they might know I was lying. Better not risk Sir Eustace.

'Mrs Blair, for one,' I said lightly. 'A friend of mine with whom I am staying.'

'I think not,' said my captor, slyly shaking his orange head. 'You have not seen her since eleven this morning. And you received our note, bidding you to come here, at lunch-time.'

His words showed me how closely my movements had been followed, but I was not going to give in without a fight.

'You are very clever,' I said. 'Perhaps you have heard of that useful invention, the telephone? Mrs Blair called me up on it when I was resting in my room after lunch. I told her then where I was going this afternoon.'

To my great satisfaction, I saw a shade of uneasiness pass over his face. Clearly he had overlooked the possibility that Suzanne might have telephoned me. I wished she really had done so!

'Enough of this,' he said harshly, rising.

'What are you going to do with me?' I asked, still endeavouring to appear composed.

'Put you where you can do no harm in case your friends come after you.'

For a moment my blood ran cold, but his next words reassured me.

'Tomorrow you'll have some questions to answer, and after you've answered them we shall know what to do with you. And I can tell you, young lady, we've more ways than one of making obstinate little fools talk.'

It was not cheering, but it was at least a respite. I had until tomorrow. This man was clearly an underling obeying the orders of a superior. Could that superior by any chance be Pagett?

He called and two Kafirs appeared. I was taken upstairs. Despite my struggles, I was gagged and then bound hand and foot. The room into which they had taken me was a kind of attic right under the roof. It was dusty and showed little signs of having been occupied. The Dutchman made a mock bow and withdrew, closing the door behind him.

I was quite helpless. Turn and twist as I would, I could not loosen my bonds in the slightest degree, and the gag prevented me from crying out. If, by any possible chance, anyone did come to the house, I could do nothing to attract their attention. Down below I heard the sound of a door shutting. Evidently the Dutchman was going out.

It was maddening not to be able to do anything. I strained again at my bonds, but the knots held. I desisted at last, and either fainted or fell asleep. When I awoke I was in pain all over. It was quite dark now, and I judged that the night must be well advanced, for the moon was high in the heavens and shining down through the dusty skylight. The gag was half choking me and the stiffness and pain were unendurable.

It was then that my eyes fell on a bit of broken glass lying in the corner. A moonbeam slanted right down on it, and its glistening had caught my attention. As I looked at it, an idea came into my head.

My arms and legs were helpless, but surely I could still *roll.* Slowly and awkwardly, I set myself in motion. It was not easy. Besides being extremely painful, since I could not guard my face with my arms, it was also exceedingly difficult to keep any particular direction.

I tended to roll in every direction except the one I wanted to go. In the end, however, I came right up against my objective. It almost touched my bound hands.

Even then it was not easy. It took an infinity of time before I could wriggle the glass into such a position, wedged against the wall, that it would rub up and down on my bonds. It was a long heart-rending process, and I almost despaired, but in the end I succeeded in sawing through the cords that bound my wrists. The rest was a matter of time. Once I had restored the circulation to my hands by rubbing the wrists vigorously, I was able to undo the gag. One or two full breaths did a lot for me.

Very soon I had undone the last knot, though even then it was some time before I could stand on my feet, but at last I stood erect, swinging my arms to and fro to restore the circulation, and wishing above all things that I could get hold of something to eat.

I waited about a quarter of an hour, to be quite sure of my recovered strength. Then I tiptoed noiselessly to the door. As I had hoped, it was not locked, only latched. I unlatched it and peeped cautiously out.

Everything was still. The moonlight came in through a window and showed me the dusty uncarpeted staircase. Cautiously I crept down it. Still no sound – but as I stood on the landing below, a faint murmur of voices reached me. I stopped dead, and stood there for some time. A clock on the wall registered the fact that it was after midnight.

I was fully aware of the risks I might run if I descended lower, but my curiosity was too much for me. With infinite precautions I prepared to explore. I crept softly down the last flight of stairs and stood in the square hall. I looked round me – and then caught my breath with a gasp. A Kafir boy was sitting by the hall door. He had not seen me, indeed I soon realized by his breathing that he was fast asleep.

Should I retreat, or should I go on? The voices came from the room I had been shown into on arrival. One of them was that of my Dutch friend, the other I could not for the moment recognize, though it seemed vaguely familiar.

In the end I decided that it was clearly my duty to hear all I could. I must risk the Kafir boy waking up. I crossed the hall noiselessly and knelt by the study door. For a moment or two I could hear no better. The voices were louder, but I could not distinguish what they said.

I applied my eye to the keyhole instead of my ear. As I had guessed, one of the speakers was the big Dutchman. The other man was sitting outside my circumscribed range of vision.

Suddenly he rose to get himself a drink. His back, blackclad and decorous, came into view. Even before he turned round I knew who he was.

Mr Chichester!

Now I began to make out the words.

'All the same, it is dangerous. Suppose her friends come after her?'

It was the big man speaking. Chichester answered him. He had dropped his clerical voice entirely. No wonder I had not recognized it.

'All bluff. They haven't an idea where she is.'

'She spoke very positively.'

'I dare say. I've looked into the matter, and we've nothing to fear. Anyway, it's the "Colonel's" orders. You don't want to go against them, I suppose?'

The Dutchman ejaculated something in his own language. I judged it to be a hasty disclaimer.

'But why not knock her on the head?' he growled. 'It would be simple. The boat is all ready. She could be taken out to sea.'

'Yes,' said Chichester meditatively. 'That is what I should do.

She knows too much, that is certain. But the "Colonel" is a man who likes to play a lone hand – though no one else must do so.' Something in his own words seemed to awaken a memory that annoyed him. 'He wants information of some kind from this girl.'

He had paused before the 'information', and the Dutchman was quick to catch him up.

'Information?'

'Something of the kind.'

'Diamonds,' I said to myself.

'And now,' continued Chichester, 'give me the lists.'

For a long time their conversation was quite incomprehensible to me. It seemed to deal with large quantities of vegetables. Dates were mentioned, prices, and various names of places which I did not know. It was quite half an hour before they had finished their checking and counting.

'Good,' said Chichester, and there was a sound as though he pushed back his chair. 'I will take these with me for the "Colonel" to see.'

'When do you leave?'

'Ten o'clock tomorrow morning will do.'

'Do you want to see the girl before you go?'

'No. There are strict orders that no one is to see her until the "Colonel" comes. Is she all right?'

'I looked in on her when I came in for dinner. She was asleep, I think. What about food?'

'A little starvation will do no harm. The "Colonel" will be here some time tomorrow. She will answer questions better if she is hungry. No one had better go near her till then. Is she securely tied up?'

The Dutchman laughed.

'What do you think?'

They both laughed. So did I, under my breath. Then, as the sounds seemed to betoken that they were about to come out of the room, I beat a hasty retreat. I was just in time. As I reached the head of the stairs, I heard the door of the room open, and at the same time the Kafir stirred and moved. My retreat by the way of the hall door was not to be thought of. I retired prudently to the attic, gathered my bonds round me and lay down again on the floor, in case they should take it into their heads to come and look at me.

They did not do so, however. After about an hour, I crept down the stairs, but the Kafir by the door was awake and humming softly to himself. I was anxious to get out of the house, but I did not quite see how to manage it.

In the end, I was forced to retreat to the attic again. The Kafir was clearly on guard for the night. I remained there patiently all through the sounds of early morning preparation. The men breakfasted in the hall, I could hear their voices distinctly floating up the stairs. I was getting thoroughly unnerved. How on earth was I to get out of the house?

I counselled myself to be patient. A rash move might spoil everything. After breakfast came the sounds of Chichester departing. To my intense relief, the Dutchman accompanied him.

I waited breathlessly. Breakfast was being cleared away, the work of the house was being done. At last, the various activities seemed to die down. I slipped out from my lair once more. Very carefully I crept down the stairs. The hall was empty. Like a flash I was across it, had unlatched the door, and was outside in the sunshine. I ran down the drive like one possessed.

Once outside, I resumed a normal walk. People stared at me curiously, and I do not wonder. My face and clothes must have been covered in dust from rolling about in the attic. At last I came to a garage. I went in.

'I have met with an accident,' I explained. 'I want a car to take me to Cape Town at once. I must catch the boat to Durban.'

I had not long to wait. Ten minutes later I was speeding along in the direction of Cape Town. I must know if Chichester was on the boat. Whether to sail on her myself or not, I could not determine, but in the end I decided to do so. Chichester would not know that I had seen him in the villa at Muizenberg. He would doubtless lay further traps for me, but I was forewarned. And he was the man I was after, the man who was seeking the diamonds on behalf of the mysterious 'Colonel'.

Alas, for my plans! As I arrived at the docks, the *Kilmorden Castle* was steaming out to sea. And I had no means of knowing whether Chichester had sailed on her or not!

CHAPTER 20

I drove to the hotel. There was no one in the lounge that I knew. I ran upstairs and tapped on Suzanne's door. Her voice bade me 'come in'. When she saw who it was she literally fell on my neck.

'Anne, dear, where have you been? I've been worried to death about you. What have you been doing?'

'Having adventures,' I replied. 'Episode III of *The Perils of Pamela.*'

I told her the whole story. She gave vent to a deep sigh when I finished.

'Why do these things always happen to you?' she demanded plaintively. 'Why does no one gag me and bind me hand and foot?'

'You wouldn't like it if they did,' I assured her. 'To tell you the truth, I'm not nearly so keen on having adventures myself as I was. A little of that sort of thing goes a long way.'

Suzanne seemed unconvinced. An hour or two of gagging and binding would have changed her view quickly enough. Suzanne likes thrills, but she hates being uncomfortable.

'And what are we all doing now?' she asked.

'I don't quite know,' I said thoughtfully. 'You still go to Rhodesia, of course, to keep an eye on Pagett –'

'And you?'

That was just my difficulty. Had Chichester gone on the *Kilmorden*, or had he not? Did he mean to carry out his original plan of going to Durban? The hour of his leaving Muizenberg seemed to point to an affirmative answer to both questions. In that case, I might go to Durban by train. I fancied that I should get there before the boat. On the other hand, if the news of my escape were wired to Chichester, and also the information that I had left Cape Town for Durban, nothing was simpler for him than to leave the boat at either Port Elizabeth or East London and so give me the slip completely.

It was rather a knotty problem.

'We'll inquire about trains to Durban anyway,' I said.

'And it's not too late for morning tea,' said Suzanne. 'We'll have it in the lounge.'

The Durban train left at 8.15 that evening, so they told me at the office. For the moment I postponed decision, and joined Suzanne for somewhat belated 'eleven-o'clock tea'.

'Do you feel that you would really recognize Chichester again – in any other disguise, I mean?' asked Suzanne.

I shook my head ruefully.

'I certainly didn't recognize him as the stewardess, and never should have but for your drawing.'

'The man's a professional actor, I'm sure of it,' said Suzanne thoughtfully. 'His make-up is perfectly marvellous. He might come off the boat as a navvy or something, and you'd never spot him.'

'You're very cheering,' I said.

At that minute Colonel Race stepped in through the window and came and joined us.

'What is Sir Eustace doing?' asked Suzanne. 'I haven't seen him about today.'

Rather an odd expression passed over the Colonel's face.

'He's got a little trouble of his own to attend to which is keeping him busy.'

'Tell us about it.'

'I mustn't tell tales out of school.'

'Tell us something – even if you have to invent it for our special benefit.'

'Well, what would you say to the famous "Man in the Brown Suit" having made the voyage with us?'

'*What?*'

I felt the colour die out of my face and then surge back again. Fortunately Colonel Race was not looking at me.

'It's a fact, I believe. Every port watched for him and he bamboozled Pedler into bringing him out as his secretary!'

'Not Mr Pagett?'

'Oh, not Pagett – the other fellow. Rayburn, he called himself.'

'Have they arrested him?' asked Suzanne. Under the table she gave my hand a reassuring squeeze. I waited breathlessly for an answer.

'He seems to have disappeared into thin air.'

'How does Sir Eustace take it?'

'Regards it as a personal insult offered him by Fate.'

An opportunity of hearing Sir Eustace's views on the matter presented itself later in the day. We were awakened from a refreshing afternoon nap by a page-boy with a note. In touching terms it requested the pleasure of our company at tea in his sitting-room.

The poor man was indeed in a pitiable state. He poured out his troubles to us, encouraged by Suzanne's sympathetic murmurs. (She does that sort of thing very well.)

'First a perfectly strange woman has the impertinence to get herself murdered in my house – on purpose to annoy me, I do believe. Why my house? Why, of all the houses in Great Britain, choose the Mill House? What harm had I ever done the woman that she must needs get herself murdered there?'

Suzanne made one of her sympathetic noises again and Sir Eustace proceeded, in a still more aggrieved tone:

'And, if that's not enough, the fellow who murdered her has the impudence, the colossal impudence, to attach himself to me as my secretary. My secretary, if you please! I'm tired of secretaries, I won't have any more secretaries. Either they're concealed murderers or else they're drunken brawlers. Have you seen Pagett's black eye? But of course you have. How can I go about with a secretary like that? And his face is such a nasty shade of yellow too – just the colour that doesn't go with a black eye. I've done with secretaries – unless I have a girl. A nice girl, with liquid eyes, who'll hold my hand when I'm feeling cross. What about you, Miss Anne? Will you take on the job?'

'How often shall I have to hold your hand?' I asked, laughing.

'All day long,' replied Sir Eustace gallantly.

'I shan't get much typing done at that rate,' I reminded him.

'That doesn't matter. All this work is Pagett's idea. He works me to death. I'm looking forward to leaving him behind in Cape Town.'

'He is staying behind?'

'Yes, he'll enjoy himself thoroughly sleuthing about after Rayburn. That's the sort of thing that suits Pagett down to the ground. He adores intrigue. But I'm quite serious in my offer. Will you come? Mrs Blair here is a competent chaperone, and you can have a half-holiday every now and again to dig for bones.'

'Thank you very much, Sir Eustace,' I said cautiously, 'but I think I'm leaving for Durban tonight.'

'Now don't be an obstinate girl. Remember, there are lots of lions in Rhodesia. You'll like lions. All girls do.'

'Will they be practising low jumps?' I asked, laughing. 'No, thank you very much, but I must go to Durban.'

Sir Eustace looked at me, sighed deeply, then opened the door of the adjoining room, and called to Pagett.

'If you've quite finished your afternoon sleep, my dear fellow, perhaps you'd do a little work for a change.'

Guy Pagett appeared in the doorway. He bowed to us both, starting slightly at the sight of me, and replied in a melancholy voice:

'I have been typing that memorandum all this afternoon, Sir Eustace.'

'Well, stop typing it then. Go down to the Trade Commissioner's Office, or the Board of Agriculture, or the Chamber of Mines, or one of those places, and ask them to lend me some kind of a woman to take to Rhodesia. She must have liquid eyes and not object to my holding her hand.'

'Yes, Sir Eustace. I will ask for a competent shorthand-typist.'

'Pagett's a malicious fellow,' said Sir Eustace, after the secretary had departed. 'I'd be prepared to bet that he'll pick out some slab-faced creature on purpose to annoy me. She must have nice feet too – I forgot to mention that.'

I clutched Suzanne excitedly by the hand and almost dragged her along to her room.

'Now, Suzanne,' I said, 'we've got to make plans – and make them quickly. Pagett is staying behind here – you heard that?'

'Yes. I suppose that means that I shan't be allowed to go to Rhodesia – which is very annoying, because I *want* to go to Rhodesia. How tiresome.'

'Cheer up,' I said. 'You're going all right. I don't see how you could back out at the last moment without its appearing frightfully suspicious. And, besides, Pagett might suddenly be summoned by Sir Eustace, and it would be far harder for you to attach yourself to him for the journey up.'

'It would hardly be respectable,' said Suzanne, dimpling. 'I should have to pretend a fatal passion for him as an excuse.'

'On the other hand, if you were there when he arrived, it would all be perfectly simple and natural. Besides, I don't think we ought to lose sight of the other two entirely.'

'Oh, Anne, you surely can't suspect Colonel Race or Sir Eustace?'

'I suspect everybody,' I said darkly, 'and if you've read any detective stories, Suzanne, you must know that it's always the most unlikely person who's the villain. Lots of criminals have been cheerful fat men like Sir Eustace.'

'Colonel Race isn't particularly fat – or particularly cheerful either.'

'Sometimes they're lean and saturnine,' I retorted. 'I don't say I seriously suspect either of them, but, after all, the woman was murdered in Sir Eustace's house –'

'Yes, yes, we needn't go over all that again. I'll watch him for you, Anne, and if he gets any fatter and any more cheerful, I'll send you a telegram at once. "Sir E. swelling highly suspicious. Come at once."'

'Really, Suzanne,' I cried, 'you seem to think all this is a game!'

'I know I do,' said Suzanne, unabashed. 'It seems like that. It's your fault, Anne. I've got imbued with your "Let's have an adventure" spirit. It doesn't seem a bit real. Dear me, if Clarence knew that I was running about Africa tracking dangerous criminals, he'd have a fit.'

'Why don't you cable him about it?' I asked sarcastically.

Suzanne's sense of humour always fails her when it comes to sending cables. She considered my suggestion in perfectly good faith.

'I might. It would have to be a very long one.' Her eyes brightened at the thought. 'But I think it's better not. Husbands always want to interfere with perfectly harmless amusements.'

'Well,' I said, summing up the situation, 'you will keep an eye on Sir Eustace and Colonel Race –'

'I know why I've got to watch Sir Eustace,' interrupted Suzanne, 'because of his figure and his humorous conversation. But I think it's carrying it rather far to suspect Colonel Race; I do indeed.

Why, he's something to do with the Secret Service. Do you know, Anne, I believe the best thing we could do would be to confide in him and tell him the whole story.'

I objected vigorously to this unsporting proposal. I recognized in it the disastrous effects of matrimony. How often have I not heard a perfectly intelligent female say, in the tone of one clinching an argument, '*Edgar* says –' And all the time you are perfectly aware that Edgar is a perfect fool. Suzanne, by reason of her married state, was yearning to lean upon some man or other.

However, she promised faithfully that she would not breathe a word to Colonel Race, and we went on with our plan-making.

'It's quite clear that I must stay here and watch Pagett, and this is the best way to do it. I must pretend to leave for Durban this evening, take my luggage down and so on, but really I shall go to some small hotel in the town. I can alter my appearance a little – wear a fair toupee and one of those thick white lace veils, and I shall have a much better chance of seeing what he's really at if he thinks I'm safely out of the way.'

Suzanne approved this plan heartily. We made due and ostentatious preparations, inquiring once more about the departure of the train at the office and packing my luggage.

We dined together in the restaurant. Colonel Race did not appear, but Sir Eustace and Pagett were at their table in the window. Pagett left the table half-way through the meal, which annoyed me, as I had planned to say goodbye to him. However, doubtless Sir Eustace would do as well. I went over to him when I had finished.

'Goodbye, Sir Eustace,' I said. 'I'm off tonight to Durban.'

Sir Eustace sighed heavily.

'So I heard. You wouldn't like me to come with you, would you?'

'I should love it.'

'Nice girl. Sure you won't change your mind and come and look for lions in Rhodesia?'

'Quite sure.'

'He must be a very handsome fellow,' said Sir Eustace plaintively. 'Some young whipper-snapper in Durban, I suppose, who puts my mature charms completely in the shade. By the way,

Pagett's going down in the car in a minute or two. He could take you to the station.'

'Oh, no, thank you,' I said hastily. 'Mrs Blair and I have got our own taxi ordered.'

To go down with Guy Pagett was the last thing I wanted! Sir Eustace looked at me attentively.

'I don't believe you like Pagett. I don't blame you. Of all the officious, interfering asses – going about with the air of a martyr, and doing everything he can to annoy and upset me!'

'What has he done now?' I inquired with some curiosity.

'He's got hold of a secretary for me. You never saw such a woman! Forty, if she's a day, wears pince-nez and sensible boots and an air of brisk efficiency that will be the death of me. A regular slab-faced woman.'

'Won't she hold your hand?'

'I devoutly hope not!' exclaimed Sir Eustace. 'That would be the last straw. Well, goodbye, liquid eyes. If I shoot a lion I shan't give you the skin – after the base way you've deserted me.'

He squeezed my hand warmly and we parted. Suzanne was waiting for me in the hall. She was to come down to see me off.

'Let's start at once,' I said hastily, and motioned to the man to get a taxi.

Then a voice behind me made me start:

'Excuse me, Miss Beddingfeld, but I'm just going down in a car. I can drop you and Mrs Blair at the station.'

'Oh, thank you,' I said hastily. 'But there's no need to trouble you. I –'

'No trouble at all, I assure you. Put the luggage in, porter.'

I was helpless. I might have protested further, but a slight warning nudge from Suzanne urged me to be on my guard.

'Thank you, Mr Pagett,' I said coldly.

We all got into the car. As we raced down the road into the town, I racked my brains for something to say. In the end Pagett himself broke the silence.

'I have secured a very capable secretary for Sir Eustace,' he observed. 'Miss Pettigrew.'

'He wasn't exactly raving about her just now,' I remarked.

Pagett looked at me coldly.

'She is a proficient shorthand-typist,' he said repressively.

We pulled up in front of the station. Here surely he would leave us. I turned with outstretched hand – but no.

'I'll come and see you off. It's just eight o'clock, your train goes in a quarter of an hour.'

He gave efficient directions to porters. I stood helpless, not daring to look at Suzanne. The man suspected. He was determined to make sure that I did go by the train. And what could I do? Nothing. I saw myself, in a quarter of an hour's time, steaming out of the station with Pagett planted on the platform waving me adieu. He had turned the tables on me adroitly. His manner towards me had changed, moreover. It was full of an uneasy geniality which sat ill upon him, and which nauseated me. The man was an oily hypocrite. First he tried to murder me, and now he paid me compliments! Did he imagine for one minute that I hadn't recognized him that night on the boat? No, it was a pose, a pose which he forced me to acquiesce in, his tongue in his cheek all the while.

Helpless as a sheep, I moved along under his expert directions. My luggage was piled in my sleeping compartment – I had a two-berth one to myself. It was twelve minutes past eight. In three minutes the train would start.

But Pagett had reckoned without Suzanne.

'It will be a terribly hot journey, Anne,' she said suddenly. 'Especially going through the Karoo tomorrow. You've got some eau-de-Cologne or lavender water with you, haven't you?'

My cue was plain.

'Oh, dear,' I cried. 'I left my eau-de-Cologne on the dressing-table at the hotel.'

Suzanne's habit of command served her well. She turned imperiously to Pagett.

'Mr Pagett. Quick. You've just time. There's a chemist almost opposite the station. Anne must have some eau-de-Cologne.'

He hesitated, but Suzanne's imperative manner was too much for him. She is a born autocrat. He went. Suzanne followed him with her eyes till he disappeared.

'Quick, Anne, get out the other side – in case he hasn't really gone but is watching us from the end of the platform. Never mind your luggage. You can telegraph about that tomorrow. Oh, if only the train starts on time!'

I opened the gate on the opposite side to the platform and climbed down. Nobody was observing me. I could just see Suzanne standing where I had left her, looking up at the train and apparently chatting to me at the window. A whistle blew, the train began to draw out. Then I heard feet racing furiously up the platform. I withdrew to the shadow of a friendly bookstall and watched.

Suzanne turned from waving her handkerchief to the retreating train.

'Too late, Mr Pagett,' she said cheerfully. 'She's gone. Is that the eau-de-Cologne? What a pity we didn't think of it sooner!'

They passed not far from me on their way out of the station. Guy Pagett was extremely hot. He had evidently run all the way to the chemist and back.

'Shall I get you a taxi, Mrs Blair?'

Suzanne did not fail in her role.

'Yes, please. Can't I give you a lift back? Have you much to do for Sir Eustace? Dear me, I wish Anne Beddingfeld was coming with us tomorrow. I don't like the idea of a young girl like that travelling off to Durban all by herself. But she was set upon it. Some little attraction there, I fancy –'

They passed out of earshot. Clever Suzanne. She had saved me.

I allowed a minute or two to elapse and then I too made my way out of the station, almost colliding as I did so with a man – an unpleasant-looking man with a nose disproportionately big for his face.

CHAPTER 21

I had no further difficulty in carrying out my plans. I found a small hotel in a back street, got a room there, paid a deposit as I had no luggage with me, and went placidly to bed.

On the following morning I was up early and went out into the town to purchase a modest wardrobe. My idea was to do nothing until after the departure of the eleven-o'clock train to Rhodesia with most of the party on board. Pagett was not likely to indulge in any nefarious activities until he had got rid of them. Accordingly

I took a train out of the town and proceeded to enjoy a country walk. It was comparatively cool, and I was glad to stretch my legs after the long voyage and my close confinement at Muizenberg.

A lot hinges on small things. My shoe-lace came untied, and I stopped to do it up. The road had just turned a corner, and as I was bending over the offending shoe a man came right round and almost walked into me. He lifted his hat, murmuring an apology, and went on. It struck me at the time that his face was vaguely familiar, but at the moment I thought no more of it. I looked at my wrist-watch. The time was getting on. I turned my feet in the direction of Cape Town.

There was a tram on the point of going and I had to run for it. I heard other footsteps running behind me. I swung myself on and so did the other runner. I recognized him at once. It was the man who had passed me on the road when my shoe came untied, and in a flash I knew why his face was familiar. It was the small man with the big nose whom I had run into on leaving the station the night before.

The coincidence was rather startling. Could it be possible that the man was deliberately following me? I resolved to test that as promptly as possible. I rang the bell and got off at the next stop. The man did not get off. I withdrew into the shadow of a shop doorway and watched. He alighted at the next stop and walked back in my direction.

The case was clear enough. I was being followed. I had crowed too soon. My victory over Guy Pagett took on another aspect. I hailed the next tram and, as I expected, my shadower also got on. I gave myself up to some very serious thinking.

It was perfectly apparent that I had stumbled on a bigger thing than I knew. The murder in the house at Marlow was not an isolated incident committed by a solitary individual. I was up against a gang, and, thanks to Colonel Race's revelations to Suzanne, and what I had overheard at the house at Muizenberg, I was beginning to understand some of its manifold activities. Systematized crime, organized by the man known to his followers as the 'Colonel'! I remembered some of the talk I had heard on board ship, of the strike on the Rand and the causes underlying it – and the belief that some secret organization was at work fomenting the agitation. That was the 'Colonel's' work, his emissaries were acting according to plan. He took no part in these things himself, I had always heard, as he limited himself to directing and organizing. The brain-work – not the dangerous labour – for him. But still it well might be that he himself was on the spot, directing affairs from an apparently impeccable position.

That, then, was the meaning of Colonel Race's presence on the *Kilmorden Castle*. He was out after the arch-criminal. Everything fitted in with that assumption. He was someone high up in the Secret Service whose business it was to lay the 'Colonel' by the heels.

I nodded to myself – things were becoming very clear to me. What of my part in the affair? Where did I come in? Was it only diamonds they were after? I shook my head. Great as the value of the diamonds might be, they hardly accounted for the desperate attempts which had been made to get me out of the way. No, I stood for more than that. In some way, unknown to myself, I was a menace, a danger! Some knowledge that I had, or that they thought I had, made them anxious to remove me at all costs – and that knowledge was bound up somehow with the diamonds. There was one person, I felt sure, who could enlighten me – if he would! 'The Man in the Brown Suit' – Harry Rayburn. He knew the other half of the story. But he had vanished into the darkness, he was a hunted creature flying from pursuit. In all probability he and I would never meet again . . .

I brought myself back with a jerk to the actualities of the moment. It was no good thinking sentimentally of Harry Rayburn. He had displayed the greatest antipathy to me from the first. Or, at least – There I was again – dreaming! The real problem was what to do – *now!*

I, priding myself upon my role of watcher, had become the watched. And I was afraid! For the first time, I began to lose my nerve. I was the little bit of grit that was impeding the smooth working of the great machine – and I fancied that the machine would have a short way with little bits of grit. Once Harry Rayburn had saved me, once I had saved myself – but I felt suddenly that the odds were heavily against me. My enemies were all around me in every direction, and they were closing in. If I continued to play a lone hand I was doomed.

I rallied myself with an effort. After all, what could they do? I was in a civilized city – with policemen every few yards. I would be wary in future. They should not trap me again as they had done in Muizenberg.

As I reached this point in my meditations, the tram arrived at Adderley Street. I got out. Undecided what to do, I walked slowly up the left-hand side of the street. I did not trouble to look if my watcher was behind me. I knew he was. I walked into Cartwright's and ordered two coffee ice-cream sodas – to steady my nerves. A man, I suppose, would have had a stiff peg; but girls derive a lot of comfort from ice-cream sodas. I applied myself to the end of the straw with gusto. The cool liquid went trickling down my throat in the most agreeable manner. I pushed the first glass aside empty.

I was sitting on one of the little high stools in front of the counter. Out of the tail of my eye, I saw my tracker come in and sit down unostentatiously at a little table near the door. I finished the second coffee soda and demanded a maple one. I can drink practically an unlimited amount of ice-cream sodas.

Suddenly the man by the door got up and went out. That surprised me. If he was going to wait ouside, why not wait outside from the beginning? I slipped down from my stool and went cautiously to the door. I drew back quickly into the shadow. The man was talking to Guy Pagett.

If I had ever had any doubts, that would have settled it. Pagett had his watch out and was looking at it. They exchanged a few brief words, and then the secretary swung on down the street towards the station. Evidently he had given his orders. But what were they?

Suddenly my heart leapt into my mouth. The man who had followed me crossed to the middle of the road and spoke to a policeman. He spoke at some length, gesticulating towards Cartwright's and evidently explaining something. I saw the plan at once. I was to be arrested on some charge or other – pocket-picking, perhaps. It would be easy enough for the gang to put through a simple little matter like that. Of what good to protest my innocence? They would have seen to every detail. Long ago they had brought a charge of robbing De Beers against Harry Rayburn, and he had not been able to disprove it, though I had little doubt but that he had been absolutely blameless. What chance had I against such a 'frame up' as the 'Colonel' could devise?

I glanced up at the clock almost mechanically, and immediately another aspect of the case struck me. I saw the point of Guy Pagett's looking at his watch. It was just on eleven, and at eleven the mail train left for Rhodesia bearing with it the influential friends who might otherwise come to my rescue. That was the reason of my immunity up to now. From last night till eleven this morning I had been safe, but now the net was closing in upon me.

I hurriedly opened my bag and paid for my drinks, and as I did so, my heart seemed to stand still, *for inside it was a man's wallet stuffed with notes!* It must have been deftly introduced into my handbag as I left the tram.

Promptly I lost my head. I hurried out of Cartwright's. The little man with the big nose and the policeman were just crossing the road. They saw me, and the little man designated me excitedly to the policeman. I took to my heels and ran. I judged him to be a slow policeman. I should get a start. But I had no plan, even then. I just ran for my life down Adderley Street. People began to stare. I felt that in another minute someone would stop me.

An idea flashed into my head.

'The station?' I asked, in a breathless gasp.

'Just down on the right.'

I sped on. It is permissible to run for a train. I turned into the station, but as I did so I heard footsteps close behind me. The little man with the big nose was a champion sprinter. I foresaw that I should be stopped before I got to the platform I was in search of. I looked up to the clock – one minute to eleven. I might just do it if my plan succeeded.

I had entered the station by the main entrance in Adderley Street. I now darted out again through the side exit. Directly opposite me was the side entrance to the post office, the main entrance to which is in Adderley Street.

As I expected, my pursuer, instead of following me in, ran down the street to cut me off when I emerged by the main entrance, or to warn the policeman to do so.

In an instant I slipped across the street again and back into the station. I ran like a lunatic. It was just eleven. The long train was moving as I appeared on the platform. A porter tried to stop me, but I wriggled myself out of his grasp and sprang upon the foot-board. I mounted the two steps and opened the gate. I was safe! The train was gathering way.

We passed a man standing by himself at the end of the platform. I waved to him.

'Goodbye Mr Pagett,' I shouted.

Never have I seen a man more taken aback. He looked as though he had seen a ghost.

In a minute or two I was having trouble with the conductor. But I took a lofty tone.

'I am Sir Eustace Pedler's secretary,' I said haughtily. 'Please take me to his private car.'

Suzanne and Colonel Race were standing on the rear observation platform. They both uttered an exclamation of utter surprise at seeing me.

'Hullo, Miss Anne,' cried Colonel Race, 'where have you turned up from? I thought you'd gone to Durban. What an unexpected person you are!'

Suzanne said nothing, but her eyes asked a hundred questions.

'I must report myself to my chief,' I said demurely. 'Where is he?'

'He's in the office – middle compartment – dictating at an incredible rate to the unfortunate Miss Pettigrew.'

'This enthusiasm for work is something new,' I commented.

'H'm!' said Colonel Race. 'His idea is, I think, to give her sufficient work to chain her to her typewriter in her own compartment for the rest of the day.'

I laughed. Then, followed by the other two, I sought out Sir Eustace. He was striding up and down the circumscribed space, hurling a flood of words at the unfortunate secretary whom I now saw for the first time. A tall, square woman in drab clothing, with pince-nez and an efficient air. I judged that she was finding it difficult to keep pace with Sir Eustace, for her pencil was flying along, and she was frowning horribly.

I stepped into the compartment.

'Come aboard, sir,' I said saucily.

Sir Eustace paused dead in the middle of a complicated sentence on the labour situation, and stared at me. Miss Pettigrew must be a nervous creature, in spite of her efficient air, for she jumped as though she had been shot.

'God bless my soul!' ejaculated Sir Eustace. 'What about the young man in Durban?'

'I prefer you,' I said softly.

'Darling,' said Sir Eustace. 'You can start holding my hand at once.'

Miss Pettigrew coughed, and Sir Eustace hastily withdrew his hand.

'Ah, yes,' he said. 'Let me see, where were we? Yes. Tylman Roos, in his speech at – What's the matter? Why aren't you taking it down?'

'I think,' said Colonel Race gently, 'that Miss Pettigrew has broken her pencil.'

He took it from her and sharpened it. Sir Eustace stared, and so did I. There was something in Colonel Race's tone that I did not quite understand.

CHAPTER 22

(EXTRACT FROM THE DIARY OF SIR EUSTACE PEDLER)

I am inclined to abandon my Reminiscences. Instead, I shall write a short article entitled 'Secretaries I have had'. As regards secretaries, I seem to have fallen under a blight. At one minute I have no secretaries, at another I have too many. At the present minute I am journeying to Rhodesia with a pack of women. Race goes off with the two best-looking, of course, and leaves me with the dud. That is what always happens to me – and, after all, this is my private car, not Race's.

Also Anne Beddingfeld is accompanying me to Rhodesia on the pretext of being my temporary secretary. But all this afternoon she has been out on the observation platform with Race exclaiming at the beauty of the Hex River Pass. It is true that I told her her principal duty would be to hold my hand. But she isn't even doing that. Perhaps she is afraid of Miss Pettigrew. I don't blame her if so. There is nothing attractive about Miss Pettigrew – she is a repellent female with large feet, more like a man than a woman.

There is something very mysterious about Anne Beddingfeld.

She jumped on board the train at the last minute, puffing like a steam-engine, for all the world as though she's been running a race – and yet Pagett told me that he'd seen her off to Durban last night! Either Pagett has been drinking again, or else the girl must have an astral body.

And she never explains. Nobody ever explains. Yes, 'Secretaries I have had'. No. 1, a murderer fleeing from justice. No. 2, a secret drinker who carries on disreputable intrigues in Italy. No. 3, a beautiful girl who possesses the useful faculty of being in two places at once. No. 4, Miss Pettigrew, who, I have no doubt, is really a particularly dangerous crook in disguise! Probably one of Pagett's Italian friends that he has palmed off on me. I shouldn't wonder if the world found some day that it had been grossly deceived by Pagett. On the whole, I think Rayburn was the best of the bunch. He never worried me or got in my way. Guy Pagett has had the impertinence to have the stationery trunk put in here. None of us can move without falling over it.

I went out on the observation platform just now, expecting my appearance to be greeted with hails of delight. Both the women were listening spellbound to one of Race's traveller's tales. I shall label this car – not 'Sir Eustace Pedler and Party', but 'Colonel Race and Harem'.

Then Mrs Blair must needs begin taking silly photographs. Every time we went round a particularly appalling curve, as we climbed higher and higher, she snapped at the engine.

'You see the point,' she cried delightedly. 'It must be some curve if you can photograph the front part of the train from the back, and with the mountain background it will look awfully dangerous.'

I pointed out to her that no one could possibly tell it had been taken from the back of the train. She looked at me pityingly.

'I shall write underneath it. "Taken from the train. Engine going round a curve."'

'You could write that under any snapshot of a train,' I said. Women never think of these simple things.

'I'm glad we've come up here in daylight,' cried Anne Beddingfeld. 'I shouldn't have seen this if I'd gone last night to Durban, should I?'

'No,' said Colonel Race, smiling. 'You'd have woken up tomorrow morning to find yourself in the Karoo, a hot, dusty desert of stones and rocks.'

'I'm glad I changed my mind,' said Anne, sighing contentedly, and looking round.

It was rather a wonderful sight. The great mountains all around, through which we turned and twisted and laboured ever steadily upwards.

'Is this the best train in the day to Rhodesia?' asked Anne Beddingfeld.

'In the day?' laughed Race. 'Why, my dear Miss Anne, there are only three trains a week. Mondays, Wednesdays, and Saturdays. Do you realize that you don't arrive at the Falls until Saturday next?'

'How well we shall know each other by that time!' said Mrs Blair maliciously. 'How long are you going to stay at the Falls, Sir Eustace?'

'That depends,' I said cautiously.

'On what?'

'On how things go at Johannesburg. My original idea was to stay a couple of days at the Falls – which I've never seen, though this is my third visit to Africa – and then go on to Jo'burg and study the conditions of things on the Rand. At home, you know, I pose as being an authority on South African politics. But from all I hear, Jo'burg will be a particularly unpleasant place to visit in about a week's time. I don't want to study conditions in the midst of a raging revolution.'

Race smiled in a rather superior manner.

'I think your fears are exaggerated, Sir Eustace. There will be no great danger in Jo'burg.'

The women immediately looked at him in the 'What a brave hero you are' manner. It annoyed me intensely. I am every bit as brave as Race – but I lack the figure. These long, lean, brown men have it all their own way.

'I suppose you'll be there,' I said coldly.

'Very possibly. We might travel together.'

'I'm not sure that I shan't stay on at the Falls a bit,' I answered non-committally. Why is Race so anxious that I should go to Jo'burg? He's got his eye on Anne, I believe. 'What are your plans, Miss Anne?'

'That depends,' she replied demurely, copying me.

'I thought you were my secretary,' I objected.

'Oh, but I've been cut out. You've been holding Miss Pettigrew's hand all the afternoon.'

'Whatever I've been doing, I can swear I've not been doing that,' I assured her.

Thursday night.

We have just left Kimberley. Race was made to tell the story of the diamond robbery all over again. Why are women so excited by anything to do with diamonds?

At last Anne Beddingfeld has shed her veil of mystery. It seems that she's a newspaper correspondent. She sent an immense cable from De Aar this morning. To judge by the jabbering that went on nearly all night in Mrs Blair's cabin she must have been reading aloud all her special articles for years to come.

It seems that all along she's been on the track of 'The Man in the Brown Suit'. Apparently she didn't spot him on the Kilmorden *– in fact, she hardly had the chance, but she's now very busy cabling home: 'How I journeyed out with the Murderer', and inventing highly fictitious stories of 'What he said to me', etc. I know how these things are done. I do them myself, in my Reminiscences when Pagett will let me. And of course one of Nasby's efficient staff will brighten up the details still more, so that when it appears in the* Daily Budget *Rayburn won't recognize himself.*

The girl's clever, though. All on her own, apparently, she's ferreted out the identity of the woman who was killed in my house. She was a Russian dancer called Nadina. I asked Anne Beddingfeld if she was sure of this. She replied that it was merely a deduction – quite in the Sherlock Holmes manner. However, I gather that she had cabled it home to Nasby as a proved fact. Women have these intuitions – I've no doubt that Anne Beddingfeld is perfectly right in her guess – but to call it a deduction is absurd.

How she ever got on the staff of the Daily Budget *is more than I can imagine. But she is the kind of young woman who does these things. Impossible to withstand her. She is full of coaxing ways that mask an invincible determination. Look how she has got into my private car!*

I am beginning to have an inkling why. Race said something about the police suspecting that Rayburn would make for Rhodesia. He might just have got off by Monday's train. They telegraphed all along the line, I presume, and no one of his description was found, but that says little. He's an astute young man and he knows Africa.

He's probably exquisitely disguised as an old Kafir woman – and the simple police continue to look for a handsome young man with a scar, dressed in the height of European fashion. I never did quite swallow that scar.

Anyway, Anne Beddingfeld is on his track. She wants the glory of discovering him for herself and the Daily Budget. *Young women are very cold-blooded nowadays. I hinted to her that it was an unwomanly action. She laughed at me. She assured me that did she run him to earth her fortune was made. Race doesn't like it, either, I can see. Perhaps Rayburn is on this train. If so, we may all be murdered in our beds. I said so to Mrs Blair – but she seemed quite to welcome the idea, and remarked that if I were murdered it would be really a terrific scoop for Anne! A scoop for Anne, indeed!*

Tomorrow we shall be going through Bechuanaland. The dust will be atrocious. Also at every station little Kafir children come and sell you quaint wooden animals that they carve themselves. Also mealie bowls and baskets. I am rather afraid that Mrs Blair may run amok. There is a primitive charm about these toys that I feel will appeal to her.

Friday evening.
As I feared. Mrs Blair and Anne have bought forty-nine wooden animals!

CHAPTER 23

(ANNE'S NARRATIVE RESUMED)

I thoroughly enjoyed the journey up to Rhodesia. There was something new and exciting to see every day. First the wonderful scenery of the Hex River valley, then the desolate grandeur of the Karoo, and finally that wonderful straight stretch of line in Bechaunaland, and the perfectly adorable toys the natives brought to sell. Suzanne and I were nearly left behind at each station – if you could call them stations. It seemed to me that the train just stopped whenever it felt like it, and no sooner had it done so than a horde of natives materialized out of the empty landscape, holding up mealie bowls and sugar canes and fur karosses and adorable carved wooden animals. Suzanne began at once to make a collection of the latter. I imitated her example – most of them cost a '*tiki*' (threepence) and each was different. There were giraffes and tigers and snakes and a melancholy-looking eland and absurd little black warriors. We enjoyed ourselves enormously.

Sir Eustace tried to restrain us – but in vain. I still think it was a miracle we were not left behind at some oasis of the line. South African trains don't hoot or get excited when they are going to start off again. They just glide quietly away, and you look up from your bargaining and run for your life.

Suzanne's amazement at seeing me climb upon the train at Cape Town can be imagined. We held an exhaustive survey of the situation on the first evening out. We talked half the night.

It had become clear to me that defensive tactics must be adopted as well as aggressive ones. Travelling with Sir Eustace Pedler and his party, I was fairly safe. Both he and Colonel Race were powerful protectors, and I judged that my enemies would not wish to stir up a hornet's nest about *my* ears. Also, as long as I was near Sir Eustace, I was more or less in touch with Guy Pagett – and Guy Pagett was the heart of the mystery. I asked Suzanne whether in her opinion it was possible that Pagett himself was the mysterious 'Colonel'. His subordinate position was, of course, against the assumption, but it had struck me once or twice that, for all his autocratic ways, Sir Eustace was really very much influenced by his secretary. He was an easy-going man, and one whom an adroit secretary might be able to twist round his little finger. The comparative obscurity of his position might in reality be useful to him, since he would be anxious to be well out of the limelight.

Suzanne, however, negatived these ideas very strongly. She refused to believe that Guy Pagett was the ruling spirit. The real head – the 'Colonel' – was somewhere in the background and had probably been already in Africa at the time of our arrival.

I agreed that there was much to be said for her view, but I was not entirely satisfied. For in each suspicious instance Pagett had been shown as the directing genius. It was true that his personality seemed to lack the assurance and decision that one would expect from a master criminal – but after all, according to Colonel Race, it was brain-work only that this mysterious leader supplied, and creative genius is often allied to a weak and timorous physical constitution.

'There speaks the Professor's daughter,' interrupted Suzanne, when I had got to this point in my argument.

'It's true, all the same. On the other hand, Pagett may be the Grand Vizier, so to speak, of the All Highest.' I was silent for a minute or two, and then went on musingly: 'I wish I knew how Sir Eustace made his money!'

'Suspecting him again?'

'Suzanne, I've got into that state that I can't help suspecting somebody! I don't really suspect him – but, after all, he *is* Pagett's employer, and he *did* own the Mill House.'

'I've always heard that he made his money in some way he isn't anxious to talk about,' said Suzanne thoughtfully. 'But that doesn't necessarily mean crime – it might be tintacks or hair restorer!'

I agreed ruefully.

'I suppose,' said Suzanne doubtfully, 'that we're not barking up the wrong tree? Being led completely astray, I mean, by assuming Pagett's complicity? Supposing that, after all, he is a perfectly honest man?'

I considered that for a minute or two, then I shook my head.

'I can't believe that.'

'After all, he has his explanations for everything.'

'Y – es, but they're not very convincing. For instance, the night he tried to throw me overboard on the *Kilmorden*, he says he followed Rayburn up on deck and Rayburn turned and knocked him down. Now we know that's not true.'

'No,' said Suzanne unwillingly. 'But we only heard the story at second-hand from Sir Eustace. If we'd heard it direct from Pagett himself, it might have been different. You know how people always get a story a little wrong when they repeat it.'

I turned the thing over in my mind.

'No,' I said at last, 'I don't see any way out. Pagett's guilty. You can't get away from the fact that he tried to throw me overboard, and everything else fits in. Why are you so persistent in this new idea of yours?'

'Because of his face.'

'His face? But –'

'Yes, I know what you're going to say. It's a sinister face. That's just it. No man with a face like that could be really sinister. It must be a colossal joke on the part of Nature.'

I did not believe much in Suzanne's argument. I know a lot about Nature in past ages. If she's got a sense of humour, she doesn't show it much. Suzanne is just the sort of person who would clothe Nature with all her own attributes.

We passed on to discuss our immediate plans. It was clear to me that I must have some kind of standing. I couldn't go on avoiding explanations for ever. The solution of all my difficulties lay ready to my hand, though I didn't think of it for some time. The *Daily Budget*! My silence or my speech could no longer affect Harry Rayburn. He was marked down as 'The Man in the Brown Suit' through no fault of mine. I could help him best by seeming to be against him. The 'Colonel' and his gang must have no suspicion that there existed any friendly feeling between me and the man they had elected to be the scapegoat of the murder at Marlow. As far as I knew, the woman killed was still unidentified. I would cable to Lord Nasby, suggesting that she was no other than the famous Russian dancer 'Nadina' who had been delighting Paris for so long. It seemed incredible to me that she had not been identified already – but when I learnt more of the case long afterwards I saw how natural it really was.

Nadina had never been to England, during her successful career in Paris. She was unknown to London audiences. The pictures in the papers of the Marlow victim were so blurred and unrecognizable that it is small wonder no one identified them. And, on the other hand, Nadina had kept her intention of visiting England a profound secret from everyone. The day after the murder, a letter had been received by her manager purporting to be from the dancer, in which she said that she was returning to Russia on urgent private affairs and that he must deal with her broken contract as best he could.

All this, of course, I only learned afterwards. With Suzanne's full approval, I sent a long cable from De Aar. It arrived at a psychological moment (this again, of course, I learnt afterwards). The *Daily Budget* was hard up for a sensation. My guess was verified and proved to be correct and the *Daily Budget* had the scoop of its lifetime. 'Victim of the Mill House Murder identified by our special reporter.' And so on. 'Our reporter makes voyage with the murderer. The Man in the Brown Suit. What he is really like.'

The main facts were, of course, cabled to the South African papers, but I only read my own lengthy articles at a much later date! I received approval and full instructions by cable at Bulawayo. I was on the staff of the *Daily Budget*, and I had a private word of congratulation from Lord Nasby himself. I was definitely accredited to hunt down the murderer, and I, and only I, knew that the murderer was not Harry Rayburn! But let the world think that it was he – best so for the present.

CHAPTER 24

We arrived at Bulawayo early on Saturday morning. I was disappointed in the place. It was very hot, and I hated the hotel. Also Sir Eustace was what I can only describe as thoroughly sulky. I think it was all our wooden animals that annoyed him – especially the big giraffe. It was a colossal giraffe with an impossible neck, a mild eye and a dejected tail. It had character. It had charm. A controversy was already arising as to whom it belonged to – me or Suzanne. We had each contributed a *tiki* to its purchase. Suzanne advanced the claims of seniority and the married state, I stuck to the position that I had been the first to behold its beauty.

In the meantime, I must admit, it occupied a good deal of this three-dimensional space of ours. To carry forty-nine wooden animals, all of awkward shape, and all of extremely brittle wood, is somewhat of a problem. Two porters were laden with a bunch of animals each – and one promptly dropped a ravishing group of ostriches and broke their heads off. Warned by this, Suzanne and I carried all we could, Colonel Race helped, and I pressed the big giraffe into Sir Eustace's arms. Even the correct Miss Pettigrew did not escape, a large hippopotamus and two black warriors fell to her share. I had a feeling Miss Pettigrew didn't like me. Perhaps she fancied I was a bold hussy. Anyway, she avoided me as much as she could. And the funny thing was, her face seemed vaguely familiar to me, though I couldn't quite place it.

We reposed ourselves most of the morning, and in the afternoon we drove out to the Matopos to see Rhodes's grave. That is to say, we were to have done so, but at the last moment Sir Eustace backed out. He was very nearly in as bad a temper as the morning we arrived at Cape Town – when he bounced the peaches on the floor and they squashed! Evidently arriving early in the morning at places is bad for his temperament. He cursed the porters, he cursed the waiter at breakfast, he cursed the whole hotel management, he would doubtless have liked to curse Miss Pettigrew, who hovered around with her pencil and pad, but I don't think even Sir Eustace would have dared to curse Miss Pettigrew. She's just like the efficient secretary in a book. I only rescued our dear giraffe just in time. I feel Sir Eustace would have liked to dash him to the ground.

To return to our expedition, after Sir Eustace had backed out, Miss Pettigrew said she would remain at home in case he might want her. And at the very last minute Suzanne sent down a message to say she had a headache. So Colonel Race and I drove off alone.

He is a strange man. One doesn't notice it so much in a crowd. But when one is alone with him the sense of his personality seems really almost overpowering. He becomes more taciturn, and yet his silence seems to say more than speech might do.

It was so that day that we drove to the Matopos through the soft yellow-brown scrub. Everything seemed strangely silent – except our car, which I should think was the first Ford ever made by man! The upholstery of it was torn to ribbons and, though I know nothing about engines, even I could guess that all was not as it should be in its interior.

By and by the character of the country changed. Great boulders appeared, piled up into fantastic shapes. I felt suddenly that I had got into a primitive era. Just for a moment Neanderthal men seemed quite as real to me as they had to Papa. I turned to Colonel Race.

'There must have been giants once,' I said dreamily. 'And their children were just like children are today – they played with handfuls of pebbles, piling them up and knocking them down, and the more cleverly they balanced them, the better pleased they were. If I were to give a name to this place I should call it The Country of Giant Children.'

'Perhaps you're nearer the mark than you know,' said Colonel Race gravely. 'Simple, primitive, big – that is Africa.'

I nodded appreciatively.

'You love it, don't you?' I asked.

'Yes. But to live in it long – well, it makes one what you would call cruel. One comes to hold life and death very lightly.'

'Yes,' I said, thinking of Harry Rayburn. He had been like that too. 'But not cruel to weak things?'

'Opinions differ as to what are and are not "weak things", Miss Anne.'

There was a note of seriousness in his voice which almost startled me. I felt that I knew very little really of this man at my side.

'I meant children and dogs, I think.'

'I can truthfully say I've never been cruel to children or dogs. So you don't class women as "weak things"?'

I considered.

'No, I don't think I do – though they are, I suppose. That is, they are nowadays. But Papa always said that in the beginning men and women roamed the world together, equal in strength – like lions and tigers –'

'And giraffes?' interpolated Colonel Race slyly.

I laughed. Everyone makes fun of that giraffe.

'And giraffes. They were nomadic, you see. It wasn't till they settled down in communities, and women did one kind of thing and men another, that women got weak. And of course, underneath, one is still the same – one *feels* the same, I mean – and that is why women worship physical strength in men: it's what they once had and have lost.'

'Almost ancestor worship, in fact?'

'Something of the kind.'

'And you really think that's true? That women worship strength, I mean?'

'I think it's quite true – if one's honest. You think you admire moral qualities, but when you fall in love, you revert to the primitive where the physical is all that counts. But I don't think that's the end; if you lived in primitive conditions it would be all right, but you don't – and so, in the end, the other thing wins after all. It's the things that are apparently conquered that always do win, isn't it? They win in the only way that counts. Like what the Bible says about losing your life and finding it.'

'In the end,' said Colonel Race thoughtfully, 'you fall in love – and you fall out of it, is that what you mean?'

'Not exactly, but you can put it that way if you like.'

'But I don't think you've ever fallen out of love, Miss Anne?'

'No, I haven't,' I admitted frankly.

'Or fallen in love, either?'

I did not answer.

The car drew up at our destination and brought the conversation to a close. We got out and began the slow ascent to the World's View. Not for the first time, I felt a slight discomfort in Colonel Race's company. He veiled his thoughts so well behind those impenetrable black eyes. He frightened me a little. He had always frightened me. I never knew where I stood with him.

We climbed in silence till we reached the spot where Rhodes lies guarded by giant boulders. A strange, eerie place, far from the haunts of men, that sings a ceaseless paean of rugged beauty.

We sat there for time in silence. Then descended once more, but diverging slightly from the path. Sometimes it was a rough scramble and once we came to a sharp slope or rock that was almost sheer.

Colonel Race went first, then turned to help me.

'Better lift you,' he said suddenly, and swung me off my feet with a quick gesture.

I felt the strength of him as he set me down and released his clasp. A man of iron, with muscles like taut steel. And again I felt afraid, especially as he did not move aside, but stood directly in front of me, staring into my face.

'What are you really doing here, Anne Beddingfeld?' he said abruptly.

'I'm a gipsy seeing the world.'

'Yes, that's true enough. The newspaper correspondent is only a pretext. You've not the soul of a journalist. You're out for your own hand – snatching at life. But that's not all.'

What was he going to make me tell him? I was afraid – afraid.

I looked him full in the face. My eyes can't keep secrets like his, but they can carry the war into the enemy's country.

'What are *you* really doing here, Colonel Race?' I asked deliberately.

For a moment I thought he wasn't going to answer. He was clearly taken aback, though. At last he spoke, and his words seemed to afford him a grim amusement.

'Pursuing ambition,' he said. 'Just that – pursuing ambition. You will remember, Miss Beddingfeld, that "by that sin fell the angels", etc.'

'They say,' I said slowly, 'that you are really connected with the Government – that you are in the Secret Service. Is that true?'

Was it my fancy, or did he hesitate for a fraction of a second before he answered?

'I can assure you, Miss Beddingfeld, that I am out here strictly as a private individual travelling for my own pleasure.'

Thinking the answer over later, it struck me as slightly ambiguous. Perhaps he meant it to be so.

We rejoined the car in silence. Half-way back to Bulawayo we stopped for tea at a somewhat primitive structure at the side of the road. The proprietor was digging in the garden, and seemed annoyed at being disturbed. But he graciously promised to see what he could do. After an interminable wait, he brought us some stale cakes and some lukewarm tea. Then disappeared to his garden again.

No sooner had he departed than we were surrounded by cats, six of them all miaowing piteously at once. The racket was deafening. I offered them some pieces of cake. They devoured them ravenously. I poured all the milk there was into a saucer and they fought each other to get it.

'Oh,' I cried indignantly, 'they're starved! It's wicked. Please, please, order some more milk and another plate of cake.'

Colonel Race departed silently to do my bidding. The cats had begun miaowing again. He returned with a big jug of milk and the cats finished it all.

I got up with determination on my face.

'I'm going to take those cats home with us – I shan't leave them here.'

'My dear child, don't be absurd. You can't carry six cats as well as fifty wooden animals round with you.'

'Never mind the wooden animals. These cats are alive. I shall take them back with me.'

'You will do nothing of the kind.' I looked at him resentfully but he went on: 'You think me cruel – but one can't go through life sentimentalizing over these things. It's no good standing out – I shan't allow you to take them. It's a primitive country, you know, and I'm stronger than you.'

I always know when I am beaten. I went down to the car with tears in my eyes.

'They're probably short of food just today,' he explained consolingly. 'That man's wife has gone into Bulawayo for stores. So it will be all right. And anyway, you know, the world's full of starving cats.'

'Don't – don't,' I said fiercely.

'I'm teaching you to realize life as it is. I'm teaching you to be hard and ruthless – like I am. That's the secret of strength – and the secret of success.'

'I'd sooner be dead than hard,' I said passionately.

We got into the car and started off. I pulled myself together again slowly. Suddenly, to my intense astonishment, he took my hand in his.

'Anne,' he said gently, 'I want you. Will you marry me?'

I was utterly taken aback.

'Oh, no,' I stammered. 'I can't.'

'Why not?'

'I don't care for you in that way. I've never thought of you like that.'

'I see. Is that the only reason?'

I had to be honest. I owed it him.

'No,' I said, 'it is not. You see – I – care for someone else.'

'I see,' he said again. 'And was that true at the beginning – when I first saw you – on the *Kilmorden?*'

'No,' I whispered. 'It was – since then.'

'I see,' he said for the third time, but this time there was a purposeful ring in his voice that made me turn and look at him. His face was grimmer than I had ever seen it.

'What – what do you mean?' I faltered.

He looked at me, inscrutable, dominating.

'Only – that I know now what I have to do.'

His words sent a shiver through me. There was a determination behind them that I did not understand – and it frightened me.

We neither of us said any more until we got back to the hotel. I went straight up to Suzanne. She was lying on her bed reading, and did not look in the least as though she had a headache.

'Here reposes the perfect gooseberry,' she remarked. '*Alias* the tactful chaperone. Why, Anne dear, what's the matter?'

For I had burst into a flood of tears.

I told her about the cats – I felt it wasn't fair to tell her about Colonel Race. But Suzanne is very sharp. I think she saw that there was something more behind.

'You haven't caught a chill, have you, Anne? Sounds absurd even to suggest such things in this heat, but you keep on shivering.'

'It's nothing,' I said. 'Nerves – or someone walking over my grave. I keep feeling something dreadful's going to happen.'

'Don't be silly,' said Suzanne, with decision. 'Let's talk of something interesting. Anne, about those diamonds –'

'What about them?'

'I'm not sure they're safe with me. It was all right before, no one could think they'd be amongst my things. But now that everyone knows we're such friends, you and I, I'll be under suspicion too.'

'Nobody knows they're in a roll of films, though,' I argued. 'It's a splendid hiding-place and I really don't think we could better it.'

She agreed doubtfully, but said we would discuss it again when we got to the Falls.

Our train went at nine o'clock. Sir Eustace's temper was still far from good, and Miss Pettigrew looked subdued. Colonel Race was completely himself. I felt that I had dreamed the whole conversation on the way back.

I slept heavily that night on my hard bunk, struggling with ill-defined, menacing dreams. I awoke with a headache and went out on the observation platform of the car. It was fresh and lovely, and everywhere, as far as one could see, were the undulating wooded hills. I loved it – loved it more than any place I had ever seen. I wished then that I could have a little hut somewhere in the heart of the scrub and live there always – always . . .

Just before half-past two, Colonel Race called me out from the 'office' and pointed to a bouquet-shaped white mist that hovered over one portion of the bush.

'The spray from the Falls,' he said. 'We are nearly there.'

I was still wrapped in that strange dream feeling of exaltation that had succeeded my troubled night. Very strongly implanted in me was the feeling that I had come home . . . Home! And yet I had never been here before – or had I in dreams?

We walked from the train to the hotel, a big white building closely wired against mosquitoes. There were no roads, no houses. We went out on the *stoep* and I uttered a gasp. There, half a mile away, facing us, were the Falls. I've never seen anything so grand and beautiful – I never shall.

'Anne, you're fey,' said Suzanne, as we sat down to lunch. 'I've never seen you like this before.'

She stared at me curiously.

'Am I?' I laughed, but I felt that my laugh was unnatural. 'It's just that I love it all.'

'It's more than that.'

A little frown crossed her brow – one of apprehension.

Yes, I was happy, but beyond that I had the curious feeling that I was waiting for something – something that would happen soon. I was excited – restless.

After tea we strolled out, got on the trolley and were pushed by smiling blacks down the little tracks of rails to the bridge.

It was a marvellous sight, the great chasm and the rushing waters below, and the veil of mist and spray in front of us that parted every now and then for one brief minute to show the cataract of water and then closed up again in its impenetrable mystery. That, to my mind, has always been the fascination of the Falls – their elusive quality. You always think you're going to see – and you never do.

We crossed the bridge and walked slowly on by the path that was marked out with white stone on either side and led round the brink of the gorge. Finally we arrived in a big clearing where on the left a path led downwards towards the chasm.

'The palm gully,' explained Colonel Race. 'Shall we go down?

Or shall we leave it until tomorrow? It will take some time, and it's a good climb up again.'

'We'll leave it until tomorrow,' said Sir Eustace with decision. He isn't at all fond of strenuous physical exercise, I have noticed.

He led the way back. As we went, we passed a fine native stalking along. Behind him came a woman who seemed to have the entire household belongings piled upon her head! The collection included a frying-pan.

'I never have my camera when I want it,' groaned Suzanne.

'That's an opportunity that will occur often enough, Mrs Blair,' said Colonel Race. 'So don't lament.'

We arrived back on the bridge.

'Shall we go into the rainbow forest?' he continued. 'Or are you afraid of getting wet?'

Suzanne and I accompanied him. Sir Eustace went back to the hotel. I was rather disappointed in the rainbow forest. There weren't nearly enough rainbows, and we got soaked to the skin, but every now and then we got a glimpse of the Falls opposite and realized how enormously wide they are. Oh, dear, dear Falls, how I love and worship you and always shall!

We got back to the hotel just in time to change for dinner. Sir Eustace seems to have taken a positive antipathy to Colonel Race. Suzanne and I rallied him gently, but didn't get much satisfaction.

After dinner he retired to his sitting-room, dragging Miss Pettigrew with him. Suzanne and I talked for a while with Colonel Race, and then she declared, with an immense yawn, that she was going to bed. I didn't want to be left alone with him, so I got up too and went to my room.

But I was far too excited to go to sleep. I did not even undress. I lay back in a chair and gave myself up to dreaming. And all the time I was conscious of something coming nearer and nearer . . .

There was a knock at the door, and I started. I got up and went to it. A little black boy held out a note. It was addressed to me in a handwriting I did not know. I took it and came back into the room. I stood there holding it. At last I opened it. It was very short!

'I must see you. I dare not come to the hotel. Will you come to the

clearing by the palm gully? In memory of Cabin 17 please come. The man you knew as Harry Rayburn.'

My heart beat to suffocation. He was here then! Oh, I had known it – I had known it all along! I had felt him near me. All unwittingly I had come to his place of retreat.

I wound a scarf round my head and stole to the door. I must be careful. He was hunted down. No one must see me meet him. I stole along to Suzanne's room. She was fast asleep. I could hear her breathing evenly.

Sir Eustace? I paused outside the door of his sitting-room. Yes, he was dictating to Miss Pettigrew, I could hear her monotonous voice repeating: 'I therefore venture to suggest, that in tackling this problem of coloured labour –' She paused for him to continue, and I heard him grunt something angrily.

I stole on again. Colonel Race's room was empty. I did not see him in the lounge. And he was the man I feared most! Still, I could waste no more time. I slipped quickly out of the hotel, and took the path to the bridge.

I crossed it and stood there waiting in the shadow. If anyone had followed me, I should see them crossing the bridge. But the minutes passed, and no one came. I had not been followed. I turned and took the path to the clearing. I took six paces or so, and then stopped. Something had rustled behind me. It could not be anyone who had followed me from the hotel. It was someone who was already here, waiting.

And immediately, without rhyme or reason, but with the sureness of instinct, I knew that it was I myself who was threatened. It was the same feeling as I had had on the *Kilmorden* that night – a sure instinct warning me of danger.

I looked sharply over my shoulder. Silence. I moved on a pace or two. Again I heard that rustle. Still walking, I looked over my shoulder again. A man's figure came out of the shadow. He saw that I saw him, and jumped forward, hard on my track.

It was too dark to recognize anybody. All I could see was that he was tall, and a European, not a native. I took to my heels and ran. I heard him pounding behind. I ran quicker, keeping my eyes fixed on the white stones that showed me where to step, for there was no moon that night.

And suddenly my foot felt nothingness. I heard the man behind me laugh, an evil, sinister laugh. It rang in my ears, as I fell headlong – down – down – down to destruction far beneath.

CHAPTER 25

I came to myself slowly and painfully. I was conscious of an aching head and a shooting pain down my left arm when I tried to move, and everything seemed dreamlike and unreal. Nightmare visions floated before me. I felt myself falling – falling again. Once Harry Rayburn's face seemed to come to me out of the mist. Almost I imagined it real. Then it floated away again, mocking me. Once, I remember, someone put a cup to my lips and I drank. A black face grinned into mine – a devil's face, I thought it, and screamed out. Then dreams again – long, troubled dreams in which I vainly sought Harry Rayburn to warn him – warn him – what of? I did not know myself. But there was some danger – some great danger – and I alone could save him. Then darkness again, merciful darkness and real sleep.

I woke at last myself again. The long nightmare was over. I remembered perfectly everything that had happened: my hurried flight from the hotel to meet Harry, the man in the shadows and the last terrible moment of falling . . .

By some miracle or other I had not been killed. I was bruised and aching, and very weak, but I was alive. But where was I? Moving my head with difficulty I looked round me. I was in a small room with rough wooden walls. On them were huge skins of animals and various tusks of ivory. I was lying on a kind of rough couch, also covered with skins, and my left arm was bandaged up and felt stiff and uncomfortable. At first I thought I was alone, and then I saw a man's figure sitting between me and the light, his head turned towards the window. He was so still that he might have been carved out of wood. Something in the close-cropped black head was familiar to me, but I did not dare to let my imagination run astray. Suddenly he turned, and I caught my breath. It was Harry Rayburn. Harry Rayburn in the flesh.

He rose and came over to me.

'Feeling better?' he said a trifle awkwardly.

I could not answer. The tears were running down my face. I was weak still, but I held his hand in both of mine. If only I could die like this, whilst he stood there looking down on me with that new look in his eyes.

'Don't cry, Anne. Please don't cry. You're safe now. No one shall hurt you.'

He went and fetched a cup and brought it to me.

'Drink some of this milk.'

I drank obediently. He went on talking, in a low coaxing tone such as he might have used to a child.

'Don't ask any more questions now. Go to sleep again. You'll be stronger by and by. I'll go away if you like.'

'No,' I said urgently. 'No, no.'

'Then I'll stay.'

He brought a small stool over beside me and sat there. He laid his hand over mine, and, soothed and comforted, I dropped off to sleep once more.

It must have been evening then, but when I woke again the sun was high in the heavens. I was alone in the hut, but as I stirred an old native woman came running in. She was hideous as sin, but she grinned at me encouragingly. She brought me water in a basin and helped me wash my face and hands. Then she brought me a large bowl of soup, and I finished it every drop! I asked her several questions, but she only grinned and nodded and chattered away in a guttural language, so I gathered she knew no English.

Suddenly she stood up and drew back respectfully as Harry Rayburn entered. He gave her a nod of dismissal and she went out, leaving us alone. He smiled at me.

'Really better today!'

'Yes, indeed, but very bewildered still. Where am I?'

'You're on a small island on the Zambesi about four miles up from the Falls.'

'Do – do my friends know I'm here?'

He shook his head.

'I must send word to them.'

'That is as you like, of course, but if I were you I should wait until you are a little stronger.'

'Why?'

He did not answer immediately, so I went on:

'How long have I been here?'

His answer amazed me.

'Nearly a month.'

'Oh!' I cried. 'I must send word to Suzanne. She'll be terribly anxious.'

'Who is Suzanne?'

'Mrs Blair. I was with her and Sir Eustace and Colonel Race at the hotel – but you knew that, surely?'

He shook his head.

'I know nothing, except that I found you, caught in the fork of a tree, unconscious and with a badly wrenched arm.'

'Where was the tree?'

'Overhanging the ravine. But for your clothes catching on the branches, you would certainly have been dashed to pieces.'

I shuddered. Then a thought struck me.

'You say you didn't know I was there. What about the note then?'

'What note?'

'The note you sent me, asking me to meet you in the clearing.'

He stared at me.

'I sent no note.'

I felt myself flushing up to the roots of my hair. Fortunately he did not seem to notice.

'How did you come to be on the spot in such a marvellous manner?' I asked, in as nonchalant a manner as I could assume. 'And what are you doing in this part of the world, anyway?'

'I live here,' he said simply.

'On this island?'

'Yes, I came here after the war. Sometimes I take parties from the hotel out in my boat, but it costs me very little to live, and mostly I do as I please.'

'You live here all alone?'

'I am not pining for society, I assure you,' he replied coldly.

'I am sorry to have inflicted mine upon you,' I retorted, 'but I seem to have had very little to say in the matter.'

To my surprise, his eyes twinkled a little.

'None whatever. I slung you across my shoulders like a sack of coal and carried you to my boat. Quite like a primitive man of the Stone Age.'

'But for a different reason,' I put in.

He flushed this time, a deep burning blush. The tan of his face was suffused.

'But you haven't told me how you came to be wandering about so conveniently for me?' I said hastily, to cover his confusion.

'I couldn't sleep. I was restless – disturbed – had the feeling something was going to happen. In the end I took the boat and came ashore and tramped down towards the Falls. I was just at the head of the palm gully when I heard you scream.'

'Why didn't you get help from the hotel instead of carting me all the way here?' I asked.

He flushed again.

'I suppose it seems an unpardonable liberty to you – but I don't think that even now you realize your danger! You think I should have informed your friends? Pretty friends, who allowed you to be decoyed out to death. No, I swore to myself that I'd take better care of you than anyone else could. Not a soul comes to this island. I got old Batani, whom I cured of a fever once, to come and look after you. She's loyal. She'll never say a word. I could keep you here for months and no one would ever know.'

I could keep you here for months and no one would ever know! How some words please one!

'You did quite right,' I said quietly. 'And I shall not send word to anyone. A day or so more anxiety doesn't make much difference. It's not as though they were my own people. They're only acquaintances really – even Suzanne. And whoever wrote that note must have known – a great deal! It was not the work of an outsider.'

I managed to mention the note this time without blushing at all.

'If you would be guided by me –' he said, hesitating.

'I don't expect I shall be,' I answered candidly. 'But there's no harm in hearing.'

'Do you always do what you like, Miss Beddingfeld?'

'Usually,' I replied cautiously. To anyone else I would have said 'Always.'

'I pity your husband,' he said unexpectedly.

'You needn't,' I retorted. 'I shouldn't dream of marrying anyone unless I was madly in love with him. And of course there is really nothing a woman enjoys so much as doing all the things she doesn't like for the sake of someone she *does* like. And the more self-willed she is, the more she likes it.'

'I'm afraid I disagree with you. The boot is on the other leg as a rule.' He spoke with a slight sneer.

'Exactly,' I cried eagerly. 'And that's why there are so many unhappy marriages. It's all the fault of the men. Either they give way to their women – and then the women despise them – or else they are utterly selfish, insist on their own way and never say "thank you". Successful husbands make their wives do just what they want, and then make a frightful fuss of them for doing it. Women like to be mastered, but they hate not to have their sacrifices appreciated. On the other hand, men don't really appreciate women who are nice to them all the time. When I am married, I shall be a devil most of the time, but every now and then, when my husband least expects it, I shall show him what a perfect angel I can be.'

Harry laughed outright.

'What a cat-and-dog life you will lead!'

'Lovers always fight,' I assured him. 'Because they don't understand each other. And by the time they do understand each other they aren't in love any more.'

'Does the reverse hold true? Are people who fight each other always lovers?'

'I – I don't know,' I said, momentarily confused.

He turned away to the fire-place.

'Like some more soup?' he asked in a casual tone.

'Yes, please. I'm so hungry that I would eat a hippopotamus.'

'That's good.'

He busied himself with the fire, I watched.

'When I can get off the couch, I'll cook for you,' I promised.

'I don't suppose you know anything about cooking.'

'I can warm up things out of tins as well as you can,' I retorted, pointing to a row of tins on the mantelpiece.

'*Touché*,' he said and laughed.

His whole face changed when he laughed. It became boyish, happy – a different personality.

I enjoyed my soup. As I ate it I reminded him that he had not, after all, tendered me his advice.

'Ah, yes, what I was going to say was this. If I were you I would stay quietly *perdu* here until you are quite strong again. Your enemies will believe you dead. They will hardly be surprised at not finding the body. It would have been dashed to pieces on the rocks and carried down with the torrent.'

I shivered.

'Once you are completely restored to health, you can journey quietly on to Beira and get a boat to take you back to England.'

'That would be very tame,' I objected scornfully.

'There speaks a foolish schoolgirl.'

'I'm not a foolish schoolgirl,' I cried indignantly. 'I'm a woman.'

He looked at me with an expression I could not fathom, as I sat up flushed and excited.

'God help me, so you are,' he muttered and went abruptly out.

My recovery was rapid. The two injuries I had sustained were a knock on the head and a badly wrenched arm. The latter was the most serious and, to begin with, my rescuer had believed it to be actually broken. A careful examination, however, convinced him that it was not so, and although it was very painful I was recovering the use of it quite quickly.

It was a strange time. We were cut off from the world, alone together as Adam and Eve might have been – but with what a difference! Old Batani hovered about, counting no more than a dog might have done. I insisted on doing the cooking, or as much of it as I could manage with one arm. Harry was out a good part of the time, but we spent long hours together lying out in the shade of the palms, talking and quarrelling – discussing everything under high heaven, quarrelling and making it up again. We bickered a good deal, but there grew up between us a real and lasting comradeship such as I could never have believed possible. That – and something else.

The time was drawing near, I knew it, when I should be well enough to leave, and I realized it with a heavy heart. Was he going to let me go? Without a word? Without a sign? He had fits of silence, long moody intervals, moments when he would spring up and tramp off by himself. One evening the crisis came. We had finished our simple meal and were sitting in the doorway of the hut. The sun was sinking.

Hairpins were necessities of life with which Harry had not been able to provide me, and my hair, straight and black, hung to my knees. I sat, my chin on my hands, lost in meditation. I felt rather than saw Harry looking at me.

'You look like a witch, Anne,' he said at last, and there was something in his voice that had never been there before.

He reached out his hand and just touched my hair. I shivered. Suddenly he sprang up with an oath.

'You must leave here tomorrow, do you hear?' he cried. 'I – I can't bear any more. I'm only a man after all. You must go, Anne. You must. You're not a fool. You know yourself that this can't go on.'

'I suppose not,' I said slowly. 'But – it's been happy, hasn't it?'

'Happy? It's been hell!'

'As bad as that!'

'What do you torment me for? Why are you mocking at me? Why do you say that – laughing into your hair?'

'I wasn't laughing. And I'm not mocking. If you want me to go, I'll go. But if you want me to stay – I'll stay.'

'Not that!' he cried vehemently. 'Not that. Don't tempt me, Anne. Do you realize what I am? A criminal twice over. A man hunted down. They know me here as Harry Parker – they think I've been away on a trek up country, but any day they may put two and two together – and then the blow will fall. You're so young, Anne, and so beautiful – with the kind of beauty that sends men mad. All the world's before you – love, life, everything. Mine's behind me – scorched, spoiled, with a taste of bitter ashes.'

'If you don't want me –'

'You know I want you. You know that I'd give my soul to pick you up in my arms and keep you here, hidden away from the world, for ever and ever. And you're tempting me, Anne. You, with your long witch's hair, and your eyes that are golden and brown and green and never stop laughing even when your mouth is grave. But I'll save you from yourself and from me. You shall go tonight. You shall go to Beira –'

'I'm not going to Beira,' I interrupted.

'You are. You shall go to Beira if I have to take you there myself and throw you on to the boat. What do you think I'm made of? Do you think I'll wake up night after night, fearing they've got you? One can't go on counting on miracles happening. You must go back to England, Anne – and – and marry and be happy.'

'With a steady man who'll give me a good home!'

'Better that than – utter disaster.'

'And what of you?'

His face grew grim and set.

'I've got my work ready to hand. Don't ask what it is. You can guess, I dare say. But I'll tell you this – I'll clear my name, or die in the attempt, and I'll choke the life out of the damned scoundrel who did his best to murder you the other night.'

'We must be fair,' I said. 'He didn't actually push me over.'

'He'd no need to. His plan was cleverer than that. I went up to the path afterwards. Everything looked all right, but by the marks on the ground I saw that the stones which outline the path had been taken up and put down again in a slightly different place. There are tall bushes growing just over the edge. He'd balanced the outside stones on them, so that you'd think you were still on the path when in reality you were stepping into nothingness. God help him if I lay my hands upon him!'

He paused a minute and then said, in a totally different tone:

'We've never spoken of these things, Anne, have we? But the time's come. I want you to hear the whole story – from the beginning.'

'If it hurts you to go over the past, don't tell me,' I said in a low voice.

'But I want you to know. I never thought I should speak of that part of my life to anyone. Funny, isn't it, the tricks Fate plays?'

He was silent for a minute or two. The sun had set, and the velvety darkness of the African night was enveloping us like a mantle.

'Some of it I know,' I said gently.

'What do you know?'

'I know that your real name is Harry Lucas.'

Still he hesitated – not looking at me, but staring straight out in front of him. I had no clue as to what was passing in his mind, but at last he jerked his head forward as though acquiescing in some unspoken decision of his own, and began his story.

CHAPTER 26

'You are right. My real name is Harry Lucas. My father was a retired soldier who came out to farm in Rhodesia. He died when I was in my second year at Cambridge.'

'Were you fond of him?' I asked suddenly.

'I – don't know.'

Then he flushed and went on with sudden vehemence:

'Why do I say that? I *did* love my father. We said bitter things to each other the last time I saw him, and we had many rows over my wildness and my debts, but I cared for the old man. I know how much now – when it's too late,' he continued more quietly. 'It was at Cambridge that I met the other fellow –'

'Young Eardsley?'

'Yes – young Eardsley. His father, as you know, was one of South Africa's most prominent men. We drifted together at once, my friend and I. We had our love of South Africa in common and we both had a taste for the untrodden places of the world. After he left Cambridge, Eardsley had a final quarrel with his father. The old man had paid his debts twice, he refused to do so again. There was a bitter scene between them. Sir Laurence declared himself at the end of his patience – he would do no more for his son. He must stand on his own legs for a while. The result was, as you know, that those two young men went off to South America together, prospecting for diamonds. I'm not going into that now, but we had a wonderful time out there. Hardships in plenty, you understand, but it was a good life – a hand-to-mouth scramble for existence far from the beaten track – and, my God that's the place to know a friend. There was a bond forged between us two out there that only death could have broken. Well, as Colonel Race told you, our efforts were crowned with success. We found a second Kimberley in the heart of the British Guiana jungles. I can't tell you our elation. It wasn't so much the actual value in money of the find – you see, Eardsley was used to money, and he knew that when his father died he would be a millionaire, and

Lucas had always been poor and was used to it. No, it was the sheer delight of discovery.'

He paused, and then added, almost apologetically.

'You don't mind my telling it this way, do you? As though I wasn't in it at all. It seems like that now when I look back and see those two boys. I almost forget that one of them was – Harry Rayburn.'

'Tell it any way you like,' I said, and he went on:

'We came to Kimberley – very cock-a-hoop over our find. We brought a magnificent selection of diamonds with us to submit to the experts. And then – in the hotel at Kimberley – we met her –'

I stiffened a little, and the hand that rested on the door-post clenched itself involuntarily.

'Anita Grünberg – that was her name. She was an actress. Quite young and very beautiful. She was South African born, but her mother was a Hungarian, I believe. There was some sort of mystery about her, and that, of course, heightened her attraction for two boys home from the wilds. She must have had an easy task. We both fell for her right away, and we both took it hard. It was the first shadow that had ever come between us – but even then it didn't weaken our friendship. Each of us, I honestly believe, was willing to stand aside for the other to go in and win. But that wasn't her game. Sometimes, afterwards, I wondered why it hadn't been, for Sir Laurence Eardsley's only son was quite a *parti*. But the truth of it was that she was married – to a sorter in De Beers – though nobody knew of it. She pretended enormous interest in our discovery, and we told her all about it and even showed her the diamonds. Delilah – that's what she should have been called – and she played her part well!

'The De Beers robbery was discovered, and like a thunderclap the police came down upon us. They seized our diamonds. We only laughed at first – the whole thing was so absurd. And then the diamonds were produced in court – and without question they were the stones stolen from De Beers. Anita Grünberg had disappeared. She had effected the substitution neatly enough, and our story that these were not the stones originally in our possession was laughed to scorn.

'Sir Laurence Eardsley had enormous influence. He succeeded

in getting the case dismissed – but it left two young men ruined and disgraced to face the world with the stigma of thief attached to their name, and it pretty well broke the old fellow's heart. He had one bitter interview with his son in which he heaped upon him every reproach imaginable. He had done what he could to save the family name, but from that day on his son was his son no longer. He cast him off utterly. And the boy, like the proud young fool that he was, remained silent, disdaining to protest his innocence in the face of his father's disbelief. He came out furious from the interview – his friend was waiting for him. A week later, war was declared. The two friends enlisted together. You know what happened. The best pal a man ever had was killed, partly through his own mad recklessness in rushing into unnecessary danger. He died with his name tarnished . . .

'I swear to you, Anne, that it was mainly on his account that I was so bitter against that woman. It had gone deeper with him than with me. I had been madly in love with her for the moment – I even think that I frightened her sometimes – but with him it was a quieter and deeper feeling. She had been the very centre of his universe – and her betrayal of him tore up the very roots of life. The blow stunned him and left him paralysed.'

Harry paused. After a minute or two he went on:

'As you know, I was reported "Missing, presumed killed". I never troubled to correct the mistake. I took the name of Parker and came to this island, which I knew of old. At the beginning of the war I had had ambitious hopes of proving my innocence, but now all that spirit seemed dead. All I felt was, "What's the good?" My pal was dead, neither he nor I had any living relations who would care. I was supposed to be dead too; let it remain at that. I led a peaceful existence here, neither happy nor unhappy – numbed of all feeling. I see now, though I did not realize it at the time, that that was partly the effect of the war.

'And then one day something occurred to wake me right up again. I was taking a party of people in my boat on a trip up the river, and I was standing at the landing-stage, helping them in, when one of the men uttered a startled exclamation. It focused my attention on him. He was a small, thin man with a beard, and he was staring at me for all he was worth as though I was a ghost. So powerful was his emotion that it awakened my curiosity.

I made inquiries about him at the hotel and learned that his name was Carton, that he came from Kimberley, and that he was a diamond-sorter employed by De Beers. In a minute all the old sense of wrong surged over me again. I left the island and went to Kimberley.

'I could find out little more about him, however. In the end, I decided that I must force an interview. I took my revolver with me. In the brief glimpse I had had of him, I had realized that he was a physical coward. No sooner were we face to face than I recognized that he was afraid of me. I soon forced him to tell me all he knew. He had engineered part of the robbery and Anita Grünberg was his wife. He had once caught sight of both of us when we were dining with her at the hotel, and, having read that I was killed, my appearance in the flesh at the Falls had startled him badly. He and Anita had married quite young, but she had soon drifted away from him. She had got in with a bad lot, he told me – and it was then for the first time that I heard of the "Colonel". Carton himself had never been mixed up in anything except this one affair – so he solemnly assured me, and I was inclined to believe him. He was emphatically not of the stuff of which successful criminals are made.

'I still had the feeling that he was keeping back something. As a test, I threatened to shoot him there and then, declaring that I cared very little what became of me now. In a frenzy of terror he poured out a further story. It seems that Anita Grünberg did not quite trust the "Colonel". Whilst pretending to hand over to him the stones she had taken from the hotel, she kept back some in her own possession. Carton advised her, with his technical knowledge, which to keep. If, at any time, these stones were produced, they were of such colour and quality as to be readily identifiable, and the experts at De Beers would admit at once that these stones had never passed through their hands. In this way, my story of a substitution would be supported, my name would be cleared, and suspicion would be diverted to the proper quarter. I gathered that, contrary to his usual practice, the "Colonel" himself had been concerned in this affair, therefore Anita felt satisfied that she had a real hold over him, should she need it. Carton now proposed that I should make a bargain with Anita Grünberg, or Nadina, as she now called herself. For a sufficient sum of money, he thought that she would be willing to give up the diamonds and betray her former employer. He would cable to her immediately.

'I was still suspicious of Carton. He was a man whom it was easy enough to frighten, but who, in his fright, would tell so many lies that to sift the truth out from them would be no easy job. I went back to the hotel and waited. By the following evening I judged that he would have received the reply to his cable. I called round to his house and was told that Mr Carton was away, but would be returning on the morrow. Instantly I became suspicious. In the nick of time I found out that he was in reality sailing for England on the *Kilmorden Castle*, which left Cape Town in two days' time. I had just time to journey down and catch the same boat.

'I had no intention of alarming Carton by revealing my presence on board. I had done a good deal of acting in my time at Cambridge, and it was comparatively easy for me to transform myself into a grave, bearded gentleman of middle age. I avoided Carton carefully on board the boat, keeping to my own cabin as far as possible under the pretence of illness.

'I had no difficulty in trailing him when we got to London. He went straight to an hotel and did not go out until the following day. He left the hotel shortly before one o'clock. I was behind him. He went straight to a house-agent in Knightsbridge. There he asked for particulars of houses to let on the river.

'I was at the next table also inquiring about houses. Then suddenly in walked Anita Grünberg, Nadina – whatever you like to call her. Superb, insolent, and almost as beautiful as ever. God! how I hated her. There she was, the woman who had ruined my life – and who had also ruined a better life than mine. At that minute I could have put my hands round her neck and squeezed the life out of her inch by inch! Just for a minute or two I saw red. I hardly took in what the agent was saying. It was her voice that I heard next, high and clear, with an exaggerated foreign accent: "The Mill House, Marlow. The property of Sir Eustace Pedler. That sounds as though it might suit me. At any rate, I will go and see it.'

'The man wrote her an order, and she walked out again in her regal insolent manner. Not by word or a sign had she recognized Carton, yet I was sure that their meeting there was a preconceived plan. Then I started to jump to conclusions. Not knowing that Sir Eustace was at Cannes, I thought that this house-hunting business was a mere pretext for meeting him in the Mill House. I knew that he had been in South Africa at the time of the robbery, and never having seen him I immediately leaped to the conclusion that he himself was the mysterious "Colonel" of whom I had heard so much.

'I followed my two suspects along Knightsbridge. Nadina went into the Hyde Park Hotel. I quickened my pace and went in also. She walked straight into the restaurant, and I decided that I would not risk her recognizing me at the moment, but would continue to follow Carton. I was in great hopes that he was going to get the diamonds, and that by suddenly appearing and making myself known to him when he least expected it I might startle the truth out of him. I followed him down into the Tube station at Hyde Park Corner. He was standing by himself at the end of the platform. There was some girl standing near, but no one else. I decided that I would accost him then and there. You know what happened. In the sudden shock of seeing a man whom he imagined far away in South Africa, he lost his head and stepped back upon the line. He was always a coward. Under the pretext of being a doctor, I managed to search his pockets. There was a wallet with some notes in it and one or two unimportant letters, there was a roll of films – which I must have dropped somewhere later – and there was a piece of paper with an appointment made on it for the 22nd on the *Kilmorden Castle*. In my haste to get away before anyone detained me, I dropped that also, but fortunately I remembered the figures.

'I hurried to the nearest cloak-room and hastily removed my make-up. I did not want to be laid by the heels for picking a dead man's pocket. Then I retraced my steps to the Hyde Park Hotel. Nadina was still having lunch. I needn't describe in detail how I followed her down to Marlow. She went into the house, and I spoke to the woman at the lodge, pretending that I was with her. Then I, too, went in.

He stopped. There was a tense silence.

'You will believe me, Anne, won't you? I swear before God that what I am going to say is true. I went into the house after her with something very like murder in my heart – and she was dead! I found her in that first-floor room – God! It was horrible. Dead – and I was not more than three minutes behind her. And there was no sign of anyone else in the house! Of course I realized at once the terrible position I was in. By one master-stroke the blackmailed had rid himself of the blackmailer, and at the same time had provided a victim to whom the crime would be ascribed. The hand of the "Colonel" was very plain. For the second time I was to be his victim. Fool that I had been to walk into the trap so easily!

'I hardly know what I did next. I managed to go out of the place looking fairly normal, but I knew that it could not be long before the crime was discovered and a description of my appearance telegraphed all over the country.

'I lay low for some days, not daring to make a move. In the end, chance came to my aid. I overheard a conversation between two middle-aged gentlemen in the street, one of whom proved to be Sir Eustace Pedler. I at once conceived the idea of attaching myself to him as his secretary. The fragment of conversation I had overheard gave me my clue. I was now no longer so sure that Sir Eustace Pedler was the "Colonel". His house might have been appointed as a rendezvous by accident, or for some obscure motive that I had not fathomed.'

'Do you know,' I interrupted, 'that Guy Pagett was in Marlow at the date of the murder?'

'That settles it then. I thought he was at Cannes with Sir Eustace.'

'He was supposed to be in Florence – but he certainly never went *there*. I'm pretty certain he was really in Marlow, but of course I can't prove it.'

'And to think I never suspected Pagett for a minute until the night he tried to throw you overboard. The man's a marvellous actor.'

'Yes, isn't he?'

'That explains why the Mill House was chosen. Pagett could probably get in and out of it unobserved. Of course he made no objection to my accompanying Sir Eustace across in the boat. He didn't want me laid by the heels immediately. You see, evidently Nadina didn't bring the jewels with her to the rendezvous, as they had counted on her doing. I fancy that Carton really had them and concealed them somewhere on the *Kilmorden Castle* – that's where he came in. They hoped that I might have some clue as to where they were hidden. As long as the "Colonel" did not recover the diamonds, he was still in danger – hence his anxiety to get them at all costs. Where the devil Carton hid them – if he did hide them – I don't know.'

'That's another story,' I quoted. 'My story. And I'm going to tell it to you now.'

CHAPTER 27

Harry listened attentively whilst I recounted all the events that I have narrated in these pages. The thing that bewildered and astonished him most was to find that all along the diamonds had been in my possession – or rather in Suzanne's. That was a fact he had never suspected. Of course, after hearing his story, I realized the point of Carton's little arrangement – or rather Nadina's, since I had no doubt that it was her brain which had conceived the plan. No surprise tactics executed against her or her husband could result in the seizure of the diamonds. The secret was locked in her own brain, and the 'Colonel' was not likely to guess that they had been entrusted to the keeping of an ocean steward!

Harry's vindication from the old charge of theft seemed assured. It was the other graver charge that paralysed all our activities. For, as things stood, he could not come out in the open to prove his case.

The one thing we came back to, again and again, was the identity of the 'Colonel'. Was he, or was he not, Guy Pagett?

'I should say he was but for one thing,' said Harry. 'It seems pretty much of a certainty that it was Pagett who murdered Anita Grünberg at Marlow – and that certainly lends colour to the supposition that he is actually the "Colonel", since Anita's business was not of the nature to be discussed with a subordinate. No – the only thing that militates against that theory is the attempt to put you out of the way the night of your arrival here. You saw Pagett left behind at Cape Town – by no possible means could he have arrived here before the following Wednesday. He is unlikely to have any emissaries in this part of the world, and all his plans were laid to deal with you in Cape Town. He might, of course, have cabled instructions to some lieutenant of his in Johannesburg, who could have joined the Rhodesian train at Mafeking, but his instructions would have had to be particularly definite to allow of that note being written.'

We sat silent for a moment, then Harry went on slowly:

'You say that Mrs Blair was asleep when you left the hotel and that you heard Sir Eustace dictating to Miss Pettigrew? Where was Colonel Race?'

'I could not find him anywhere.'

'Had he any reason to believe that – you and I might be friendly with each other?'

'He might have had,' I answered thoughtfully, remembering our conversation on the way back from the Matopos. 'He's a very powerful personality,' I continued, 'but not at all my idea of the "Colonel". And, anyway, such an idea would be absurd. He's in the Secret Service.'

'How do we know that he is? It's the easiest thing in the world to throw out a hint of that kind. No one contradicts it, and the rumour spreads until everyone believes it as gospel truth. It provides an excuse for all sorts of doubtful doings. Anne, do you like Race?'

'I do – and I don't. He repels me and at the same time fascinates me; but I know one thing, I'm always a little afraid of him.'

'He was in South Africa, you know, at the time of the Kimberley robbery,' said Harry slowly.

'But it was he who told Suzanne all about the "Colonel" and how he had been in Paris trying to get on his track.'

'*Camouflage* – of a particularly clever kind.'

'But where does Pagett come in? Is he in Race's pay?'

'Perhaps,' said Harry slowly, 'he doesn't come in at all.'

'What?'

'Think back, Anne. Did you ever hear Pagett's own account of that night on the *Kilmorden?*'

'Yes – through Sir Eustace.'

I repeated it. Harry listened closely.

'He saw a man coming from the direction of Sir Eustace's cabin and followed him up on deck. Is that what he says? Now, who had the cabin opposite to Sir Eustace? Colonel Race. Supposing

Colonel Race crept up on deck, and, foiled in his attack on you, fled round the deck and met Pagett just coming through the saloon door. He knocks him down and springs inside, closing the door. We dash round and find Pagett lying there. How's that?'

'You forget that he declares positively it was you who knocked him down.'

'Well, suppose that just as he regains consciousness he sees me disappearing in the distance? Wouldn't he take it for granted that I was his assailant? Especially as he thought all along it was I he was following?'

'It's possible, yes,' I said slowly. 'But it alters all our ideas. And there are other things.'

'Most of them are open to explanation. The man who followed you in Cape Town spoke to Pagett, and Pagett looked at his watch. The man might have merely asked him the time.'

'It was just a coincidence, you mean?'

'Not exactly. There's a method in all this, connecting Pagett with the affair. Why was the Mill House chosen for the murder? Was it because Pagett had been in Kimberley when the diamonds were stolen? Would *he* have been made the scapegoat if I had not appeared so providentially upon the scene?'

'Then you think he may be entirely innocent?'

'It looks like it, but, if so, we've got to find out what he was doing in Marlow. If he's got a reasonable explanation of that, we're on the right tack.'

He got up.

'It's past midnight. Turn in, Anne, and get some sleep. Just before dawn I'll take you over in the boat. You must catch the train at Livingstone. I've got a friend there who will keep you hidden away until the train starts. You go to Bulawayo and catch the Beira train there. I can find out from my friend in Livingstone what's going on at the hotel and where your friends are now.'

'Beira,' I said meditatively.

'Yes, Anne, it's Beira for you. This is man's work. Leave it to me.'

We had had a momentary respite from emotion whilst we talked the situation out, but it was on us again now. We did not even look at each other.

'Very well,' I said, and passed into the hut.

I lay down on the skin-covered couch, but I didn't sleep, and outside I could hear Harry Rayburn pacing up and down, up and down through the long dark hours. At last he called me:

'Come, Anne, it's time to go.'

I got up and came out obediently. It was still quite dark, but I knew that dawn was not far off.

'We'll take the canoe, not the motor-boat –' Harry began, when suddenly he stopped dead and held up his hand.

'Hush! What's that?'

I listened, but could hear nothing. His ears were sharper than mine, however, the ears of a man who has lived long in the wilderness. Presently I heard it too – the faint splash of paddles in the water coming from the direction of the right bank of the river and rapidly approaching our little landing-stage.

We strained our eyes in the darkness, and could make out a dark blur on the surface of the water. It was a boat. Then there was a momentary spurt of flame. Someone had struck a match. By its light I recognized one figure, the red-bearded Dutchman of the villa at Muizenberg. The others were natives.

'Quick – back to the hut.'

Harry swept me back with him. He took down a couple of rifles and a revolver from the wall.

'Can you load a rifle?'

'I never have. Show me how.'

I grasped his instructions well enough. We closed the door and Harry stood by the window which overlooked the landing-stage. The boat was just about to run alongside it.

'Who's that?' called out Harry, in a ringing voice.

Any doubt we might have had as to our visitors' intentions was swiftly resolved. A hail of bullets splattered round us. Fortunately neither of us was hit. Harry raised the rifle. It spat murderously, and again and again. I heard two groans and a splash.

'That's given 'em something to think about,' he muttered grimly, as he reached for the second rifle. 'Stand well back, Anne, for God's sake. And load quickly.'

More bullets. One just grazed Harry's cheek. His answering fire was more deadly than theirs. I had the rifle reloaded when he turned for it. He caught me close with his left arm and kissed me once savagely before he turned to the window again. Suddenly he uttered a shout.

'They're going – had enough of it. They're a good mark out there on the water, and they can't see how many of us there are. They're routed for the moment – but they'll come back. We'll have to get ready for them.' He flung down the rifle and turned to me.

'Anne! You beauty! You wonder! You little queen! As brave as a lion. Black-haired witch!'

He caught me in his arms. He kissed my hair, my eyes, my mouth.

'And now to business,' he said, suddenly releasing me. 'Get out those tins of paraffin.'

I did as I was told. He was busy inside the hut. Presently I saw him on the roof of the hut, crawling along with something in his arms. He rejoined me in a minute or two.

'Go down to the boat. We'll have to carry it across the island to the other side.'

He picked up the paraffin as I disappeared.

'They're coming back,' I called softly. I had seen the blur moving out from the opposite shore.

He ran down to me.

'Just in time. Why – where the hell's the boat?'

Both had been cut adrift. Harry whistled softly.

'We're in a tight place, honey. Mind?'

'Not with you.'

'Ah, but dying together's not much fun. We'll do better than that. See – they've got two boat-loads this time. Going to land at two different points. Now for my little scenic effect.'

Almost as he spoke a long flame shot up from the hut. Its light illuminated two crouching figures huddled together on the roof.

'My old clothes – stuffed with rags – but they won't tumble to it for some time. Come, Anne, we've got to try desperate means.'

Hand in hand, we raced across the island. Only a narrow channel of water divided it from the shore on that side.

'We've got to swim for it. Can you swim at all, Anne? Not that it matters. I can get you across. It's the wrong side for a boat – too many rocks, but the right side for swimming, and the right side for Livingstone.'

'I can swim a little – further than that. What's the danger, Harry?' For I had seen the grim look on his face. 'Sharks?'

'No, you little goose. Sharks live in the sea. But you're sharp, Anne. Crocs, that's the trouble.'

'Crocodiles?'

'Yes, don't think of them – or say your prayers, whichever you feel inclined.'

We plunged in. My prayers must have been efficacious, for we reached the shore without adventure, and drew ourselves up wet and dripping on the bank.

'Now for Livingstone. It's rough going, I'm afraid, and wet clothes won't make it any better. But it's got to be done.'

That walk was a nightmare. My wet skirts flapped round my legs, and my stockings were soon torn off by the thorns. Finally, I stopped, utterly exhausted. Harry came back to me.

'Hold up, honey. I'll carry you for a bit.'

That was the way I came into Livingstone, slung across his shoulder like a sack of coals. How he did it for all that way, I don't know. The first faint light of dawn was just breaking. Harry's friend was a young man of twenty years old who kept a store of native curios. His name was Ned – perhaps he had another, but I never heard it. He didn't seem in the least surprised to see Harry walk in, dripping wet, holding an equally dripping female by the hand. Men are very wonderful.

He gave us food to eat, and hot coffee, and got our clothes dried for us whilst we rolled ourselves in Manchester blankets of gaudy hue. In the tiny back room of the hut we were safe from observation whilst he departed to make judicious inquiries as to what had become of Sir Eustace's party, and whether any of them were still at the hotel.

It was then that I informed Harry that nothing would induce me to go to Beira. I never meant to, anyway, but now all reason for such proceedings had vanished. The point of the plan had been that my enemies believed me dead. Now that they knew I wasn't dead, my going to Beira would do no good whatever. They could easily follow me there and murder me quietly. I should have no one to protect me. It was finally arranged that I should join Suzanne, wherever she was, and devote all my energies to taking care of myself. On no account was I to seek adventures or endeavour to checkmate the 'Colonel'.

I was to remain quietly with her and await instructions from Harry. The diamonds were to be deposited in the bank at Kimberley under the name of Parker.

'There's one thing,' I said thoughtfully, 'we ought to have a code of some kind. We don't want to be hoodwinked again by messages purporting to come from one to the other.'

'That's easy enough. Any message that comes *genuinely* from me will have the word "and" crossed out in it.'

'Without trade-mark, none genuine,' I murmured. 'What about wires?'

'Any wires from me will be signed "Andy".'

'Train will be in before long, Harry,' said Ned, putting his head in, and withdrawing it immediately.

I stood up.

'And shall I marry a nice steady man if I find one?' I asked demurely.

Harry came close to me.

'My God! Anne, if you ever marry anyone else but me, I'll wring his neck. And as for you –'

'Yes,' I said, pleasurably excited.

'I shall carry you away and beat you black and blue!'

'What a delightful husband I have chosen!' I said satirically. 'And doesn't he change his mind overnight!'

CHAPTER 28

(EXTRACT FROM THE DIARY OF SIR EUSTACE PEDLER)

As I remarked once before, I am essentially a man of peace. I yearn for a quiet life – and that's just the one thing I don't seem able to have. I am always in the middle of storms and alarms. The relief of getting away from Pagett with his incessant nosing out of intrigues was enormous, and Miss Pettigrew is certainly a useful creature. Although there is nothing of the houri about her, one or two of her accomplishments are invaluable. It is true that I had a touch of liver at Bulawayo and behaved like a bear in consequence, but I had had a disturbed night in the train. At 3 a.m. an exquisitely dressed young man looking like a musical-comedy hero of the Wild West entered my compartment and asked where I was going. Disregarding my first murmur of 'Tea – and for God's sake don't put sugar in it,' he repeated his question, laying stress on the fact that he was not a waiter but an Immigration officer. I finally succeeded in satisfying him that I was suffering from no infectious disease, that I was visiting Rhodesia from the purest of motives, and further gratified him with my full Christian names and my place of birth. I then endeavoured to snatch a little sleep, but some officious ass aroused me at 5.30 with a cup of liquid sugar which he called tea. I don't think I threw it at him, but I know that that was what I wanted to do. He brought me unsugared tea, stone cold, at 6, and I then fell asleep utterly exhausted, to awaken just outside Bulawayo and be landed with a beastly wooden giraffe, all legs and neck!

But for these small contretemps, all had been going smoothly. And then fresh calamity befell.

It was the night of our arrival at the Falls. I was dictating to Miss Pettigrew in my sitting-room, when suddenly Mrs Blair burst in without a word of excuse and wearing most compromising attire.

'Where's Anne?' she cried.

A nice question to ask. As though I were responsible for the girl. What did she expect Miss Pettigrew to think? That I was in the habit of producing Anne Beddingfeld from my pocket at midnight or thereabouts? Very compromising for a man in my position.

'I presume,' I said coldly, 'that she is in her bed.'

I cleared my throat and glanced at Miss Pettigrew, to show that I was ready to resume dictating. I hoped Mrs Blair would take the hint. She did nothing of the kind. Instead she sank into a chair, and waved a slippered foot in an agitated manner.

'She's not in her room. I've been there. I had a dream – a terrible dream – that she was in some awful danger, and I got up and went to her room, just to reassure myself, you know. She wasn't there and her bed hadn't been slept in.'

She looked at me appealingly.

'What shall I do, Sir Eustace?'

Repressing the desire to reply, 'Go to bed, and don't worry over nothing. An able-bodied young woman like Anne Beddingfeld is perfectly well able to take care of herself,' I frowned judicially.

'What does Race say about it?'

Why should Race have it all his own way? Let him have some of the disadvantages as well as the advantages of female society.

'I can't find him anywhere.'

She was evidently making a night of it. I sighed, and sat down in a chair.

'I don't quite see the reason for your agitation,' I said patiently.

'My dream –'

'That curry we had for dinner!'

'Oh, Sir Eustace!'

The woman was quite indignant. And yet everybody knows that nightmares are a direct result of injudicious eating.

'After all,' I continued persuasively, 'why shouldn't Anne Beddingfeld and Race go out for a little stroll without having the whole hotel aroused about it?'

'You think they've just gone out for a stroll together? But it's after midnight?'

'One does these foolish things when one is young,' I murmured, 'though Race is certainly old enough to know better.'

'Do you really think so?'

'I dare say they've run away to make a match of it,' I continued soothingly, though fully aware that I was making an idiotic suggestion. For, after all, at a place like this, where is there to run away to?

I don't know how much longer I should have gone on making feeble remarks, but at that moment Race himself walked in upon us. At any rate, I had been partly right – he had been out for a stroll, but he hadn't taken Anne with him. However, I had been quite wrong in my way of dealing with the situation. I was soon shown that. Race had the whole hotel turned upside-down in three minutes. I've never seen a man more upset.

The thing is very extraordinary. Where did the girl go? She walked out of the hotel, fully dressed, about ten minutes past eleven, and she was never seen again. The idea of suicide seems impossible. She was one of these energetic young women who are in love with life, and have not the faintest intention of quitting it. There was no train either way until midday on the morrow, so she can't have left the place. Then where the devil is she?

Race is almost beside himself, poor fellow. He has left no stone unturned. All the D.C.s, or whatever they call themselves, for hundreds of miles round have been pressed into the service. The native trackers have run about on all fours. Everything that can be done is being done – but no sign of Anne Beddingfeld. The accepted theory is that she walked in her sleep. There are signs on the path near the bridge which seem to show that the girl walked deliberately off the edge. If so, of course, she must have been dashed to pieces on the rocks below. Unfortunately, most of the footprints were obliterated by a party of tourists who chose to walk that way early on the Monday morning.

I don't know that it's a very satisfactory theory. In my young days, I was always told that sleep-walkers couldn't hurt themselves – that their own sixth sense took care of them. I don't think the theory satisfies Mrs Blair either.

I can't make that woman out. Her whole attitude towards Race has changed. She watches him now like a cat a mouse, and she makes obvious efforts to bring herself to be civil to him. And they used to be such friends. Altogether she is unlike herself, nervous, hysterical, starting and jumping at the least sound. I am beginning to think that it is high time I went to Jo'burg.

A rumour came along yesterday of a mysterious island somewhere up the river, with a man and a girl on it. Race got very excited. It turned out to be all a mare's nest, however. The man had been there for years, and is well known to the manager of the hotel. He takes parties up and down the river in the season and points out crocodiles and a stray hippopotamus or so to them. I believe that he keeps a tame one which is trained to bite pieces out of the boat on occasions. Then he fends it off with a boathook, and the party feel they have really got to the back of beyond at last. How long the girl has been there is not definitely known, but it seems pretty clear that she can't be Anne, and there is a certain delicacy in interfering in other people's affairs. If I were this young fellow, I should certainly kick Race off the island if he came asking questions about my love affairs.

Later.

It is definitely settled that I go to Jo'burg tomorrow. Race urges me to do so. Things are getting unpleasant there, by all I hear, but I might as well go before they get worse. I dare say I shall be shot by a striker, anyway. Mrs Blair was to have accompanied me, but at the last minute she changed her mind and decided to stay on at the

Falls. It seems as though she couldn't bear to take her eyes off Race. She came to me tonight, and said, with some hesitation, that she had a favour to ask. Would I take charge of her souvenirs for her?

'Not the animals?' I asked, in lively alarm. I always felt that I should get stuck with those beastly animals sooner or later.

In the end, we effected a compromise. I took charge of two small wooden boxes for her which contained fragile articles. The animals are to be packed by the local store in vast crates and sent to Cape Town by rail, where Pagett will see to their being stored.

The people who are packing them say that they are of a particularly awkward shape (!), and that special cases will have to be made. I pointed out to Mrs Blair that by the time she has got them home those animals will have cost her easily a pound apiece!

Pagett is straining at the leash to rejoin me in Jo'burg. I shall make an excuse of Mrs Blair's cases to keep him in Cape Town. I have written him that he must receive the cases and see to their safe disposal, as they contain rare curios of immense value.

So all is settled, and I and Miss Pettigrew go off into the blue together. And anyone who has seen Miss Pettigrew will admit that it is perfectly respectable.

CHAPTER 29

Johannesburg, March 6th.

There is something about the state of things here that is not at all healthy. To use the well-known phrase that I have so often read, we are all living on the edge of a volcano. Bands of strikers, or so-called strikers, patrol the streets and scowl at one in a murderous fashion. They are picking out the bloated capitalists ready for when the massacres begin, I suppose. You can't ride in a taxi – if you do, strikers pull you out again. And the hotels hint pleasantly that when the food gives out they will fling you out on the mat!

I met Reeves, my Labour friend of the Kilmorden, *last night. He has cold feet worse than any man I ever saw. He's like all the rest of these people; they make inflammatory speeches of enormous length, solely for political purposes, and then wish they hadn't. He's busy now going about and saying he didn't really do it. When I met him, he was just off to Cape Town, where he meditates making a three days' speech in Dutch, vindicating himself, and pointing out that the things he said really meant something entirely different. I am thankful that I do not have to sit in the Legislative Assembly of South Africa. The House of Commons is bad enough, but at least we have only one language, and some slight restriction as to length of speeches. When I went to the Assembly before leaving Cape Town, I listened to a grey-haired gentleman with a drooping moustache who looked exactly like the Mock Turtle in* Alice in Wonderland. *He dropped out his words one by one in a particularly melancholy fashion. Every now and then he galvanized himself to further efforts by ejaculating something that sounded like 'Platt Skeet', uttered* fortissimo *and in marked contrast to the rest of his delivery. When he did this, half his audience yelled 'whoof, whoof!' which is possibly Dutch for 'Hear, hear', and the other half woke up with a start from the pleasant nap they had been having. I was given to understand that the gentleman had been speaking for at least three days. They must have a lot of patience in South Africa.*

I have invented endless jobs to keep Pagett in Cape Town, but at last the fertility of my imagination has given out, and he joins me tomorrow in the spirit of the faithful dog who comes to die by his master's side. And I was getting on so well with my Reminiscences too! I had invented some extraordinarily witty things that the strike leaders said to me and I said to the strike leaders.

This morning I was interviewed by a Government official. He was urbane, persuasive and mysterious in turn. To begin with, he alluded to my exalted position and importance, and suggested that I should remove myself, or be removed by him, to Pretoria.

'You expect trouble, then?' I asked.

His reply was so worded as to have no meaning whatsoever, so I gathered that they were expecting serious trouble. I suggested to him that his Government were letting things go rather too far.

'There is such a thing as giving a man enough rope, and letting him hang himself, Sir Eustace.'

'Oh, quite so, quite so.'

'It is not the strikers themselves who are causing the trouble. There is some organization at work behind them. Arms and explosives have been pouring in, and we have made a haul of certain documents which throw a good deal of light on the methods adopted to import them. There is a regular code. Potatoes mean

"detonators", cauliflower, "rifles", other vegetables stand for various explosives.'

'That's very interesting,' I commented.

'More than that, Sir Eustace, we have every reason to believe that the man who runs the whole show, the directing genius of the affair, is at this minute in Johannesburg.'

He stared at me so hard that I began to fear that he suspected me of being the man. I broke out into a cold perspiration at the thought, and began to regret that I had ever conceived the idea of inspecting a miniature revolution at first hand.

'No trains are running from Jo'burg to Pretoria,' he continued. 'But I can arrange to send you over by private car. In case you should be stopped on the way, I can provide you with two separate passes, one issued by the Union Government, and the other stating that you are an English visitor who has nothing whatsoever to do with the Union.'

'One for your people, and one for the strikers, eh?'

'Exactly.'

The project did not appeal to me – I know what happens in a case of that kind. You get flustered and mix the things up. I should hand the wrong pass to the wrong person, and it would end in my being summarily shot by a bloodthirsty rebel, or one of the supporters of law and order whom I notice guarding the streets wearing bowler hats and smoking pipes, with rifles tucked carelessly under their arms. Besides, what should I do with myself in Pretoria? Admire the architecture of the Union buildings, and listen to the echoes of the shooting round Johannesburg? I should be penned up there God knows how long. They've blown up the railway line already, I hear. It isn't even as if one could get a drink there. They put the place under martial law two days ago.

'My dear fellow,' I said, 'you don't seem to realize that I'm studying conditions on the Rand. How the devil am I going to study them from Pretoria? I appreciate your care for my safety, but don't worry about me, I shall be all right.'

'I warn you, Sir Eustace, that the food question is already serious.'

'A little fasting will improve my figure,' I said, with a sigh.

We were interrupted by a telegram being handed to me. I read it with amazement.

'Anne is safe. Here with me at Kimberley. Suzanne Blair.'

I don't think I ever really believed in the annihilation of Anne. There is something peculiarly indestructible about that young woman – she is like the patent balls that one gives to terriers. She has an extraordinary knack of turning up smiling. I still don't see why it was necessary for her to walk out of the hotel in the middle of the night in order to get to Kimberley. There was no train, anyway. She must have put on a pair of angel's wings and flown there. And I don't suppose she will ever explain. Nobody does – to me. I always have to guess. It becomes monotonous after a while. The exigencies of journalism are at the bottom of it, I suppose. 'How I shot the rapids,' by our Special Correspondent.

I refolded the telegram and got rid of my Governmental friend. I don't like the prospect of being hungry, but I'm not alarmed for my personal safety. Smuts is perfectly capable of dealing with the revolution. But I would give a considerable sum of money for a drink! I wonder if Pagett will have the sense to bring a bottle of whisky with him when he arrives tomorrow?

I put on my hat and went out, intending to buy a few souvenirs. The curio-shops in Jo'burg are rather pleasant. I was just studying a window full of imposing karosses, when a man coming out of the shop cannoned into me. To my surprise it turned out to be Race.

I can't flatter myself that he looked pleased to see me. As a matter of fact, he looked distinctly annoyed, but I insisted on his accompanying me back to the hotel. I get tired of having no one but Miss Pettigrew to talk to.

'I had no idea you were in Jo'burg,' I said chattily. 'When did you arrive?'

'Last night.'

'Where are you staying?'

'With friends.'

He was disposed to be extraordinarily taciturn, and seemed to be embarrassed by my questions.

'I hope they keep poultry,' I remarked. 'A diet of new-laid eggs, and the occasional slaughtering of an old cock, will be decidedly agreeable soon, from all I hear.'

'By the way,' I said, when we were back in the hotel, 'have you heard that Miss Beddingfeld is alive and kicking?'

He nodded.

'She gave us quite a fright,' I said airily. 'Where the devil did she go to that night, that's what I'd like to know.'

'She was on the island all the time.'

'Which island? Not the one with the young man on it?'

'Yes.'

'How very improper,' I said. 'Pagett will be quite shocked. He always did disapprove of Anne Beddingfeld. I suppose that was the young man she originally intended to meet in Durban?'

'I don't think so.'

'Don't tell me anything if you don't want to,' I said, by way of encouraging him.

'I fancy that this is a young man we should all be very glad to lay our hands on.'

'Not –?' I cried, in rising excitement.

He nodded.

'Harry Rayburn, alias *Harry Lucas – that's his real name, you know. He's given us all the slip once more, but we're bound to rope him in soon.'*

'Dear me, dear me,' I murmured.

'We don't suspect the girl of complicity in any case. On her side it's – just a love affair.'

I always did think Race was in love with Anne. The way he said those last words made me feel sure of it.

'She's gone to Beira,' he continued rather hastily.

'Indeed,' I said, staring. 'How do you know?'

'She wrote to me from Bulawayo, telling me she was going home that way. The best thing she can do, poor child.'

'Somehow, I don't fancy she is in Beira,' I said meditatively.

'She was just starting when she wrote.'

I was puzzled. Somebody was clearly lying. Without stopping to reflect that Anne might have excellent reasons for her misleading statements, I gave myself up to the pleasure of scoring off Race. He is always so cocksure. I took the telegram from my pocket and handed it to him.

'Then how do you explain this?' I asked nonchalantly.

He seemed dumbfounded. 'She said she was just starting for Beira,' he said, in a dazed voice.

I know that Race is supposed to be clever. He is, in my opinion, rather a stupid man. It never seemed to occur to him that girls do not always tell the truth.

'Kimberley too. What are they doing there?' he muttered.

'Yes, that surprised me. I should have thought Miss Anne would have been in the thick of it here, gathering copy for the Daily Budget.'

'Kimberley,' he said again. The place seemed to upset him. 'There's nothing to see there – the pits aren't being worked.'

'You know what women are,' I said vaguely.

He shook his head and went off. I have evidently given him something to think about.

No sooner had he departed than my Government official reappeared.

'I hope you will forgive me for troubling you again, Sir Eustace,' he apologized. 'But there are one or two questions I should like to ask you.'

'Certainly, my dear fellow,' I said cheerfully. 'Ask away.'

'It concerns your secretary –'

'I know nothing about him,' I said hastily. 'He foisted himself upon me in London, robbed me of valuable papers – for which I shall be hauled over the coals – and disappeared like a conjuring trick at Cape Town. It's true that I was at the Falls at the same time as he was, but I was at the hotel, and he was on an island. I can assure you that I never set eyes upon him the whole time that I was there.'

I paused for breath.

'You misunderstand me. It was of your other secretary that I spoke.'

'What? Pagett?' I cried, in lively astonishment. 'He's been with me eight years – a most trustworthy fellow.'

My interlocutor smiled.

'We are still at cross-purposes. I refer to the lady.'

'Miss Pettigrew?' I exclaimed.

'Yes. She has been seen coming out of Agrasato's Native Curio-shop.'

'God bless my soul!' I interrupted. 'I was going into that place myself this afternoon. You might have caught me *coming out!'*

There doesn't seem to be any innocent thing that one can do in Jo'burg without being suspected for it.

'Ah! but she has been seen there more than once – and in rather doubtful circumstances. I may as well tell you – in confidence, Sir Eustace – that the place is suspected of being a well-known rendezvous used by the secret organization behind this revolution. That is why I

should be glad to hear all that you can tell me about this lady. Where and how did you come to engage her?'

'She was lent to me,' I replied coldly, 'by your own Government.'

He collapsed utterly.

CHAPTER 30

(ANNE'S NARRATIVE RESUMED)

I

As soon as I got to Kimberlely I wired to Suzanne. She joined me there with the utmost dispatch, heralding her arrival with telegrams sent off *en route*. I was awfully surprised to find that she really was fond of me – I thought I had been just a new sensation, but she positively fell on my neck and wept when we met.

When we had recovered from our emotion a little, I sat down on the bed and told her the whole story from A to Z.

'You always did suspect Colonel Race,' she said thoughtfully, when I had finished. 'I didn't until the night you disappeared. I liked him so much all along and thought he would make such a nice husband for you. Oh, Anne, dear, don't be cross, but how do you know that this young man of yours is telling the truth? You believe every word he says.'

'Of course I do,' I cried indignantly.

'But what is there in him that attracts you so? I don't see that there's anything in him at all except his rather reckless good looks and his modern Sheik-cum-Stone-Age love-making.'

I poured out the vials of my wrath upon Suzanne for some minutes.

'Just because you're comfortably married and getting fat, you've forgotten that there's any such thing as romance,' I ended.

'Oh, I'm not getting fat, Anne. All the worry I've had about you lately must have worn me to a shred.'

'You look particularly well nourished,' I said coldly. 'I should say you must have put on about half a stone.'

'And I don't know that I'm so comfortably married either,' continued Suzanne in a melancholy voice. 'I've been having the most dreadful cables from Clarence ordering me to come home at once. At last I didn't answer them, and now I haven't heard for over a fortnight.'

I'm afraid I didn't take Suzanne's matrimonial troubles very seriously. She will be able to get round Clarence all right when the time comes. I turned the conversation to the subject of the diamonds.

Suzanne looked at me with a dropped jaw.

'I must explain, Anne. You see, as soon as I began to suspect Colonel Race, I was terribly upset about the diamonds. I wanted to stay on at the Falls in case he might have kidnapped you somewhere close by, but didn't know what to do about the diamonds. I was afraid to keep them in my possession –'

Suzanne looked round her uneasily, as though she feared the walls might have ears, and then whispered vehemently in my ear.

'A distinctly good idea,' I approved. 'At the time, that is. It's a bit awkward now. What did Sir Eustace do with the cases?'

'The big ones were sent down to Cape Town. I heard from Pagett before I left the Falls, and he enclosed the receipt for their storage. He's leaving Cape Town today by the by, to join Sir Eustace in Johannesburg.'

'I see,' I said thoughtfully. 'And the small ones, where are they?'

'I suppose Sir Eustace has got them with him.'

I turned the matter over in my mind.

'Well,' I said at last, 'it's awkward – but it's safe enough. We'd better do nothing for the present.'

Suzanne looked at me with a little smile.

'You don't like doing nothing, do you, Anne?'

'Not very much,' I replied honestly.

The one thing I could do was to get hold of a time-table and see what time Guy Pagett's train would pass through Kimberley. I found that it would arrive at 5.40 on the following afternoon and depart again at 6. I wanted to see Pagett as soon as possible, and that seemed to me a good opportunity. The situation on the Rand was getting very serious, and it might be a long time before I got another chance.

The only thing that livened up the day was a wire dispatched from Johannesburg. A most innocent-sounding telegram:

'Arrived safely. All going well. Eric here, also Eustace, but not Guy. Remain where you are for the present. Andy.'

II

Eric was our pseudonym for Race. I chose it because it is a name I dislike exceedingly. There was clearly nothing to be done until I could see Pagett. Suzanne employed herself in sending off a long, soothing cable to the far-off Clarence. She became quite sentimental over him. In her way – which of course is quite different from me and Harry – she is really fond of Clarence.

'I do wish he was here, Anne,' she gulped. 'It's such a long time since I've seen him.'

'Have some face-cream,' I said soothingly.

Suzanne rubbed a little on the tip of her charming nose.

'I shall want some more face-cream soon too,' she remarked, 'and you can only get this kind in Paris.' She sighed. 'Paris!'

'Suzanne,' I said, 'very soon you'll have had enough of South Africa and adventure.'

'I should like a really nice hat,' admitted Suzanne wistfully. 'Shall I come with you to meet Guy Pagett tomorrow?'

'I prefer to go alone. He'd be shyer speaking before two of us.'

So it came about that I was standing in the doorway of the hotel on the following afternoon, struggling with a recalcitrant parasol that refused to go up, whilst Suzanne lay peacefully on her bed with a book and a basket of fruit.

According to the hotel porter, the train was on its good behaviour today and would be almost on time, though he was extremely doubtful whether it would ever get through to Johannesburg. The line had been blown up, so he solemnly assured me. It sounded cheerful!

The train drew in just ten minutes late. Everybody tumbled out on the platform and began walking up and down feverishly. I had no difficulty in espying Pagett. I accosted him eagerly. He gave his usual nervous start at seeing me – somewhat accentuated this time.

'Dear me, Miss Beddingfeld, I understood that you had disappeared.'

'I have reappeared again,' I told him solemnly. 'And how are you, Mr Pagett?'

'Very well, thank you – looking forward to taking up my work again with Sir Eustace.'

'Mr Pagett,' I said, 'there is something I want to ask you. I hope that you won't be offended, but a lot hangs on it, more than you can possibly guess. I want to know what you were doing at Marlow on the 8th of January last?'

He started violently.

'Really, Miss Beddingfeld – I – indeed –'

'You *were* there, weren't you?'

'I – for reasons of my own I was in the neighbourhood, yes.'

'Won't you tell me what those reasons were?'

'Sir Eustace has not already told you?'

'Sir Eustace? Does he know?'

'I am almost sure that he does. I hoped he had not recognized me, but from the hints he has let drop, and his remarks, I fear it is only too certain. In any case, I meant to make a clean breast of the matter and offer my resignation. He is a peculiar man, Miss Beddingfeld, with an abnormal sense of humour. It seems to amuse him to keep me on tenterhooks. All the time, I dare say, he was perfectly well aware of the true facts. Possibly he has known them for years.'

I hoped that sooner or later I should be able to understand what Pagett was talking about. He went on fluently:

'It is difficult for a man of Sir Eustace's standing to put himself in my position. I know that I was in the wrong, but it seemed a harmless deception. I would have thought it better taste on his part to have tackled me outright – instead of indulging in covert jokes at my expense.'

A whistle blew, and the people began to surge back into the train.

'Yes, Mr Pagett,' I broke in, 'I'm sure I quite agree with all you're saying about Sir Eustace. *But why did you go to Marlow?*'

'It was wrong of me, but natural under the circumstances – yes, I still feel natural under the circumstances.'

'What circumstances?' I cried desperately.

For the first time, Pagett seemed to recognize that I was asking him a question. His mind detached itself from the peculiarities of Sir Eustace, and his own justification, and came to rest on me.

'I beg your pardon, Miss Beddingfeld,' he said stiffly, 'but I fail to see your concern in the matter.'

He was back in the train now, leaning down to speak to me. I felt desperate. What could one do with a man like that?

'Of course, if it's so dreadful that you'd be ashamed to speak of it to me –' I began spitefully.

At last I had found the right stop. Pagett stiffened and flushed.

'Dreadful? Ashamed? I don't understand you.'

'Then tell me.'

In three short sentences he told me. At last I knew Pagett's secret! It was not in the least what I expected.

I walked slowly back to the hotel. There a wire was handed to me. I tore it open. It contained full and definite instructions for me to proceed forthwith to Johannesburg, or rather to a station this side of Johannesburg, where I should be met by a car. It was signed, not Andy, but Harry.

I sat down in a chair to do some very serious thinking.

CHAPTER 31

(EXTRACT FROM THE DIARY OF SIR EUSTACE PEDLER)

Johannesburg, March 7th.

Pagett has arrived. He is in a blue funk, of course. Suggested at once that we should go off to Pretoria. Then, when I had told him kindly but firmly that we were going to remain here, he went to the other extreme, wished he had his rifle here, and began bucking about some bridge he guarded during the Great War. A railway bridge at Little Puddecombe junction, or something of that sort.

I soon cut that short by telling him to unpack the big typewriter. I thought that that would keep him employed for some time, because the typewriter was sure to have gone wrong – it always does – and he would have to take it somewhere to be mended. But I had forgotten Pagett's powers of being in the right.

'I've already unpacked all the cases, Sir Eustace. The typewriter is in perfect condition.'

'What do you mean – all the cases?'

'The two small cases as well.'

'I wish you wouldn't be so officious, Pagett. Those small cases were no business of yours. They belong to Mrs Blair.'

Pagett looked crestfallen. He hates to make a mistake.

'So you can just pack them up again neatly,' I continued. 'After that you can go out and look around you. Jo'burg will probably be a heap of smoking ruins by tomorrow, so it may be your last chance.'

I thought that that would get rid of him successfully for the morning, at any rate.

'There is something I want to say to you when you have the leisure, Sir Eustace.'

'I haven't got it now,' I said hastily. 'At this minute I have absolutely no leisure whatsoever.'

Pagett retired.

'By the way,' I called after him, 'what was there in those cases of Mrs Blair's?'

'Some fur rugs, and a couple of fur – hats, I think.'

'That's right,' I assented. 'She bought them on the train. They are *hats – of a kind – though I hardly wonder at your not recognizing them. I dare say she's going to wear one of them at Ascot. What else was there?'*

'Some rolls of films, and some baskets – a lot of baskets –'

'There would be,' I assured him. 'Mrs Blair is the kind of woman who never buys less than a dozen or so of anything.'

'I think that's all, Sir Eustace, except some miscellaneous odds and ends, a motor-veil and some odd gloves – that sort of thing.'

'If you hadn't been a born idiot, Pagett, you would have seen from the start that those couldn't possibly be my belongings.'

'I thought some of them might belong to Miss Pettigrew.'

'Ah, that reminds me – what do you mean by picking me out such a doubtful character as a secretary?'

And I told him about the searching cross-examination I had been put through. Immediately I was sorry, I saw a glint in his eye that I know only too well. I changed the conversation hurriedly. But it was too late. Pagett was on the war-path.

He next proceeded to bore me with a long pointless story about the Kilmorden. *It was about a roll of films and a wager. The roll of films being thrown through a port-hole in the middle of the night by some steward who ought to have known better. I hate horse-play.*

I told Pagett so, and he began to tell me the story all over again. He tells a story extremely badly, anyway. It was a long time before I could make head or tail of this one.

I did not see him again until lunch-time. Then he came in brimming over with excitement, like a bloodhound on the scent. I never have cared for bloodhounds. The upshot of it all was that he had seen Rayburn.

'What?' I cried, startled.

Yes, he had caught sight of someone whom he was sure was Rayburn crossing the street. Pagett had followed him.

'And who do you think I saw him stop and speak to? Miss Pettigrew!'

'What?'

'Yes, Sir Eustace. And that's not all. I've been making inquiries about her –'

'Wait a bit. What happened to Rayburn?'

'He and Miss Pettigrew went into that corner curio-shop –'

I uttered an involuntary exclamation. Pagett stopped inquiringly.

'Nothing,' I said. 'Go on.'

'I waited outside for ages – but they didn't come out. At last I went in. Sir Eustace, there was no one in the shop! There must be another way out.'

I stared at him.

'As I was saying, I came back to the hotel and made some inquiries about Miss Pettigrew.' Pagett lowered his voice and breathed hard as he always does when he wants to be confidential. 'Sir Eustace, a man was seen coming out of her room last night.'

I raised my eyebrows.

'And I always regarded her as a lady of such eminent respectability,' I murmured.

Pagett went on without heeding.

'I went straight up and searched her room. What do you think I found?'

I shook my head.

'This!'

Pagett held up a safety razor and a stick of shaving soap.

'What should a woman want with these?'

I don't suppose Pagett ever reads the advertisements in the high-class ladies' papers. I do. Whilst not proposing to argue with him on the subject, I refused to accept the presence of the razor as proof positive of Miss Pettigrew's sex. Pagett is so hopelessly behind the times. I should not have been at all surprised if he had produced a cigarette-case to support his theory. However, even Pagett has his limits.

'You're not convinced, Sir Eustace. What do you say to this?'

I inspected the article which he dangled aloft triumphantly.

'It looks like hair,' I remarked distastefully.

'It is hair. I think it's what they call a toupee.'

'Indeed,' I commented.

'Now are you convinced that that Pettigrew woman is a man in disguise?'

'Really, my dear Pagett, I think I am. I might have known it by her feet.'

'Then that's that. And now, Sir Eustace, I want to speak to you about my private affairs. I cannot doubt, from your hints and your continual allusions to the time I was in Florence, that you have found me out.'

At last the mystery of what Pagett did in Florence is going to be revealed!

'Make a clean breast of it, my dear fellow,' I said kindly. 'Much the best way.'

'Thank you, Sir Eustace.'

'Is it her husband? Annoying fellows, husbands. Always turning up when they're least expected.'

'I fail to follow you, Sir Eustace. Whose husband?'

'The lady's husband.'

'What lady?'

'God bless my soul, Pagett, the lady you met in Florence. There must have been a lady. Don't tell me that you merely robbed a church or stabbed an Italian in the back because you didn't like his face.'

'I am quite at a loss to understand you, Sir Eustace. I suppose you are joking.'

'I am an amusing fellow sometimes, when I take the trouble, but I can assure you that I am not trying to be funny this minute.'

'I hoped that as I was a good way off you had not recognized me, Sir Eustace.'

'Recognized you where?'

'At Marlow, Sir Eustace?'

'At Marlow? What the devil were you doing at Marlow?'

'I thought you understood that –'

'I'm beginning to understand less and less. Go back to the beginning of the story and start again. You went to Florence –'

'Then you don't know after all – and you didn't recognize me!'

'As far as I can judge, you seem to have given yourself away needlessly – made a coward of by your conscience. But I shall be able to tell better when I've heard the whole story. Now, then, take a deep breath and start again. You went to Florence –'

'But I didn't go to Florence. That is just it.'

'Well, where did you go, then?'

'I went home – to Marlow.'

'What the devil did you want to go to Marlow for?'

'I wanted to see my wife. She was in delicate health and expecting –'

'Your wife? But I didn't know you were married!'

'No, Sir Eustace, that is just what I am telling you. I deceived you in this matter.'

'How long have you been married?'

'Just over eight years. I had been married just six months when I became your secretary. I did not want to lose the post. A resident secretary is not supposed to have a wife, so I suppressed the fact.'

'You take my breath away,' I remarked. 'Where has she been all these years?'

'We have had a small bungalow on the river at Marlow, quite close to the Mill House, for over five years.'

'God bless my soul,' I muttered. 'Any children?'

'Four children, Sir Eustace.'

I gazed at him in a kind of stupor. I might have known, all along, that a man like Pagett couldn't have a guilty secret. The respectability of Pagett has always been my bane. That's just the kind of secret he would have – a wife and four children.

'Have you told this to anyone else?' I demanded at last, when I had gazed at him in fascinated interest for quite a long while.

'Only Miss Beddingfeld. She came to the station at Kimberley.'

I continued to stare at him. He fidgeted under my glance.

'I hope, Sir Eustace, that you are not seriously annoyed?'

'My dear fellow,' I said, 'I don't mind telling you here and now that you've blinking well torn it!'

I went out seriously ruffled. As I passed the corner curio-shop, I was assailed by a sudden irresistible temptation and went in. The proprietor came forward obsequiously, rubbing his hands.

'Can I show you something? Furs, curios?'

'I want something quite out of the ordinary,' I said. 'It's for a special occasion. Will you show me what you've got?'

'Perhaps you will come into my back room? We have many specialities there.'

That is where I made a mistake. And I thought I was going to be so clever. I followed him through the swinging portières.

CHAPTER 32

(ANNE'S NARRATIVE RESUMED)

I had great trouble with Suzanne. She argued, she pleaded, she even wept before she would let me carry out my plan. But in the end I got my own way. She promised to carry out my instructions to the letter and came down to the station to bid me a tearful farewell.

I arrived at my destination the following morning early. I was met by a short, black-bearded Dutchman whom I had never seen before. He had a car waiting and we drove off. There was a queer booming in the distance, and I asked him what it was. 'Guns,' he answered laconically. So there was fighting going on in Jo'burg!

I gathered that our objective was a spot somewhere in the suburbs of the city. We turned and twisted and made several detours to get there, and every minute the guns were nearer. It was an exciting time. At last we stopped before a somewhat ramshackle building. The door was opened by a Kafir boy. My guide signed to me to enter. I stood irresolute in the dingy square hall. The man passed me and threw open a door.

'The young lady to see Mr Harry Rayburn,' he said, and laughed.

Thus announced, I passed in. The room was sparsely furnished and smelt of cheap tobacco smoke. Behind a desk a man sat writing. He looked up and raised his eyebrows.

'Dear me,' he said, 'if it isn't Miss Beddingfeld!'

'I must be seeing double,' I apologized. 'Is it Mr Chichester, or is it Miss Pettigrew? There is an extraordinary resemblance to both of them.'

'Both characters are in abeyance for the moment. I have doffed my petticoats – and my cloth likewise. Won't you sit down?'

I accepted a seat composedly.

'It would seem,' I remarked, 'that I have come to the wrong address.'

'From your point of view, I am afraid you have. Really, Miss Beddingfeld, to fall into the trap a second time!'

'It was not very bright of me,' I admitted meekly.

Something about my manner seemed to puzzle him.

'You hardly seem upset by the occurrence,' he remarked dryly.

'Would my going into heroics have any effect upon you?' I asked.

'It certainly would not.'

'My Great-aunt Jane always used to say that a true lady was neither shocked nor surprised at anything that might happen,' I murmured dreamily. 'I endeavour to live up to her precepts.'

I read Mr Chichester-Pettigrew's opinion so plainly written on his face that I hastened into speech once more.

'You really are positively marvellous at make-up,' I said generously. 'All the time you were Miss Pettigrew I never recognized you – even when you broke your pencil in the shock of seeing me climb upon the train at Cape Town.'

He tapped upon the desk with the pencil he was holding in his hand at the minute.

'All this is very well in its way, but we must get to business. Perhaps, Miss Beddingfeld, you can guess why we required your presence here?'

'You will excuse me,' I said, 'but I never do business with anyone but principals.'

I had read the phrase or something like it in a moneylender's circular, and I was rather pleased with it. It certainly had a devastating effect upon Mr Chichester-Pettigrew. He opened his mouth and then shut it again. I beamed upon him.

'My Great-uncle George's maxim,' I added, as an afterthought. 'Great-aunt Jane's husband, you know. He made knobs for brass beds.'

I doubt if Chichester-Pettigrew had ever been ragged before. He didn't like it at all.

'I think you would be wise to alter your tone, young lady.'

I did not reply, but yawned – a delicate little yawn that hinted at intense boredom.

'What the devil –' he began forcibly.

I interrupted him.

'I can assure you it's no good shouting at me. We are only wasting time here. I have no intention of talking with underlings. You will save a lot of time and annoyance by taking me straight to Sir Eustace Pedler.'

'To –'

He looked dumbfounded.

'Yes,' I said. 'Sir Eustace Pedler.'

'I – I – excuse me –'

He bolted from the room like a rabbit. I took advantage of the respite to open my bag and powder my nose thoroughly. Also I settled my hat at a more becoming angle. Then I settled myself to wait with patience for my enemy's return.

He reappeared in a subtly chastened mood.

'Will you come this way, Miss Beddingfeld?'

I followed him up the stairs. He knocked at the door of a room, a brisk 'Come in' sounded from inside, and he opened the door and motioned to me to pass inside.

Sir Eustace Pedler sprang up to greet me, genial and smiling.

'Well, well, Miss Anne.' He shook me warmly by the hand. 'I'm delighted to see you. Come and sit down. Not tired after your journey? That's good.'

He sat down facing me, still beaming. It left me rather at a loss. His manner was so completely natural.

'Quite right to insist on being brought straight to me,' he went on. 'Minks is a fool. A clever actor – but a fool. That was Minks you saw downstairs.'

'Oh, really,' I said feebly.

'And now,' said Sir Eustace cheerfully, 'let's get down to facts. How long have you known that I was the "Colonel"?'

'Ever since Mr Pagett told me that he had seen you in Marlow when you were supposed to be in Cannes.'

Sir Eustace nodded ruefully.

'Yes, I told the fool he'd blinking well torn it. He didn't understand, of course. His whole mind was set on whether *I'd* recognized *him*. It never occurred to him to wonder what I was doing down there. A piece of sheer bad luck, that was. I arranged it all so carefully, too, sending him off to Florence, telling the hotel I was going over to Nice for one night or possibly two. Then, by the time the murder was discovered, I was back again in Cannes, with nobody dreaming that I'd ever left the Riviera.'

He still spoke quite naturally and unaffectedly. I had to pinch myself to understand that this was all real – that the man in front of me was really that deep-dyed criminal, the 'Colonel'. I followed things out in my mind.

'Then it was you who tried to throw me overboard on the *Kilmorden*,' I said slowly. 'It was you that Pagett followed up on deck that night?'

He shrugged his shoulders.

'I apologize, my dear child, I really do. I always liked you – but you were so confoundedly interfering. I couldn't have all my plans brought to naught by a chit of a girl.'

'I think your plan at the Falls was really the cleverest,' I said, endeavouring to look at the thing in a detached fashion. 'I would have been ready to swear anywhere that you were in the hotel when I went out. Seeing is believing in future.'

'Yes, Minks had one of his greatest successes, as Miss Pettigrew, and he can imitate my voice quite creditably.'

'There is one thing I should like to know.'

'Yes?'

'How did you induce Pagett to engage her?'

'Oh, that was quite simple. She met Pagett in the doorway of the Trade Commissioner's office or the Chamber of Mines, or wherever it was he went – told him I had 'phoned down in a hurry, and that she had been selected by the Government department in question. Pagett swallowed it like a lamb.'

'You're very frank,' I said, studying him.

'There's no earthly reason why I shouldn't be.'

I didn't like the sound of that. I hastened to put my own interpretation on it.

'You believe in the success of this revolution? You've burnt your boats.'

'For an otherwise intelligent young woman, that's a singularly unintelligent remark. No, my dear child, I do not believe in this revolution. I give it a couple of days longer and it will fizzle out ignominiously.'

'Not one of your successes, in fact?' I said nastily.

'Like all women, you've no idea of business. The job I took on was to supply certain explosives and arms – heavily paid for – to foment feeling generally, and to incriminate certain people up to the hilt. I've carried out my contract with complete success, and I was careful to be paid in advance. I took special care over the whole thing, as I intended it be my last contract before retiring from business. As for burning my boats, as you call it, I simply don't know what you mean. I'm not the rebel chief, or anything of that kind – I'm a distinguished English visitor, who had the misfortune to go nosing into a certain curio-shop – and saw a little more than he was meant to, and so the poor fellow was kidnapped. Tomorrow, or the day after, when circumstances permit, I shall be found tied up somewhere, in a pitiable state of terror and starvation.'

'Ah!' I said slowly. 'But what about me?'

'That's just it,' said Sir Eustace softly. 'What about you? I've got you here – I don't want to rub it in in any way – but I've got you here very neatly. The question is, what am I going to do with you? The simplest way of disposing of you – and, I may add, the pleasantest to myself – is the way of marriage. Wives can't accuse their husbands, you know, and I'd rather like a pretty young wife to hold my hand and glance at me out of liquid eyes – don't flash them at me so! You quite frighten me. I see that the plan does not commend itself to you?'

'It does not.'

Sir Eustace sighed.

'A pity! But I am no Adelphi villain. The usual trouble, I suppose. You love another, as the books say.'

'I love another.'

'I thought as much – first I thought it was that long-legged, pompous ass, Race, but I suppose it's the young hero who fished you out of the Falls that night. Women have no taste. Neither of those two have half the brains that I have. I'm such an easy person to underestimate.'

I think he was right about that. Although I knew well enough the kind of man he was and must be, I could not bring myself to realize it. He had tried to kill me on more than one occasion, he had actually killed another woman, and he was responsible for endless other deeds of which I knew nothing, and yet I was quite unable to bring myself into the frame of mind for appreciating his deeds as they deserved. I could not think of him as other than our amusing, genial travelling companion. I could not even feel frightened of him – and yet I knew he was capable of having me murdered in cold blood if it struck him as necessary. The only parallel I can think of is the case of Stevenson's Long John Silver. He must have been much the same kind of man.

'Well, well,' said this extraordinary person, leaning back in his chair. 'It's a pity that the idea of being Lady Pedler doesn't appeal to you. The other alternatives are rather crude.'

I felt a nasty feeling going up and down my spine. Of course I had known all along that I was taking a big risk, but the prize had seemed worth it. Would things turn out as I had calculated, or would they not?

'The fact of the matter is,' Sir Eustace was continuing, 'I've a weakness for you. I really don't want to proceed to extremes. Suppose you tell me the whole story, from the very beginning, and let's see what we can make of it. But no romancing, mind – I want the truth.'

I was not going to make any mistake over that. I had a great deal of respect for Sir Eustace's shrewdness. It was a moment for the truth, the whole truth, and nothing but the truth. I told him the whole story, omitting nothing, up to the moment of my rescue by Harry. When I had finished, he nodded his head in approval.

'Wise girl. You've made a clean breast of the thing. And let me tell you I should soon have caught you out if you hadn't. A lot of people wouldn't believe your story, anyway, expecially the beginning part, but I do. You're the kind of girl who would start off like that – at a moment's notice, on the slenderest of motives. You've had amazing luck, of course, but sooner or later the amateur runs up against the professional and then the result is a foregone conclusion. I am the professional. I started on this business when I was quite a youngster. All things considered, it seemed to me a good way of getting rich quickly. I always could think things out and devise ingenious schemes – and I never made the mistake of trying to carry out my schemes myself. Always employ the expert – that has been my motto. The one time I departed from it I came to grief – but I couldn't trust anyone to do that job for me. Nadina knew too much. I'm an easy-going man, kind-hearted and good-tempered so long as I'm not thwarted. Nadina both thwarted me and threatened me – just as I was at the apex of a successful career. Once she was dead and the diamonds were in my possession, I was safe. I've come to the conclusion now that I bungled the job. That idiot Pagett, with his wife and family! My fault – it tickled my sense of humour to employ the fellow, with his Cinquecento poisoner's face and his mid-Victorian soul. A maxim for you, my dear Anne. Don't let your sense of humour carry you away. For years I've had an instinct that it would be wise to get rid of Pagett, but the fellow was so hard-working and conscientious that I honestly couldn't find an excuse for sacking him. So I let things drift.

'But we're wandering from the point. The question is what to do with you. Your narrative was admirably clear, but there is one thing that still escapes me. Where are the diamonds now?'

'Harry Rayburn has them,' I said, watching him.

His face did not change, it retained its expression of sardonic good-humour.

'H'm. I want those diamonds.'

'I don't see much chance of your getting them,' I replied.

'Don't you? Now I do. I don't want to be unpleasant, but I should like you to reflect that a dead girl or so found in this quarter of the city will occasion no surprise. There's a man downstairs who does those sort of jobs very neatly. Now, you're a sensible young woman. What I propose is this: you will sit down and write to Harry Rayburn, telling him to join you here and bring the diamonds with him –'

'I won't do anything of the kind.'

'Don't interrupt your elders. I propose to make a bargain with you. The diamonds in exchange for your life. And don't make any mistake about it, your life is absolutely in my power.'

'And Harry?'

'I'm far too tender-hearted to part two young lovers. He shall go free too – on the understanding, of course, that neither of you interfere with me in the future.'

'And what guarantee have I that you will keep your side of the bargain?'

'None whatever, my dear girl. You'll have to trust me and hope for the best. Of course, if you're in an heroic mood and prefer annihilation, that's another matter.'

This was what I had been playing for. I was careful not to jump at the bait. Gradually I allowed myself to be bullied and cajoled into yielding. I wrote at Sir Eustace's dictation:

'Dear Harry,

I think I see a chance of establishing your innocence beyond any possible doubt. Please follow my instructions minutely. Go to Agrasato's curio-shop. Ask to see something "out of the ordinary", "for a special occasion". The man will then ask you to "come into the back room". Go with him. You will find a messenger who will bring you to me. Do exactly as he tells you. Be sure and bring the diamonds with you. Not a word to anyone.'

Sir Eustace stopped.

'I leave the fancy touches to your own imagination,' he remarked. 'But be careful to make no mistakes.'

'"Yours for ever and ever, Anne," will be sufficient,' I remarked.

I wrote in the words. Sir Eustace stretched out his hand for the letter and read it through.

'That seems all right. Now the address.'

I gave it him. It was that of a small shop which received letters and telegrams for a consideration.

He struck the bell upon the table with his hand. Chichester-Pettigrew, *alias* Minks, answered the summons.

'This letter is to go immediately – the usual route.'

'Very well, Colonel.'

He looked at the name on the envelope. Sir Eustace was watching him keenly.

'A friend of yours, I think?'

'Of mine?' The man seemed startled.

'You had a prolonged conversation with him in Johannesburg yesterday.'

'A man came up and questioned me about your movements and those of Colonel Race. I gave him misleading information.'

'Excellent, my dear fellow, excellent,' said Sir Eustace genially. 'My mistake.'

I chanced to look at Chichester-Pettigrew as he left the room. He was white to the lips, as though in deadly terror. No sooner was he outside, than Sir Eustace picked up a speaking-tube that rested by his elbow, and spoke down it. 'That you, Schwart? Watch Minks. He's not to leave the house without orders.'

He put the speaking-tube down again, and frowned, slightly tapping the table with his hand.

'May I ask you a few questions, Sir Eustace?' I said, after a minute or two of silence.

'Certainly. What excellent nerves you have, Anne! You are capable of taking an intelligent interest in things when most girls would be sniffling and wringing their hands.'

'Why did you take Harry as your secretary instead of giving him up to the police?'

'I wanted those cursed diamonds. Nadina, the little devil, was playing off your Harry against me. Unless I gave her the price she wanted, she threatened to sell them back to him. That was another mistake I made – I thought she'd have them with her that day. But she was too clever for that. Carton, her husband, was dead too – I'd no clue whatsoever as to where the diamonds were hidden. Then I managed to get a copy of a wireless message sent to Nadina by someone on board the *Kilmorden* – either Carton or Rayburn, I didn't know which. It was a duplicate of that piece of paper you picked up. "Seventeen one twenty-two", it ran. I took it to be an appointment with Rayburn, and when he was so desperate to get aboard the *Kilmorden* I was convinced that I was right. So I pretended to swallow his statements, and let him come. I kept a pretty sharp watch upon him and hoped that I should learn more. Then I found Minks trying to play a lone hand, and interfering with me. I soon stopped that. He came to heel all right. It was annoying not getting Cabin 17, and it worried me not being able to place you. Were you the innocent young girl you seemed, or were you not? When Rayburn set out to keep the appointment that night, Minks was told off to intercept him. Minks muffed it, of course.'

'But why did the wireless message say "seventeen" instead of "seventy-one"?'

'I've thought that out. Carton must have given that wireless operator his own memorandum to copy off on to a form, and he never read the copy through. The operator made the same mistake we all did, and read it as 17.1.22 instead of 1.71.22. The thing I don't know is how Minks got on to Cabin 17. It must have been sheer instinct.'

'And the dispatch to General Smuts? Who tampered with that?'

'My dear Anne, you don't suppose I was going to have a lot of my plans given away, without making an effort to save them? With an escaped murderer as a secretary, I had no hesitation whatever in substituting blanks. Nobody would think of suspecting poor old Pedler.'

'What about Colonel Race?'

'Yes, that was a nasty jar. When Pagett told me he was a Secret Service fellow, I had an unpleasant feeling down the spine. I remembered that he'd been nosing around Nadina in Paris during the war – and I had a horrible suspicion that he was out after *me*! I don't like the way he's stuck to me ever since. He's one of those strong, silent men who have always got something up their sleeve.'

A whistle sounded. Sir Eustace picked up the tube, listened for a minute or two, then answered:

'Very well, I'll see him now.'

'Business,' he remarked. 'Miss Anne, let me show you your room.'

He ushered me into a small shabby apartment, a Kafir boy brought up my small suitcase, and Sir Eustace, urging me to ask for anything I wanted, withdrew, the picture of a courteous host. A can of hot water was on the wash-stand, and I proceeded to unpack a few necessaries. Something hard and unfamiliar in my sponge-bag puzzled me greatly. I untied the string and looked inside.

To my utter amazement I drew out a small pearl-handled revolver. It hadn't been there when I started from Kimberley. I examined the thing gingerly. It appeared to be loaded.

I handled it with a comfortable feeling. It was a useful thing to have in a house such as this. But modern clothes are quite unsuited to the carrying of fire-arms. In the end I pushed it gingerly into the top of my stocking. It made a terrible bulge, and I expected every minute that it would go off and shoot me in the leg, but it really seemed the only place.

CHAPTER 33

I was not summoned to Sir Eustace's presence until late in the afternoon. Eleven-o'clock tea and a substantial lunch had been served to me in my own apartment, and I felt fortified for further conflict.

Sir Eustace was alone. He was walking up and down the room, there was a gleam in his eye and a restlessness in his manner which did not escape me. He was exultant about something. There was a subtle change in his manner towards me.

'I have news for you. Your young man is on his way. He will be here in a few minutes. Moderate your transports – I have something more to say. You attempted to deceive me this morning. I warned you that you would be wise to stick to the truth, and up to a certain point you obeyed me. Then you ran off the rails. You attempted to make me believe that the diamonds were in Harry Rayburn's possession. At the time I accepted your statement because it facilitated my task – the task of inducing you to decoy Harry Rayburn here. But, my dear Anne, the diamonds have been in my possession ever since I left the Falls – though I only discovered the fact yesterday.'

'You know!' I gasped.

'It may interest you to hear that it was Pagett who gave the show away. He insisted on boring me with a long pointless story about a wager and a tin of films. It didn't take me long to put two and two together – Mrs Blair's distrust of Colonel Race, her agitation, her entreaty that I would take care of her souvenirs for her. The excellent Pagett had already unfastened the cases through an excess of zeal. Before leaving the hotel, I simply transferred all the rolls of films to my own pocket. They are in the corner there. I admit that I haven't had time to examine them yet, but I notice that one is of a totally different weight to the others, rattles in a peculiar fashion, and has evidently been stuck down with seccotine, which will necessitate the use of a tin-opener. The case seems clear, does it not? And now, you see, I have you both nicely in the trap . . . It's a pity that you didn't take kindly to the idea of becoming Lady Pedler.'

I did not answer. I stood looking at him.

There was the sound of feet on the stairs, the door was flung open, and Harry Rayburn was hustled into the room between two men. Sir Eustace flung me a look of triumph.

'According to plan,' he said softly. 'You amateurs *will* pit yourselves against professionals.'

'What's the meaning of this?' cried Harry hoarsely.

'It means that you have walked into my parlour – said the spider to the fly,' remarked Sir Eustace facetiously. 'My dear Rayburn, you are extraordinarily unlucky.'

'You said I could come safely, Anne.'

'Do not reproach her, my dear fellow. That note was written at my dictation, and the lady could not help herself. She would have been wiser not to write it, but I did not tell her so at the time. You followed her instructions, went to the curio-shop, were taken through the secret passage from the back room – and found yourself in the hands of your enemies!'

Harry looked at me. I understood his glance and edged nearer to Sir Eustace.

'Yes,' murmured the latter, 'decidedly you are not lucky! This is – let me see, the third encounter.'

'You are right,' said Harry. 'This is the third encounter. Twice you have worsted me – have you never heard that the third time the luck changes? This is my round – cover him, Anne.'

I was all ready. In a flash I had whipped the pistol out of my stocking and was holding it to his head. The two men guarding Harry sprang forward, but his voice stopped them.

'Another step – and he dies! If they come any nearer, Anne, pull the trigger – don't hesitate.'

'I shan't,' I replied cheerfully. 'I'm rather afraid of pulling it, anyway.'

I think Sir Eustace shared my fears. He was certainly shaking like a jelly.

'Stay where you are,' he commanded, and the men stopped obediently.

'Tell them to leave the room,' said Harry.

Sir Eustace gave the order. The men filed out, and Harry shot the bolt across the door behind them.

'Now we can talk,' he observed grimly, and, coming across the room, he took the revolver out of my hand.

Sir Eustace uttered a sigh of relief and wiped his forehead with a handkerchief.

'I'm shockingly out of condition,' he observed. 'I think I must have a weak heart. I am glad that revolver is in competent hands. I didn't trust Miss Anne with it. Well, my young friend, as you say, now we can talk. I'm willing to admit that you stole a march upon me. Where the devil that revolver came from I don't know. I had the girl's luggage searched when she arrived. And where did you produce it from now? You hadn't got it on you a minute ago?'

'Yes, I had,' I replied. 'It was in my stocking.'

'I don't know enough about women. I ought to have studied them more,' said Sir Eustace sadly. 'I wonder if Pagett would have known that?'

Harry rapped sharply on the table.

'Don't play the fool. If it weren't for your grey hairs, I'd throw you out of the window. You damned scoundrel! Grey hairs, or no grey hairs, I –'

He advanced a step or two, and Sir Eustace skipped nimbly behind the table.

'The young are always so violent,' he said reproachfully. 'Unable to use their brains, they rely solely on their muscles. Let us talk sense. For the moment you have the upper hand. But that state of affairs cannot continue. The house is full of my men. You are hopelessly outnumbered. Your momentary ascendancy has been gained by an accident –'

'Has it?'

Something in Harry's voice, a grim raillery, seemed to attract Sir Eustace's attention. He stared at him.

'Has it?' said Harry again. 'Sit down, Sir Eustace, and listen to what I have to say.' Still covering him with the revolver, he went on: 'The cards are against you this time. To begin with, listen to *that*!'

That was a dull banging at the door below. There were shouts, oaths, and then a sound of firing. Sir Eustace paled.

'What's that?'

'Race – and his people. You didn't know, did you, Sir Eustace, that Anne had an arrangement with me by which we should know whether communications from one to the other were genuine? Telegrams were to be signed "Andy", letters were to have the word "and" crossed out somewhere in them. Anne knew that your telegram was a fake. She came here of her own free will, walked deliberately into the snare, in the hope that she might catch you in your own trap. Before leaving Kimberley she wired both to me and to Race. Mrs Blair has been in communication with us ever since. I received the letter written at your dictation, which was just what I expected. I had already discussed the probabilities of a secret passage leading out of the curio-shop with Race, and he had discovered the place where the exit was situated.'

There was a screaming, tearing sound, and a heavy explosion which shook the room.

'They're shelling this part of the town. I must get you out of here, Anne.'

A bright light flared up. The house opposite was on fire. Sir Eustace had risen and was pacing up and down. Harry kept him covered with the revolver.

'So you see, Sir Eustace, the game is up. It was you yourself who very kindly provided us with the clue of your whereabouts. Race's men were watching the exit of the secret passage. In spite of the precautions you took, they were successful in following me here.'

Sir Eustace turned suddenly.

'Very clever. Very creditable. But I've still a word to say. If I've lost the trick, so have you. You'll never be able to bring the murder of Nadina home to me. I was in Marlow on that day, that's all you've got against me. No one can prove that I even knew the woman. But you knew her, you had a motive for killing her – and your record's against you. You're a thief, remember, a thief. There's one thing you don't know, perhaps. *I've got the diamonds.* And here goes –'

With an incredibly swift movement, he stooped, swung up his arm and threw. There was a tinkle of breaking glass, as the object went through the window and disappeared into the blazing mass opposite.

'There goes your only hope of establishing your innocence over the Kimberley affair. And now we'll talk. I'll drive a bargain with you. You've got me cornered. Race will find all he needs in this house. There's a chance for me if I can get away. I'm done for if I stay, but so are you, young man! There's a skylight in the next room. A couple of minutes' start and I shall be all right. I've got one or two little arrangements all ready made. You let me out of the way, and give me a start – and I leave you a signed confession that I killed Nadina.'

'*Yes*, Harry,' I cried. 'Yes, yes, yes!'

He turned a stern face on me.

'No, Anne, a thousand times, no. You don't know what you're saying.'

'I do. It solves everything.'

'I'd never be able to look Race in the face again. I'll take my chance, but I'm damned if I'll let this slippery old fox get away. It's no good, Anne. I won't do it.'

Sir Eustace chuckled. He accepted defeat without the least emotion.

'Well, well,' he remarked. 'You seem to have met your master, Anne. But I can assure you both that moral rectitude does not always pay.'

There was a crash of rending wood, and footsteps surged up the stairs. Harry drew back the bolt. Colonel Race was the first to enter the room. His face lit at the sight of us.

'You're safe, Anne. I was afraid –' He turned to Sir Eustace. 'I've been after you for a long time, Pedler – and at last I've got you.'

'Everybody seems to have gone completely mad,' declared Sir Eustace airily. 'These young people have been threatening me with revolvers and accusing me of the most shocking things. I don't know what it's all about.'

'Don't you? It means that I've found the "Colonel". It means that on January 8th last you were not at Cannes, but at Marlow. It means that when your tool, Madame Nadina, turned against you, you planned to do away with her – and at last we shall be able to bring the crime home to you.'

'Indeed? And from whom did you get all this interesting information? From the man who is even now being looked for by the police? His evidence will be very valuable.'

'We have other evidence. There is someone else who knew that Nadina was going to meet you at the Mill House.'

Sir Eustace looked surprised. Colonel Race made a gesture with his hand. Arthur Minks *alias* the Rev. Edward Chichester *alias* Miss Pettigrew stepped forward. He was pale and nervous, but he spoke clearly enough:

'I saw Nadina in Paris the night before she went over to England. I was posing at the time as a Russian Count. She told me of her purpose. I warned her, knowing what kind of man she had to deal with, but she did not take my advice. There was a wireless message on the table. I read it. Afterwards I thought I would have a try for the diamonds myself. In Johannesburg Mr Rayburn accosted me. He persuaded me to come over to his side.'

Sir Eustace looked at him. He said nothing, but Minks seemed visibly to wilt.

'Rats always leave a sinking ship,' observed Sir Eustace. 'I don't care for rats. Sooner or later, I destroy vermin.'

'There's just one thing I'd like to tell you, Sir Eustace,' I remarked. 'That tin you threw out of the window didn't contain the diamonds. It had common pebbles in it. The diamonds are in a perfectly safe place. As a matter of fact they're in the big giraffe's stomach. Suzanne hollowed it out, put the diamonds in with cotton wool, so that they wouldn't rattle, and plugged it up again.'

Sir Eustace looked at me for some time. His reply was characteristic:

'I always did hate that blinking giraffe,' he said. 'It must have been instinct.'

CHAPTER 34

We were not able to return to Johannesburg that night. The shells were coming over pretty fast, and I gathered that we were now more or less cut off, owing to the rebels having obtained possession of a new part of the suburbs.

Our place of refuge was a farm some twenty miles or so from Johannesburg – right out on the veld. I was dropping with fatigue. All the excitement and anxiety of the last two days had left me little better than a limp rag.

I kept repeating to myself, without being able to believe it, that our troubles were really over. Harry and I were together and we should never be separated again. Yet all through I was conscious of some barrier between us – a constraint on his part, the reason for which I could not fathom.

Sir Eustace had been driven off in an opposite direction accompanied by a strong guard. He waved his hand airily to us on departing.

I came out on to the *stoep* early on the following morning and looked across the veld in the direction of Johannesburg. I could see the great dumps glistening in the pale morning sunshine, and I could hear the low rumbling mutter of the guns. The revolution was not over yet.

The farmer's wife came out and called me in to breakfast. She was a kind, motherly soul, and I was already very fond of her. Harry had gone out at dawn and had not yet returned, so she informed me. Again I felt a stir of uneasiness pass over me. What was this shadow of which I was so conscious between us?

After breakfast I sat out on the *stoep*, a book in my hand which I did not read. I was so lost in my own thoughts that I never saw Colonel Race ride up and dismount from his horse. It was not until he said 'Good morning, Anne,' that I became aware of his presence.

'Oh,' I said, with a flush, 'it's you.'

'Yes. May I sit down?'

He drew a chair up beside me. It was the first time we had been alone together since that day at the Matopos. As always, I felt that curious mixture of fascination and fear that he never failed to inspire in me.

'What is the news?' I asked.

'Smuts will be in Johannesburg tomorrow. I give this outbreak three days more before it collapses utterly. In the meantime the fighting goes on.'

'I wish,' I said, 'that one could be sure that the right people were the ones to get killed. I mean the ones who wanted to fight – not just all the poor people who happen to live in the parts where the fighting is going on.'

He nodded.

'I know what you mean, Anne. That's the unfairness of war. But I've other news for you.'

'Yes?'

'A confession of incompetency on my part. Pedler has managed to escape.'

'What?'

'Yes. No one knows how he managed it. He was securely locked up for the night – in an upper-storey room of one of the farms roundabouts which the Military have taken over, but this morning the room was empty and the bird had flown.'

Secretly, I was rather pleased. Never, to this day, have I been able to rid myself of a sneaking fondness for Sir Eustace. I dare say it's reprehensible, but there it is. I admired him. He was a thorough-going villain, I dare say – but he was a pleasant one. I've never met anyone half so amusing since.

I concealed my feelings, of course. Naturally Colonel Race would feel quite differently about it. He wanted Sir Eustace brought to justice. There was nothing very surprising in his escape when one came to think of it. All round Jo'burg he must have innumerable spies and agents. And, whatever Colonel Race might think, I was exceedingly doubtful that they would ever catch him. He probably had a well-planned line of retreat. Indeed, he had said as much to us.

I expressed myself suitably, though in a rather lukewarm manner, and the conversation languished. Then Colonel Race asked suddenly for Harry. I told him that he had gone off at dawn and that I hadn't seen him this morning.

'You understand, don't you, Anne, that apart from formalities, he is completely cleared? There are technicalities, of course, but Sir Eustace's guilt is well assured. There is nothing now to keep you apart.'

He said this without looking at me, in a slow, jerky voice.

'I understand,' I said gratefully.

'And there is no reason why he should not at once resume his real name.'

'No, of course not.'

'You know his real name?'

The question surprised me.

'Of course I do. Harry Lucas.'

He did not answer, and something in the quality of his silence struck me as peculiar.

'Anne, do you remember that, as we drove home from the Matopos that day, I told you that I knew what I had to do?'

'Of course I remember.'

'I think that I may fairly say I have done it. The man you love is cleared of suspicion.'

'Was that what you meant?'

'Of course.'

I hung my head, ashamed of the baseless suspicion I had entertained. He spoke again in a thoughtful voice:

'When I was a mere youngster, I was in love with a girl who jilted me. After that I thought only of my work. My career meant everything to me. Then I met you, Anne – and all that seemed worth nothing. But youth calls to youth . . . I've still got my work.'

I was silent. I suppose one can't really love two men at once – but you can feel like it. The magnetism of this man was very great. I looked up at him suddenly.

'I think that you'll go very far,' I said dreamily. 'I think that you've got a great career ahead of you. You'll be one of the world's big men.'

I felt as though I was uttering a prophecy.

'I shall be alone, though.'

'All the people who do really big things are.'

'You think so?'

'I'm sure of it.'

He took my hand, and said in a low voice:

'I'd rather have had – the other.'

Then Harry came striding round the corner of the house. Colonel Race rose.

'Good morning – Lucas,' he said.

For some reason Harry flushed up to the roots of his hair.

'Yes,' I said gaily, 'you must be known by your real name now.'

But Harry was still staring at Colonel Race.

'So you know, sir,' he said at last.

'I never forget a face. I saw you once as a boy.'

'What's all this about?' I asked, puzzled, looking from one to the other.

It seemed a conflict of wills between them. Race won. Harry turned slightly away.

'I suppose you're right, sir. Tell her my real name.'

'Anne, this isn't Harry Lucas. Harry Lucas was killed in the War. This is John Harold Eardsley.'

CHAPTER 35

With his last words, Colonel Racc had swung away and left us. I stood staring after him. Harry's voice recalled me to myself.

'Anne, forgive me, say you forgive me.'

He took my hand in his and almost mechanically I drew it away.

'Why did you deceive me?'

'I don't know that I can make you understand. I was afraid of all that sort of thing – the power and fascination of wealth. I wanted you to care for me just for myself – for the man I was – without ornaments and trappings.'

'You mean you didn't trust me?'

'You can put it that way if you like, but it isn't quite true. I'd become embittered, suspicious – always prone to look for ulterior motives – and it was so wonderful to be cared for in the way you cared for me.'

'I see,' I said slowly. I was going over in my own mind the story he had told me. For the first time I noted discrepancies in it which I had disregarded – an assurance of money, the power to buy back the diamonds of Nadina, the way in which he had preferred to speak of both men from the point of view of an outsider. And when he had said 'my friend' he had meant not Eardsley, but Lucas. It was Lucas, the quiet fellow, who had loved Nadina so deeply.

'How did it come about?' I asked.

'We were both reckless – anxious to get killed. One night we exchanged identification discs – for luck! Lucas was killed the next day – blown to pieces.'

I shuddered.

'But why didn't you tell me now? This morning? You couldn't have doubted my caring for you by this time?'

'Anne, I didn't want to spoil it all. I wanted to take you back to the island. What's the good of money? It can't buy happiness. We'd have been happy on the island. I tell you I'm afraid of that other life – it nearly rotted me through once.'

'Did Sir Eustace know who you really were?'

'Oh, yes.'

'And Carton?'

'No. He saw us both with Nadina at Kimberley one night, but he didn't know which was which. He accepted my statement that I was Lucas, and Nadina was deceived by his cable. She was never afraid of Lucas. He was a quiet chap – very deep. But I always had the devil's own temper. She'd have been scared out of her life if she'd known that I'd come to life again.'

'Harry, if Colonel Race hadn't told me, what did you mean to do?'

'Say nothing. Go on as Lucas.'

'And your father's millions?'

'Race was welcome to them. Anyway, he would make a better use of them than I ever shall. Anne, what are you thinking about? You're frowning so.'

'I'm thinking,' I said slowly, 'that I almost wish Colonel Race hadn't made you tell me.'

'No. He was right. I owed you the truth.'

He paused, then said suddenly:

'You know, Anne, I'm jealous of Race. He loves you too – and he's a bigger man than I am or ever shall be.'

I turned to him, laughing.

'Harry, you idiot. It's you I want – and that's all that matters.'

As soon as possible we started for Cape Town. There Suzanne was waiting to greet me, and we disembowelled the big giraffe together. When the revolution was finally quelled, Colonel Race came down to Cape Town and at his suggestion the big villa at Muizenberg that had belonged to Sir Laurence Eardsley was reopened and we all took up our abode in it.

There we made our plans. I was to return to England with Suzanne and to be married from her house in London. And the trousseau was to be bought in Paris! Suzanne enjoyed planning all these details enormously. So did I. And yet the future seemed curiously unreal. And sometimes, without knowing why, I felt absolutely stifled – as though I couldn't breathe.

It was the night before we were to sail. I couldn't sleep. I was miserable, and I didn't know why. I hated leaving Africa. When I came back to it, would it be the same thing? Would it ever be the same thing again?

And then I was startled by an authoritative rap on the shutter. I sprang up. Harry was on the *stoep* outside.

'Put some clothes on, Anne, and come out. I want to speak to you.'

I huddled on a few garments, and stepped out into the cool night air – still and scented, with its velvety feel. Harry beckoned me out of earshot of the house. His face looked pale and determined and his eyes were blazing.

'Anne, do you remember saying to me once that women enjoyed doing things they disliked for the sake of someone they liked?'

'Yes,' I said, wondering what was coming.

He caught me in his arms.

'Anne, come away with me – now – tonight. Back to Rhodesia – back to the island. I can't stand all this tomfoolery. I can't wait for you any longer.'

I disengaged myself a minute.

'And what about my French frocks?' I lamented mockingly.

To this day, Harry never knows when I'm in earnest, and when I'm only teasing him.

'Damn your French frocks. Do you think I want to put frocks on you? I'm a damned sight more likely to want to tear them off you. I'm not going to let you go, do you hear? You're my woman. If I let you go away, I may lose you. I'm never sure of you. You're coming with me now – tonight – and damn everybody.'

He held me to him, kissing me until I could hardly breathe.

'I can't do without you any longer, Anne. I can't indeed. I hate all this money. Let Race have it. Come on. Let's go.'

'My toothbrush?' I demurred.

'You can buy one. I know I'm a lunatic, but for God's sake, *come*!'

He stalked off at a furious pace. I followed him as meekly as the Barotsi woman I had observed at the Falls. Only I wasn't carrying a frying-pan on my head. He walked so fast that it was very difficult to keep up with him.

'Harry,' I said at last, in a meek voice, 'are we going to walk all the way to Rhodesia?'

He turned suddenly, and with a great shout of laughter gathered me up in his arms.

'I'm mad, sweetheart, I know it. But I do love you so.'

'We're a couple of lunatics. And, oh, Harry, you never asked me, but I'm not making a sacrifice at all! I *wanted* to come!'

CHAPTER 36

That was two years ago. We still live on the island. Before me, on the rough wooden table, is the letter that Suzanne wrote me.

Dear Babes in the Wood – Dear Lunatics in Love,

I'm not surprised – not at all. All the time we've been talking Paris and frocks I felt that it wasn't a bit real – that you'd vanish into the blue some day to be married over the tongs in the good old gipsy fashion. But you are *a couple of lunatics! This idea of renouncing a vast fortune is absurd. Colonel Race wanted to argue the matter, but I have persuaded him to leave the argument to time. He can administer the estate for Harry – and none better. Because, after all, honeymoons don't last for ever – you're not here, Anne, so I can safely say that without having you fly out at me like a little wild-cat – Love in the wilderness will last a good while, but one day you will suddenly begin to dream of houses in Park Lane, sumptuous furs, Paris frocks, the largest thing in motors and the latest thing in perambulators, French maids and Norland nurses! Oh, yes, you will!*

But have your honeymoon, dear lunatics, and let it be a long one. And think of me sometimes, comfortably putting on weight amidst the fleshpots!

Your loving friend,
Suzanne Blair

P.S. – *I am sending you an assortment of frying-pans as a wedding present, and an enormous* terrine *of* pâté de foie gras *to remind you of me.*

There is another letter that I sometimes read. It came a good while after the other and was accompanied by a bulky parcel. It appeared to be written from somewhere in Bolivia.

My dear Anne Beddingfeld,

I can't resist writing to you, not so much for the pleasure it gives me to write, as for the enormous pleasure I know it will give you to hear from me. Our friend Race wasn't quite as clever as he thought himself, was he?

I think I shall appoint you my literary executor. I'm sending you my diary. There's nothing in it that would interest Race and his crowd, but I fancy that there are passages in it which may amuse you. Make use of it in any way you like. I suggest an article for the Daily Budget, *'Criminals I have met.' I only stipulate that I shall be the central figure.*

By this time I have no doubt that you are no longer Anne Beddingfeld, but Lady Eardsley, queening it in Park Lane. I should just like to say that I bear you no malice whatever. It is hard, of course, to have to begin all over again at my time of life, but, entre nous, *I had a little reserve fund carefully put aside for such a contingency. It has come in very usefully and I am getting together a nice little connexion. By the way, if you ever come across that funny friend of yours, Arthur Minks, just tell him that I haven't forgotten him, will you? That will give him a nasty jar.*

On the whole I think I have displayed a most Christian and forgiving spirit. Even to Pagett. I happened to hear that he – or rather Mrs Pagett – had brought a sixth child into the world the other day. England will be entirely populated by Pagetts soon. I sent the child a silver mug, and, on a postcard, declared my willingness to act as godfather. I can see Pagett taking both mug and postcard straight to Scotland Yard without a smile on his face!

Bless you, liquid eyes. Some day you will see what a mistake you have made in not marrying me.

Yours ever
Eustace Pedler

Harry was furious. It is the one point on which he and I do not see eye to eye. To him, Sir Eustace was the man who tried to murder me and whom he regards as responsible for the death of his friend. Sir Eustace's attempts on my life have always puzzled me. They are not in the picture, so to speak. For I am sure that he always had a genuinely kindly feeling towards me.

Then why did he twice attempt to take my life? Harry says 'because he's a damned scoundrel', and seems to think that settles the matter. Suzanne was more discriminating. I talked it over with her, and she put it down to a 'fear complex'. Suzanne goes in rather for psycho-analysis. She pointed out to me that Sir Eustace's whole life was actuated by a desire to be safe and comfortable. He had an acute sense of self-preservation. And the murder of Nadina removed certain inhibitions. His actions did not represent the state of his feeling towards me, but were the result of his acute fears for his own safety. I think Suzanne is right. As for Nadina, she was the kind of woman who deserved to die. Men do all sorts of questionable things in order to get rich, but women shouldn't pretend to be in love when they aren't for ulterior motives.

I can forgive Sir Eustace easily enough, but I shall never forgive Nadina. Never, never, never!

The other day I was unpacking some tins that were wrapped in bits of an old *Daily Budget*, and I suddenly came upon the words, 'The Man in the Brown Suit'. How long ago it seemed! I had, of course, severed my connexion with the *Daily Budget* long ago – I had done with it sooner than it had done with me. MY ROMANTIC WEDDING was given a halo of publicity.

My son is lying in the sun, kicking his legs. There's a 'man in a brown suit' if you like. He's wearing as little as possible, which is the best costume for Africa, and is as brown as a berry. He's always burrowing in the earth. I think he takes after Papa. He'll have that same mania for Pleistocene clay.

Suzanne sent me a cable when he was born:

Congratulations and love to the latest arrival on Lunatics' Island. Is his head dolichocephalic or brachycephalic?

I wasn't going to stand that from Suzanne. I sent her a reply of one word, economical and to the point:

Platycephalic!

THE SECRET OF CHIMNEYS

To my nephew

In memory of an inscription
at Compton Castle and a day
at the zoo

CHAPTER 1

ANTHONY CADE SIGNS ON

'Gentleman Joe!'

'Why, if it isn't old Jimmy McGrath!'

Castle's Select Tour, represented by seven depressed-looking females and three perspiring males, looked on with considerable interest. Evidently their Mr Cade had met an old friend. They all admired Mr Cade so much, his tall, lean figure, his sun-tanned face, the light-hearted manner with which he settled disputes and cajoled them all into good temper. This friend of his now – surely rather a peculiar-looking man. About the same height as Mr Cade, but thickset and not nearly so good-looking. The sort of man one read about in books, who probably kept a saloon. Interesting though. After all, that was what one came abroad for – to see all these peculiar things one read about in books. Up to now they had been rather bored with Bulawayo. The sun was unbearably hot, the hotel was uncomfortable, there seemed to be nowhere particular to go until the moment should arrive to motor to the Matopos. Very fortunately, Mr Cade had suggested picture postcards. There was an excellent supply of picture postcards.

Anthony Cade and his friend had stepped a little apart.

'What the hell are you doing with this pack of females?' demanded McGrath. 'Starting a harem?'

'Not with this little lot,' grinned Anthony. 'Have you taken a good look at them?'

'I have that. Thought maybe you were losing your eyesight.'

'My eyesight's as good as ever it was. No, this is a Castle's Select Tour. I'm Castle – the local Castle, I mean.'

'What the hell made you take on a job like that?'

'A regrettable necessity for cash. I can assure you it doesn't suit my temperament.'

Jimmy grinned.

'Never a hog for regular work, were you?'

Anthony ignored this aspersion.

'However, something will turn up soon, I expect,' he remarked hopefully. 'It usually does.'

Jimmy chuckled.

'If there's any trouble brewing, Anthony Cade is sure to be in it sooner or later, I know that,' he said. 'You've an absolute instinct for rows – *and* the nine lives of a cat. When can we have a yarn together?'

Anthony sighed.

'I've got to take these cackling hens to see Rhodes's grave.'

'That's the stuff,' said Jimmy approvingly. 'They'll come back bumped black and blue with the ruts in the road, and clamouring for bed to rest the bruises on. Then you and I will have a spot or two and exchange the news.'

'Right. So long, Jimmy.'

Anthony rejoined his flock of sheep. Miss Taylor, the youngest and most skittish of the party, instantly attacked him.

'Oh, Mr Cade, was that an old friend of yours?'

'It was, Miss Taylor. One of the friends of my blameless youth.'

Miss Taylor giggled.

'I thought he was such an interesting-looking man.'

'I'll tell him you said so.'

'Oh, Mr Cade, how can you be so naughty! The very idea! What was that name he called you?'

'Gentleman Joe?'

'Yes. Is your name Joe?'

'I thought you knew it was Anthony, Miss Taylor.'

'Oh, go on with you!' cried Miss Taylor coquettishly.

Anthony had by now well mastered his duties. In addition to making the necessary arrangements of travel, they included soothing down irritable old gentlemen when their dignity was ruffled, seeing that elderly matrons had ample opportunities to buy picture postcards, and flirting with everything under a catholic forty years of age. The last task was rendered easier for him by the extreme readiness of the ladies in question to read a tender meaning into his most innocent remarks.

Miss Taylor returned to the attack.

'Why does he call you Joe, then?'

'Oh, just because it isn't my name.'

'And why Gentleman Joe?'

'The same kind of reason.'

'Oh, Mr Cade,' protested Miss Taylor, much distressed, 'I'm sure you shouldn't say that. Papa was only saying last night what gentlemanly manners you had.'

'Very kind of your father, I'm sure, Miss Taylor.'

'And we are all agreed that you are quite the gentleman.'

'I'm overwhelmed.'

'No, really, I mean it.'

'Kind hearts are more than coronets,' said Anthony vaguely, without a notion of what he meant by the remark, and wishing fervently it was lunch-time.

'That's such a beautiful poem, I always think. Do you know much poetry, Mr Cade?'

'I might recite "The boy stood on the burning deck" at a pinch. "The boy stood on the burning deck, whence all but he had fled." That's all I know, but I can do that bit with action if you like. "The boy stood on the burning deck" – whoosh – whoosh – whoosh – (the flames, you see) "Whence all but he had fled" – for that bit I run to and fro like a dog.'

Miss Taylor screamed with laughter.

'Oh, do look at Mr Cade! Isn't he funny?'

'Time for morning tea,' said Anthony briskly. 'Come this way. There is an excellent café in the next street.'

'I presume,' said Mrs Caldicott in her deep voice, 'that the expense is included in the Tour?'

'Morning tea, Mrs Caldicott,' said Anthony, assuming his professional manner, 'is an extra.'

'Disgraceful.'

'Life is full of trials, isn't it?' said Anthony cheerfully.

Mrs Caldicott's eyes gleamed, and she remarked with the air of one springing a mine:

'I suspected as much, and in anticipation I poured off some tea into a jug at breakfast this morning! I can heat that up on the spirit-lamp. Come, Father.'

Mr and Mrs Caldicott sailed off triumphantly to the hotel, the lady's back complacent with successful forethought.

'Oh, Lord,' muttered Anthony, 'what a lot of funny people it does take to make a world.'

He marshalled the rest of the party in the direction of the café. Miss Taylor kept by his side, and resumed her catechism.

'Is it a long time since you saw your friend?'

'Just over seven years.'

'Was it in Africa you knew him?'

'Yes, not this part, though. The first time I ever saw Jimmy McGrath he was all trussed up ready for the cooking pot. Some of the tribes in the interior are cannibals, you know. We got there just in time.'

'What happened?'

'Very nice little shindy. We potted some of the beggars, and the rest took to their heels.'

'Oh, Mr Cade, what an adventurous life you must have led.'

'Very peaceful, I assure you.'

But it was clear that the lady did not believe him.

It was about ten o'clock that night when Anthony Cade walked into the small room where Jimmy McGrath was busy manipulating various bottles.

'Make it strong, James,' he implored. 'I can tell you, I need it.'

'I should think you did, my boy. I wouldn't take on that job of yours for anything.'

'Show me another, and I'll jump out of it fast enough.'

McGrath poured out his own drink, tossed it off with a practised hand and mixed a second one. Then he said slowly:

'Are you in earnest about that, old son?'

'About what?'

'Chucking this job of yours if you could get another?'

'Why? You don't mean to say that you've got a job going begging? Why don't you grab it yourself?'

'I have grabbed it – but I don't much fancy it, that's why I'm trying to pass it on to you.'

Anthony became suspicious.

'What's wrong with it? They haven't engaged you to teach in a Sunday school, have they?'

'Do you think anyone would choose me to teach in a Sunday school?'

'Not if they knew you well, certainly.'

'It's a perfectly good job – nothing wrong with it whatsoever.'

'Not in South America by any lucky chance? I've rather got my eye on South America. There's a very tidy little revolution coming off in one of those little republics soon.'

McGrath grinned.

'You always were keen on revolutions – anything to be mixed up in a really good row.'

'I feel my talents might be appreciated out there. I tell you, Jimmy, I can be jolly useful in a revolution – to one side or the other. It's better than making an honest living any day.'

'I think I've heard that sentiment from you before, my son. No, the job isn't in South America – it's in England.'

'England? Return of hero to his native land after many long years. They can't dun you for bills after seven years, can they, Jimmy?'

'I don't think so. Well, are you on for hearing more about it?'

'I'm on all right. The thing that worries me is why you're not taking it on yourself.'

'I'll tell you. I'm after gold, Anthony – far up in the interior.'

Anthony whistled and looked at him.

'You've always been after gold, Jimmy, ever since I knew you. It's your weak spot – your own particular little hobby. You've followed up more wild-cat trails than anyone I know.'

'And in the end I'll strike it. You'll see.'

'Well, every one his own hobby. Mine's rows, yours is gold.'

'I'll tell you the whole story. I suppose you know all about Herzoslovakia?'

Anthony looked up sharply.

'Herzoslovakia?' he said, with a curious ring in his voice.

'Yes. Know anything about it?'

There was quite an appreciable pause before Anthony answered. Then he said slowly:

'Only what everyone knows. It's one of the Balkan States, isn't it? Principal rivers, unknown. Principal mountains, also unknown, but fairly numerous. Capital, Ekarest. Population, chiefly brigands. Hobby, assassinating kings and having revolutions. Last King, Nicholas IV, assassinated about seven years ago. Since then it's been a republic. Altogether a very likely spot. You might have mentioned before that Herzoslovakia came into it.'

'It doesn't, except indirectly.'

Anthony gazed at him more in sorrow than in anger.

'You ought to do something about this, James,' he said. 'Take a correspondence course, or something. If you'd told a story like this in the good old Eastern days, you'd have been hung up by the heels and bastinadoed or something equally unpleasant.'

Jimmy pursued this course quite unmoved by these strictures.

'Ever heard of Count Stylptitch?'

'Now you're talking,' said Anthony. 'Many people who have never heard of Herzoslovakia would brighten at the mention of Count Stylptitch. The Grand Old Man of the Balkans. The Greatest Statesman of Modern Times. The biggest villain unhung. The point of view all depends on which newspaper you take in. But be sure of this, Count Stylptitch will be remembered long after you and I are dust and ashes, James. Every move and counter-move in the Near East for the last twenty years has had Count Stylptitch at the bottom of it. He's been a dictator and a patriot and a statesman – and nobody knows exactly what he has been, except that he's been a perfect king of intrigue. Well, what about him?'

'He was Prime Minister of Herzoslovakia – that's why I mentioned it first.'

'You've no sense of proportion, Jimmy. Herzoslovakia is of no importance at all compared to Stylptitch. It just provided him with a birthplace and a post in public affairs. But I thought he was dead?'

'So he is. He died in Paris about two months ago. What I'm telling you about happened some years ago.'

'The question is,' said Anthony, 'what *are* you telling me about?'

Jimmy accepted the rebuke and hastened on.

'It was like this. I was in Paris – just four years ago, to be exact. I was walking along one night in rather a lonely part, when I saw half a dozen French toughs beating up a respectable-looking old gentleman. I hate a one-sided show, so I promptly butted in and proceeded to beat up the toughs. I guess they'd never been hit really hard before. They melted like snow!'

'Good for you, James,' said Anthony softly. 'I'd like to have seen that scrap.'

'Oh, it was nothing much,' said Jimmy modestly. 'But the old boy was no end grateful. He'd had a couple, no doubt about that, but he was sober enough to get my name and address out of me, and he came along and thanked me next day. Did the thing in style, too. It was then that I found out it was Count Stylptitch I'd rescued. He'd got a house up by the Bois.'

Anthony nodded.

'Yes, Stylptitch went to live in Paris after the assassination of King Nicholas. They wanted him to come back and be president later, but he wasn't taking any. He remained sound to his monarchical principles, though he was reported to have his finger in all the backstairs pies that went on in the Balkans. Very deep, the late Count Stylptitch.'

'Nicholas IV was the man who had a funny taste in wives, wasn't he?' said Jimmy suddenly.

'Yes,' said Anthony. 'And it did for him, too, poor beggar. She was some little guttersnipe of a music-hall artiste in Paris – not even suitable for a morganatic alliance. But Nicholas had a frightful crush on her, and she was all out for being a Queen. Sounds fantastic, but they managed it somehow. Called her the Countess Popoffsky, or something, and pretended she had Romanoff blood in her veins. Nicholas married her in the cathedral at Ekarest with a couple of unwilling archbishops to do the job, and she was crowned as Queen Varaga. Nicholas squared his ministers, and I suppose he thought that was all that mattered – but he forgot to reckon with the populace. They're very aristocratic and reactionary in Herzoslovakia. They like their kings and queens to be the genuine article. There were mutterings and discontent, and the usual ruthless suppressions, and the final uprising which stormed the palace, murdered the King and Queen, and proclaimed a republic. It's been a republic ever since – but things still manage to be pretty lively there, so I've heard. They've assassinated a president or two, just to keep their hand in. But *revenons à nos moutons*. You had got to where Count Stylptitch was hailing you as his preserver.'

'Yes. Well, that was the end of that business. I came back to Africa and never thought of it again until about two weeks ago I got a queer-looking parcel which had been following me all over the place for the Lord knows how long. I'd seen in a paper that Count Stylptitch had recently died in Paris. Well, this parcel contained his memoirs – or reminiscences, or whatever you call the things. There was a note enclosed to the effect that if I delivered the manuscript at a certain firm of publishers in London on or before October 13th, they were instructed to hand me a thousand pounds.'

'A thousand pounds? Did you say a thousand pounds, Jimmy?'

'I did, my son. I hope to God it's not a hoax. Put not your trust in princes or politicians, as the saying goes. Well, there it is. Owing to the way the manuscript had been following me around, I had no time to lose. It was a pity, all the same. I'd just fixed up this trip to the interior, and I'd set my heart on going. I shan't get such a good chance again.'

'You're incurable, Jimmy. A thousand pounds in the hand is worth a lot of mythical gold.'

'And supposing it's all a hoax? Anyway, here I am, passage booked and everything, on the way to Cape Town – and then you blow along!'

Anthony got up and lit a cigarette.

'I begin to perceive your drift, James. You go gold-hunting as planned, and I collect the thousand pounds for you. How much do I get out of it?'

'What do you say to a quarter?'

'Two hundred and fifty pounds free of income tax, as the saying goes?'

'That's it.'

'Done, and just to make you gnash your teeth I'll tell you that I would have gone for a hundred! Let me tell you, James McGrath, *you* won't die in your bed counting up your bank balance.'

'Anyway, it's a deal?'

'It's a deal all right. I'm on. And confusion to Castle's Select Tours.'

They drank the toast solemnly.

CHAPTER 2

A LADY IN DISTRESS

'So that's that,' said Anthony, finishing off his glass and replacing it on the table. 'What boat were you going on?'

'*Granarth Castle.*'

'Passage booked in your name, I suppose, so I'd better travel as James McGrath. We've outgrown the passport business, haven't we.

'No odds either way. You and I are totally unlike, but we'd probably have the same description on one of those blinking things. Height six feet, hair brown, eyes blue, nose ordinary, chin ordinary –'

'Not so much of this "ordinary" stunt. Let me tell you that Castle's selected me out of several applicants solely on account of my pleasing appearance and nice manners.'

Jimmy grinned.

'I noticed your manners this morning.'

'The devil you did.'

Anthony rose and paced up and down the room. His brow was slightly wrinkled, and it was some minutes before he spoke.

'Jimmy,' he said at last. 'Stylptitch died in Paris. What's the point of sending a manuscript from Paris to London via Africa?'

Jimmy shook his head helplessly.

'I don't know.'

'Why not do it up in a nice little parcel and send it by post?'

'Sounds a damn sight more sensible, I agree.'

'Of course,' continued Anthony, 'I know that kings and queens and government officials are prevented by etiquette from doing anything in a simple, straightforward fashion. Hence King's Messengers and all that. In medieval days you gave a fellow a signet ring as a sort of open sesame. "The King's Ring! Pass, my lord!" And usually it was the other fellow who had stolen it. I always wonder why some bright lad never hit on the expedient of copying the ring – making a dozen or so, and selling them at a hundred ducats apiece. They seem to have had no initiative in the Middle Ages.'

Jimmy yawned.

'My remarks on the Middle Ages don't seem to amuse you. Let us get back to Count Stylptitch. From France to England via Africa seems a bit thick even for a diplomatic personage. If he merely wanted to ensure that you should get a thousand pounds he could have left it you in his will. Thank God neither you nor I are too proud to accept a legacy! Stylptitch must have been barmy.'

'You'd think so, wouldn't you?'

Anthony frowned and continued his pacing.

'Have you read the thing at all?' he asked suddenly.

'Read what?'

'The manuscript.'

'Good Lord, no. What do you think I want to read a thing of that kind for?'

Anthony smiled.

'I just wondered, that's all. You know a lot of trouble has been caused by memoirs. Indiscreet revelations, that sort of thing. People who have been close as an oyster all their lives seem positively to relish causing trouble when they themselves shall be comfortably dead. It gives them a kind of malicious glee. Jimmy, what sort of a man was Count Stylptitch? You met him and talked to him, and you're a pretty good judge of raw human nature. Could you imagine him being a vindictive old devil?'

Jimmy shook his head.

'It's difficult to tell. You see, that first night he was distinctly canned, and the next day he was just a high-toned old boy with the most beautiful manners overwhelming me with compliments till I didn't know where to look.'

'And he didn't say anything interesting when he was drunk?'

Jimmy cast his mind back, wrinkling his brows as he did so.

'He said he knew where the Koh-i-noor was,' he volunteered doubtfully.

'Oh, well,' said Anthony, 'we all know that. They keep it in the Tower, don't they? Behind thick plate-glass and iron bars, with a lot of gentlemen in fancy dress standing round to see you don't pinch anything.'

'That's right,' agreed Jimmy.

'Did Stylptitch say anything else of the same kind? That he knew which city the Wallace Collection was in, for instance?'

Jimmy shook his head.

'Hm!' said Anthony.

He lit another cigarette, and once more began pacing up and down the room.

'You never read the papers, I suppose, you heathen?' he threw out presently.

'Not very often,' said McGrath simply. 'They're not about anything that interests me as a rule.'

'Thank heaven I'm more civilized. There have been several mentions of Herzoslovakia lately. Hints at a royalist restoration.'

'Nicholas IV didn't leave a son,' said Jimmy. 'But I don't suppose for a minute that the Obolovitch dynasty is extinct. There are probably shoals of young 'uns knocking about, cousins and second cousins and third cousins once removed.'

'So that there wouldn't be any difficulty in finding a king?'

'Not in the least, I should say,' replied Jimmy. 'You know, I don't wonder at their getting tired of republican institutions. A full-blooded, virile people like that must find it awfully tame to pot at presidents after being used to kings. And talking of kings, that reminds me of something else old Stylptitch let out that night. He said he knew the gang that was after him. They were King Victor's people, he said.'

'What?' Anthony wheeled round suddenly.

A short grin widened on McGrath's face.

'Just a mite excited, aren't you, Gentleman Joe?' he drawled.

'Don't be an ass, Jimmy. You've just said something rather important.'

He went over to the window and stood there looking out.

'Who is this King Victor, anyway?' demanded Jimmy. 'Another Balkan monarch?'

'No,' said Anthony slowly. 'He isn't that kind of a king.'

'What is he, then?'

There was a pause, and then Anthony spoke.

'He's a crook, Jimmy. The most notorious jewel thief in the world. A fantastic, daring fellow, not to be daunted by anything. King Victor was the nickname he was known by in Paris. Paris was the headquarters of his gang. They caught him there and put him away for seven years on a minor charge. They couldn't prove the more important things against him. He'll be out soon – or he may be out already.'

'Do you think Count Stylptitch had anything to do with putting him away? Was that why the gang went for him? Out of revenge?'

'I don't know,' said Anthony. 'It doesn't seem likely on the face of it. King Victor never stole the crown jewels of Herzoslovakia as far as I've heard. But the whole thing seems rather suggestive, doesn't it? The death of Stylptitch, the memoirs, and the rumours in the papers – all vague but interesting. And there's a further rumour to the effect that they've found oil in Herzoslovakia. I've a feeling in my bones, James, that people are getting ready to be interested in that unimportant little country.'

'What sort of people?'

'Hebraic people. Yellow-faced financiers in city offices.'

'What are you driving at with all this?'

'Trying to make an easy job difficult, that's all.'

'You can't pretend there's going to be any difficulty in handing over a simple manuscript at a publisher's office?'

'No,' said Anthony regretfully. 'I don't suppose there'll be anything difficult about that. But shall I tell you, James, where I propose to go with my two hundred and fifty pounds?'

'South America?'

'No, my lad, Herzoslovakia. I shall stand in with the republic, I think. Very probably I shall end up as president.'

'Why not announce yourself as the principal Obolovitch and be a king whilst you're about it?'

'No, Jimmy. Kings are for life. Presidents only take on the job for four years or so. It would quite amuse me to govern a kingdom like Herzoslovakia for four years.'

'The average for kings is even less, I should say,' interpolated Jimmy.

'It will probably be a serious temptation to me to embezzle your share of the thousand pounds. You won't want it, you know, when you get back weighed down with nuggets. I'll invest it for you in Herzoslovakian oil shares. You know, James, the more I think of it, the more pleased I am with this idea of yours. I should never have thought of Herzoslovakia if you hadn't mentioned it. I shall spend one day in London, collecting the booty, and then away by the Balkan Express!'

'You won't get off quite as fast as that. I didn't mention it before, but I've got another little commission for you.'

Anthony sank into a chair and eyed him severely.

'I knew all along that you were keeping something dark. This is where the catch comes in.'

'Not a bit. It's just something that's got to be done to help a lady.'

'Once and for all, James, I refuse to be mixed up in your beastly love affairs.'

'It's not a love affair. I've never seen the woman. I'll tell you the whole story.'

'If I've got to listen to more of your long, rambling stories, I shall have to have another drink.'

His host complied hospitably with this demand, then began the tale.

'It was when I was up in Uganda. There was a dago there whose life I had saved –'

'If I were you, Jimmy, I should write a short book entitled "Lives I have Saved". This is the second I've heard of this evening.'

'Oh, well, I didn't really do anything this time. Just pulled the dago out of the river. Like all dagos, he couldn't swim.'

'Wait a minute, has this story anything to do with the other business?'

'Nothing whatever, though, oddly enough, now I remember it, the man was a Herzoslovakian. We always called him Dutch Pedro, though.'

Anthony nodded indifferently.

'Any name's good enough for a dago,' he remarked. 'Get on with the good work, James.'

'Well, the fellow was sort of grateful about it. Hung around like a dog. About six months later he died of fever. I was with him. Last thing, just as he was pegging out, he beckoned me and whispered some excited jargon about a secret – a gold mine, I thought he said. Shoved an oilskin packet into my hand which he'd always worn next his skin. Well, I didn't think much of it at the time. It wasn't until a week afterwards that I opened the packet. Then I was curious, I must confess. I shouldn't have thought that Dutch Pedro would have had the sense to know a gold mine when he saw it – but there's no accounting for luck –'

'And at the mere thought of gold, your heart beat pitterpat as always,' interrupted Anthony.

'I was never so disgusted in my life. Gold mine, indeed! I dare say it may have been a gold mine to him, the dirty dog. Do you know what it was? A woman's letters – yes, a woman's letters, and an Englishwoman at that. The skunk had been blackmailing her – and he had the impudence to pass on his dirty bag of tricks to me.'

'I like to see your righteous heat, James, but let me point out to you that dagos will be dagos. He meant well. You had saved his life, he bequeathed to you a profitable source of raising money – your high-minded British ideals did not enter his horizon.'

'Well, what the hell was I to do with the things? Burn 'em, that's what I thought at first. And then it occurred to me that there would be that poor dame, not knowing they'd been destroyed, and always living in a quake and a dread lest that dago should turn up again one day.'

'You've more imagination than I gave you credit for, Jimmy,' observed Anthony, lighting a cigarette. 'I admit that the case presented more difficulties than were at first apparent. What about just sending them to her by post?'

'Like all women, she'd put no date and no address on most of the letters. There was a kind of address on one – just one word. "Chimneys."'

Anthony paused in the act of blowing out his match, and he dropped it with a quick jerk of the wrist as it burned his finger.

'Chimneys?' he said. 'That's rather extraordinary.'

'Why, do you know it?'

'It's one of the stately homes of England, my dear James. A place where kings and queens go for weekends, and diplomatists forgather and diplome.'

'That's one of the reasons why I'm so glad that you're going to England instead of me. You know all these things,' said Jimmy simply. 'A josser like myself from the backwoods of Canada would be making all sorts of bloomers. But someone like you who's been to Eton and Harrow –'

'Only one of them,' said Anthony modestly.

'Will be able to carry it through. Why didn't I send them to her, you say? Well, it seemed to me dangerous. From what I could make out, she seemed to have a jealous husband. Suppose he opened the letter by mistake. Where would the poor dame be then? Or she might be dead – the letters looked as though they'd been written some time. As I figured it out, the only thing was for someone to take them to England and put them into her own hands.'

Anthony threw away his cigarette, and coming across to his friend, clapped him affectionately on the back.

'You're a real knight-errant, Jimmy,' he said. 'And the backwoods of Canada should be proud of you. I shan't do the job half as prettily as you would.'

'You'll take it on, then?'

'Of course.'

McGrath rose, and going across to a drawer, took out a bundle of letters and threw them on the table.

'Here you are. You'd better have a look at them.'

'Is it necessary? On the whole, I'd rather not.'

'Well, from what you say about this Chimneys place, she may have been staying there only. We'd better look through the letters and see if there's any clue as to where she really hangs out.'

'I suppose you're right.'

They went through the letters carefully, but without finding what they had hoped to find. Anthony gathered them up again thoughtfully.

'Poor little devil,' he remarked. 'She was scared stiff.'

Jimmy nodded.

'Do you think you'll be able to find her all right?' he asked anxiously.

'I won't leave England till I have. You're very concerned about this unknown lady, James?'

Jimmy ran his finger thoughtfully over the signature.

'It's a pretty name,' he said apologetically. '*Virginia Revel.*'

CHAPTER 3

ANXIETY IN HIGH PLACES

'Quite so, my dear fellow, quite so,' said Lord Caterham.

He had used the same words three times already, each time in the hope that they would end the interview and permit him to escape. He disliked very much being forced to stand on the steps of the exclusive London club to which he belonged and listen to the interminable eloquence of the Hon. George Lomax.

Clement Edward Alistair Brent, ninth Marquis of Caterham, was a small gentleman, shabbily dressed, and entirely unlike the popular conception of a marquis. He had faded blue eyes, a thin melancholy nose, and a vague but courteous manner.

The principal misfortune of Lord Caterham's life was to have succeeded his brother, the eighth marquis, four years ago. For the previous Lord Caterham had been a man of mark, a household word all over England. At one time Secretary of State for Foreign Affairs, he had always bulked largely in the counsels of the Empire, and his country seat, Chimneys, was famous for its hospitality. Ably seconded by his wife, a daughter of the Duke of Perth, history had been made and unmade at informal weekend parties at Chimneys, and there was hardly anyone of note in England – or indeed in Europe – who had not, at one time or another, stayed there.

That was all very well. The ninth Marquis of Caterham had the utmost respect and esteem for the memory of his brother. Henry had done that kind of thing magnificently. What Lord Caterham objected to was the assumption that Chimneys was a national possession rather than a private country house. There was nothing that bored Lord Caterham more than politics – unless it was politicians. Hence his impatience under the continued eloquence of George Lomax. A robust man, George Lomax, inclined to *embonpoint*, with a red face and protuberant eyes, and an immense sense of his own importance.

'You see the point, Caterham? We can't – we simply can't afford a scandal of any kind just now. The position is one of the utmost delicacy.'

'It always is,' said Lord Caterham, with a flavour of irony.

'My dear fellow, I'm in a position to *know*!'

'Oh, quite so, quite so,' said Lord Caterham, falling back upon his previous line of defence.

'One slip over this Herzoslovakian business and we're done. It is most important that the oil concessions should be granted to a British company. You must see that?'

'Of course, of course.'

'Prince Michael Obolovitch arrives the end of the week, and the whole thing can be carried through at Chimneys under the guise of a shooting party.'

'I was thinking of going abroad this week,' said Lord Caterham.

'Nonsense, my dear Caterham, no one goes abroad in early October.'

'My doctor seems to think I'm in rather a bad way,' said Lord Caterham, longingly eyeing a taxi that was crawling past.

He was quite unable to make a dash for liberty, however, since Lomax had the unpleasant habit of retaining a hold upon a person with whom he was engaged in serious conversation – doubtless the result of long experience. In this case, he had a firm grip of the lapel of Lord Caterham's coat.

'My dear man, I put it to you imperially. In a moment of national crisis, such as is fast approaching –'

Lord Caterham wriggled uneasily. He felt suddenly that he would rather give any number of house parties than listen to George Lomax quoting from one of his own speeches. He knew by experience that Lomax was quite capable of going on for twenty minutes without a stop.

'All right,' he said hastily, 'I'll do it. You'll arrange the whole thing, I suppose.'

'My dear fellow, there's nothing to arrange. Chimneys, quite apart from its historic associations, is ideally situated. I shall be at the Abbey, less than seven miles away. It wouldn't do, of course, for me to be actually a member of the house party.'

'Of course not,' agreed Lord Caterham, who had no idea why it would not do, and was not interested to learn.

'Perhaps you wouldn't mind having Bill Eversleigh, though. He'd be useful to run messages.'

'Delighted,' said Lord Caterham, with a shade more animation. 'Bill's quite a decent shot, and Bundle likes him.'

'The shooting, of course, is not really important. It's only the pretext, as it were.'

Lord Caterham looked depressed again.

'That will be all, then. The Prince, his suite, Bill Eversleigh, Herman Isaacstein –'

'Who?'

'Herman Isaacstein. The representative of the syndicate I spoke to you about.'

'The all-British syndicate?

'Yes. Why?'

'Nothing – nothing – I only wondered, that's all. Curious names these people have.'

'Then, of course, there ought to be one or two outsiders – just to give the thing a *bona fide* appearance. Lady Eileen could see to that – young people, uncritical, and with no idea of politics.'

'Bundle would attend to that all right, I'm sure.'

'I wonder now.' Lomax seemed struck by an idea. 'You remember the matter I was speaking about just now?'

'You've been speaking about so many things.'

'No, no, I mean this unfortunate contretemps' – he lowered his voice to a mysterious whisper – 'the memoirs – Count Stylptitch's memoirs.'

'I think you're wrong about that,' said Lord Caterham, suppressing a yawn. 'People *like* scandal. Damn it all, I read reminiscences myself – and enjoy 'em too.'

'The point is not whether people will read them or not – they'll read them fast enough – but their publication at this juncture might ruin everything – everything. The people of Herzoslovakia wish to restore the monarchy, and are prepared to offer the crown to Prince Michael, who has the support and encouragement of His Majesty's Government –'

'And who is prepared to grant concessions to Mr Ikey Hermanstein and Co in return for the loan of a million or so to set him on the throne –'

'Caterham, Caterham,' implored Lomax in an agonized whisper. 'Discretion, I beg of you. Above all things, discretion.'

'And the point is,' continued Lord Caterham, with some relish, though he lowered his voice in obedience to the other's appeal, 'that some of Stylptitch's reminiscences may upset the apple-cart. Tyranny and misbehaviour of the Obolovitch family generally, eh? Questions asked in the House. Why replace the present broad-minded and democratic form of government by an obsolete tyranny? Policy dictated by the blood-sucking capitalists. Down with the Government. That kind of thing – eh?'

Lomax nodded.

'And there might be worse still,' he breathed. 'Suppose – only suppose that some reference should be made to – to that unfortunate disappearance – you know what I mean.'

Lord Caterham stared at him.

'No, I don't. What disappearance?'

'You must have heard of it? Why, it happened while they were at Chimneys. Henry was terribly upset about it. It almost ruined his career.'

'You interest me enormously,' said Lord Caterham. 'Who or what disappeared?'

Lomax leant forward and put his mouth to Lord Caterham's ear. The latter withdrew it hastily.

'For God's sake, don't hiss at me.'

'You heard what I said?'

'Yes, I did,' said Lord Caterham reluctantly. 'I remember now hearing something about it at the time. Very curious affair. I wonder who did it. It was never recovered?'

'Never. Of course we had to go about the matter with the utmost discretion. No hint of the loss could be allowed to leak out. But Stylptitch was there at the time. He knew something. Not all, but something. We were at loggerheads with him once or twice over the Turkish question. Suppose that in sheer malice he has set the whole thing down for the world to read. Think of the scandal – of the far-reaching results. Everyone would say – why was it hushed up?'

'Of course they would,' said Lord Caterham, with evident enjoyment.

Lomax, whose voice had risen to a high pitch, took a grip on himself.

'I must keep calm,' he murmured. 'I must keep calm. But I ask you this, my dear fellow. If he didn't mean mischief, why did he send the manuscript to London in this roundabout way?'

'It's odd, certainly. You are sure of your facts?'

'Absolutely. We – er – had our agents in Paris. The memoirs were conveyed away secretly some weeks before his death.'

'Yes, it looks as though there's something in it,' said Lord Caterham, with the same relish he had displayed before.

'We have found out that they were sent to a man called Jimmy, or James, McGrath, a Canadian at present in Africa.'

'Quite an Imperial affair, isn't it?' said Lord Caterham cheerily.

'James McGrath is due to arrive by the *Granarth Castle* tomorrow – Thursday.'

'What are you going to do about it?'

'We shall, of course, approach him at once, point out the possibly serious consequences, and beg him to defer publication of the memoirs for at least a month, and in any case to permit them to be judiciously – er – edited.'

'Supposing that he says "No, sir," or "I'll goddarned well see you in hell first," or something bright and breezy like that?' suggested Lord Caterham.

'That's just what I'm afraid of,' said Lomax simply. 'That's why it suddenly occurred to me that it might be a good thing to ask him down to Chimneys as well. He'd be flattered, naturally, at being asked to meet Prince Michael, and it might be easier to handle him.'

'I'm not going to do it,' said Lord Caterham hastily. 'I don't get on with Canadians, never did – especially those that have lived much in Africa!'

'You'd probably find him a splendid fellow – a rough diamond, you know.'

'No, Lomax. I put my foot down there absolutely. Somebody else has got to tackle him.'

'It has occurred to me,' said Lomax, 'that a woman might be very useful here. Told enough and not too much, you understand. A woman could handle the whole thing delicately and with tact – put the position before him, as it were, without getting his back up. Not that I approve of women in politics – St Stephen's is ruined, absolutely ruined, nowadays. But woman in her own sphere can do wonders. Look at Henry's wife and what she did for him. Marcia was magnificent, unique, a perfect political hostess.'

'You don't want to ask Marcia down for this party, do you?'

asked Lord Caterham faintly, turning a little pale at the mention of his redoubtable sister-in-law.

'No, no, you misunderstand me. I was speaking of the influence of women in general. No, I suggest a young woman, a woman of charm, beauty, intelligence?'

'Not Bundle? Bundle would be no use at all. She's a red-hot Socialist if she's anything at all, and she'd simply scream with laughter at the suggestion.'

'I was not thinking of Lady Eileen. Your daughter, Caterham, is charming, simply charming, but quite a child. We need some one with *savoir faire*, poise, knowledge of the world – Ah, of course, the very person. My cousin Virginia.'

'Mrs Revel?' Lord Caterham brightened up. He began to feel that he might possibly enjoy the party after all. 'A very good suggestion of yours, Lomax. The most charming woman in London.'

'She is well up in Herzoslovakian affairs too. Her husband was at the Embassy there, you remember. And, as you say, a woman of great personal charm.'

'A delightful creature,' murmured Lord Caterham.

'That is settled, then.'

Mr Lomax relaxed his hold on Lord Caterham's lapel, and the latter was quick to avail himself of the chance.

'Bye-bye, Lomax, you'll make all the arrangements, won't you?'

He dived into a taxi. As far as it is possible for one upright Christian gentleman to dislike another upright Christian gentleman, Lord Caterham disliked the Hon. George Lomax. He disliked his puffy red face, his heavy breathing, and his prominent earnest blue eyes. He thought of the coming week-end and sighed. A nuisance, an abominable nuisance. Then he thought of Virginia Revel and cheered up a little.

'A delightful creature,' he murmured to himself. 'A most delightful creature.'

CHAPTER 4

INTRODUCING A VERY CHARMING LADY

George Lomax returned straightway to Whitehall. As he entered the sumptuous apartment in which he transacted affairs of State, there was a scuffling sound.

Mr Bill Eversleigh was assiduously filing letters, but a large arm-chair near the window was still warm from contact with a human form.

A very likeable young man, Bill Eversleigh. Age at a guess, twenty-five, big and rather ungainly in his movements, a pleasantly ugly face, a splendid set of white teeth and a pair of honest brown eyes.

'Richardson sent up that report yet?'

'No, sir. Shall I get on to him about it?'

'It doesn't matter. Any telephone messages?'

'Miss Oscar is dealing with most of them. Mr Isaacstein wants to know if you can lunch with him at the Savoy tomorrow.'

'Tell Miss Oscar to look in my engagement book. If I'm not engaged, she can ring up and accept.'

'Yes, sir.'

'By the way, Eversleigh, you might ring up a number for me now. Look it up in the book. Mrs Revel, 487 Pont Street.'

'Yes, sir.'

Bill seized the telephone book, ran an unseeing eye down a column of Ms, shut the book with a bang and moved to the instrument on the desk. With his hand upon it, he paused, as though in sudden recollection.

'Oh, I say, sir, I've just remembered. Her line's out of order. Mrs Revel's, I mean. I was trying to ring her up just now.'

George Lomax frowned.

'Annoying,' he said, 'distinctly annoying.' He tapped the table undecidedly.

'If it's anything important, sir, perhaps I might go round there now in a taxi. She is sure to be in at this time in the morning.'

George Lomax hesitated, pondering the matter. Bill waited expectantly, poised for instant flight, should the reply be favourable.

'Perhaps that would be the best plan,' said Lomax at last. 'Very well, then, take a taxi there, and ask Mrs Revel if she will be at home this afternoon at four o'clock as I am very anxious to see her about an important matter.'

'Right, sir.'

Bill seized his hat and departed.

Ten minutes later, a taxi deposited him at 487 Pont Street. He rang the bell and executed a loud rat-tat on the knocker. The door was opened by a grave functionary to whom Bill nodded with the ease of long acquaintance.

'Morning, Chilvers, Mrs Revel in?'

'I believe, sir, that she is just going out.'

'Is that you, Bill?' called a voice over the banisters. 'I thought I recognized that muscular knock. Come up and talk to me.'

Bill looked up at the face that was laughing down on him, and which was always inclined to reduce him – and not him alone – to a state of babbling incoherency. He took the stairs two at a time and clasped Virginia Revel's outstretched hands tightly in his.

'Hullo, Virginia!'

'Hullo, Bill!'

Charm is a very peculiar thing; hundreds of young women, some of them more beautiful than Virginia Revel, might have said 'Hullo, Bill,' with exactly the same intonation, and yet have produced no effect whatever. But those two simple words, uttered by Virginia, had the most intoxicating effect upon Bill.

Virginia Revel was just twenty-seven. She was tall and of an exquisite slimness – indeed, a poem might have been written to her slimness, it was so exquisitely proportioned. Her hair was of real bronze, with the greenish tint in its gold; she had a determined little chin, a lovely nose, slanting blue eyes that showed a gleam of deepest cornflower between the half-closed lids, and a delicious and quite indescribable mouth that tilted ever so slightly at one corner in what is known as 'the signature of Venus'. It was a wonderfully expressive face, and there was a sort of radiant vitality about her that always challenged attention. It would have been quite impossible ever to ignore Virginia Revel.

She drew Bill into the small drawing-room, which was all pale mauve and green and yellow, like crocuses surprised in a meadow.

'Bill, darling,' said Virginia, 'isn't the Foreign Office missing you? I thought they couldn't get on without you?'

'I've brought a message for you from Codders.'

Thus irreverently did Bill allude to his chief.

'And by the way, Virginia, in case he asks, remember that your telephone was out of order this morning.'

'But it hasn't been.'

'I know that. But I said it was.'

'Why? Enlighten me as to this Foreign Office touch.' Bill threw her a reproachful glance.

'So that I could get here and see you, of course.'

'Oh, darling Bill, how dense of me! And how perfectly sweet of you!'

'Chilvers said you were going out.'

'So I was – to Sloane Street. There's a place there where they've got a perfectly wonderful new hip band.'

'A hip band?'

'Yes, Bill, H-I-P hip, B-A-N-D band. A band to confine the hips. You wear it next the skin.'

'I blush for you Virginia. You shouldn't describe your underwear to a young man to whom you are not related. It isn't delicate.'

'But, Bill dear, there's nothing indelicate about hips. We've all got hips – although we poor women are trying awfully hard to pretend we haven't. This hip band is made of red rubber and comes to just above the knees, and it's simply impossible to walk in it.'

'How awful!' said Bill. 'Why do you do it?'

'Oh, because it gives one such a noble feeling to suffer for one's silhouette. But don't let's talk about my hip band. Give me George's message.'

'He wants to know whether you'll be in at four o'clock this afternoon.'

'I shan't. I shall be at Ranelagh. Why this sort of formal call? Is he going to propose to me, do you think?'

'I shouldn't wonder.'

'Because, if so, you can tell him that I much prefer men who propose on impulse.'

'Like me?'

'It's not an impulse with you, Bill. It's habit.'

'Virginia, won't you ever –'

'No, no, no, Bill. I won't have it in the morning before lunch. Do try and think of me as a nice motherly person approaching middle age who has your interests thoroughly at heart.'

'Virginia, I do love you so.'

'I know, Bill, I know. And I simply love being loved. Isn't it wicked and dreadful of me? I should like every nice man in the world to be in love with me.'

'Most of them are, I expect,' said Bill gloomily.

'But I hope George isn't in love with me. I don't think he can be. He's so wedded to his career. What else did he say?'

'Just that it was very important.'

'Bill, I'm getting intrigued. The things that George thinks important are so awfully limited. I think I must chuck Ranelagh. After all, I can go to Ranelagh any day. Tell George that I shall be awaiting him meekly at four o'clock.'

Bill looked at his wristwatch.

'It seems hardly worthwhile to go back before lunch. Come out and chew something, Virginia.'

'I'm going out to lunch somewhere or other.'

'That doesn't matter. Make a day of it, and chuck everything all round.'

'It would be rather nice,' said Virginia, smiling at him.

'Virginia, you're a darling. Tell me, you do like me rather, don't you? Better than other people.'

'Bill, I adore you. If I had to marry someone – simply had to – I mean if it was in a book and a wicked mandarin said to me, "Marry someone or die by slow torture," I should choose you at once – I should indeed: I should say, "Give me little Bill".'

'Well, then –'

'Yes, but I haven't got to marry anyone. I love being a wicked widow.'

'You could do all the same things still. Go about, and all that. You'd hardly notice me about the house.'

'Bill, you don't understand. I'm the kind of person who marries enthusiastically if they marry at all.'

Bill gave a hollow groan.

'I shall shoot myself one of these days, I expect,' he murmured gloomily.

'No, you won't, Bill darling. You'll take a pretty girl out to supper – like you did the night before last.'

Mr Eversleigh was momentarily confused.

'If you mean Dorothy Kirkpatrick, the girl who's in *Hooks and Eyes*, I – well, dash it all, she's a thoroughly nice girl, straight as they make 'em. There was no harm in it.'

'Bill darling, of course there wasn't. I love you to enjoy yourself. But don't pretend to be dying of a broken heart, that's all.'

Mr Eversleigh recovered his dignity.

'You don't understand at all, Virginia,' he said severely. 'Men –'

'Are polygamous! I know they are. Sometimes I have a shrewd suspicion that I am polyandrous. If you really love me, Bill, take me out to lunch quickly.'

CHAPTER 5

FIRST NIGHT IN LONDON

There is often a flaw in the best-laid plans. George Lomax had made one mistake – there was a weak spot in his preparations. The weak spot was Bill.

Bill Eversleigh was an extremely nice lad. He was a good cricketer and a scratch golfer, he had pleasant manners and an amiable disposition, but his position in the Foreign Office had been gained not by brains, but by good connexions. For the work he had to do he was quite suitable. He was more or less George's dog. He did no responsible or brainy work. His part was to be constantly at George's elbow, to interview unimportant people whom George didn't want to see, to run errands, and generally to make himself useful. All this Bill carried out faithfully enough. When George was absent, Bill stretched himself out in the biggest chair and read the sporting news, and in so doing he was merely carrying out a time-honoured tradition.

Being accustomed to send Bill on errands, George had dispatched him to the Union Castle offices to find out when the

Granarth Castle was due in. Now, in common with most well-educated young Englishmen, Bill had a pleasant but quite inaudible voice. Any elocution master would have found fault with his pronunciation of the word Granarth. It might have been anything. The clerk took it to be Carnfrae.

The *Carnfrae Castle* was due in on the following Thursday. He said so. Bill thanked him and went out. George Lomax accepted the information and laid his plans accordingly. He knew nothing about Union Castle liners, and took it for granted that James McGrath would duly arrive on Thursday.

Therefore, at the moment he was buttonholing Lord Caterham on the steps of the club on Wednesday morning, he would have been greatly surprised to learn that the *Granarth Castle* had docked at Southampton the preceding afternoon. At two o'clock that afternoon Anthony Cade, travelling under the name of Jimmy McGrath, stepped out of the boat train at Waterloo, hailed a taxi, and, after a moment's hesitation, ordered the driver to proceed to the Blitz Hotel.

'One might as well be comfortable,' said Anthony to himself as he looked with some interest out of the taxi windows.

It was exactly fourteen years since he had been in London.

He arrived at the hotel, booked a room, and then went for a short stroll along the Embankment. It was rather pleasant to be back in London again. Everything was changed of course. There had been a little restaurant there – just past Blackfriars Bridge – where he had dined fairly often, in company with other earnest lads. He had been a Socialist then, and worn a flowing red tie. Young – very young.

He retraced his steps back to the Blitz. Just as he was crossing the road, a man jostled against him, nearly making him lose his balance. They both recovered themselves, and the man muttered an apology, his eyes scanning Anthony's face narrowly. He was a short, thick-set man of the working classes, with something foreign in his appearance.

Anthony went on into the hotel, wondering, as he did so, what had inspired that searching glance. Nothing in it probably. The deep tan of his face was somewhat unusual looking amongst these pallid Londoners and it had attracted the fellow's attention. He went up to his room and, led by a sudden impulse, crossed to the looking-glass and stood studying his face in it. Of the few friends of the old days – just a chosen few – was it likely that any of them would recognize him now if they were to meet him face to face? He shook his head slowly.

When he had left London he had been just eighteen – a fair, slightly chubby boy, with a misleadingly seraphic expression. Small chance that that boy would be recognized in the lean, brown-faced man with the quizzical expression.

The telephone beside the bed rang, and Anthony crossed to the receiver.

'Hullo!'

The voice of the desk clerk answered him.

'Mr James McGrath?'

'Speaking.'

'A gentleman has called to see you.'

Anthony was rather astonished.

'To see *me*?'

'Yes, sir, a foreign gentleman.'

'What's his name?'

There was a slight pause, and then the clerk said:

'I will send up a page-boy with his card.'

Anthony replaced the receiver and waited. In a few minutes there was a knock on the door and a small page appeared bearing a card upon a salver.

Anthony took it. The following was the name engraved upon it.

Baron Lolopretjzyl

He now fully appreciated the desk clerk's pause.

For a moment or two he stood studying the card, and then made up his mind.

'Show the gentleman up.'

'Very good, sir.'

In a few minutes the Baron Lolopretjzyl was ushered into the room, a big man with an immense fan-like black beard and a high, bald forehead.

He brought his heels together with a click, and bowed.

'Mr McGrath,' he said.

Anthony imitated his movements as nearly as possible.

'Baron,' he said. Then, drawing forward a chair, 'Pray sit down. I have not, I think had the pleasure of meeting you before?'

'That is so,' agreed the Baron, seating himself. 'It is my misfortune,' he added politely.

'And mine also,' responded Anthony, on the same note.

'Let us now to business come,' said the Baron. 'I represent in London the Loyalist Party of Herzoslovakia.'

'And represent it admirably, I am sure,' murmured Anthony.

The Baron bowed in acknowledgment of the compliment.

'You are too kind,' he said stiffly. 'Mr McGrath, I will not from you conceal anything. The moment has come for the restoration of the monarchy, in abeyance since the martyrdom of His Most Gracious Majesty King Nicholas IV of blessed memory.'

'Amen,' murmured Anthony. 'I mean hear, hear.'

'On the throne will be placed His Highness Prince Michael, who the support of the British Government has.'

'Splendid,' said Anthony. 'It's very kind of you to tell me all this.'

'Everything arranged is – when you come here to trouble make.'

The Baron fixed him with a stern eye.

'My dear Baron,' protested Anthony.

'Yes, yes, I know what I am talking about. You have with you the memoirs of the late Count Stylptitch.'

He fixed Anthony with an accusing eye.

'And if I have? What have the memoirs of Count Stylptitch to do with Prince Michael?'

'They will cause scandals.'

'Most memoirs do that,' said Anthony soothingly.

'Of many secrets he the knowledge had. Should he reveal but the quarter of them, Europe into war plunged may be.'

'Come, come,' said Anthony. 'It can't be as bad as all that.'

'An unfavourable opinion of the Obolovitch will abroad be spread. So democratic is the English spirit.'

'I can quite believe,' said Anthony, 'that the Obolovitch may have been a trifle high-handed now and again. It runs in the blood. But people in England expect that sort of thing from the Balkans. I don't know why they should, but they do.'

'You do not understand,' said the Baron. 'You do not understand at all. And my lips sealed are.' He sighed.

'What exactly are you afraid of?' asked Anthony.

'Until I have read the memoirs I do not know,' explained the Baron simply. 'But there is sure to be something. These great diplomats are always indiscreet. The apple-cart upset will be, as the saying goes.'

'Look here,' said Anthony kindly. 'I'm sure you're taking altogether too pessimistic a view of the thing. I know all about publishers – they sit on manuscripts and hatch 'em like eggs. It will be at least a year before the thing is published.'

'Either a very deceitful or a very simple young man you are. All is arranged for the memoirs in a Sunday newspaper to come out immediately.

'Oh!' Anthony was somewhat taken aback. 'But you can always deny everything,' he said hopefully.

The Baron shook his head sadly.

'No, no, through the hat you talk. Let us to business come. One thousand pounds you are to have, is it not so? You see, I have the good information got.'

'I certainly congratulate the Intelligence Department of the Loyalists.'

'Then I to you offer fifteen hundred.'

'Anthony stared at him in amazement, then shook his head ruefully.

'I'm afraid it can't be done,' he said, with regret.

'Good. I to you offer two thousand.'

'You tempt me, Baron, you tempt me. But I still say it can't be done.'

'Your own price name, then.'

'I'm afraid you don't understand the position. I'm perfectly willing to believe that you are on the side of the angels, and that these memoirs may damage your cause. Nevertheless, I've undertaken the job, and I've got to carry it through. See? I can't allow myself to be bought off by the other side. That kind of thing isn't done.'

The Baron listened very attentively. At the end of Anthony's speech he nodded his head several times.

'I see. Your honour as an Englishman it is?'

'Well, we don't put it that way ourselves,' said Anthony. 'But I dare say, allowing for a difference in vocabulary, that we both mean much the same thing.'

The Baron rose to his feet.

'For the English honour I much respect have,' he announced. 'We must another way try. I wish you good morning.'

He drew his heels together, clicked, bowed and marched out of the room, holding himself stiffly erect.

'Now I wonder what he meant by that,' mused Anthony. 'Was it a threat? Not that I'm in the least afraid of old Lollipop. Rather a good name for him, that, by the way. I shall call him Baron Lollipop.'

He took a turn or two up and down the room, undecided on his next course of action. The date stipulated upon for delivering the manuscript was a little over a week ahead. Today was the 5th of October. Anthony had no intention of handing it over before the last moment. Truth to tell, he was by now feverishly anxious to read these memoirs. He had meant to do so on the boat coming over, but had been laid low with a touch of fever, and not at all in the mood for deciphering crabbed and illegible handwriting, for none of the manuscript was typed. He was now more than ever determined to see what all the fuss was about.

There was the other job too.

On an impulse, he picked up the telephone book and looked up the name of Revel. There were six Revels in the book: Edward Henry Revel, surgeon, of Harley Street; and James Revel and Co., saddlers; Lennox Revel of Abbotbury Mansions, Hampstead; Miss Mary Revel with an address in Ealing; Hon. Mrs Timothy Revel of 487 Pont Street; and Mrs Willis Revel of 42 Cadogan Square. Eliminating the saddlers and Miss Mary Revel, that gave him four names to investigate – and there was no reason to suppose that the lady lived in London at all! He shut up the book with a short shake of the head.

'For the moment I'll leave it to chance,' he said. 'Something usually turns up.'

The luck of the Anthony Cades of this world is perhaps in some measure due to their own belief in it. Anthony found what he was after not half an hour later, when he was turning over the pages of an illustrated paper. It was a representation of some tableaux organized by the Duchess of Perth. Below the central figure, a woman in Eastern dress, was the inscription:

> *The Hon. Mrs Timothy Revel as Cleopatra. Before her marriage, Mrs Revel was the Hon. Virginia Cawthron, a daughter of Lord Edgbaston.*

Anthony looked at the picture some time, slowly pursing up his lips as though to whistle. Then he tore out the whole page, folded it up and put it in his pocket. He went upstairs again, unlocked his suitcase and took out the packet of letters. He took out the folded page from his pocket and slipped it under the string that held them together.

Then, at a sudden sound behind him, he wheeled round sharply. A man was standing in the doorway, the kind of man whom Anthony had fondly imagined existed only in the chorus of a comic opera. A sinister-looking figure, with a squat brutal head and lips drawn back in an evil grin.

'What the devil are you doing here?' asked Anthony. 'And who let you come up?'

'I pass where I please,' said the stranger. His voice was guttural and foreign, though his English was idiomatic enough.

'Another dago,' thought Anthony.

'Well, get out, do you hear?' he went on aloud.

The man's eyes were fixed on the packet of letters which Anthony had caught up.

'I will get out when you have given me what I have come for.'

'And what's that, may I ask?'

The man took a step nearer.

'The memoirs of Count Stylptitch,' he hissed.

'It's impossible to take you seriously,' said Anthony. 'You're so completely the stage villain. I like your get-up very much. Who sent you here? Baron Lollipop?'

'Baron? –' The man jerked out a string of harsh-sounding consonants.

'So that's how you pronounce it, is it? A cross between gargling and barking like a dog. I don't think I could say it myself – my throat's not made that way. I shall have to go on calling him Lollipop. So he sent you, did he?'

But he received a vehement negative. His visitor went so far as to spit upon the suggestion in a very realistic manner. Then he drew from his pocket a sheet of paper which he threw upon the table.

'Look,' he said. 'Look and tremble, accursed Englishman.'

Anthony looked with some interest, not troubling to fulfil the latter part of the command. On the paper was traced the crude design of a human hand in red.

'It looks like a hand,' he remarked. 'But, if you say so, I'm quite prepared to admit that it's a cubist picture of Sunset at the North Pole.'

'It is the sign of the Comrades of the Red Hand. I am a Comrade of the Red Hand.'

'You don't say so,' said Anthony, looking at him with much interest. 'Are the others all like you? I don't know what the Eugenic Society would have to say about it.'

The man snarled angrily.

'Dog,' he said. 'Worse than dog. Paid slave of an effete monarchy. Give me the memoirs, and you shall go unscathed. Such is the clemency of the Brotherhood.'

'It's very kind of them, I'm sure,' said Anthony, 'but I'm afraid that both they and you are labouring under a misapprehension. My instructions are to deliver the manuscript – not to your amiable society, but to a certain firm of publishers.'

'Pah!' laughed the other. 'Do you think you will ever be permitted to reach that office alive? Enough of this fool's talk. Hand over the papers, or I shoot.'

He drew a revolver from his pocket and brandished it in the air.

But there he misjudged his Anthony Cade. He was not used to men who could act as quickly – or quicker than they could think. Anthony did not wait to be covered by the revolver. Almost as soon as the other got it out of his pocket, Anthony had sprung forward and knocked it out of his hand. The force of the blow sent the man swinging round, so that he presented his back to his assailant.

The chance was too good to be missed. With one mighty, well-directed kick, Anthony sent the man flying through the doorway into the corridor, where he collapsed in a heap.

Anthony stepped out after him, but the doughty Comrade of the Red Hand had had enough. He got nimbly to his feet and fled down the passage. Anthony did not pursue him, but went back into his own room.

'So much for the Comrades of the Red Hand,' he remarked. 'Picturesque appearance, but easily routed by direct action. How the hell did that fellow get in, I wonder? There's one thing that stands out pretty clearly – this isn't going to be quite such a soft job as I thought. I've already fallen foul of both the Loyalist and the Revolutionary parties. Soon, I suppose, the Nationalists and the Independent Liberals will be sending up a delegation. One thing's fixed. I start on that manuscript tonight.'

Looking at his watch, Anthony discovered that it was nearly nine o'clock, and he decided to dine where he was. He did not anticipate any more surprise visits, but he felt that it was up to him to be on his guard. He had no intention of allowing his suitcase to be rifled whilst he was downstairs in the Grill Room. He rang the bell and asked for the menu, selected a couple of dishes and ordered a bottle of Chambertin. The waiter took the order and withdrew.

Whilst he was waiting for the meal to arrive, he got out the package of manuscript and put it on the table with the letters.

There was a knock at the door, and the waiter entered with a small table and the accessories of the meal. Anthony had strolled over to the mantelpiece. Standing there with his back to the room, he was directly facing the mirror, and idly glancing in it he noticed a curious thing.

The waiter's eyes were glued on the parcel of manuscript. Shooting little glances sideways at Anthony's immovable back, he moved softly round the table. His hands were twitching and he kept passing his tongue over his dry lips. Anthony observed him more closely. He was a tall man, supple like all waiters, with a clean-shaven, mobile face. An Italian, Anthony thought, not a Frenchman.

At the critical moment Anthony wheeled round abruptly. The waiter started slightly, but pretended to be doing something with the salt-cellar.

'What's your name?' asked Anthony abruptly.

'Giuseppe, monsieur.'

'Italian, eh?'

'Yes, monsieur.'

Anthony spoke to him in that language, and the man answered fluently enough. Finally Anthony dismissed him with a nod, but all the while he was eating the excellent meal which Giuseppe served to him, he was thinking rapidly.

Had he been mistaken? Was Giuseppe's interest in the parcel just ordinary curiosity? It might be so, but remembering the feverish intensity of the man's excitement, Anthony decided against that theory. All the same, he was puzzled.

'Dash it all,' said Anthony to himself, 'everyone can't be after the blasted manuscript. Perhaps I'm fancying things.'

Dinner concluded and cleared away, he applied himself to the perusal of the memoirs. Owing to the illegibility of the late Count's handwriting, the business was a slow one. Anthony's yawns succeeded one another with suspicious rapidity. At the end of the fourth chapter, he gave it up.

So far, he had found the memoirs insufferably dull, with no hint of scandal of any kind.

He gathered up the letters and the wrapping of the manuscript which were lying in a heap together on the table and locked them up in the suitcase. Then he locked the door, and as an additional precaution put a chair against it. On the chair he placed the water-bottle from the bathroom.

Surveying these preparations with some pride, he undressed and got into bed. He had one more shot at the Count's memoirs, but felt his eyelids drooping, and stuffing the manuscript under his pillow, he switched out the light and fell asleep almost immediately.

It must have been some four hours later that he awoke with a start. What had awakened him he did not know – perhaps a sound, perhaps only the consciousness of danger which in men who have led an adventurous life is very fully developed.

For a moment he lay quite still, trying to focus his impressions. He could hear a very stealthy rustle, and then he became aware of a denser blackness somewhere between him and the window – on the floor by the suitcase.

With a sudden spring, Anthony jumped out of bed, switching

the light on as he did so. A figure sprang up from where it had been kneeling by the suitcase.

It was the waiter, Giuseppe. In his right hand gleamed a long thin knife. He hurled himself straight upon Anthony, who was by now fully conscious of his own danger. He was unarmed and Giuseppe was evidently thoroughly at home with his own weapon.

Anthony sprang to one side, and Giuseppe missed him with the knife. The next minute the two men were rolling on the floor together, locked in a close embrace. The whole of Anthony's faculties were centred on keeping a close grip of Giuseppe's right arm so that he would be unable to use the knife. He bent it slowly back. At the same time he felt the Italian's other hand clutching at his windpipe, stifling him, choking. And still, desperately, he bent the right arm back.

There was a sharp tinkle as the knife fell on the floor. At the same time, the Italian extricated himself with a swift twist from Anthony's grasp. Anthony sprang up too, but made the mistake of moving towards the door to cut off the other's retreat. He saw, too late, that the chair and the water-bottle were just as he had arranged them.

Giuseppe had entered by the window, and it was the window he made for now. In the instant's respite given him by Anthony's move towards the door, he had sprung out on the balcony, leaped over to the adjoining balcony and had disappeared through the adjoining window.

Anthony knew well enough that it was of no use to pursue him. His way of retreat was doubtless fully assured. Anthony would merely get himself into trouble.

He walked over to the bed, thrusting his hand beneath the pillow and drawing out the memoirs. Lucky that they had been there and not in the suitcase. He crossed over to the suitcase and looked inside, meaning to take out the letters.

Then he swore softly under his breath.

The letters were gone.

CHAPTER 6

THE GENTLE ART OF BLACKMAIL

It was exactly five minutes to four when Virginia Revel, rendered punctual by a healthy curiosity, returned to the house in Pont Street. She opened the door with her latchkey, and stepped into the hall to be immediately confronted by the impassive Chilvers.

'I beg pardon, ma'am, but a – a person has called to see you –'

For the moment, Virginia did not pay attention to the subtle phraseology whereby Chilvers cloaked his meaning.

'Mr Lomax? Where is he? In the drawing-room?'

'Oh, no, ma'am, not Mr Lomax.' Chilvers's tone was faintly reproachful. 'A person – I was reluctant to let him in, but he said his business was most important – connected with the late Captain, I understood him to say. Thinking therefore that you might wish to see him, I put him – er – in the study.'

Virginia stood thinking for a minute. She had been a widow now for some years, and the fact that she rarely spoke of her husband was taken by some to indicate that below her careless demeanour was a still-aching wound. By others it was taken to mean the exact opposite, that Virginia had never really cared for Tim Revel, and that she found it insincere to profess a grief she did not feel.

'I should have mentioned, ma'am,' continued Chilvers, 'that the man appears to be some kind of foreigner.'

Virginia's interest heightened a little. Her husband had been in the Diplomatic Service, and they had been together in Herzoslovakia just before the sensational murder of the King and Queen. This man might probably be a Herzoslovakian, some old servant who had fallen on evil days.

'You did quite right, Chilvers,' she said with a quick, approving nod. 'Where did you say you put him? In the study?'

She crossed the hall with her light, buoyant step, and opened the door of the small room that flanked the dining-room.

The visitor was sitting in a chair by the fire-place. He rose on her entrance and stood looking at her. Virginia had an excellent memory for faces, and she was at once quite sure that she had never seen the man before. He was tall and dark, supple in figure, and quite unmistakably a foreigner; but she did not think he was of Slavonic origin. She put him down as Italian or possibly Spanish.

'You wish to see me?' she asked. 'I am Mrs Revel.'

The man did not answer for a minute or two. He was looking her slowly over, as though appraising her narrowly. There was a veiled insolence in his manner which she was quick to feel.

'Will you please state your business?' she said, with a touch of impatience.

'You are Mrs Revel? Mrs Timothy Revel?'

'Yes. I told you so just now.'

'Quite so. It is a good thing that you consented to see me, Mrs Revel. Otherwise, as I told your butler, I should have been compelled to do business with your husband.'

Virginia looked at him in astonishment, but some impulse quelled the retort that sprang to her lips. She contented herself by remarking dryly:

'You might have found some difficulty in doing that.'

'I think not. I am very persistent. But I will come to the point. Perhaps you recognize this?'

He flourished something in his hand. Virginia looked at it without much interest.

'Can you tell me what it is, madame?'

'It appears to be a letter,' replied Virginia, who was by now convinced that she had to do with a man who was mentally unhinged.

'And perhaps you note to whom it is addressed,' said the man significantly, holding it out to her.

'I can read,' Virginia informed him pleasantly. 'It is addressed to a Captain O'Neill at Rue de Quenelles No. 15, Paris.'

The man seemed searching her face hungrily for something he did not find.

'Will you read it, please?'

Virginia took the envelope from him, drew out the enclosure and glanced at it, but almost immediately she stiffened and held it out to him again.

'This is a private letter – certainly not meant for my eyes.'

The man laughed sardonically.

'I congratulate you, Mrs Revel, on your admirable acting. You play your part to perfection. Nevertheless, I think that you will hardly be able to deny the signature!'

'The signature?'

Virginia turned the letter over – and was struck dumb with astonishment. The signature, written in a delicate slanting hand, was Virginia Revel. Checking the exclamation of astonishment that rose to her lips, she turned again to the beginning of the letter and deliberately read the whole thing through. Then she stood a minute lost in thought. The nature of the letter made it clear enough what was in prospect.

'Well, madame?' said the man. 'That is your name, is it not?'

'Oh, yes,' said Virginia. 'It's my name.'

'But not my handwriting,' she might have added.

Instead she turned a dazzling smile upon her visitor.

'Supposing,' she said sweetly, 'we sit down and talk it over?'

He was puzzled. Not so had he expected her to behave. His instinct told him that she was not afraid of him.

'First of all, I should like to know how you found me out?'

'That was easy.'

He took from his pocket a page torn from an illustrated paper, and handed it to her. Anthony Cade would have recognized it.

She gave it back to him with a thoughtful little frown.

'I see,' she said. 'It was very easy.'

'Of course you understand, Mrs Revel, that that is not the only letter. There are others.'

'Dear me,' said Virginia, 'I seem to have been frightfully indiscreet.'

Again she could see that her light tone puzzled him. She was by now thoroughly enjoying herself.

'At any rate,' she said, smiling sweetly at him, 'it's very kind of you to call and give them back to me.'

There was a pause as he cleared his throat.

'I am a poor man, Mrs Revel,' he said at last, with a good deal of significance in his manner.

'As such you will doubtless find it easier to enter the Kingdom of Heaven, or so I have always heard.'

'I cannot afford to let you have these letters for nothing.'

'I think you are under a misapprehension. Those letters are the property of the person who wrote them.'

'That may be the law, madame, but in this country you have a saying: "Possession is nine points of the law." And, in any case, are you prepared to invoke the aid of the law?'

'The law is a severe one for blackmailers,' Virginia reminded him.

'Come, Mrs Revel, I am not quite a fool. I have read these letters – the letters of a woman to her lover, one and all breathing dread of discovery by her husband. Do you want me to take them to your husband?'

'You have overlooked one possibility. Those letters were written some years ago. Supposing that since then – I have become a widow.'

He shook his head with confidence.

'In that case – if you had nothing to fear – you would not be sitting here making terms with me.'

Virginia smiled.

'What is your price?' she asked in a business-like manner.

'For one thousand pounds I will hand the whole packet over to you. It is very little that I am asking there; but, you see, I do not like the business.'

'I shouldn't dream of paying you a thousand pounds,' said Virginia with decision.

'Madame, I never bargain. A thousand pounds, and I will place the letters in your hands.'

Virginia reflected.

'You must give me a little time to think it over. It will not be easy for me to get such a sum together.'

'A few pounds on account perhaps – say fifty – and I will call again.'

Virginia looked up at the clock. It was five minutes past four, and she fancied that she had heard the bell.

'Very well,' she said hurriedly. 'Come back tomorrow, but later than this. About six.'

She crossed over to a desk that stood against the wall, unlocked one of the drawers, and took out an untidy handful of notes.

'There is about forty pounds here. That will have to do for you.'

He snatched at it eagerly.

'And now go at once, please,' said Virginia.

He left the room obediently enough. Through the open door, Virginia caught a glimpse of George Lomax in the hall, just being ushered upstairs by Chilvers. As the front door closed, Virginia called to him.

'Come in here, George. Chilvers, bring us tea in here, will you please?'

She flung open both windows, and George Lomax came into the room to find her standing erect with dancing eyes and wind-blown hair.

'I'll shut them in a minute, George, but I felt the room ought to be aired. Did you fall over the blackmailer in the hall?'

'The what?'

'Blackmailer, George. B-L-A-C-K-M-A-I-L-E-R: blackmailer. One who blackmails.'

'My dear Virginia, you can't be serious!'

'Oh, but I am, George.'

'But who did he come here to blackmail?'

'Me, George.'

'But, my dear Virginia, what have you been doing?'

'Well, just for once, as it happens, I hadn't been doing anything. The good gentleman mistook me for someone else.'

'You rang up the police, I suppose?'

'No, I didn't. I suppose you think I ought to have done so.'

'Well –' George considered weightily. 'No, no, perhaps not – perhaps you acted wisely. You might be mixed up in some unpleasant publicity in connexion with the case. You might even have had to give evidence –'

'I should have liked that,' said Virginia. 'I would love to be summoned, and I should like to see if judges really do make all the rotten jokes you read about. It would be most exciting. I was at Vine Street the other day to see about a diamond brooch I had lost, and there was the most perfectly lovely inspector – the nicest man I ever met.'

George, as was his custom, let all irrelevancies pass.

'But what did you do about this scoundrel?'

'Well, George, I'm afraid I let him do it.'

'Do what?'

'Blackmail me.'

George's face of horror was so poignant that Virginia had to bite her under-lip.

'You mean – do I understand you to mean – that you did not correct the misapprehension under which he was labouring?'

Virginia shook her head, shooting a sideways glance at him.

'Good heavens, Virginia, you must be mad.'

'I suppose it would seem that way to you.'

'But why? In God's name, why?'

'Several reasons. To begin with, he was doing it so beautifully – blackmailing me, I mean – I hate to interrupt an artist when he's doing his job really well. And then, you see, I'd never been blackmailed –'

'I should hope not, indeed.'

'And I wanted to see what it felt like.'

'I am quite at a loss to comprehend you, Virginia.'

'I knew you wouldn't understand.'

'You did not give him money, I hope?'

'Just a trifle,' said Virginia apologetically.

'How much?'

'Forty pounds.'

'Virginia!'

'My dear George, it's only what I pay for an evening dress. It's just as exciting to buy a new experience as it is to buy a new dress – more so, in fact.'

George Lomax merely shook his head, and Chilvers appearing at that moment with the tea urn, he was saved from having to express his outraged feelings. When tea had been brought in, and Virginia's deft fingers were manipulating the heavy silver teapot, she spoke again on the subject.

'I had another motive too, George – a brighter and better one. We women are usually supposed to be cats, but at any rate I've done another woman a good turn this afternoon. This man isn't likely to go off looking for another Virginia Revel. He thinks he's found his bird all right. Poor little devil, she was in a blue funk when she wrote that letter. Mr Blackmailer would have had the easiest job in his life there. Now, though he doesn't know it, he's up against a tough proposition. Starting with the great advantage of having led a blameless life, I shall toy with him to his undoing – as they say in books. Guile, George, lots of guile.'

George still shook his head.

'I don't like it,' he persisted. 'I don't like it.'

'Well, never mind, George dear. You didn't come here to talk about blackmailers. What did you come here for, by the way? Correct answer: "To see *you*!" Accent on the you, and press her hand with significance unless you happen to have been eating heavily buttered muffin, in which case it must all be done with the eyes.'

'I did come to see you,' replied George seriously. 'And I am glad to find you alone.'

'"Oh, George, this is so sudden." Says she, swallowing a currant.'

'I wanted to ask a favour of you. I have always considered you, Virginia, as a woman of considerable charm.'

'Oh, George!'

'And also as a woman of intelligence!'

'Not really? How well the man knows me.'

'My dear Virginia, there is a young fellow arriving in England tomorrow whom I should like you to meet.'

'All right, George, but it's your party – let that be clearly understood.'

'You could, I feel sure, if you chose, exercise your considerable charm.'

Virginia cocked her head a little on one side.

'George dear, I don't "charm" as a profession, you know. Often I like people – and then, well, they like me. But I don't think I could set out in cold blood to fascinate a helpless stranger. That sort of thing isn't done, George, it really isn't. There are professional sirens who would do it much better than I should.'

'That is out of the question, Virginia. This young man, he is a Canadian, by the way, of the name of McGrath –'

'"A Canadian of Scottish descent." Says she, deducing brilliantly.'

'Is probably quite unused to the higher walks of English society. I should like him to appreciate the charm and distinction of a real English gentlewoman.'

'Meaning me?'

'Exactly.'

'Why?'

'I beg your pardon?'

'I said why? You don't boon the real English gentlewoman with every stray Canadian who sets foot upon our shores. What is the deep idea, George? To put it vulgarly, what do *you* get out of it?'

'I cannot see that that concerns you, Virginia.'

'I couldn't possibly go out for an evening and fascinate unless I knew all the whys and wherefores.'

'You have a most extraordinary way of putting things, Virginia. Anyone would think –'

'Wouldn't they? Come on, George, part with a little more information.'

'My dear Virginia, matters are likely to be a little strained shortly in a certain Central European nation. It is important, for reasons which are immaterial, that this – Mr – er – McGrath should be brought to realize that the restoring of the monarchy in Herzoslovakia is imperative to the peace of Europe.'

'The part about the peace of Europe is all bosh,' said Virginia calmly, 'but I'm all for monarchies every time, especially for a picturesque people like the Herzoslovakians. So you're running a King in the Herzoslovakian Stakes, are you? Who is he?

George was reluctant to answer, but did not see his way to avoid the question. The interview was not going at all as he had planned. He had foreseen Virginia as a willing, docile tool, receiving his hints gratefully, and asking no awkward questions. This was far from being the case. She seemed determined to know all about it, and this George, ever doubtful of female discretion, was determined at all costs to avoid. He had made a mistake. Virginia was not the woman for the part. She might, indeed, cause serious trouble. Her account of her interview with the blackmailer had caused him grave apprehension. A most undependable creature, with no idea of treating serious matters seriously.

'Prince Michael Obolovitch,' he replied, as Virginia was obviously waiting for an answer to her question. 'But please let that go no further.'

'Don't be absurd, George. There are all sorts of hints in the papers already, and articles cracking up the Obolovitch dynasty and talking about the murdered Nicholas IV as though he were a cross between a saint and a hero instead of a stupid little man besotted by a third-rate actress.'

George winced. He was more than ever convinced that he had made a mistake in enlisting Virginia's aid. He must stave her off quickly.

'You are right, my dear Virginia,' he said hastily, as he rose to his feet to bid her farewell. 'I should not have made the suggestion I did to you. But we are anxious for the Dominions to see eye to eye with us on this Herzoslovakian crisis, and McGrath has, I believe, influence in journalistic circles. As an ardent monarchist, and with your knowledge of the country, I thought it a good plan for you to meet him.'

'So that's the explanation, is it?'

'Yes, but I dare say you wouldn't have cared for him.'

Virginia looked at him for a second and then she laughed.

'George,' she said, 'you're a rotten liar.'

'Virginia!'

'Rotten, absolutely rotten! If I had had your training, I could have managed a better one than that – one that had a chance of being believed. But I shall find out all about it, my poor George. Rest assured of that. The Mystery of Mr McGrath. I shouldn't wonder if I got a hint or two at Chimneys this weekend.'

'At Chimneys? You are going to Chimneys?'

George could not conceal his perturbation. He had hoped to reach Lord Caterham in time for the invitation to remain un-issued.

'Bundle rang up and asked me this morning.'

George made a last effort.

'Rather a dull party, I believe,' he said. 'Hardly in your line, Virginia.'

'My poor George, why didn't you tell me the truth and trust me? It's still not too late.'

George took her hand and dropped it again limply.

'I have told you the truth,' he said coldly, and he said it without a blush.

'That's a better one,' said Virginia approvingly. 'But it's still not good enough. Cheer up, George, I shall be at Chimneys all right, exerting my considerable charm – as you put it. Life has become suddenly very much more amusing. First a blackmailer, and then George in diplomatic difficulties. Will he tell all to the beautiful woman who asks for his confidence so pathetically? No, he will reveal nothing until the last chapter. Goodbye, George. One last fond look before you go? No? Oh, George, dear, don't be sulky about it!'

Virginia ran to the telephone as soon as George had departed with a heavy gait through the front door.

She obtained the number she required and asked to speak to Lady Eileen Brent.

'Is that you, Bundle? I'm coming to Chimneys all right tomorrow. What? Bore me? No, it won't. Bundle, wild horses wouldn't keep me away! So there!'

CHAPTER 7

MR McGRATH REFUSES AN INVITATION

The letters were gone!

Having once made up his mind to the fact of their disappearance, there was nothing to do but accept it. Anthony realized very well that he could not pursue Giuseppe through the corridors of the Blitz Hotel. To do so was to court undesired publicity, and in all probability to fail in his object all the same.

He came to the conclusion that Giuseppe had mistaken the packets of letters, enclosed as they were in the other wrappings, for the memoirs themselves. It was likely therefore that when he discovered his mistake he would make another attempt to get hold of the memoirs. For this attempt Anthony intended to be fully prepared.

Another plan that occurred to him was to advertise discreetly for the return of the package of letters. Supposing Giuseppe to be an emissary of the Comrades of the Red Hand, or, which seemed to Anthony more probable, to be employed by the Loyalist Party, the letters could have no possible interest for either employer and he would probably jump at the chance of obtaining a small sum of money for their return.

Having thought out all this, Anthony returned to bed and slept peacefully until morning. He did not fancy that Giuseppe would be anxious for a second encounter that night.

Anthony got up with his plan of campaign fully thought out. He had a good breakfast, glanced at the papers which were full of the new discoveries of oil in Herzoslovakia, and then demanded an interview with the manager and being Anthony Cade, with a gift for getting his own way by means of quiet determination, he obtained what he asked for.

The manager, a Frenchman with an exquisitely suave manner, received him in his private office.

'You wished to see me, I understand, Mr – er – McGrath?'

'I did. I arrived at your hotel yesterday afternoon and I had dinner served to me in my own rooms by a waiter whose name was Giuseppe.'

He paused.

'I dare say we have a waiter of that name,' agreed the manager indifferently.

'I was struck by something unusual in the man's manner, but thought nothing more of it at the time. Later, in the night, I was awakened by the sound of someone moving softly about the room. I switched on the light, and found this same Giuseppe in the act of rifling my leather suitcase.'

The manager's indifference had completely disappeared now.

'But I have heard nothing of this,' he exclaimed. 'Why was I not informed sooner?'

'The man and I had a brief struggle – he was armed with a knife, by the way. In the end he succeeded in making off by way of the window.'

'What did you do then, Mr McGrath?'

'I examined the contents of my suitcase.'

'Had anything been taken?'

'Nothing of – importance,' said Anthony slowly.

The manager leaned back with a sigh.

'I am glad of that,' he remarked. 'But you will allow me to say, Mr McGrath, that I do not quite understand your attitude in the matter. You made no attempt to arouse the hotel? To pursue the thief?'

Anthony shrugged his shoulders.

'Nothing of value had been taken, as I tell you. I am aware, of course, that strictly speaking it is a case for the police –'

He paused, and the manager murmured without any particular enthusiasm:

'For the police – of course –'

'In any case, I was fairly certain that the man would manage to make good his escape, and since nothing was taken, why bother with the police?'

The manager smiled a little.

'I see that you realize, Mr McGrath, that I am not at all anxious to have the police called in. From my point of view it is always disastrous. If the newspapers can get hold of anything connected with a big fashionable hotel such as this, they always run it for all it is worth, no matter how insignificant the real subject may be.'

'Quite so,' agreed Anthony. 'Now I told you that nothing of value had been taken, and that was perfectly true in a sense. Nothing of any value to the thief was taken, but he got hold of something which is of considerable value to me.'

'Ah?'

'Letters, you understand.'

An expression of superhuman discretion, only to be achieved by a Frenchman, settled down upon the manager's face.

'I comprehend,' he murmured. 'But perfectly. Naturally, it is not a matter for the police.'

'We are quite agreed upon that point. But you will understand that I have every intention of recovering these letters. In the part of the world where I come from, people are used to doing things for themselves. What I require from you therefore is the fullest possible information you can give me about this waiter, Giuseppe.'

'I see no objection to that,' said the manager after a moment or two's pause. 'I cannot give you the information offhand, of course, but if you will return in half an hour's time I will have everything ready to lay before you.'

'Thank you very much. That will suit me admirably.'

In half an hour's time, Anthony returned to the office again to find that the manager had been as good as his word. Jotted down on a piece of paper were all the relevant facts known about Giuseppe Manelli.

'He came to us, you see, about three months ago. A skilled and experienced waiter. Has given complete satisfaction. He has been in England about five years.'

Together the two men ran over a list of the hotels and restaurants where the Italian had worked. One fact struck Anthony as being possibly of significance. At two of the hotels in question there had been serious robberies during the time that Giuseppe was employed there, though no suspicion of any kind had attached to him in either case. Still, the fact was significant.

Was Giuseppe merely a clever hotel thief? Had his search of Anthony's suitcase been only part of his habitual professional tactics? He might just possibly have had the packet of letters in his hand at the moment when Anthony switched on the light, and have shoved it into his pocket mechanically so as to have his hands free. In that case, the thing was mere plain or garden robbery.

Against that, there was to be put the man's excitement of the evening before when he had caught sight of the papers lying on the table. There had been no money or object of value there such as would excite the cupidity of an ordinary thief.

No, Anthony felt convinced that Giuseppe had been acting as a tool for some outside agency. With the information supplied to him by the manager, it might be possible to learn something about Giuseppe's private life and so finally track him down. He gathered up the sheet of paper and rose.

'Thank you very much indeed. It's quite unnecessary to ask, I suppose, whether Giuseppe is still in the hotel?'

The manager smiled.

'His bed was not slept in, and all his things have been left behind. He must have rushed straight out after his attack upon you. I don't think there is much chance of our seeing him again.'

'I imagine not. Well, thank you very much indeed. I shall be staying on here for the present.'

'I hope you will be successful in your task, but I confess that I am rather doubtful.'

'I always hope for the best.'

One of Anthony's first proceedings was to question some of the other waiters who had been friendly with Giuseppe, but he obtained very little to go upon. He wrote out an advertisement on the lines he had planned, and had it sent to five of the most widely read newspapers. He was just about to go out and visit the restaurant at which Giuseppe had been previously employed when the telephone rang. Anthony took up the receiver.

'Hullo, what is it?'

A toneless voice replied.

'Am I speaking to Mr McGrath?'

'You are. Who are you?'

'This is Messrs Balderson and Hodgkins. Just a minute, please. I will put you through to Mr Balderson.'

'Our worthy publishers,' thought Anthony. 'So they are getting worried too, are they? They needn't. There's a week to run still.'

A hearty voice struck suddenly upon his ear.

'Hullo! That Mr McGrath?'

'Speaking.'

'I'm Mr Balderson of Balderson and Hodgkins. What about that manuscript, Mr McGrath?'

'Well,' said Anthony, 'what about it?'

'Everything about it. I understand, Mr McGrath, that you have just arrived in this country from South Africa. That being so, you can't possibly understand the position. There's going to be trouble about that manuscript, Mr McGrath, big trouble. Sometimes I wish we'd never said we'd handle it.'

'Indeed?'

'I assure you it's so. At present I'm anxious to get it into my possession as quickly as possible, so as to have a couple of copies made. Then, if the original is destroyed – well, no harm will be done.'

'Dear me,' said Anthony.

'Yes, I expect it sounds absurd to you, Mr McGrath. But, I assure you, you don't appreciate the situation. There's a determined effort being made to prevent its ever reaching this office. I say to you quite frankly and without humbug that if you attempt to bring it yourself it's ten to one that you'll never get here.'

'I doubt that,' said Anthony. 'When I want to get anywhere, I usually do.'

'You're up against a very dangerous lot of people. I wouldn't have believed it myself a month ago. I tell you, Mr McGrath, we've been bribed and threatened and cajoled by one lot and another until we don't know whether we're on our heads or our heels. My suggestion is that you do not attempt to bring the manuscript here. One of our people will call upon you at the hotel and take possession of it.'

'And supposing the gang does him in?' asked Anthony.

'The responsibility would then be ours – not yours. You would have delivered it to our representative and obtained a written discharge. The cheque for – er – a thousand pounds which we are instructed to hand to you will not be available until Wednesday next by the terms of our agreement with the executors of the late – er – author – you know whom I mean, but if you insist I will send my own cheque for that amount by the messenger.'

Anthony reflected for a minute or two. He had intended to keep the memoirs until the last day of grace, because he was anxious to see for himself what all the fuss was about. Nevertheless, he realized the force of the publisher's arguments.

'All right,' he said, with a little sigh. 'Have it your own way. Send your man along. And if you don't mind sending that cheque as well I'd rather have it now, as I may be going out of England before next Wednesday.'

'Certainly, Mr McGrath. Our representative will call upon you first thing tomorrow morning. It will be wiser not to send anyone direct from the office. Our Mr Holmes lives in South London. He will call in on his way to us, and will give you a receipt for the package. I suggest that tonight you should place a dummy packet in the manager's safe. Your enemies will get to hear of this, and it will prevent any attack being made upon your apartments tonight.'

'Very well, I will do as you direct.'

Anthony hung up the receiver with a thoughtful face.

Then he went on with his interrupted plan of seeking news of the slippery Giuseppe. He drew a complete blank, however. Giuseppe had worked at the restaurant in question, but nobody seemed to know anything of his private life or associates.

'But I'll get you, my lad,' murmured Anthony, between his teeth. 'I'll get you yet. It's only a matter of time.'

His second night in London was entirely peaceful.

At nine o'clock the following morning, the card of Mr Holmes from Messrs Balderson and Hodgkins was sent up, and Mr Holmes followed it. A small, fair man with a quiet manner.

Anthony handed over the manuscript, and received in exchange a cheque for a thousand pounds. Mr Holmes packed up the manuscript in the small brown bag he carried, wished Anthony good morning, and departed. The whole thing seemed very tame.

'But perhaps he'll be murdered on the way there,' Anthony murmured aloud, as he stared idly out of the window. 'I wonder now – I very much wonder.'

He put the cheque in an envelope, enclosed a few lines of writing with it, and sealed it up carefully. Jimmy, who had been more or less in funds at the time of his encounter with Anthony at Bulawayo, had advanced him a substantial sum of money which was, as yet, practically untouched.

'If one job's done with, the other isn't,' said Anthony to himself. 'Up to now, I've bungled it. But never say die. I think that, suitably disguised, I shall go and have a look at 487 Pont Street.'

He packed his belongings, went down and paid his bill, and ordered his luggage to be put on a taxi. Suitably rewarding those who stood in his path, most of whom had done nothing whatever materially to add to his comfort, he was on the point of being driven off, when a small boy rushed down the steps with a letter.

'Just come for you, this very minute, sir.'

With a sigh, Anthony produced yet another shilling. The taxi groaned heavily and jumped forward with a hideous crashing of gears, and Anthony opened the letter.

It was rather a curious document. He had to read it four times before he could be sure of what it was all about. Put in plain English (the letter was not in plain English, but in the peculiar involved style common to missives issued by Government officials) it presumed that Mr McGrath was arriving in England from South Africa today – Thursday, it referred obliquely to the memoirs of Count Stylptitch, and begged Mr McGrath to do nothing in the matter until he had had a confidential conversation with Mr George Lomax, and certain other parties whose magnificence was vaguely hinted at. It also contained a definite invitation to go down to Chimneys as the guest of Lord Caterham, on the following day, Friday.

A mysterious and thoroughly obscure communication. Anthony enjoyed it very much.

'Dear old England,' he murmured affectionately. 'Two days behind the times, as usual. Rather a pity. Still, I can't go down to Chimneys under false pretences. I wonder, though, if there's an inn handy? Mr Anthony Cade might stay at the inn without anyone being the wiser.'

He leaned out of the window, and gave new directions to the taxi driver, who acknowledged them with a snort of contempt.

The taxi drew up before one of London's more obscure hostelries. The fare, however, was paid on a scale befitting its point of departure.

Having booked a room in the name of Anthony Cade, Anthony passed into a dingy writing-room, took out a sheet of notepaper stamped with the legend Hotel Blitz, and wrote rapidly.

He explained that he had arrived on the preceding Tuesday, that he had handed over the manuscript in question to Messrs Balderson and Hodgkins, and he regretfully declined the kind invitation of Lord Caterham as he was leaving England almost immediately. He signed the letter 'Yours faithfully, James McGrath'.

And now,' said Anthony, as he affixed the stamp to the envelope. 'To business. Exit James McGrath, and Enter Anthony Cade.'

CHAPTER 8

A DEAD MAN

On that same Thursday afternoon Virginia Revel had been playing tennis at Ranelagh. All the way back to Pont Street, as she lay back in the long, luxurious limousine, a little smile played upon her lips as she rehearsed her part in the forthcoming interview. Of course it was within the bounds of possibility that the blackmailer might not reappear, but she felt pretty certain that he would. She had shown herself an easy prey. Well, perhaps this time there would be a little surprise for him!

When the car drew up at the house, she turned to speak to the chauffeur before going up the steps.

'How's your wife, Walton? I forgot to ask.'

'Better I think, ma'am. The doctor said he'd look in and see her about half-past six. Will you be wanting the car again?'

Virginia reflected for a minute.

'I shall be away for the weekend. I'm going by the 6.40 from Paddington, but I shan't need you again – a taxi will do for that. I'd rather you saw the doctor. If he thinks it would do your wife good to go away for the week-end, take her somewhere, Walton. I'll stand the expense.'

Cutting short the man's thanks with an impatient nod of the head, Virginia ran up the steps, delved into her bag in search of her latch-key, remembered she hadn't got it with her, and hastily rang the bell.

It was not answered at once, but as she waited there a young man came up the steps. He was shabbily dressed, and carried in his hand a sheaf of leaflets. He held one out to Virginia with the legend on it plainly visible: 'Why Did I Serve My Country?' In his left hand he held a collecting box.

'I can't buy two of those awful poems in one day,' said Virginia pleadingly. 'I bought one this morning. I did, indeed, honour bright.'

The young man threw back his head and laughed. Virginia laughed with him. Running her eyes carelessly over him, she thought him a more pleasing specimen than usual of London's unemployed. She liked his brown face, and the lean hardness of him. She went so far as to wish she had a job for him.

But at that moment the door opened, and immediately Virginia forgot all about the problem of the unemployed, for to her astonishment the door was opened by her own maid, Elise.

'Where's Chilvers?' she demanded sharply, as she stepped into the hall.

'But he is gone, madame, with the others.'

'What others? Gone where?'

'But to Datchet, madame – to the cottage, as your telegram said.'

'My telegram?' said Virginia, utterly at sea.

'Did not madame send a telegram? Surely there can be no mistake. It came but an hour ago.'

'I never sent any telegram. What did it say?'

'I believe it is still on the table *là-bas*.'

Elise retired, pouncing upon it, and brought it to her mistress in triumph.

'*Voilà*, madame!'

The telegram was addressed to Chilvers and ran as follows:

Please take household down to cottage at once, and make preparations for week-end party there. Catch 5.49 train.

There was nothing unusual about it, it was just the sort of message she herself had frequently sent before, when she had arranged a party at her riverside bungalow on the spur of the moment. She always took the whole household down, leaving an old woman as caretaker. Chilvers would not have seen anything wrong with the message, and like a good servant had carried out his orders faithfully enough.

'Me, I remained,' explained Elise, 'knowing that madame would wish me to pack for her.'

'It's a silly hoax,' cried Virginia, flinging down the telegram angrily. 'You know perfectly well, Elise, that I am going to Chimneys. I told you so this morning.'

'I thought madame had changed her mind. Sometimes that does happen, does it not, madame?'

Virginia admitted the truth of the accusation with a half-smile. She was busy trying to find a reason for this extraordinary practical joke. Elise put forward a suggestion.

'*Mon Dieu*!' she cried, clasping her hands. 'If it should be the malefactors, the thieves! They send the bogus telegram and get the *domestiques* all out of the house, and then they rob it.'

'I suppose that might be it,' said Virginia doubtfully.

'Yes, yes madame, that is without a doubt. Every day you read in the papers of such things. Madame will ring up the police at once – at once – before they arrive and cut our throats.'

'Don't get so excited, Elise. They won't come and cut our throats at six o'clock in the afternoon.'

'Madame, I implore you, let me run out and fetch a policeman now, at once.'

'What on earth for? Don't be silly, Elise. Go up and pack my things for Chimneys, if you haven't already done it. The new Cailleaux evening dress, and the white *crêpe marocain*, and – yes, the black velvet – black velvet is so political, is it not?'

'Madame looks ravishing in the *eau de nil satin*,' suggested

Elise, her professional instincts reasserting themselves.

'No, I won't take that. Hurry up, Elise, there's a good girl. We've got very little time. I'll send a wire to Chilvers at Datchet, and I'll speak to the policeman on the beat as we go out and tell him to keep an eye on the place. Don't start rolling your eyes again, Elise – if you get so frightened before anything has happened, what would you do if a man jumped out from some dark corner and stuck a knife into you?'

Elise gave vent to a shrill squeak, and beat a speedy retreat up the stairs, darting nervous glances over her shoulder as she went.

Virginia made a face at her retreating back, and crossed the hall to the little study where the telephone was. Elise's suggestion of ringing up the police station seemed to her a good one, and she intended to act upon it without any further delay.

She opened the study door and crossed to the telephone. Then, with her hand on the receiver, she stopped. A man was sitting in the big armchair, sitting in a curious huddled position. In the stress of the moment, she had forgotten all about her expected visitor. Apparently he had fallen asleep whilst waiting for her.

She came right up to the chair, a slightly mischievous smile upon her face. And then suddenly the smile faded.

The man was not asleep. *He was dead.*

She knew it at once, knew it instinctively even before her eyes had seen and noted the small shining pistol lying on the floor, the little-singed hole just above the heart with the dark stain round it, and the horrible dropped jaw.

She stood quite still, her hands pressed to her sides. In the silence she heard Elise running down the stairs.

'Madame! Madame!'

'Well, what is it?'

She moved quickly to the door. Her whole instinct was to conceal what had happened – for the moment anyway – from Elise. Elise would promptly go into hysterics, she knew that well enough, and she felt a great need for calm and quiet in which to think things out.

'Madame, would it not be better if I should draw the chain across the door? These malefactors, at any minute they may arrive.'

'Yes, if you like. Anything you like.'

She heard the rattle of the chain, and then Elise running upstairs again, and drew a long breath of relief.

She looked at the man in the chair and then at the telephone. Her course was quite clear, she must ring up the police at once.

But still she did not do so. She stood quite still, paralysed with horror and with a host of conflicting ideas rushing through her brain. The bogus telegram! Had it something to do with this? Supposing Elise had not stayed behind? She would have let herself in – that is, presuming she had had her latch-key with her as usual, to find herself alone in the house with a murdered man – a man whom she had permitted to blackmail her on a former occasion. Of course she had an explanation of that; but thinking of that explanation she was not quite easy in her mind. She remembered how frankly incredible George had found it. Would other people think the same? Those letters now – of course, she hadn't written them, but would it be so easy to prove that?

She put her hands on her forehead, squeezing them tight together.

'I must think,' said Virginia. 'I simply must think.'

Who had let the man in? Surely not Elise. If she had done so, she would have been sure to have mentioned the fact at once. The whole thing seemed more and more mysterious as she thought about it. There was really only one thing to be done – ring up the police.

She stretched out her hand to the telephone, and suddenly she thought of George. A man – that was what she wanted – an ordinary level-headed, unemotional man who would see things in their proper proportion and point out to her the best course to take.

Then she shook her head. Not George. The first thing George would think of would be his own position. He would hate being mixed up in this kind of business. George wouldn't do at all.

Then her face softened. Bill, of course! Without more ado, she rang up Bill.

She was informed that he had left half an hour ago for Chimneys.

'Oh, damn!' cried Virginia, jamming down the receiver. It was horrible to be shut up with a dead body and to have no one to speak to.

And at that minute the front door bell rang.

Virginia jumped. In a few minutes it rang again. Elise, she knew, was upstairs packing and wouldn't hear it.

Virginia went out in the hall, drew back the chain, and undid all the bolts that Elise had fastened in her zeal. Then, with a long breath, she threw open the door. On the steps was the unemployed young man.

Virginia plunged headlong with a relief born of overstrung nerves.

Come in,' she said. 'I think perhaps I've got a job for you.'

She took him into the dining-room, pulled forward a chair for him, sat herself facing him, and stared at him very attentively.

'Excuse me,' she said, 'but are you – I mean –'

'Eton and Oxford,' said the young man. 'That's what you wanted to ask me, wasn't it?'

'Something of the kind,' admitted Virginia.

'Come down in the world entirely through my own incapacity to stick to regular work. This isn't regular work you're offering me, I hope?'

A smile hovered for a moment on her lips.

'It's very irregular.'

'Good,' said the young man in a tone of satisfaction.

Virginia noted his bronzed face and long lean body with approval.

'You see,' she explained. 'I'm in rather a hole, and most of my friends are – well, rather high up. They've all got something to lose.'

'I've nothing whatever to lose. So go ahead. What's the trouble?'

'There's a dead man in the next room,' said Virginia. 'He's been murdered, and I don't know what to do about it.'

She blurted out the words as simply as a child might have done. The young man went up enormously in her estimation by the way he accepted her statement. He might have been used to hearing a similar announcement made every day of his life.

'Excellent,' he said, with a trace of enthusiasm. 'I've always wanted to do a bit of amateur detective work. Shall we go and view the body, or will you give me the facts first?'

'I think I'd better give you the facts.' She paused for a moment to consider how best to condense her story, and then began speaking quietly and concisely:

'This man came to the house for the first time yesterday and asked to see me. He had certain letters with him – love letters, signed with my name –'

'But which weren't written by you,' put in the young man quietly.

Virginia looked at him in some astonishment.

'How did you know that?'

'Oh, I deduced it. But go on.'

'He wanted to blackmail me – and I – well, I don't know if you'll understand, but I – let him.'

She looked at him appealingly, and he nodded his head reassuringly.

'Of course I understand. You wanted to see what it felt like.'

'How frightfully clever of you! That's just what I did feel.'

'I *am* clever,' said the young man modestly. 'But, mind you, very few people would understand that point of view. Most people, you see, haven't got any imagination.'

'I suppose that's so. I told this man to come back today – at six o'clock. I arrived home from Ranelagh to find that a bogus telegram had got all the servants except my maid out of the house. Then I walked into the study and found the man shot.'

'Who let him in?'

'I don't know. I think if my maid had done so she would have told me.'

'Does she know what has happened?'

'I have told her nothing.'

The young man nodded, and rose to his feet.

'And now to view the body,' he said briskly. 'But I'll tell you this – on the whole it's always best to tell the truth. One lie involves you in such a lot of lies – and continuous lying is so monotonous.'

'Then you advise me to ring up the police?'

'Probably. But we'll just have a look at the fellow first.'

Virginia led the way out of the room. On the threshold she paused, looking back at him.

'By the way,' she said, 'you haven't told me your name yet?'

'My name? My name's Anthony Cade.'

CHAPTER 9

ANTHONY DISPOSES OF A BODY

Anthony followed Virginia out of the room, smiling a little to himself. Events had taken quite an unexpected turn. But as he bent over the figure in the chair he grew grave again.

'He's still warm,' he said sharply. 'He was killed less than half an hour ago.'

'Just before I came in?'

'Exactly.'

He stood upright, drawing his brows together in a frown. Then he asked a question of which Virginia did not at once see the drift:

'Your maid's not been in this room, of course?'

'No.'

'Does she know that you've been into it?'

'Why – yes. I came to the door to speak to her.'

'After you'd found the body?'

'Yes.'

'And you said nothing?'

'Would it have been better if I had? I thought she would go into hysterics – she's French, you know, and easily upset – I wanted to think over the best thing to do.'

Anthony nodded, but did not speak.

'You think it a pity, I can see?'

'Well, it was rather unfortunate, Mrs Revel. If you and the maid had discovered the body together, immediately on your return, it would have simplified matters very much. The man would then definitely have been shot *before* your return to the house.'

'Whilst now they might say he was shot *after* – I see –'

He watched her taking in the idea, and was confirmed in his first impression of her, formed when she had spoken to him on the steps outside. Besides beauty, she possessed courage and brains.

Virginia was so engrossed in the puzzle presented to her that it did not occur to her to wonder at this strange man's ready use of her name.

'Why didn't Elise hear the shot, I wonder?' she murmured.

Anthony pointed to the open window, as a loud backfire came from a passing car.

'There you are. London's not the place to notice a pistol shot.'

Virginia turned with a little shudder to the body in the chair.

'He looks like an Italian,' she remarked curiously.

'He is an Italian,' said Anthony. 'I should say that his regular profession was that of a waiter. He only did blackmailing in his spare time. His name might very possibly be Giuseppe.'

'Good heavens!' cried Virginia. 'Is this Sherlock Holmes?'

'No,' said Anthony regretfully. 'I'm afraid it's just plain or garden cheating. I'll tell you all about it presently. Now you say this man showed you some letters and asked you for money. Did you give him any?'

'Yes, I did.'

'How much?'

'Forty pounds.'

'That's bad,' said Anthony, but without manifesting any undue surprise. 'Now let's have a look at the telegram.'

Virginia picked it up from the table and gave it to him. She saw his face grow grave as he looked at it.

'What's the matter?'

He held it out, pointing silently to the place of origin.

'Barnes,' he said. 'And you were at Ranelagh this afternoon. What's to prevent you having sent it off yourself?'

Virginia felt fascinated by his words. It was as though a net was closing tighter and tighter round her. He was forcing her to see all the things which she had felt dimly at the back of her mind.

Anthony took out his handkerchief and wound it round his hand, then he picked up the pistol.

'We criminals have to be so careful,' he said apologetically. 'Fingerprints, you know.'

Suddenly she saw his whole figure stiffen. His voice, when he spoke, had altered. It was terse and curt.

'Mrs Revel,' he said, 'have you ever seen this pistol before?'

'No,' said Virginia wonderingly.

'Are you sure of that?'

'Quite sure.'

'Have you a pistol of your own?'

'No.'

'Have you ever had one?'

'No, never.'

'You are sure of that?'

'Quite sure.'

He stared at her steadily for a minute, and Virginia stared back in complete surprise at his tone.

Then, with a sigh, he relaxed.

'That's odd,' he said. 'How do you account for this?'

He held out the pistol. It was a small, dainty article, almost a toy – though capable of doing deadly work. Engraved on it was the name Virginia.

'Oh, it's impossible!' cried Virginia.

Her astonishment was so genuine that Anthony could but believe in it.

'Sit down,' he said quietly. 'There's more in this than there seemed to be first go off. To begin with, what's our hypothesis? There are only two possible ones. There is, of course, the real Virginia of the letters. She may have somehow or other tracked him down, shot him, dropped the pistol, stolen the letters, and taken herself off. That's quite possible, isn't it?'

'I suppose so,' said Virginia unwillingly.

'The other hypothesis is a good deal more interesting. Whoever wished to kill Giuseppe, wished also to incriminate you – in fact, that may have been their main object. They could get *him* easily enough anywhere, but they took extraordinary pains and trouble to get him *here*, and whoever they were they knew all about you, your cottage at Datchet, your usual household arrangements, and the fact that you were at Ranelagh this afternoon. It seems an absurd question, but have you any enemies, Mrs Revel?'

'Of course I haven't – not that kind, anyway.'

'The question is,' said Anthony, 'what are we going to do now? There are two courses open to us. A: ring up the police, tell the whole story, and trust to your unassailable position in the world and your hitherto blameless life. B: an attempt on my part to dispose successfully of the body. Naturally my private inclinations urge me to B. I've always wanted to see if I couldn't conceal a crime with the necessary cunning, but have had a squeamish objection to shedding blood. On the whole, I expect A's the soundest. Then here's a sort of bowdlerized A. Ring up the police, etc., but suppress the pistol and the blackmailing letters – that is, if they are on him still.'

Anthony ran rapidly through the dead man's pockets.

'He's been stripped clean,' he announced. 'There's not a thing on him. There'll be dirty work at the cross-roads over those letters yet. Hullo, what's this? Hole in the lining – something got caught there, torn roughly out, and a scrap of paper left behind.'

He drew out the scrap of paper as he spoke, and brought it over to the light. Virginia joined him.

'Pity we haven't got the rest of it,' he muttered. 'Chimneys 11.45 Thursday – Sounds like an appointment.'

'Chimneys?' cried Virginia. 'How extraordinary!'

'Why extraordinary? Rather high-toned for such a low fellow?'

'I'm going to Chimneys this evening. At least I was.'

Anthony wheeled round on her.

'What's that? Say that again.'

'I was going to Chimneys this evening,' repeated Virginia.

Anthony stared at her.

'I begin to see. At least, I may be wrong – but it's an idea. Suppose someone wanted badly to prevent your going to Chimneys?'

'My cousin George Lomax does,' said Virginia with a smile. 'But I can't seriously suspect George of murder.'

Anthony did not smile. He was lost in thought.

'If you ring up the police, its goodbye to any idea of getting to Chimneys today – or even tomorrow. And I should like you to go to Chimneys. I fancy it will disconcert our unknown friends. Mrs Revel, will you put yourself in my hands?'

'It's to be Plan B, then?'

'It's to be Plan B. The first thing is to get that maid of yours out of the house. Can you manage that?'

'Easily.'

Virginia went out in the hall and called up the stairs.

'Elise. Elise.'

'Madame?'

Anthony heard a rapid colloquy, and then the front door opened and shut. Virginia came back into the room.

'She's gone. I sent her for some special scent – told her the shop in question was open until eight. It won't be, of course. She's to follow after me by the next train without coming back here.'

'Good,' said Anthony approvingly. 'We can now proceed to the disposal of the body. It's a timeworn method, but I'm afraid I shall have to ask you if there's such a thing in the house as a trunk?'

'Of course there is. Come down to the basement and take your choice.'

There was a variety of trunks in the basement. Anthony selected a solid affair of suitable size.

'I'll attend to this part of it,' he said tactfully. 'You go upstairs and get ready to start.'

Virginia obeyed. She slipped out of her tennis kit, put on a soft brown travelling dress and a delightful little orange hat, and came down to find Anthony waiting in the hall with a neatly strapped trunk beside him.

'I should like to tell you the story of my life,' he remarked, 'but it's going to be rather a busy evening. Now this is what you've got to do. Call a taxi, have your luggage put on it, including the trunk. Drive to Paddington. There have the trunk put in the Left Luggage Office. I shall be on the platform. As you pass me, drop the cloakroom ticket. I will pick it up and return it to you, but in reality I shall keep it. Go on to Chimneys, and leave the rest to me.'

'It's awfully good of you,' said Virginia. 'It's really dreadful of me saddling a perfect stranger with a dead body like this.'

'I like it,' returned Anthony nonchalantly. 'If one of my friends, Jimmy McGrath, were here, he'd tell you that anything of this kind suits me down to the ground.'

Virginia was staring at him.

'What name did you say? Jimmy McGrath?'

Anthony returned her glance keenly.

'Yes. Why? Have you heard of him?'

'Yes – and quite lately.' She paused irresolutely, and then went on. 'Mr Cade, I must talk to you. Can't you come down to Chimneys?'

'You'll see me before very long, Mrs Revel – I'll tell you

that. Now, exit Conspirator A by back door slinkingly. Exit Conspirator B in blaze of glory by front door to taxi.'

The plan went through without a hitch. Anthony, having picked up a second taxi, was on the platform and duly retrieved the fallen ticket. He then departed in search of a somewhat battered second-hand Morris Cowley which he had acquired earlier in the day in case it should be necessary to his plans.

Returning to Paddington in this, he handed the ticket to the porter, who got the trunk out of the cloak-room and wedged it securely at the back of the car. Anthony drove off.

His objective now was out of London. Through Notting Hill, Shepherd's Bush, down Goldhawk Road, through Brentford and Hounslow till he came to the long stretch of road midway between Hounslow and Staines. It was a well-frequented road, with motors passing continuously. No footmarks or tyremarks were likely to show. Anthony stopped the car at a certain spot. Getting down, he first obscured the number-plate with mud. Then, waiting until he heard no car coming in either direction, he opened the trunk, heaved out Giuseppe's body, and laid it neatly down by the side of the road, on the inside of a curve, so that the headlights of passing motors would not strike on it.

Then he entered the car again and drove away. The whole business had occupied exactly one minute and a half. He made a detour to the right, returning to London by way of Burnham Beeches. There again he halted the car, and choosing a giant of the forest he deliberately climbed the huge tree. It was something of a feat, even for Anthony. To one of the topmost branches he affixed a small brown paper parcel, concealing it in a little niche close to the bole.

'A very clever way of disposing of the pistol,' said Anthony to himself with some approval. 'Everybody hunts about on the ground, and drags ponds. But there are very few people in England who could climb that tree.'

Next, back to London and Paddington Station. Here he left the trunk – at the other cloak-room this time, the one on the Arrivals side. He thought longingly of such things as good rump steaks, juicy chops, and large masses of fried potatoes. But he shook his head ruefully, glancing at his wrist-watch. He fed the Morris with a fresh supply of petrol, and then took the road once more. North this time.

It was just after half-past eleven that he brought the car to rest in the road adjoining the park of Chimneys. Jumping out he scaled the wall easily enough, and set out towards the house. It took him longer than he thought, and presently he broke into a run. A great grey mass loomed up out of the darkness – the venerable pile of Chimneys. In the distance a stable clock chimed the three-quarters.

11.45 – the time mentioned on the scrap of paper. Anthony was on the terrace now, looking up at the house. Everything seemed dark and quiet.

'They go to bed early, these politicians,' he murmured to himself.

And suddenly a sound smote upon his ears – the sound of a shot. Anthony spun round quickly. The sound had come from within the house – he was sure of that. He waited a minute, but everything was still as death. Finally he went up to one of the long French windows from where he judged the sound that had startled him had come. He tried the handle. It was locked. He tried some of the other windows, listening intently all the while. But the silence remained unbroken.

In the end he told himself that he must have imagined the sound, or perhaps mistaken a stray shot coming from a poacher in the woods. He turned and retraced his steps across the park, vaguely dissatisfied and uneasy.

He looked back at the house, and whilst he looked a light sprang up in one of the windows on the first floor. In another minute it went out again, and the whole place was in darkness once more.

CHAPTER 10

CHIMNEYS

Inspector Badgworthy in his office. Time, 8.30 a.m. A tall portly man, Inspector Badgworthy, with a heavy regulation tread. Inclined to breathe hard in moments of professional strain. In attendance Constable Johnson, very new to the Force, with a downy unfledged look about him, like a human chicken.

The telephone on the table rang sharply, and the inspector took it up with his usual portentous gravity of action.

'Yes. Police station Market Basing. Inspector Badgworthy speaking. What?'

Slight alteration in the inspector's manner. As he is greater than Johnson, so others are greater than Inspector Badgworthy.

'Speaking, my lord. I beg your pardon, my lord? I didn't quite hear what you said?'

Long pause, during which the inspector listens, quite a variety of expressions passing over his usually impassive countenance. Finally he lays down the receiver, after a brief 'At once, my lord.'

He turned to Johnson, seeming visibly swelled with importance.

'From his lordship – at Chimneys – murder.'

'Murder,' echoed Johnson, suitably impressed.

'Murder it is,' said the inspector, with great satisfaction.

'Why, there's never been a murder here – not that I've ever heard of – except the time that Tom Pearse shot his sweetheart.'

'And that, in a manner of speaking, wasn't murder at all, but drink,' said the inspector, deprecatingly.

'He weren't hanged for it,' agreed Johnson gloomily. 'But this is the real thing, is it, sir?'

'It is, Johnson. One of his lordship's guests, a foreign gentleman, discovered shot. Open window, and footprints outside.'

'I'm sorry it were a foreigner,' said Johnson, with some regret.

It made the murder seem less real. Foreigners, Johnson felt, were liable to be shot.

'His lordship's in a rare taking,' continued the inspector. 'We'll get hold of Dr Cartwright and take him up with us right away. I hope to goodness no one will get messing with those footprints.'

Badgworthy was in a seventh heaven. A murder! At Chimneys! Inspector Badgworthy in charge of the case. The police have a clue. Sensational arrest. Promotion and kudos for the aforementioned inspector.

'That is,' said Inspector Badgworthy to himself, 'if Scotland Yard doesn't come butting in.'

The thought damped him momentarily. It seemed so extremely likely to happen under the circumstances.

They stopped at Dr Cartwright's, and the doctor, who was a comparatively young man, displayed a keen interest. His attitude was almost exactly that of Johnson.

'Why, bless my soul,' he exclaimed. 'We haven't had a murder here since the time of Tom Pearse.'

All three of them got into the doctor's little car, and started off briskly for Chimneys. As they passed the local inn, the Jolly Cricketers, the doctor noticed a man standing in the doorway.

'Stranger,' he remarked. 'Rather a nice-looking fellow. Wonder how long he's been here, and what he's doing staying at the Cricketers? I haven't seen him about at all. He must have arrived last night.'

'He didn't come by train,' said Johnson.

Johnson's brother was the local railway porter, and Johnson was therefore always well up in arrivals and departures.

'Who was here for Chimneys yesterday?' asked the inspector.

'Lady Eileen, she come down by the 3.40, and two gentlemen with her, an American gent and a young Army chap – neither of them with valets. His lordship come down with a foreign gentleman, the one that's been shot as likely as not, by the 5.40, and the foreign gentleman's valet. Mr Eversleigh come by the same train. Mrs Revel came by the 7.25, and another foreign-looking gentleman came by it too, one with a bald head and a hook nose. Mrs Revel's maid came by the 8.56.'

Johnson paused, out of breath.

'And there was no one for the Cricketers?'

Johnson shook his head.

'He must have come by car then,' said the inspector. 'Johnson, make a note to institute inquiries at the Cricketers on your way back. We want to know all about any strangers. He was very sunburnt, that gentleman. Likely as not, he's come from foreign parts too.'

The inspector nodded his head with great sagacity, as though to imply that that was the sort of wide-awake man he was – not to be caught napping under any consideration.

The car passed in through the park gates of Chimneys. Descriptions of that historic place can be found in any guidebook. It is also No. 3 in *Historic Homes of England*, price 21*s*. On Thursday, coaches come over from Middlingham and view those portions of it which are open to the public. In view of all these facilities, to describe Chimneys would be superfluous.

They were received at the door by a white-headed butler whose demeanour was perfect.

'We are not accustomed,' it seemed to say, 'to having murder committed within these walls. But these are evil days. Let us meet disaster with perfect calm, and pretend with our dying breath that nothing out of the usual has occurred.'

'His lordship,' said the butler, 'is expecting you. This way, if you please.'

He led them to a small cosy room which was Lord Caterham's refuge from the magnificence elsewhere, and announced them.

'The police, my lord, and Dr Cartwright.'

Lord Caterham was pacing up and down in a visibly agitated state.

'Ha! Inspector, you've turned up at last. I'm thankful for that. How are you, Cartwright? This is the very devil of a business, you know. The very devil of a business.'

And Lord Caterham, running his hands through his hair in a frenzied fashion until it stood upright in little tufts, looked even less like a peer of the realm than usual.

'Where's the body?' asked the doctor, in curt business-like fashion.

Lord Caterham turned to him as though relieved at being asked a direct question.

'In the Council Chamber – just where it was found – I wouldn't have it touched. I believed – er – that that was the correct thing to do.'

'Quite right, my lord,' said the inspector approvingly.

He produced a notebook and pencil.

'And who discovered the body? Did you?'

'Good Lord, no,' said Lord Caterham. 'You don't think I usually get up at this unearthly hour in the morning, do you? No, a housemaid found it. She screamed a good deal, I believe. I didn't hear her myself. Then they came to me about it, and of course I got up and came down – and there it was, you know.'

'You recognized the body as that of one of your guests?'

'That's right, Inspector.'

'By name?'

This perfectly simple question seemed to upset Lord Caterham. He opened his mouth once or twice, and then shut it again. Finally he asked feebly:

'Do you mean – do you mean – what was his name?'

'Yes, my lord.'

'Well,' said Lord Caterham, looking slowly round the room, as though hoping to gain inspiration. 'His name was – I should say it was – yes, decidedly so – Count Stanislaus.'

There was something so odd about Lord Caterham's manner, that the inspector ceased using his pencil and stared at him instead. But at that moment a diversion occurred which seemed highly welcome to the embarrassed peer.

The door opened and a girl came into the room. She was tall, slim and dark, with an attractive boyish face and a very determined manner. This was Lady Eileen Brent, commonly known as Bundle, Lord Caterham's eldest daughter. She nodded to the others, and addressed her father directly.

'I've got him,' she announced.

For a moment the inspector was on the point of starting forward under the impression that the young lady had captured the murderer red-handed, but almost immediately he realized that her meaning was quite different.

Lord Caterham uttered a sigh of relief.

'That's a good job. What did he say?'

'He's coming over at once. We are to "use the utmost discretion".'

Her father made a sound of annoyance.

'That's just the sort of idiotic thing George Lomax would say. However, once he comes, I shall wash my hands of the whole affair.'

He appeared to cheer up a little at the prospect.

'And the name of the murdered man was Count Stanislaus?' queried the doctor.

A lightning glance passed between father and daughter, and then the former said with some dignity:

'Certainly. I said so just now.'

'I asked because you didn't seem quite sure about it before,' explained Cartwright.

There was a faint twinkle in his eye, and Lord Caterham looked at him reproachfully.

'I'll take you to the Council Chamber,' he said more briskly.

They followed him, the inspector bringing up the rear and darting sharp glances all around him as he went, much as though he expected to find a clue in a picture frame, or behind a door.

Lord Caterham took a key from his pocket and unlocked a door, flinging it open. They all passed into a big room panelled in oak, with three French windows giving on the terrace. There was a long refectory table and a good many oak chests, and some beautiful old chairs. On the walls were various paintings of dead and gone Caterhams and others.

Near the left-hand wall, about half-way between the door and the window, a man was lying on his back, his arms flung wide.

Dr Cartwright went over and knelt down by the body. The inspector strode across to the windows, and examined them in turn. The centre one was closed, but not fastened. On the steps outside were footprints leading up to the window, and a second set going away again.

'Clear enough,' said the inspector, with a nod. 'But there ought to be footprints on the inside as well. They'd show up plain on this parquet floor.'

'I think I can explain that,' interposed Bundle. 'The housemaid had polished half the floor this morning before she saw the body. You see, it was dark when she came in here. She went straight across to the windows, drew the curtains, and began on the floor, and naturally didn't see the body which is hidden from that side of the room by the table. She didn't see it until she came right on top of it.'

The inspector nodded.

'Well,' said Lord Caterham, eager to escape. 'I'll leave you here, Inspector. You'll be able to find me if you – er – want me. But Mr George Lomax is coming over from Wyvern Abbey shortly, and he'll be able to tell you far more than I could. It's his business really. I can't explain, but he will when he comes.'

Lord Caterham beat a precipitate retreat without waiting for a reply.

'Too bad of Lomax,' he complained. 'Letting me in for this. What's the matter, Tredwell?'

The white-haired butler was hovering deferentially at his elbow.

'I have taken the liberty, my lord, of advancing the breakfast hour as far as you are concerned. Everything is ready in the dining-room.'

'I don't suppose for a minute I can eat anything,' said Lord Caterham gloomily, turning his footsteps in that direction. 'Not for a moment.'

Bundle slipped her hand through his arm, and they entered the dining-room together. On the sideboard were half a score of heavy silver dishes, ingeniously kept hot by patent arrangements.

'Omelet,' said Lord Caterham, lifting each lid in turn. 'Eggs and bacon, kidneys, devilled bird, haddock, cold ham, cold pheasant. I don't like any of these things, Tredwell. Ask the cook to poach me an egg, will you?'

'Very good, my lord.'

Tredwell withdrew. Lord Caterham, in an absent-minded fashion, helped himself plentifully to kidneys and bacon, poured himself out a cup of coffee, and sat down at the long table. Bundle was already busy with a plateful of eggs and bacon.

'I'm damned hungry,' said Bundle with her mouth full. 'It must be the excitement.'

'It's all very well for you,' complained her father. 'You young people like excitement. But I'm in a very delicate state of health. Avoid all worry, that's what Sir Abner Willis said – avoid all worry. So easy for a man sitting in his consulting-room in Harley Street to say that. How can I avoid worry when that ass Lomax lands me with a thing like this? I ought to have been firm at the time. I ought to have put my foot down.'

With a sad shake of the head, Lord Caterham rose and carved himself a plate of ham.

'Codders has certainly done it this time,' observed Bundle cheerfully. 'He was almost incoherent over the telephone. He'll be here in a minute or two, spluttering nineteen to the dozen about discretion and hushing it up.'

Lord Caterham groaned at the prospect.

'Was he up?' he asked.

'He told me,' replied Bundle, 'that he had been up and dictating letters and memoranda ever since seven o'clock.'

'Proud of it, too,' remarked her father. 'Extraordinarily selfish, these public men. They make their wretched secretaries get up at the most unearthly hours in order to dictate rubbish to them. If a law was passed compelling them to stop in bed until eleven, what a benefit it would be to the nation! I wouldn't mind so much if they didn't talk such balderdash. Lomax is always talking to me of my "position". As if I had any. Who wants to be a peer nowadays?'

'Nobody,' said Bundle. 'They'd much rather keep a prosperous public-house.'

Tredwell reappeared silently with two poached eggs in a little silver dish which he placed on the table in front of Lord Caterham.

'What's that, Tredwell?' said the latter, looking at them with faint distaste.

'Poached eggs, my lord.'

'I hate poached eggs,' said Lord Caterham peevishly. 'They're so insipid. I don't like to look at them even. Take them away, will you, Tredwell?'

'Very good, my lord.'

Tredwell and the poached eggs withdrew as silently as they came.

'Thank God no one gets up early in this house,' remarked Lord Caterham devoutly. 'We shall have to break this to them when they do, I suppose.'

He sighed.

'I wonder who murdered him,' said Bundle. 'And why?'

'That's not our business, thank goodness,' said Lord Caterham. 'That's for the police to find out. Not that Badgworthy will ever find anything. On the whole I rather hope it was Nosystein.'

'Meaning –'

'The all-British syndicate.'

'Why should Mr Isaacstein murder him when he'd come down here on purpose to meet him?'

'High finance,' said Lord Caterham vaguely. 'And that reminds me, I shouldn't be at all surprised if Isaacstein wasn't an early riser. He may blow in upon us at any minute. It's a habit in the city. I believe that, however rich you are, you always catch the 9.17.'

The sound of a motor being driven at great speed was heard through the open window.

'Codders,' cried Bundle.

Father and daughter leaned out of the window and hailed the occupant of the car as it drew up before the entrance.

'In here, my dear fellow, in here,' cried Lord Caterham, hastily swallowing his mouthful of ham.

George had no intention of climbing in through the window. He disappeared through the front door, and reappeared ushered in by Tredwell, who withdrew at once.

'Have some breakfast,' said Lord Caterham, shaking him by the hand. 'What about a kidney?'

George waved the kidney aside impatiently.

'This is a terrible calamity, terrible, terrible.'

'It is indeed. Some haddock?'

'No, no. It must be hushed up – at all costs it must be hushed up.'

As Bundle had prophesied, George began to splutter.

'I understand your feelings,' said Lord Caterham sympathetically. 'Try an egg and bacon, or some haddock.'

'A totally unforeseen contingency – national calamity – concessions jeopardized –'

'Take time,' said Lord Caterham. 'And take some food. What you need is some food, to pull you together. Poached eggs now? There were some poached eggs here a minute or two ago.'

'I don't want any food,' said George. 'I've had breakfast, and even if I hadn't had any I shouldn't want it. We must think what is to be done. You have told no one as yet?'

'Well, there's Bundle and myself. And the local police. And Cartwright. And all the servants of course.'

George groaned.

'Pull yourself together, my dear fellow,' said Lord Caterham kindly. '(I wish you'd have some breakfast.) You don't seem to realize that you can't hush up a dead body. It's got to be buried and all that sort of thing. Very unfortunate, but there it is.'

George became suddenly calm.

'You are right, Caterham. You have called in the local police, you say? That will not do. We must have Battle.'

'Battle, murder and sudden death,' inquired Lord Caterham, with a puzzled face.

'No, no, you misunderstand me. I referred to Superintendent Battle of Scotland Yard. A man of the utmost discretion.

He worked with us in that deplorable business of the Party funds.'

'What was that?' asked Lord Caterham, with some interest.

But George's eye had fallen upon Bundle, as she sat half in and half out of the window, and he remembered discretion just in time. He rose.

'We must waste no time. I must send off some wires at once.'

'If you write them out, Bundle will send them through the telephone.'

George pulled out a fountain pen and began to write with incredible rapidity. He handed the first one to Bundle, who read it with a great deal of interest.

'God! what a name,' she remarked. 'Baron How Much?'

'Baron Lolopretjzyl.'

Bundle blinked.

'I've got it, but it will take some conveying to the post office.'

George continued to write. Then he handed his labours to Bundle and addressed the master of the house:

'The best thing that you can do, Caterham –'

'Yes,' said Lord Caterham apprehensively.

'Is to leave everything in my hands.'

'Certainly,' said Lord Caterham, with alacrity. 'Just what I was thinking myself. You'll find the police and Dr Cartwright in the Council Chamber. With the – er – with the body, you know. My dear Lomax, I place Chimneys unreservedly at your disposal. Do anything you like.'

'Thank you,' said George. 'If I should want to consult you –'

But Lord Caterham had faded unobtrusively through the farther door. Bundle had observed his retreat with a grim smile.

'I'll send off those telegrams at once,' she said. 'You know your way to the Council Chamber?'

'Thank you, Lady Eileen.'

George hurried from the room.

CHAPTER 11

SUPERINTENDENT BATTLE ARRIVES

So apprehensive was Lord Caterham of being consulted by George that he spent the whole morning making a tour of his estate. Only the pangs of hunger drew him homeward. He also reflected that by now the worst would surely be over.

He sneaked into the house quietly by a small side door. From there he slipped neatly into his sanctum. He flattered himself that his entrance had not been observed, but there he was mistaken. The watchful Tredwell let nothing escape him. He presented himself at the door.

'You'll excuse me, my lord –'

'What is it, Tredwell?'

'Mr Lomax, my lord, is anxious to see you in the library as soon as you return.'

By this delicate method Tredwell conveyed that Lord Caterham had not yet returned unless he chose to say so.

Lord Caterham sighed, and then rose.

'I suppose it will have to be done sooner or later. In the library, you say?'

'Yes, my lord.'

Sighing again, Lord Caterham crossed the wide spaces of his ancestral home, and reached the library door. The door was locked. As he rattled the handle, it was unlocked from inside, opened a little way, and the face of George Lomax appeared, peering out suspiciously.

His face changed when he saw who it was.

'Ah, Caterham, come in. We were just wondering what had become of you.'

Murmuring something vague about duties on the estate, repairs for tenants, Lord Caterham sidled in apologetically. There were two other men in the room. One was Colonel Melrose, the chief constable. The other was a squarely built middle-aged man with a face so singularly devoid of expression as to be quite remarkable.

'Superintendent Battle arrived half an hour ago,' explained George. 'He has been round with Inspector Badgworthy, and seen Dr Cartwright. He now wants a few facts from us.'

They all sat down, after Lord Caterham had greeted Melrose and acknowledged his introduction to Superintendent Battle.

'I need hardly tell you, Battle,' said George, 'that this is a case in which we must use the utmost discretion.'

The superintendent nodded in an offhand manner that rather took Lord Caterham's fancy.

'That will be all right, Mr Lomax. But no concealments from us. I understand that the dead gentleman was called Count Stanislaus – at least, that that is the name by which the household knew him. Now was that his real name?'

'It was not.'

'What was his real name?'

'Prince Michael of Herzoslovakia.'

Battle's eyes opened just a trifle, otherwise he gave no sign.

'And what, if I may ask the question, was the purpose of his visit here? Just pleasure?'

'There was a further object, Battle. All this in the strictest confidence, of course.'

'Yes, yes, Mr Lomax.'

'Colonel Melrose?'

'Of course.'

'Well, then, Prince Michael was here for the express purpose of meeting Mr Herman Isaacstein. A loan was to be arranged on certain terms.'

'Which were?'

'I do not know the exact details. Indeed, they had not yet been arranged. But in the event of coming to the throne, Prince Michael pledged himself to grant certain oil concessions to those companies in which Mr Isaacstein is interested. The British Government was prepared to support the claim of Prince Michael to the throne in view of his pronounced British sympathies.'

'Well,' said Superintendent Battle, 'I don't suppose I need go further into it than that. Prince Michael wanted the money, Mr Isaacstein wanted oil, and the British Government was ready to do the heavy father. Just one question. Was anyone else after those concessions?'

'I believe an American group of financiers had made overtures to His Highness.'

'And been turned down, eh?'

But George refused to be drawn.

'Prince Michael's sympathies were entirely pro-British,' he repeated.

Superintendent Battle did not press the point.

'Lord Caterham, I understand that this is what occurred yesterday. You met Prince Michael in town and journeyed down here in company with him. The Prince was accompanied by his valet, a Herzoslovakian named Boris Anchoukoff, but his equerry, Captain Andrassy, remained in town. The Prince, on arriving, declared himself greatly fatigued, and retired to the apartments set aside for him. Dinner was served to him there, and he did not meet the other members of the house party. Is that correct?'

'Quite correct.'

'This morning a housemaid discovered the body at approximately 7.45 a.m. Dr Cartwright examined the dead man and found that death was the result of a bullet fired from a revolver. No revolver was found, and no one in the house seems to have heard the shot. On the other hand the dead man's wrist-watch was smashed by the fall, and marks the crime as having been committed at exactly a quarter to twelve. Now, what time did you retire to bed last night?'

'We went early. Somehow or other the party didn't seem to "go", if you know what I mean, Superintendent. We went up about half-past ten, I should say.'

'Thank you. Now I will ask you, Lord Caterham, to give me a description of all the people staying in the house.'

'But, excuse me, I thought the fellow who did it came from outside?'

Superintendent Battle smiled.

'I dare say he did. I dare say he did. But all the same I've got to know who was in the house. Matter of routine, you know.'

'Well, there was Prince Michael and his valet and Mr Herman Isaacstein. You know all about them. Then there was Mr Eversleigh –'

'Who works in my department,' put in George condescendingly.

'And who was acquainted with the real reason of Prince Michael's being here?'

'No, I should not say that,' replied George weightily. 'Doubtless he realized that something was in the wind, but I did not think it necessary to take him fully into my confidence.'

'I see. Will you go on, Lord Caterham?'

'Let me see, there was Mr Hiram Fish.'

'Who is Mr Hiram Fish?'

'Mr Fish is an American. He brought over a letter of introduction from Mr Lucius Gott – you've heard of Lucius Gott?'

Superintendent Battle smiled acknowledgement. Who had not heard of Lucius C. Gott, the multi-millionaire?

'He was specially anxious to see my first editions. Mr Gott's collection is, of course, unequalled, but I've got several treasures myself. This Mr Fish was an enthusiast. Mr Lomax had suggested that I ask one or two extra people down here this week-end to make things seem more natural, so I took the opportunity of asking Mr Fish. That finishes the men. As for the ladies, there is only Mrs Revel – and I expect she brought a maid or something like that. Then there was my daughter, and of course the children and their nurses and governesses and all the servants.'

Lord Caterham paused and took a breath.

'Thank you,' said the detective. 'A mere matter of routine, but necessary as such.'

'There is no doubt, I suppose,' asked George ponderously, 'that the murderer entered by the window?'

Battle paused for a minute before replying slowly.

'There were footsteps leading up to the window, and footsteps leading away from it. A car stopped outside the park at 11.40 last night. At twelve o'clock a young man arrived at the Jolly Cricketers in a car, and engaged a room. He put his boots outside to be cleaned – they were very wet and muddy, as though he had been walking through the long grass in the park.'

George leant forward eagerly.

'Could not the boots be compared with the footprints?'

'They were.'

'Well?'

'They exactly correspond.'

'That settles it,' cried George. 'We have the murderer. This young man – what is his name, by the way?'

'At the inn he gave the name of Anthony Cade.'

'This Anthony Cade must be pursued at once, and arrested.'

'You won't need to pursue him,' said Superintendent Battle.

'Why?'

'Because he's still there.'

'What?'

'Curious, isn't it?'

Colonel Melrose eyed him keenly.

'What's in your mind, Battle? Out with it.'

'I just say it's curious, that's all. Here's a young man who ought to cut and run, but he doesn't cut and run. He stays here, and gives us every facility for comparing footmarks.'

'What do you think, then?'

'I don't know what to think. And that's a very disturbing state of mind.'

'Do you imagine –' began Colonel Melrose, but broke off as a discreet knock came at the door.

George rose and went to it. Tredwell, inwardly suffering from having to knock at doors in this low fashion, stood dignified upon the threshold, and addressed his master.

'Excuse me, my lord, but a gentleman wishes to see you on urgent and important business, connected, I understand, with this morning's tragedy.'

'What's his name?' asked Battle suddenly.

'His name, sir, is Mr Anthony Cade, but he said it wouldn't convey anything to anybody.'

It seemed to convey something to the four men present. They all sat up in varying degrees of astonishment.

Lord Caterham began to chuckle.

'I'm really beginning to enjoy myself. Show him in, Tredwell. Show him in at once.'

CHAPTER 12

ANTHONY TELLS HIS STORY

'Mr Anthony Cade,' announced Tredwell. 'Enter suspicious stranger from village inn,' said Anthony.

He made his way towards Lord Caterham with a kind of instinct rare in strangers. At the same time he summed up the other three men in his own mind thus: '1, Scotland Yard. 2, local dignitary – probably chief constable. 3, harassed gentleman on the verge of apoplexy – possibly connected with the Government.'

'I must apologize,' continued Anthony, still addressing Lord Caterham. 'For forcing my way in like this, I mean. But it was rumoured round the Jolly Dog, or whatever the name of your local pub may be, that you had had a murder up here, and as I thought I might be able to throw some light upon it I came along.'

For a moment or two, no one spoke. Superintendent Battle because he was a man of ripe experience who knew how infinitely better it was to let everyone else speak if they could be persuaded upon to do so, Colonel Melrose because he was habitually taciturn, George because he was in the habit of having notice given to him of the question, Lord Caterham because he had not the least idea of what to say. The silence of the other three, however, and the fact that he had been directly addressed, finally forced speech upon the last-named.

'Er – quite so – quite so,' he said nervously. 'Won't – you – er – sit down?'

'Thank you,' said Anthony.

George cleared his throat portentously.

'Er – when you say you can throw light upon this matter, you mean? –'

'I mean,' said Anthony, 'that I was trespassing upon Lord Caterham's property (for which I hope he will forgive me) last night at about 11.45, and that I actually heard the shot fired. I can at any rate fix the time of the crime for you.'

He looked round at the three in turn, his eyes resting longest on Superintendent Battle, the impassivity of whose face he seemed to appreciate.

'But I hardly think that that's news to you,' he added gently.

'Meaning by that, Mr Cade?' asked Battle.

'Just this. I put on shoes when I got up this morning. Later, when I asked for my boots, I couldn't have them. Some nice young constable had called round for them. So I naturally put two and two together, and hurried up here to clear my character if possible.'

'A very sensible move,' said Battle non-committally.

Anthony's eyes twinkled a little.

'I appreciate your reticence, Inspector. It is Inspector, isn't it?'

Lord Caterham interposed. He was beginning to take a fancy to Anthony.

'Superintendent Battle of Scotland Yard. This is Colonel Melrose, our chief constable, and Mr Lomax.'

Anthony looked sharply at George.

'Mr George Lomax?'

'Yes.'

'I think, Mr Lomax,' said Anthony, 'that I had the pleasure of receiving a letter from you yesterday.'

George stared at him.

'I think not,' he said coldly.

But he wished that Miss Oscar were here. Miss Oscar wrote all his letters for him, and remembered who they were to and what they were about. A great man like George could not possibly remember all these annoying details.

'I think, Mr Cade,' he hinted, 'that you were about to give us some – er – explanation of what you were doing in the grounds last night at 11.45?'

His tone said plainly: 'And whatever it may be, we are not likely to believe it.'

'Yes, Mr Cade, what *were* you doing?' said Lord Caterham with lively interest.

'Well,' said Anthony regretfully, 'I'm afraid it's rather a long story.'

He drew out his cigarette-case.

'May I?'

Lord Caterham nodded, and Anthony lit a cigarette, and braced himself for the ordeal.

He was aware, none better, of the peril in which he stood. In the short space of twenty-four hours, he had become embroiled in two separate crimes. His actions in connexion with the first would not bear looking into for a second. After deliberately disposing of one body and so defeating the aims of justice, he had arrived upon the scene of the second crime at the exact moment when it was being committed. For a young man looking for trouble, he could hardly have done better.

'South America,' thought Anthony to himself, 'simply isn't in it with this!'

He had already decided upon his course of action. He was going to tell the truth – with one trifling alteration, and one grave suppression.

'The story begins,' said Anthony, 'about three weeks ago – in Bulawayo. Mr Lomax, of course, knows where that is – outpost of the Empire – "What do we know of England who only England know?" all that sort of thing. I was conversing with a friend of mine, a Mr James McGrath –'

He brought out the name slowly, with a thoughtful eye on George. George bounded in his seat and repressed an exclamation with difficulty.

'The upshot of our conversation was that I came to England to carry out a little commission for Mr McGrath, who was unable to go himself. Since the passage was booked in his name, I travelled as James McGrath. I don't know what particular kind of offence that was – the superindendent can tell me, I dare say, and run me in for so many months' hard if necessary.'

'We'll get on with the story, if you please, sir,' said Battle, but his eyes twinkled a little.

'On arrival in London I went to the Blitz Hotel, still as James McGrath. My business in London was to deliver a certain manuscript to a firm of publishers, but almost immediately I received deputations from the representatives of two political parties of a foreign kingdom. The methods of one were strictly constitutional, the methods of the other were not. I dealt with them both accordingly. But my troubles were not over. That night my room was broken into, and an attempt at burglary was made by one of the waiters at the hotel.'

'That was not reported to the police, I think?' said Superintendent Battle.

'You are right. It was not. Nothing was taken, you see. But I did report the occurrence to the manager of the hotel, and he will confirm my story, and tell you that the waiter in question decamped rather abruptly in the middle of the night. The next day, the publishers rang me up, and suggested that one of their representatives would call upon me and receive the manuscript. I agreed to this, and the arrangement was duly carried out on the following morning. Since I have heard nothing further, I presume the manuscript reached them safely. Yesterday, still as James McGrath, I received a letter from Mr Lomax –'

Anthony paused. He was by now beginning to enjoy himself. George shifted uneasily.

'I remember,' he murmured. 'Such a large correspondence. The name, of course, being different, I could not be expected to know. And I may say,' George's voice rose a little, firm in assurance of moral stability, 'that I consider this – this – masquerading as another man in the highest degree improper. I have no doubt, no doubt whatever that you have incurred a severe legal penalty.'

'In this letter,' continued Anthony, unmoved, 'Mr Lomax made various suggestions concerning the manuscript in my charge. He also extended an invitation to me from Lord Caterham to join the house party here.'

'Delighted to see you, my dear fellow,' said the nobleman. 'Better late than never – eh?'

George frowned at him.

Superintendent Battle bent an unmoved eye upon Anthony.

'And is that your explanation of your presence here last night, sir?' he asked.

'Certainly not,' said Anthony warmly. 'When I am asked to stay at a country house, I don't scale the wall late at night, tramp across the park, and try the downstairs windows. I drive up to the front door, ring the bell and wipe my feet on the mat. I will proceed. I replied to Mr Lomax's letter, explaining that the manuscript had passed out of my keeping, and therefore regretfully declining Lord Caterham's kind invitation. But after I had done so, I remembered something which had up till then escaped my memory.' He paused. The moment had come for skating over thin ice. 'I must tell you that in my struggle with the waiter Giuseppe, I had wrested from him a small bit of paper with some words scribbled on it. They had conveyed nothing to me at the time, but I still had them, and the mention of Chimneys recalled them to me. I got the torn scrap out and looked at it. It was as I had thought. Here is the piece of paper, gentlemen, you can see for yourselves. The words on it are "*Chimneys 11.45 Thursday*".'

Battle examined the paper attentively.

'Of course,' continued Anthony, 'the word Chimneys might have nothing whatever to do with this house. On the other hand, it might. And undoubtedly this Giuseppe was a thieving rascal. I made up my mind to motor down here last night, satisfy myself that all was as it should be, put up at the inn, and call upon Lord Caterham in the morning and put him on his guard in case some mischief should be intended during the weekend.'

'Quite so,' said Lord Caterham encouragingly. 'Quite so.'

'I was late getting here – had not allowed enough time. Consequently I stopped the car, climbed over the wall and ran across the park. When I arrived on the terrace, the whole house was dark and silent. I was just turning away when I heard a shot. I fancied that it came from inside the house, and I ran back, crossed the terrace, and tried the windows. But they were fastened, and there was no sound of any kind from inside the house. I waited a while, but the whole place was as still as the grave, so I made up my mind that I had made a mistake, and that what I had heard was a stray poacher – quite a natural conclusion to come to under the circumstances, I think.'

'Quite natural,' said Superintendent Battle expressionlessly.

'I went on to the inn, put up as I said – and heard the news this morning. I realized, of course, that I was a suspicious character – bound to be under the circumstances, and came up here to tell my story, hoping it wasn't going to be handcuffs for one.'

There was a pause. Colonel Melrose looked sideways at Superintendent Battle.

'I think the story seems clear enough,' he remarked.

'Yes,' said Battle. 'I don't think we'll be handing out any handcuffs this morning.'

'Any questions, Battle?'

'There's one thing I'd like to know. What was this manuscript?'

He looked across at George, and the latter replied with a trace of unwillingness:

'The memoirs of the late Count Stylptitch. You see –'

'You needn't say anything more,' said Battle. 'I see perfectly.'

He turned to Anthony.

'Do you know who it was that was shot, Mr Cade?'

'At the Jolly Dog it was understood to be a Count Stanislaus or some such name.'

'Tell him,' said Battle laconically to George Lomax.

George was clearly reluctant, but he was forced to speak:

'The gentleman who was staying here incognito as Count Stanislaus was His Highness Prince Michael of Herzoslovakia.'

Anthony whistled.

'That must be deuced awkward,' he remarked.

Superintendent Battle, who had been watching Anthony closely, gave a short grunt as though satisfied of something, and rose abruptly to his feet.

'There are one or two questions I'd like to ask Mr Cade,' he announced. 'I'll take him into the Council Chamber with me if I may.'

'Certainly, certainly,' said Lord Caterham. 'Take him anywhere you like.'

Anthony and the detective went out together.

The body had been moved from the scene of the tragedy. There was a dark stain on the floor where it had lain, but otherwise there was nothing to suggest that a tragedy had ever occurred. The sun poured in through the three windows, flooding the room with light, and bringing out the mellow tone of the old panelling. Anthony looked around him with approval.

'Very nice,' he commented. 'Nothing much to beat old England, is there?'

'Did it seem to you at first that it was in this room the shot was fired?' asked the superintendent, not replying to Anthony's eulogium.

'Let me see.'

Anthony opened the window and went out on the terrace, looking up at the house.

'Yes, that's the room all right,' he said. 'It's built out, and occupies all the corner. If the shot had been fired anywhere else, it would have sounded from the *left*, but this was from behind me or to the right if anything. That's why I thought of poachers. It's at the extremity of the wing, you see.'

He stepped back across the threshold, and asked suddenly, as though the idea had just struck him:

'But why do you ask? You know he was shot here, don't you?'

'Ah!' said the superintendent. 'We never know as much as we'd like to know. But, yes, he was shot here all right. Now you said something about trying the windows, didn't you?'

'Yes. They were fastened from the inside.'

'How many of them did you try?'

'All three of them.'

'Sure of that, sir?'

'I'm in the habit of being sure. Why do you ask?'

'That's a funny thing,' said the superintendent.

'What's a funny thing?'

'When the crime was discovered this morning, the middle one was open – not latched, that is to say.'

'Whew!' said Anthony, sinking down on the window-seat, and taking out his cigarette-case. 'That's rather a blow. That opens up quite a different aspect of the case. It leaves us two alternatives. Either he was killed by someone in the house, and that someone unlatched the window after I had gone to make it look like an outside job – incidentally with me as Little Willie – or else, not to mince matters, I'm lying. I dare say you incline to the second possibility, but, upon my honour, you're wrong.'

'Nobody's going to leave this house until I'm through with them, I can tell you that,' said Superintendent Battle grimly.

Anthony looked at him keenly.

'How long have you had the idea that it might be an inside job?' he asked.

Battle smiled.

'I've had a notion that way all along. Your trail was a bit too – flaring, if I may put it that way. As soon as your boots fitted the footmarks, I began to have my doubts.'

'I congratulate Scotland Yard,' said Anthony lightly.

But at that moment, the moment when Battle apparently admitted Anthony's complete absence of complicity in the crime, Anthony felt more than ever the need of being upon his guard. Superintendent Battle was a very astute officer. It would not do to make any slip with Superintendent Battle about.

'That's where it happened, I suppose?' said Anthony, nodding towards the dark patch upon the floor.

'Yes.'

'What was he shot with – a revolver?'

'Yes, but we shan't know what make until they get the bullet out at the autopsy.'

'It wasn't found then?'

'No, it wasn't found.'

'No clues of any kind?'

'Well, we've got this.'

Rather after the manner of a conjurer, Superintendent Battle produced a half-sheet of notepaper. And, as he did so, he again watched Anthony closely without seeming to do so.

But Anthony recognized the design upon it without any sign of consternation.

'Aha! Comrades of the Red Hand again. If they're going to scatter this sort of thing about, they ought to have it lithographed. It must be a frightful nuisance doing every one separately. Where was this found?'

'Underneath the body. You've seen it before, sir?'

Anthony recounted to him in detail his short encounter with that public-spirited association.

'The idea is, I suppose, that the Comrades did him in.'

'Do you think it likely, sir?'

'Well, it would be in keeping with their propaganda. But I've always found that those who talk most about blood have never actually seen it run. I shouldn't have said the Comrades had the guts myself. And they're such picturesque people too. I don't see one of them disguising himself as a suitable guest for a country house. Still, one never knows.'

'Quite right, Mr Cade. One never knows.'

Anthony looked suddenly amused.

'I see the big idea now. Open window, trail of footprints, suspicious stranger at the village inn. But I can assure you, my dear Superintendent, that whatever I am, I am not the local agent of the Red Hand.'

Superintendent Battle smiled a little. Then he played his last card.

'Would you have any objection to seeing the body?' he shot out suddenly.

'None whatever,' rejoined Anthony.

Battle took a key from his pocket, and preceding Anthony down the corridor, paused at a door and unlocked it. It was one of the smaller drawing-rooms. The body lay on a table covered with a sheet.

Superintendent Battle waited until Anthony was beside him, and then whisked away the sheet suddenly.

An eager light sprang into his eyes at the half-uttered exclamation and the start of surprise which the other gave.

'So you *do* recognize him, Mr Cade?' he said, in a voice that he strove to render devoid of triumph.

'I've seen him before, yes,' said Anthony, recovering himself. 'But not as Prince Michael Obolovitch. He purported to come from Messrs Balderson and Hodgkins, and he called himself Mr Holmes.'

CHAPTER 13

THE AMERICAN VISITOR

Superintendent Battle replaced the sheet with the slightly crestfallen air of a man whose best point has fallen flat. Anthony stood with his hands in his pockets lost in thought.

'So that's what old Lollipop meant when he talked about "other means",' he murmured at last.

'I beg your pardon, Mr Cade?'

'Nothing, Superintendent. Forgive my abstraction. You see I – or rather my friend, Jimmy McGrath, has been very neatly done out of a thousand pounds.'

'A thousand pounds is a nice sum of money,' said Battle.

'It isn't the thousand pounds so much,' said Anthony, 'though I agree with you that it's a nice sum of money. It's being done that maddens me. I handed over that manuscript like a little woolly lamb. It hurts, Superintendent, indeed it hurts.'

The detective said nothing.

'Well, well,' said Anthony. 'Regrets are vain, and all may not yet be lost. I've only got to get hold of dear old Stylptitch's reminiscences between now and next Wednesday and all will be gas and gaiters.'

'Would you mind coming back to the Council Chamber, Mr Cade? There's one little thing I want to point out to you.'

Back in the Council Chamber, the detective strode over at once to the middle window.

'I've been thinking, Mr Cade. This particular window is very stiff; very stiff indeed. You might have been mistaken in thinking that it was fastened. It might just have stuck. I'm sure – yes, I'm almost sure, that you *were* mistaken.'

Anthony eyed him keenly.

'And supposing I say that I'm quite sure I was not?'

'Don't you think you could have been?' said Battle, looking at him very steadily.

'Well, to oblige you, Superintendent, yes.'

Battle smiled in a satisfied fashion.

'You're quick in the uptake, sir. And you'll have no objection to saying so, careless like, at a suitable moment?'

'None whatever. I –'

He paused, as Battle gripped his arm. The superintendent was bent forward, listening.

Enjoining silence on Anthony with a gesture, he tiptoed noiselessly to the door, and flung it suddenly open.

On the threshold stood a tall man with black hair neatly parted in the middle, china-blue eyes with a particularly innocent expression, and a large, placid face.

'Your pardon, gentlemen,' he said in a slow drawling voice with a pronounced transatlantic accent. 'But is it permitted to inspect the scene of the crime? I take it that you are both gentlemen from Scotland Yard?'

'I have not that honour,' said Anthony. 'But this gentleman is Superintendent Battle of Scotland Yard.'

'Is that so?' said the American gentleman, with a great appearance of interest. 'Pleased to meet you, sir. My name is Hiram P. Fish, of New York City.'

'What was it you wanted to see, Mr Fish?' asked the detective.

The American walked gently into the room, and looked with much interest at the dark patch on the floor.

'I am interested in crime, Mr Battle. It is one of my hobbies. I have contributed a monograph to one of our weekly periodicals on the subject "Degeneracy and the Criminal".'

As he spoke, his eyes went gently round the room, seeming to note everything in it. They rested just a shade longer on the window.

'The body,' said Superintendant Battle, stating a self-evident fact, 'has been removed.'

'Surely,' said Mr Fish. His eyes went on to the panelled walls. 'Some remarkable pictures in this room, gentlemen. A Holbein, two Van Dycks, and, if I am not mistaken, a Velazquez. I am interested in pictures – and likewise in first editions. It was to see his first editions that Lord Caterham was so kind as to invite me down here.'

He sighed gently.

'I guess that's all off now. It would show a proper feeling, I suppose, for the guests to return to town immediately?'

'I'm afraid that can't be done, sir,' said Superintendent Battle. 'Nobody must leave the house until after the inquest.'

'Is that so? And when is the inquest?'

'May be tomorrow, may not be until Monday. We've got to arrange for the autopsy and see the coroner.'

'I get you,' said Mr Fish. 'Under the circumstances, though it will be a melancholy party.'

Battle led the way to the door.

'We'd best get out of here,' he said. 'We're keeping it locked still.'

He waited for the other two to pass through, and then turned the key and removed it.

'I opine,' said Mr Fish, 'that you are seeking for finger-prints?'

'Maybe,' said the superintendent laconically.

'I should say too, that, on a night such as last night, an intruder would have left footprints on the hardwood floor.'

'None inside, plenty outside.'

'Mine,' explained Anthony cheerfully.

The innocent eyes of Mr Fish swept over him.

'Young man,' he said, 'you surprise me.'

They turned a corner, and came out into the big wide hall, panelled like the Council Chamber in old oak, and with a wide gallery above it. Two other figures came into sight at the far end.

'Aha!' said Mr Fish. 'Our genial host.'

This was such a ludicrous description of Lord Caterham that Anthony had to turn his head away to conceal a smile.

'And with him,' continued the American, 'is a lady whose name I did not catch last night. But she is bright – she is very bright.'

With Lord Caterham was Virginia Revel.

Anthony had been anticipating this meeting all along. He had no idea how to act. He must leave it to Virginia. Although he had full confidence in her presence of mind, he had not the slightest idea what line she would take. He was not long left in doubt.

'Why, it's Mr Cade,' said Virginia. She held out both hands to him. 'So you found you could come down after all?'

'My dear Mrs Revel, I had no idea Mr Cade was a friend of yours,' said Lord Caterham.

'He's a very old friend,' said Virginia, smiling at Anthony, with a mischievous glint in her eye. 'I ran across him in London unexpectedly yesterday, and told him I was coming down here.'

Anthony was quick to give her her pointer.

'I explained to Mrs Revel,' he said, 'that I had been forced to refuse your kind invitation – since it had really been extended to quite a different man. And I couldn't very well foist a perfect stranger on you under false pretences.'

'Well, well, my dear fellow,' said Lord Caterham, 'that's all over and done with now. I'll send down to the Cricketers for your bag.'

'It's very kind of you, Lord Caterham, but –'

'Nonsense, of course you must come to Chimneys. Horrible place, the Cricketers – to stay in, I mean.'

'Of course, you must come, Mr Cade,' said Virginia softly.

Anthony realized the altered tone of his surroundings. Already Virginia had done much for him. He was no longer an ambiguous stranger. Her position was so assured and unassailable that anyone for whom she vouched was accepted as a matter of course. He thought of the pistol in the tree at Burnham Beeches, and smiled inwardly.

'I'll send for your traps,' said Lord Caterham to Anthony. 'I suppose, in the circumstances, we can't have any shooting. A pity. But there it is. And I don't know what the devil to do with Isaacstein. It's all very unfortunate.'

The depressed peer sighed heavily.

'That's settled, then,' said Virginia. 'You can begin to be useful right away, Mr Cade, and take me out on the lake. It's very peaceful there and far from crime and all that sort of thing. Isn't it awful for poor Lord Caterham having a murder done in his house? But it's George's fault really. This is George's party, you know.'

'Ah!' said Lord Caterham. 'But I should never have listened to him!'

He assumed the air of a strong man betrayed by a single weakness.

'One can't help listening to George,' said Virginia. 'He always holds you so that you can't get away. I'm thinking of patenting a detachable lapel.'

'I wish you would,' chuckled her host. 'I'm glad you're coming to us, Cade. I need support.'

'I appreciate your kindness very much, Lord Caterham,' said Anthony. 'Especially,' he added, 'when I'm such a suspicious character. But my staying here makes it easier for Battle.'

'In what way, sir?' asked the superintendent.

'It won't be so difficult to keep an eye on me,' explained Anthony gently.

And by the momentary flicker of the superintendent's eyelids he knew that his shot had gone home.

CHAPTER 14

MAINLY POLITICAL AND FINANCIAL

Except for that involuntary twitch of the eyelids, Superintendent Battle's impassivity was unimpaired. If he had been surprised at Virginia's recognition of Anthony, he did not show it. He and Lord Caterham stood together and watched those two go out through the garden door. Mr Fish also watched them.

'Nice young fellow, that,' said Lord Caterham.

'Vurry nice for Mrs Revel to meet an old friend,' murmured the American. 'They have been acquainted some time, presoomably?'

'Seems so,' said Lord Caterham. 'But I've never heard her mention him before. Oh, by the way, Battle, Mr Lomax has been asking for you. He's in the blue morning-room.'

'Very good, Lord Caterham. I'll go there at once.'

Battle found his way to the blue morning-room without difficulty. He was already familiar with the geography of the house.

'Ah, there you are, Battle,' said Lomax.

He was striding impatiently up and down the carpet. There was one other person in the room, a big man sitting in a chair by the fire-place. He was dressed in very correct English shooting clothes which nevertheless sat strangely upon him. He had a fat yellow face, and black eyes, as impenetrable as those of a cobra. There was a generous curve to the big nose and power in the square lines of the vast jaw.

'Come in, Battle,' said Lomax irritably. 'And shut the door behind you. This is Mr Herman Isaacstein.'

Battle inclined his head respectfully.

He knew all about Mr Herman Isaacstein, and though the great financier sat there silent, whilst Lomax strode up and down and talked, he knew who was the real power in the room.

'We can speak more freely now,' said Lomax. 'Before Lord Caterham and Colonel Melrose, I was anxious not to say too much. You understand, Battle? These things mustn't get about.'

'Ah!' said Battle. 'But they always do, more's the pity.'

Just for a second he saw a trace of a smile on the fat yellow face. It disappeared as suddenly as it had come.

'Now, what do you really think of this young fellow – this Anthony Cade?' continued George. 'Do you still assume him to be innocent?'

Battle shrugged his shoulders very slightly.

'He tells a straight story. Part of it we shall be able to verify. On the face of it, it accounts for his presence here last night. I shall cable to South Africa, of course, for information about his antecedents.'

'Then you regard him as cleared of all complicity?'

Battle raised a large square hand.

'Not so fast, sir. I never said that.'

'What is your idea about the crime, Superintendent Battle?' asked Isaacstein, speaking for the first time.

His voice was deep and rich, and had a certain compelling quality about it. It had stood him in good stead at board meetings in his younger days.

'It's rather too soon to have ideas, Mr Isaacstein. I've not got beyond asking myself the first question.'

'What is that?'

'Oh, it's always the same. Motive. Who benefits by the death of Prince Michael? We've got to answer that before we can get anywhere.'

'The Revolutionary Party of Herzoslovakia –' began George.

Superintendent Battle waved him aside with something less than his usual respect.

'It wasn't the Comrades of the Red Hand, sir, if you're thinking of them.'

'But the paper – with the scarlet hand on it?'

'Put there to suggest the obvious solution.'

George's dignity was a little ruffled.

'Really, Battle, I don't see how you can be so sure of that.'

'Bless you, Mr Lomax, we know all about the Comrades of the Red Hand. We've had our eye on them ever since Prince Michael landed in England. That sort of thing is the elementary work of the department. They'd never be allowed to get within a mile of him.'

'I agree with Superintendent Battle,' said Isaacstein. 'We must look elsewhere.'

'You see, sir,' said Battle, encouraged by this support, 'we do know a little about the case. If we don't know who gains by his death, we do know who loses by it.'

'Meaning?' said Isaacstein.

His black eyes were bent upon the detective. More than ever, he reminded Battle of a hooded cobra.

'You and Mr Lomax, not to mention the Loyalist Party of Herzoslovakia. If you'll pardon the expression, sir, you're in the soup.'

'Really, Battle,' interposed George, shocked to the core.

'Go on, Battle,' said Isaacstein. 'In the soup describes the situation very accurately. You're an intelligent man.'

'You've got to have a King. You've lost your King – like that!' He snapped his large fingers. 'You've got to find another in a hurry, and that's not an easy job. No, I don't want to know the details of your scheme, the bare outline is enough for me, but, I take it, it's a big deal?'

Isaacstein bent his head slowly.

'It's a very big deal.'

'That brings me to my second question. Who is the next heir to the throne of Herzoslovakia?'

Isaacstein looked across at Lomax. The latter answered the question, with a certain reluctance, and a good deal of hesitation:

'That would be – I should say – yes, in all probability Prince Nicholas would be the next heir.'

'Ah!' said Battle. 'And who is Prince Nicholas?'

'A first cousin of Prince Michael's.'

'Ah!' said Battle. 'I should like to hear all about Prince Nicholas, especially where he is at present.'

'Nothing much is known of him,' said Lomax. 'As a young man, he was most peculiar in his ideas, consorted with Socialists and Republicans, and acted in a way highly unbecoming to his position. He was sent down from Oxford, I believe, for some wild escapade. There was a rumour of his death two years later in the Congo, but it was only a rumour. He turned up a few months ago when news of the royalist reaction got about.'

'Indeed?' said Battle. 'Where did he turn up?'

'In America.'

'America!'

Battle turned to Isaacstein with one laconic word:

'Oil?'

The financier nodded.

'He represented that if the Herzoslovakians chose a King, they would prefer him to Prince Michael as being more in sympathy with modern enlightened ideas, and he drew attention to his early democratic views and his sympathy with Republican ideals. In return for financial support, he was prepared to grant concessions to a certain group of American financiers.'

Superintendent Battle so far forgot his habitual impassivity as to give vent to a prolonged whistle.

'So that is it,' he muttered. 'In the meantime, the Loyalist Party supported Prince Michael, and you felt sure you'd come out on top. And then this happens!'

'You surely don't think –' began George.

'It was a big deal,' said Battle. 'Mr Isaacstein says so. And I should say that what he calls a big deal *is* a big deal.'

'There are always unscrupulous tools to be got hold of,' said Isaacstein quietly. 'For the moment, Wall Street wins. But they've not done with me yet. Find out who killed Prince Michael, Superintendent Battle, if you want to do your country a service.'

'One thing strikes me as highly suspicious,' put in George. 'Why did the equerry, Captain Andrassy, not come down with the Prince yesterday?'

'I've inquired into that,' said Battle. 'It's perfectly simple. He stayed in town to make arrangements with a certain lady, on behalf of Prince Michael, for next week-end. The Baron rather frowned on such things, thinking them injudicious at the present stage of affairs, so His Highness had to go about them in a hole-and-corner manner. He was, if I may say so, inclined to be a rather – er – dissipated young man.'

'I'm afraid so,' said George ponderously. 'Yes, I'm afraid so.'

'There's one other point we ought to take into account, I think,' said Battle, speaking with a certain amount of hesitation. 'King Victor's supposed to be in England.'

'King Victor?'

Lomax frowned in an effort at recollection.

'Notorious French crook, sir. We've had a warning from the Sûreté in Paris.'

'Of course,' said George. 'I remember now. Jewel thief, isn't he? Why, that's the man –'

He broke off abruptly. Isaacstein, who had been frowning abstractedly at the fire-place, looked up just too late to catch the warning glance telegraphed from Superintendent Battle to the other. But being a man sensitive to vibrations in the atmosphere, he was conscious of a sense of strain.

'You don't want me any longer, do you, Lomax?' he inquired.

'No, thank you, my dear fellow.'

'Would it upset your plans if I returned to London, Superintendent Battle?'

'I'm afraid so, sir,' said the superintendent civilly. 'You see, if you go, there will be others who'll want to go also. And that would never do.'

'Quite so.'

The great financier left the room, closing the door behind him.

'Splendid fellow, Isaacstein,' murmured George Lomax perfunctorily.

'Very powerful personality,' agreed Superintendent Battle.

George began to pace up and down again.

'What you say disturbs me greatly,' he began. 'King Victor! I thought he was in prison?'

'Came out a few months ago. French police meant to keep on his heels, but he managed to give them the slip straight away. He would too. One of the coolest customers that ever lived. For some reason or other, they believe he's in England, and have notified us to that effect.'

'But what should he be doing in England?'

'That's for you to say, sir,' said Battle significantly.

'You mean? – You think? – You know the story, of course – ah, yes, I can see you do. I was not in office, of course, at the time, but I heard the whole story from the late Lord Caterham. An unparalleled catastrophe.'

'The Koh-i-noor,' said Battle reflectively.

'Hush, Battle!' George glanced suspiciously round him. 'I beg of you, mention no names. Much better not. If you must speak of it, call it the K.'

The superintendent looked wooden again.

'You don't connect King Victor with this crime, do you, Battle?'

'It's just a possibility, that's all. If you cast your mind back, sir, you'll remember that there were four places where a – er – certain royal visitor might have concealed the jewel. Chimneys was one of them. King Victor was arrested in Paris three days after the – disappearance, if I may call it that, of the K. It was always hoped that he would some day lead us to the jewel.'

'But Chimneys has been ransacked and overhauled a dozen times.'

'Yes,' said Battle sapiently. 'But it's never much good looking when you don't know where to look. Only suppose now, that this King Victor came here to look for the thing, was surprised by Prince Michael, and shot him.'

'It's possible,' said George. 'A most likely solution of the crime.'

'I wouldn't go as far as that. It's possible, but not much more.'

'Why is that?'

'Because King Victor has never been known to take a life,' said Battle seriously.

'Oh, but a man like that – a dangerous criminal –'

But Battle shook his head in a dissatisfied manner.

'Criminals always act true to type, Mr Lomax. It's surprising. All the same –'

'Yes?'

'I'd rather like to question the Prince's servant. I've left him purposely to the last. We'll have him in here, sir, if you don't mind.'

George signified his assent. The superintendent rang the bell. Tredwell answered it, and departed with his instructions.

He returned shortly accompanied by a tall fair man with high cheekbones, and very deep-set blue eyes, and an impassivity of countenance which almost rivalled Battle's.

'Boris Anchoukoff?'

'Yes.'

'You were valet to Prince Michael?'

'I was His Highness's valet, yes.'

The man spoke good English, though with a markedly harsh foreign accent.

'You know that your master was murdered last night?'

A deep snarl, like the snarl of a wild beast, was the man's only answer. It alarmed George, who withdrew prudently towards the window.

'When did you see your master last?'

'His Highness retired to bed at half-past ten. I slept, as always, in the anteroom next to him. He must have gone down to the room downstairs by the other door, the door that gave on the corridor. I did not hear him go. It may be that I was drugged. I have been an unfaithful servant, I slept while my master woke. I am accursed.'

George gazed at him, fascinated.

'You loved your master, eh?' said Battle, watching the man closely.

Boris's features contracted painfully. He swallowed twice. Then his voice came, harsh with emotion.

'I say this to you, English policeman, I would have died for him!

And since he is dead, and I still live, my eyes shall not know sleep, or my heart rest, until I have avenged him. Like a dog will I nose out his murderer and when I have discovered him – Ah!' His eyes lit up. Suddenly he drew an immense knife from beneath his coat and brandished it aloft. 'Not all at once will I kill him – oh no! – first I will slit his nose, and cut off his ears and put out his eyes, and then – then, into his black heart, I will thrust this knife.'

Swiftly he replaced the knife, and turning, left the room. George Lomax, his eyes always protuberant, but now goggling almost out of his head, stared at the closed door.

'Pure-bred Herzoslovakian, of course,' he muttered. 'Most uncivilized people. A race of brigands.'

Superindentent Battle rose alertly to his feet.

'Either that man's sincere,' he remarked, 'or he's the best bluffer I've ever seen. And if it's the former, God help Prince Michael's murderer when that human bloodhound gets hold of him.'

CHAPTER 15

THE FRENCH STRANGER

Virginia and Anthony walked side by side down the path which led to the lake. For some minutes after leaving the house they were silent. It was Virginia who broke the silence at last with a little laugh.

'Oh, dear,' she said, 'isn't it dreadful? Here I am so bursting with the things I want to tell you, and the things I want to know, that I simply don't know where to begin. First of all' – she lowered her voice – '*What have you done with the body?* How awful it sounds, doesn't it! I never dreamt that I should be so steeped in crime.'

'I suppose it's quite a novel sensation for you,' agreed Anthony.

'But not for you?'

'Well, I've never disposed of a corpse before, certainly.'

'Tell me about it.'

Briefly and succinctly, Anthony ran over the steps he had taken on the previous night. Virginia listened attentively.

'I think you were very clever,' she said approvingly when he had finished. 'I can pick up the trunk again when I go back to

Paddington. The only difficulty that might arise is if you had to give an account of where you were yesterday evening.'

'I can't see that can arise. The body can't have been found until late last night – or possibly this morning. Otherwise there would have been something about it in this morning's papers. And whatever you may imagine from reading detective stories, doctors aren't such magicians that they can tell you exactly how many hours a man has been dead. The exact time of his death will be pretty vague. An alibi for last night would be far more to the point.'

'I know. Lord Caterham was telling me all about it. But the Scotland Yard man is quite convinced of your innocence now, isn't he?'

Anthony did not reply at once.

'He doesn't look particularly astute,' continued Virginia.

'I don't know about that,' said Anthony slowly. 'I've an impression that there are no flies on Superintendent Battle. He appears to be convinced of my innocence – but I'm not sure. He's stumped at present by my apparent lack of motive.'

'Apparent?' cried Virginia. 'But what possible reason could you have for murdering an unknown foreign count?'

Anthony darted a sharp glance at her.

'You were at one time or other in Herzoslovakia, weren't you?' he asked.

'Yes. I was there with my husband, for two years, at the Embassy.'

'That was just before the assassination of the King and Queen. Did you ever run across Prince Michael Obolovitch?'

'Michael? Of course I did. Horrid little wretch! He suggested, I remember, that I should marry him morganatically.'

'Did he really? And what did he suggest you should do about your existing husband?'

'Oh, he had a sort of David and Uriah scheme all made out.'

'And how did you respond to this amiable offer?'

'Well,' said Virginia, 'unfortunately one had to be diplomatic. So poor little Michael didn't get it as straight from the shoulder as he might have done. But he retired hurt all the same. Why all this interest about Michael?'

'Something I'm getting at in my own blundering fashion. I take it that you didn't meet the murdered man?'

'No. To put it like a book he "retired to his own apartments immediately on arrival".'

'And of course you haven't seen the body?'

Virginia, eyeing him with a good deal of interest, shook her head.

'Could you get to see it, do you think?'

'By means of influence in high places – meaning Lord Caterham – I dare say I could. Why? Is it an order?'

'Good Lord, no,' said Anthony, horrified. 'Have I been as dictatorial as all that? No, it's simply this. Count Stanislaus was the incognito of Prince Michael of Herzoslovakia.'

Virginia's eyes opened very wide.

'I see.' Suddenly her face broke into its fascinating one-sided smile. 'I hope you don't suggest that Michael went to his rooms simply to avoid seeing me?'

'Something of the kind,' admitted Anthony. 'You see, if I'm right in my mind that someone wanted to prevent your coming to Chimneys, the reason seems to lie in your knowing Herzoslovakia. Do you realize that you're the only person here who knew Prince Michael by sight?'

'Do you mean that this man who was murdered was an imposter?' asked Virginia abruptly.

'That is the possibility that crossed my mind. If you can get Lord Caterham to show you the body, we can clear up that point at once.'

'He was shot at 11.45,' said Virginia thoughtfully. 'The time mentioned on that scrap of paper. The whole thing's horribly mysterious.'

'That reminds me. Is that your window up there? The second from the end over the Council Chamber?'

'No, my room is in the Elizabethan wing, the other side. Why?'

'Simply because as I walked away last night, after thinking I heard a shot, the light went up in that room.'

'How curious! I don't know who has that room, but I can find out by asking Bundle. Perhaps they heard the shot?'

'If so, they haven't come forward to say so. I understood from

Battle that nobody in the house heard the shot fired. It's the only clue of any kind that I've got, and I dare say it's a pretty rotten one, but I mean to follow it up for what it's worth.'

'It's curious, certainly,' said Virginia thoughtfully.

They had arrived at the boathouse by the lake, and had been leaning against it as they talked.

'And now for the whole story,' said Anthony. 'We'll paddle gently about on the lake, secure from the prying ears of Scotland Yard, American visitors, and curious housemaids.'

'I've heard something from Lord Caterham,' said Virginia. 'But not nearly enough. To begin with, which are you really, Anthony Cade or Jimmy McGrath?'

For the second time that morning, Anthony unfolded the history of the last six weeks of his life – with this difference that the account given to Virginia needed no editing. He finished up with his own astonished recognition of 'Mr Holmes'.

'By the way, Mrs Revel,' he ended, 'I've never thanked you for imperilling your mortal soul by saying that I was an old friend of yours.'

'Of course you're an old friend,' cried Virginia. 'You don't suppose I'd lumber you with a corpse, and then pretend you were a mere acquaintance next time I met you? No, indeed!'

She paused.

'Do you know one thing that strikes me about all this?' she went on. 'That there's some extra mystery about those memoirs that we haven't fathomed yet.'

'I think you're right,' agreed Anthony. 'There's one thing I'd like you to tell me,' he continued.

'What's that?'

'Why did you seem so surprised when I mentioned the name of Jimmy McGrath to you yesterday at Pont Street? Had you heard it before?'

'I had, Sherlock Holmes. George – my cousin, George Lomax, you know – came to see me the other day, and suggested a lot of frightfully silly things. His idea was that I should come down here and make myself agreeable to this man, McGrath, and Delilah the memoirs out of him somehow. He didn't put it like that, of course. He talked a lot of nonsense about English gentlewomen, and things like that, but his real meaning was never obscure for a moment. It was just the sort of rotten thing poor old George would think of. And then I wanted to know too much, and he tried to put me off with lies that wouldn't have deceived a child of two.'

'Well, his plan seems to have succeeded, anyhow,' observed Anthony. 'Here am I, the James McGrath he had in mind, and here are you being agreeable to me.'

'But alas, for poor old George, no memoirs! Now I've got a question for you. When I said I hadn't written those letters, you said you knew I hadn't – you couldn't know any such thing?'

'Oh, yes, I could,' said Anthony, smiling. 'I've got a good working knowledge of psychology.'

'You mean your belief in the sterling worth of my moral character was such that –'

But Anthony was shaking his head vigorously.

'Not at all. I don't know anything about your moral character. You might have a lover, and you might write to him. But you'd never lie down to be blackmailed. The Virginia Revel of those letters was scared stiff. You'd have fought.'

'I wonder who the real Virginia Revel is – where she is, I mean. It makes me feel as though I had a double somewhere.'

Anthony lit a cigarette.

'You know that one of the letters was written from Chimneys?' he asked at last.

'What?' Virginia was clearly startled. 'When was it written?'

'It wasn't dated. But it's odd, isn't it?'

'I'm perfectly certain no other Virginia Revel has ever stayed at Chimneys. Bundle or Lord Caterham would have said something about the coincidence of the name if she had.'

'Yes. It's rather queer. Do you know, Mrs Revel, I am beginning to disbelieve profoundly in this other Virginia Revel.'

'She's very elusive,' agreed Virginia.

'Extraordinarily elusive. I am beginning to think that the person who wrote those letters deliberately used your name.'

'But why?' cried Virginia. 'Why should they do such a thing?'

'Ah, that's just the question. There's the devil of a lot to find out about everything.'

'Who do you really think killed Michael?' asked Virginia suddenly. 'The Comrades of the Red Hand?'

'I suppose they might have done so,' said Anthony in a dissatisfied voice. 'Pointless killing would be rather characteristic of them.'

'Let's get to work,' said Virginia. 'I see Lord Caterham and Bundle strolling together. The first thing to do is to find out definitely whether the dead man is Michael or not.'

Anthony paddled to shore and a few moments later they had joined Lord Caterham and his daughter.

'Lunch is late,' said his lordship in a depressed voice.

'Battle has insulted the cook, I expect.'

'This is a friend of mine, Bundle,' said Virginia. 'Be nice to him.'

Bundle looked earnestly at Anthony for some minutes, and then addressed a remark to Virginia as though he had not been there.

'Where do you pick up these nice-looking men, Virginia? "How do you do it?" says she enviously.'

'You can have him,' said Virginia generously. 'I want Lord Caterham.'

She smiled upon the flattered peer, slipped her hand through his arm and they moved off together.

'Do you talk?' asked Bundle. 'Or are you just strong and silent?'

'Talk?' said Anthony. 'I babble. I murmur. I burble – like the running brook, you know. Sometimes I even ask questions.'

'As, for instance?'

'Who occupies the second room on the left from the end?'

He pointed to it as he spoke.

'What an extraordinary question!' said Bundle. 'You intrigue me greatly. Let me see – yes – that's Mademoiselle Brun's room. The French governess. She endeavours to keep my young sisters in order. Dulcie and Daisy – like the song, you know. I dare say they'd have called the next one Dorothy May. But mother got tired of having nothing but girls and died. Thought someone else could take on the job of providing an heir.'

'Mademoiselle Brun,' said Anthony thoughtfully. 'How long has she been with you?'

'Two months. She came to us when we were in Scotland.'

'Ha!' said Anthony. 'I smell a rat.'

'I wish I could smell some lunch,' said Bundle. 'Do I ask the

Scotland Yard man to have lunch with us, Mr Cade? You're a man of the world, you know about the etiquette of such things. We've never had a murder in the house before. Exciting, Isn't it? I'm sorry your character was so completely cleared this morning. I've always wanted to meet a murderer and see for myself if they're as genial and charming as the Sunday papers always say they are. God! What's that?'

'That' seemed to be a taxi approaching the house. Its two occupants were a tall man with a bald head and a black beard, and a smaller and younger man with a black moustache. Anthony recognized the former, and guessed that it was he – rather than the vehicle which contained him – that had rung the exclamation of astonishment from his companion's lips.

'Unless I am much mistaken,' he remarked, 'that is my old friend, Baron Lollipop.'

'Baron what?'

'I call him Lollipop for convenience. The pronouncing of his own name tends to harden the arteries.'

'It nearly wrecked the telephone this morning,' remarked Bundle. 'So that's the Baron, is it? I foresee he'll be turned on to me this afternoon – and I've had Isaacstein all the morning. Let George do his own dirty work, say I, and to hell with politics. Excuse me leaving you, Mr Cade, but I must stand by poor old Father.'

Bundle retreated rapidly to the house.

Anthony stood looking after her for a minute or two and thoughtfully lighted a cigarette. As he did so, his ear was caught by a stealthy sound quite near him. He was standing by the boathouse, and the sound seemed to come from just round the corner. The mental picture conveyed to him was that of a man vainly trying to stifle a sudden sneeze.

'Now I wonder – I very much wonder who's behind the boathouse,' said Anthony to himself. 'We'd better see, I think.'

Suiting the action to the word, he threw away the match he had just blown out, and ran lightly and noiselessly round the corner of the boathouse.

He came upon a man who had evidently been kneeling on the ground and was just struggling to rise to his feet. He was tall, wore a light-coloured overcoat and glasses, and for the rest, had a short, pointed black beard and slightly foppish manner. He was between thirty and forty years of age, and altogether of a most respectable appearance.

'What are you doing here?' asked Anthony.

He was pretty certain that the man was not one of Lord Caterham's guests.

'I ask your pardon,' said the stranger, with a marked foreign accent and what was meant to be an engaging smile. 'It is that I wish to return to the Jolly Cricketers and I have lost my way. Would monsieur be so good as to direct me?'

'Certainly,' said Anthony. 'But you don't go there by water, you know.'

'Eh?' said the stranger, with the air of one at a loss.

'I said,' repeated Anthony, with a meaning glance at the boathouse, 'that you won't get there by water. There's a right of way across the park – some distance away, but all this is the private part. You're trespassing.'

'I am most sorry,' said the stranger. 'I lost my direction entirely. I thought I would come up here and inquire.'

Anthony refrained from pointing out that kneeling behind a boathouse was a somewhat peculiar manner of prosecuting inquiries. He took the stranger kindly by the arm.

'You go this way, he said. 'Right round the lake and straight on – you can't miss the path. When you get on it, turn to the left, and it will lead you to the village. You're staying at the Cricketers, I suppose?'

'I am, monsieur. Since this morning. Many thanks for your kindness in directing me.'

'Don't mention it,' said Anthony. 'I hope you haven't caught cold.'

'Eh?' said the stranger.

'From kneeling on the damp ground, I mean,' explained Anthony. 'I fancied I heard you sneezing.'

'I may have sneezed,' admitted the other.

'Quite so,' said Anthony. 'But you shouldn't suppress a sneeze, you know. One of the most eminent doctors said so only the other day. It's frightfully dangerous. I don't remember exactly what it does to you – whether it's an inhibition or whether it hardens your arteries, but you must never do it. Good morning.'

'Good morning, and thank you, monsieur, for setting me on the right road.'

'Second suspicious stranger from village inn,' murmured Anthony to himself, as he watched the other's retreating form. 'And one that I can't place, either. Appearance that of a French commercial traveller. I don't quite see him as a Comrade of the Red Hand. Does he represent yet a third party in the harassed state of Herzoslovakia? The French governess has the second window from the end. A mysterious Frenchman is found slinking round the grounds, listening to conversations that are not meant for his ears. I'll bet my hat there's something in it.'

Musing thus, Anthony retraced his steps to the house. On the terrace, he encountered Lord Caterham, looking suitably depressed, and two new arrivals. He brightened a little at the sight of Anthony.

'Ah, there you are,' he remarked. 'Let me introduce you to Baron – er – er – and Captain Andrassy. Mr Anthony Cade.'

The Baron stared at Anthony with growing suspicion.

'Mr Cade?' he said stiffly. 'I think not.'

'A word alone with you, Baron,' said Anthony. 'I can explain everything.'

The Baron bowed, and the two men walked down the terrace together.

'Baron,' said Anthony. 'I must throw myself upon your mercy. I have so far strained the honour of an English gentleman as to travel to this country under an assumed name. I represented myself to you as Mr James McGrath – but you must see for yourself that the deception involved was infinitesimal. You are doubtless acquainted with the works of Shakespeare, and his remarks about the unimportance of the nomenclature of roses? This case is the same. The man you wanted to see was the man in possession of the memoirs. I was that man. As you know only too well, I am no longer in possession of them. A neat trick, Baron, a very neat trick. Who thought of it, you or your principal?'

'His Highness's own idea it was. And for anyone but him to carry it out he would not permit.'

'He did it jolly well,' said Anthony, with approval. 'I never took him for anything but an Englishman.'

'The education of an English gentleman did the Prince receive,' explained the Baron. 'The custom of Herzoslovakia it is.'

'No professional could have pinched those papers better,' said Anthony. 'May I ask, without indiscretion, what has become of them?'

'Between gentlemen,' began the Baron.

'You are too kind, Baron,' murmured Anthony. 'I've never been called a gentleman so often as I have in the last forty-eight hours.'

'I to you say this – I believe them to be burnt.'

'You believe, but you don't know, eh? Is that it?'

'His Highness in his own keeping retained them. His purpose it was to read them and then by the fire destroy them.'

'I see,' said Anthony. 'All the same, they are not the kind of light literature you'd skim through in half an hour.'

'Among the effects of my martyred master they have not discovered been. It is clear, therefore, that burnt they are.'

'Hm!' said Anthony. 'I wonder?'

He was silent for a minute or two and then went on.

'I have asked you these questions, Baron, because, as you may have heard, I myself have been implicated in the crime. I must clear myself absolutely, so that no suspicion attaches to me.'

'Undoubtedly,' said the Baron. 'Your honour demands it.'

'Exactly,' said Anthony. 'You put these things so well. I haven't got the knack of it. To continue, I can only clear myself by discovering the real murderer, and to do that I must have all the facts. This question of the memoirs is very important. It seems to me possible that to gain possession of them might be the motive of the crime. Tell me, Baron, is that a very far-fetched idea?'

The Baron hesitated for a moment or two.

'You yourself the memoirs have read?' he asked cautiously at length.

'I think I am answered,' said Anthony, smiling. 'Now, Baron, there's just one thing more. I should like to give you fair warning that it is still my intention to deliver that manuscript to the publishers on Wednesday next, the 13th of October.'

The Baron stared at him.

'But you have no longer got it?'

'On Wednesday next, I said. Today is Friday. That gives me five days to get hold of it again.'

'But if it is burnt?'

'I don't think it is burnt. I have good reasons for not believing so.'

As he spoke they turned the corner of the terrace. A massive figure was advancing towards them. Anthony, who had not yet seen the great Mr Herman Isaacstein, looked at him with considerable interest.

'Ah, Baron,' said Isaacstein, waving a big black cigar he was smoking, 'this is a bad business – a very bad business.'

'My good friend, Mr Isaacstein, it is indeed,' cried the Baron. 'All our noble edifice in ruins is.'

Anthony tactfully left the two gentlemen to their lamentations, and retraced his steps along the terrace.

Suddenly he came to a halt. A thin spiral of smoke was rising into the air apparently from the very centre of the yew hedge.

'It must be hollow in the middle,' reflected Anthony 'I've heard of such things before.'

He looked swiftly to right and left of him. Lord Caterham was at the farther end of the terrace with Captain Andrassy. Their backs were towards him. Anthony bent down and wriggled his way through the massive yew.

He had been quite right in his supposition. The yew hedge was really not one, but two, a narrow passage divided them. The entrance to this was about halfway up, on the side of the house. There was no mystery about it, but no one seeing the yew hedge from the front would have guessed at the probability.

Anthony looked down the narrow vista. About half-way down, a man was reclining in a basket chair. A half-smoked cigar rested on the arm of the chair, and the gentleman himself appeared to be asleep.

'Hm!' said Anthony to himself. 'Evidently Mr Hiram Fish prefers sitting in the shade.'

CHAPTER 16

TEA IN THE SCHOOLROOM

Anthony regained the terrace with the feeling uppermost in his mind that the only safe place for private conversations was the middle of the lake.

The resonant boom of a gong sounded from the house, and Tredwell appeared in a stately fashion from a side door

'Luncheon is served, my lord.'

'Ah!' said Lord Caterham, brisking up a little. 'Lunch!'

At that moment two children burst out of the house. They were high-spirited young women of twelve and ten, and though their names might be Dulcie and Daisy, as Bundle had affirmed, they appeared to be more generally known as Guggle and Winkle. They executed a kind of war dance, interspersed with shrill whoops, till Bundle emerged and quelled them.

'Where's Mademoiselle?' she demanded.

'She's got the migraine, the migraine, the migraine!' chanted Winkle.

'Hurrah!' said Guggle, joining in.

Lord Caterham had succeeded in shepherding most of his guests into the house. Now he laid a restraining hand on Anthony's arm.

'Come to my study,' he breathed. 'I've got something rather special there.'

Slinking down the hall, far more like a thief than like the master of the house, Lord Caterham gained the shelter of his sanctum. Here he unlocked a cupboard and produced various bottles.

'Talking to foreigners always makes me so thirsty,' he explained apologetically. 'I don't know why it is.'

There was a knock on the door, and Virginia popped her head round the corner of it.

'Got a special cocktail for me?' she demanded.

'Of course,' said Lord Caterham hospitably. 'Come in.'

The next few minutes were taken up with serious rites.

'I needed that,' said Lord Caterham with a sigh, as he replaced his glass on the table. 'As I said just now, I find talking to foreigners particularly fatiguing. I think it's because they're so polite. Come along. Let's have some lunch.'

He led the way to the dining-room. Virginia put her hand on Anthony's arm, and drew him back a little.

'I've done my good deed for the day,' she whispered. 'I got Lord Caterham to take me to see the body.'

'Well?' demanded Anthony eagerly.

One theory of his was to be proved or disproved.

Virginia was shaking her head.

'You were wrong,' she whispered. 'It's Prince Michael all right.'

'Oh!' Anthony was deeply chagrined.

'And Mademoiselle had the migraine,' he added aloud, in a dissatisfied tone.

'What has that got to do with it?'

'Probably nothing, but I wanted to see her. You see, I've found out that Mademoiselle has the second room from the end – the one where I saw the light go up last night.'

'That's interesting.'

'Probably there's nothing in it. All the same, I mean to see Mademoiselle before the day is out.'

Lunch was somewhat of an ordeal. Even the cheerful impartiality of Bundle failed to reconcile the heterogeneous assembly. The Baron and Andrassy were correct, formal, full of etiquette, and had the air of attending a meal in a mausoleum. Lord Catherham was lethargic and depressed. Bill Eversleigh stared longingly at Virginia. George, very mindful of the trying position in which he found himself, conversed weightily with the Baron and Mr Isaacstein. Guggle and Winkle, completely beside themselves with joy at having a murder in the house, had to be continually checked and kept under, whilst Mr Hiram Fish slowly masticated his food, and drawled out dry remarks in his own peculiar idiom. Superintendent Battle had considerately vanished, and nobody knew what had become of him.

'Thank God that's over,' murmured Bundle to Anthony, as they left the table. 'And George is taking the foreign contingent over to the Abbey this afternoon to discuss State secrets.'

'That will possibly relieve the atmosphere,' agreed Anthony.

'I don't mind the American so much,' continued Bundle.

'He and Father can talk first editions together quite happily in some secluded spot. Mr Fish' – as the object of their conversation drew near – 'I'm planning a peaceful afternoon for you.'

The American bowed.

'That's too kind of you, Lady Eileen.'

'Mr Fish,' said Anthony, 'had quite a peaceful morning.'

Mr Fish shot a quick glance at him.

'Ah, you observed me, then, in my secluded retreat? There are moments, sir, when far from the madding crowd is the only motto for a man of quiet tastes.'

Bundle had drifted on, and the American and Anthony were left together. The former dropped his voice a little.

'I opine,' he said, 'that there is considerable mystery about this little dust-up?'

'Any amount of it,' said Anthony.

'That guy with the bald head was perhaps a family connexion?'

'Something of the kind.'

'These Central European nations beat the band,' declared Mr Fish. 'It's kind of being rumoured around that the deceased gentleman was a Royal Highness. Is that so, do you know?'

'He was staying here as Count Stanislaus,' replied Anthony evasively.

To this Mr Fish offered no further rejoinder than the somewhat cryptic:

'Oh, boy!'

After which he relapsed into silence for some moments.

'This police captain of yours,' he observed at last. 'Battle, or whatever his name is, is he the goods all right?'

'Scotland Yard think so,' replied Anthony dryly.

'He seems kind of hidebound to me,' remarked Mr Fish. 'No hustle to him. This big idea of his, letting no one leave the house, what is there to it?'

He darted a very sharp look at Anthony as he spoke.

'Everyone's got to attend the inquest tomorrow morning, you see.'

'That's the idea is it? No more to it than that? No question of Lord Caterham's guests being suspected?'

'My dear Mr Fish!'

'I was getting a mite uneasy – being a stranger in this country. But of course it was an outside job – I remember now. Window found unfastened, wasn't it?'

'It was,' said Anthony, looking straight in front of him.

Mr Fish sighed. After a minute or two he said in a plaintive tone:

'Young man, do you know how they get the water out of a mine?'

'How?'

'By pumping – but it's almighty hard work! I observe the figure of my genial host detaching itself from the group over yonder. I must join him.'

Mr Fish walked gently away, and Bundle drifted back again.

'Funny Fish, isn't he?' she remarked.

'He is.'

'It's no good looking for Virginia,' said Bundle sharply.

'I wasn't.'

'You were. I don't know how she does it. It isn't what she says, I don't even believe it's what she looks. But, oh, boy! she gets there every time. Anyway, she's on duty elsewhere for the time. She told me to be nice to you, and I'm going to be nice to you – by force if necessary.'

'No force required,' Anthony assured her. 'But, if it's all the same to you, I'd rather you were nice to me on the water, in a boat.'

'It's not a bad idea,' said Bundle meditatively.

They strolled down to the lake together.

'There's just one question I'd like to ask you,' said Anthony as he paddled gently out from the shore, 'before we turn to really interesting topics. Business before pleasure.'

'Whose bedroom do you want to know about now?' asked Bundle with weary patience.

'Nobody's bedroom for the moment. But I would like to know where you got your French governess from.'

'The man's bewitched,' said Bundle. 'I got her from an agency, and I pay her a hundred pounds a year, and her Christian name is Geneviève. Anything more you want to know?'

'We'll assume the agency,' said Anthony. 'What about her references?'

'Oh, glowing! She lived for ten years with the Countess of What Not.'

'What Not being? –'

'The Comtesse de Breteuil, Château de Breteuil, Dinard.'

'You didn't actually see the Comtesse yourself? It was all done by letter?'

'Exactly.'

'Hm!' said Anthony.

'You intrigue me,' said Bundle. 'You intrigue me enormously. Is it love or crime?'

'Probably sheer idiocy on my part. Let's forget it.'

'"Let's forget it," says he negligently, having extracted all the information he wants. Mr Cade, who do you suspect? I rather suspect Virginia as being the most unlikely person. Or possibly Bill.'

'What about you?'

'Member of the aristocracy joins in secret the Comrades of the Red Hand. It would create a sensation all right.'

Anthony laughed. He liked Bundle, though he was a little afraid of the shrewd penetration of her sharp grey eyes.

'You must be proud of all this,' he said suddenly, waving his hand towards the great house in the distance.

Bundle screwed up her eyes and tilted her head on one side.

'Yes – it means something, I suppose. But one's too used to it. Anyway, we're not here very much – too deadly dull. We've been at Cowes and Deauville all the summer after town, and then up to Scotland. Chimneys has been swathed in dust-sheets for about five months. Once a week they take the dust-sheets off and coaches full of tourists come and gape and listen to Tredwell. "On your right is the portrait of the fourth Marchioness of Caterham, painted by Sir Joshua Reynolds," etc. and Ed or Bert, the humorist of the party, nudges his girl and says, "Eh! Gladys, they've got two pennyworth of pictures here, right enough." And then they go and look at more pictures and yawn and shuffle their feet and wish it was time to go home.'

'Yet history has been made here once or twice, by all accounts.'

'You've been listening to George,' said Bundle sharply. 'That's the kind of thing he's always saying.'

But Anthony had raised himself on his elbow, and was staring at the shore.

'Is that a third suspicious stranger I see standing disconsolately by the boathouse? Or is it one of the house party?'

Bundle lifted her head from the scarlet cushion.

'It's Bill,' she said.

'He seems to be looking for something.'

'He's probably looking for me,' said Bundle, without enthusiasm.

'Shall we row quickly in the opposite direction?'

'That's quite the right answer, but it should be delivered with more enthusiasm.'

'I shall row with double vigour after that rebuke.'

'Not at all,' said Bundle. 'I have my pride. Row me to where that young ass is waiting. Somebody's got to look after him, I suppose. Virginia must have given him the slip. One of these days, inconceivable as it seems, I might want to marry George, so I might as well practise being "one of our well-known political hostesses".'

Anthony pulled obediently towards the shore.

'And what's to become of me, I should like to know?' he complained. 'I refuse to be the unwanted third. Is that the children I see in the distance?'

'Yes. Be careful, or they'll rope you in.'

'I'm rather fond of children,' said Anthony. 'I might teach them some nice quiet intellectual game.'

'Well, don't say I didn't warn you.'

Having relinquished Bundle to the care of the disconsolate Bill, Anthony strolled off to where various shrill cries disturbed the peace of the afternoon. He was received with acclamation.

'Are you any good at playing Red Indians?' asked Guggle sternly.

'Rather,' said Anthony. 'You should hear the noise I make when I'm being scalped. Like this.' He illustrated.

'Not so bad,' said Winkle grudgingly. 'Now do the scalper's yell.'

Anthony obliged with a blood-curdling noise. In another minute the game of Red Indians was in full swing.

About an hour later, Anthony wiped his forehead, and ventured to inquire after Mademoiselle's migraine. He was pleased to hear that that lady had entirely recovered. So popular had he become that he was urgently invited to come and have tea in the schoolroom.

'And then you can tell us about the man you saw hung,' urged Guggle.

'Did you say you'd got a bit of the rope with you?' asked Winkle.

'It's in my suitcase,' said Anthony solemnly. 'You shall each have a piece of it.'

Winkle immediately let out a wild Indian yell of satisfaction.

'We'll have to go and get washed, I suppose,' said Guggle gloomily. 'You will come to tea, won't you? You won't forget?'

Anthony swore solemnly that nothing should prevent him keeping the engagement. Satisfied, the youthful pair beat a retreat towards the house. Anthony stood for a minute looking after them, and, as he did so, he became aware of a man leaving the other side of a little copse of trees and hurrying away across the park. He felt almost sure that it was the same black-bearded stranger he had encountered that morning. Whilst he was hesitating whether to go after him or not the trees just ahead of him were parted and Mr Hiram Fish stepped out into the open. He started slightly when he saw Anthony.

'A peaceful afternoon, Mr Fish?' inquired the latter.

'I thank you, yes.'

Mr Fish did not look as peaceful as usual, however. His face was flushed, and he was breathing hard as though he had been running. He drew out his watch and consulted it.

'I guess,' he said softly, 'it's just about time for your British institution of afternoon tea.'

Closing his watch with a snap, Mr Fish ambled gently away in the direction of the house.

Anthony stood in a brown study and awoke with a start to the fact that Superintendent Battle was standing beside him. Not the faintest sound had heralded his approach, and he seemed literally to have materialized from space.

'Where did you spring from?' asked Anthony irritably.

With a slight jerk of his head, Battle indicated the little copse of trees behind them.

'It seems a popular spot this afternoon,' remarked Anthony.

'You were very lost in thought, Mr Cade.'

'I was indeed. Do you know what I was doing, Battle? I was trying to put two and one and five and three together so as to make four. And it can't be done, Battle, it simply can't be done.'

'There's difficulties that way,' agreed the detective.

'But you're just the man I wanted to see. Battle, I want to go away. Can it be done?'

True to his creed, Superintendent Battle showed neither emotion nor surprise. His reply was easy and matter of fact.

'That depends, sir, as to where you want to go.'

'I'll tell you exactly, Battle. I'll lay my cards upon the table. I want to go Dinard, to the château of Madame la Comtesse de Breteuil. Can it be done?'

'When do you want to go, Mr Cade?'

'Say tomorrow after the inquest. I could be back here by Sunday evening.'

'I see,' said the superintendent, with peculiar solidity.

'Well, what about it?'

'I've no objection, provided you go where you say you're going, and come straight back here.'

'You're a man in a thousand, Battle. Either you have taken an extraordinary fancy to me or else you're extraordinarily deep. Which is it?'

Superintendent Battle smiled a little, but did not answer.

'Well, well,' said Anthony, 'I expect you'll take your precautions. Discreet minions of the law will follow my suspicious footsteps. So be it. But I do wish I knew what it was all about.'

'I don't get you, Mr Cade.'

'The memoirs – what all the fuss is about. Were they only memoirs? Or have you got something up your sleeve?'

Battle smiled again.

'Take it like this. I'm doing you a favour because you've made a favourable impression on me, Mr Cade. I'd like you to work in with me over this case. The amateur and the professional, they go well together. The one has the intimacy, so to speak, and the other the experience.'

'Well,' said Anthony slowly, 'I don't mind admitting that I've always wanted to try my hand at unravelling a murder mystery.'

'Any ideas about the case at all, Mr Cade?'

'Plenty of them,' said Anthony. 'But they're mostly questions.'

'As, for instance?'

'Who steps into the murdered Michael's shoes? It seems to me that that is important?'

A rather wry smile came over Superintendent Battle's face.

'I wondered if you'd think of that, sir. Prince Nicholas Obolovitch is the next heir – first cousin of this gentleman.'

'And where is he at the present moment?' asked Anthony, turning away to light a cigarette. 'Don't tell me you don't know, Battle, because I shan't believe you.'

'We've reason to believe that he's in the United States. He was until quite lately, at all events. Raising money on his expectations.'

Anthony gave vent to a surprised whistle.

'I get you,' said Anthony. 'Michael was backed by England, Nicholas by America. In both countries a group of financiers are anxious to obtain the oil concessions. The Loyalist Party adopted Michael as their candidate – now they'll have to look elsewhere. Gnashing of teeth on the part of Isaacstein and Co. and Mr George Lomax. Rejoicings in Wall Street. Am I right?'

'You're not far off,' said Superintendent Battle.

'Hm!' said Anthony. 'I almost dare swear that I know what you were doing in that copse.'

The detective smiled, but made no reply.

'International politics are very fascinating,' said Anthony, 'but I fear I must leave you. I have an appointment in the schoolroom.'

He strode briskly away towards the house. Inquiries of the dignified Tredwell showed him the way to the schoolroom. He tapped on the door and entered, to be greeted by squeals of joy.

Guggle and Winkle immediately rushed at him and bore him in triumph to be introduced to Mademoiselle.

For the first time, Anthony felt a qualm. Mademoiselle Brun was a small, middle-aged woman with a sallow face, pepper-and-salt hair, and a budding moustache!

As the notorious foreign adventuress she did not fit into the picture at all.

'I believe,' said Anthony to himself, 'I'm making the most utter fool of myself. Never mind, I must go through with it now.'

He was extremely pleasant to Mademoiselle, and she, on her part, was evidently delighted to have a good-looking young man invade her schoolroom. The meal was a great success.

But that evening, alone in the charming bedchamber that had been allotted to him, Anthony shook his head several times.

'I'm wrong,' he said to himself. 'For the second time, I'm wrong. Somehow or other, I can't get the hang of this thing.'

He stopped in his pacing of the floor.

'What the devil –' began Anthony.

The door was being softly opened. In another minute a man had slipped into the room, and stood deferentially by the door.

He was a big fair man, squarely built, with high Slavonic cheekbones, and dreamy fanatic eyes.

'Who the devil are you?' asked Anthony, staring at him.

The man replied in perfect English.

'I am Boris Anchoukoff.'

'Prince Michael's servant, eh?'

'That is so. I served my master. He is dead. Now I serve you.'

'It's very kind of you,' said Anthony. 'But I don't happen to want a valet.'

'You are my master now. I will serve you faithfully.'

'Yes – but – look – here – I don't need a valet. I can't afford one.'

Boris Anchoukoff looked at him with a touch of scorn.

'I do not ask for money. I served my master. So will I serve you – to the death!'

Stepping quickly forward, he dropped on one knee, caught Anthony's hand and placed it on his forehead. Then he rose swiftly and left the room as suddenly as he had come.

Anthony stared after him, his face a picture of astonishment.

'That's damned odd,' he said to himself. 'A faithful sort of dog. Curious the instincts these fellows have.'

He rose and paced up and down.

'All the same,' he muttered, 'it's awkward – damned awkward – just at present.'

CHAPTER 17

A MIDNIGHT ADVENTURE

The inquest took place on the following morning. It was extraordinarily unlike the inquests as pictured in sensational fiction. It satisfied even George Lomax in its rigid suppression of all interesting details. Superintendent Battle and the coroner, working together with the support of the chief constable, had reduced the proceedings to the lowest level of boredom.

Immediately after the inquest, Anthony took an unostentatious departure.

His departure was the one bright spot in the day for Bill Eversleigh. George Lomax, obsessed with the fear that something damaging to his department might leak out, had been exceedingly trying. Miss Oscar and Bill had been in constant attendance. Everything useful and interesting had been done by Miss Oscar. Bill's part had been to run to and fro with countless messages, to decode telegrams, and to listen by the hour to George's repeating himself.

It was a completely exhausted young man who retired to bed on Saturday night. He had had practically no chance to talk to Virginia all day, owing to George's exactions, and he felt injured and ill-used. Thank goodness, that Colonial fellow had taken himself off. He had monopolized far too much of Virginia's society, anyway. And of course if George Lomax went on making an ass of himself like this – His mind seething with resentment, Bill fell asleep. And, in dreams, came consolation. For he dreamt of Virginia.

It was an heroic dream, a dream of burning timbers in which he played the part of the gallant rescuer. He brought down Virginia from the topmost storey in his arms. She was unconscious. He laid her on the grass. Then he went off to find a packet of sandwiches. It was most important that he should find that packet of sandwiches. George had it but instead of giving it up to Bill, he began to dictate telegrams. They were now in the vestry of a church, and any minute Virginia might arrive to be married to him. Horror! He was wearing pyjamas. He must get home at once and find his proper clothes. He rushed out to the car. The car would not start. No petrol in the tank! He was getting desperate. And then a big General bus drew up and Virginia got out of it on the arm of the bald-headed Baron. She was deliciously cool, and exquisitely dressed in grey. She came over to him and shook him by the shoulders playfully. 'Bill,' she said. 'Oh, Bill.' She shook him harder. 'Bill,' she said. 'Wake up. Oh, do wake up!'

Very dazed, Bill woke up. He was in his bedroom at Chimneys. But part of the dream was with him still. Virginia was leaning over him, and was repeating the same words with variations.

'Wake up, Bill. Oh, do wake up! Bill.'

'Hullo!' said Bill, sitting up in bed. 'What's the matter?'

Virginia gave a sigh of relief.

'Thank goodness. I thought you'd never wake up. I've been shaking you and shaking you. Are you properly awake now?'

'I think so,' said Bill doubtfully.

'You great lump,' said Virginia. 'The trouble I've had! My arms are aching.'

'These insults are uncalled for,' said Bill, with dignity. 'Let me say, Virginia, that I consider your conduct most unbecoming. Not at all that of a pure young widow.'

'Don't be an idiot, Bill. Things are happening.'

'What kind of things?'

'Queer things. In the Council Chamber. I thought I heard a door bang somewhere, and I came down to see. And then I saw a light in the Council Chamber. I crept along the passage, and peeped through the crack of the door. I couldn't see much, but what I could see was so extraordinary that I felt I must see more. And then, all of a sudden, I felt that I should like a nice, big strong man with me. And you were the nicest and biggest and strongest man I could think of, so I came in and tried to wake you up quietly. But I've been ages doing it.'

'I see,' said Bill. 'And what do you want me to do now? Get up and tackle the burglars?'

Virginia wrinkled her brows.

'I'm not sure that they are burglars. Bill, it's very queer – But don't let's waste time talking. Get up.'

Bill slipped obediently out of bed.

'Wait while I don a pair of boots – the big ones with nails in them. However big and strong I am. I'm not going to tackle hardened criminals with bare feet.'

'I like your pyjamas, Bill,' said Virginia dreamily. 'Brightness without vulgarity.'

'While we're on the subject,' remarked Bill, reaching for his second boot, 'I like that thingummybob of yours. It's a pretty shade of green. What do you call it? It's not just a dressing-gown, is it?'

'It's a negligé,' said Virginia.. 'I'm glad you've led such a pure life, Bill.'

'I haven't,' said Bill indignantly.

'You've just betrayed the fact. You're very nice, Bill, and I like you. I dare say that tomorrow morning – say about ten o'clock, a good safe hour for not unduly exciting the emotions – I might even kiss you.'

'I always think these things are best carried out on the spur of the moment,' suggested Bill.

'We've other fish to fry,' said Virginia. 'If you don't want to put on a gasmask and a shirt of chain-mail, shall we start?'

'I'm ready,' said Bill.

He wriggled into a lurid silk dressing-gown, and picked up a poker.

'The orthodox weapon,' he observed.

'Come on,' said Virginia, 'and don't make a noise.'

They crept out of the room and along the corridor, and then down the wide double staircase. Virginia frowned as they reached the bottom of it.

'Those boots of yours aren't exactly domes of silence, are they, Bill?'

'Nails will be nails,' said Bill. 'I'm doing my best.'

'You'll have to take them off,' said Virginia firmly.

Bill groaned.

'You can carry them in your hand. I want to see if you can make out what's going on in the Council Chamber. Bill, it's awfully mysterious. Why should burglars take a man in armour to pieces?'

'Well, I suppose they can't take him away whole very well. They disarticulate him, and pack him neatly.'

Virginia shook her head, dissatisfied.

'What should they want to steal a mouldy old suit of armour

for? Why, Chimneys is full of treasures that are much easier to take away.'

Bill shook his head.

'How many of them are there?' he asked, taking a firmer grip of his poker.

'I couldn't see properly. You know what a keyhole is. And they only had a flashlight.'

'I expect they've gone by now,' said Bill hopefully.

He sat on the bottom stair and drew off his boots. Then, holding them in his hand, he crept along the passage that led to the Council Chamber, Virginia close behind him. They halted outside the massive oak door. All was silent within, but suddenly Virginia pressed his arm, and he nodded. A bright light had shown for a minute through the keyhole.

Bill went down on his knees, and applied his eye to the orifice. What he saw was confusing in the extreme. The scene of the drama that was being enacted inside was evidently just to the left, out of his line of vision. A subdued chink every now and then seemed to point to the fact that the invaders were still dealing with the figure in armour. There were two of these, Bill remembered. They stood together by the wall just under the Holbein portrait. The light of the electric torch was evidently being directed upon the operations in progress. It left the rest of the room nearly in darkness. Once a figure flitted across Bill's line of vision, but there was not sufficient light to distinguish anything about it. It might have been that of a man or a woman. In a minute or two it flitted back again and then the subdued chinking sounded again. Presently there came a new sound, a faint tap-tap as of knuckles on wood.

Bill sat back on his heels suddenly.

'What is it?' whispered Virginia.

'Nothing. It's no good going on like this. We can't see anything, and we can't guess what they're up to. I must go in and tackle them.'

He drew on his boots and stood up.

'Now, Virginia, listen to me. We'll open the door as softly as possible. You know where the switch of the electric light is?'

'Yes, just by the door.'

'I don't think there are more than two of them. There may be only one. I want to get well into the room. Then, when I say "Go" I want you to switch on the lights. Do you understand?'

'Perfectly.'

'And don't scream or faint or anything. I won't let anyone hurt you.'

'My hero!' murmured Virginia.

Bill peered at her suspiciously through the darkness. He heard a faint sound which might have been either a sob or a laugh. Then he grasped the poker firmly and rose to his feet. He felt that he was fully alive to the situation.

Very softly, he turned the handle of the door. It yielded and swung gently inwards. Bill felt Virginia close beside him. Together they moved noiselessly into the room.

At the farther end of the room, the torch was playing upon the Holbein picture. Silhouetted against it was the figure of a man, standing on a chair and gently tapping on the panelling. His back, of course, was to them, and he merely loomed up as a monstrous shadow.

What more they might have seen cannot be told, for at that moment Bill's nails squeaked upon the parquet floor. The man swung round, directing the powerful torch full upon them and almost dazzling them with the sudden glare.

Bill did not hesitate.

'Go,' he roared to Virginia, and sprang for his man, as she obediently pressed down the switch of the electric lights.

The big chandelier should have been flooded with light; but instead, all that happened was the click of the switch. The room remained in darkness.

Virginia heard Bill curse freely. The next minute the air was filled with panting, scuffling sounds. The torch had fallen to the ground and extinguished itself in the fall. There was the sound of a desperate struggle going on in the darkness, but as to who was getting the better of it, and indeed as to who was taking part in it, Virginia had no idea. Had there been anyone else in the room besides the man who was tapping the panelling? There might have been. Their glimpse had been only a momentary one.

Virginia felt paralysed. She hardly knew what to do. She dared not try to join in the struggle. To do so might hamper and not aid Bill. Her one idea was to stay in the doorway, so that anyone trying to escape should not leave the room that way. At the same time, she disobeyed Bill's express instructions and screamed loudly and repeatedly for help.

She heard doors opening upstairs, and a sudden gleam of light from the hall and the big staircase. If only Bill could hold his man until help came.

But at that minute there was a final terrific upheaval. They must have crashed into one of the figures in armour, for it fell to the ground with a deafening noise. Virginia saw dimly a figure springing for the window, and at the same time heard Bill cursing and disengaging himself from fragments of armour.

For the first time, she left her post, and rushed wildly for the figure at the window. But the window was already unlatched. The intruder had no need to stop and fumble for it. He sprang out and raced away down the terrace and round the corner of the house. Virginia raced after him. She was young and athletic, and she turned the corner of the terrace not many seconds after her quarry.

But there she ran headlong into the arms of a man who was emerging from a small side door. It was Mr Hiram P. Fish.

'Gee! It's a lady,' he exclaimed. 'Why, I beg your pardon, Mrs Revel. I took you for one of the thugs fleeing from justice.'

'He's just passed this way,' cried Virginia breathlessly. 'Can't we catch him?'

But even as she spoke, she knew it was too late. The man must have gained the park by now, and it was a dark night with no moon. She retraced her steps to the Council Chamber, Mr Fish by her side, discoursing in a soothing monotone upon the habits of burglars in general, of which he seemed to have a wide experience.

Lord Caterham, Bundle and various frightened servants were standing in the doorway of the Council Chamber.

'What the devil's the matter?' asked Bundle. 'Is it burglars? What are you and Mr Fish doing, Virginia? Taking a midnight stroll?'

Virginia explained the events of the evening.

'How frightfully exciting,' commented Bundle. 'You don't usually get a murder and a burglary crowded into one week-end.

What's the matter with the lights in here? They're all right everywhere else.'

That mystery was soon explained. The bulbs had simply been removed and laid in a row against the wall. Mounted on a pair of steps, the dignified Tredwell, dignified even in undress, restored illumination to the stricken apartment.

'If I am not mistaken,' said Lord Caterham in his sad voice as he looked around him, 'this room has recently been the centre of somewhat violent activity.'

There was some justice in the remark. Everything that could have been knocked over had been kocked over. The floor was littered with splintered chairs, broken china, and fragments of armour.

'How many of them were there?' asked Bundle. 'It seems to have been a desperate fight.'

'Only one, I think,' said Virginia. But, even as she spoke she hesitated a little. Certainly only one person – a man – had passed out through the window. But as she had rushed after him, she had a vague impression of a rustle somewhere close at hand. If so, the second occupant of the room could have escaped through the door. Perhaps, though, the rustle had been an effect of her own imagination.

Bill appeared suddenly at the window. He was out of breath and panting hard.

'Damn the fellow!' he exclaimed wrathfully. 'He's escaped. I've been hunting all over the place. Not a sign of him.'

'Cheer up, Bill,' said Virginia, 'better luck next time.'

'Well,' said Lord Caterham, 'what do you think we'd better do now? Go back to bed? I can't get hold of Badgworthy at this time of night. Tredwell, you know the sort of thing that's necessary. Just see to it, will you?'

'Very good, my lord.'

With a sigh of relief, Lord Caterham prepared to retreat.

'That beggar, Isaacstein, sleeps soundly,' he remarked, with a touch of envy. 'You'd have thought all this row would have brought him down.' He looked across at Mr Fish. 'You found time to dress, I see,' he added.

'I flung on a few articles of clothing, yes,' admitted the American.

'Very sensible of you,' said Lord Caterham. 'Damned chilly things, pyjamas.'

He yawned. In a rather depressed mood, the house party retired to bed.

CHAPTER 18

SECOND MIDNIGHT ADVENTURE

The first person that Anthony saw as he alighted from his train on the following afternoon was Superintendent Battle. His face broke into a smile.

'I've returned according to contract,' he remarked. 'Did you come down here to assure yourself of the fact?'

Battle shook his head.

'I wasn't worrying about that, Mr Cade. I happen to be going to London, that's all.'

'You have such a trustful nature, Battle.'

'Do you think so, sir?'

'No. I think you're deep – very deep. Still waters, you know, and all that sort of thing. So you're going to London?'

'I am, Mr Cade.'

'I wonder why?'

The detective did not reply.

'You're so chatty,' remarked Anthony. 'That's what I like about you.'

A far-off twinkle showed in Battle's eyes.

'What about your own little job, Mr Cade?' he inquired. 'How did that go off?'

'I've drawn blank, Battle. For the second time I've been proved hopelessly wrong. Galling, isn't it?'

'What was the idea, sir, if I may ask?'

'I suspected the French governess, Battle. A: upon the grounds of her being the most unlikely person, according to the canons of the best fiction. B: because there was a light in her room on the night of the tragedy.'

'That wasn't much to go upon.'

'You are quite right. It was not. But I discovered that she had only been here a short time, and I also found a suspicious

Frenchman spying round the place. You know all about him, I suppose?'

'You mean the man who calls himself M. Chelles? Staying at the Cricketers? A traveller in silk.'

'That's it, is it? What about him? What does Scotland Yard think?'

'His actions have been suspicious,' said Superintendent Battle expressionlessly.

'Very suspicious, I should say. Well, I put two and two together. French governess in the house, French stranger outside. I decided that they were in league together, and I hurried off to interview the lady with whom Mademoiselle Brun had lived for the last ten years. I was fully prepared to find that she had never heard of any such person as Mademoiselle Brun, but I was wrong, Battle. Mademoiselle is the genuine article.'

Battle nodded.

'I must admit,' said Anthony, 'that as soon as I spoke to her I had an uneasy conviction that I was barking up the wrong tree. She seemed so absolutely the governess.'

Again Battle nodded.

'All the same, Mr Cade, you can't always go by that. Women especially can do a lot with make-up. I've seen quite a pretty girl with the colour of her hair altered, a sallow complexion stain, slightly reddened eyelids and, most efficacious of all, dowdy clothes, who would fail to be identified by nine people out of ten who had seen her in her former character. Men haven't got quite the same pull. You can do something with the eyebrows, and of course different sets of false teeth alter the whole expression. But there are always the ears – there's an extraordinary lot of character in ears, Mr Cade.'

'Don't look so hard at mine, Battle,' complained Anthony. 'You make me quite nervous.'

'I'm not talking of false beards and grease-paint,' continued the superintendent. 'That's only for books. No, there are very few men who can escape identification and put it over on you. In fact there's only one man I know who has a positive genius for impersonation. King Victor. Ever heard of King Victor, Mr Cade?'

There was something so sharp and sudden about the way the

detective put the question that Anthony checked the words that were rising to his lips.

'King Victor?' he said reflectively instead. 'Somehow, I seem to have heard the name.'

'One of the most celebrated jewel thieves in the world. Irish father, French mother. Can speak five languages at least. He's been serving a sentence, but his time was up a few months ago.'

'Really? And where is he supposed to be now?'

'Well, Mr Cade, that's what we'd rather like to know.'

'The plot thickens,' said Anthony lightly. 'No chance of his turning up here, is there? But I suppose he wouldn't be interested in political memoirs – only in jewels.'

'There's no saying,' said Superintendent Battle. 'For all we know, he may be here already.'

'Disguised as the second footman? Splendid. You'll recognize him by his ears and cover yourself with glory.'

'Quite fond of your little joke, aren't you, Mr Cade? By the way, what do you think of that curious business at Staines?'

'Staines?' said Anthony. 'What's been happening at Staines?'

'It was in Saturday's papers. I thought you might have seen about it. Man found by the roadside shot. A foreigner. It was in the papers again today, of course.'

'I did see something about it,' said Anthony carelessly. 'Not suicide, apparently.'

'No. There was no weapon. As yet the man hasn't been identified.'

'You seem very interested,' said Anthony, smiling. 'No connexion with Prince Michael's death, is there?'

His hand was quite steady. So were his eyes. Was it his fancy that Superintendent Battle was looking at him with peculiar intentness?

'Seems to be quite an epidemic of that sort of thing,' said Battle. 'But, well, I dare say there's nothing in it.'

He turned away, beckoning to a porter as the London train came thundering in. Anthony drew a faint sigh of relief.

He strolled across the park in an unusually thoughtful mood. He purposely chose to approach the house from the same direction as that from which he had come on the fateful Thursday night, and as he drew near to it he looked up at the windows cudgelling his brains to make sure of the one where he had seen the light. Was he quite sure that it was the second from the end?

And, doing so, he made a discovery. There was an angle at the corner of the house in which was a window set farther back. Standing on one spot, you counted this window as the first, and the first one built out over the Council Chamber as the second, but move a few yards to the right and the part built out over the Council Chamber appeared to be the end of the house. The first window was invisible, and the two windows of the rooms over the Council Chamber would have appeared the first and second from the end. Where exactly had he been standing when he had seen the light flash up?

Anthony found the question very hard to determine. A matter of a yard or so made all the difference. But one point was made abundantly clear. It was quite possible that he had been mistaken in describing the light as ocurring in the second room from the end. It might equally well have been the *third*.

Now who occupied the third room? Anthony was determined to find that out as soon as possible. Fortune favoured him. In the hall Tredwell had just set the massive silver urn in its place on the tea-tray. Nobody else was there.

'Hullo, Tredwell,' said Anthony. 'I wanted to ask you something. Who has the third room from the end on the west side? Over the Council Chamber, I mean.'

Tredwell reflected for a minute or two.

'That would be the American gentleman's room, sir. Mr Fish.'

'Oh, is it? Thank you.'

'Not at all, sir.'

Tredwell prepared to depart, then paused. The desire to be the first to impart news makes even pontifical butlers human.

'Perhaps you have heard, sir, of what occurred last night?'

'Not a word,' said Anthony. 'What did occur last night?'

'An attempt at robbery, sir!'

'Not really? Was anything taken?'

'No, sir. The thieves were dismantling the suits of armour in the Council Chamber when they were surprised and forced to flee. Unfortunately they got clear away.'

'That's very extraordinary,' said Anthony. 'The Council Chamber again. Did they break in that way?'

'It is supposed, sir, that they forced the window.'

Satisfied with the interest his information had aroused, Tredwell resumed his retreat, but brought up short with a dignified apology.

'I beg your pardon, sir. I didn't hear you come in, and didn't know you were standing just behind me.'

Mr Isaacstein, who had been the victim of the impact, waved his hand in a friendly fashion.

'No harm done, my good fellow. I assure you no harm done.'

Tredwell retired looking contemptuous, and Isaacstein came forward and dropped into an easy-chair.

'Hullo, Cade, so you're back again. Been hearing all about last night's little show?'

'Yes,' said Anthony. 'Rather an exciting week-end, isn't it?'

'I should imagine that last night was the work of local men,' said Isaacstein. 'It seems a clumsy, amateurish affair.'

'Is there anyone about here who collects armour?' asked Anthony. 'It seems a curious thing to select.'

'Very curious,' agreed Mr Isaacstein. He paused a minute, and then said slowly: 'The whole position here is very unfortunate.'

There was something almost menacing in his tone.

'I don't quite understand,' said Anthony.

'Why are we all being kept here in this way? The inquest was over yesterday. The Prince's body will be removed to London, where it is being given out that he died of heart failure. And still nobody is allowed to leave the house. Mr Lomax knows no more than I do. He refers me to Superintendent Battle.'

'Superintendent Battle has something up his sleeve,' said Anthony thoughtfully. 'And it seems the essence of his plan that nobody should leave.'

'But, excuse me, Mr Cade, you have been away.'

'With a string tied to my leg. I've no doubt that I was shadowed the whole time. I shouldn't have been given a chance of disposing of the revolver or anything of that kind.'

'Ah, the revolver,' said Isaacstein thoughtfully. 'That has not yet been found, I think?'

'Not yet.'

'Possibly thrown into the lake in passing.'

'Very possibly.'

'Where is Superintendent Battle? I have not seen him this afternoon.'

'He's gone to London. I met him at the station.'

'Gone to London? Really? Did he say when he would be back?'

'Early tomorrow, so I understand.'

Virginia came in with Lord Caterham and Mr Fish. She smiled a welcome at Anthony.

'So you're back, Mr Cade. Have you heard all about our adventures last night?'

'Why, trooly, Mr Cade,' said Hiram Fish. 'It was a night of strenuous excitement. Did you hear that I mistook Mrs Revel for one of the thugs?'

'And in the meantime,' said Anthony, 'the thug –?'

'Got clear away,' said Mr Fish mournfully.

'Do pour out,' said Lord Caterham to Virginia. 'I don't know where Bundle is.'

Virginia officiated. Then she came and sat down near Anthony.

'Come to the boathouse after tea,' she said in a low voice. 'Bill and I have got a lot to tell you.'

Then she joined lightly in the general conversation.

The meeting at the boathouse was duly held.

Virginia and Bill were bubbling over with their news. They agreed that a boat in the middle of the lake was the only safe place for confidential conversation. Having paddled out a sufficient distance, the full story of last night's adventure was related to Anthony. Bill looked a little sulky. He wished Virginia would not insist on bringing this Colonial fellow into it.

'It's very odd,' said Anthony, when the story was finished. 'What do you make of it?' he asked Virginia.

'I think they were looking for something,' she returned promptly. 'The burglar idea is absurd.'

'They thought the something, whatever it was, might be concealed in the suits of armour, that's clear enough. But why tap the panelling? That looks more as though they were looking for a secret staircase, or something of that kind.'

'There's a priest's hole at Chimneys, I know,' said Virginia. 'And I believe there's a secret staircase as well. Lord Caterham would tell us all about it. What I want to know is, what can they have been looking for?'

'It can't be the memoirs,' said Anthony. 'They're a great bulky package. It must have been something small.'

'George knows, I expect,' said Virginia. 'I wonder whether I could get it out of him. All along I've felt there was something behind all this.'

'You say there was only one man,' pursued Anthony, 'but that there might possibly be another, as you thought you heard someone going towards the door as you sprang to the window.'

'The sound was very slight,' said Virginia. 'It might have been just my imagination.'

'That's quite possible, but in case it wasn't your imagination the second person must have been an inmate of the house. I wonder now –'

'What are you wondering at?' asked Virginia.

'The thoroughness of Mr Hiram Fish, who dresses himself completely when he hears screams for help downstairs.'

'There's something in that,' agreed Virginia. 'And then there's Isaacstein, who sleeps through it all. That's suspicious too. Surely he couldn't?'

'There's that fellow Boris,' suggested Bill. 'He looks an unmitigated ruffian. Michael's servant, I mean.'

'Chimneys is full of suspicious characters,' said Virginia. 'I dare say the others are just as suspicious of us. I wish Superintendent Battle hadn't gone to London. I think it's rather stupid of him. By the way, Mr Cade, I've seen that peculiar-looking Frenchman about once or twice, spying round the park.'

'It's a mix-up,' confessed Anthony. 'I've been away on a wild-goose chase. Made a thorough ass of myself. Look here, to me the whole question seems to resolve itself into this: did the men find what they were looking for last night?'

'Supposing they didn't?' said Virginia. 'I'm pretty sure they didn't, as a matter of fact.'

'Just this, I believe they'll come again. They know, or they soon will know, that Battle's in London. They'll take the risk and come again tonight.'

'Do you really think so?'

'It's a chance. Now we three will form a little syndicate.

Eversleigh and I will conceal ourselves with due precautions in the Council Chamber –'

'What about me?' interrupted Virginia. 'Don't think you're going to leave me out of it.'

'Listen to me, Virginia,' said Bill. 'This is men's work –'

'Don't be an idiot, Bill. I'm in on this. Don't you make any mistake about it. The syndicate will keep watch tonight.'

It was settled thus, and the details of the plan were laid. After the party had retired to bed, first one and then another of the syndicate crept down. They were all armed with powerful electric torches, and in the pocket of Anthony's coat lay a revolver.

Anthony had said that he believed another attempt to resume the search would be made. Nevertheless, he did not expect that the attempt would be made from outside. He believed that Virginia had been correct in her guess that someone had passed her in the dark the night before, and as he stood in the shadow of an old oak dresser it was towards the door and not the window that his eyes were directed. Virginia was crouching behind a figure in armour on the opposite wall, and Bill was by the window.

The minutes passed, at interminable length. One o'clock chimed, then the half-hour, then two, then half-hour. Anthony felt stiff and cramped. He was coming slowly to the conclusion that he had been wrong. No attempt would be made tonight.

And then he stiffened suddenly, all his senses on the alert. He had heard a footstep on the terrace outside. Silence again, and then a low scratching noise at the window. Suddenly it ceased, and the window swung open. A man stepped across the still into the room. He stood quite still for a moment, peering round as though listening. After a minute or two, seemingly satisfied, he switched on a torch he carried, and turned it rapidly round the room. Apparently he saw nothing unusual. The three watchers held their breath.

He went over to the same bit of panelled wall he had been examining the night before.

And then a terrible knowledge smote Bill. He was going to sneeze! The wild race through the dew-laden park the night before had given him a chill. All day he had sneezed intermittently. A sneeze was due now, and nothing on earth would stop it.

He adopted all the remedies he could think of. He pressed his upper lip, swallowed hard, threw back his head and looked at the ceiling. As a last resort he held his nose and pinched it violently. It was of no avail. He sneezed.

A stifled, checked, emasculated sneeze, but a startling sound in the deadly quiet of the room.

The stranger sprang round, and in the same minute, Anthony acted. He flashed on his torch, and jumped full for the stranger. In another minute they were down on the floor together.

'Lights,' shouted Anthony.

Virginia was ready at the switch. The lights came on true and full tonight. Anthony was on top of his man. Bill leant down to give him a hand.

'And now,' said Anthony, 'let's see who you are, my fine fellow.'

He rolled his victim over. It was the neat, dark-bearded stranger from the Cricketers.

'Very nice indeed,' said an approving voice.

They all looked up startled. The bulky form of Superintendent Battle was standing in the open doorway.

'I thought you were in London, Superintendent Battle,' said Anthony.

Battle's eyes twinkled.

'Did you sir?' he said. 'Well, I thought it would be a good thing if I was thought to be going.'

'And it has been,' agreed Anthony, looking down at his prostrate foe.

To his surprise there was a slight smile on the stranger's face.

'May I get up, gentlemen?' he inquired. 'You are three to one.'

Anthony kindly hauled him on to his legs. The stranger settled his coat, pulled up his collar, and directed a keen look at Battle.

'I demand pardon,' he said, 'but do I understand that you are a representative from Scotland Yard?'

'That's right,' said Battle.

'Then I will present to you my credentials.' He smiled rather ruefully. 'I would have been wise to do so before.'

He took some papers from his pocket and handed them to the

Scotland Yard detective. At the same time, he turned back the lapel of his coat and showed something pinned there.

Battle gave an exclamation of astonishment. He looked through the papers and handed them back with a little bow.

'I'm sorry you've been man-handled, monsieur,' he said, 'but you brought it on yourself, you know.'

He smiled, noting the astonished expression on the faces of the others.

'This is a colleague we have been expecting for some time,' he said. 'M. Lemoine, of the Sûreté in Paris.'

CHAPTER 19

SECRET HISTORY

They all stared at the French detective, who smiled back at them.

'But yes,' he said, 'it is true.'

There was a pause for a general readjusting of ideas. Then Virginia turned to Battle.

'Do you know what I think, Superintendent Battle?'

'What do you think, Mrs Revel?'

'I think the time has come to enlighten us a little.'

'To enlighten you? I don't quite understand, Mrs Revel.'

'Superintendent Battle, you understand perfectly. I dare say Mr Lomax has hedged you about with recommendations of secrecy – George would, but surely it's better to tell us than have us stumbling on the secret all by ourselves, and perhaps doing untold harm. M. Lemoine, don't you agree with me?'

'Madame, I agree with you entirely.'

'You can't go on keeping things dark for ever,' said Battle, 'I've told Mr Lomax so. Mr Eversleigh is Mr Lomax's secretary, there's no objection to his knowing what there is to know. As for Mr Cade, he's been brought into the thing willy-nilly, and I consider he's a right to know where he stands. But –'

Battle paused.

'I know,' said Virginia. 'Women are so indiscreet! I've often heard George say so.'

Lemoine had been studying Virginia attentively. Now he turned to the Scotland Yard man.

'Did I hear you just now address Madame by the name of Revel?'

'That is my name,' said Virginia.

'Your husband was in the Diplomatic Service, was he not? And you were with him in Herzoslovakia just before the assassination of the late King and Queen.'

'Yes.'

Lemoine turned again.

'I think Madame has a right to hear the story. She is indirectly concerned. Moreover' – his eyes twinkled a little – 'Madame's reputation for discretion stands very high in diplomatic circles.'

'I'm glad they give me a good character,' said Virginia, laughing. 'And I'm glad I'm not going to be left out of it.'

'What about refreshments?' said Anthony. 'Where does the conference take place? Here?'

'If you please, sir,' said Battle, 'I've a fancy for not leaving this room until morning. You'll see why when you've heard the story.'

'Then I'll go and forage,' said Anthony.

Bill went with him and they returned with a tray of glasses, siphons and other necessaries of life.

The augmented syndicate established itself comfortably in the corner by the window, being grouped round a long oak table.

'It's understood, of course,' said Battle, 'that anything that's said here is said in strict confidence. There must be no leakage. I've always felt it would come out one of these days. Gentlemen like Mr Lomax who want everything hushed up take bigger risks than they think. The start of this business was just over seven years ago. There was a lot of what they call reconstruction going on – especially in the Near East. There was a good deal going on in England, strictly on the QT, with that old gentleman, Count Stylptitch, pulling the strings. All the Balkan States were interested parties, and there were a lot of royal personages in England just then. I'm not going into details but Something disappeared – disappeared in a way that seemed incredible unless you admitted two things – that the thief was a royal personage and that at the same time it was the work of a high-class professional. M. Lemoine here will tell you how that well might be.'

The Frenchman bowed courteously and took up the tale.

'It is possible that you in England may not even have heard of our famous and fantastic King Victor. What his real name is, no one knows, but he is a man of singular courage and daring, one who speaks five languages and is unequalled in the art of disguise. Though his father is known to have been either English or Irish, he himself has worked chiefly in Paris. It was there, nearly eight years ago, that he was carrying out a daring series of robberies and living under the name of Captain O'Neill.'

A faint exclamation escaped Virginia. M. Lemoine darted a keen glance at her.

'I think I understand what agitates madame. You will see in a minute. Now we of the Sûreté had our suspicions that this Captain O'Neill was none other than "King Victor", but we could not obtain the necessary proof. There was also in Paris at the time a clever young actress, Angèle Mory, of the Folies Bergères. For some time we had suspected that she was associated with the operations of King Victor. But again no proof was forthcoming.

'About that time, Paris was preparing for the visit of the young King Nicholas IV of Herzoslovakia. At the Sûreté we were given special instructions as to the course to be adopted to ensure the safety of His Majesty. In particular we were warned to superintend the activities of a certain Revolutionary organization which called itself the Comrades of the Red Hand. It is fairly certain now that the Comrades approached Angèle Mory and offered her a huge sum if she would aid them in their plans. Her part was to infatuate the young King, and decoy him to some spot agreed upon with them. Angèle Mory accepted the bribe and promised to perform her part.

'But the young lady was cleverer and more ambitious than her employers suspected. She succeeded in captivating the King, who fell desperately in love with her and loaded her with jewels. It was then that she conceived the idea of being – not a King's mistress, but a Queen! As everyone knows, she realized her ambition. She was introduced into Herzoslovakia as the Countess Varaga Popoleffsky, an offshoot of the Romanoffs, and became eventually Queen Veraga of Herzoslovakia. Not bad for a little Parisian actress! I have always heard that she played the part extremely well. But her triumph was not to be long-lived. The Comrades of the Red Hand, furious at her betrayal, twice attempted her life. Finally they worked up the country to such a pitch that a revolution broke out in which both the King and Queen perished. Their bodies, horribly mutilated and hardly recognizable, were recovered, attesting to the fury of the populace against the low-born foreign Queen.

'Now, in all this, it seems certain that Queen Varaga still kept in with her confederate, King Victor. It is possible that the bold plan was his all along. What is known is that she continued to correspond with him, in a secret code, from the Court of Herzoslovakia. For safety the letters were written in English, and signed with the name of an English lady then at the Embassy. If any inquiry had been made, and the lady in question had denied her signature, it is possible that she would not have been believed, for the letters were those of a guilty woman to her lover. It was your name she used, Mrs Revel.'

'I know,' said Virginia. Her colour was coming and going unevenly. 'So that is the truth of the letters! I have wondered and wondered.'

'What a blackguardly trick,' cried Bill indignantly.

'The letters were addressed to Captain O'Neill at his rooms in Paris, and their principal purpose may have light shed upon it by a curious fact which came to light later. After the assassination of the King and Queen, many of the crown jewels which had fallen, of course, into the hands of the mob, found their way to Paris, and it was discovered that in nine cases out of ten the principal stones had been replaced by paste – and mind you, there were some very famous stones among the jewels of Herzoslovakia. So as a Queen, Angèle Mory still practised her former activities.

'You see now where we have arrived. Nicholas IV and Queen Varaga came to England and were the guests of the late Marquis of Caterham, then Secretary of State for Foreign Affairs. Herzoslovakia is a small country, but it could not be left out. Queen Varaga was necessarily received. And there we have a royal personage and at the same time an expert thief. There is also no doubt that the – er – substitute which was so wonderful as to deceive anyone but an expert could only have been fashioned by

King Victor, and indeed the whole plan, in its daring and audacity, pointed to him as the author.'

'What happened?' asked Virginia.

'Hushed up,' said Superintendent Battle laconically. 'Not a mention of it's ever been made public to this day. We did all that could be done on the quiet – and that was a good deal more than you'd ever imagine, by the way. We've got methods of our own that would surprise. That jewel didn't leave England with the Queen of Herzoslovakia – I can tell you that much. No, Her Majesty hid it somewhere – but where we've never been able to discover. But I shouldn't wonder' – Superintendent Battle let his eyes wander gently round – 'if it wasn't somewhere in this room.'

Anthony leapt to his feet.

'What? After all these years?' he cried incredulously. 'Impossible.'

'You do not know the peculiar circumstances, monsieur,' said the Frenchman quickly. 'Only a fortnight later, the revolution in Herzoslovakia broke out, and the King and Queen were murdered. Also, Captain O'Neill was arrested in Paris and sentenced on a minor charge. We hoped to find the packet of code letters in his house, but it appears that this had been stolen by some Herzoslovakian go-between. The man turned up in Herzoslovakia just before the revolution, and then disappeared completely.'

'He probably went abroad,' said Anthony thoughtfully. 'To Africa as likely as not. And you bet he hung on to that packet. It was as good as a gold mine to him. It's odd how things come about. They probably called him Dutch Pedro or something like that out there.'

He caught Superintendent Battle's expressionless glance bent upon him, and smiled.

'It's not really clairvoyance, Battle,' he said, 'though it sounds like it. I'll tell you presently.'

'There is one thing that you have not explained,' said Virginia. 'Where does this link up with the memoirs? There must be a link, surely?'

'Madame is very quick,' said Lemoine approvingly. 'Yes, there is a link. Count Stylptitch was also staying at Chimneys at the time.'

'So that he might have known about it?'

'*Parfaitement.*'

'And, of course,' said Battle, 'if he's blurted it out in his precious memoirs, the fat will be in the fire. Especially after the way the whole thing was hushed up.'

Anthony lit a cigarette.

'There's no possibility of there being a clue in the memoirs as to where the stone was hidden?' he asked.

'Very unlikely,' said Battle decisively. 'He was never in with the Queen – opposed the marriage tooth and nail. She's not likely to have taken him into her confidence.'

'I wasn't suggesting such a thing for a minute,' said Anthony. 'But by all accounts he was a cunning old boy. Unknown to her, he may have discovered where she hid the jewel. In that case, what would he have done, do you think?'

'Sat tight,' said Battle, after a moment's reflection.

'I agree,' said the Frenchman. 'It was a ticklish moment, you see. To return the stone anonymously would have presented great difficulties. Also, the knowledge of its whereabouts would give him great power – and he liked power, that strange old man. Not only did he hold the Queen in the hollow of his hand, but he had a powerful weapon to negotiate with at any time. It was not the only secret he possessed – oh, no! – he collected secrets like some men collect rare pieces of china. It is said that, once or twice before his death, he boasted to people of the things he could make public if the fancy took him. And once at least he declared that he intended to make some startling revelations in his memoirs. Hence' – the Frenchman smiled rather dryly – 'the general anxiety to get hold of them. Our own secret police intended to seize them, but the Count took the precaution to have them conveyed away before his death.'

'Still, there's no real reason to believe that he knew this particular secret,' said Battle.

'I beg your pardon,' said Anthony quietly. 'There are his own words.'

'What?'

Both detectives stared at him as though unable to believe their ears.

'When Mr McGrath gave me that manuscript to bring to

England, he told me the circumstances of his one meeting with Count Stylptitch. It was in Paris. At some considerable risk to himself. Mr McGrath rescued the Count from a band of Apaches. He was, I understand – shall we say a trifle – exhilarated? Being in that condition, he made two rather interesting remarks. One of them was to the effect that he knew where the Koh-i-noor was – a statement to which my friend paid very little attention. He also said that the gang in question were King Victor's men. Taken together, those two remarks are very significant.'

'Good lord,' ejaculated Superintendent Battle. 'I should say they were. Even the murder of Prince Michael wears a different aspect.'

'King Victor has never taken a life,' the Frenchman reminded him.

'Supposing he were surprised when he was searching for the jewel?'

'Is he in England, then?' asked Anthony sharply. 'You say that he was released a few months ago. Didn't you keep track of him?'

A rather rueful smile overspread the French detective's face.

'We tried to, monsieur. But he is a devil, that man. He gave us the slip at once – at once. We thought, of course, that he would make straight for England. But no. He went – where do you think?'

'Where?' said Anthony.

He was staring intently at the Frenchman, and absent-mindedly his fingers played with a box of matches.

'To America. To the United States.'

'What?'

There was sheer amazement in Anthony's tone.

'Yes, and what do you think he called himself? What part do you think he played over there? The part of Prince Nicholas of Herzoslovakia.'

The matchbox fell from Anthony's hand, but his amazement was fully equalled by that of Battle.

'Impossible.'

'Not so, my friend. You, too, will get the news in the morning. It has been the most colossal bluff. As you know, Prince Nicholas was rumoured to have died in the Congo years ago. Our friend,

King Victor, seizes on that – difficult to prove a death of that kind. He resurrects Prince Nicholas, and plays him to such purpose that he gets away with a tremendous haul of American dollars – all on account of the supposed oil concessions. But by a mere accident, he was unmasked, and had to leave the country hurriedly. This time he did come to England. And that is why I am here. Sooner or later he will come to Chimneys. That is, if he is not already here!'

'You think – that?'

'I think he was here the night Prince Michael died, and again last night.'

'It was another attempt, eh?' said Battle.

'It was another attempt.'

'What has bothered me,' continued Battle, 'was wondering what had become of M. Lemoine here. I'd had word from Paris that he was on his way over to work with me, and couldn't make out why he hadn't turned up.'

'I must indeed apologize,' said Lemoine. 'You see, I arrived on the morning after the murder. It occurred to me at once that it would be as well for me to study things from an unofficial standpoint without appearing officially as your colleague. I thought that great possibilities lay that way. I was, of course, aware that I was bound to be an object of suspicion, but that in a way furthered my plan since it would not put the people I was after on their guard. I can assure you that I have seen a good deal that is interesting on the last two days.'

'But look here,' said Bill, 'what really did happen last night?'

'I am afraid,' said M. Lemoine, 'that I gave you rather violent exercise.'

'It was you I chased, then?'

'Yes. I will recount things to you. I came up here to watch, convinced that the secret had to do with this room since the Prince had been killed here. I stood outside on the terrace. Presently I became aware that someone was moving about in this room. I could see the flash of a torch now and again. I tried the middle window and found it unlatched. Whether the man had entered that way earlier, or whether he had left it so as a blind in case he was disturbed, I do not know. Very gently, I pushed it back and slipped inside the room. Step by step I felt my way until I was in a spot where I could watch operations without likelihood of being discovered myself. The man himself I could not see clearly. His back was to me, of course, and he was silhouetted against the light of the torch so that his outline only could be seen. But his actions filled me with surprise. He took to pieces first one and then the other of those two suits of armour, examining each one piece by piece. When he had convinced himself that what he sought was not there, he began tapping the panelling of the wall under that picture. What he would have done next, I do not know. The interruption came. *You* burst in –' He looked at Bill.

'Our well-meant interference was really rather a pity,' said Virginia thoughtfully.

'In a sense, madame, it was. The man switched out his torch, and I, who had no wish as yet to be forced to reveal my identity, sprang for the window. I collided with the other two in the dark, and fell headlong. I sprang up and out through the window. Mr Eversleigh, taking me for his assailant, followed.'

'I followed you first,' said Virginia. 'Bill was only second in the race.'

'And the other fellow had the sense to stay still and sneak out through the door. I wonder he didn't meet the rescuing crowd.'

'That would present no difficulties,' said Lemoine. 'He would be a rescuer in advance of the rest, that was all.'

'Do you really think this Arsène Lupin fellow is actually among the household now?' asked Bill, his eyes sparkling.

'Why not?' said Lemoine. 'He could pass perfectly as a servant. For all we may know, he may be Boris Anchoukoff, the trusted servant of the late Prince Michael.'

'He is an odd-looking bloke,' agreed Bill.

But Anthony was smiling.

'That's hardly worthy of you, M. Lemoine,' he said gently.

The Frenchman smiled too.

'You've taken him on as your valet now, haven't you, Mr Cade?' asked Superintendent Battle.

'Battle, I take off my hat to you. You know everything. But just as a matter of detail, he's taken me on, not I him.'

'Why was that, I wonder, Mr Cade?'

'I don't know,' said Anthony lightly. 'It's a curious taste, but perhaps he may have liked my face. Or he may think I murdered his master and wish to establish himself in a handy position for executing revenge upon me.'

He rose and went over to the windows, pulling the curtains.

'Daylight,' he said, with a slight yawn. 'There won't be any more excitements now.'

Lemoine rose also.

'I will leave you,' he said. 'We shall perhaps meet again later in the day.'

With a graceful bow to Virginia, he stepped out of the window.

'Bed,' said Virginia, yawning. 'It's all been very exciting. Come on, Bill, go to bed like a good little boy. The breakfast-table will see us not, I fear.'

Anthony stayed at the window looking after the retreating form of M. Lemoine.

'You wouldn't think it,' said Battle behind him, 'but that's supposed to be the cleverest detective in France.'

'I don't know that I wouldn't,' said Anthony thoughtfully. 'I rather think I would.'

'Well,' said Battle, 'he was right about the excitements of this night being over. By the way, do you remember my telling you about that man they'd found shot near Staines?'

'Yes. Why?'

'Nothing. They've identified him, that's all. It seems he was called Giuseppe Manuelli. He was a waiter at the Blitz in London. Curious, isn't it?'

CHAPTER 20

BATTLE AND ANTHONY CONFER

Anthony said nothing. He continued to stare out of the window. Superintendent Battle looked for some time at his motionless back.

'Well, goodnight, sir,' he said at last, and moved to the door.

Anthony stirred.

'Wait a minute, Battle.'

The superintendent halted obediently. Anthony left the window. He drew out a cigarette from his case and lighted it.

Then, between two puffs of smoke, he said:

'You seem very interested in this business at Staines?'

'I wouldn't go as far as that, sir. It's unusual, that's all.'

'Do you think the man was shot where he was found, or do you think he was killed elsewhere and the body brought to that particular spot afterwards?'

'I think he was shot somewhere else, and the body brought there in a car.'

'I think so too,' said Anthony.

Something in the emphasis of his tone made the detective look up sharply.

'Any ideas of your own, sir? Do you know who brought him there?'

'Yes,' said Anthony. 'I did.'

He was a little annoyed at the absolutely unruffled calm preserved by the other.

'I must say you take these shocks very well, Battle,' he remarked.

'"Never display emotion." That was a rule that was given to me once, and I've found it very useful.'

'You live up to it, certainly,' said Anthony. 'I can't say I've ever seen you ruffled. Well, do you want to hear the whole story?'

'If you please, Mr Cade.'

Anthony pulled up two of the chairs, both men sat down, and Anthony recounted the events of the preceding Thursday night.

Battle listened immovably. There was a far-off twinkle in his eyes as Anthony finished.

'You know, sir,' he said, 'you'll get into trouble one of these days.'

'Then, for the second time, I'm not to be taken into custody?'

'We always like to give a man plenty of rope,' said Superintendent Battle.

'Very delicately put,' said Anthony. 'Without unduly stressing the end of the proverb.'

'What I can't make out, sir,' said Battle, 'is why you decided to come across with this now?'

'It's rather difficult to explain,' said Anthony. 'You see, Battle, I've come to have really a very high opinion of your abilities. When the moment comes, you're always there. Look at tonight. And it occurred to me that, in withholding this knowledge of mine, I was seriously cramping your style. You deserve to have access to all the facts. I've done what I could, and up to now I've made a mess of things. Until tonight, I couldn't speak for Mrs Revel's sake. But now that those letters have been definitely proved to have nothing whatever to do with her, any idea of her complicity becomes absurd. Perhaps I advised her badly in the first place, but it struck me that her statement of having paid this man money to suppress the letters, simply as a whim, might take a bit of believing.'

'It might, by a jury,' agreed Battle. 'Juries never have any imagination.'

'But you accept it quite easily?' said Anthony, looking curiously at him.

'Well, you see, Mr Cade, most of my work has lain amongst these people. What they call the upper classes, I mean. You see, the majority of people are always wondering what the neighbours will think. But tramps and aristocrats don't – they just do the first thing that comes into their heads, and they don't bother to think what anyone thinks of them. I'm not meaning just the idle rich, the people who give big parties, and so on. I mean those that have had it born and bred in them for generations that nobody else's opinion counts but their own. I've always found the upper classes the same – fearless, truthful, and sometimes extraordinarily foolish.'

'This is a very interesting lecture, Battle. I suppose you'll be writing your reminiscences one of these days. They ought to be worth reading too.'

The detective acknowledged the suggestion with a smile, but said nothing.

'I'd like rather to ask you one question,' continued Anthony. 'Did you connect me at all with the Staines affair? I fancied, from your manner, that you did.'

'Quite right. I had a hunch that way. But nothing definite to go upon. Your manner was very good, if I may say so, Mr Cade. You never overdid the carelessness.'

'I'm glad of that,' said Anthony. 'I've a feeling that ever since I met you you've been laying little traps for me. On the whole I've managed to avoid falling into them, but the strain has been acute.'

Battle smiled grimly.

'That's how you get a crook in the end, sir. Keep him on the run, to and fro, turning and twisting. Sooner or later, his nerve goes, and you've got him.'

'You're a cheerful fellow, Battle. When will you get me, I wonder?'

'Plenty of rope, sir,' quoted the superintendent, 'plenty of rope.'

'In the meantime,' said Anthony. 'I am still the amateur assistant?'

'That's it, Mr Cade.'

'Watson to your Sherlock, in fact?'

'Detective stories are mostly bunkum,' said Battle unemotionally. 'But they amuse people,' he added, as an afterthought. 'And they're useful sometimes.'

'In what way?' asked Anthony curiously.

'They encourage the universal idea that the police are stupid. When we get an amateur crime, such as a murder, that's very useful indeed.'

Anthony looked at him for some minutes in silence. Battle sat quite still, blinking now and then, with no expression whatsoever on his square placid face. Presently he rose.

'Not much good going to bed now,' he observed. 'As soon as he's up, I want to have a few words with his lordship. Anyone who wants to leave the house can do so now. At the same time I should be much obliged to his lordship if he'll extend an informal invitation to his guests to stay on. You'll accept it, sir, if you please, and Mrs Revel also.'

'Have you ever found the revolver?' asked Anthony suddenly.

'You mean the one Prince Michael was shot with? No, I haven't. Yet it must be in the house or grounds. I'll take a hint from you, Mr Cade, and send some boys up bird's-nesting. If I could get hold of the revolver, we might get forward a bit. That, and the bundle of letters. You say that a letter with the heading "Chimneys" was amongst them? Depend upon it that was the last one written. The instructions for finding the diamond are written in code in that letter.'

'What's your theory of the killing of Giuseppe?' asked Anthony.

'I should say he was a regular thief, and that he was got hold of, either by King Victor or by the Comrades of the Red Hand, and employed by them. I shouldn't wonder at all if the Comrades and King Victor aren't working together. The organization has plenty of money and power, but it isn't very strong in brains. Giuseppe's task was to steal the memoirs – they couldn't have known that you had the letters – it's a very odd coincidence that you should have, by the way.'

'I know,' said Anthony. 'It's amazing when you come to think of it.'

'Giuseppe gets hold of the letters instead. Is at first vastly chagrined. Then sees the cutting from the paper and has the brilliant idea of turning them to account on his own by blackmailing the lady. He has, of course, no idea of their real significance. The Comrades find out what he is doing, believe that he is deliberately double-crossing them, and decree his death. They're very fond of executing traitors. It has a picturesque element which seems to appeal to them. What I can't quite make out is the revolver with "Virginia" engraved upon it. There's too much finesse about that for the Comrades. As a rule, they enjoy plastering their Red Hand sign about – in order to strike terror into other would-be traitors. No, it looks to me as though King Victor had stepped in there. But what his motive was, I don't know. It looks like a very deliberate attempt to saddle Mrs Revel with the murder, and, on the surface, there doesn't seem any particular point in that.'

'I had a theory,' said Anthony. 'But it didn't work out according to plan.'

He told Battle of Virginia's recognition of Michael. Battle nodded his head.

'Oh, yes, no doubt as to his identity. By the way, that old Baron has a very high opinion of you. He speaks of you in most enthusiastic terms.'

'That's very kind of him,' said Anthony. 'Especially as I've given him full warning that I mean to do my utmost to get hold of the missing memoirs before Wednesday next.'

'You'll have a job to do that,' said Battle.

'Y-es. You think so? I suppose King Victor and Co. have got the letters.'

Battle nodded.

'Pinched them off Giuseppe that day in Pont Street. Prettily planned piece of work, that. Yes, they've got 'em all right, and they've decoded them, and they know where to look.'

Both men were on the point of passing out of the room.

'In here?' said Anthony, jerking his head back.

'Exactly, in here. But they haven't found the prize yet, and they're going to run a pretty risk trying to get it.'

'I suppose,' said Anthony, 'that you've got a plan in that subtle head of yours?'

Battle returned no answer. He looked particularly stolid and unintelligent. Then, very slowly, he winked.

'Want my help?' asked Anthony.

'I do. And I shall want someone else's.'

'Who is that?'

'Mrs Revel's. You may have noticed it, Mr Cade, but she's a lady who has a particularly beguiling way with her.'

'I've noticed it all right,' said Anthony.

He glanced at his watch.

'I'm inclined to agree with you about bed, Battle. A dip in the lake and a hearty breakfast will be far more to the point.'

He ran lightly upstairs to his bedroom. Whistling to himself, he discarded, his evening clothes, and picked up a dressing-gown and a bath towel.

Then suddenly he stopped dead in front of the dressing-table, staring at the object that reposed demurely in front of the looking-glass.

For a moment he could not believe his eyes. He took it up, examined it closely. Yes, there was no mistake.

It was the bundle of letters signed Virginia Revel. They were intact. Not one missing.

Anthony dropped into a chair, the letters in his hand.

'My brain must be cracking,' he murmured. 'I can't understand a quarter of what is going on in this house. Why should the letters reappear like a damned conjuring trick? Who put them on my dressing-table? Why?'

And to all these very pertinent questions he could find no satisfactory reply.

CHAPTER 21

MR ISAACSTEIN'S SUIT-CASE

At ten o'clock that morning, Lord Caterham and his daughter were breakfasting. Bundle was looking very thoughtful.

'Father,' she said at last.

Lord Caterham, absorbed in *The Times*, did not reply.

'Father,' said Bundle again, more sharply.

Lord Caterham, torn from his interested perusal of forthcoming sales of rare books, looked up absent-mindedly.

'Eh?' he said. 'Did you speak?'

'Yes. Who is it who's had breakfast?'

She nodded towards a place that had evidently been occupied. The rest were all expectant.

'Oh, what's-his-name.'

'Fat Iky?'

Bundle and her father had enough sympathy between them to comprehend each other's somewhat misleading observations.

'That's it.'

'Did I see you talking to the detective this morning before breakfast?'

Lord Caterham sighed.

'Yes, he buttonholed me in the hall. I do think the hours before breakfast should be sacred. I shall have to go abroad. The strain on my nerves –'

Bundle interrupted unceremoniously.

'What did he say?'

'Said everyone who wanted to could clear out.'

'Well,' said Bundle, 'that's all right. That's what you've been wanting.'

'I know. But he didn't leave it at that. He went on to say that nevertheless he wanted me to ask everyone to stay on.'

'I don't understand,' said Bundle, wrinkling her nose.

'So confusing and contradictory,' complained Lord Caterham. 'And before breakfast too.'

'What did you say?'

'Oh, I agreed, of course. It's never any good arguing with these people. Especially before breakfast,' continued Lord Caterham, reverting to his principal grievance.

'Who have you asked so far?'

'Cade. He was up very early this morning. He's going to stop on. I don't mind that. I can't quite make the fellow out; but I like him – I like him very much.'

'So does Virginia,' said Bundle, drawing a pattern on the table with her fork.

'Eh?'

'And so do I. But that doesn't seem to matter.'

'And I asked Isaacstein,' continued Lord Caterham.

'Well?'

'But fortunately he's got to go back to town. Don't forget to order the car for the 10.50, by the way.'

'All right.'

'Now if I can only get rid of Fish too,' continued Lord Caterham, his spirits rising.

'I thought you liked talking to him about your mouldy old books.'

'So I do, so I do. So I did, rather. But it gets monotonous when one finds that one is always doing all the talking. Fish is very interested, but he never volunteers any statements of his own.'

'It's better than doing all the listening,' said Bundle. 'Like one does with George Lomax.'

Lord Caterham shuddered at the remembrance.

'George is all very well on platforms,' said Bundle. 'I've clapped him myself, though of course I know all the time that he's talking balderdash. And anyway, I'm a Socialist –'

'I know, my dear, I know,' said Lord Caterham hastily.

'It's all right,' said Bundle. 'I'm not going to bring politics into the home. That's what George does – public speaking in private life. It ought to be abolished by Act of Parliament.'

'Quite so,' said Lord Caterham.

'What about Virginia?' asked Bundle. 'Is she to be asked to stop on?'

'Battle said everybody.'

'Says he firmly! Have you asked her to be my stepma yet?'

'I don't think it would be any good,' said Lord Caterham mournfully. 'Although she did call me a darling last night. But that's the worst of these attractive young women with affectionate dispositions. They'll say anything, and they mean absolutely nothing by it.'

'No,' agreed Bundle. 'It would have been much more hopeful if she'd thrown a boot at you or tried to bite you.'

'You modern young people seem to have such unpleasant ideas about love-making,' said Lord Caterham plaintively.

'It comes from reading *The Sheik*,' said Bundle. 'Desert love. Throw her about, etc.'

'What is *The Sheik*?' asked Lord Caterham simply. 'Is it a poem?'

Bundle looked at him with commiserating pity. Then she rose and kissed the top of his head.

'Dear old Daddy,' she remarked, and sprang lightly out of the window.

Lord Caterham went back to the salerooms.

He jumped when addressed suddenly by Mr Hiram Fish, who had made his usual noiseless entry.

'Good morning, Lord Caterham.'

'Oh, good morning,' said Lord Caterham. 'Good morning. Nice day.'

'The weather is delightful,' said Mr Fish.

He helped himself to coffee. By way of food, he took a piece of dry toast.

'Do I hear correctly that the embargo is removed?' he asked after a minute or two. 'That we are all free to depart?'

'Yes – er – yes,' said Lord Caterham 'As a matter of fact, I hoped, I mean, that I shall be delighted' – his conscience drove him on – 'only too delighted if you will stay on for a little.'

'Why, Lord Caterham –'

'It's been a beastly visit, I know,' Lord Caterham hurried on. 'Too bad. Shan't blame you for wanting to run away.'

'You misjudge me, Lord Caterham. The associations have been painful, no one could deny that point. But the English country life, as lived in the mansions of the great, has a powerful attraction for me. I am interested in the study of those conditions. It is a thing we lack completely in America. I shall be only too delighted to accept your vurry kind invitation and stay on.'

'Oh, well,' said Lord Caterham, 'that's that. Absolutely delighted, my dear fellow, absolutely delighted.'

Spurring himself on to a false geniality of manner, Lord Caterham murmured something about having to see his bailiff and escaped from the room.

In the hall, he saw Virginia just descending the staircase.

'Shall I take you in to breakfast?' asked Lord Caterham tenderly.

'I've had it in bed, thank you, I was frightfully sleepy this morning.'

She yawned.

'Had a bad night, perhaps?'

'Not exactly a bad night. From one point of view decidedly a good night. Oh, Lord Caterham' – she slipped her hand inside his arm and gave it a squeeze – 'I *am* enjoying myself. You were a darling to ask me down.'

'You'll stop on for a bit then, won't you? Battle is lifting the – the embargo, but I want you to stay particularly. So does Bundle.'

'Of course I'll stay. It's sweet of you to ask me.'

'Ah!' said Lord Caterham.

He sighed.

'What is your secret sorrow?' asked Virginia. 'Has anyone bitten you?'

'That's just it,' said Lord Caterham mournfully.

Virginia looked puzzled.

'You don't feel, by any chance, that you want to throw a boot at me? No, I can see you don't. Oh, well, it's of no consequence.'

Lord Caterham drifted sadly away, and Virginia passed out through a side door into the garden.

She stood there for a moment, breathing in the crisp October air which was infinitely refreshing to one in her slightly jaded state.

She started a little to find Superintendent Battle at her elbow. The man seemed to have an extraordinary knack of appearing out of space without the least warning.

'Good morning, Mrs Revel. Not too tired, I hope?'

Virginia shook her head.

'It was a most exciting night,' she said. 'Well worth the loss of a little sleep. The only thing is, today seems a trifle dull after it.'

'There's a nice shady place down under that cedar tree,' remarked the superintendent. 'Shall I take a chair down to it for you?'

'If you think it's the best thing for me to do,' said Virginia solemnly.

'You're very quick, Mrs Revel. Yes, it's quite true, I do want a word with you.'

He picked up a long wicker chair and carried it down the lawn. Virginia followed him with a cushion under her arm.

'Very dangerous place, that terrace,' remarked the detective. 'That is, if you want to have a private conversation.'

'I'm getting excited again, Superintendent Battle.'

'Oh, it's nothing important.' He took out a big watch and glanced at it. 'Half-past ten. I'm starting for Wyvern Abbey in ten minutes to report to Mr Lomax. Plenty of time. I only wanted to know if you could tell me a little more about Mr Cade.'

'About Mr Cade?'

Virginia was startled.

'Yes, where you first met him, and how long you've known him and so forth.'

Battle's manner was easy and pleasant enough. He even refrained from looking at her and the fact that he did so made her vaguely uneasy.

'It's more difficult than you think,' she said at last. 'He did me a great service once –'

Battle interrupted her.

'Before you go any further, Mrs Revel, I'd just like to say something. Last night, after you and Mr Eversleigh had gone to bed, Mr Cade told me all about the letters and the man who was killed in your house.'

'He did?' gasped Virginia.

'Yes, and very wisely too. It clears up a lot of misunderstanding. There's only one thing he didn't tell me – how long he had known you. Now I've a little idea of my own about that. You shall tell me if I'm right or wrong. I think that the day he came to your house in Pont Street was the first time you had ever seen him. Ah! I see I'm right. It was so.'

Virginia said nothing. For the first time she felt afraid of this stolid man with the expressionless face. She understood what Anthony had meant when he said there were no flies on Superintendent Battle.

'Has he ever told you anything about his life?' the detective continued. 'Before he was in South Africa, I mean. Canada? Or before that, the Sudan? Or about his boyhood?'

Virginia merely shook her head.

'And yet I'd bet he's got something worth telling. You can't mistake the face of a man who's led a life of daring and adventure. He could tell you some interesting tales if he cared to.'

'If you want to know about his past life, why don't you cable to that friend of his, Mr McGrath?' Virginia asked.

'Oh, we have. But it seems he's up-country somewhere. Still, there's no doubt Mr Cade was in Bulawayo when he said he was. But I wondered what he'd been doing before he came to South Africa. He'd only had that job with Castle's about a month.' He took out his watch again. 'I must be off. The car will be waiting.'

Virginia watched him retreat to the house. But she did not move from her chair. She hoped that Anthony might appear and join her. Instead came Bill Eversleigh, with a prodigious yawn.

'Thank God, I've got a chance to speak to you at last, Virginia,' he complained.

'Well, speak to me very gently, Bill darling, or I shall burst into tears.'

'Has someone been bullying you?'

'Not exactly bullying me. Getting inside my mind and turning it inside out. I feel as though I'd been jumped on by an elephant.'

'Not Battle?'

'Yes, Battle. He's a terrible man really.'

'Well, never mind Battle. I say, Virginia, I do love you so awfully –'

'Not this morning, Bill. I'm not strong enough. Anyway, I've always told you the best people don't propose before lunch.'

'Good Lord,' said Bill. 'I could propose to you before breakfast.'

Virginia shuddered.

'Bill, be sensible and intelligent for a minute. I want to ask your advice.'

'If you'd once make up your mind to it, and say you'd marry me, you'd feel miles better, I'm sure. Happier, you know, and more settled down.'

'Listen to me, Bill. Proposing to me is your *idée fixe*. All men propose when they're bored and can't think of anything to say. Remember my age and my widowed state, and go and make love to a pure young girl.'

'My darling Virginia – Oh, blast! Here's that French idiot bearing down on us.'

It was indeed M. Lemoine, black-bearded and correct of demeanour as ever.

'Good morning, madame. You are not fatigued, I trust?'

'Not in the least.'

'That is excellent. Good morning, Mr Eversleigh.'

'How would it be if we promenaded ourselves a little, the three of us?' suggested the Frenchman.

'How about it, Bill?' said Virginia.

'Oh, all right,' said the unwilling young gentleman by her side.

He heaved himself up from the grass, and the three of them walked slowly along, Virginia between the two men. She was sensible at once of a strange undercurrent of excitement in the Frenchman, though she had no clue as to what caused it.

Soon, with her usual skill, she was putting him at his ease, asking him questions, listening to his answers, and gradually drawing him out. Presently he was telling them anecdotes of the famous King Victor. He talked well, albeit with a certain bitterness as he described the various ways in which the detective bureau had been outwitted.

But all the time, despite the real absorption of Lemoine in his own narrative, Virginia had a feeling that he had some other object in view. Moreover, she judged that Lemoine, under cover of his story, was deliberately striking out his own course across the park. They were not just strolling idly. He was deliberately guiding them in a certain direction.

Suddenly, he broke off his story and looked round. They were standing just where the drive intersected the park before turning an abrupt corner by a clump of trees. Lemoine was staring at a vehicle approaching them from the direction of the house.

Virginia's eyes followed his.

'It's the luggage cart,' she said, 'taking Isaacstein's luggage and his valet to the station.'

'Is that so?' said Lemoine. He glanced down at his own watch and started. 'A thousand pardons. I have been longer here than I meant – such charming company. Is it possible, do you think, that I might have a lift to the village?'

He stepped out on to the drive and signalled with his arm. The luggage cart stopped, and after a word or two of explanation Lemoine climbed in behind. He raised his hat politely to Virginia, and drove off.

The other two stood and watched the cart disappearing with puzzled expressions. Just as the cart swung round the bend, a suitcase fell off into the drive. The cart went on.

'Come on,' said Virginia to Bill. 'We're going to see something interesting. That suitcase was thrown out.'

'Nobody's noticed it,' said Bill.

They ran down the drive towards the fallen piece of luggage. Just as they reached it, Lemoine came round the corner of the bend on foot. He was hot from walking fast.

'I was obliged to descend,' he said pleasantly. 'I found that I had left something behind.'

'This?' said Bill, indicating the suitcase.

It was a handsome case of heavy pigskin, with the initials H. I. on it.

'What a pity!' said Lemoine gently. 'It must have fallen out. Shall we lift it from the road?'

Without waiting for a reply, he picked up the suitcase, and carried it over to the belt of trees. He stooped over it, something flashed in his hand, and the lock slipped back.

He spoke, and his voice was totally different, quick and commanding.

'The car will be here in a minute,' he said. 'Is it in sight?'

Virginia looked back towards the house.

'No.'

'Good.'

With deft fingers he tossed the things out of the suitcase. Gold-topped bottle, silk pyjamas, a variety of socks. Suddenly his whole figure stiffened. He caught up what appeared to be a bundle of silk underwear, and unrolled it rapidly.

A slight exclamation broke from Bill. In the centre of the bundle was a heavy revolver.

'I hear the horn,' said Virginia.

Like lightning, Lemoine repacked the suitcase. The revolver he wrapped in a silk handkerchief of his own, and slipped into his pocket. He snapped the locks of the suitcase, and turned quickly to Bill.

'Take it. Madame will be with you. Stop the car, and explain that it fell off the luggage cart. Do not mention me.'

Bill stepped quickly down to the drive just as the big Lanchester limousine with Isaacstein inside it came round the corner. The chauffeur slowed down, and Bill swung the suitcase up to him.

'Fell off the luggage cart,' he explained. 'We happened to see it.'

He caught a momentary glimpse of a startled yellow face as the financier stared at him, and then the car swept on again.

They went back to Lemoine. He was standing with the revolver in his hand, and a look of gloating satisfaction in his face.

'A long shot,' he said. 'A very long shot. But it came off.'

CHAPTER 22

THE RED SIGNAL

Superintendent Battle was standing in the library at Wyvern Abbey.

George Lomax, seated before a desk overflowing with papers, was frowning portentously.

Superintendent Battle had opened proceedings by making a brief and business-like report. Since then, the conversation had lain almost entirely with George, and Battle had contented himself with making brief and usually monosyllabic replies to the other's questions.

On the desk, in front of George, was the packet of letters Anthony had found on his dressing-table.

'I can't understand it at all,' said George irritably, as he picked up the packet. 'They're in code, you say?'

'Just so, Mr Lomax.'

'And where does he say he found them – on his dressing-table?'

Battle repeated, word for word, Anthony Cade's account of how he had come to regain possession of the letters.

'And he brought them at once to you? That was quite proper – quite proper. But who could have placed them in his room?'

Battle shook his head.

'That's the sort of thing you ought to know,' complained George. 'It sounds to me very fishy – very fishy indeed. What do we know about this man Cade, anyway? He appears in a most mysterious manner – under highly suspicious circumstances – and we know nothing whatever about him. I may say that I, personally, don't care for his manner at all. You've made inquiries about him, I suppose?'

Superintendent Battle permitted himself a patient smile.

'We wired at once to South Africa, and his story has been confirmed on all points. He was in Bulawayo with Mr McGrath at the time he stated. Previous to their meeting, he was employed by Messrs Castle, the tourist agents.'

'Just what I should have expected,' said George. 'He has the kind of cheap assurance that succeeds in a certain type of employment. But about these letters – steps must be taken at once – at once –'

The great man puffed himself out and swelled importantly.

Superintendent Battle opened his mouth, but George forestalled him.

'There must be no delay. These letters must be decoded without any loss of time. Let me see, who is the man? There is a man – connected with the British Museum. Knows all there is to know about ciphers. Ran the department for us during the war. Where is Miss Oscar? She will know. Name something like Win – Win –'

'Professor Wynwood,' said Battle.

'Exactly. I remember perfectly now. He must be wired to immediately.'

'I have done so, Mr Lomax, an hour ago. He will arrive by the 12.10.'

'Oh, very good, very good. Thank heaven, something is off my mind. I shall have to be in town today. You can get along without me, I suppose?'

'I think so, sir.'

'Well, do your best, Battle, do your best. I am terribly rushed just at present.'

'Just so, sir.'

'By the way, why did not Mr Eversleigh come over with you?'

'He was still asleep, sir. We've been up all night, as I told you.'

'Oh, quite so. I am frequently up nearly the whole night myself. To do the work of thirty-six hours in twenty-four, that is my constant task! Send Mr Eversleigh over at once when you get back, will you, Battle?'

'I will give him your message, sir.'

'Thank you, Battle. I realize perfectly that you had to repose a certain amount of confidence in him. But do you think it was strictly necessary to take my cousin, Mrs Revel, into your confidence also?'

'In view of the name signed to those letters, I do, Mr Lomax.'

'An amazing piece of effrontery,' murmured George, his brow darkened as he looked at the bundle of letters. 'I remember the late King of Herzoslovakia. A charming fellow, but weak – deplorably weak. A tool in the hands of an unscrupulous woman. Have you any theory as to how these letters came to be restored to Mr Cade?'

'It's my opinion,' said Battle, 'that if people can't get a thing one way – they try another.'

'I don't quite follow you,' said George.

'This crook, this King Victor, he's well aware by now that the Council Chamber is watched. So he'll let us have the letters, and let us do the decoding, and let us find the hiding-place. And then – trouble! But Lemoine and I between us will attend to that.'

'You've got a plan, eh?'

'I wouldn't go so far as to say I've got a plan. But I've got an idea. It's a very useful thing sometimes, an idea.'

Thereupon Superintendent Battle took his departure.

He had no intention of taking George any further into his confidence.

On the way back, he passed Anthony on the road and stopped.

'Going to give me a lift back to the house?' asked Anthony. 'That's good.'

'Where have you been, Mr Cade?'

'Down to the station to inquire about trains.'

Battle raised his eyebrows.

'Thinking of leaving us again?' he inquired.

'Not just at present,' laughed Anthony. 'By the way, what's upset Isaacstein? He arrived in the car just as I left, and he looked as though something had given him a nasty jolt.'

'Mr Isaacstein?'

'Yes.'

'I can't say, I'm sure. I fancy it would take a good deal to jolt him.'

'So do I,' agreed Anthony. 'He's quite one of the strong, silent, yellow men of finance.'

Suddenly Battle leant forward and touched the chauffeur on the shoulder.

'Stop, will you? And wait for me here.'

He jumped out of the car, much to Anthony's surprise. But in a minute or two, the latter perceived M. Lemoine advancing to meet the English detective, and gathered that it was a signal from him which had attracted Battle's attention.

There was a rapid colloquy between them, and then the superintendent returned to the car and jumped in again, bidding the chauffeur drive on.

His expression had completely changed.

'They've found the revolver,' he said suddenly and curtly.

'What?'

Anthony gazed at him in great surprise.

'Where?'

'In Isaacstein's suitcase.'

'Oh, impossible!'

'Nothing's impossible,' said Battle. 'I ought to have remembered that.'

He sat perfectly still, tapping his knee with his hand.

'Who found it?'

Battle jerked his head over his shoulder.

'Lemoine. Clever chap. They think no end of him at the Sûreté.'

'But doesn't this upset all your ideas?'

'No,' said Superintendent Battle very slowly. 'I can't say it does. It was a bit of a surprise, I admit, at first. But it fits in very well with one idea of mine.'

'Which is?'

But the superintendent branched off on to a totally different subject.

'I wonder if you'd mind finding Mr Eversleigh for me, sir? There's a message for him from Mr Lomax. He's to go over to the Abbey at once.'

'All right,' said Anthony. The car had just drawn up at the great door. 'He's probably in bed still.'

'I think not,' said the detective. 'If you'll look, you'll see him walking under the trees there with Mrs Revel.'

'Wonderful eyes you have, haven't you, Battle?' said Anthony as he departed on his errand.

He delivered the message to Bill, who was duly disgusted.

'Damn it all,' grumbled Bill to himself, as he strode off to the house, 'why can't Codders sometimes leave me alone? And why can't these blasted Colonials stay in their Colonies? What do they want to come over here for, and pick out all the best girls? I'm fed up to the teeth with everything.'

'Have you heard about the revolver?' asked Virginia breathlessly, as Bill left them.

'Battle told me. Rather staggering, isn't it? Isaacstein was in a frightful state yesterday to get away, but I thought it was just nerves. He's about the one person I'd have pitched upon as being above suspicion. Can you see any motive for his wanting Prince Michael out of the way?'

'It certainly doesn't fit in,' agreed Virginia thoughtfully.

'Nothing fits in anywhere,' said Anthony discontentedly. 'I rather fancied myself as an amateur detective to begin with, and so far all I've done is to clear the character of the French governess at vast trouble and some little expense.'

'Is that what you went to France for?' inquired Virginia.

'Yes, I went to Dinard and had an interview with the Comtesse de Breteuil, awfully pleased with my own cleverness, and fully expecting to be told that no such person as Mademoiselle Brun had ever been heard of. Instead of which I was given to understand that the lady in question had been the mainstay of the household for the last seven years. So, unless the Comtesse is also a crook, that ingenious theory of mine falls to the ground.'

Virginia shook her head.

'Madame de Breteuil is quite above suspicion. I know her quite well, and I fancy I must have come across Mademoiselle at the château. I certainly knew her face quite well – in that vague way one does know governesses and companions and people one sits opposite to in trains. It's awful, but I never really look at them properly. Do you?'

'Only if they're exceptionally beautiful,' admitted Anthony.

'Well, in this case –' she broke off. 'What's the matter?'

Anthony was staring at a figure which detached itself from the clump of trees and stood there rigidly at attention. It was the Herzoslovakian, Boris.

'Excuse me,' said Anthony to Virginia, 'I must just speak to my dog a minute.'

He went across to where Boris was standing.

'What's the matter? What do you want?'

'Master,' said Boris, bowing.

'Yes, that's all very well, but you mustn't keep following me about like this. It looks odd.'

Without a word, Boris produced a soiled scrap of paper, evidently torn from a letter, and handed it to Anthony.

'What's this?' said Anthony.

There was an address scrawled on the paper, nothing else.

'He dropped it,' said Boris. 'I bring it to the master.'

'Who dropped it?'

'The foreign gentleman.'

'But why bring it to me?'

Boris looked at him reproachfully.

'Well, anyway, go away now,' said Anthony. 'I'm busy.'

Boris saluted, turning sharply on his heel, and marched away. Anthony rejoined Virginia, thrusting the piece of paper into his pocket.

'What did he want?' she asked curiously. 'And why do you call him your dog?'

'Because he acts like one,' said Anthony, answering the last question first. 'He must have been a retriever in his last incarnation, I think. He's just brought me a piece of a letter which he says the foreign gentleman dropped. I suppose he means Lemoine.'

'I suppose so,' acquiesced Virginia.

'He's always following me round,' continued Anthony. 'Just like a dog. Says next to nothing. Just looks at me with his big round eyes. I can't make him out.'

'Perhaps he meant Isaacstein,' suggested Virginia. 'Isaacstein looks foreign enough, heaven knows.'

'Isaacstein,' muttered Anthony impatiently. 'Where the devil does he come in?'

'Are you ever sorry that you've mixed yourself up in all this?' asked Virginia suddenly.

'Sorry? Good Lord, no. I love it. I've spent most of my life looking for trouble, you know. Perhaps, this time, I've got a little more than I bargained for.'

'But you're well out of the wood now,' said Virginia, a little surprised by the unusual gravity of his tone.

'Not quite.'

They strolled on for a minute or two in silence.

'There are some people,' said Anthony, breaking the silence, 'who don't conform to the signals. An ordinary well-regulated locomotive slows down or pulls up when it sees the red light hoisted against it. Perhaps I was born colour-blind. When I see the red signal – I can't help forging ahead. And in the end, you know, that spells disaster. Bound to. And quite right really. That sort of thing is bad for traffic generally.'

He still spoke very seriously.

'I suppose,' said Virginia, 'that you have taken a good many risks in your life?'

'Pretty nearly every one there is – except marriage.'

'That's rather cynical.'

'It wasn't meant to be. Marriage, the kind of marriage I mean, would be the biggest adventure of the lot.'

'I like that,' said Virginia, flushing eagerly.

'There's only one kind of woman I'd want to marry – the kind who is worlds removed from my type of life. What would we do about it? Is she to lead my life, or am I to lead hers?'

'If she loved you –'

'Sentimentality, Mrs Revel. You know it is. Love isn't a drug that you take to blind you to your surroundings – you can make it that, yes, but it's a pity – love can be a lot more than that. What do you think the King and his beggarmaid thought of married life after they'd been married a year or two? Didn't she regret her rags and her bare feet and her carefree life? You bet she did. Would it have been any good his renouncing his crown for her sake? Not a bit of good, either. He'd have made a damned bad beggar, I'm sure. And no woman respects a man when he's doing a thing thoroughly badly.'

'Have you fallen in love with a beggarmaid, Mr Cade?' inquired Virginia softly.

'It's the other way about with me, but the principle's the same.'

'And there's no way out?' asked Virginia.

'There's always a way out,' said Anthony gloomily. 'I've got a theory that one can always get anything one wants if one will pay the price. And do you know what the price is, nine times out of ten? Compromise. A beastly thing, compromise, but it steals upon you as you near middle age. It's stealing upon me now. To get the woman I want I'd – I'd even take up regular work.'

Virginia laughed.

'I was brought up to a trade, you know,' continued Anthony.

'And you abandoned it?'

'Yes.'

'Why?'

'A matter of principle.'

'Oh!'

'You're a very unusual woman,' said Anthony suddenly, turning and looking at her.

'Why?'

'You can refrain from asking questions.'

'You mean that I haven't asked you what your trade was?'

'Just that.'

Again they walked on in silence. They were nearing the house now, passing close by the scented sweetness of the rose garden.

'You understand well enough, I dare say,' said Anthony, breaking the silence. 'You know when a man's in love with you. I don't suppose you care a hang for me – or for anyone else – but, by God, I'd like to make you care.'

'Do you think you could?' asked Virginia, in a low voice.

'Probably not, but I'd have a damned good try.'

'Are you sorry you ever met me?' she said suddenly.

'Lord, no. It's the red signal again. When I first saw you – that day in Pont Street, I knew I was up against something that was going to hurt like fun. Your face did that to me – just your face. There's magic in you from head to foot – some women are like that, but I've never known a woman who had so much of it as you have. You'll marry someone respectable and prosperous, I suppose, and I shall return to my disreputable life, but I'll kiss you once before I go – I swear I will.'

'You can't do it now,' said Virginia softly. 'Superintendent Battle is watching us out of the library window.'

Anthony looked at her.

'You're rather a devil, Virginia,' he said dispassionately. 'But rather a dear too.'

Then he waved his hand airily to Superintendent Battle.

'Caught any criminals this morning, Battle?'

'Not as yet, Mr Cade.'

'That sounds hopeful.'

Battle, with an agility surprising in so stolid a man, vaulted out of the library window and joined them on the terrace.

'I've got Professor Wynwood down here,' he announced in a whisper. 'Just this minute arrived. He's decoding the letters now. Would you like to see him at work?'

His tone suggested that of the showman speaking of some pet exhibit. Receiving a reply in the affirmative, he led them up to the window and invited them to peep inside.

Seated at a table, the letters spread out in front of him and writing busily on a big sheet of paper, was a small red-haired man of middle age. He grunted irritably to himself as he wrote and every now and then rubbed his nose violently until its hue almost rivalled that of his hair.

Presently he looked up.

'That you, Battle? What do you want me down here to unravel

this tomfoolery for? A child in arms could do it. A baby of two could do it on his head. Call this thing a cipher? It leaps to the eye, man.'

'I'm glad of that, Professor,' said Battle mildly. 'But we're not all so clever as you are, you know.'

'It doesn't need cleverness,' snapped the professor. 'It's routine work. Do you want the whole bundle done? It's a long business, you know – requires diligent application and close attention and absolutely no intelligence. I've done the one dated "Chimneys" which you said was important. I might as well take the rest back to London and hand 'em over to one of my assistants. I really can't afford the time myself. I've come away now from a real teaser, and I want to get back to it.'

His eyes glistened a little.

'Very well, Professor,' assented Battle. 'I'm sorry we're such small fry. I'll explain to Mr Lomax. It's just this one letter that all the hurry is about. Lord Caterham is expecting you to stay for lunch, I believe.'

'Never have lunch,' said the professor. 'Bad habit, lunch. A banana and a water biscuit is all any sane and healthy man should need in the middle of the day.'

He seized his overcoat, which lay across the back of a chair. Battle went round to the front of the house, and a few minutes later Anthony and Virginia heard the sound of a car driving away.

Battle rejoined them, carrying in his hand the half-sheet of paper which the Professor had given him.

'He's always like that,' said Battle, referring to the departed Professor. 'In the very deuce of a hurry. Clever man, though. Well, here's the kernel of Her Majesty's letter. Care to have a look at it?'

Virginia stretched out a hand, and Anthony read it over her shoulder. It had been, he remembered, a long epistle, breathing mingled passion and despair. The genius of Professor Wynwood had transformed it into an essentially business-like communication.

Operations carried out successfully, but S double-crossed us. Has removed stone from hiding-place. Not in his room. I have searched.

Found following memorandum which I think refers to it: RICHMOND SEVEN STRAIGHT EIGHT LEFT THREE RIGHT.

'S?' said Anthony. 'Stylptitch, of course. Cunning old dog. He changed the hiding-place.'

'Richmond,' said Virginia thoughtfully. 'Is the diamond concealed somewhere at Richmond, I wonder?'

'It's a favourite spot for royalties,' agreed Anthony.

Battle shook his head.

'I still think it's a reference to something in this house.'

'I know,' cried Virginia suddenly.

Both men turned to look at her.

'The Holbein portrait in the Council Chamber. They were tapping on the wall just below it. And it's a portrait of the Earl of Richmond!'

'You've got it,' said Battle, and slapped his leg.

He spoke with an animation quite unwonted.

'That's the starting-point, the picture, and the crooks know no more than we do what the figures refer to. Those two men in armour stand directly underneath the picture, and their first idea was that the diamond was hidden in one of them. The measurements might have been inches. That failed, and their next idea was a secret passage or stairway, or a sliding panel. Do you know of any such thing, Mrs Revel?'

Virginia shook her head.

'There's a priest's hole, and at least one secret passage, I know,' she said. 'I believe I've been shown them once, but I can't remember much about them now. Here's Bundle, she'll know.'

Bundle was coming quickly along the terrace towards them.

'I'm taking the Panhard up to town after lunch,' she remarked. 'Anyone want a lift? Wouldn't you like to come, Mr Cade? We'll be back by dinner-time.'

'No, thanks,' said Anthony. 'I'm quite happy and busy down here.'

'The man fears me,' said Bundle. 'Either my driving or my fatal fascination! Which is it?'

'The latter,' said Anthony. 'Every time.'

'Bundle, dear,' said Virginia, 'is there any secret passage leading out of the Council Chamber?'

'Rather. But it's only a mouldy one. Supposed to lead from Chimneys to Wyvern Abbey. So it did in the old, old days, but it's all blocked up now. You can only get along it for about a hundred yards from this end. The one upstairs in the White Gallery is ever so much more amusing, and the priest's hole isn't half bad.'

'We're not regarding them from an artistic standpoint,' explained Virginia. 'It's business. How do you get into the Council Chamber one?'

'Hinged panel. I'll show it you after lunch if you like.'

'Thank you,' said Superintendent Battle. 'Shall we say at 2.30?'

Bundle looked at him with lifted eyebrows.

'Crook stuff?' she inquired.

Tredwell appeared on the terrace.

'Luncheon is served, my lady,' he announced.

CHAPTER 23

ENCOUNTER IN THE ROSE GARDEN

At 2.30 a little party met together in the Council Chamber: Bundle, Virginia, Superintendent Battle, M. Lemoine and Anthony Cade.

'No good waiting until we can get hold of Mr Lomax,' said Battle. 'This is the kind of business one wants to get on with quickly.'

'If you've got any idea that Prince Michael was murdered by someone who got in this way, you're wrong,' said Bundle. 'It can't be done. The other end's blocked completely.'

'There is no question of that, milady,' said Lemoine quickly. 'It is quite a different search that we make.'

'Looking for something, are you?' asked Bundle quickly. 'Not the historic what-not, by any chance?'

Lemoine looked puzzled.

'Explain yourself, Bundle,' said Virginia encouragingly. 'You can when you try.'

'The thingummybob,' said Bundle. 'The historic diamond of purple princes that was pinched in the dark ages before I grew to years of discretion.'

'Who told you this, Lady Eileen?' asked Battle.

'I've always known. One of the footmen told me when I was twelve years old.'

'A footman,' said Battle. 'Lord! I'd like Mr Lomax to have heard that!'

'Is it one of George's closely guarded secrets?' asked Bundle. 'How perfectly screaming! I never really thought it was true. George always was an ass – he must know that servants know everything.'

She went across to the Holbein portrait, touched a spring concealed somewhere at the side of it, and immediately, with a creaking noise, a section of the panelling swung inwards, revealing a dark opening.

'*Entrez, messieurs et mesdames*,' said Bundle dramatically. 'Walk up, walk up, walk up, dearies. Best show of the season, and only a tanner.'

Both Lemoine and Battle were provided with torches. They entered the dark aperture first, the others close on their heels.

'Air's nice and fresh,' remarked Battle. 'Must be ventilated somehow.'

He walked on ahead. The floor was rough uneven stone, but the walls were bricked. As Bundle had said, the passage extended for a bare hundred yards. Then it came to an abrupt end with a fallen heap of masonry. Battle satisfied himself that there was no way of egress beyond, and then spoke over his shoulder.

'We'll go back, if you please. I wanted just to spy out the land, so to speak.'

In a few minutes they were back again at the panelled entrance.

'We'll start from here,' said Battle. 'Seven straight, eight left, three right. Take the first as paces.'

He paced seven steps carefully, and bending down examined the ground.

'About right, I should fancy. At one time or another, there's been a chalk mark made here. Now then, eight left. That's not paces, the passage is only wide enough to go Indian file, anyway.'

'Say it in bricks,' suggested Anthony.

'Quite right, Mr Cade. Eight bricks from the bottom or the top on the left-hand side. Try from the bottom first – it's easier.'

He counted up eight bricks.

'Now three to the right of that. One, two, three – Hullo – Hullo, what's this?'

'I shall scream in a minute,' said Bundle, 'I know I shall. *What* is it?'

Superintendent Battle was working at the brick with the point of his knife. His practised eye had quickly seen that this particular brick was different from the rest. A minute or two's work, and he was able to pull it right out. Behind was a small dark cavity. Battle thrust in his hand.

Everyone waited in breathless expectancy.

Battle drew out his hand again.

He uttered an exclamation of surprise and anger.

The others crowded round and stared uncomprehendingly at the three articles he held. For a moment it seemed as though their eyes must have deceived them.

A card of small pearl buttons, a square of coarse knitting, and a piece of paper on which were inscribed a row of capital Es!

'Well,' said Battle. 'I'm – I'm danged. What's the meaning of this?'

'*Mon Dieu*,' muttered the Frenchman. '*Ça, c'est un peu trop fort!*'

'But what does it mean?' cried Virginia, bewildered.

'Mean?' said Anthony. 'There's only one thing it can mean. The late Count Stylptitch must have had a sense of humour! This is an example of that humour. I may say that I don't consider it particularly funny myself.'

'Do you mind explaining your meaning a little more clearly, sir?' said the Superintendent Battle.

'Certainly. This was the Count's little joke. He must have suspected that his memorandum had been read. When the crooks came to recover the jewel, they were to find instead this extremely clever conundrum. It's the sort of thing you pin on to yourself at Book Teas, when people have to guess what you are.'

'It has a meaning, then?'

'I should say, undoubtedly. If the Count had meant to be merely offensive, he would have put a placard with "Sold" on it, or a picture of a donkey or something crude like that.'

'A bit of knitting, some capital Es, and a lot of buttons,' muttered Battle discontendedly.

'*C'est inouï*,' said Lemoine angrily.

'Cipher No. 2,' said Anthony. 'I wonder whether Professor Wynwood would be any good at this one?'

'When was this passage last used, milady?' asked the Frenchman of Bundle.

Bundle reflected.

'I don't believe anyone's been into it for over two years. The priest's hole is the show exhibit for Americans and tourists generally.'

'Curious,' murmured the Frenchman.

'Why curious?'

Lemoine stooped and picked up a small object from the floor.

'Because of this,' he said. 'This match has not lain here for two years – not even two days.'

'Any of you ladies or gentlemen drop this, by any chance?' he asked.

He received a negative all round.

'Well, then,' said Superintendent Battle, 'we've seen all there is to see. We might as well get out of here.'

The proposal was assented to by all. The panel had swung to, but Bundle showed them how it was fastened from the inside. She unlatched it, swung it noiselessly open, and sprang through the opening, alighting in the Council Chamber with a resounding thud.

'Damn!' said Lord Caterham, springing up from an arm-chair in which he appeared to have been taking forty winks.

'Poor old Father,' said Bundle. 'Did I startle you?'

'I can't think,' said Lord Caterham, 'why nobody nowadays ever sits still after a meal. It's a lost art. God knows Chimneys is big enough, but even here there doesn't seem to be a single room where I can be sure of a little peace. Good Lord, how many of you are there? Reminds me of the pantomimes I used to go to as a boy when hordes of demons used to pop up out of trapdoors.'

'Demon No. 7,' said Virginia, approaching him, and patting him on the head. 'Don't be cross. We're just exploring secret passages, that's all.'

'There seems to be a positive boom in secret passages today,' grumbled Lord Caterham, not yet completely mollified. 'I've had to show that fellow Fish round them all this morning.'

'When was that?' asked Battle quickly.

'Just before lunch. It seems he'd heard of the one in here. I showed him that, and then took him up to the White Gallery, and we finished up with the priest's hole. But his enthusiasm was waning by that time. He looked bored to death. But I made him go through with it.' Lord Caterham chuckled at the remembrance.

Anthony put a hand on Lemoine's arm.

'Come outside,' he said softly. 'I want to speak to you.'

The two men went out together through the window. When they had gone a sufficient distance from the house, Anthony drew from his pocket the scrap of paper that Boris had given him that morning.

'Look here,' he said. 'Did you drop this?'

Lemoine took it and examined it with some interest.

'No,' he said. 'I have never seen it before. Why?'

'Quite sure?'

'Absolutely sure, monsieur.'

'That's very odd.'

He repeated to Lemoine what Boris had said. The other listened with close attention.

'No, I did not drop it. You say he found it in that clump of trees?'

'Well, I assumed so, but he did not actually say so.'

'It is just possible that it might have fluttered out of M. Isaacstein's suitcase. Question Boris again.' He handed the paper back to Anthony. After a minute or two he said: 'What exactly do you know of this man Boris?'

Anthony shrugged his shoulders.

'I understood he was the late Prince Michael's trusted servant.'

'It may be so, but make it your business to find out. Ask someone who knows, such as the Baron Lolopretjzyl. Perhaps this man was engaged but a few weeks ago. For myself, I have believed him honest. But who knows? King Victor is quite capable of making himself into a trusted servant at a moment's notice.'

'Do you really think –'

Lemoine interrupted him.

'I will be quite frank. With me, King Victor is an obsession. I see him everywhere. At this moment even I ask myself – this man who is talking to me, this M. Cade, is he, perhaps, King Victor?'

'Good Lord,' said Anthony, 'you have got it badly.'

'What do I care for the diamond? For the discovery of the murderer of Prince Michael? I leave those affairs to my colleague of Scotland Yard whose business it is. Me, I am in England for one purpose, and one purpose only, to capture King Victor and capture him red-handed. Nothing else matters.'

'Think you'll do it?' asked Anthony, lighting a cigarette.

'How should I know?' said Lemoine, with sudden despondency.

'Hm!' said Anthony.

They had regained the terrace. Superintendent Battle was standing near the French window in a wooden attitude.

'Look at poor old Battle,' said Anthony. 'Let's go and cheer him up.' He paused a minute, and said, 'You know, you're an odd fish in some ways, M. Lemoine.'

'In what ways, M. Cade?'

'Well,' said Anthony, 'in your place, I should have been inclined to note down that address that I showed you. It may be of no importance – quite conceivably. On the other hand, it might be very important indeed.'

Lemoine looked at him for a minute or two steadily. Then, with a slight smile, he drew back the cuff of his left coat-sleeve. Pencilled on the white shirt-cuff beneath were the words 'Hurstmere, Langly Road, Dover.'

'I apologize,' said Anthony. 'And I retire worsted.'

He joined Superintendent Battle.

'You look very pensive, Battle,' he remarked.

'I've got a lot to think about, Mr Cade.'

'Yes, I expect you have.'

'Things aren't dovetailing. They're not dovetailing at all.'

'Very trying,' sympathized Anthony. 'Never mind, Battle, if the worst comes to the worst, you can always arrest me. You've got my guilty footprints to fall back upon, remember.'

But the superintendent did not smile.

'Got any enemies here that you know of, Mr Cade?' he asked.

'I've an idea that the third footman doesn't like me,' replied Anthony lightly. 'He does his best to forget to hand me the choicest vegetables. Why?'

'I've been getting anonymous letters,' said Superintendent Battle. 'Or rather an anonymous letter, I should say.'

'About me?'

Without answer Battle took a folded sheet of cheap notepaper from his pocket, and handed it to Anthony. Scrawled on it in an illiterate handwriting were the words:

Look out for Mr Cade. He isn't wot he seems.

Anthony handed it back with a light laugh.

'That all? Cheer up, Battle. I'm really a King in disguise, you know.'

He went into the house, whistling lightly as he walked along. But as he entered his bedroom and shut the door behind him, his face changed. It grew set and stern. He sat down on the edge of the bed and stared moodily at the floor.

'Things are getting serious,' said Anthony to himself. 'Something must be done about it. It's all damned awkward . . .'

He sat there for a minute or two, then strolled to the window. For a moment or two he stood looking out aimlessly and then his eyes became suddenly focused on a certain spot, and his face lightened.

'Of course,' he said. 'The rose garden! That's it! The rose garden.'

He hurried downstairs again and out into the garden by a side door. He approached the rose garden by a circuitous route. It had a little gate at either end. He entered by the far one, and walked up to the sundial which was on a raised hillock in the exact centre of the garden.

Just as Anthony reached it, he stopped dead and stared at another occupant of the rose garden who seemed equally surprised to see him.

'I didn't know that you were interested in roses, Mr Fish,' said Anthony gently.

'Sir,' said Mr Fish, 'I am considerably interested in roses.'

They looked at each other warily, as antagonists seek to measure their opponent's strength.

'So am I,' said Anthony.

'Is that so?'

'In fact, I dote upon roses,' said Anthony airily.

A very slight smile hovered upon Mr Fish's lips, and at the same time Anthony also smiled. The tension seemed to relax.

'Look at this beauty now,' said Mr Fish, stooping to point out a particularly fine bloom. 'Madame Abel Chatenay, I pressoom it to be. Yes, I am right. This white rose, before the war, was known as Frau Carl Drusky. They have, I believe, renamed it. Over-sensitive, perhaps, but truly patriotic. The La France is always popular. Do you care for red roses at all, Mr Cade? A bright scarlet rose now –'

Mr Fish's slow, drawling voice was interrupted. Bundle was leaning out of a first-floor window.

'Care for a spin to town, Mr Fish? I'm just off.'

'Thank you, Lady Eileen, but I am vurry happy here.'

'Sure you won't change your mind, Mr Cade?'

Anthony laughed and shook his head. Bundle disappeared.

'Sleep is more in my line,' said Anthony, with a wide yawn. 'A good after-luncheon nap!' He took out a cigarette. 'You haven't got a match, have you?'

Mr Fish handed him a matchbox. Anthony helped himself, and handed back the box with a word of thanks.

'Roses,' said Anthony, 'are all very well. But I don't feel particularly horticultural this afternoon.'

With a disarming smile, he nodded cheerfully.

A thundering noise sounded from just outside the house.

'Pretty powerful engine she's got in that car of hers,' remarked Anthony. 'There, off she goes.'

They had a view of the car speeding down the long drive.

Anthony yawned again, and strolled towards the house.

He passed in through the door. Once inside, he seemed as though changed to quicksilver. He raced across the hall, out through one of the windows on the farther side, and across the park. Bundle, he knew, had to make a big detour by the lodge gates, and through the village.

He ran desperately. It was a race against time. He reached the park wall just as he heard the car outside. He swung himself up and dropped into the road.

'Hi!' cried Anthony.

In her astonishment, Bundle swerved half across the road. She managed to pull up without accident. Anthony ran after the car, opened the door, and jumped in beside Bundle.

'I'm coming to London with you,' he said. 'I meant to all along.'

'Extraordinary person,' said Bundle. 'What's that you've got in your hand?'

'Only a match,' said Anthony.

He regarded it thoughtfully. It was pink, with a yellow head. He threw away his unlighted cigarette, and put the match carefully into his pocket.

CHAPTER 24

THE HOUSE AT DOVER

'You don't mind, I suppose,' said Bundle after a minute or two, 'if I drive rather fast? I started later than I meant to do.'

It had seemed to Anthony that they were proceeding at a terrific speed already, but he soon saw that that was nothing compared to what Bundle could get out of the Panhard if she tried.

'Some people,' said Bundle, as she slowed down momentarily to pass through a village, 'are terrified of my driving. Poor old Father, for instance. Nothing would induce him to come up with me in this old bus.'

Privately, Anthony thought Lord Caterham was entirely justified. Driving with Bundle was not a sport to be indulged in by nervous, middle-aged gentlemen.

'But you don't seem nervous a bit,' continued Bundle approvingly, as she swept round a corner on two wheels.

'I'm in pretty good training, you see,' explained Anthony gravely. 'Also,' he added, as an afterthought, 'I'm rather in a hurry myself.'

'Shall I speed her up a bit more?' asked Bundle kindly.

'Good Lord, no,' said Anthony hastily. 'We're averaging about fifty as it is.'

'I'm burning with curiosity to know the reason for this sudden departure,' said Bundle, after executing a fanfare upon the klaxon which must temporarily have deafened the neighbourhood. 'But I suppose I mustn't ask? You're not escaping from justice, are you?'

'I'm not quite sure,' said Anthony. 'I shall know soon.'

'That Scotland Yard man isn't as much of a rabbit as I thought,' said Bundle thoughtfully.

'Battle's a good man,' agreed Anthony.

'You ought to have been in diplomacy,' remarked Bundle. 'You don't part with much information, do you?'

'I was under the impression that I babbled.'

'Oh! Boy! You're not eloping with Mademoiselle Brun, by any chance?'

'Not guilty!' said Anthony with fervour.

There was a pause of some minutes during which Bundle caught up and passed three other cars. Then she asked suddenly:

'How long have you known Virginia?'

'That's a difficult question to answer,' said Anthony, with perfect truth. 'I haven't actually met her very often, and yet I seem to have known her a long time.'

Bundle nodded.

'Virginia's got brains,' she remarked abruptly. 'She's always talking nonsense, but she's got brains all right. She was frightfully good out in Herzoslovakia, I believe. If Tim Revel had lived he'd have had a fine career – and mostly owing to Virginia. She worked for him tooth and nail. She did everything in the world she could for him – and I know why, too.'

'Because she cared for him?' Anthony sat looking very straight ahead of him.

'No, because she didn't. Don't you see? She didn't love him – she never loved him, and so she did everything on earth she could to make up. That's Virginia all over. But don't you make any mistake about it. Virginia was never in love with Tim Revel.'

'You seem very positive,' said Anthony, turning to look at her.

Bundle's little hands were clenched on the steering wheel, and her chin was stuck out in a determined manner.

'I know a thing or two. I was only a kid at the time of her marriage, but I heard one or two things, and knowing Virginia I can put them together easily enough. Tim Revel was bowled over by Virginia – he was Irish, you know, and most attractive, with a genius for expressing himself well. Virginia was quite young – eighteen. She couldn't go anywhere without seeing Tim in a state of picturesque misery, vowing he'd shoot himself or take to drink if she didn't marry him. Girls believe these things – or used to – we've advanced a lot in the last eight years. Virginia was carried away by the feeling she thought she'd inspired. She married him – and she was an angel to him always. She wouldn't have been half as much of an angel if she'd loved him. There's a lot of the devil in Virginia. But I can tell you one thing – she enjoys her freedom. And anyone will have a hard time persuading her to give it up.'

'I wonder why you tell me all this?' said Anthony slowly.

'It's interesting to know about people, isn't it? Some people, that is.'

'I've wanted to know,' he acknowledged.

'And you'd never have heard from Virginia. But you can trust me for an inside tip from the stables. Virginia's a darling. Even women like her because she isn't a bit of a cat. And anyway,' Bundle ended, somewhat obscurely, 'one must be a sport, mustn't one?'

'Oh, certainly,' Anthony agreed. But he was still puzzled. He had no idea what had prompted Bundle to give him so much information unasked. That he was glad of it, he did not deny.

'Here are the trams,' said Bundle, with a sigh. 'Now, I suppose, I shall have to drive carefully.'

'It might be as well,' agreed Anthony.

His ideas and Bundle's on the subject of careful driving hardly coincided. Leaving indignant suburbs behind them they finally emerged into Oxford Street.

'Not bad going, eh?' said Bundle, glancing at her wrist-watch.

Anthony assented fervently.

'Where do you want to be dropped?'

'Anywhere. Which way are you going?'

'Knightsbridge way.'

'All right, drop me at Hyde Park Corner.'

'Goodbye,' said Bundle, as she drew up at the place indicated. 'What about the return journey?'

'I'll find my own way back, thanks very much.'

'I *have* scared him,' remarked Bundle.

'I shouldn't recommend driving with you as a tonic for nervous old ladies, but personally I've enjoyed it. The last time I was in equal danger was when I was charged by a herd of wild elephants.'

'I think you're extremely rude,' remarked Bundle. 'We've not even had one bump today.'

'I'm sorry if you've been holding yourself in on my account,' retorted Anthony.

'I don't think men are really very brave,' said Bundle.

'That's a nasty one,' said Anthony. 'I retire, humiliated.' Bundle nodded and drove on. Anthony hailed a passing taxi. 'Victoria Station,' he said to the driver as he got in.

When he got to Victoria he paid off the taxi and inquired for the next train to Dover. Unfortunately he had just missed one.

Resigning himself to a wait of something over an hour, Anthony paced up and down, his brows knit. Once or twice he shook his head impatiently.

The journey to Dover was uneventful. Arrived there, Anthony passed quickly out of the station and then, as though suddenly remembering, he turned back again. There was a slight smile on his lips as he asked to be directed to Hurstmere, Langly Road.

The road in question was a long one, leading right out of the town. According to the porter's instructions, Hurstmere was the last house. Anthony trudged along steadily. The little pucker had reappeared between his eyes. Nevertheless there was a new elation in his manner, as always when danger was near at hand.

Hurstmere was, as the porter had said, the last house in Langly Road. It stood well back, enclosed in its own grounds, which were ragged and overgrown. The place, Anthony judged, must have been empty for many years. A large iron gate swung rustily on its hinges, and the name on the gate-post was half obliterated.

'A lonely spot,' muttered Anthony to himself, 'and a good one to choose.'

He hesitated a minute or two, glanced quickly up and down the road – which was quite deserted – and then slipped quietly past the creaking gate into the overgrown drive. He walked up it a little way, and then stood listening. He was still some distance from the house. Not a sound could be heard anywhere. Some fast-yellowing leaves detached themselves from one of the trees overhead and fell with a soft rustling sound that was almost sinister in the stillness. Anthony started; then smiled.

'Nerves,' he murmured to himself. 'Never knew I had such things before.'

He went on up the drive. Presently, as the drive curved, he slipped into the shrubbery and so continued his way unseen from the house. Suddenly he stood still, peering out through the leaves. Some distance away a dog was barking, but it was a sound nearer at hand that had attracted Anthony's attention.

His keen hearing had not been mistaken. A man came rapidly round the corner of the house, a short, square, thick-set man, foreign in appearance. He did not pause but walked steadily on, circling the house and disappearing again.

Anthony nodded to himself.

'Sentry,' he murmured. 'They do the thing quite well.'

As soon as he had passed, Anthony went on, diverging to the left, and so following in the footsteps of the sentry.

His own footsteps were quite noiseless.

The wall of the house was on his right, and presently he came to where a broad blur of light fell on the gravelled walk. The sound of several men talking together was clearly audible.

'My God! What double-dyed idiots,' murmured Anthony to himself. 'It would serve them right to be given a fright.'

He stole up to the window, stooping a little so that he should not be seen. Presently he lifted his head very carefully to the level of the sill and looked in.

Half a dozen men were sprawling round a table. Four of them were big thick-set men, with high cheekbones, and eyes set in Magyar slanting fashion. The other two were rat-like little men with quick gestures. The language that was being spoken was French, but the four big men spoke it with uncertainty and a hoarse guttural intonation.

'The boss?' growled one of these. 'When will he be here?'

One of the smaller men shrugged his shoulders.

'Any time now.'

'About time, too,' growled the first man. 'I have never seen him, this boss of yours, but, oh, what great and glorious work might we not have accomplished in these days of idle waiting!'

'Fool,' said the other little man bitingly. 'Getting nabbed by the police is all the great and glorious work you and your precious lot would have been likely to accomplish. A lot of blundering gorillas!'

'Aha!' roared another big thick-set fellow. 'You insult the Comrades? I will soon set the sign of the Red Hand round your throat.'

He half rose, glaring ferociously at the Frenchman, but one of his companions pulled him back again.

'No quarrelling,' he grunted. 'We're to work together. From all I heard, this King Victor doesn't stand for being disobeyed.'

In the darkness, Anthony heard the footsteps of the sentry coming his round again, and he drew back behind a bush.

'Who's that?' said one of the men inside.

'Carlo – going his rounds.'

'Oh! What about the prisoner?'

'He's all right – coming round pretty fast now. He's recovered well from the crack on the head we gave him.'

Anthony moved gently away.

'God! What a lot,' he muttered. 'They discuss their affairs with an open window, and that fool Carlo goes his round with the tread of an elephant – and the eyes of a bat. And to crown all, the Herzoslovakians and the French are on the point of coming to blows. King Victor's headquarters seem to be in a parlous condition. It would amuse me, it would amuse me very much, to teach them a lesson.'

He stood irresolute for a minute, smiling to himself.

From somewhere above his head came a stifled groan.

Anthony looked up. The groan came again.

Anthony glanced quickly from left to right. Carlo was not due round again just yet. He grasped the heavy virginia creeper and climbed nimbly till he reached the sill of a window. The window was shut, but with a tool from his pocket he soon succeeded in forcing up the catch.

He paused a minute to listen, then sprang lightly inside the room. There was a bed in the far corner and on that bed a man was lying, his figure barely discernible in the gloom.

Anthony went over to the bed, and flashed his pocket torch on the man's face. It was a foreign face, pale and emaciated, and the head was swathed in heavy bandages.

The man was bound hand and foot. He stared up at Anthony like one dazed.

Anthony bent over him, and as he did so he heard a sound

behind him and swung round, his hand travelling to his coat pocket.

But a sharp command arrested him.

'Hands up, sonny. You didn't expect to see me here, but I happened to catch the same train as you at Victoria.'

It was Mr Hiram Fish who was standing in the doorway. He was smiling and in his hand was a big blue automatic.

CHAPTER 25

TUESDAY NIGHT AT CHIMNEYS

Lord Caterham, Virginia and Bundle were sitting in the library after dinner. It was Tuesday evening. Some thirty hours had elapsed since Anthony's rather dramatic departure.

For at least the seventh time Bundle repeated Anthony's parting words, as spoken at Hyde Park Corner.

'I'll find my own way back,' echoed Virginia thoughtfully. 'That doesn't look as though he expected to be away as long as this. And he's left all his things here.'

'He didn't tell you where he was going?'

'No,' said Virginia, looking straight in front of her. 'He told me nothing.'

After this, there was a silence for a minute or two. Lord Caterham was the first to break it.

'On the whole,' he said, 'keeping an hotel has some advantages over keeping a country house.'

'Meaning –'

'That little notice they always hang up in your room. Visitors intending departure must give notice before twelve o'clock.'

Virginia smiled.

'I dare say,' he continued, 'that I am old-fashioned and unreasonable. It's the fashion, I know, to pop in and out of a house. Same idea as an hotel – perfect freedom of action, and no bill at the end!'

'You are an old grouser,' said Bundle. 'You've had Virginia and me. What more do you want?'

'Nothing more, nothing more,' Lord Caterham assured them hastily. 'That's not it at all. It's the principle of the thing. It gives one such a restless feeling. I'm quite willing to admit that it's been an almost ideal twenty-four hours. Peace – perfect peace. No burglaries or other crimes of violence, no detectives, no Americans. What I complain of is that I should have enjoyed it all so much more if I'd felt really secure. As it is, all the time, I've been saying to myself, "One or the other of them is bound to turn up in a minute." And that spoilt the whole thing.'

'Well, nobody has turned up,' said Bundle. 'We've been left severely alone – neglected, in fact. It's odd the way Fish disappeared. Didn't he say anything?'

'Not a word. Last time I saw him he was pacing up and down the rose garden yesterday afternoon, smoking one of those unpleasant cigars of his. After that he seems to have just melted into the landscape.'

'Somebody must have kidnapped him,' said Bundle hopefully.

'In another day or two, I expect we shall have Scotland Yard dragging the lake to find his dead body,' said her father gloomily. 'It serves me right. At my time of life, I ought to have gone quietly abroad and taken care of my health, and not allowed myself to be drawn into George Lomax's wild-cat schemes. I –'

He was interrupted by Tredwell.

'Well,' said Lord Caterham, irritably, 'what is it?'

'The French detective is here, my lord, and would be glad if you could spare him a few minutes.'

'What did I tell you?' said Lord Caterham. 'I knew it was too good to last. Depend up on it, they've found Fish's dead body doubled up in the goldfish pond.'

Tredwell, in a strictly respectful manner, steered him back to the point at issue.

'Am I to say that you will see him, my lord?'

'Yes, yes. Bring him in here.'

Tredwell departed. He returned a minute or two later announcing in a lugubrious voice:

'Monsieur Lemoine.'

The Frenchman came in with a quick, light step. His walk, more than his face, betrayed the fact that he was excited about something.

'Good evening, Lemoine,' said Lord Caterham. 'Have a drink, won't you?'

'I thank you, no.' He bowed punctiliously to the ladies. 'At last I make progress. As things are, I felt that you should be acquainted with the discoveries – the very grave discoveries that I have made in the course of the last twenty-four hours.'

'I thought there must be something important going on somewhere,' said Lord Caterham.

'My lord, yesterday afternoon one of your guests left this house in a curious manner. From the beginning, I must tell you, I have had my suspicions. Here is a man who comes from the wilds. Two months ago he was in South Africa. Before that – where?'

Virginia drew a sharp breath. For a moment the Frenchman's eyes rested on her doubtfully. Then he went on:

'Before that – where? None can say. And he is just such a one as the man I am looking for – gay, audacious, reckless, one who would dare anything. I send cable after cable, but I can get no word as to his past life. Ten years ago he was in Canada, yes, but since then – silence. My suspicions grow stronger. Then I pick up one day a scrap of paper where he has lately passed along. It bears an address – the address of a house in Dover. Later, as though by chance, I drop that same piece of paper. Out of the tail of my eye, I see this Boris, the Herzoslovakian, pick it up and take it to his master. All along I have been sure that this Boris is an emissary of the Comrades of the Red Hand. We know that the Comrades are working in with King Victor over this affair. If Boris recognized his chief in Mr Anthony Cade, would he not do just what he has done – transferred his allegiance? Why should he attach himself otherwise to an insignificant stranger? It was suspicious, I tell you, very suspicious.

'But almost I am disarmed, for Anthony Cade brings this same paper to me at once and asks me if I have dropped it. As I say, almost I am disarmed – but not quite! For it may mean that he is innocent, or it may mean that he is very, very clever. I deny, of course, that it is mine or that I dropped it. But in the meantime I have set inquiries on foot. Only today I have news. The house at Dover has been precipitately abandoned, but up till yesterday afternoon it was occupied by a body of foreigners. Not a doubt but that it was King Victor's headquarters. Now see the significance of these points. Yesterday afternoon, Mr Cade clears out from here precipitately. Ever since he dropped that paper, he must know that the game is up. He reaches Dover and immediately the gang is disbanded. What the next move will be, I do not know. What is quite certain is that Mr Anthony Cade will not return here. But knowing King Victor as I do, I am certain that he will not abandon the game without having one more try for the jewel. And that is when I shall get him!'

Virginia stood up suddenly. She walked across to the mantelpiece and spoke in a voice that rang cold like steel.

'You are leaving one thing out of account, I think, M. Lemoine,' she said. 'Mr Cade is not the only guest who disappeared yesterday in a suspicious manner.'

'You mean, madame? –'

'That all you have said applies equally well to another person. What about Mr Hiram Fish?'

'Oh, Mr Fish!'

'Yes, Mr Fish. Did you not tell us that first night that King Victor had lately come to England from America? So has Mr Fish come to England from America. It is true that he brought a letter of introduction from a very well-known man, but surely that would be a simple thing for a man like King Victor to manage. He is certainly not what he pretends to be. Lord Caterham has commented on the fact that when it is a question of the first editions he is supposed to have come here to see he is always the listener, never the talker. And there are several suspicious facts against him. There was a light in his window the night of the murder. Then take that evening in the Council Chamber. When I met him on the terrace he was fully dressed. *He* could have dropped the paper. You didn't actually *see* Mr Cade do so. Mr Cade may have gone to Dover. If he did it was simply to investigate. He may have been kidnapped there. I say that there is far more suspicion attaching to Mr Fish's actions than to Mr Cade's.'

The Frenchman's voice rang out sharply:

'From your point of view, that well may be, madame. I do not dispute it. And I agree that Mr Fish is not what he seems.'

'Well, then?'

'But that makes no difference. *You see, madame, Mr Fish is a Pinkerton's man.*'

'What?' cried Lord Caterham.

'Yes, Lord Caterham. He came over here to trail King Victor. Superintendent Battle and I have known this for some time.'

Virginia said nothing. Very slowly she sat down again. With those few words the structure that she had built up so carefully was scattered in ruins about her feet.

'You see,' Lemoine was continuing, 'we have all known that eventually King Victor would come to Chimneys. It was the one place we were sure of catching him.'

Virginia looked up with an odd light in her eyes, and suddenly she laughed.

'You've not caught him yet,' she said.

Lemoine looked at her curiously.

'No, madame. But I shall.'

'He's supposed to be rather famous for outwitting people, isn't he?'

The Frenchman's face darkened with anger.

'This time, it will be different,' he said between his teeth.

'He's a very attractive fellow,' said Lord Caterham. 'Very attractive. But surely – why, you said he was an old friend of yours, Virginia?'

'That is why,' said Virginia composedly, 'I think M. Lemoine must be making a mistake.'

And her eyes met the detective's steadily, but he appeared in no wise discomfited.

'Time will show, madame,' he said.

'Do you pretend that it was he who shot Prince Michael?' she asked presently.

'Certainly.'

But Virginia shook her head.

'Oh no!' she said, 'Oh, no! That is one thing I am quite sure of. Anthony Cade never killed Prince Michael.'

Lemoine was watching her intently.

'There is a possibility that you are right, madame,' he said slowly. 'A possibility, that is all. It may have been the Herzoslovakian, Boris, who exceeded his orders and fired that shot. Who knows, Prince Michael may have done him some great wrong, and the man sought revenge.'

'He looks a murderous sort of fellow,' agreed Lord Caterham.

'The housemaids, I believe, scream when he passes them in the passages.'

'Well,' said Lemoine. 'I must be going now. I felt it was due to you, my lord, to know exactly how things stand.'

'Very kind of you, I'm sure,' said Lord Caterham. 'Quite certain you won't have a drink? All right, then. Good night.'

'I hate that man with his prim little black beard and his eyeglasses,' said Bundle, as soon as the door had shut behind him. 'I hope Anthony *does* snoo him. I'd love to see him dancing with rage. What do you think about it all, Virginia?'

'I don't know,' said Virginia. 'I'm tired. I shall go up to bed.'

'Not a bad idea,' said Lord Caterham. 'It's half-past eleven.'

As Virginia was crossing the wide hall, she caught sight of a broad back that seemed familiar to her discreetly vanishing through a side door.

'Superintendent Battle,' she called imperiously.

The superintendent, for it was indeed he, retraced his steps with a shade of unwillingness.

'Yes, Mrs Revel?'

'M. Lemoine has been here. He says – Tell me, is it true, really true, that Mr Fish is an American detective?'

Superintendent Battle nodded.

'That's right.'

'You have known it all along?'

Again Superintendent Battle nodded.

Virginia turned away towards the staircase.

'I see,' she said. 'Thank you.'

Until that minute she had refused to believe.

And now? –

Sitting down before her dressing-table in her own room, she faced the question squarely. Every word that Anthony had said came back to her fraught with a new significance.

Was this the 'trade' that he had spoken of?

The trade that he had given up. But then –

An unusual sound disturbed the even tenor of her meditations. She lifted her head with a start. Her little gold clock showed the hour to be after one. Nearly two hours she had sat here thinking.

Again the sound was repeated. A sharp tap on the windowpane.

Virginia went to the window and opened it. Below on the pathway was a tall figure which even as she looked stooped for another handful of gravel.

For a moment Virginia's heart beat faster – then she recognized the massive strength and square-cut outline of the Herzoslovakian, Boris.

'Yes,' she said in a low voice. 'What is it?'

At the moment it did not strike her as strange that Boris should be throwing gravel at her window at this hour of the night.

'What is it?' she repeated impatiently.

'I come from the master,' said Boris in a low tone which nevertheless carried perfectly. 'He has sent for you.'

He made the statement in a perfectly matter-of-fact tone.

'Sent for me?'

'Yes, I am to bring you to him. There is a note. I will throw it up to you.'

Viriginia stood back a little, and a slip of paper, weighted with a stone, fell accurately at her feet. She unfolded it and read:

> *My dear* (Anthony had written) – *I'm in a tight place, but I mean to win through. Will you trust me and come to me?*

For quite two minutes Virginia stood there, immovable, reading those few words over and over again.

She raised her head, looking round the well-appointed luxury of the bedroom as though she saw it with new eyes.

Then she leaned out of the window again.

'What am I to do?' she asked.

'The detectives are the other side of the house, outside the Council Chamber. Come down and out through the side door. I will be there. I have a car waiting outside in the road.'

Virginia nodded. Quickly she changed her dress for one of fawn tricot, and pulled on a little fawn leather hat.

Then, smiling a little, she wrote a short note, addressed it to Bundle and pinned it to the pin-cushion.

She stole quietly downstairs and undid the bolts of the side door. Just a moment she paused, then, with a little gallant toss of the head, the same toss of the head with which her ancestors had gone into action in the Crusades, she passed through.

CHAPTER 26

THE 13TH OF OCTOBER

At ten o'clock on the morning of Wednesday, the 13th of October, Anthony Cade walked into Harridge's Hotel and asked for Baron Lolopretjzyl who was occupying a suite there.

After suitable and imposing delay, Anthony was taken to the suite in question. The Baron was standing on the hearthrug in a correct and stiff fashion. Little Captain Andrassy, equally correct as to demeanour, but with a slightly hostile attitude, was also present.

The usual bows, clicking of heels, and other formal greetings of etiquette took place. Anthony was, by now, thoroughly conversant with the routine.

'You will forgive this early call, I trust, Baron,' he said cheerfully, laying down his hat and stick on the table. 'As a matter of fact, I have a little business proposition to make to you.'

'Ha! Is that so?' said the Baron.

Captain Andrassy, who had never overcome his initial distrust of Anthony, looked suspicious.

'Business,' said Anthony, 'is based on the well-known principle of supply and demand. You want something, the other man has it. The only thing left to settle is the price.'

The Baron looked at him attentively, but said nothing.

'Between a Herzoslovakian nobleman and an English gentleman the terms should be easily arranged,' said Anthony rapidly.

He blushed a little as he said it. Such words do not rise easily to an Englishman's lips, but he had observed on previous occasions the enormous effect of such phraseology upon the Baron's mentality. True enough, the charm worked.

'That is so,' said the Baron approvingly, nodding his head. 'That is entirely so.'

Even Captain Andrassy appeared to unbend a little, and nodded his head also.

'Very good,' said Anthony. 'I won't beat about the bush any more –'

'What is that, you say?' interrupted the Baron. 'To beat about the bush? I do not comprehend.'

'A mere figure of speech, Baron. To speak in plain English, *you* want the goods, *we* have them! The ship is all very well, but it lacks a figurehead. By the ship, I mean the Loyalist Party of Herzoslovakia. At the present minute you lack the principal plank of your political programme. You are minus a Prince! Now supposing – only supposing, that I could supply you with a Prince?'

The Baron stared.

'I do not comprehend you in the least,' he declared.

'Sir,' said Captain Andrassy, twirling his moustache fiercely, 'you are insulting!'

'Not at all,' said Anthony. 'I'm trying to be helpful. Supply and demand, you understand. It's all perfectly fair and square. No Princes supplied unless genuine – see trademark. If we come to terms, you'll find it's quite all right. I'm offering you the real genuine article – out of the bottom drawer.'

'Not in the least,' the Baron declared again, 'do I comprehend you.'

'It doesn't really matter,' said Anthony kindly. 'I just want you to get used to the idea. To put it vulgarly, I've got something up my sleeve. Just get hold of this. You want a Prince. Under certain conditions, I will undertake to supply you with one.'

The Baron and Andrassy stared at him. Anthony took up his hat and stick again and prepared to depart.

'Just think it over. Now, Baron, there is one thing further. You must come down to Chimneys this evening – Captain Andrassy also. Several very curious things are likely to happen there. Shall we make an appointment? Say in the Council Chamber at nine o'clock? Thank you, gentlemen, I may rely upon you to be there?'

The Baron took a step forward and looked searchingly in Anthony's face.

'Mr Cade,' he said, not without dignity, 'it is not, I hope, that you wish to make fun of me?'

Anthony returned his gaze steadily.

'Baron,' he said, and there was a curious note in his voice, 'when this evening is over, I think you will be the first to admit that there is more earnest than jest about this business.'

Bowing to both men, he left the room.

His next call was in the City where he sent in his card to Mr Herman Isaacstein.

After some delay, Anthony was received by a pale and exquisitely dressed underling with an engaging manner and a military title.

'You wanted to see Mr Isaacstein, didn't you?' said the young man. 'I'm afraid he's most awfully busy this morning – board meetings and all that sort of thing, you know. Is it anything that I can do?'

'I must see him personally,' said Anthony, and added carelessly, 'I've just come up from Chimneys.'

The young man was slightly staggered by the mention of Chimneys.

'Oh!' he said doubtfully. 'Well, I'll see.'

'Tell him it's important,' said Anthony.

'Message from Lord Caterham?' suggested the young man.

'Something of the kind,' said Anthony, 'but it's imperative that I should see Mr Isaacstein at once.'

Two minutes later Anthony was conducted into a sumptuous inner sanctum where he was principally impressed by the immense size and roomy depths of the leather-covered armchairs.

Mr Isaacstein rose to greet him.

'You must forgive my looking you up like this,' said Anthony. 'I know that you're a busy man, and I'm not going to waste more of your time than I can help. It's just a little matter of business that I want to put before you.'

Isaacstein looked at him attentively for a minute or two out of his beady black eyes.

'Have a cigar,' he said unexpectedly, holding out an open box.

'Thank you,' said Anthony. 'I don't mind if I do.'

He helped himself.

'It's about this Herzoslovakian business,' continued Anthony as he accepted a match. He noted the momentary flickering of the other's steady gaze. 'The murder of Prince Michael must have rather upset the apple-cart.'

Mr Isaacstein raised one eyebrow, murmured. 'Ah?' interrogatively and transferred his gaze to the ceiling.

'Oil,' said Anthony, thoughtfully surveying the polished surface of the desk. 'Wonderful thing, oil.'

He felt the slight start the financier gave.

'Do you mind coming to the point, Mr Cade?'

'Not at all. I imagine, Mr Isaacstein, that if those oil concessions are granted to another company you won't be exactly pleased about it?'

'What's the proposition?' asked the other, looking straight at him.

'A suitable claimant to the throne, full of pro-British sympathies.'

'Where have you got him?'

'That's my business.'

Isaacstein acknowledged the retort by a slight smile, his glance had grown hard and keen.

'The genuine article? I can't stand for any funny business?'

'The absolute genuine article.'

'Straight?'

'Straight.'

'I'll take your word for it.'

'You don't seem to take much convincing?' said Anthony, looking curiously at him.

Herman Isaacstein smiled.

'I shouldn't be where I am now if I hadn't learnt to know whether a man is speaking the truth or not,' he replied simply. What terms do you want?'

'The same loan, on the same conditions, that you offered to Prince Michael.'

'What about yourself?'

'For the moment, nothing, except that I want you to come down to Chimneys tonight.'

'No,' said Isaacstein, with some decision. 'I can't do that.'

'Why?'

'Dining out – rather an important dinner.'

'All the same, I'm afraid you'll have to cut it out – for your own sake.'

'What do you mean?'

Anthony looked at him for a full minute before he said slowly:

'Do you know that they've found the revolver, the one Michael was shot with? Do you know where they found it? In your suitcase.'

'What?'

Isaacstein almost leapt from his chair. His face was frenzied.

'What are you saying? What do you mean?'

'I'll tell you.'

Very obligingly, Anthony narrated the occurrences in connexion with the finding of the revolver. As he spoke the other's face assumed a greyish tinge of absolute terror.

'But it's false,' he screamed out as Anthony finished. 'I never put it there. I know nothing about it. It is a plot.'

'Don't excite yourself,' said Anthony soothingly. 'If that's the case you'll easily be able to prove it.'

'Prove it? How can I prove it?'

'If I were you,' said Anthony gently, 'I'd come to Chimneys tonight.'

Isaacstein looked at him doubtfully.

'You advise it?'

Anthony leant forward and whispered to him. The financier fell back in amazement, staring at him.

'You actually mean –'

'Come and see,' said Anthony.

CHAPTER 27

THE 13TH OF OCTOBER (*cont'd*)

The clock in the Council Chamber struck nine.

'Well,' said Lord Caterham, with a deep sigh. 'Here they all are, just like little Bo-Peep's flock, back again and wagging their tails behind them.'

He looked sadly round the room.

'Organ grinder complete with monkey,' he murmured, fixing the Baron with his eye. 'Nosy Parker of Throgmorton Street –'

'I think you're rather unkind to the Baron,' protested Bundle, to whom these confidences were being poured out. 'He told me that he considered you the perfect example of English hospitality among the *haute noblesse*.'

'I dare say,' said Lord Caterham. 'He's always saying things like that. It makes him most fatiguing to talk to. But I can tell you I'm not nearly as much of the hospitable English gentleman as I was. As soon as I can I shall let Chimneys to an enterprising American, and go and live in an hotel. There, if anyone worries you, you can just ask for your bill and go.'

'Cheer up,' said Bundle. 'We seem to have lost Mr Fish for good.'

'I always found him rather amusing,' said Lord Caterham, who was in a contradictory temper. 'It's that precious young man of yours who has let me in for this. Why should I have this board meeting called in my house? Why doesn't he rent The Larches or Elmhurst, or some nice villa residence like that at Streatham, and hold his company meetings there?'

'Wrong atmosphere,' said Bundle.

'No one is going to play any tricks on us, I hope?' said her father nervously. 'I don't trust that French fellow, Lemoine. The French police are up to all sorts of dodges. Put india-rubber bands round your arm, and then reconstruct the crime and make you jump, and it's registered on a thermometer. I know that when they call out "Who killed Prince Michael?" I shall register a hundred and twenty-two or something perfectly frightful, and they'll haul me off to jail at once.'

The door opened and Tredwell announced:

'Mr George Lomax. Mr Eversleigh.'

'Enter Codders, followed by faithful dog,' murmured Bundle.

Bill made a beeline for her, whilst George greeted Lord Caterham in the genial manner he assumed for public occasions.

'My dear Caterham,' said George, shaking him by the hand, 'I got your message and came over, of course.'

'Very good of you, my dear fellow, very good of you. Delighted to see you.' Lord Caterham's conscience always drove him on to an excess of geniality when he was conscious of feeling none. 'Not that it was my message, but that doesn't matter at all.'

In the meantime Bill was attacking Bundle in an undertone.

'I say. What's it all about? What's this I hear about Virginia bolting off in the middle of the night? She's not been kidnapped, has she?'

'Oh, no,' said Bundle. 'She left a note pinned to the pin-cushion in the orthodox fashion.'

'She's not gone off with anyone, has she? Not with that Colonial Johnny? I never liked the fellow, and, from all I hear, there seems to be an idea floating around that he himself is the super-crook. But I don't quite see how that can be?'

'Why not?'

'Well, this King Victor was a French fellow, and Cade's English enough.'

'You don't happen to have heard that King Victor was an accomplished linguist, and, moreover, was half Irish?'

'Oh, Lord! Then that's why he's made himself scarce, is it?'

'I don't know about his making himself scarce. He disappeared the day before yesterday, as you know. But this morning we got a wire from him saying he would be down here at 9 p.m. tonight, and suggesting that Codders should be asked over. All these other people have turned up as well – asked by Mr Cade.'

'It is a gathering,' said Bill, looking round. 'One French detective by window, one English ditto by fire-place. Strong foreign element. The Stars and Stripes don't seem to be represented?'

Bundle shook her head.

'Mr Fish has disappeared into the blue. Virginia's not here either. But everyone else is assembled, and I have a feeling in my bones, Bill, that we are drawing very near to the moment when somebody says "James, the footman", and everything is revealed. We're only waiting now for Anthony Cade to arrive.'

'He'll never show up,' said Bill.

'Then why call this company meeting, as Father calls it?'

'Ah, there's some deep idea behind that. Depend upon it. Wants us all here while he's somewhere else – you know the sort of thing.'

'You don't think he'll come, then?'

'No fear. Run his head into the lion's mouth? Why, the room's bristling with detectives and high officials.'

'You don't know much about King Victor, if you think that would deter him. By all accounts, it's the kind of situation he loves above all, and he always manages to come out on top.'

Mr Eversleigh shook his head doubtfully.

'That would take some doing – with the dice loaded against him. He'll never –'

The door opened again and Tredwell announced:

'Mr Cade.'

Anthony came straight across to his host.

'Lord Caterham,' he said, 'I'm giving you a frightful lot of trouble, and I'm awfully sorry about it. But I really do think that tonight will see the clearing up of the mystery.'

Lord Caterham looked mollified. He had always had a secret liking for Anthony.

'No trouble at all,' he said heartily.

'It's very kind of you,' said Anthony. 'We're all here, I see. Then I can get on with the good work.'

'I don't understand,' said George Lomax weightily. 'I don't understand in the least. This is all very irregular. Mr Cade has no standing – no standing whatever. The position is a very difficult and delicate one. I am strongly of the opinion –'

George's flood of eloquence was arrested. Moving unobtrusively to the great man's side, Superintendent Battle whispered a few words in his ear. George looked perplexed and baffled.

'Very well, if you say so,' he remarked grudgingly. Then added in a louder tone, 'I'm sure we are all willing to listen to what Mr Cade has to say.'

Anthony ignored the palpable condescension of the other's tone.

'It's just a little idea of mine, that's all,' he said cheerfully. 'Probably all of you know that we got hold of a certain message in cipher the other day. There was a reference to Richmond, and some numbers.' He paused. 'Well, we had a shot at solving it – and we failed. Now in the late Count Stylptitch's memoirs (which I happen to have read) there is a reference to a certain dinner – a "flower" dinner which everyone attended wearing a badge representing a flower. The Count himself wore the exact duplicate of that curious device we found in the cavity in the secret passage. It represented a rose. If you remember, it was all *rows* of things – buttons, letter Es, and finally rows of knitting. Now, gentlemen, what is there in this house that is arranged in rows? Books, isn't that so? Add to that, that in the catalogue of Lord Caterham's library there is a book called *The Life of the Earl of Richmond*, and I think you will get a very fair idea of the hiding-place. Starting at the volume in question, and using the numbers to denote shelves and books, I think you will find that the – er – object of our search is concealed in a dummy book, or in a cavity behind a particular book.'

Anthony looked round modestly, obviously waiting for applause.

'Upon my word, that's very ingenious,' said Lord Caterham.

'Quite ingenious,' admitted George condescendingly. 'But it remains to be seen –'

Anthony laughed.

'The proof of the pudding's in the eating – eh? Well, I'll soon settle that for you.' He sprang to his feet. 'I'll go to the library –'

He got no farther. M. Lemoine moved forward from the window.

'Just one moment, Mr Cade. You permit, Lord Caterham?'

He went to the writing-table, and hurriedly scribbled a few lines. He sealed them up in an envelope, and then rang the bell. Tredwell appeared in answer to it. Lemoine handed him the note.

'See that that is delivered at once, if you please.'

'Very good, sir,' said Tredwell.

With his usual dignified tread he withdrew.

Anthony, who had been standing, irresolute, sat down again.

'What's the big idea, Lemoine?' he asked gently.

There was a sudden sense of strain in the atmosphere.

'If the jewel is where you say it is – well, it has been there for over seven years – a quarter of an hour more does not matter.'

'Go on,' said Anthony. 'That wasn't all you wanted to say?'

'No, it was not. At this juncture it is – unwise to permit any one person to leave the room. Especially if that person has rather questionable antecedents.'

Anthony raised his eyebrows and lighted a cigarette.

'I suppose a vagabond life is not very respectable,' he mused.

'Two months ago, Mr Cade, you were in South Africa. That is admitted. Where were you before that?'

Anthony leaned back in his chair, idly blowing smoke rings.

'Canada. Wild North-west.'

'Are you sure you were not in prison? A French prison?'

Automatically, Superintendent Battle moved a step nearer the door, as if to cut off a retreat that way, but Anthony showed no signs of doing anything dramatic.

Instead, he stared at the French detective, and then burst out laughing.

'My poor Lemoine. It is a monomania with you! You do indeed see King Victor everywhere. So you fancy that I am that interesting gentleman?'

'Do you deny it?'

Anthony brushed a fleck of ash from his coat-sleeve.

'I never deny anything that amuses me,' he said lightly. 'But the accusation is really too ridiculous.'

'Ah! You think so?' The Frenchman leant forward. His face was twitching painfully, and yet he seemed perplexed and baffled – as though something in Anthony's manner puzzled him. 'What if I tell you, monsieur, that this time – this time – I am out to get King Victor, and nothing shall stop me!'

'Very laudable,' was Anthony's comment. 'You've been out to get him before, though, haven't you, Lemoine? And he's got the better of you. Aren't you afraid that that may happen again? He's a slippery fellow, by all accounts.'

The conversation had developed into a duel between the detective and Anthony. Everyone else in the room was conscious of the tension. It was a fight to a finish between the Frenchman, painfully in earnest, and the man who smoked so calmly and whose words seemed to show that he had not a care in the world.

'If I were you, Lemoine,' continued Anthony, 'I should be very, very careful. Watch your step, and all that sort of thing.'

'This time,' said Lemoine grimly, 'there will be no mistake.'

'You seem very sure about it all,' said Anthony. 'But there's such a thing as evidence, you know.'

Lemoine smiled, and something in his smile seemed to attract Anthony's attention. He sat up and stubbed out his cigarette.

'You saw that note I wrote just now?' said the French detective. 'It was to my people at the inn. Yesterday I received from France the fingerprints and the Bertillon measurements of King Victor – the so-called Captain O'Neill. I have asked for them to be sent up to me here. In a few minutes we shall *know* whether you are the man!'

Anthony stared steadily at him. Then a little smile crept over his face.

'You're really rather clever, Lemoine. I never thought of that.

The documents will arrive, you will induce me to dip my fingers in the ink, or something equally unpleasant, and you will measure my ears and look for my distinguishing marks. And if they agree –'

'Well,' said Lemoine, 'if they agree – eh?'

Anthony leaned forward in his chair.

'Well, if they do agree,' he said very gently, 'what then?'

'What then?' The detective seemed taken aback. 'But – I shall have proved then that you are King Victor!'

But for the first time, a shade of uncertainty crept into his manner.

'That will doubtless be a great satisfaction to you,' said Anthony. 'But I don't quite see where it's going to hurt me. I'm not admitting anything, but supposing, just for the sake of argument, that I was King Victor – I might be trying to repent, you know.'

'Repent?'

'That's the idea. Put yourself in King Victor's place, Lemoine. Use your imagination. You've just come out of prison. You're getting on in life. You've lost the first fine rapture of the adventurous life. Say, even, that you meet a beautiful girl. You think of marrying and settling down somewhere in the country where you can grow vegetable marrows. You decide henceforth to lead a blameless life. Put yourself in King Victor's place. Can't you imagine feeling like that?'

'I do not think that I should feel like that,' said Lemoine with a sardonic smile.

'Perhaps you wouldn't,' admitted Anthony. 'But then you're not King Victor, are you? You can't possibly know what he feels like.'

'But it is nonsense, what you are saying there,' spluttered the Frenchman.

'Oh, no, it isn't. Come now, Lemoine, if I'm King Victor, what have you against me after all? You could never get the necessary evidence in the old, old days, remember. I've served my sentence, and that's all there is to it. I suppose you could arrest me for the French equivalent of "Loitering with intent to commit a felony", but that would be poor satisfaction, wouldn't it?'

'You forget,' said Lemoine. 'America! How about this business of obtaining money under false pretences, and passing yourself off as Prince Nicholas Obolovitch?'

'No good, Lemoine,' said Anthony, 'I was nowhere near America at the time. And I can prove that easily enough. If King Victor impersonated Prince Nicholas in America, then I'm not King Victor. You're sure he *was* impersonated? That it wasn't the man himself?'

Superintendent Battle suddenly interposed.

'The man was an imposter all right, Mr Cade.'

'I wouldn't contradict you, Battle,' said Anthony. 'You have such a habit of being always right. Are you equally sure that Prince Nicholas died in the Congo?'

Battle looked at him curiously.

'I wouldn't swear to that, sir. But it's generally believed.'

'Careful man. What's your motto? Plenty of rope, eh? I've taken a leaf out of your book. I've given M. Lemoine plenty of rope. I've not denied his accusations. But, all the same, I'm afraid he's going to be disappointed. You see I always believe in having something up one's sleeve. Anticipating that some little unpleasantness might arise here, I took the precaution to bring a trump card along with me. It – or rather he – is upstairs.'

'Upstairs?' said Lord Caterham, very interested.

'Yes, he's been having rather a trying time of it lately, poor fellow. Got a nasty bump on the head from someone. I've been looking after him.'

Suddenly the deep voice of Mr Isaacstein broke in: 'Can we guess who he is?'

'If you like,' said Anthony, 'but –'

Lemoine interrupted with sudden ferocity:

'All this is foolery. You think to outwit me yet again. It may be true what you say – that you were not in America. You are too clever to say it if it were not true. But there is something else. Murder! Yes, murder. The murder of Prince Michael. He interfered with you that night as you were looking for the jewel.'

'Lemoine, have you ever known King Victor do murder?' Anthony's voice rang out sharply. 'You know as well – better than I do – that he has never shed blood.'

'Who else but you could have murdered him?' cried Lemoine. 'Tell me that!'

The last word died on his lips, as a shrill whistle sounded from the terrace outside. Anthony sprang up, all his assumed nonchalance laid aside.

'You ask me who murdered Prince Michael?' he cried. 'I won't tell you – I'll *show* you. That whistle was the signal I've been waiting for. The murderer of Prince Michael is in the library now.'

He sprang out through the window, and the others followed him as he led the way round the terrace until they came to the library window. He pushed the window, and it yielded to his touch.

Very softly he held aside the thick curtain, so that they could look into the room.

Standing by the bookcase was a dark figure, hurriedly pulling out and replacing volumes, so absorbed in the task that no outside sound was heeded.

And then, as they stood watching, trying to recognize the figure that was vaguely silhouetted against the light of the electric torch it carried, someone sprang past them with a sound like the roar of a wild beast.

The torch fell to the ground, was extinguished, and the sounds of a terrific struggle filled the room. Lord Caterham groped his way to the lights and switched them on.

Two figures were swaying together. And as they looked the end came. The short, sharp crack of a pistol shot, and the small figure crumbled up and fell. The other figure turned and faced them – it was Boris, his eyes alight with rage.

'She killed my master,' he growled. 'Now she tries to shoot me. I would have taken the pistol from her and shot her, but it went off in the struggle. St Michael directed it. The evil woman is dead.'

'A woman?' cried George Lomax.

They drew nearer. On the floor, the pistol still clasped in her hand, and an expression of deadly malignity on her face, lay – Mademoiselle Brun.

CHAPTER 28

KING VICTOR

'I suspected her from the first,' explained Anthony. 'There was a light in her room on the night of the murder. Afterwards, I wavered. I made inquiries about her in Brittany, and came back satisfied that she was what she represented herself to be. I was a fool. Because the Comtesse de Breteuil had employed a Mademoiselle Brun and spoke highly of her, it never occurred to me that the real Mademoiselle Brun might have been kidnapped on her way to her new post, and that it might be a substitute taking her place. Instead I shifted my suspicions to Mr Fish. It was not until he had followed me to Dover, and we had had a mutual explanation, that I began to see clearly. Once I knew that he was a Pinkerton's man, trailing King Victor, my suspicions swung back again to their original object.

'The thing that worried me most was that Mrs Revel had definitely recognized the woman. Then I remembered that it was only *after* I had mentioned her being Madame de Breteuil's governess. And all she had said was that that accounted for the fact that the woman's face was familiar to her. Superintendent Battle will tell you that a deliberate plot was formed to keep Mrs Revel from coming to Chimneys. Nothing more nor less than a dead body, in fact. And though the murder was the work of the Comrades of the Red Hand, punishing supposed treachery on the part of the victim, the staging of it, and the absence of the Comrade's sign-manual, pointed to some abler intelligence directing operations. From the first, I suspected some connexion with Herzoslovakia. Mrs Revel was the only member of the house party who had been to the country. I suspected at first that someone was impersonating Prince Michael, but that proved to be a totally erroneous idea. When I realized the possibility of Mademoiselle Brun's being an impostor, and added to that the fact that her face was familiar to Mrs Revel, I began to see daylight. It was evidently very important that she should not be recognized, and Mrs Revel was the only person likely to do so.'

'But who was she?' said Lord Caterham. 'Someone Mrs Revel had known in Herzoslovakia?'

'I think the Baron might be able to tell us,' said Anthony.

'I?' The Baron stared at him, then down at the motionless figure.

'Look well,' said Anthony. 'Don't be put off by the make-up. She was an actress once, remember.'

The Baron stared again. Suddenly he started.

'God in heaven,' he breathed, 'it is not possible.'

'What is not possible?' asked George. 'Who is the lady? You recognize her, Baron?'

'No, no, it is not possible.' The Baron continued to mutter. 'She was killed. They were both killed. On the steps of the palace. Her body was recovered.'

'Mutilated and unrecognizable,' Anthony reminded him. 'She managed to put up a bluff. I think she escaped to America, and has spent a good many years lying low in deadly terror of the Comrades of the Red Hand. They promoted the revolution, remember, and, to use an expressive phrase, they always had it in for her. Then King Victor was released, and they planned to recover the diamond together. She was searching for it that night when she came suddenly upon Prince Michael, and he recognized her. There was never much fear of her meeting him in the ordinary way of things. Royal guests don't come in contact with governesses, and she could always retire with a convenient migraine, as she did the day the Baron was here.

'However, she met Prince Michael face to face when she least expected it. Exposure and disgrace stared her in the face. She shot him. It was she who placed the revolver in Isaacstein's suitcase, so as to confuse the trail, and she who returned the letters.'

Lemoine moved forward.

'She was coming down to search for the jewel that night, you say,' he said. 'Might she not have been going to meet her accomplice, King Victor, who was coming from outside? Eh? What do you say to that?'

Anthony sighed.

'Still at it, my dear Lemoine? How persistent you are! You won't take my hint that I've got a trump card up my sleeve?'

But George, whose mind worked slowly, now broke in.

'I am still completely at sea. Who was this lady, Baron? You recognize her, it seems?'

But the Baron drew himself up and stood very straight and stiff.

'You are in error, Mr Lomax. To my knowledge I have not this lady seen before. A complete stranger she is to me.'

'But –'

George stared at him – bewildered.

The Baron took him into a corner of the room, and murmured something into his ear. Anthony watched with a good deal of enjoyment, George's face turning slowly purple, his eyes bulging, and all the incipient symptoms of apoplexy. A murmur of George's throaty voice came to him.

'Certainly . . . certainly . . . by all means . . . no need at all . . . complicate situation . . . utmost discretion.'

'Ah!' Lemoine hit the table sharply with his hand. 'I do not care about all this! The murder of Prince Michael – that was not my affair. I want King Victor.'

Anthony shook his head gently.

'I'm sorry for you, Lemoine. You're really a very able fellow. But, all the same, you're going to lose the trick. I'm about to play my trump card.'

He stepped across the room and rang the bell. Tredwell answered it.

'A gentlemen arrived with me this evening, Tredwell.'

'Yes, sir, a foreign gentleman.'

'Quite so. Will you kindly ask him to join us here as soon as possible?'

'Yes, sir.'

Tredwell withdrew.

'Entry of the trump card, the mysterious Monsieur X,' remarked Anthony. '*Who is he?* Can anyone guess?'

'Putting two and two together,' said Herman Isaacstein, 'what with your mysterious hints this morning, and your attitude this afternoon, I should say there was no doubt about it. Somehow or other you've managed to get hold of Prince Nicholas of Herzoslovakia.'

'You think the same, Baron?'

'I do. Unless yet another impostor you have put forward. But that I will not believe. With me, your dealings most honourable have been.'

'Thank you, Baron. I shan't forget those words. So you are all agreed?'

His eyes swept round the circle of waiting faces. Only Lemoine did not respond, but kept his eyes fixed sullenly on the table.

Anthony's quick ears had caught the sound of footsteps outside in the hall.

'And yet, you know,' he said with a queer smile, 'you're all wrong!'

He crossed swiftly to the door and flung it open.

A man stood on the threshold – a man with a neat black beard, eyeglasses, and a foppish appearance slightly marred by a bandage round the head.

'Allow me to present to you the real Monsieur Lemoine of the Sûreté.'

There was a rush and a scuffle, and then the nasal tones of Mr Hiram Fish rose bland and reassuring from the window:

'No, you don't, sonny – not this way. I have been stationed here this whole evening for the particular purpose of preventing your escape. You will observe that I have you covered well and good with this gun of mine. I came over to get you, and I've got you – but you sure are some lad!'

CHAPTER 29

FURTHER EXPLANATIONS

'You owe us an explanation, I think, Mr Cade,' said Herman Isaacstein, somewhat later in the evening.

'There's nothing much to explain,' said Anthony modestly. 'I went to Dover and Fish followed me under the impression that I was King Victor. We found a mysterious stranger imprisoned there, and as soon as we heard his story we knew where we were. The same idea again, you see. The real man kidnapped, and the false one – in this case King Victor himself – takes his place. But it seems that Battle here always thought there was something fishy about his French colleague, and wired to Paris for his fingerprints and other means of identification.'

'Ah!' cried the Baron. 'The fingerprints. The Bertillon measurements that that scoundrel talked about?'

'It was a clever idea,' said Anthony. 'I admired it so much that I felt forced to play it up. Besides, my doing so puzzled the false Lemoine enormously. You see, as soon as I had given the tip about the "rows" and where the jewel really was, he was keen to pass on the news to his accomplice, and at the same time to keep us all in that room. The note was really to Mademoiselle Brun. He told Tredwell to deliver it at once, and Tredwell did so by taking it upstairs to the schoolroom. Lemoine accused me of being King Victor, by that means creating a diversion and preventing anyone from leaving the room. By the time all that had been cleared up and we adjourned to the library to look for the stone, he flattered himself that the stone would be no longer there to find!'

George cleared his throat.

'I must say, Mr Cade,' he said pompously, 'that I consider your action in that matter highly reprehensible. If the slightest hitch had occurred in your plans, one of our national possessions might have disappeared beyond the hope of recovery. It was foolhardy, Mr Cade, reprehensibly foolhardy.'

'I guess you haven't tumbled to the little idea, Mr Lomax,' said the drawling voice of Mr Fish. 'That historic diamond was never behind the books in the library.'

'Never?'

'Not on your life.'

'You see,' explained Anthony, 'that little device of Count Stylptitch's stood for what it had originally stood for – a rose. When that dawned upon me on Monday afternoon, I went straight to the rose garden. Mr Fish had already tumbled to the same idea. If, standing with your back to the sundial, you take seven paces straight forward, then eight to the left and three to the right, you come to some bushes of a bright red rose called Richmond. The house has been ransacked to find the hiding-place, but nobody has thought of digging in the garden. I suggest a little digging party tomorrow morning.'

'Then the story about the books in the library –'

'An invention of mine to trap the lady. Mr Fish kept watch on the terrace, and whistled when the psychological moment had arrived. I may say that Mr Fish and I established martial law at the Dover house, and prevented the Comrades from communicating with the false Lemoine. He sent them an order to clear out, and word was conveyed to him that this had been done. So he went happily ahead with his plans for denouncing me.'

'Well, well,' said Lord Caterham cheerfully, 'everything seems to have been cleared up most satisfactorily.'

'Everything but one thing,' said Mr Isaacstein.

'What is that?'

The great financier looked steadily at Anthony.

'What did you get me down here for? Just to assist at a dramatic scene as an interested onlooker?'

Anthony shook his head.

'No, Mr Isaacstein. You are a busy man whose time is money. Why did you come down here originally?'

'To negotiate a loan.'

'With whom?'

'Prince Michael of Herzoslovakia.'

'Exactly. Prince Michael is dead. Are your prepared to offer the same loan on the same terms to his cousin Nicholas?'

'Can you produce him? I thought he was killed in the Congo?'

'He was killed all right. I killed him. Oh, no, I'm not a murderer. When I say I killed him, I mean that I spread the report of his death. I promise you a Prince, Mr Isaacstein. Will *I* do?'

'You?'

'Yes, I'm the man. Nicholas Sergius Alexander Ferdinand Obolovitch. Rather long for the kind of life I proposed to live, so I emerged from the Congo as plain Anthony Cade.'

Little Captain Andrassy sprang up.

'But this is incredible – incredible,' he spluttered. 'Have a care, sir, what you say.'

'I can give you plenty of proofs,' said Anthony quietly. 'I think I shall be able to convince the Baron here.'

The Baron lifted his hand.

'Your proofs I will examine, yes. But of them for me there is no need. Your word alone sufficient for me is. Besides, your English mother you much resemble. All along have I said: "This young man on one side or the other most highly born is."'

'You have always trusted my word, Baron,' said Anthony. 'I can assure you that in the days to come I shall not forget.'

Then he looked over at Superintendent Battle, whose face had remained perfectly expressionless.

'You can understand,' said Anthony with a smile, 'that my position has been extremely precarious. Of all of those in the house I might be supposed to have the best reason for wishing Michael Obolovitch out of the way, since I was the next heir to the throne. I've been extraordinarily afraid of Battle all along. I always felt that he suspected me, but that he was held up by lack of motive.'

'I never believed for a minute that you'd shot him, sir,' said Superintendent Battle. 'We've got a feeling in such matters. But I knew that you were afraid of something, and you puzzled me. If I'd known sooner who you really were I dare say I'd have yielded to the evidence, and arrested you.'

'I'm glad I managed to keep one guilty secret from you. You wormed everything else out of me all right. You're a damned good man at your job Battle. I shall always think of Scotland Yard with respect.'

'Most amazing,' muttered George. 'Most amazing story I ever heard. I – I can really hardly believe it. You are quite sure, Baron, that –'

'My dear Mr Lomax,' said Anthony, with a slight hardness in his tone, 'I have no intention of asking the British Foreign Office to support my claim without bringing forward the most convincing documentary evidence. I suggest that we adjourn now, and that you, the Baron, Mr Isaacstein and myself discuss the terms of the proposed loan.'

The Baron rose to his feet, and clicked his heels together.

'It will be the proudest moment of my life, sir,' he said solemnly, 'when I see you King of Herzoslovakia.'

'Oh, by the way, Baron,' said Anthony carelessly, slipping his hand through the other's arm, 'I forgot to tell you. There's a string tied to this. I'm married, you know.'

The Baron retreated a step or two. Dismay overspread his countenance.

'Something wrong I knew there would be,' he boomed. 'Merciful God in heaven! He has married a black woman in Africa!'

'Come, come, it's not so bad as all that,' said Anthony laughing. 'She's white enough – white all through, bless her.'

'Good. A respectable morganatic affair it can be, then.'

'Not a bit of it. She's to play Queen to my King. It's no

use shaking your head. She's fully qualified for the post. She's the daughter of an English peer who dates back to the time of the Conqueror. It's very fashionable just now for royalties to marry into the aristocracy – and she knows something of Herzoslovakia.'

'My God!' cried George Lomax, startled out of his usual careful speech. 'Not – not – Virginia Revel?'

'Yes,' said Anthony. 'Virginia Revel.'

'My dear fellow,' cried Lord Caterham, 'I mean – sir, I congratulate you. I do indeed. A delightful creature.'

'Thank you, Lord Caterham,' said Anthony. 'She's all you say and more.'

But Mr Isaacstein was regarding him curiously.

'You'll excuse my asking your Highness, but when did this marriage take place?'

Anthony smiled back at him.

'As a matter of fact,' he said, 'I married her this morning.'

CHAPTER 30

ANTHONY SIGNS ON FOR A NEW JOB

'If you will go on, gentlemen, I will follow you in a minute,' said Anthony.

He waited while the others filed out, and then turned to where Superintendent Battle was standing apparently absorbed in examining the panelling.

'Well, Battle? Want to ask me something, don't you?'

'Well, I do, sir, though I don't know how you knew I did. But I always marked you out as being specially quick in the uptake. I take it that the lady who is dead was the late Queen Varaga?'

'Quite right, Battle. It'll be hushed up, I hope. You can understand what I feel about family skeletons.'

'Trust Mr Lomax for that, sir. No one will ever know. That is, a lot of people will know, but it won't get about.'

'Was that what you wanted to ask me about?'

'No, sir – that was only in passing. I was curious to know just what made you drop your own name – if I'm not taking too much of a liberty?'

'Not a bit of it. I'll tell you. I killed myself for the purest motives, Battle. My mother was English, I'd been educated in England, and I was far more interested in England than in Herzoslovakia. And I felt an absolute fool knocking about the world with a comic-opera title tacked on to me. You see, when I was very young, I had democratic ideas. Believed in the purity of ideals, and the equality of all men. I especially disbelieved in Kings and Princes.'

'And since then?' asked Battle shrewdly.

'Oh, since then, I've travelled and seen the world. There's damned little equality going about. Mind you, I still believe in democracy. But you've got to force it on people with a strong hand – ram it down their throats. Men don't want to be brothers – they may some day, but they don't now. My belief in the brotherhood of man died the day I arrived in London last week, when I observed people standing in a Tube train resolutely refuse to move up and make room for those who entered. You won't turn people into angels by appealing to their better natures just yet awhile – but by judicious force you can coerce them into behaving more or less decently to one another to go on with. I still believe in the brotherhood of man, but it's not coming yet awhile. Say another ten thousand years or so. It's no good being impatient. Evolution is a slow process.'

'I'm very interested in these views of yours, sir,' said Battle with a twinkle. 'And if you'll allow me to say so, I'm sure you'll make a very fine King out there.'

'Thank you, Battle,' said Anthony with a sigh.

'You don't seem very happy about it, sir?'

'Oh, I don't know. I dare say it will be rather fun. But it's tying oneself down to regular work. I've always avoided that before.'

'But you consider it your duty, I suppose, sir?'

'Good Lord, no! What an idea. It's a woman – it's always a woman, Battle. I'd do more than be a King for her sake.'

'Quite so, sir.'

'I've arranged it so that the Baron and Isaacstein can't kick. The one wants a King, and the other wants oil. They'll both get what they want, and I've got – oh, Lord, Battle, have you ever been in love?'

'I am much attached to Mrs Battle, sir.'

'Much attached to Mrs – oh, you don't know what I'm talking about! It's entirely different!'

'Excuse me, sir, that man of yours is waiting outside the window.'

'Boris? So he is. He's a wonderful fellow. It's a mercy that pistol went off in the struggle and killed the lady. Otherwise Boris would have wrung her neck as sure as Fate, and then you would have wanted to hang him. His attachment to the Obolovitch dynasty is remarkable. The queer thing was that as soon as Michael was dead he attached himself to me – and yet he couldn't possibly have known who I really was.'

'Instinct,' said Battle. 'Like a dog.'

'Very awkward instinct I thought it at the time. I was afraid it might give the show away to you. I suppose I'd better see what he wants.'

He went out through the window. Superintendent Battle, left alone, looked after him for a minute, then apparently addressed the panelling.

'He'll do,' said Superintendent Battle.

Outside Boris explained himself.

'Master,' he said, and led the way along the terrace.

Anthony followed him, wondering what was forward.

Presently Boris stopped and pointed with his forefinger. It was moonlight, and in front of them was a stone seat on which sat two figures.

'He *is* a dog,' said Anthony to himself. 'And what's more a pointer!'

He strode forward. Boris melted into the shadows.

The two figures rose to meet him. One of them was Virginia – the other –

'Hullo, Joe,' said a well-remembered voice. 'This is a great girl of yours.'

'Jimmy McGrath, by all that's wonderful,' cried Anthony. 'How in the name of fortune did you get here?'

'That trip of mine into the interior went phut. Then some dagos came monkeying around. Wanted to buy that manuscript off me. Next thing I as near as nothing got a knife in the back one night. That made me think that I'd handed you out a bigger job than

I knew. I thought you might need help, and I came along after you by the very next boat.'

'Wasn't it splendid of him?' said Virginia. She squeezed Jimmy's arm. 'Why didn't you ever tell me how frightfully nice he was? You are, Jimmy, you're a perfect dear.'

'You two seem to be getting along all right,' said Anthony.

'Sure thing,' said Jimmy. 'I was snooping round for news of you, when I connected with this dame. She wasn't at all what I thought she'd be – some swell haughty society lady that'd scare the life out of me.'

'He told me all about the letters,' said Virginia. 'And I feel almost ashamed not to have been in real trouble over them when he was such a knight-errant.'

'If I'd known what you were like,' said Jimmy gallantly, 'I'd not have given him the letters. I'd have brought them to you myself. Say, young man, is the fun really over? Is there nothing for me to do?'

'By Jove,' said Anthony, 'there is! Wait a minute.'

He disappeared into the house. In a minute or two he returned with a paper package which he cast into Jimmy's arms.

'Go round to the garage and help yourself to a likely looking car. Beat it to London and deliver that parcel at 17 Everdean Square. That's Mr Balderson's private address. In exchange he'll hand you a thousand pounds.'

'What? It's not the memoirs? I understood that they'd been burnt.'

'What do you take me for?' demanded Anthony. 'You don't think I'd fall for a story like that, do you? I rang up the publishers at once, found out that the other was a fake call, and arranged accordingly. I made up a dummy package as I'd been directed to do. But I put the real package in the manager's safe and handed over the dummy. The memoirs have never been out of my possession.'

'Bully for you, my son,' said Jimmy.

'Oh, Anthony,' cried Virginia. 'You're not going to let them be published?'

'I can't help myself. I can't let a pal like Jimmy down. But you needn't worry. I've had time to wade through them, and I see now why people always hint that bigwigs don't write their own reminiscences but hire someone to do it for them. As a writer, Stylptitch is an insufferable bore. He proses on about statecraft, and doesn't go in for any racy and indiscreet anecdotes. His ruling passion of secrecy held strong to the end. There's not a word in the memoirs from beginning to end to flutter the susceptibilities of the most difficult politician. I rang up Balderson today, and arranged with him that I'd deliver the manuscript tonight before midnight. But Jimmy can do his own dirty work now that he's here.'

'I'm off,' said Jimmy. 'I like the idea of that thousand pounds – especially when I'd made up my mind it was down and out.'

'Half a second,' said Anthony. 'I've got a confession to make to you, Virginia. Something that everyone else knows, but that I haven't yet told you.'

'I don't mind how many strange women you've loved so long as you don't tell me about them.'

'Women!' said Anthony, with a virtuous air. 'Women indeed? You ask James here what kind of women I was going about with the last time he saw me.'

'Frumps,' said Jimmy solemnly. 'Utter frumps. Not one a day under forty-five.'

'Thank you, Jimmy,' said Anthony, 'you're a true friend. No, it's much worse than that. I've deceived you as to my real name.'

'Is it very dreadful?' said Virginia, with interest. 'It isn't something silly like Pobbles, is it? Fancy being called Mrs Pobbles.'

'You are always thinking the worst of me.'

'I admit that I did once think you were King Victor, but only for about a minute and a half.'

'By the way, Jimmy, I've got a job for you – gold prospecting in the rocky fastnesses of Herzoslovakia.'

'Is there gold there?' asked Jimmy eagerly.

'Sure to be,' said Anthony. 'It's a wonderful country.'

'So you're taking my advice and going there?'

'Yes,' said Anthony. 'Your advice was worth more than you knew. Now for the confession. I wasn't changed at nurse, or anything romantic like that, but nevertheless I am really Prince Nicholas Obolovitch of Herzoslovakia.'

'Oh, Anthony,' cried Virginia. 'How perfectly screaming! And I have married you! What are we going to do about it?'

'We'll go to Herzoslovakia and pretend to be Kings and Queens. Jimmy McGrath once said that the average life of a King or Queen out there is under four years. I hope you don't mind?'

'Mind?' cried Virginia. 'I shall love it!'

'Isn't she great?' murmured Jimmy.

Then, discreetly, he faded into the night. A few minutes later the sound of a car was heard.

'Nothing like letting a man do his own dirty work,' said Anthony with satisfaction. 'Besides, I didn't know how else to get rid of him. Since we were married I've not had one minute alone with you.'

'We'll have a lot of fun,' said Virginia. 'Teaching the brigands not to be brigands, and the assassins not to assassinate, and generally improving the moral tone of the country.'

'I like to hear these pure ideals,' said Anthony. 'It makes me feel my sacrifice has not been in vain.'

'Rot,' said Virginia calmly, 'you'll enjoy being a King. It's in your blood, you know. You were brought up to the trade of royalty, and you've got a natural aptitude for it, just like plumbers have a natural bent for plumbing.'

'I never think they have,' said Anthony. 'But, damn it all, don't let's waste time talking about plumbers. Do you know that at this very minute I'm supposed to be deep in conference with Isaacstein and old Lollipop? They want to talk about oil. Oil, my God! They can just await my kingly pleasure. Virginia, do you remember my telling you once that I'd have a damned good try to make you care for me?'

'I remember,' said Virginia softly. 'But Superintendent Battle was looking out of the window.'

'Well, he isn't now,' said Anthony.

He caught her suddenly to him, kissing her eyelids, her lips, the green gold of her hair . . .

'I do love you so, Virginia,' he whispered. 'I do love you so. Do you love me?'

He looked down at her – sure of the answer.

Her head rested against his shoulder, and very low, in a sweet shaken voice, she answered:

'Not a bit!'

'You little devil,' cried Anthony, kissing her again. 'Now I know for certain that I shall love you until I die . . .'

CHAPTER 31

SUNDRY DETAILS

Scene – Chimneys, 11 a.m. Thursday morning.

Johnson, the police constable, with his coat off, digging.

Something in the nature of a funeral feeling seems to be in the air. The friends and relations stand round the grave that Johnson is digging.

George Lomax has the air of the principal beneficiary under the will of the deceased. Superintendent Battle, with his immovable face, seems pleased that the funeral arrangements have gone so nicely. As the undertaker, it reflects credit upon him. Lord Caterham has that solemn and shocked look which Englishmen assume when a religious ceremony is in progress.

Mr Fish does not fit into the picture so well. He is not sufficiently grave.

Johnson bends to his task. Suddenly he straightens up. A little stir of excitement passes round.

'That'll do, sonny,' said Mr Fish. 'We shall do nicely now.'

One perceives at once that he is really the family physician.

Johnson retires. Mr Fish, with due solemnity, stoops over the excavation. The surgeon is about to operate.

He brings out a small canvas package. With much ceremony he hands it to Superintendent Battle. The latter, in his turn, hands it to George Lomax. The etiquette of the situation has now been carefully complied with.

George Lomax unwraps the package, slits up the oilsilk inside it, burrows into further wrapping. For a moment he holds something on the palm of his hand – then quickly shrounds it once more in cottonwool.

He clears his throat.

'At this auspicious moment,' he begins, with the clear delivery of the practised speaker.

Lord Caterham beats a precipitate retreat. On the terrace he finds his daughter.

'Bundle, is that car of yours in order?'

'Yes. Why?'

'Then take me up to town in it immediately. I'm going abroad at once – today.'

'But, Father –'

'Don't argue with me, Bundle. George Lomax told me when he arrived this morning that he was anxious to have a few words with me privately on a matter of the utmost delicacy. He added that the King of Timbuctoo was arriving in London shortly. I won't go through it again, Bundle, do you hear? Not for fifty George Lomaxes! If Chimneys is so valuable to the nation, let the nation buy it. Otherwise I shall sell it to a syndicate and they can turn it into an hotel.'

'Where is Codders now?'

Bundle is rising to the situation.

'At the present minute,' replied Lord Caterham, looking at his watch, 'he is good for at least fifteen minutes about the Empire.'

Another picture.

Mr Bill Eversleigh, not invited to be present at the graveside ceremony, at the telephone.

'No, really, I mean it . . . I say, don't be huffy . . . Well, you will have supper tonight, anyway? . . . No, I haven't. I've been kept to it with my nose at the grindstone. You've no idea what Codders is like . . . I say, Dolly, you know jolly well what I think about you . . . You know I've never cared for anyone but you . . . Yes, I'll come to the show first. How does the old wheeze go? "And the little girl tries, Hooks and Eyes" . . .'

Unearthly sounds. Mr Eversleigh trying to hum the refrain in question.

And now George's peroration draws to a close.

'. . . the lasting peace and prosperity of the British Empire!'

'I guess,' said Mr Hiram Fish *sotto voce* to himself and the world at large, 'that this has been a great little old week.'

THE SEVEN DIALS MYSTERY

CHAPTER 1

ON EARLY RISING

That amiable youth, Jimmy Thesiger, came racing down the big staircase at Chimneys two steps at a time. So precipitate was his descent that he collided with Tredwell, the stately butler, just as the latter was crossing the hall bearing a fresh supply of hot coffee. Owing to the marvellous presence of mind and masterly agility of Tredwell, no casualty occurred.

'Sorry,' apologized Jimmy. 'I say, Tredwell, am I the last down?'

'No, sir. Mr Wade has not come down yet.'

'Good,' said Jimmy, and entered the breakfast room.

The room was empty save for his hostess, and her reproachful gaze gave Jimmy the same feeling of discomfort he always experienced on catching the eye of a defunct codfish exposed on a fisherman's slab. Yet, hang it all, why should the woman look at him like that? To come down at a punctual nine-thirty when staying in a country house simply wasn't done. To be sure, it was now a quarter past eleven which was, perhaps, the outside limit, but even then –

'Afraid I'm a bit late, Lady Coote. What?'

'Oh, it doesn't matter,' said Lady Coote in a melancholy voice.

As a matter of fact, people being late for breakfast worried her very much. For the first ten years of her married life, Sir Oswald Coote (then plain Mr) had, to put it baldly, raised hell if his morning meal were even a half-minute later than eight o'clock. Lady Coote had been disciplined to regard unpunctuality as a deadly sin of the most unpardonable nature. And habit dies hard. Also, she was an earnest woman, and she could not help asking herself what possible good these young people would ever do in the world without early rising. As Sir Oswald so often said, to reporters and others: 'I attribute my success entirely to my habits of early rising, frugal living, and methodical habits.'

Lady Coote was a big, handsome woman in a tragic sort of fashion. She had large, mournful eyes and a deep voice. An artist looking for a model for 'Rachel mourning for her children' would have hailed Lady Coote with delight. She would have done well, too, in melodrama, staggering through the falling snow as the deeply wronged wife of the villain.

She looked as though she had some terrible secret sorrow in her life, and yet if the truth be told, Lady Coote had had no trouble in her life whatever, except the meteoric rise to prosperity of Sir Oswald. As a young girl she had been a jolly flamboyant creature, very much in love with Oswald Coote, the aspiring young man in the bicycle shop next to her father's hardware store. They had lived very happily, first in a couple of rooms, and then in a tiny house, and then in a larger house, and then in successive houses of increasing magnitude, but always within a reasonable distance of 'the Works', until now Sir Oswald had reached such an eminence that he and 'the Works' were no longer interdependent, and it was his pleasure to rent the very largest and most magnificent mansions available all over England. Chimneys was an historic place, and in renting it from the Marquis of Caterham for two years, Sir Oswald felt that he had attained the top notch of his ambition.

Lady Coote was not nearly so happy about it. She was a lonely woman. The principal relaxation of her early married life had been talking to 'the girl' – and even when 'the girl' had been multiplied by three, conversation with her domestic staff had still been the principal distraction of Lady Coote's day. Now, with a pack of housemaids, a butler like an archbishop, several footmen of imposing proportions, a bevy of scuttling kitchen and scullery maids, a terrifying foreign chef with a 'temperament', and a housekeeper of immense proportions who alternately creaked and rustled when she moved, Lady Coote was as one marooned on a desert island.

She sighed now, heavily, and drifted out through the open window, much to the relief of Jimmy Thesiger, who at once helped himself to more kidneys and bacon on the strength of it.

Lady Coote stood for a few moments tragically on the terrace and then nerved herself to speak to MacDonald, the head gardener, who was surveying the domain over which he ruled with an autocratic eye. MacDonald was a very chief and prince among head gardeners. He knew his place – which was to rule. And he ruled – despotically.

Lady Coote approached him nervously.

'Good morning, MacDonald.'

'Good morning, m'lady.'

He spoke as head gardeners should speak – mournfully, but with dignity – like an emperor at a funeral.

'I was wondering – could we have some of those late grapes for dessert tonight?'

'They're no fit for picking yet,' said MacDonald.

He spoke kindly but firmly.

'Oh!' said Lady Coote.

She plucked up courage.

'Oh! But I was in the end house yesterday, and I tasted one and they seemed very good.'

MacDonald looked at her, and she blushed. She was made to feel that she had taken an unpardonable liberty. Evidently the late Marchioness of Caterham had never committed such a solecism as to enter one of her own hothouses and help herself to grapes.

'If you had given orders, m'lady, a bunch should have been cut and sent in to you,' said MacDonald severely.

'Oh, thank you,' said Lady Coote. 'Yes, I will do that another time.'

'But they're no properly fit for picking yet.'

'No,' murmured Lady Coote, 'no, I suppose not. We'd better leave it then.'

MacDonald maintained a masterly silence. Lady Coote nerved herself once more.

'I was going to speak to you about the piece of lawn at the back of the rose garden. I wondered if it could be used as a bowling green. Sir Oswald is very fond of a game of bowls.'

'And why not?' thought Lady Coote to herself. She had been instructed in her history of England. Had not Sir Francis Drake and his knightly companions been playing a game of bowls when the Armada was sighted? Surely a gentlemanly pursuit and one to which MacDonald could not reasonably object. But she had reckoned without the predominant trait of a good head gardener, which is to oppose any and every suggestion made to him.

'Nae doot it could be used for that purpose,' said MacDonald non-committally.

He threw a discouraging flavour into the remark, but its real object was to lure Lady Coote on to her destruction.

'If it was cleared up and – er – cut – and – er – all that sort of thing,' she went on hopefully.

'Aye,' said MacDonald slowly. 'It could be done. But it would mean taking William from the lower border.'

'Oh!' said Lady Coote doubtfully. The words 'lower border' conveyed absolutely nothing to her mind – except a vague suggestion of a Scottish song – but it was clear that to MacDonald they constituted an insuperable objection.

'And that would be a pity,' said MacDonald.

'Oh, of course,' said Lady Coote. 'It *would*.' And wondered why she agreed so fervently.

MacDonald looked at her very hard.

'Of course,' he said, 'if it's your *orders*, m'lady –'

He left it like that. But his menacing tone was too much for Lady Coote. She capitulated at once.

'Oh, no,' she said. 'I see what you mean, MacDonald. N–no – William had better get on with the lower border.'

'That's what I thocht meself, m'lady.'

'Yes,' said Lady Coote. 'Yes, certainly.'

'I thocht you'd agree, m'lady,' said MacDonald.

'Oh, certainly,' said Lady Coote again.

MacDonald touched his hat and moved away.

Lady Coote sighed unhappily and looked after him. Jimmy Thesiger, replete with kidneys and bacon, stepped out on to the terrace beside her, and sighed in quite a different manner.

'Topping morning, eh?' he remarked.

'Is it?' said Lady Coote absently. 'Oh, yes, I suppose it is. I hadn't noticed.'

'Where are the others? Punting on the lake?'

'I expect so. I mean, I shouldn't wonder if they were.'

Lady Coote turned and plunged abruptly into the house again. Tredwell was just examining the coffee pot.

'Oh, dear,' said Lady Coote. 'Isn't Mr – Mr –'

'Wade, m'lady?'

'Yes, Mr Wade. Isn't he down *yet*?'

'No, m'lady.'

'It's very late.'

'Yes, m'lady.'

'Oh, dear. I suppose he will come down *sometime*, Tredwell?'

'Oh, undoubtedly, m'lady. It was eleven-thirty yesterday morning when Mr Wade came down, m'lady.'

Lady Coote glanced at the clock. It was now twenty minutes to twelve. A wave of human sympathy rushed over her.

'It's very hard luck on you, Tredwell. Having to clear and then get lunch on the table by one o'clock.'

'I am accustomed to the ways of young gentlemen, m'lady.'

The reproof was dignified, but unmistakable. So might a prince of the Church reprove a Turk or an infidel who had unwittingly committed a solecism in all good faith.

Lady Coote blushed for the second time that morning. But a welcome interruption occurred. The door opened and a serious, spectacled young man put his head in.

'Oh, there you are, Lady Coote. Sir Oswald was asking for you.'

'Oh, I'll go to him at once, Mr Bateman.'

Lady Coote hurried out.

Rupert Bateman, who was Sir Oswald's private secretary, went out the other way, through the window where Jimmy Thesiger was still lounging amiably.

''Morning, Pongo,' said Jimmy. 'I suppose I shall have to go and make myself agreeable to those blasted girls. You coming?'

Bateman shook his head and hurried along the terrace and in at the library window. Jimmy grinned pleasantly at his retreating back. He and Bateman had been at school together, when Bateman had been a serious, spectacled boy, and had been nicknamed Pongo for no earthly reason whatever.

Pongo, Jimmy reflected, was very much the same sort of ass now that he had been then. The words 'Life is real, life is earnest' might have been written specially for him.

Jimmy yawned and strolled slowly down to the lake. The girls were there, three of them – just the usual sort of girls, two with dark shingled heads and one with a fair shingled head. The one that giggled most was (he thought) called Helen – and there was another called Nancy – and the third one was, for some reason, addressed as Socks. With them were his two friends, Bill Eversleigh and Ronny Devereux, who were employed in a purely ornamental capacity at the Foreign Office.

'Hallo,' said Nancy (or possibly Helen). 'It's Jimmy. Where's what's-his-name?'

'You don't mean to say,' said Bill Eversleigh, 'that Gerry Wade's not up *yet*? Something ought to be done about it.'

'If he's not careful,' said Ronny Devereux, 'he'll miss his breakfast altogether one day – find it's lunch or tea instead when he rolls down.'

'It's a shame,' said the girl called Socks. 'Because it worries Lady Coote so. She gets more and more like a hen that wants to lay an egg and can't. It's too bad.'

'Let's pull him out of bed,' suggested Bill. 'Come on, Jimmy.'

'Oh! Let's be more subtle than that,' said the girl called Socks. Subtle was a word of which she was rather fond. She used it a great deal.

'I'm not subtle,' said Jimmy. 'I don't know how.'

'Let's get together and do something about it tomorrow morning,' suggested Ronny vaguely. 'You know, get him up at seven. Stagger the household. Tredwell loses his false whiskers and drops the tea urn. Lady Coote has hysterics and faints in Bill's arms – Bill being the weight carrier. Sir Oswald says "Ha!" and steel goes up a point and five-eighths. Pongo registers emotion by throwing down his spectacles and stamping on them.'

'You don't know Gerry,' said Jimmy. 'I daresay enough cold water *might* wake him – judiciously applied, that is. But he'd only turn over and go to sleep again.'

'Oh! We must think of something more subtle than cold water,' said Socks.

'Well, what?' asked Ronny bluntly. And nobody had any answer ready.

'We ought to be able to think of something,' said Bill. 'Who's got any brains?'

'Pongo,' said Jimmy. 'And here he is, rushing along in a harried manner as usual. Pongo was always the one for brains. It's been his misfortune from his youth upwards. Let's turn Pongo on to it.'

Mr Bateman listened patiently to a somewhat incoherent statement. His attitude was that of one poised for flight. He delivered his solution without loss of time.

'I should suggest an alarum clock,' he said briskly. 'I always use one myself for fear of oversleeping. I find that early tea brought in in a noiseless manner is sometimes powerless to awaken one.'

He hurried away.

'An alarum clock.' Ronny shook his head. '*One* alarum clock. It would take about a dozen to disturb Gerry Wade.'

'Well, why not?' Bill was flushed and earnest. 'I've got it. Let's all go into Market Basing and buy an alarum clock each.'

There was laughter and discussion. Bill and Ronny went off to get hold of cars. Jimmy was deputed to spy upon the dining-room. He returned rapidly.

'He's here right enough. Making up for lost time and wolfing down toast and marmalade. How are we going to prevent him coming along with us?'

It was decided that Lady Coote must be approached and instructed to hold him in play. Jimmy and Nancy and Helen fulfilled this duty. Lady Coote was bewildered and apprehensive.

'A rag? You will be careful, won't you, my dears? I mean, you won't smash the furniture and wreck things or use too much water. We've got to hand this house over next week, you know. I shouldn't like Lord Caterham to think –'

Bill, who had returned from the garage, broke in reassuringly.

'That's all right, Lady Coote. Bundle Brent – Lord Caterham's daughter – is a great friend of mine. And there's nothing she'd stick at – absolutely nothing! You can take it from me. And anyway there's not going to be any damage done. This is quite a quiet affair.'

'Subtle,' said the girl called Socks.

Lady Coote went sadly along the terrace just as Gerald Wade emerged from the breakfast room. Jimmy Thesiger was a fair, cherubic young man, and all that could be said of Gerald Wade was that he was fairer and more cherubic, and that his vacuous expression made Jimmy's face quite intelligent by contrast.

''Morning, Lady Coote,' said Gerald Wade. 'Where are all the others?'

'They've all gone to Market Basing,' said Lady Coote.

'What for?'

'Some joke,' said Lady Coote in her deep, melancholy voice.

'Rather early in the morning for jokes,' said Mr Wade.

'It's not so very early in the morning,' said Lady Coote pointedly.

'I'm afraid I was a bit late coming down,' said Mr Wade with engaging frankness. 'It's an extraordinary thing, but wherever I happen to be staying, I'm always last to be down.'

'Very extraordinary,' said Lady Coote.

'I don't know why it is,' said Mr Wade, meditating. 'I can't think, I'm sure.'

'Why don't you just get up?' suggested Lady Coote.

'Oh!' said Mr Wade. The simplicity of the solution rather took him aback.

Lady Coote went on earnestly.

'I've heard Sir Oswald say so many times that there's nothing for getting a young man on in the world like punctual habits.'

'Oh, I know,' said Mr Wade. 'And I have to when I'm in town. I mean, I have to be round at the jolly old Foreign Office by eleven o'clock. You mustn't think I'm always a slacker, Lady Coote. I say, what awfully jolly flowers you've got down in that lower border. I can't remember the names of them, but we've got some at home – those mauve thingummybobs. My sister's tremendously keen on gardening.'

Lady Coote was immediately diverted. Her wrongs rankled within her.

'What kind of gardeners do you have?'

'Oh just one. Rather an old fool, I believe. Doesn't know much, but he does what he's told. And that's a great thing, isn't it?'

Lady Coote agreed that it was with a depth of feeling in her voice that would have been invaluable to her as an emotional actress. They began to discourse on the iniquities of gardeners.

Meanwhile the expedition was doing well. The principal emporium of Market Basing had been invaded and the sudden demand for alarum clocks was considerably puzzling the proprietor.

'I wish we'd got Bundle here,' murmured Bill. 'You know her, don't you, Jimmy? Oh, you'd like her. She's a splendid girl – a real good sport – and mark you, she's got brains too. You know her, Ronny?'

Ronny shook his head.

'Don't know Bundle? Where have you been vegetating? She's simply it.'

'Be a bit more subtle, Bill,' said Socks. 'Stop blethering about your lady friends and get on with the business.'

Mr Murgatroyd, owner of Murgatroyd's Stores, burst into eloquence.

'If you'll allow me to advise you, Miss, I should say – *not* the 7/11 one. It's a good clock – I'm not running it down, mark you, but I should strongly advise this kind at 10/6. Well worth the extra money. Reliability, you understand. I shouldn't like you to say afterwards –'

It was evident to everybody that Mr Murgatroyd must be turned off like a tap.

'We don't want a reliable clock, said Nancy.

'It's got to go for one day, that's all,' said Helen.

'We don't want a subtle one,' said Socks. 'We want one with a good loud ring.'

'We want –' began Bill, but was unable to finish, because Jimmy, who was of a mechanical turn of mind, had at last grasped the mechanism. For the next five minutes the shop was hideous with the loud raucous ringing of many alarum clocks.

In the end six excellent starters were selected.

'And I'll tell you what,' said Ronny handsomely, 'I'll get one for Pongo. It was his idea, and it's a shame that he should be out of it. He shall be represented among those present.'

'That's right,' said Bill. 'And I'll take an extra one for Lady Coote. The more the merrier. And she's doing some of the spade work. Probably gassing away to old Gerry now.'

Indeed at this precise moment Lady Coote was detailing a long story about MacDonald and a prize peach and enjoying herself very much.

The clocks were wrapped up and paid for. Mr Murgatroyd watched the cars drive away with a puzzled air. Very spirited the young people of the upper classes nowadays, very spirited indeed, but not at all easy to understand. He turned with relief to attend to the vicar's wife, who wanted a new kind of dripless teapot.

CHAPTER 2

CONCERNING ALARUM CLOCKS

'Now where shall we put them?'

Dinner was over. Lady Coote had been once more detailed for duty. Sir Oswald had unexpectedly come to the rescue by suggesting bridge – not that suggesting is the right word. Sir Oswald, as became one of 'Our Captains of Industry' (No. 7 of Series I), merely expressed a preference and those around him hastened to accommodate themselves to the great man's wishes.

Rupert Bateman and Sir Oswald were partners against Lady Coote and Gerald Wade, which was a very happy arrangement. Sir Oswald played bridge, like he did everything else, extremely well, and liked a partner to correspond. Bateman was as efficient a bridge player as he was a secretary. Both of them confined themselves strictly to the matter in hand, merely uttering in curt short barks, 'Two no trumps,' 'Double,' 'Three spades.' Lady Coote and Gerald Wade were amiable and discursive, and the young man never failed to say at the conclusion of each hand, 'I say, partner, you played that simply splendidly,' in tones of simple admiration which Lady Coote found both novel and extremely soothing. They also held very good cards.

The others were supposed to be dancing to the wireless in the big ballroom. In reality they were grouped around the door of Gerald Wade's bedroom, and the air was full of subdued giggles and the loud ticking of clocks.

'Under the bed in a row,' suggested Jimmy in answer to Bill's question.

'And what shall we set them at? What time, I mean? All together so that there's one glorious whatnot, or at intervals?'

The point was hotly disputed. One party argued that for a champion sleeper like Gerry Wade the combined ringing of eight alarum clocks was necessary. The other party argued in favour of steady and sustained effort.

In the end the latter won the day. The clocks were set to go off one after the other, starting at 6.30 a.m.

'And I hope,' said Bill virtuously, 'that this will be a lesson to him.'

'Hear, hear,' said Socks.

The business of hiding the clocks was just being begun when there was a sudden alarm.

'Hist,' cried Jimmy. 'Somebody's coming up the stairs.'

There was a panic.

'It's all right,' said Jimmy. 'It's only Pongo.'

Taking advantage of being dummy, Mr Bateman was going to his room for a handkerchief. He paused on his way and took in the situation at a glance. He then made a comment, a simple and practical one.

'He will hear them ticking when he goes to bed.'

The conspirators looked at each other.

'What did I tell you?' said Jimmy in a reverent voice. 'Pongo always *did* have brains!'

The brainy one passed on.

'It's true,' admitted Ronny Devereux, his head on one side. 'Eight clocks all ticking at once do make a devil of a row. Even old Gerry, ass as he is, couldn't miss it. He'll guess something's up.'

'I wonder if he is,' said Jimmy Thesiger.

'Is what?'

'Such an ass as we all think.'

Ronny stared at him.

'We all know old Gerald.'

'Do we?' said Jimmy. 'I've sometimes thought that – well, that it isn't possible for anyone to be quite the ass old Gerry makes himself out to be.'

They all stared at him. There was a serious look on Ronny's face.

'Jimmy,' he said, 'you've got brains.'

'A second Pongo,' said Bill encouragingly.

'Well, it just occurred to me, that's all,' said Jimmy, defending himself.

'Oh! don't let's all be subtle,' cried Socks. 'What are we to do about these clocks?'

'Here's Pongo coming back again. Let's ask him,' suggested Jimmy.

Pongo, urged to bring his great brain to bear upon the matter, gave his decision.

'Wait till he's gone to bed and got to sleep. Then enter the room very quietly and put the clocks down on the floor.'

'Little Pongo's right again,' said Jimmy. 'On the word one all park clocks, and then we'll go downstairs and disarm suspicion.'

Bridge was still proceeding – with a slight difference. Sir Oswald was now playing with his wife and was conscientiously pointing out to her the mistakes she had made during the play of each hand. Lady Coote accepted reproof good-humouredly, and with a complete lack of any real interest. She reiterated, not once, but many times:

'I see, dear. It's so kind of you to tell me.'

And she continued to make exactly the same errors.

At intervals, Gerald Wade said to Pongo:

'Well played, partner, jolly well played.'

Bill Eversleigh was making calculations with Ronny Devereux.

'Say he goes to bed about twelve – what do you think we ought to give him – about an hour?'

He yawned.

'Curious thing – three in the morning is my usual time for bye-bye, but tonight, just because I know we've got to sit up a bit, I'd give anything to be a mother's boy and turn in right away.'

Everyone agreed that they felt the same.

'My dear Maria,' rose the voice of Sir Oswald in mild irritation. 'I have told you over and over again not to hesitate when you are wondering whether to finesse or not. You give the whole table information.'

Lady Coote had a very good answer to this – namely that as Sir Oswald was dummy, he had no right to comment on the play of the hand. But she did not make it. Instead she smiled kindly, leaned her ample chest well forward over the table, and gazed firmly into Gerald Wade's hand where he sat on her right.

Her anxieties lulled to rest by perceiving the queen, she played the knave and took the trick and proceeded to lay down her cards.

'Four tricks and the rubber,' she announced. 'I think I was very lucky to get four tricks there.'

'Lucky,' murmured Gerald Wade, as he pushed back his chair and came over to the fireside to join the others. 'Lucky, she calls it. That woman wants watching.'

Lady Coote was gathering up notes and silver.

'I know I'm not a good player,' she announced in a mournful tone which nevertheless held an undercurrent of pleasure in it. 'But I'm really very lucky at the game.'

'You'll never be a bridge player, Maria,' said Sir Oswald.

'No, dear,' said Lady Coote. 'I know I shan't. You're always telling me so. And I do try so hard.'

'She does,' said Gerald Wade *sotto voce*. 'There's no subterfuge about it. She'd put her head right down on your shoulder if she couldn't see into your hand any other way.'

'I know you try,' said Sir Oswald. 'It's just that you haven't any card sense.'

'I know, dear,' said Lady Coote. 'That's what you're always telling me. And you owe me another ten shillings, Oswald.'

'Do I?' Sir Oswald looked surprised.

'Yes. Seventeen hundred – eight pounds ten. You've only given me eight pounds.'

'Dear me,' said Sir Oswald. 'My mistake.'

Lady Coote smiled at him sadly and took up the extra ten-shilling note. She was very fond of her husband, but she had no intention of allowing him to cheat her out of ten shillings.

Sir Oswald moved over to a side table and became hospitable with whisky and soda. It was half-past twelve when general good-nights were said.

Ronny Devereux, who had the room next door to Gerald Wade's, was told off to report progress. At a quarter to two he crept round tapping at doors. The party, pyjamaed and dressing-gowned, assembled with various scuffles and giggles and low whispers.

'His light went out twenty minutes ago,' reported Ronny in a hoarse whisper. 'I thought he'd never put it out. I opened the door just now and peeped in, and he seems sound off. What about it?'

Once more the clocks were solemnly assembled. Then another difficulty arose.

'We can't all go barging in. Make no end of a row. One person's got to do it and the others can hand him the whatnots from the door.'

Hot discussion then arose as to the proper person to be selected.

The three girls were rejected on the grounds that they would giggle. Bill Eversleigh was rejected on the grounds of his height, weight and heavy tread, also for his general clumsiness, which latter clause he fiercely denied. Jimmy Thesiger and Ronny Devereux were considered possibles, but in the end an overwhelming majority decided in favour of Rupert Bateman.

'Pongo's the lad,' agreed Jimmy. 'Anyway, he walks like a cat – always did. And then, if Gerry should waken up, Pongo will be able to think of some rotten silly thing to say to him. You know, something plausible that'll calm him down and not rouse his suspicions.'

'Something subtle,' suggested the girl Socks thoughtfully.

'Exactly,' said Jimmy.

Pongo performed his job neatly and efficiently. Cautiously opening the bedroom door, he disappeared into the darkness inside bearing the two largest clocks. In a minute or two he reappeared on the threshold and two more were handed to him and then again twice more. Finally he emerged. Everyone held their breath and listened. The rhythmical breathing of Gerald Wade could still be heard, but drowned, smothered and buried beneath the triumphant, impassioned ticking of Mr Murgatroyd's eight alarum clocks.

CHAPTER 3

THE JOKE THAT FAILED

'Twelve o'clock,' said Socks despairingly.

The joke – as a joke – had not gone off any too well. The alarum clocks, on the other hand, had performed their part. *They* had gone off – with a vigour and *élan* that could hardly have been surpassed and which had sent Ronny Devereux leaping out of bed with a confused idea that the Day of Judgment had come. If such had been the effect in the room next door, what must it have been at close quarters? Ronny hurried out in the passage and applied his ear to the crack of the door.

He expected profanity – expected it confidently and with intelligent anticipation. But he heard nothing at all. That is to say, he heard nothing of what he expected. The clocks were ticking all right – ticking in a loud, arrogant, exasperating manner. And presently another went off, ringing with a crude, deafening note that would have aroused acute irritation in a deaf man.

There was no doubt about it; the clocks had performed their part faithfully. They did all and more than Mr Murgatroyd had claimed for them. But apparently they had met their match in Gerald Wade.

The syndicate was inclined to be despondent about it.

'The lad isn't human,' grumbled Jimmy Thesiger.

'Probably thought he heard the telephone in the distance and rolled over and went to sleep again,' suggested Helen (or possibly Nancy).

'It seems to me very remarkable,' said Rupert Bateman seriously. 'I think he ought to see a doctor about it.'

'Some disease of the eardrums,' suggested Bill hopefully.

'Well, if you ask me,' said Socks, 'I think he's just spoofing us. Of course they woke him up. But he's just going to do us down by pretending that he didn't hear anything.'

Everyone looked at Socks with respect and admiration.

'It's an idea,' said Bill.

'He's subtle, that's what it is,' said Socks. 'You'll see, he'll be extra late for breakfast this morning – just to show us.'

And since the clock now pointed to some minutes past twelve the general opinion was that Socks's theory was a correct one. Only Ronny Devereux demurred.

'You forget, I was outside the door when the first one went off. Whatever old Gerry decided to do later, the first one must have surprised him. He'd have let out something about it. Where did you put it, Pongo?'

'On a little table close by his ear,' said Mr Bateman.

'That was thoughtful of you, Pongo,' said Ronny. 'Now, tell me.' He turned to Bill. 'If a whacking great bell started ringing within a few inches of your ear at half-past six in the morning, what would you say about it?'

'Oh, Lord,' said Bill. 'I should say –' He came to a stop.

'Of course you would,' said Ronny. 'So would I. So would anyone. What they call the natural man would emerge. Well, it didn't. So I say that Pongo is right – as usual – and that Gerry has got an obscure disease of the eardrums.'

'It's now twenty past twelve,' said one of the other girls sadly.

'I say,' said Jimmy slowly, 'that's a bit beyond anything, isn't it? I mean a joke's a joke. But this is carrying it a bit far. It's a shade hard on the Cootes.'

Bill stared at him.

'What are you getting at?'

'Well,' said Jimmy. 'Somehow or other – it's not like old Gerry.'

He found it hard to put into words just what he meant to say. He didn't want to say too much, and yet – He saw Ronny looking at him. Ronny was suddenly alert.

It was at that moment Tredwell came into the room and looked around him hesitatingly.

'I thought Mr Bateman was here,' he explained apologetically.

'Just gone out this minute through the window,' said Ronny. 'Can I do anything?'

Tredwell's eyes wandered from him to Jimmy Thesiger and then back again. As though singled out, the two young men left the room with him. Tredwell closed the dining-room door carefully behind him.

'Well,' said Ronny. 'What's up?'

'Mr Wade not having yet come down, sir, I took the liberty of sending Williams up to his room.'

'Yes?'

'Williams has just come running down in a great state of agitation, sir.' Tredwell paused – a pause of preparation. 'I am afraid, sir, the poor young gentleman must have died in his sleep.'

Jimmy and Ronny stared at him.

'Nonsense,' cried Ronny at last. 'It's – it's impossible. Gerry –' His face worked suddenly. 'I'll – I'll run up and see. That fool Williams may have made a mistake.'

Tredwell stretched out a detaining hand. With a queer, unnatural feeling of detachment, Jimmy realized that the butler had the whole situation in hand.

'No, sir, Williams has made no mistake. I have already sent for Dr Cartwright, and in the meantime I have taken the liberty of locking the door, preparatory to informing Sir Oswald of what has occurred. I must now find Mr Bateman.'

Tredwell hurried away. Ronny stood like a man dazed.

'Gerry,' he muttered to himself.

Jimmy took his friend by the arm and steered him out through a side door on to a secluded portion of the terrace. He pushed him down on to a seat.

'Take it easy, old son,' he said kindly. 'You'll get your wind in a minute.'

But he looked at him rather curiously. He had no idea that Ronny was such a friend of Gerry Wade's.

'Poor old Gerry,' he said thoughtfully. 'If ever a man looked fit, he did.'

Ronny nodded.

'All that clock business seems so rotten now,' went on Jimmy. 'It's odd, isn't it, why farce so often seems to get mixed up with tragedy?'

He was talking more or less at random, to give Ronny time to recover himself. The other moved restlessly.

'I wish that doctor would come. I want to know –'

'Know what?'

'What he – died of.'

Jimmy pursed up his lips.

'Heart?' he hazarded.

Ronny gave a short, scornful laugh.

'I say, Ronny,' said Jimmy.

'Well?'

Jimmy found a difficulty in going on.

'You don't mean – you aren't thinking – I mean, you haven't got it into your head – that, well I mean he wasn't biffed on the head or anything? Tredwell's locking the door and all that.'

It seemed to Jimmy that his words deserved an answer, but Ronny continued to stare straight out in front of him.

Jimmy shook his head and relapsed into silence. He didn't see that there was anything to do except just wait. So he waited.

It was Tredwell who disturbed them.

'The doctor would like to see you two gentlemen in the library, if you please, sir.'

Ronny sprang up. Jimmy followed him.

Dr Cartwright was a thin, energetic young man with a clever

face. He greeted them with a brief nod. Pongo, looking more serious and spectacled than ever, performed introductions.

'I understand you were a great friend of Mr Wade's,' the doctor said to Ronny.

'His greatest friend.'

'H'm. Well, this business seems straightforward enough. Sad, though. He looked a healthy young chap. Do you know if he was in the habit of smoking stuff to make him sleep?'

'Make him *sleep*.' Ronny stared. 'He always slept like a top.'

'You never heard him complain of sleeplessness?'

'Never.'

'Well, the facts are simple enough. There'll have to be an inquest, I'm afraid, nevertheless.'

'How did he die?'

'There's not much doubt; I should say an overdose of chloral. The stuff was by his bed. And a bottle and glass. Very sad, these things are.'

It was Jimmy who asked the question which he felt was trembling on his friend's lips, and yet which the other could somehow or other not get out.

'There's no question of – foul play?'

The doctor looked at him sharply.

'Why do you say that? Any cause to suspect it, eh?'

Jimmy looked at Ronny. If Ronny knew anything now was the time to speak. But to his astonishment Ronny shook his head.

'No cause whatever,' he said clearly.

'And suicide – eh?'

'Certainly not.'

Ronny was emphatic. The doctor was not so clearly convinced.

'No troubles that you know of? Money troubles? A woman?'

Again Ronny shook his head.

'Now about his relations. They must be notified.'

'He's got a sister – a half-sister rather. Lives at Deane Priory. About twenty miles from here. When he wasn't in town Gerry lived with her.'

'H'm,' said the Doctor. 'Well, she must be told.'

'I'll go,' said Ronny. 'It's a rotten job, but somebody's got to do it.' He looked at Jimmy. 'You know her, don't you?'

'Slightly. I've danced with her once or twice.'

'Then we'll go in your car. You don't mind, do you? I can't face it alone.'

'That's all right,' said Jimmy reassuringly. 'I was going to suggest it myself. I'll go and get the old bus cranked up.'

He was glad to have something to do. Ronny's manner puzzled him. What did he know or suspect? And why had he not voiced his suspicions, if he had them, to the doctor?

Presently the two friends were skimming along in Jimmy's car with a cheerful disregard for such things as speed limits.

'Jimmy,' said Ronny at last, 'I suppose you're about the best pal I have – now.'

'Well' said Jimmy, 'what about it?'

He spoke gruffly.

'There's something I'd like to tell you. Something you ought to know.'

'About Gerry Wade?'

'Yes, about Gerry Wade.'

Jimmy waited.

'Well?' he inquired at last.

'I don't know that I ought to,' said Ronny.

'Why?'

'I'm bound by a kind of promise.'

'Oh! Well then, perhaps you'd better not.'

There was a silence.

'And yet, I'd like – You see, Jimmy, your brains are better than mine.'

'They could easily be that,' said Jimmy unkindly.

'No, I can't,' said Ronny suddenly.

'All right,' said Jimmy. 'Just as you like.'

After a long silence, Ronny said:

'What's she like?'

'Who?'

'This girl. Gerry's sister.'

Jimmy was silent for some minutes, then he said in a voice that had somehow or other altered:

'She's all right. In fact – well, she's a corker.'

'Gerry was very devoted to her, I knew. He often spoke of her.'

'She was very devoted to Gerry. It – it's going to hit her hard.'

'Yes, a nasty job.'

They were silent till they reached Deane Priory.

Miss Loraine, the maid told them, was in the garden. Unless they wanted to see Mrs Coker.

Jimmy was eloquent that they did not want to see Mrs Coker.

'Who's Mrs Coker?' asked Ronny as they went round into the somewhat neglected garden.

'The old trout who lives with Loraine.'

They had stepped out into a paved walk. At the end of it was a girl with two black spaniels. A small girl, very fair, dressed in shabby old tweeds. Not at all the girl that Ronny had expected to see. Not, in fact, Jimmy's usual type.

Holding one dog by the collar, she came down the pathway to meet them.

'How do you do,' she said. 'You mustn't mind Elizabeth. She's just had some puppies and she's very suspicious.'

She had a supremely natural manner and, as she looked up smiling, the faint wild-rose flush deepened in her cheeks. Her eyes were a very dark blue – like cornflowers.

Suddenly they widened – was it with alarm? As though, already, she guessed.

Jimmy hastened to speak.

'This is Ronny Devereux, Miss Wade. You must often have heard Gerry speak of him.'

'Oh, yes.' She turned a lovely, warm, welcoming smile on him. 'You've both been staying at Chimneys, haven't you? Why didn't you bring Gerry over with you?'

'We – er – couldn't,' said Ronny, and then stopped.

Again Jimmy saw the look of fear flash into her eyes.

'Miss Wade,' he said, 'I'm afraid – I mean, we've got bad news for you.'

She was on the alert in a moment.

'Gerry?'

'Yes – Gerry. He's –'

She stamped her foot with sudden passion.

'Oh! Tell me – tell me –' She turned suddenly on Ronny. '*You'll* tell me.'

Jimmy felt a pang of jealousy, and in that moment he knew what up to now he had hesitated to admit to himself. He knew why Helen and Nancy and Socks were just 'girls' to him and nothing more.

He only *half* heard Ronny's voice saying bravely:

'Yes, Miss Wade, I'll tell you. Gerry is dead.'

She had plenty of pluck. She gasped and drew back, but in a minute or two she was asking eager, searching questions. How? When?

Ronny answered her as gently as he could.

'*Sleeping* draught? Gerry?'

The incredulity in her voice was plain. Jimmy gave her a glance. It was almost a glance of warning. He had a sudden feeling that Loraine in her innocence might say too much.

In his turn he explained as gently as possible the need for an inquest. She shuddered. She declined their offer of taking her back to Chimneys with them, but explained she would come over later. She had a two-seater of her own.

'But I want to be – be alone a little first,' she said piteously.

'I know,' said Ronny.

'That's all right,' said Jimmy.

They looked at her, feeling awkward and helpless.

'Thank you both ever so much for coming.'

They drove back in silence and there was something like constraint between them.

'My God! That girl's plucky,' said Ronny once.

Jimmy agreed.

'Gerry was my friend,' said Ronny. 'It's up to me to keep an eye on her.'

'Oh! Rather. Of course.'

On returning to Chimneys Jimmy was waylaid by a tearful Lady Coote.

'That poor boy,' she kept repeating. 'That poor boy.'

Jimmy made all the suitable remarks he could think of.

Lady Coote told him at great length various details about the decease of various dear friends of hers. Jimmy listened with a show of sympathy and at last managed to detach himself without actual rudeness.

He ran lightly up the stairs. Ronny was just emerging from

Gerald Wade's room. He seemed taken aback at the sight of Jimmy.

'I've been in to see him,' he said. 'Are you going in?'

'I don't think so,' said Jimmy, who was a healthy young man with a natural dislike of being reminded of death.

'I think all his friends ought to.'

'Oh! Do you?' said Jimmy, and registered to himself an impression that Ronny Devereux was damned odd about it all.

'Yes. It's a sign of respect.'

Jimmy sighed, but gave in.'

'Oh! Very well,' he said, and passed in, setting his teeth a little.

There were white flowers arranged on the coverlet, and the room had been tidied and set to rights.

Jimmy gave one quick, nervous glance at the still, white face. Could that be cherubic, pink Gerry Wade? That still, peaceful figure. He shivered.

As he turned to leave the room, his glance swept the mantelshelf and he stopped in astonishment. The alarum clocks had been ranged along it neatly in a row.

He went out sharply. Ronny was waiting for him.

'Looks very peaceful and all that. Rotten luck on him,' mumbled Jimmy.

Then he said:

'I say, Ronny, who arranged all those clocks like that in a row?'

'How should I know? One of the servants, I suppose.'

'The funny thing is,' said Jimmy, 'that there are seven of them, not eight. One of them's missing. Did you notice that?'

Ronny made an inaudible sound.

'Seven instead of eight,' said Jimmy, frowning. 'I wonder why.'

CHAPTER 4

A LETTER

'Inconsiderate, that's what I call it,' said Lord Caterham.

He spoke in a gentle, plaintive voice and seemed pleased with the adjective he had found.

'Yes, distinctly inconsiderate. I often find these self-made men *are* inconsiderate. Very possibly that is why they amass such large fortunes.'

He looked mournfully out over his ancestral acres, of which he had today regained possession.

His daughter, Lady Eileen Brent, known to her friends and society in general as 'Bundle', laughed.

'You'll certainly never amass a large fortune,' she observed dryly, 'though you didn't do so badly out of old Coote, sticking him for this place. What was he like? Presentable?'

'One of those large men,' said Lord Caterham, shuddering slightly, 'with a red, square face and iron-grey hair. Powerful, you know. What they call a forceful personality. The kind of man you'd get if a steam-roller were turned into a human being.'

'Rather tiring?' suggested Bundle sympathetically.

'Frightfully tiring, full of all the most depressing virtues like sobriety and punctuality. I don't know which are the worst, powerful personalities or earnest politicians. I do so prefer the cheerful inefficient.'

'A cheerful inefficient wouldn't have been able to pay you the price you asked for this old mausoleum,' Bundle reminded him.

Lord Caterham winced.

'I wish you wouldn't use that word, Bundle. We were just getting away from the subject.'

'I don't see why you're so frightfully sensitive about it,' said Bundle. 'After all, people must die somewhere.'

'They needn't die in my house,' said Lord Caterham.

'I don't see why not. Lots of people have. Masses of stuffy old great-grandfathers and grandmothers.'

'That's different,' said Lord Caterham. 'Naturally I expect Brents to die here – they don't count. But I do object to strangers. And I especially object to inquests. The thing will become a habit soon. This is the second. You remember all that fuss we had four years ago? For which, by the way, I hold George Lomax entirely to blame.'

'And now you're blaming poor old steam-roller Coote. I'm sure he was quite as annoyed about it as anyone.'

'Very inconsiderate,' said Lord Caterham obstinately. 'People who are likely to do that sort of thing oughtn't to be asked to stay.

And you may say what you like, Bundle, I don't like inquests. I never have and I never shall.'

'Well, this wasn't the same sort of thing as the last one,' said Bundle soothingly. 'I mean, it wasn't a murder.'

'It might have been – from the fuss that thickhead of an inspector made. He's never got over that business four years ago. He thinks every death that takes place here must necessarily be a case of foul play fraught with grave political significance. You've no idea the fuss he made. I've been hearing about it from Tredwell. Tested everything imaginable for fingerprints. And of course they only found the dead man's own. The clearest case imaginable – though whether it was suicide or accident is another matter.'

'I met Gerry Wade once,' said Bundle. 'He was a friend of Bill's. You'd have liked him, Father. I never saw anyone more cheerfully inefficient than he was.'

'I don't like anyone who comes and dies in my house on purpose to annoy me,' said Lord Caterham obstinately.

'But I certainly can't imagine anyone murdering him,' continued Bundle. 'The idea's absurd.'

'Of course it is,' said Lord Caterham. 'Or would be to anyone but an ass like Inspector Raglan.'

'I daresay looking for fingerprints made him feel important,' said Bundle soothingly. 'Anyway, they brought it in "Death by misadventure", didn't they?'

Lord Caterham acquiesced.

'They had to show some consideration for the sister's feelings?'

'Was there a sister. I didn't know.'

'Half-sister, I believe. She was much younger. Old Wade ran away with her mother – he was always doing that sort of thing. No woman appealed to him unless she belonged to another man.'

'I'm glad there's one bad habit you haven't got,' said Bundle.

'I've always led a very respectable God-fearing life,' said Lord Caterham. 'It seems extraordinary, considering how little harm I do to anybody, that I can't be let alone. If only –'

He stopped as Bundle made a sudden excursion through the window.

'MacDonald,' called Bundle in a clear, autocratic voice.

The emperor approached. Something that might possibly have been taken for a smile of welcome tried to express itself on his countenance, but the natural gloom of gardeners dispelled it.

'Your ladyship?' said MacDonald.

'How are you?' said Bundle.

'I'm no verra grand,' said MacDonald.

'I wanted to speak to you about the bowling green. It's shockingly overgrown. Put someone on to it, will you?'

MacDonald shook his head dubiously.

'It would mean taking William from the lower border, m'lady.'

'Damn the lower border,' said Bundle. 'Let him start at once. And MacDonald –'

'Yes, m'lady?'

'Let's have some of those grapes in from the far house. I know it's the wrong time to cut them because it always is, but I want them all the same. See?'

Bundle re-entered the library.

'Sorry, Father,' she said. 'I wanted to catch MacDonald. Were you speaking?'

'As a matter of fact I was,' said Lord Caterham. 'But it doesn't matter. What were you saying to MacDonald?'

'Trying to cure him of thinking he's God Almighty. But that's an impossible task. I expect the Cootes have been bad for him. MacDonald wouldn't care one hoot, or even two hoots, for the largest steam-roller that ever was. What's Lady Coote like?'

Lord Caterham considered the question.

'Very like my idea of Mrs Siddons,' he said at last. 'I should think she went in a lot for amateur theatricals. I gather she was very upset about the clock business.'

'What clock business?'

'Tredwell has just been telling me. It seems the house party had some joke on. They bought a lot of alarum clocks and hid them about this young Wade's room. And then, of course, the poor chap was dead. Which made the whole thing rather beastly.'

Bundle nodded.

'Tredwell told me something else rather odd about the clocks,' continued Lord Caterham, who was now quite enjoying himself. 'It seems that somebody collected them all and put them in a row on the mantelpiece after the poor fellow was dead.'

'Well, why not?' said Bundle.

'I don't see why not myself,' said Lord Caterham. 'But apparently there was some fuss about it. No one would own up to having done it, you see. All the servants were questioned and swore they hadn't touched the beastly things. In fact, it was rather a mystery. And then the coroner asked questions at the inquest, and you know how difficult it is to explain things to people of that class.'

'Perfectly foul,' agreed Bundle.

'Of course,' said Lord Caterham, 'it's very difficult to get the hang of things afterwards. I didn't quite see the point of half the things Tredwell told me. By the way, Bundle, the fellow died in your room.'

Bundle made a grimace.

'Why need people die in my room?' she asked with some indignation.

'That's just what I've been saying,' said Lord Caterham, in triumph. 'Inconsiderate. Everybody's damned inconsiderate nowadays.'

'Not that I mind,' said Bundle valiantly. 'Why should I?'

'I should,' said her father. 'I should mind very much. I should dream things, you know – spectral hands and clanking chains.'

'Well,' said Bundle. 'Great-aunt Louisa died in *your* bed. I wonder you don't see her spook hovering over you.'

'I do sometimes,' said Lord Caterham, shuddering. 'Especially after lobster.'

'Well, thank heaven I'm not superstitious,' declared Bundle.

Yet that evening, as she sat in front of her bedroom fire, a slim, pyjamaed figure, she found her thoughts reverting to that cheery, vacuous young man, Gerry Wade. Impossible to believe that anyone so full of the joy of living could deliberately have committed suicide. No, the other solution must be the right one. He had taken a sleeping draught and by a pure mistake had swallowed an overdose. That *was* possible. She did not fancy that Gerry Wade had been overburdened in an intellectual capacity.

Her gaze shifted to the mantelpiece and she began thinking about the story of the clocks. Her maid had been full of that, having just been primed by the second housemaid. She had added a detail which apparently Tredwell had not thought worth while retailing to Lord Caterham, but which had piqued Bundle's curiosity.

Seven clocks had been neatly ranged on the mantelpiece; the last and remaining one had been found on the lawn outside, where it had obviously been thrown from the window.

Bundle puzzled over that point now. It seemed such an extraordinarily purposeless thing to do. She could imagine that one of the maids might have tidied the clocks and then, frightened by the inquisition into the matter, have denied doing so. But surely no maid would have thrown a clock into the garden?

Had Gerry Wade done so when its first sharp summons woke him? But no; that again was impossible. Bundle remembered hearing that his death must have taken place in the early hours of the morning, and he would have been in a comatose condition for some time before that.

Bundle frowned. This business of the clocks *was* curious. She must get hold of Bill Eversleigh. He had been there, she knew.

To think was to act with Bundle. She got up and went over to the writing-desk. It was an inlaid affair with a lid that rolled back. Bundle sat down at it, pulled a sheet of notepaper towards her and wrote.

Dear Bill, –

She paused to pull out the lower part of the desk. It had stuck half-way, as she remembered it often did. Bundle tugged at it impatiently but it did not move. She recalled that on a former occasion an envelope had been pushed back with it and had jammed it for the time being. She took a thin paper-knife and slipped it into the narrow crack. She was so far successful that a corner of white paper showed. Bundle caught hold of it and drew it out. It was the first sheet of a letter, somewhat crumpled.

It was the date that first caught Bundle's eye. A big flourishing date that leaped out from the paper. September 21st.

'September 21st,' said Bundle slowly. 'Why, surely that was –'

She broke off. Yes, she was sure of it. The 22nd was the day Gerry Wade was found dead. This, then, was a letter he must have been writing on the very evening of the tragedy.

Bundle smoothed it out and read it. It was unfinished.

'My Darling Loraine, – I will be down on Wednesday. Am feeling awfully fit and rather pleased with myself all round. It will be heavenly to see you. Look here, do forget what I said about that Seven Dials business. I thought it was going to be more or less a joke – but it isn't – anything but. I'm sorry I ever said anything about it – it's not the kind of business kids like you ought to be mixed up in. So forget about it, see?

'Something else I wanted to tell you – but I'm so sleepy I can't keep my eyes open.

'Oh, about Lurcher; I think –'

Here the letter broke off.

Bundle sat frowning. Seven Dials. Where was that? Some rather slummy district of London, she fancied. The words Seven Dials reminded her of something else, but for the moment she couldn't think of what. Instead her attention fastened on two phrases. 'Am feeling awfully fit . . .' and 'I'm so sleepy I can't keep my eyes open.'

That didn't fit in. That didn't fit in at all. For it was that very night that Gerry Wade had taken such a heavy dose of chloral that he never woke again. And if what he had written in that letter were true, why should he have taken it?

Bundle shook her head. She looked round the room and gave a slight shiver. Supposing Gerry Wade were watching her now. In this room he had died . . .

She sat very still. The silence was unbroken save for the ticking of her little gold clock. That sounded unnaturally loud and important.

Bundle glanced towards the mantelpiece. A vivid picture rose before her mind's eyes. The dead man lying on the bed, and seven clocks ticking on the mantelpiece – ticking loudly, ominously . . . ticking . . . ticking . . .

CHAPTER 5

THE MAN IN THE ROAD

'Father,' said Bundle, opening the door of Lord Caterham's special sanctum and putting her head in, 'I'm going up to town in the Hispano. I can't stand the monotony down here any longer.'

'We only got home yesterday,' complained Lord Caterham.

'I know. It seems like a hundred years. I'd forgotten how dull the country could be.'

'I don't agree with you,' said Lord Caterham. 'It's peaceful, that's what it is – peaceful. And extremely comfortable. I appreciate getting back to Tredwell more than I can tell you. That man studies my comfort in the most marvellous manner. Somebody came round only this morning to know if they could hold a tally for Girl Guides here –'

'A rally,' interrupted Bundle.

'Rally or tally – it's all the same. Some silly word meaning nothing whatever. But it would have put me in a very awkward position – having to refuse – in fact, I probably shouldn't have refused. But Tredwell got me out of it. I've forgotten what he said – something damned ingenious which couldn't hurt anybody's feelings and which knocked the idea on the head absolutely.'

'Being comfortable isn't enough for me,' said Bundle. 'I want excitement.'

Lord Caterham shuddered.

'Didn't we have enough excitement four years ago?' he demanded plaintively.

'I'm about ready for some more,' said Bundle. 'Not that I expect I shall find any in town. But at any rate I shan't dislocate my jaw with yawning.'

'In my experience,' said Lord Caterham, 'people who go about looking for trouble usually find it.' He yawned. 'All the same,' he added, 'I wouldn't mind running up to town myself.'

'Well, come on,' said Bundle. 'But be quick, because I'm in a hurry.'

Lord Caterham, who had begun to rise from his chair, paused.

'Did you say you were in a hurry?' he asked suspiciously.

'In the devil of a hurry,' said Bundle.

'That settles it,' said Lord Caterham. 'I'm not coming. To be driven by you in the Hispano when you're in a hurry – no, it's not fair on any elderly man. I shall stay here.'

'Please yourself,' said Bundle, and withdrew.

Tredwell took her place.

'The vicar, my lord, is most anxious to see you, some unfortunate controversy having arisen about the status of the Boys' Brigade.'

Lord Caterham groaned.

'I rather fancied, my lord, that I had heard you mention at breakfast that you were strolling down to the village this morning to converse with the vicar on the subject.'

'Did you tell him so?' asked Lord Caterham eagerly.

'I did, my lord. He departed, if I may say so, hot foot. I hope I did right, my lord?'

'Of course you did, Tredwell. You are always right. You couldn't go wrong if you tried.'

Tredwell smiled benignly and withdrew.

Bundle meanwhile was sounding the Klaxon impatiently before the lodge gates, while a small child came hastening out with all speed from the lodge, admonishment from her mother following her.

'Make haste, Katie. That be her ladyship in a mortal hurry as always.'

It was indeed characteristic of Bundle to be in a hurry, especially when driving a car. She had skill and nerve and was a good driver; had it been otherwise her reckless pace would have ended in disaster more than once.

It was a crisp October day, with a blue sky and a dazzling sun. The sharp tang of the air brought the blood to Bundle's cheeks and filled her with the zest of living.

She had that morning sent Gerald Wade's unfinished letter to Loraine Wade at Deane Priory, enclosing a few explanatory lines. The curious impression it had made upon her was somewhat dimmed in the daylight, yet it still struck her as needing explanation. She intended to get hold of Bill Eversleigh sometime and extract from him fuller details of the house party which had ended so tragically. In the meantime, it was a lovely morning and she felt particularly well and the Hispano was running like a dream.

Bundle pressed her foot down on the accelerator and the Hispano responded at once. Mile after mile vanished, traffic was few and far between and Bundle had a clear stretch of road in front of her.

And then, without any warning whatever, a man reeled out of the hedge and on to the road right in front of the car. To stop in time was out of the question. With all her might Bundle wrenched at the steering wheel and swerved out to the right. The car was nearly in the ditch – nearly, but not quite. It was a dangerous manoeuvre; but it succeeded. Bundle was almost certain that she had missed the man.

She looked back and felt a sickening sensation in the middle of her anatomy. The car had not passed over the man, but nevertheless it must have struck him in passing. He was lying face downwards on the road, and he lay ominously still.

Bundle jumped out and ran back. She had never yet run over anything more important than a stray hen. The fact that the accident was hardly her fault did not weigh with her at the minute. The man had seemed drunk, but drunk or not, she had killed him. She was quite sure she had killed him. Her heart beat sickeningly in great pounding thumps, sounding right up in her ears.

She knelt down by the prone figure and turned him very gingerly over. He neither groaned nor moaned. He was young, she saw, rather a pleasant-faced young man, well dressed and wearing a small toothbrush moustache.

There was no external mark of injury that she could see, but she was quite positive that he was either dead or dying. His eyelids flickered and the eyes half opened. Piteous eyes, brown and suffering, like a dog's. He seemed to be struggling to speak. Bundle bent right over.

'Yes,' she said. 'Yes?'

There was something he wanted to say, she could see that. Wanted to say badly. And she couldn't help him, couldn't do anything.

At last the words came, a mere sighing breath:

'*Seven Dials . . . tell . . .*'

'Yes,' said Bundle again. It was a name he was trying to get out – trying with all his failing strength. 'Yes. Who am I to tell?'

'*Tell . . . Jimmy Thesiger . . .*' He got it out at last, and then, suddenly, his head fell back and his body went limp.

Bundle sat back on her heels, shivering from head to foot. She could never have imagined that anything so awful could have happened to her. He was dead – and she had killed him.

She tried to pull herself together. What must she do now? A doctor – that was her first thought. It was possible – just possible – that the man might only be unconscious, not dead. Her instinct cried out against the possibility, but she forced herself to act upon it. Somehow or other she must get him into the car and take him to the nearest doctor's. It was a deserted stretch of country road and there was no one to help her.

Bundle, for all her slimness, was strong. She had muscles of whipcord. She brought the Hispano as close as possible, and then exerting all her strength, she dragged and pulled the inanimate figure into it. It was a horrid business, and one that made her set her teeth, but at last she managed it.

Then she jumped into the driver's seat and set off. A couple of miles brought her into a small town and on inquiring she was quickly directed to the doctor's house.

Dr Cassell, a kindly, middle-aged man, was startled to come into his surgery and find a girl there who was evidently on the verge of collapse.

Bundle spoke abruptly.

'I – I think I've killed a man. I ran over him. I brought him along in the car. He's outside now. I – I was driving too fast, I suppose. I've always driven too fast.'

The doctor cast a practised glance over her. He stepped over to a shelf and poured something into a glass. He brought it over to her.

'Drink this down,' he said, 'and you'll feel better. You've had a shock.'

Bundle drank obediently and a tinge of colour came into her pallid face. The doctor nodded approvingly.

'That's right. Now I want you to sit quietly here. I'll go out and attend to things. After I've made sure there's nothing to be done for the poor fellow, I'll come back and we'll talk about it.'

He was away some time. Bundle watched the clock on the

mantelpiece. Five minutes, ten minutes, a quarter of an hour, twenty minutes – would he ever come?

Then the door opened and Dr Cassell reappeared. He looked different – Bundle noticed that at once – grimmer and at the same time more alert. There was something else in his manner that she did not quite understand, a suggestion of repressed excitement.

'Now then, young lady,' he said. 'Let's have this out. You ran over this man, you say. Tell me just how the accident happened?'

Bundle explained to the best of her ability. The doctor followed her narrative with keen attention.

'Just so; the car didn't pass over his body?'

'No. In fact, I thought I'd missed him altogether.'

'He was reeling, you say?'

'Yes, I thought he was drunk.'

'And he came from the hedge?'

'There was a gate just there, I think. He must have come through the gate.'

The doctor nodded, then he leaned back in his chair and removed his pince-nez.

'I've no doubt at all,' he said, 'that you're a very reckless driver, and that you'll probably run over some poor fellow and do for him one of these days – but you haven't done it this time.'

'But –'

'The car never touched him. *This man was shot.*'

CHAPTER 6

SEVEN DIALS AGAIN

Bundle stared at him. And very slowly the world, which for the last three-quarters of an hour had been upside down, shifted till it stood once more the right way up. It was quite two minutes before Bundle spoke, but when she did it was no longer the panic-stricken girl but the real Bundle, cool, efficient and logical.

'How could he be shot?' she said.

'I don't know how he could,' said the doctor dryly. 'But he was. He's got a rifle bullet in him all right. He bled internally, that's why you didn't notice anything.'

Bundle nodded.

'The question is,' the doctor continued, 'who shot him? You saw nobody about?'

Bundle shook her head.

'It's odd,' said the doctor. 'If it was an accident, you'd expect the fellow who did it would come running to the rescue – unless just possibly he didn't know what he'd done.'

'There was no one about,' said Bundle. 'On the road, that is.'

'It seems to me,' said the doctor, 'that the poor lad must have been running – the bullet got him just as he passed through the gate and he came reeling on to the road in consequence. You didn't hear a shot?'

Bundle shook her head.

'But I probably shouldn't anyway,' she said, 'with the noise of the car.'

'Just so. He didn't say anything before he died?'

'He muttered a few words.'

'Nothing to throw light on the tragedy?'

'No. He wanted something – I don't know what – told to a friend of his. Oh! Yes, and he mentioned Seven Dials.'

'H'm,' said Doctor Cassell. 'Not a likely neighbourhood for one of his class. Perhaps his assailant came from there. Well, we needn't worry about that now. You can leave it in my hands. I'll notify the police. You must, of course, leave your name and address, as the police are sure to want to question you. In fact, perhaps you'd better come round to the police station with me now. They might say I ought to have detained you.'

They went together in Bundle's car. The police inspector was a slow-speaking man. He was somewhat overawed by Bundle's name and address when she gave it to him, and he took down her statement with great care.

'Lads!' he said. 'That's what it is. Lads practising! Cruel stupid, them young varmints are. Always loosing off at birds with no consideration for anyone as may be the other side of a hedge.'

The doctor thought it a most unlikely solution, but he realized that the case would soon be in abler hands and it did not seem worth while to make objections.

'Name of deceased?' asked the sergeant, moistening his pencil.

'He had a card-case on him. He appeared to have been a Mr Ronald Devereux, with an address in the Albany.'

Bundle frowned. The name Ronald Devereux awoke some chord of rememberance. She was sure she had heard it before.

It was not until she was half-way back to Chimneys in the car that it came to her. Of course! Ronny Devereux. Bill's friend in the Foreign Office. He and Bill and – yes – Gerald Wade.

As this last realization came to her, Bundle nearly went into the hedge. First Gerald Wade – then Ronny Devereux. Gerry Wade's death might have been natural – the result of carelessness – but Ronny Devereux's surely bore a more sinister interpretation.

And then Bundle remembered something else. Seven Dials! When the dying man had said it, it had seemed vaguely familiar. Now she knew why. Gerald Wade had mentioned Seven Dials in that last letter of his written to his sister on the night before his death. And that again connected up with something else that escaped her.

Thinking all these things over, Bundle had slowed down to such a sober pace that nobody would have recognized her. She drove the car round to the garage and went in search of her father.

Lord Caterham was happily reading a catalogue of a forthcoming sale of rare editions and was immeasurably astonished to see Bundle.

'Even you,' he said, 'can't have been to London and back in this time.'

'I haven't been to London,' said Bundle. 'I ran over a man.'

'What?'

'Only I didn't really. He was shot.'

'How could he have been?'

'I don't know how he could have been, but he was.'

'But why did you shoot him?'

'*I* didn't shoot him.'

'You shouldn't shoot people,' said Lord Caterham in a tone of mild remonstrance. 'You shouldn't really. I daresay some of them richly deserve it – but all the same it will lead to trouble.'

'I tell you I didn't shoot him.'

'Well, who did?'

'Nobody knows,' said Bundle.

'Nonsense,' said Lord Caterham. 'A man can't be shot and run over without anyone having done it.'

'He wasn't run over,' said Bundle.

'I thought you said he was.'

'I said I thought I had.'

'A tyre burst, I suppose,' said Lord Caterham. 'That does sound like a shot. It says so in detective stories.'

'You really are perfectly impossible, Father. You don't seem to have the brains of a rabbit.'

'Not at all,' said Lord Caterham. 'You come in with a wildly impossible tale about men being run over and shot and I don't know what, and then you expect me to know all about it by magic.'

Bundle sighed wearily.

'Just attend,' she said. 'I'll tell you all about it in words of one syllable.'

'There,' she said when she had concluded. 'Now have you got it?'

'Of course. I understand perfectly now. I can make allowances for your being a little upset, my dear. I was not far wrong when I remarked to you before starting out that people looking for trouble usually found it. I am thankful,' finished Lord Caterham with a slight shiver, 'that I stayed quietly here.'

He picked up the catalogue again.

'Father, where is Seven Dials?'

'In the East End somewhere, I fancy. I have frequently observed buses going there – or do I mean Seven Sisters? I have never been there myself, I'm thankful to say. Just as well, because I don't fancy it is the sort of spot I should like. And yet, curiously enough, I seem to have heard of it in some connection just lately.'

'You don't know a Jimmy Thesiger, do you?'

Lord Caterham was now engrossed in his catalogue once more. He had made an effort to be intelligent on the subject of Seven Dials. This time he made hardly any effort at all.

'Thesiger,' he murmured vaguely. 'Thesiger. One of the Yorkshire Thesigers?'

'That's what I'm asking you. Do attend, Father. This is important.'

Lord Caterham made a desperate effort to look intelligent without really having to give his mind to the matter.

'There *are* some Yorkshire Thesigers,' he said earnestly. 'And unless I am mistaken some Devonshire Thesigers also. Your Great-aunt Selina married a Thesiger.'

'What good is that to me?' cried Bundle.

Lord Caterham chuckled.

'It was very little good to her, if I remember rightly.'

'You're impossible,' said Bundle, rising. 'I shall have to get hold of Bill.'

'Do, dear,' said her father absently as he turned a page. 'Certainly. By all means. Quite so.'

Bundle rose to her feet with an impatient sigh.

'I wish I could remember what that letter said,' she murmured, more to herself than aloud. 'I didn't read it very carefully. Something about a joke, that the Seven Dials business wasn't a joke.'

Lord Caterham emerged suddenly from his catalogue.

'Seven Dials?' he said. 'Of course. I've got it now.'

'Got what?'

'I know why it sounded so familiar. George Lomax has been over. Tredwell failed for once and let him in. He was on his way up to town. It seems he's having some political party at the Abbey next week and he got a warning letter.'

'What do you mean by a warning letter?'

'Well, I don't really know. He didn't go into details. I gather it said "Beware" and "Trouble is at hand", and all those sorts of things. But anyway it was written from Seven Dials, I distinctly remember his saying so. He was going up to town to consult Scotland Yard about it. You know George?'

Bundle nodded. She was well acquainted with that public-spirited Cabinet Minister, George Lomax, His Majesty's Permanent Under Secretary of State for Foreign Affairs, who was shunned by many because of his inveterate habit of quoting from his public speeches in private. In allusion to his bulging eyeballs, he was known to many – Bill Eversleigh among others – as Codders.

'Tell me,' she said, 'was Codders interested at all in Gerald Wade's death?'

'Not that I heard of. He may have been, of course.'

Bundle said nothing for some minutes. She was busily engaged in trying to remember the exact wording of the letter she had sent on to Loraine Wade, and at the same time she was trying to picture the girl to whom it had been written. What sort of a girl was this to whom, apparently, Gerald Wade was so devoted? The more she thought over it, the more it seemed to her that it was an unusual letter for a brother to write.

'Did you say the Wade girl was Gerry's half-sister?' she asked suddenly.

'Well, of course, strictly speaking, I suppose she isn't – wasn't, I mean – his sister at all.'

'But her name's Wade?'

'Not really. She wasn't old Wade's child. As I was saying, he ran away with his second wife, who was married to a perfect blackguard. I suppose the Courts gave the rascally husband the custody of the child, but he certainly didn't avail himself of the privilege. Old Wade got very fond of the child and insisted that she should be called by his name.'

'I see,' said Bundle. 'That explains it.'

'Explains what?'

'Something that puzzled me about that letter.'

'She's rather a pretty girl, I believe,' said Lord Caterham. 'Or so I've heard.'

Bundle went upstairs thoughtfully. She had several objects in view. First she must find this Jimmy Thesiger. Bill, perhaps, would be helpful there. Ronny Devereux had been a friend of Bill's. If Jimmy Thesiger was a friend of Ronny's, the chances were that Bill would know him too. Then there was the girl, Loraine Wade. It was possible that she could throw some light on the problem of Seven Dials. Evidently Gerry Wade had said something to her about it. His anxiety that she should forget the fact had a sinister suggestion.

CHAPTER 7

BUNDLE PAYS A CALL

Getting hold of Bill presented few difficulties. Bundle motored up to town on the following morning – this time without adventures on the way – and rang him up. Bill responded with alacrity and made various suggestions as to lunch, tea, dinner and dancing. All of which suggestions Bundle turned down as made.

'In a day or two, I'll come and frivol with you, Bill. But for the moment I'm up on business.'

'Oh,' said Bill. 'What a beastly bore.'

'It's not that kind,' said Bundle. 'It's anything but boring. Bill, do you know anyone called Jimmy Thesiger?'

'Of course. So do you.'

'No, I don't,' said Bundle.

'Yes, you do. You must. Everyone knows old Jimmy.'

'Sorry,' said Bundle. 'Just for once I don't seem to be everyone.'

'Oh! But you must know Jimmy – pink-faced chap. Looks a bit of an ass. But really he's got as many brains as I have.'

'You don't say so,' said Bundle. 'He must feel a bit top-heavy when he walks about.'

'Was that meant for sarcasm?'

'It was a feeble effort at it. What does Jimmy Thesiger do?'

'How do you mean, what does he do?'

'Does being at the Foreign Office prevent you from understanding your native language?'

'Oh! I see, you mean, has he got a job? No, he just fools around. Why should he do anything?'

'In fact, more money than brains?'

'Oh! I wouldn't say that. I told you just now that he had more brains than you'd think.'

Bundle was silent. She was feeling more and more doubtful. This gilded youth did not sound a very promising ally. And yet it was his name that had come first to the dying man's lips. Bill's voice chimed in suddenly with singular appropriateness.

'Ronny always thought a lot of his brains. You know, Ronny Devereux. Thesiger was his greatest pal.'

'Ronny –'

Bundle stopped, undecided. Clearly Bill knew nothing of the other's death. It occurred to Bundle for the first time that it was odd the morning papers had contained nothing of the tragedy. Surely it was the kind of spicy item of news that would never be passed over. There could be one explanation, and one explanation only. The police, for reasons of their own, were keeping the matter quiet.

Bill's voice was continuing.

'I haven't seen Ronny for an age – not since that week-end down at your place. You know, when poor old Gerry Wade passed out.'

He paused and then went on.

'Rather a foul business that altogether. I expect you've heard about it. I say, Bundle – are you there still?'

'Of course I'm here.'

'Well, you haven't said anything for an age. I began to think that you had gone away.'

'No, I was just thinking over something.'

Should she tell Bill of Ronny's death? She decided against it – it was not the sort of thing to be said over the telephone. But soon, very soon, she must have a meeting with Bill. In the meantime –

'Bill?'

'Hullo.'

'I might dine with you tomorrow night.'

'Good, and we'll dance afterwards. I've got a lot to talk to you about. As a matter of fact I've been rather hard hit – the foulest luck –

'Well, tell me about it tomorrow,' said Bundle, cutting him short rather unkindly. 'In the meantime, what is Jimmy Thesiger's address?'

'Jimmy Thesiger?'

'That's what I said.'

'He's got rooms in Jermyn Street – do I mean Jermyn Street or the other one?'

'Bring that class A brain to bear upon it.'

'Yes, Jermyn Street. Wait a bit and I'll give you the number.'

There was a pause.

'Are you still there?'

'I'm always here.'

'Well, one never knows with these dashed telephones. The number is 103. Got it?'

'103. Thank you, Bill.'

'Yes, but, I say – what do you want it for? You said you didn't know him.'

'I don't, but I shall in half an hour.'

'You're going round to his rooms?'

'Quite right, Sherlock.'

'Yes, but, I say – well, for one thing he won't be up.'

'Won't be up?'

'I shouldn't think so. I mean, who would be if they hadn't got to? Look at it that way. You've no idea what an effort it is for me to get here at eleven every morning, and the fuss Codders makes if I'm behind time is simply appalling. You haven't the least idea, Bundle, what a dog's life this is –'

'You shall tell me all about it tomorrow night,' said Bundle hastily.

She slammed down the receiver and took stock of the situation. First she glanced at the clock. It was five and twenty minutes to twelve. Despite Bill's knowledge of his friend's habits, she inclined to her belief that Mr Thesiger would by now be in a fit state to receive visitors. She took a taxi to 103 Jermyn Street.

The door was opened by a perfect example of the retired gentleman's gentleman. His face, expessionless and polite, was such a face as may be found by the score in that particular district of London.

'Will you come this way, madam?'

He ushered her upstairs into an extremely comfortable sitting-room containing leather-covered arm-chairs of immense dimensions. Sunk in one of those monstrosities was another girl, rather younger than Bundle. A small, fair girl, dressed in black.

'What name shall I say, madam?'

'I won't give any name,' said Bundle. 'I just want to see Mr Thesiger on important business.'

The grave gentleman bowed and withdrew, shutting the door noiselessly behind him.

There was a pause.

'It's a nice morning,' said the fair girl timidly.

'It's an awfully nice morning,' agreed Bundle.

There was another pause.

'I motored up from the country this morning,' said Bundle, plunging once more into speech. 'And I thought it was going to be one of those foul fogs. But it wasn't.'

'No,' said the other girl. 'It wasn't.' And she added: 'I've come up from the country too.'

Bundle eyed her more attentively. She had been slightly annoyed at finding the other there. Bundle belonged to the energetic order of people who liked 'to get on with it', and she foresaw that the second visitor would have to be disposed of and got rid of before she could broach her own business. It was not a topic she could introduce before a stranger.

Now, as she looked more closely, an extraordinary idea rose to her brain. Could it be? Yes, the girl was in deep mourning; her black-clad ankles showed that. It was a long shot, but Bundle was convinced that her idea was right. She drew a long breath.

'Look here,' she said, 'are you by any chance Loraine Wade?'

Loraine's eyes opened wide.

'Yes, I am. How clever of you to know. We've never met, have we?'

'I wrote to you yesterday, though. I'm Bundle Brent.'

'It was so very kind of you to send me Gerry's letter,' said Loraine. 'I've written to thank you. I never expected to see you here.'

'I'll tell you why I'm here,' said Bundle. 'Did you know Ronny Devereux?'

Loraine nodded.

'He came over the day that Gerry – you know. And he's been to see me two or three times since. He was one of Gerry's greatest friends.'

'I know. Well – he's dead.'

Loraine's lips parted in surprise.

'*Dead*! But he always seemed so fit.'

Bundle narrated the events of the preceding day as briefly as possible. A look of fear and horror came into Loraine's face.

'Then it *is* true. It *is* true.'

'What's true?'

'What I've thought – what I've been thinking all these weeks. Gerry didn't die a natural death. He was killed.'

'You've thought that, have you?'

'Yes. Gerry would never have taken things to make him sleep.' She gave the little ghost of a laugh. 'He slept much too well to need them. I always thought it queer. And *he* thought so too – I know he did.'

'Who?'

'Ronny. And now this happens. Now he's killed too.' She paused and then went on: 'That's what I came for today. That letter of Gerry's you sent me – as soon as I read it, I tried to get hold of Ronny, but they said he was away. So I thought I'd come and see Jimmy – he was Ronny's other great friend. I thought perhaps he'd tell me what I ought to do.'

'You mean –' Bundle paused. 'About – Seven Dials.'

Loraine nodded.

'You see –' she began.

But at that moment Jimmy Thesiger entered the room.

CHAPTER 8

VISITORS FOR JIMMY

We must at this point go back to some twenty minutes earlier, to a moment when Jimmy Thesiger, emerging from the mists of sleep, was conscious of a familiar voice speaking unfamiliar words.

His sleep-ridden brain tried for a moment to cope with the situation, but failed. He yawned and rolled over again.

'A young lady, sir, has called to see you.'

The voice was implacable. So prepared was it to go on repeating the statement indefinitely that Jimmy resigned himself to the inevitable. He opened his eyes and blinked.

'Eh, Stevens?' he said. 'Say that again.'

'A young lady, sir, has called to see you.'

'Oh!' Jimmy strove to grasp the situation. 'Why?'

'I couldn't say, sir.'

'No, I suppose not. No,' he thought it over. 'I suppose you couldn't.'

Stevens swooped down upon a tray by the bedside.

'I will bring you some fresh tea, sir. This is cold.'

'You think that I ought to get up and – er – see the lady?'

Stevens made no reply, but he held his back very stiff and Jimmy read the signs correctly.

'Oh! Very well,' he said. 'I suppose I'd better. She didn't give her name?'

'No, sir.'

'M'm. She couldn't be by any possible chance my Aunt Jemima, could she? Because if so, I'm damned if I'm going to get up.'

'The lady, sir, could not possibly be anyone's aunt, I should say, unless the youngest of a large family.'

'Aha,' said Jimmy. 'Young and lovely. Is she – what kind is she?'

'The young lady, sir, is most undoubtedly strictly *comme il faut*, if I may use the expression.'

'You may use it,' said Jimmy graciously. 'Your French pronunciation, Stevens, if I may say so, is very good. Much better than mine.'

'I am gratified to hear it, sir. I have lately been taking a correspondence course in French.'

'Have you really? You're a wonderful chap, Stevens.'

Stevens smiled in a superior fashion and left the room. Jimmy lay trying to recall the names of any young and lovely girls strictly *comme il faut* who might be likely to come and call upon him.

Stevens re-entered with fresh tea, and as Jimmy sipped it he felt a pleasurable curiosity.

'You've given her the paper and all that, I hope, Stevens,' he said.

'I supplied her with the *Morning Post* and *Punch*, sir.'

A ring at the bell took him away. In a few minutes he returned.

'Another young lady, sir.'

'What?'

Jimmy clutched his head.

'Another young lady; she declines to give her name, sir, but says her business is important.'

Jimmy stared at him.

'This is damned odd, Stevens. Damned odd. Look here, what time did I come home last night?'

'Just upon five o'clock, sir.'

'And was I – er – how was I?'

'Just a little cheerful, sir – nothing more. Inclined to sing "Rule Britannia".'

'What an extraordinary thing,' said Jimmy. '"Rule Britannia", eh? I cannot imagine myself in a sober state ever singing "Rule Britannia". Some latent patriotism must have emerged under the stimulus of – er – just a couple too many. I was celebrating at the Mustard and Cress, I remember. Not nearly such an innocent spot as it sounds, Stevens.' He paused. 'I was wondering –'

'Yes, sir?'

'I was wondering whether under the aforementioned stimulus I had put an advertisement in a newspaper asking for a nursery governess or something of that sort.'

Stevens coughed.

'*Two* girls turning up. It looks odd. I shall eschew the Mustard and Cress in future. That's a good word, Stevens – *eschew* – I met it in a crossword the other day and took a fancy to it.'

Whilst he was talking Jimmy was rapidly apparelling himself. At the end of ten minutes he was ready to face his unknown guests. As he opened the door of his sitting-room the first person he saw was a dark, slim girl who was totally unknown to him. She was standing by the mantelpiece, leaning against it. Then his glance went on to the big leather-covered arm-chair, and his heart missed a beat. Loraine!

It was she who rose and spoke first a little nervously.

'You must be very surprised to see me. But I had to come. I'll explain in a minute. This is Lady Eileen Brent.'

'Bundle – that's what I'm usually known as. You've probably heard of me from Bill Eversleigh.'

'Oh, rather, of course I have,' said Jimmy, endeavouring to cope with the situation. 'I say, do sit down and let's have a cocktail or something.'

Both girls declined.

'As a matter of fact,' continued Jimmy, 'I'm only just out of bed.'

'That's what Bill said,' remarked Bundle. 'I told him I was coming round to see you, and he said you wouldn't be up.'

'Well, I'm up now,' said Jimmy encouragingly.

'It's about Gerry,' said Loraine. 'And now about Ronny –'

'What do you mean by "and now about Ronny"?'

'He was shot yesterday.'

'What?' cried Jimmy.

Bundle told her story for the second time. Jimmy listened like a man in a dream.

'Old Ronny – shot,' he murmured. 'What *is* this damned business?'

He sat down on the edge of a chair, thinking for a minute or two, and then spoke in a quiet, level voice.

'There's something I think I ought to tell you.'

'Yes,' said Bundle encouragingly.

'It was on the day Gerry Wade died. On the way over to break the news to *you*' – he nodded at Loraine – 'in the car Ronny said something to me. That is to say, he started to tell me something. There was something he wanted to tell me, and he began about it, and then he said he was bound by a promise and couldn't go on.'

'Bound by a promise,' said Loraine thoughtfully.

'That's what he said. Naturally I didn't press him after that. But he was odd – damned odd – all through. I got the impression then that he suspected – well, foul play. I thought he'd tell the doctor so. But no, not even a hint. So I thought I'd been mistaken. And afterwards, with the evidence and all – well, it seemed such a very clear case. I thought my suspicions had been all bosh.'

'But you think Ronny still suspected?' asked Bundle.

Jimmy nodded.

'That's what I think now. Why, none of us has seen anything of him since. I believe he was playing a lone hand – trying to find out the truth about Gerry's death, and what's more, I believe he *did* find out. That's why the devils shot him. And then he tried to send word to me, but could only get out those two words.'

'Seven Dials,' said Bundle, and shivered a little.

'Seven Dials,' said Jimmy gravely. 'At any rate we've got that to go on with.'

Bundle turned to Loraine.

'You were just going to tell me –'

'Oh! Yes. First, about the letter.' She spoke to Jimmy. 'Gerry left a letter. Lady Eileen –'

'Bundle.'

'Bundle found it.' She explained the circumstances in a few words.

Jimmy listened, keenly interested. This was the first he had heard of the letter. Loraine took it from her bag and handed it to him. He read it, then looked across at her.

'This is where you can help us. What was it Gerry wanted you to forget?'

Loraine's brows wrinkled a little in perplexity.

'It's so hard to remember exactly now. I opened a letter of Gerry's by mistake. It was written on cheap sort of paper, I remember, and very illiterate handwriting. It had some address in Seven Dials at the head of it. I realized it wasn't for me, so I put it back in the envelope without reading it.'

'Sure?' asked Jimmy very gently.

Loraine laughed for the first time.

'I know what you think, and I admit that women *are* curious. But, you see, this didn't even look interesting. It was a kind of list of names and dates.'

'Names and dates,' said Jimmy thoughtfully.

'Gerry didn't seem to mind much,' continued Loraine. 'He laughed. He asked me if I had ever heard of the Mafia, and then said it would be queer if a society like the Mafia started in England – but that that kind of secret society didn't take on much with English people. "Our criminals," he said, "haven't got a picturesque imagination."'

Jimmy pursued up his lips into a whistle.

'I'm beginning to see,' he said. 'Seven Dials must be the headquarters for some secret society. As he says in his letter to you. He thought it rather a joke to start with. But evidently it wasn't a joke – he says as much. And there's something else: his anxiety that you should forget what he's told you. There can be only one reason for that – if that society suspected that you had any knowledge of its activity, you too would be in danger. Gerald realized the peril, and he was terribly anxious – for you.'

He stopped, then he went on quietly:

'I rather fancy that we're all going to be in danger – if we go on with this.'

'If –?' cried Bundle indignantly.

'I'm talking of you two. It's different for me. I was poor old Ronny's pal.' He looked at Bundle. 'You've done your bit. You've delivered the message he sent me. No; for God's sake keep out of it, you and Loraine.'

Bundle looked questioningly at the other girl. Her own mind was definitely made up, but she gave no indication of it just then. She had no wish to push Loraine Wade into a dangerous undertaking.

But Loraine's small face was alight at once with indignation.

'You say that! Do you think for one minute I'd be contented to keep out of it – when they killed Gerry – my own dear Gerry, the best and dearest and kindest brother any girl ever had? The only person belonging to me I had in the whole world!'

Jimmy cleared his throat uncomfortably. Loraine, he thought, was wonderful; simply wonderful.

'Look here,' he said awkwardly. 'You mustn't say that. About being alone in the world – all that rot. You've got lots of friends – only too glad to do what they can. See what I mean?'

It is possible that Loraine did, for she suddenly blushed, and to cover her confusion began to talk nervously.

'That's settled,' she said. 'I'm going to help. Nobody's going to stop me.'

'And so am I, of course,' said Bundle.

They both looked at Jimmy.

'Yes,' he said slowly. 'Yes, quite so.'

They looked at him inquiringly.

'I was just wondering,' said Jimmy, 'how we were going to begin.'

CHAPTER 9

PLANS

Jimmy's words lifted the discussion at once into a more practical sphere.

'All things considered,' he said, 'we haven't got much to go on. In fact, just the words Seven Dials. As a matter of fact I don't even know exactly where Seven Dials is. But, anyway, we can't very well comb out the whole of that district, house by house.'

'We could,' said Bundle.

'Well, perhaps we could eventually – though I'm not so sure. I imagine it's a well-populated area. But it wouldn't be very subtle.'

The word reminded him of the girl Socks and he smiled.

'Then, of course, there's the part of the country where Ronny was shot. We could nose around there. But the police are probably doing everything we could do, and doing it much better.'

'What I like about you,' said Bundle sarcastically, 'is your cheerful and optimistic disposition.'

'Never mind her, Jimmy,' said Loraine softly. 'Go on.'

'Don't be so impatient,' said Jimmy to Bundle. 'All the best sleuths approach a case this way, by eliminating unnecessary and unprofitable investigation. I'm coming now to the third alternative – Gerald's death. Now that we know it was murder – by the way, you do both believe that, don't you?'

'Yes,' said Loraine.

'Yes,' said Bundle.

'Good. So do I. Well, it seems to me that there we do stand some faint chance. After all, if Gerry didn't take the chloral himself, someone must have got into his room and put it there – dissolved it in the glass of water, so that when he woke up he drank it off. And of course left the empty box or bottle or whatever it was. You agree with that?'

'Ye–es,' said Bundle slowly. 'But –'

'Wait. And that someone must have been in the house at the time. It couldn't very well have been someone from outside.'

'No,' agreed Bundle, more readily this time.

'Very well. Now, that narrows down things considerably. To begin with, I suppose a good many of the servants are family ones – they're your lot, I mean.'

'Yes,' said Bundle. 'Practically all the staff stayed when we let it. All the principal ones are there still – of course there have been changes among the under-servants.'

'Exactly – that's what I am getting at. *You*' – he addressed Bundle – 'must go into all that. Find out when new servants were engaged – what about footmen, for instance?'

'One of the footmen is new. John, his name is.'

'Well, make inquiries about John. And about the others who have only come recently.'

'I suppose,' said Bundle slowly, 'it must have been a servant. It couldn't have been one of the guests?'

'I don't see how that's possible.'

'Who were there exactly?'

'Well, there were three girls – Nancy and Helen and Socks –'

'Socks Daventry? I know her.'

'May have been. Girl who was always saying things were subtle.'

'That's Socks all right. Subtle is one of her words.'

'And then there was Gerry Wade and me and Bill Eversleigh and Ronny. And, of course, Sir Oswald and Lady Coote. Oh! and Pongo.'

'Who's Pongo?'

'Chap called Bateman – secretary to old Coote. Solemn sort of cove but very conscientious. I was at school with him.'

'There doesn't seem anything very suspicious there,' remarked Loraine.

'No, there doesn't,' said Bundle. 'As you say, we'll have to look amongst the servants. By the way, you don't suppose that clock being thrown out of the window had anything to do with it?'

'A clock thrown out of the window,' said Jimmy, staring. It was the first he had heard of it.

'I can't see how it can have anything to do with it,' said Bundle. 'But it's odd somehow. There seems no sense in it.'

'I remember,' said Jimmy slowly. 'I went in to – to see poor old Gerry, and, there were the clocks ranged along the mantelpiece. I remember noticing there were only seven – not eight.'

He gave a sudden shiver and explained himself apologetically.

'Sorry, but somehow those clocks have always given me the shivers. I dream of them sometimes. I'd hate to go into that room in the dark and see them there in a row.'

'You wouldn't be able to see them if it was dark,' said Bundle practically. 'Not unless they had luminous dials – Oh!' She gave a sudden gasp and the colour rushed into her cheeks. 'Don't you see! *Seven Dials!*'

The others looked at her doubtfully, but she insisted with increasing vehemence.

'It must be. It can't be a coincidence.'

There was a pause.

'You may be right,' said Jimmy Thesiger at last. 'It's – it's dashed odd.'

Bundle started questioning him eagerly.

'Who bought the clocks?'

'All of us.'

'Who thought of them?'

'All of us.'

'Nonsense, somebody must have thought of them first.'

'It didn't happen that way. We were discussing what we could do to get Gerry up, and Pongo said an alarum clock, and somebody said one would be no good, and somebody else – Bill Eversleigh, I think – said why not get a dozen. And we all said good egg and hoofed off to get them. We got one each and an extra one for Pongo and one for Lady Coote – just out of the generosity of our hearts. There was nothing premeditated about it – it just happened.'

Bundle was silenced, but not convinced.

Jimmy proceeded to sum up methodically.

'I think we can say we're sure of certain facts. There's a secret society, with points of resemblance to the Mafia, in existence. Gerry Wade came to know about it. At first he treated it as rather a joke – as an absurdity, shall we say. He couldn't believe in its being really dangerous. But later something happened to convince him, and then he got the wind up in earnest. I rather fancy he must have said something to Ronny Devereux about it. Anyway, when he was put out of the way, Ronny suspected, and he must have known enough to get on the same track himself. The unfortunate thing is that we've got to start quite from the outer darkness. We haven't got the knowledge the other two had.'

'Perhaps that's an advantage,' said Loraine coolly. 'They won't suspect us and therefore they won't be trying to put us out of the way.'

'I wish I felt sure about that,' said Jimmy in a worried voice. 'You know, Loraine, old Gerry himself wanted you to keep out of it. Don't you think you could –'

'No, I couldn't,' said Loraine. 'Don't let's start discussing that again. It's only a waste of time.'

At the mention of the word time, Jimmy's eyes rose to the clock and he uttered an exclamation of astonishment. He rose and opened the door.

'Stevens.'

'Yes, sir?'

'What about a spot of lunch, Stevens? Could it be managed?'

'I anticipated that it would be required, sir. Mrs Stevens has made preparations accordingly.'

'That's a wonderful man,' said Jimmy, as he returned, heaving a sigh of relief. 'Brain, you know. Sheer brain. He takes correspondence courses. I sometimes wonder if they'd be any good to me.'

'Don't be silly,' said Loraine.

Stevens opened the door and proceeded to bring in a most *recherché* meal. An omelette was followed by quails and the very lightest thing in soufflés.

'Why are men so happy when they're single?' said Loraine tragically. 'Why are they so much better looked after by other people than by us?'

'Oh! But that's rot, you know,' said Jimmy. 'I mean, they're not. How could they be? I often think –'

He stammered and stopped. Loraine blushed again.

Suddenly Bundle let out a whoop and both the others started violently.

'Idiot,' said Bundle. 'Imbecile. Me, I mean. I knew there was something I'd forgotten.'

'What?'

'You know Codders – George Lomax, I mean?'

'I've heard of him a good deal,' said Jimmy. 'From Bill and Ronny, you know.'

'Well, Codders is giving some sort of a dry party next week – and he's had a warning letter from Seven Dials.'

'What?' cried Jimmy excitedly, leaning forward. 'You can't mean it?'

'Yes, I do. He told Father about it. Now what do you think that points to?'

Jimmy leant back in his chair. He thought rapidly and carefully. At last he spoke. His speech was brief and to the point.

'Something's going to happen at that party,' he said.

'That's what I think,' said Bundle.

'It all fits in,' said Jimmy almost dreamily.

He turned to Loraine.

'How old were you when the war was on?' he asked unexpectedly.

'Nine – no, eight.'

'And Gerry, I suppose, was about twenty. Most lads of twenty fought in the war. Gerry didn't.'

'No,' said Loraine, after thinking a minute or two. 'No, Gerry wasn't a soldier. I don't know why.'

'I can tell you why,' said Jimmy. 'Or at least I can make a very shrewd guess. He was out of England from 1915 to 1918. I've taken the trouble to find that out. And nobody seems to know exactly where he was. I think he was in Germany.'

The colour rose in Loraine's cheeks. She looked at Jimmy with admiration.

'How clever of you.'

'He spoke German well, didn't he?'

'Oh, yes, like a native.'

'I'm sure I'm right. Listen you two. Gerry Wade was at the Foreign Office. He appeared to be the same sort of amiable idiot – excuse the term, but you know what I mean – as Bill Eversleigh and Ronny Devereux. A purely ornamental excrescence. But in reality he was something quite different. I think Gerry Wade was the real thing. Our Secret Service is supposed to be the best in the world. I think Gerry Wade was pretty high up in that service. And that explains everything! I remember saying idly that last evening at Chimneys that Gerry couldn't be quite such an ass as he made himself out to be.'

'And if you're right?' said Bundle, practical as ever.

'Then the thing's bigger than we thought. This Seven Dials business isn't merely criminal – it's international. One thing's certain, somebody has got to be at this house party of Lomax's.'

Bundle made a slight grimace.

'I know George well – but he doesn't like me. He'd never think of asking me to a serious gathering. All the same, I might –'

She remained a moment lost in thought.

'Do you think *I* could work it through Bill?' asked Jimmy. 'He's bound to be there as Codders's right-hand man. He might bring me along somehow or other.'

'I don't see why not,' said Bundle. 'You'll have to prime Bill and make him say the right things. He's incapable of thinking of them for himself.'

'What do you suggest?' asked Jimmy humbly.

'Oh! It's quite easy. Bill describes you as a rich young man – interested in politics, anxious to stand for Parliament. George will fall at once. You know what these political parties are: always looking for new rich young men. The richer Bill says you are, the easier it will be to manage.'

'Short of being described as Rothschild, I don't mind,' said Jimmy.

'Then I think that's practically settled. I'm dining with Bill tomorrow night, and I'll get a list of who is to be there. That will be useful.'

'I'm sorry you can't be there,' said Jimmy. 'But on the whole I think it's all for the best.'

'I'm not sure I shan't be there,' said Bundle. 'Codders hates me like poison – but there are other ways.'

She became meditative.

'And what about me?' asked Loraine in a small, meek voice.

'You're not on in this act,' said Jimmy instantly. 'See? After all, we've got to have someone outside to – er –'

'To what?' said Loraine.

Jimmy decided not to pursue this tack. He appealed to Bundle.

'Look here,' he said, 'Loraine must keep out of this, mustn't she?'

'I certainly think she'd better.'

'Next time,' said Jimmy kindly.

'And suppose there isn't a next time?' said Loraine.

'Oh, there probably will be. Not a doubt of it.'

'I see. I'm just to go home and – wait?'

'That's it,' said Jimmy, with every appearance of relief. 'I thought you'd understand.'

'You see,' explained Bundle, 'three of us forcing our way in might look rather suspicious. And you would be particularly difficult. You do see that, don't you?'

'Oh, yes,' said Loraine.

'Then it's settled – you do nothing,' said Jimmy.

'I do nothing,' said Loraine meekly.

Bundle looked at her in sudden suspicion. The tameness with which Loraine was taking it seemed hardly natural. Loraine looked at her. Her eyes were blue and guileless. They met Bundle's without a quiver even of the lashes. Bundle was only partly satisfied. She found the meekness of Loraine Wade highly suspicious.

CHAPTER 10

BUNDLE VISITS SCOTLAND YARD

Now it may be said at once that in the foregoing conversation each one of the three participants had, as it were, held something in reserve. That 'Nobody tells everything' is a very true motto.

It may be questioned, for instance, if Loraine Wade was perfectly sincere in her account of the motives which had led her to seek out Jimmy Thesiger.

In the same way, Jimmy Thesiger himself had various ideas and plans connected with the forthcoming party at George Lomax's which he had no intention of revealing to – say, Bundle.

And Bundle herself had a fully-fledged plan which she proposed to put into immediate execution and which she had said nothing whatever about.

On leaving Jimmy Thesiger's rooms, she drove to Scotland Yard, where she asked for Superintendent Battle.

Superintendent Battle was rather a big man. He worked almost entirely on cases of a delicate political nature. On such a case he had come to Chimneys four years ago, and Bundle was frankly trading on his remembering this fact.

After a short delay, she was taken along several corridors and into the Superintendent's private room. Battle was a stolid-looking man with a wooden face. He looked supremely unintelligent and more like a commissionaire than a detective.

He was standing by the window when she entered, gazing in an expressionless manner at some sparrows.

'Good afternoon, Lady Eileen,' he said. 'Sit down, won't you?'

'Thank you,' said Bundle. 'I was afraid you mightn't remember me.'

'Always remember people,' said Battle. He added: 'Got to in my job.'

'Oh!' said Bundle, rather damped.

'And what can I do for you?' inquired the superintendent.

Bundle came straight to the point.

'I've always heard that you people at Scotland Yard have lists of all secret societies and things like that that are formed in London.'

'We try to keep up to date,' said Superintendent Battle cautiously.

'I suppose a great many of them aren't really dangerous?'

'We've got a very good rule to go by,' said Battle. 'The more they talk, the less they'll do. You'd be surprised how well that works out.'

'And I've heard that very often you let them go on?'

Battle nodded.

'That's so. Why shouldn't a man call himself a Brother of Liberty and meet twice a week in a cellar and talk about rivers of blood – it won't hurt either him or us? And if there *is* trouble any time, we know where to lay our hands on him.'

'But sometimes, I suppose,' said Bundle slowly, 'a society may be more dangerous than anyone imagines?'

'Very likely,' said Battle.

'But it *might* happen,' persisted Bundle.

'Oh, it *might*,' admitted the superintendent.

There was a moment or two's silence. Then Bundle said quietly:

'Superintendent Battle, could you give me a list of secret societies that have their headquarters in Seven Dials?'

It was Superintendent Battle's boast that he had never been seen to display emotion. But Bundle could have sworn that just for a moment his eyelids flickered and he looked taken aback. Only for a moment, however. He was his usual wooden self as he said:

'Strictly speaking, Lady Eileen, there's no such place as Seven Dials nowadays.'

'No?'

'No. Most of it is pulled down and rebuilt. It was rather a low quarter once, but it's very respectable and high class nowadays.

Not at all a romantic spot to poke about in for mysterious secret societies.'

'Oh!' said Bundle, rather nonplussed.

'But all the same I should very much like to know what put that neighbourhood into your head, Lady Eileen.'

'Have I got to tell you?'

'Well, it saves trouble, doesn't it? We know where we are, so to speak.'

Bundle hesitated for a minute.

'There was a man shot yesterday,' she said slowly. 'I thought I had run over him –'

'Mr Ronald Devereux?'

'You know about it, of course. Why has there been nothing in the papers?'

'Do you really want to know that, Lady Eileen?'

'Yes, please.'

'Well, we just thought we should like to have a clear twenty-four hours – see? It will be in the papers tomorrow.'

'Oh!' Bundle studied him, puzzled.

What was hidden behind that immovable face? Did he regard the shooting of Ronald Devereux as an ordinary crime or as an extraordinary one?

'He mentioned Seven Dials when he was dying,' said Bundle slowly.

'Thank you,' said Battle. 'I'll make a note of that.'

He wrote a few words on the blotting pad in front of him.

Bundle started on another tack.

'Mr Lomax, I understand, came to see you yesterday about a threatening letter he had had?'

'He did.'

'And that was written from Seven Dials?'

'It had Seven Dials written at the top if it, I believe.'

Bundle felt as though she was battering hopelessly on a locked door.

'If you'll let me advise you, Lady Eileen –'

'I know what you're going to say.'

'I should go home and – well, think no more about these matters.'

'Leave it to you, in fact?'

'Well,' said Superintendent Battle, 'after all, we *are* the professionals.'

'And I'm only an amateur? Yes, but you forget one thing – I mayn't have your knowledge and skill – but I have one advantage over you. I can work in the dark.'

She thought that the Superintendent seemed a little taken aback, as though the force of her words struck home.

'Of course,' said Bundle, 'if you won't give me a list of secret societies –'

'Oh! I never said that. You shall have a list of the whole lot.'

He went to the door, put his head through and called out something, then came back to his chair. Bundle, rather unreasonably, felt baffled. The ease with which he acceded to her request seemed to her suspicious. He was looking at her now in a placid fashion.

'Do you remember the death of Mr Gerald Wade?' she asked abruptly.

'Down at your place, wasn't it? Took an overdraught of sleeping mixture.'

'His sister says he never took things to make him sleep.'

'Ah!' said the Superintendent. 'You'd be surprised what a lot of things there are that sisters don't know.'

Bundle again felt baffled. She sat in silence till a man came in with a typewritten sheet of paper, which he handed to the superintendent.

'Here you are,' said the latter when the other had left the room. 'The Blood Brothers of St Sebastian. The Wolf Hounds. The Comrades of Peace. The Comrades Club. The Friends of Oppression. The Children of Moscow. The Red Standard Bearers. The Herrings. The Comrades of the Fallen – and half a dozen more.'

He handed it to her with a distinct twinkle in his eye.

'You give it to me,' said Bundle, 'because you know it's not going to be the slightest use to me. Do you want me to leave the whole thing alone?'

'I should prefer it,' said Battle. 'You see – if you go messing around all these places – well, it's going to give us a lot of trouble.'

'Looking after me, you mean?'

'Looking after you, Lady Eileen.'

Bundle had risen to her feet. Now she stood undecided. So far the honours lay with Superintendent Battle. Then she remembered one slight incident, and she based her last appeal upon it.

'I said just now that an amateur could do some things which a professional couldn't. You didn't contradict me. That's because you're an honest man, Superintendent Battle. You knew I was right.'

'Go on,' said Battle quickly.

'At Chimneys you let me help. Won't you let me help now?'

Battle seemed to be turning the thing over in his mind. Emboldened by his silence, Bundle continued.

'You know pretty well what I'm like, Superintendent Battle. I butt into things. I'm a Nosy Parker. I don't want to get in your way or to try and do things that you're doing and can do a great deal better. But if there's a chance for an amateur, let me have it.'

Again there was a pause, and then Superintendent Battle said quietly:

'You couldn't have spoken fairer than you have done, Lady Eileen. But I'm just going to say this to you. What you propose is dangerous. And when I say dangerous, I *mean* dangerous.'

'I've grasped that,' said Bundle. 'I'm not a fool.'

'No,' said Superintendent Battle. 'Never knew a young lady who was less so. What I'll do for you, Lady Eileen, is this. I'll just give you one little hint. And I'm doing it because I never have thought much of the motto "Safety First". In my opinion all the people who spend their lives avoiding being run over by buses had much better be run over and put safely out of the way. They're no good.'

This remarkable utterance issuing from the conventional lips of Superintendent Battle quite took Bundle's breath away.

'What was that hint you were going to give me?' she asked at last.

'You know Mr Eversleigh, don't you?'

'Know Bill? Why, of course, But what –?'

'I think Mr Bill Eversleigh will be able to tell you all you want to know about Seven Dials.'

'Bill knows about it? *Bill?*'

'I didn't say that. Not at all. But I think, being a quick-witted young lady, you'll get what you want from him.

'And now,' said Superintendent. Battle firmly, 'I'm not going to say another word.'

CHAPTER 11

DINNER WITH BILL

Bundle set out to keep her appointment with Bill on the following evening full of expectation.

Bill greeted her with every sign of elation.

'Bill really *is* rather nice,' thought Bundle to herself. 'Just like a large, clumsy dog that wags its tail when it's pleased to see you.'

The large dog was uttering short staccato yelps of comment and information.

'You look tremendously fit, Bundle. I can't tell you how pleased I am to see you. I've ordered oysters – you do like oysters, don't you? And how's everything? What did you want to go mouldering about abroad so long? Were you having a very gay time?'

'No, deadly,' said Bundle. 'Perfectly foul. Old diseased colonels creeping about in the sun, and active, wizened spinsters running libraries and churches.'

'Give me England,' said Bill. 'I bar this foreign business – except Switzerland. Switzerland's all right. I'm thinking of going this Christmas. Why don't you come along?'

'I'll think about it,' said Bundle. 'What have you been doing with yourself lately, Bill?'

It was an incautious query. Bundle had merely made it out of politeness and as a preliminary to introducing her own topics of conversation. It was, however, the opening for which Bill had been waiting.

'That's just what I've been wanting to tell you about. You're brainy, Bundle, and I want your advice. You know that musical show, "Damn Your Eyes"?'

'Yes.'

'Well, I'm going to tell you about one of the dirtiest pieces of work imaginable. My God! the theatrical crowd. There's a girl – a Yankee girl – a perfect stunner –'

Bundle's heart sank. The grievances of Bill's lady friends were always interminable – they went on and on and there was no stemming them.

'This girl, Babe St Maur her name is –'

'I wonder how she got her name?' said Bundle sarcastically.

Bill replied literally.

'She got it out of *Who's Who*. Opened it and jabbed her finger down on a page without looking. Pretty nifty, eh? Her real name's Goldschmidt or Abrameier – something quite impossible.'

'Oh, quite,' agreed Bundle.

'Well, Babe St Maur is pretty smart. And she's got muscles. She was one of the eight girls who made the living bridge –'

'Bill,' said Bundle desperately. 'I went to see Jimmy Thesiger yesterday morning.'

'Good old Jimmy,' said Bill. 'Well, as I was telling you, Babe's pretty smart. You've got to be nowadays. She can put it over on most theatrical people. If you want to live, be high-handed, that's what Babe says. And mind you, she's the goods all right. She can act – it's marvellous how that girl can act. She'd not much chance in "Damn Your Eyes" – just swamped in a pack of good-looking girls. I said why not try the legitimate stage – you know, Mrs Tanqueray – that sort of stuff – but Babe just laughed –'

'Have you seen Jimmy at all?'

'Saw him this morning. Let me see, where was I? Oh, yes, I hadn't got to the rumpus yet. And mind you it was jealousy – sheer, spiteful jealousy. The other girl wasn't a patch on Babe for looks and she knew it. So she went behind her back –'

Bundle resigned herself to the inevitable and heard the whole story of the unfortunate circumstances which had led up to Babe St Maur's summary disappearance from the cast of 'Damn Your Eyes.' It took a long time. When Bill finally paused for breath and sympathy, Bundle said:

'You're quite right, Bill, it's a rotten shame. There must be a lot of jealousy about –'

'The whole theatrical world's rotten with it.'

'It must be. Did Jimmy say anything to you about coming down to the Abbey next week?'

For the first time, Bill gave his attention to what Bundle was saying.

'He was full of a long rigmarole he wanted me to stuff Codders with. About wanting to stand in the Conservative interest. But you know, Bundle, it's too damned risky.'

'Stuff,' said Bundle. 'If George *does* find him out, he won't blame you. You'll just have been taken in, that's all.'

'That's not it at all,' said Bill. 'I mean it's too damned risky for Jimmy. Before he knows where he is, he'll be parked down somewhere like Tooting East, pledged to kiss babies and make speeches. You don't know how thorough Codders is and how frightfully energetic.'

'Well, we'll have to risk that,' said Bundle. 'Jimmy can take care of himself all right.'

'You don't know Codders,' repeated Bill.

'Who's coming to this party, Bill? Is it anything very special?'

'Only the usual sort of muck. Mrs Macatta for one.'

'The M.P.?'

'Yes, you know, always going off the deep end about Welfare and Pure Milk and Save the Children. Think of poor Jimmy being talked to by her.'

'Never mind, Jimmy. Go on telling me.'

'Then there's the Hungarian, what they call a Young Hungarian. Countess something unpronounceable. She's all right.'

He swallowed as though embarrassed, and Bundle observed that he was crumbling his bread nervously.

'Young and beautiful?' she inquired delicately.

'Oh, rather.'

'I didn't know George went in for female beauty much.'

'Oh, he doesn't. She runs baby feeding in Buda Pesth – something like that. Naturally she and Mrs Macatta want to get together.'

'Who else?'

'Sir Stanley Digby –'

'The Air Minister?'

'Yes. And his secretary, Terence O'Rourke. He's rather a lad, by the way – or used to be in his flying days. Then there's a perfectly poisonous German chap called Herr Eberhard. I don't know who he is, but we're all making the hell of a fuss about him. I've been twice told off to take him out to lunch, and I can tell you, Bundle, it was no joke. He's not like the Embassy chaps, who are all very decent. This man sucks in soup and eats peas with a knife. Not only that, but the brute is always biting his finger-nails – positively gnaws at them.'

'Pretty foul.'

'Isn't it? I believe he invents things – something of the kind. Well, that's all. Oh, yes, Sir Oswald Coote.'

'And Lady Coote?'

'Yes, I believe she's coming too.'

Bundle sat lost in thought for some minutes. Bill's list was suggestive, but she hadn't time to think out various possibilities just now. She must get on to the next point.

'Bill,' she said, 'what's all this about Seven Dials?'

Bill at once looked horribly embarrassed. He blinked and avoided her glance.

'I don't know what you mean,' he said.

'Nonsense,' said Bundle. 'I was told you know all about it.'

'About what?'

This was rather a poser. Bundle shifted her ground.

'I don't see what you want to be so secretive for,' she complained.

'Nothing to be secretive about. Nobody goes there much now. It was only a craze.'

This sounded puzzling.

'One gets so out of things when one is away,' said Bundle in a sad voice.

'Oh, you haven't missed much,' said Bill. 'Everyone went there just to say they had been. It was boring really, and, my God, you *can* get tired of fried fish.'

'Where did everyone go?'

'To the Seven Dials Club, of course,' said Bill, staring. 'Wasn't that what you were asking about?'

'I didn't know it by that name,' said Bundle.

'Used to be a slummy sort of district round about Tottenham Court Road way. It's all pulled down and cleaned up now. But the Seven Dials Club keeps to the old atmosphere. Fried fish and chips. General squalor. Kind of East End stunt, but awfully handy to get at after a show.'

'It's a night club, I suppose,' said Bundle. 'Dancing and all that?'

'That's it. Awfully mixed crowd. Not a posh affair. Artists, you know, and all sorts of odd women and a sprinkling of our lot. They say quite a lot of things, but I think that that's all bunkum myself, just said to make the place go.'

'Good,' said Bundle. 'We'll go there tonight.'

'Oh! I shouldn't do that,' said Bill. His embarrassment had returned. 'I tell you it's played out. Nobody goes there now.'

'Well, we're going.'

'You wouldn't care for it, Bundle. You wouldn't really.'

'You're going to take me to the Seven Dials Club and nowhere else, Bill. And I should like to know why you are so unwilling?'

'I? Unwilling?'

'Painfully so. What's the guilty secret?'

'Guilty secret?'

'Don't keep repeating what I say. You do it to give yourself time.'

'I don't,' said Bill indignantly. 'It's only –'

'Well? I know there's something. You never can conceal anything.'

'I've got nothing to conceal. It's only –'

'Well?'

'It's a long story – You see, I took Babe St Maur there one night –'

'Oh! Babe St Maur again.'

'Why not?'

'I didn't know it was about her –' said Bundle, stifling a yawn.

'As I say, I took Babe there. She rather fancied a lobster. I had a lobster under my arm –'

The story went on – When the lobster had been finally dismembered in a struggle between Bill and a fellow who was a rank outsider, Bundle brought her attention back to him.

'I see,' she said. 'And there was a row?'

'Yes, but it was *my* lobster. I'd bought it and paid for it. I had a perfect right –'

'Oh, you had, you had,' said Bundle hastily. 'But I'm sure that's all forgotten now. And I don't care for lobsters anyway. So let's go.'

'We may be raided by the police. There's a room upstairs where they play baccarat.'

'Father will have to come and bail me out, that's all. Come on, Bill.'

Bill still seemed rather reluctant, but Bundle was adamant and they were soon speeding to their destination in a taxi.

The place, when they got to it, was much as she imagined it would be. It was a tall house in a narrow street, 14 Hunstanton Street; she noted the number.

A man whose face was strangely familiar opened the door. She thought he started slightly when he saw her, but he greeted Bill with respectful recognition. He was a tall man, with fair hair, a rather weak, anaemic face and slightly shifty eyes. Bundle puzzled to herself where she could have seen him before.

Bill had recovered his equilibrium now and quite enjoyed doing showman. They danced in the cellar, which was very full of smoke – so much so that you saw everyone through a blue haze. The smell of fried fish was almost overpowering.

On the wall were rough charcoal sketches, some of them executed with real talent. Thc company was extremely mixed. There were portly foreigners, opulent Jewesses, a sprinkling of the really smart, and several ladies belonging to the oldest profession in the world.

Soon Bill led Bundle upstairs. There the weak-faced man was on guard, watching all those admitted to the gambling room with a lynx eye. Suddenly recognition came to Bundle.

'Of course,' she said. 'How stupid of me. It's Alfred who used to be second footman at Chimneys. How are you, Alfred?'

'Nicely, thank you, your Ladyship.'

'When did you leave Chimneys, Alfred? Was it long before we got back?'

'It was about a month ago, m'lady. I got a chance of bettering myself, and it seemed a pity not to take it.'

'I suppose they pay you very well here,' remarked Bundle.

'Very fair, m'lady.'

Bundle passed in. It seemed to her that in this room the real life of the club was exposed. The stakes were high, she saw that at once, and the people gathered round the two tables were of the true type. Hawk-eyed, haggard, with the gambling fever in their blood.

She and Bill stayed here for about half an hour. Then Bill grew restive.

'Let's get out of this place, Bundle, and go on dancing.'

Bundle agreed. There was nothing to be seen here. They went down again. They danced for another half-hour, had fish and chips, and then Bundle declared herself ready to go home.

'But it's so early,' Bill protested.

'No, it isn't. Not really. And, anyway, I've got a long day in front of me tomorrow.'

'What are you going to do?'

'That depends,' said Bundle mysteriously. 'But I can tell you this, Bill, the grass is not going to grow under my feet.'

'It never does,' said Mr Eversleigh.

CHAPTER 12

INQUIRIES AT CHIMNEYS

Bundle's temperament was certainly not inherited from her father, whose prevailing characteristic was a wholly amiable inertia. As Bill Eversleigh had very justly remarked, the grass never did grow under Bundle's feet.

On the morning following her dinner with Bill, Bundle woke full of energy. She had three distinct plans which she meant to put into operation that day, and she realized that she was going to be slightly hampered by the limits of time and space.

Fortunately she did not suffer from the affliction of Gerry Wade, Ronny Devereux and Jimmy Thesiger – that of not being able to get up in the morning. Sir Oswald Coote himself would have had no fault to find with her on the score of early rising. At half-past eight Bundle had breakfasted and was on her way to Chimneys in the Hispano.

Her father seemed mildly pleased to see her.

'I never know when you're going to turn up,' he said. 'But this will save me ringing up, which I hate. Colonel Melrose was here yesterday about the inquest.'

Colonel Melrose was chief constable of the county, and an old friend of Lord Caterham.

'You mean the inquest of Ronny Devereux? When is it to be?'

'Tomorrow. Twelve o'clock. Melrose will call for you. Having found the body, you'll have to give evidence, but he said you needn't be at all alarmed.'

'Why on earth should I be alarmed?'

'Well, you know,' said Lord Caterham apologetically, 'Melrose is a bit old-fashioned.'

'Twelve o'clock,' said Bundle. 'Good. I shall be here, if I'm still alive.'

'Have you any reason to anticipate not being alive?'

'One never knows,' said Bundle. 'The strain of modern life – as the newspapers say.'

'Which reminds me that George Lomax asked me to come over to the Abbey next week. I refused, of course.'

'Quite right,' said Bundle. 'We don't want you mixed up in any funny business.'

'Is there going to be any funny business?' asked Lord Caterham with a sudden awakening of interest.

'Well – warning letters and all that, you know,' said Bundle.

'Perhaps George is going to be assassinated,' said Lord Caterham hopefully. 'What do you think, Bundle – perhaps I'd better go after all.'

'You curb your bloodthirsty instincts and stay quietly at home,' said Bundle. 'I'm going to talk to Mrs Howell.'

Mrs Howell was the housekeeper, that dignified, creaking lady who struck terror to the heart of Lady Coote. She had no terror for Bundle, whom, indeed, she always called Miss Bundle, a relic of the days when Bundle had stayed at Chimneys, a long-legged, impish child, before her father had succeeded to the title.

'Now, Howelly,' said Bundle, 'let's have a cup of rich cocoa together, and let me hear all the household news.'

She gleaned what she wanted without much difficulty, making mental notes as follows:

'Two new scullery maids – village girls – doesn't seem much there. New third housemaid – head housemaid's niece. That sounds all right. Howelly seems to have bullied poor Lady Coote a good deal. She would.'

'I never thought the day would come when I should see Chimneys inhabited by strangers, Miss Bundle.'

'Oh! One must go with the times,' said Bundle. 'You'll be lucky,

Howelly, if you never see it converted into desirable flats with use of superb pleasure grounds.'

Mrs Howells shivered all down her reactionary aristocratic spine.

'I've never seen Sir Oswald Coote,' remarked Bundle.

'Sir Oswald is no doubt a very clever gentleman,' said Mrs Howells distantly.

Bundle gathered that Sir Oswald had not been liked by his staff.

'Of course, it was Mr Bateman who saw to everything,' continued the housekeeper. 'A very efficient gentleman. A very efficient gentleman indeed, and one who knew the way things ought to be done.'

Bundle led the talk on to the topic of Gerald Wade's death. Mrs Howell was only too willing to talk about it, and was full of pitying ejaculations about the poor young gentleman, but Bundle gleaned nothing new. Presently she took leave of Mrs Howell and came downstairs again, where she promptly rang for Tredwell.

'Tredwell, when did Arthur leave?'

'It would be about a month ago now, my lady.'

'Why did he leave?'

'It was by his own wish, my lady. I believe he has gone to London. I was not dissatisfied with him in any way. I think you will find the new footman, John, very satisfactory. He seems to know his work and to be most anxious to give satisfaction.'

'Where did he come from?'

'He had excellent references, my lady. He had lived last with Lord Mount Vernon.'

'I see,' said Bundle thoughtfully.

She was remembering that Lord Mount Vernon was at present on a shooting trip in East Africa.

'What's his last name, Tredwell?'

'Bower, my lady.'

Tredwell paused for a minute or two and then, seeing that Bundle had finished, he quietly left the room. Bundle remained lost in thought.

John had opened the door to her on her arrival that day, and she had taken particular notice of him without seeming to do so. Apparently he was the perfect servant, well trained, with an expressionless face. He had, perhaps, a more soldierly bearing than most footmen and there was something a little odd about the shape of the back of his head.

But these details, as Bundle realized, were hardly relevant to the situation. She sat frowning down at the blotting paper in front of her. She had a pencil in her hand and was idly tracing the name Bower over and over again.

Suddenly an idea struck her and she stopped dead, staring at the word. Then she summoned Tredwell once more.

'Tredwell, how is the name Bower spelt?'

'B-A-U-E-R, my lady.'

'That's not an English name.'

'I believe he is of Swiss extraction, my lady.'

'Oh! That's all, Tredwell, thank you.'

Swiss extraction? No. German! That martial carriage, that flat back to the head. And he had come to Chimneys a fornight before Gerry Wade's death.

Bundle rose to her feet. She had done all she could here. Now to get on with things! She went in search of her father.

'I'm off again,' she said. 'I've got to go and see Aunt Marcia.'

'Got to see Marcia?' Lord Caterham's voice was full of astonishment. 'Poor child, how did you get let in for that?'

'Just for once,' said Bundle, 'I happen to be going of my own free will.'

Lord Caterham looked at her in amazement. That anyone could have a genuine desire to face his redoubtable sister-in-law was quite incomprehensible to him. Marcia, Marchioness of Caterham, the widow of his late brother Henry, was a very prominent personality. Lord Caterham admitted that she had made Henry an admirable wife and that but for her in all probability he would never have held the office of Secretary of State for Foreign Affairs. On the other hand, he had always looked upon Henry's early death as a merciful release.

It seemed to him that Bundle was foolishly putting her head into the lion's mouth.

'Oh! I say,' he said. 'You know, I shouldn't do that. You don't know what it may lead to.'

'I know what I hope it's going to lead to,' said Bundle. 'I'm all right, Father, don't you worry about me.'

Lord Caterham sighed and settled himself more comfortably in his chair. He went back to his perusal of *The Field*. But in a minute or two Bundle suddenly put her head in again.

'Sorry,' she said. 'But there's one other thing I wanted to ask you. What is Sir Oswald Coote?'

'I told you – a steam-roller.'

'I don't mean your personal impression of him. How did he make his money – trouser buttons or brass beds or what?'

'Oh, I see. He's steel. Steel and iron. He's got the biggest steel works, or whatever you call it, in England. He doesn't, of course, run the show personally now. It's a company or companies. He got me in as a director of something or other. Very good business for me – nothing to do except go down to the city once or twice a year to one of those hotel places – Cannon Street or Liverpool Street – and sit around a table where they have very nice new blotting paper. Then Coote or some clever Johnny makes a speech simply bristling with figures, but fortunately you needn't listen to it – and I can tell you, you often get a jolly good lunch out of it.'

Uninterested in Lord Caterham's lunches, Bundle had departed again before he had finished speaking. On the way back to London, she tried to piece together things to her satisfaction.

As far as she could see, steel and infant welfare did not go together. One of the two, then, was just padding – presumably the latter. Mrs Macatta and the Hungarian countess could be ruled out of court. They were *camouflage*. No, the pivot of the whole thing seemed to be the unattractive Herr Eberhard. He did not seem to be the type of man whom George Lomax would normally invite. Bill had said vaguely that he invented. Then there was the Air Minister, and Sir Oswald Coote, who was steel. Somehow that seemed to hang together.

Since it was useless speculating further, Bundle abandoned the attempt and concentrated on her forthcoming interview with Lady Caterham.

The lady lived in a large gloomy house in one of London's higher-class squares. Inside it smelt of sealing wax, bird seed and slightly decayed flowers. Lady Caterham was a large woman – large in every way. Her proportions were majestic, rather than ample. She had a large, beaked nose, wore gold-rimmed pince-nez and her upper lip bore just the faintest suspicion of a moustache.

She was somewhat surprised to see her niece, but accorded her a frigid cheek, which Bundle duly kissed.

'This is quite an unexpected pleasure, Eileen,' she observed coldly.

'We've only just got back, Aunt Marcia.'

'I know. How is your father? Much as usual?'

Her tone conveyed disparagement. She had a poor opinion of Alastair Edward Brent, ninth Marquis of Caterham. She would have called him, had she known the term, a 'poor fish'.

'Father is very well. He's down at Chimneys.'

'Indeed. You know, Eileen, I never approved of the letting of Chimneys. The place is in many ways an historical monument. It should not be cheapened.'

'It must have been wonderful in Uncle Henry's days,' said Bundle with a slight sigh.

'Henry realized his responsibilities,' said Henry's widow.

'Think of the people who stayed there,' went on Bundle ecstatically. 'All the principal statesmen of Europe.'

Lady Caterham sighed.

'I can truly say that history has been made there more than once,' she observed. 'If only your father –'

She shook her head sadly.

'Politics bore father,' said Bundle, 'and yet they are about the most fascinating study there is, I should say. Especially if one knew about them from the inside.'

She made this extravagantly untruthful statement of her feelings without even a blush. Her aunt looked at her with some surprise.

'I am pleased to hear you say so,' she said. 'I always imagined, Eileen, that you cared for nothing but this modern pursuit of pleasure.'

'I used to,' said Bundle.

'It is true that you are still very young,' said Lady Caterham thoughtfully. 'But with your advantages, and if you were to marry suitably, you might be one of the leading political hostesses of the day.'

Bundle felt slightly alarmed. For a moment she feared that her aunt might produce a suitable husband straight away.

'But I feel such a fool,' said Bundle. 'I mean, I know so little.'

'That can easily be remedied,' said Lady Caterham briskly. 'I have any amount of literature I can lend you.'

'Thank you, Aunt Marcia,' said Bundle, and proceeded hastily to her second line of attack.

'I wondered if you knew Mrs Macatta, Aunt Marcia?'

'Certainly I know her. A most estimable woman with a brilliant brain. I may say that as a general rule I do not hold with women standing for Parliament. They can make their influence felt in a more womanly fashion.' She paused, doubtless to recall the womanly way in which she had forced a reluctant husband into the political arena and the marvellous success which had crowned his and her efforts. 'But still, times change. And the work Mrs Macatta is doing is of truly national importance, and of the utmost value to all women. It is, I think I may say, true womanly work. You must certainly meet Mrs Macatta.'

Bundle gave a rather dismal sigh.

'She's going to be at a house party at George Lomax's next week. He asked Father, who, of course, won't go, but he never thought of asking me. Thinks I'm too much of an idiot, I suppose.'

It occurred to Lady Caterham that her niece was really wonderfully improved. Had she, perhaps, had an unfortunate love affair? An unfortunate love affair, in Lady Caterham's opinion, was so often highly beneficial to young girls. It made them take life seriously.

'I don't suppose George Lomax realizes for a moment that you have – shall we say, grown up? Eileen dear' she said, 'I must have a few words with him.'

'He doesn't like me,' said Bundle. 'I know he won't ask me.'

'Nonsense,' said Lady Caterham. 'I shall make a point of it. I knew George Lomax when he was so high.' She indicated a quite impossible height. 'He will be only too pleased to do me a favour. And he will be sure to see for himself that it is vitally important that the present-day young girls of our own class should take an intelligent interest in the welfare of their country.'

Bundle nearly said: 'Hear, hear,' but checked herself.

'I will find you some literature now,' said Lady Caterham, rising.

She called in a piercing voice: 'Miss Connor.'

A very neat secretary with a frightened expression came running. Lady Caterham gave her various directions. Presently Bundle was driving back to Brook Street with an armful of the driest-looking literature imaginable.

Her next proceeding was to ring up Jimmy Thesiger. His first words were full of triumph.

'I've managed it,' he said. 'Had a lot of trouble with Bill, though. He'd got it into his thick head that I should be a lamb among wolves. But I made him see sense at last. I've got a lot of thingummybobs now and I'm studying them. You know, blue books and white papers. Deadly dull – but one must do the thing properly. Have you ever heard of the Santa Fé boundary dispute?'

'Never,' said Bundle.

'Well, I'm taking special pains with that. It went on for years and was very complicated. I'm making it my subject. Nowadays one has to specialize.'

'I've got a lot of the same sort of things,' said Bundle. 'Aunt Marcia gave them to me.'

'Aunt who?'

'Aunt Marcia – Father's sister-in-law. She's very political. In fact, she's going to get me invited to George's party.'

'No? Oh, I say, that will be splendid.' There was a pause and then Jimmy said:

'I say, I don't think we'd better tell Loraine that – eh?'

'Perhaps not.'

'You see, she mayn't like being out of it. And she really must be kept out of it.'

'Yes.'

'I mean you can't let a girl like that run into danger!'

Bundle reflected that Mr Thesiger was slightly deficient in tact. The prospect of *her* running into danger did not seem to give him any qualms whatever.

'Have you gone away?' asked Jimmy.

'No, I was only thinking.'

'I see. I say, are you going to the inquest tomorrow?'

'Yes, are you?'

'Yes. By the way, it's in the evening papers. But tucked away in a corner. Funny – I should have thought they'd have made rather a splash about it.'

'Yes – so should I.'

'Well,' said Jimmy, 'I must be getting on with my task. I've just got to where Bolivia sent us a Note.'

'I suppose I must get on with my little lot,' said Bundle. 'Are you going to swot at it all the evening?'

'I think so. Are you?'

'Oh, probably. Good night.'

They were both liars of the most unblushing order. Jimmy Thesiger knew perfectly well that he was taking Loraine Wade out to dinner.

As for Bundle, no sooner had she rung off than she attired herself in various nondescript garments belonging, as a matter of fact, to her maid. And having donned them she sallied out on foot deliberating whether bus or Tube would be the best route by which to reach the Seven Dials Club.

CHAPTER 13

THE SEVEN DIALS CLUB

Bundle reached 14 Hunstanton Street about 6 p.m. At that hour, as she rightly judged, the Seven Dials Club was a dead spot. Bundle's aim was a simple one. She intended to get hold of the ex-footman Alfred. She was convinced that once she had got hold of him the rest would be easy. Bundle had a simple autocratic method of dealing with retainers. It seldom failed, and she saw no reason why it should fail now.

The only thing of which she was not certain was how many people inhabited the club premises. Naturally she wished to disclose her presence to as few people as possible.

Whilst she was hesitating as to the best line of attack, the problem was solved for her in a singularly easy fashion. The door of No. 14 opened and Alfred himself came out.

'Good afternoon, Alfred,' said Bundle pleasantly.

Alfred jumped.

'Oh! good afternoon, your ladyship. I – I didn't recognize your ladyship just for a moment.'

Paying a tribute in her own mind to her maid's clothing, Bundle proceeded to business.

'I want a few words with you, Alfred. Where shall we go?'

'Well – really, my lady – I don't know – it's not what you might call a nice part round here – I don't know, I'm sure –'

Bundle cut him short.

'Who's in the club?'

'No one at present, my lady.'

'Then we'll go in there.'

Alfred produced a key and opened the door. Bundle passed in. Alfred, troubled and sheepish, followed her. Bundle sat down and looked straight at the uncomfortable Alfred.

'I suppose you know,' she said crisply, 'that what you're doing here is dead against the law?'

Alfred shifted uncomfortably from one foot to the other.

'It's true as we've been raided twice,' he admitted. 'But nothing compromising was found, owing to the neatness of Mr Mosgorovsky's arrangements.'

'I'm not talking of the gambling only,' said Bundle. 'There's more than that – probably a great deal more than you know. I'm going to ask you a direct question, Alfred, and I should like the truth, please. *How much were you paid for leaving Chimneys?*'

Alfred looked twice round the cornice as though seeking for inspiration, swallowed three or four times, and then took the inevitable course of a weak will opposed to a strong one.

'It was this way, your ladyship. Mr Mosgorovsky, he come with a party to visit Chimneys on one of the show days. Mr Tredwell, he was indisposed like – an ingrowing toe-nail as a matter of fact – so it fell to me to show the parties over. At the end of the tour Mr Mosgorovsky, he stays behind the rest, and after giving me something handsome, he falls into conversation.'

'Yes,' said Bundle encouragingly.

'And the long and the short of it was,' said Alfred, with a sudden acceleration of his narrative, 'that he offers me a hundred pound down to leave that instant and to look after this here club. He wanted someone as was used to the best families – to give the place a tone, as he put it. And, well, it seemed flying in the face of providence to refuse – let alone that the wages I get here are just three times what they were as second footman.'

'A hundred pounds,' said Bundle. 'That's a very large sum, Alfred. Did they say anything about who was to fill your place at Chimneys?'

'I demurred a bit, my lady, about leaving at once. As I pointed out, it wasn't usual and might cause inconvenience. But Mr Mosgorovsky he knew of a young chap – been in good service and ready to come any minute. So I mentioned his name to Mr Tredwell and everything was settled pleasant like.'

Bundle nodded. Her own suspicions had been correct and the *modus operandi* was much as she had thought it to be. She essayed a further inquiry.

'Who is Mr Mosgorovsky?'

'Gentleman as runs this club. Russian gentleman. A very clever gentleman too.'

Bundle abandoned the getting of information for the moment and proceeded to other matters.

'A hundred pounds is a very large sum of money, Alfred.'

'Larger than I ever handled, my lady,' said Alfred with simple candour.

'Did you ever suspect that there was something wrong?'

'Wrong, my lady?'

'Yes. I'm not talking about the gambling. I mean something far more serious. You don't want to be sent to penal servitude, do you, Alfred?'

'Oh, Lord! My lady, you don't mean it?'

'I was at Scotland Yard the day before yesterday,' said Bundle impressively. 'I heard some very curious things. I want you to help me, Alfred, and if you do, well – if things go wrong, I'll put in a good word for you.'

'Anything I can do, I shall be only too pleased, my lady. I mean I would anyway.'

'Well, first,' said Bundle, 'I want to go all over this place – from top to bottom.'

Accompanied by a mystified and scared Alfred, she made a very thorough tour of inspection. Nothing struck her eye till she came to the gaming room. There she noticed an inconspicuous door in the corner, and the door was locked.

Alfred explained readily.

'That's used as a getaway, your ladyship. There's a room and a door on to a staircase what comes out in the next street. That's the way the gentry goes when there's a raid.'

'But don't the police know about it?'

'It's a cunning door, you see, my lady. Looks like a cupboard, that's all.'

Bundle felt a rising excitement.

'I must get in there,' she said.

Alfred shook his head.

'You can't, my lady; Mr Mosgorovsky, he has the key.'

'Well,' said Bundle, 'there are other keys.'

She perceived that the lock was a perfectly ordinary one which probably could be easily unlocked by the key of one of the other doors. Alfred, rather troubled, was sent to collect likely specimens. The fourth that Bundle tried fitted. She turned it, opened the door and passed through.

She found herself in a small, dingy apartment. A long table occupied the centre of the room with chairs ranged round it. There was no other furniture in the room. Two built-in cupboards stood on either side of the fire-place. Alfred indicated the nearer one with a nod.

'That's it,' he explained.

Bundle tried the cupboard door, but it was locked, and she saw at once that this lock was a very different affair. It was of the patent kind that would only yield to its own key.

''Ighly ingenious, it is,' explained Alfred. 'It looks all right when opened. Shelves, you know, with a few ledgers and that on 'em. Nobody'd ever suspect, but you touch the right spot and the whole things swings open.'

Bundle had turned round and was surveying the room thoughtfully. The first thing she noticed was that the door by which they had entered was carefully fitted round with baize. It must be completely sound-proof. Then her eyes wandered to the chairs. There were seven of them, three each side and one rather more imposing in design at the head of the table.

Bundle's eyes brightened. She had found what she was looking for. This, she felt sure, was the meeting place of the secret organization. The place was almost perfectly planned. It looked so innocent – you could reach it just by stepping through from the gaming room, or you could arrive there by the secret entrance – and any secrecy, any precautions were easily explained by the gaming going on in the next room.

Idly, as these thoughts passed through her mind, she drew a finger across the marble of the mantelpiece. Alfred saw and misinterpreted the action.

'You won't find no dirt, not to speak of,' he said. 'Mr Mosgorovsky, he ordered the place to be swept out this morning, and I did it while he waited.'

'Oh!' said Bundle, thinking very hard. 'This morning, eh?

'Has to be done sometimes,' said Alfred. 'Though the room's never what you might call used.'

Next minute he received a shock.

'Alfred,' said Bundle, 'you've got to find me a place in this room where I can hide.'

Alfred looked at her in dismay.

'But it's impossible, my lady. You'll get me into trouble and I'll lose my job.'

'You'll lose it anyway when you go to prison,' said Bundle unkindly. 'But as a matter of fact, you needn't worry, nobody will know anything about it.'

'And there ain't no place,' wailed Alfred. 'Look round for yourself, your ladyship, if you don't believe me.'

Bundle was forced to admit that there was something in this argument. But she had the true spirit of one undertaking adventures.

'Nonsense,' she said with determination. 'There has *got* to be a place.'

'But there ain't one,' wailed Alfred.

Never had a room shown itself more unpropitious for concealment. Dingy blinds were drawn down over the dirty window panes, and there were no curtains. The window sill outside, which Bundle examined, was about four inches wide! Inside the room there were the table, the chairs and the cupboards.

The second cupboard had a key in the lock. Bundle went across and pulled it open. Inside were shelves covered with an odd assortment of glasses and crockery.

'Surplus stuff as we don't use,' explained Alfred. 'You can

see for yourself, my lady, there's no place here as a cat could hide.'

But Bundle was examining the shelves.

'Flimsy work,' she said. 'Now then, Alfred, have you got a cupboard downstairs where you could shove all this glass? You have? Good. Then get a tray and start to carry it down at once. Hurry – there's no time to lose.'

'You can't, my lady. And it's getting late, too. The cooks will be here any minute now.'

'Mr Mosgo – whatnot doesn't come till later, I suppose?'

'He's never here much before midnight. But oh, my lady –'

'Don't talk so much, Alfred,' said Bundle. 'Get that tray. If you stay here arguing, you *will* get into trouble.'

Doing what is familiarly known as 'wringing his hands', Alfred departed. Presently he returned with a tray, and having by now realized that his protests were useless, he worked with a nervous energy quite surprising.

As Bundle had seen, the shelves were easily detachable. She took them down, ranged them upright against the wall, and then stepped in.

'H'm,' she remarked. 'Pretty narrow. It's going to be a tight fit. Shut the door on me carefully, Alfred – that's right. Yes, it can be done. Now I want a gimlet.'

'A gimlet, my lady?'

'That's what I said.'

'I don't know –'

'Nonsense, you must have a gimlet – perhaps you've got an auger as well. If you haven't got what I want, you'll have to go out and buy it, so you'd better try hard to find the right thing.'

Alfred departed and returned presently with quite a creditable assortment of tools. Bundle seized what she wanted and proceeded swiftly and efficiently to bore a small hole at the level of her right eye. She did this from the outside so that it should be less noticeable, and she dared not make it too large lest it should attract attention.

'There, that'll do,' she remarked at last.

'Oh, but, my lady, my lady –'

'Yes?'

'But they'll find you – if they should open the door.'

'They won't open the door,' said Bundle. 'Because you are going to lock it and take the key away.'

'And if by chance Mr Mosgorovsky should ask for the key?'

'Tell him it's lost,' said Bundle briskly. 'But nobody's going to worry about this cupboard – it's only here to attract attention from the other one and make it a pair. Go on, Alfred, someone might come at any time. Lock me in and take the key and come and let me out when everyone's gone.'

'You'll be taken bad, my lady. You'll faint –'

'I never faint,' said Bundle. 'But you might as well get me a cocktail. I shall certainly need it. Then lock the door of the room again – don't forget – and take the door keys back to their proper doors. And Alfred – don't be too much of a rabbit. Remember, if anything goes wrong, I'll see you through.'

'And that's that,' said Bundle to herself, when having served the cocktail, Alfred had finally departed.

She was not nervous lest Alfred's nerve should fail and he should give her away. She knew that his sense of self-preservation was far too strong for that. His training alone helped him to conceal private emotions beneath the mask of a well-trained servant.

Only one thing worried Bundle. The interpretation she had chosen to put upon the cleaning of the room that morning might be all wrong. And if so – Bundle sighed in the narrow confines of the cupboard. The prospect of spending long hours in it for nothing was not attractive.

CHAPTER 14

THE MEETING OF THE SEVEN DIALS

It would be as well to pass over the sufferings of the next four hours as quickly as possible. Bundle found her position extremely cramped. She had judged that the meeting, if meeting there was to be, would take place at a time when the club was in full swing – somewhere probably between the hours of midnight and 2 a.m.

She was just deciding that it must be at least six o'clock in the morning when a welcome sound come to her ears, the sound of the unlocking of a door.

In another minute the electric light was switched on. The hum of voices, which had come to her for a minute or two, rather like the far-off roar of sea waves, ceased as suddenly as it had begun, and Bundle heard the sound of a bolt being shot. Clearly someone had come in from the gaming room next door, and she paid tribute to the thoroughness with which the communicating door had been rendered sound-proof.

In another minute the intruder came into her line of vision – a line of vision that was necessarily somewhat incomplete but which yet answered its purpose. A tall man, broad-shouldered and powerful-looking, with a long black beard, Bundle remembered having seen him sitting at one of the baccarat tables on the preceding night.

This, then, was Alfred's mysterious Russian gentleman, the proprietor of the club, the sinister Mr Mosgorovsky. Bundle's heart beat faster with excitement. So little did she resemble her father that at this minute she fairly gloried in the extreme discomfort of her position.

The Russian remained for some minutes standing by the table, stroking his beard. Then he drew a watch from his pocket and glanced at the time. Nodding his head as though satisfied, he again thrust his hand into his pocket and, pulling out something that Bundle could not see, he moved out of the line of vision.

When he reappeared she could hardly help giving a gasp of surprise.

His face was now covered by a mask – but hardly a mask in the conventional sense. It was not shaped to the face. It was a mere piece of material hanging in front of the features like a curtain in which two slits were pierced for the eyes. In shape it was round and on it was the representation of a clock face, with the hands pointing to six o'clock.

'The Seven Dials!' said Bundle to herself.

And at that minute there came a new sound – seven muffled taps.

Mosgorovsky strode across to where Bundle knew was the other cupboard door. She heard a sharp click, and then the sound of greetings in a foreign tongue.

Presently she had a view of the newcomers.

They also wore clock masks, but in their case the hands were in a different position – four o'clock and five o'clock respectively. Both men were in evening dress – but with a difference. One was an elegant, slender young man wearing evening clothes of exquisite cut. The grace with which he moved was foreign rather than English. The other man could be better described as wiry and lean. His clothes fitted him sufficiently well, but no more, and Bundle guessed at his nationality even before she heard his voice.

'I reckon we're the first to arrive at this little meeting.'

A full pleasant voice with a slight American drawl, and an inflection of Irish behind it.

The elegant young man said in good, but slightly stilted English:

'I had much difficulty in getting away tonight. These things do not always arrange themselves fortunately. I am not, like No. 4 here, my own master.'

Bundle tried to guess at his nationality. Until he spoke, she had thought he might be French, but the accent was not a French one. He might possibly, she thought, be an Austrian, or a Hungarian, or even a Russian.

The American moved to the other side of the table, and Bundle heard a chair being pulled out.

'One o'clock's being a great success,' he said. 'I congratulate you on taking the risk.'

Five o'clock shrugged his shoulders.

'Unless one takes risks –' He left the sentence unfinished.

Again seven taps sounded and Mosgorovsky moved across to the secret door.

She failed to catch anything definite for some moments since the whole company were out of sight, but presently she heard the bearded Russian's voice upraised.

'Shall we begin proceedings?'

He himself came round the table and took the seat next to the arm-chair at the top. Sitting thus, he was directly facing Bundle's cupboard. The elegant five o'clock took the place next to him. The third chair that side was out of Bundle's sight, but the American, No. 4, moved into her line of vision for a moment or two before he sat down.

On the near side of the table also, only two chairs were visible, and as she watched a hand turned the second – really the middle chair – down. And then with a swift movement, one of the newcomers brushed past the cupboard and took the chair opposite Mosgorovsky. Whoever sat there had, of course, their back directly turned to Bundle – and it was at that back that Bundle was staring with a good deal of interest, for it was the back of a singularly beautiful woman very much *décolleté*.

It was she who spoke first. Her voice was musical, foreign – with a deep, seductive note in it. She was glancing towards the empty chair at the head of the table.

'So we are not to see No. 7 tonight?' she said. 'Tell me, my friends, shall we ever see him?'

'That's darned good,' said the American. 'Darned good! As for seven o'clock – *I'm* beginning to believe there is no such person.'

'I should not advise you to think that, my friend,' said the Russian pleasantly.

There was a silence – rather an uncomfortable silence, Bundle felt.

She was still staring as though fascinated at the beautiful back in front of her. There was a tiny black mole just below the right shoulder-blade that enhanced the whiteness of the skin. Bundle felt that at last the term 'beautiful adventuress', so often read, had a real meaning for her. She was quite certain that this woman had a beautiful face – a dark Slavonic face with passionate eyes.

She was recalled from her imagining by the voice of the Russian, who seemed to act as master of ceremonies.

'Shall we get on with our business? First to our absent comrade! No. 2!'

He made a curious gesture with his hand towards the turned-down chair next to the woman, which everyone present imitated, turning to the chair as they did so.

'I wish No. 2 were with us tonight,' he continued. 'There are many things to be done. Unsuspected difficulties have arisen.'

'Have you had his report?' It was the American who spoke.

'As yet – I have nothing from him.' There was a pause. 'I cannot understand it.'

'You think it may have – gone astray?'

'That is – a possibility.'

'In other words,' said five o'clock softly, 'there is – danger.'

He spoke the word delicately – and yet with relish.

The Russian nodded emphatically.

'Yes – there's danger. Too much is getting known about us – about this place. I know of several people who suspect.' He added coldly: 'They must be silenced.'

Bundle felt a little cold shiver pass down her spine. If she were to be found, would she be silenced? She was recalled suddenly to attention by a word.

'So nothing has come to light about Chimneys?'

Mosgorovsky shook his head.

'Nothing.'

Suddenly No. 5 leant forward.

'I agree with Anna; where is our president – No. 7? He who called us into being. Why do we never see him?'

'No. 7,' said the Russian, 'has his own ways of working.'

'So you always say.'

'I will say no more,' said Mosgorovsky. 'I pity the man – or woman – who comes up against him.'

There was an awkward silence.

'We must get on with our business,' said Mosgorovsky quietly. 'No. 3, you have the plans of Wyvern Abbey?'

Bundle strained her ears. So far she had neither caught a glimpse of No. 3, nor had she heard his voice. She heard it now and recognized it as unmistakable. Low, pleasant, indistinct – the voice of a well-bred Englishman.

'I've got them here, sir.'

Some papers were shoved across the table. Everyone bent forward. Presently Mosgorovsky raised his head again.

'And the list of guests?'

'Here.'

The Russian read them.

'Sir Stanley Digby. Mr Terence O'Rourke. Sir Oswald and Lady Coote. Mr Bateman. Countess Anna Radzky. Mrs Macatta. Mr James Thesiger –' He paused and then asked sharply:

'Who is Mr James Thesiger?'

The American laughed.

'I guess you needn't worry any about him. The usual complete young ass.'

The Russian continued reading.

'Herr Eberhard and Mr Eversleigh. That completes the list.'

'Does it?' said Bundle silently. 'What about that sweet girl, Lady Eileen Brent?'

'Yes, there seems nothing to worry about there,' said Mosgorovsky. He looked across the table. 'I suppose there's no doubt whatever about the value of Eberhard's invention?'

Three o'clock made a laconic British reply.

'None whatever.'

'Commercially it should be worth millions,' said the Russian. 'And internationally – well, one knows only too well the greed of nations.'

Bundle had an idea that behind his mask he was smiling unpleasantly.

'Yes,' he went on. 'A gold mine.'

'Well worth a few lives,' said No. 5, cynically, and laughed.

'But you know what inventors are,' said the American. 'Sometimes these darned things won't work.'

'A man like Sir Oswald Coote will have made no mistake,' said Mosgorovsky.

'Speaking as an aviator myself,' said No. 5, 'the thing is perfectly feasible. It has been discussed for years – but it needed the genius of Eberhard to bring it to fruition.'

'Well,' said Mosgorovsky, 'I don't think we need discuss matters any further. You have all seen the plans. I do not think our original scheme can be bettered. By the way, I hear something about a letter of Gerald Wade's that has been found – a letter that mentions this organization. Who found it?'

'Lord Caterham's daughter – Lady Eileen Brent.'

'Bauer should have been on to that,' said Mosgorovsky. 'It was careless of him. Who was the letter written to?'

'His sister, I believe,' said No. 3.

'Unfortunate,' said Mosgorovsky. 'But it cannot be helped. The inquest on Ronald Devereux is tomorrow. I suppose that has been arranged for?'

'Reports as to local lads having been practising with rifles have been spread everywhere,' said the American.

'That should be all right then. I think there is nothing further to be said. I think we must all congratulate our dear one o'clock and wish her luck in the part she has to play.'

'Hurrah!' cried No. 5. 'To Anna!'

All hands flew out in the same gesture which Bundle had noticed before.

'To Anna!'

One o'clock acknowledged the salutation with a typically foreign gesture. Then she rose to her feet and the others followed suit. For the first time, Bundle caught a glimpse of No. 3 as he came to put Anna's cloak round her – a tall, heavily built man.

Then the party filed out through the secret door. Mosgorovsky secured it after them. He waited a few moments and then Bundle heard him unbolt the other door and pass through after extinguishing the electric light.

It was not until two hours later that a white and anxious Alfred came to release Bundle. She almost fell into his arms and he had to hold her up.

'Nothing,' said Bundle. 'Just stiff, that's all. Here, let me sit down.'

'Oh, Gord, my lady, it's been awful.'

'Nonsense,' said Bundle. 'It all went off splendidly. Don't get the wind up now it's all over. It might have gone wrong, but thank goodness it didn't.'

'Thank goodness, as you say, my lady. I've been in a twitter all the evening. They're a funny crowd, you know.'

'A damned funny crowd,' said Bundle, vigorously massaging her arms and legs. 'As a matter of fact, they're the sort of crowd I always imagined until tonight only existed in books. In this life, Alfred, one never stops learning.'

CHAPTER 15

THE INQUEST

Bundle reached home about 6 a.m. She was up and dressed by half-past nine, and rang up Jimmy Thesiger on the telephone.

The promptitude of his reply somewhat surprised her, till he explained that he was going down to attend the inquest.

'So am I,' said Bundle. 'And I've got a lot to tell you.'

'Well, suppose you let me drive you down and we can talk on the way. How about that?'

'All right. But allow a bit extra because you'll have to take me to Chimneys. The chief constable's picking me up there.'

'Why?'

'Because he's a kind man,' said Bundle.

'So am I,' said Jimmy. 'Very kind.'

'Oh! You – you're an ass,' said Bundle. 'I heard somebody say so last night.'

'Who?'

'To be strictly accurate – a Russian Jew. No, it wasn't. It was –'

But an indignant protest drowned her words.

'I may be an ass,' said Jimmy. 'I daresay I am – but I won't have Russian Jews saying so. What were you doing last night, Bundle?'

'That's what I'm going to talk about,' said Bundle. 'Goodbye for the moment.'

She rang off in a tantalizing manner which left Jimmy pleasantly puzzled. He had the highest respect for Bundle's capabilities, though there was not the slightest trace of sentiment in his feeling towards her.

'She's been up to something,' he opined, as he took a last hasty drink of coffee. 'Depend upon it, she's been up to something.'

Twenty minutes later, his little two-seater drew up before the Brook Street house and Bundle, who had been waiting, came tripping down the steps. Jimmy was not ordinarily an observant young man, but he noticed that there were black rings round Bundle's eyes and that she had all the appearance of having had a late night the night before.

'Now then,' he said, as the car began to nose her way through the suburbs, 'what dark deeds have you been up to?'

'I'll tell you,' said Bundle. 'But don't interrupt until I've finished.'

It was a somewhat long story, and Jimmy had all he could do to keep sufficient attention on the car to prevent an accident. When Bundle had finished he sighed – then looked at her searchingly.

'Bundle?'

'Yes?'

'Look here, you're not pulling my leg?'

'What do you mean?'

'I'm sorry,' apologized Jimmy, 'but it seems to me as though I'd heard it all before – in a dream, you know.'

'I know,' said Bundle sympathetically.

'It's impossible,' said Jimmy, following out his own train of thought. 'The beautiful foreign adventuress, the international gang, the mysterious No. 7, whose identity nobody knows – I've read it all a hundred times in books.'

'Of course you have. So have I. But it's no reason why it shouldn't really happen.'

'I suppose not,' admitted Jimmy.

'After all – I suppose fiction is founded on the truth. I mean unless things did happen, people couldn't think of them.'

'There is something in what you say,' agreed Jimmy. 'But all the same I can't help pinching myself to see if I'm awake.'

'That's how I felt.'

Jimmy gave a deep sigh.

'Well, I suppose we are awake. Let me see, a Russian, an American, an Englishman – a possible Austrian or Hungarian – and the lady who may be any nationality – for choice Russian or Polish – that's a pretty representative gathering.'

'And a German,' said Bundle. 'You've forgotten the German.'

'Oh!' said Jimmy slowly. 'You think –?'

'The absent No. 2. No. 2 is Bauer – our footman. That seems to me quite clear from what they said about expecting a report which hadn't come in – though what there can be to report about Chimneys, I can't think.'

'It must be something to do with Gerry Wade's death,' said Jimmy. 'There's something there we haven't fathomed yet. You say they actually mentioned Bauer by name?'

Bundle nodded.

'They blamed him for not having found that letter.'

'Well, I don't see what you could have clearer than that. There's no going against it. You'll have to forgive my first incredulity, Bundle – but you know, it was rather a tall story. You say they knew about my going down to Wyvern Abbey next week?'

'Yes, that's when the American – it was him, not the Russian

– said they needn't worry – you were only the usual kind of ass.'

'Ah!' said Jimmy. He pressed his foot down on the accelerator viciously and the car shot forward. 'I'm very glad you told me that. It gives me what you might call a personal interest in the case.'

He was silent for a minute or two and then he said:

'Did you say that German inventor's name was Eberhard?'

'Yes. Why?'

'Wait a minute. Something's coming back to me. Eberhard, Eberhard – yes, I'm sure that was the name.'

'Tell me.'

'Eberhard was a Johnny who'd got some patent process he applied to sell. I can't put the thing properly because I haven't got the scientific knowledge – but I know the result was that it became so toughened that a wire was as strong as a steel bar had previously been. Eberhard had to do with aeroplanes and his idea was that the weight would be so enormously reduced that flying would be practically revolutionized – the cost of it, I mean. I believe he offered his invention to the German Government, and they turned it down, pointed out some undeniable flaw in it – but they did it rather nastily. He set to work and circumvented the difficulty, whatever it was, but he'd been offended by their attitude and swore they shouldn't have his ewe lamb. I always thought the whole thing was probably bunkum, but now – it looks differently.'

'That's it,' said Bundle eagerly. 'You must be right, Jimmy. Eberhard must have offered his invention to our Government. They've been taking, or are going to take, Sir Oswald Coote's expert opinion on it. There's going to be an unofficial conference at the Abbey. Sir Oswald, George, the Air Minister and Eberhard. Eberhard will have the plans or the process or whatever you call it –'

'Formula,' suggested Jimmy. 'I think "formula" is a good word myself.'

'He'll have the formula with him, and the Seven Dials are out to steal the formula. I remember the Russian saying it was worth millions.'

'I suppose it would be,' said Jimmy.

'And well worth a few lives – that's what the other man said.'

'Well, it seems to have been,' said Jimmy, his face clouding over. 'Look at this damned inquest today. Bundle, are you sure Ronny said nothing else?'

'No,' said Bundle. 'Just that. *Seven Dials. Tell Jimmy Thesiger*. That's all he could get out, poor lad.'

'I wish we knew what he knew,' said Jimmy. 'But we've found out one thing. I take it that the footman, Bauer, must almost certainly have been responsible for Gerry's death. You know, Bundle –'

'Yes?'

'Well, I'm a bit worried sometimes. Who's going to be the next one! It really isn't the sort of business for a girl to be mixed up in.'

Bundle smiled in spite of herself. It occurred to her that it had taken Jimmy a long time to put her in the same category as Loraine Wade.

'It's far more likely to be you than me,' she remarked cheerfully.

'Hear, hear,' said Jimmy. 'But what about a few casualties on the other side for a change? I'm feeling rather bloodthirsty this morning. Tell me, Bundle, would you recognize any of these people if you saw them?'

Bundle hesitated.

'I think I should recognize No. 5,' she said at last. 'He's got a queer way of speaking – a kind of venomous, lisping way – that I think I'd know again.'

'What about the Englishman?'

Bundle shook her head.

'I saw him least – only a glimpse – and he's got a very ordinary voice. Except that he's a big man, there's nothing much to go by.'

'There's the woman, of course,' continued Jimmy. 'She ought to be easier. But then, you're not likely to run across her. She's probably putting in the dirty work, being taken out to dinner by amorous Cabinet Ministers and getting State secrets out of them when they've had a couple. At least, that's how it's done in books. As a matter of fact, the only Cabinet Minister I know drinks hot water with a dash of lemon in it.'

'Take George Lomax, for instance, can you imagine him

being amorous with beautiful foreign women?' said Bundle with a laugh.

Jimmy agreed with her criticism.

'And now about the man of mystery – No. 7,' went on Jimmy. 'You've no idea who he could be?'

'None whatever.'

'Again – by book standards, that is – he ought to be someone we all know. What about George Lomax himself?'

Bundle reluctantly shook her head.

'In a book it would be perfect,' she agreed. 'But knowing Codders –' And she gave herself up to sudden uncontrollable mirth. 'Codders, the great criminal organizer,' she gasped. 'Wouldn't it be marvellous?'

Jimmy agreed that it would. Their discussion had taken some time and his driving had slowed down involuntarily once or twice. They arrived at Chimneys, to find Colonel Melrose already there waiting. Jimmy was introduced to him and they all three proceeded to the inquest together.

As Colonel Melrose had predicted, the whole affair was very simple. Bundle gave her evidence. The doctor gave his. Evidence was given of rifle practice in the neighbourhood. A verdict of death by misadventure was brought in.

After the proceedings were over, Colonel Melrose volunteered to drive Bundle back to Chimneys, and Jimmy Thesiger returned to London.

For all his lighthearted manner, Bundle's story had impressed him profoundly. He set his lips closely together.

'Ronny, old boy,' he murmured, 'I'm going to be up against it. And you're not here to join in the game.'

Another thought flashed into his mind. Loraine! Was she in danger?

After a minute or two's hesitation, he went over to the telephone and rang her up.

'It's me – Jimmy. I thought you'd like to know the result of the inquest. Death by misadventure.'

'Oh, but –'

'Yes, but I think there's something behind that. The coroner had had a hint. Someone's at work to hush it up. I say, Loraine –'

'Yes?'

'Look here. There's – there's some funny business going about. You'll be very careful, won't you? For my sake.'

He heard the quick note of alarm that sprang into her voice.

'Jimmy – but then it's dangerous – for *you*.'

He laughed.

'Oh, *that's* all right. I'm the cat that had nine lives. Bye-bye, old thing.'

He rang off and remained a minute or two lost in thought. Then he summoned Stevens.

'Do you think you could go out and buy me a pistol, Stevens?'

'A pistol, sir?'

True to his training, Stevens betrayed no hint of surprise.

'What kind of a pistol would you be requiring?'

'The kind where you put your finger on the trigger and the thing goes on shooting until you take it off again.'

'An automatic, sir.'

'That's it,' said Jimmy. 'An automatic. And I should like it to be a blue-nosed one – if you and the shopman know what that is. In American stories, the hero always takes his blue-nosed automatic from his hip pocket.'

Stevens permitted himself a faint, discreet smile.

'Most American gentlemen that I have known, sir, carry something very different in their hip pockets,' he observed.

Jimmy Thesiger laughed.

CHAPTER 16

THE HOUSE PARTY AT THE ABBEY

Bundle drove over to Wyvern Abbey just in time for tea on Friday afternoon. George Lomax came forward to welcome her with considerable *empressement*.

'My dear Eileen,' he said, 'I can't tell you how pleased I am to see you here. You must forgive my not having invited you when I asked your father, but to tell the truth I never dreamed that a party of this kind would apeal to you. I was both – er – surprised and – er – delighted when Lady Caterham told me of your – er – interest in – er – politics.'

'I wanted to come so much,' said Bundle in a simple, ingenuous manner.

'Mrs Macatta will not arrive till the later train,' explained George. 'She was speaking at a meeting in Manchester last night. Do you know Thesiger? Quite a young fellow, but a remarkable grasp of foreign politics. One would hardly suspect it from his appearance.'

'I know Mr Thesiger,' said Bundle, and she shook hands solemnly with Jimmy, who she observed had parted his hair in the middle in the endeavour to add earnestness to his expression.

'Look here,' said Jimmy in a low hurried voice, as George temporarily withdrew. 'You mustn't be angry, but I've told Bill about our little stunt.'

'Bill?' said Bundle, annoyed.

'Well, after all,' said Jimmy, 'Bill is one of the lads, you know. Ronny was a pal of his and so was Gerry.'

'Oh! I know,' said Bundle.

'But you think it's a pity? Sorry.'

'Bill's all right, of course. It isn't that,' said Bundle. 'But he's – well, Bill's a born blunderer.'

'Not mentally very agile?' suggested Jimmy. 'But you forget one thing – Bill's got a very hefty fist. And I've an idea that a hefty fist is going to come in handy.'

'Well, perhaps you're right. How did he take it?'

'Well, he clutched his head a good bit, but – I mean the facts took some driving home. But by repeating the thing patiently in words of one syllable I at last got it into his thick head. And, naturally, he's with us to the death, as you might say.'

George reappeared suddenly.

'I must make some introductions, Eileen. This is Sir Stanley Digby – Lady Eileen Brent. Mr O'Rourke.' The Air Minister was a little round man with a cheerful smile. Mr O'Rourke, a tall young man with laughing blue eyes and a typical Irish face, greeted Bundle with enthusiasm.

'And I thinking it was going to be a dull political party entirely,' he murmured in an adroit whisper.

'Hush,' said Bundle. 'I'm political – very political.'

'Sir Oswald and Lady Coote you know,' continued George.

'We've never actually met,' said Bundle, smiling.

She was mentally applauding her father's descriptive powers.

Sir Oswald took her hand in an iron grip and she winced slightly.

Lady Coote, after a somewhat mournful greeting, had turned to Jimmy Thesiger, and appeared to be registering something closely akin to pleasure. Despite his reprehensible habit of being late for breakfast, Lady Coote had a fondness for this amiable, pink-faced young man. His air of irrepressible good nature fascinated her. She had a motherly wish to cure him of his bad habits and form him into one of the world's workers. Whether, once formed, he would be as attractive was a question she had never asked herself. She began now to tell him of a very painful motor accident which had happened to one of her friends.

'Mr Bateman,' said George briefly, as one who would pass on to better things.

A serious, pale-faced young man bowed.

'And now,' continued George, 'I must introduce you to Countess Radzky.'

Countess Radzky had been conversing with Mr Bateman. Leaning very far back on a sofa, with her legs crossed in a daring manner, she was smoking a cigarette in an incredibly long turquoise-studded holder.

Bundle thought she was one of the most beautiful women she had ever seen. Her eyes were very large and blue, her hair was coal black, she had a matte skin, the slightly flattened nose of the Slav, and a sinuous, slender body. Her lips were reddened to a degree with which Bundle was sure Wyvern Abbey was totally unacquainted.

She said eagerly: 'This is Mrs Macatta – yes?'

On George's replying in the negative and introducing Bundle, the countess gave her a careless nod, and at once resumed her conversation with the serious Mr Bateman.

Bundle heard Jimmy's voice in her ear:

'Pongo is absolutely fascinated by the lovely Slav,' he said. 'Pathetic, isn't it? Come and have some tea.'

They drifted once more into the neighbourhood of Sir Oswald Coote.

'That's a fine place of yours, Chimneys,' remarked the great man.

'I'm glad you liked it,' said Bundle meekly.

'Wants new plumbing,' said Sir Oswald. 'Bring it up to date, you know.'

He ruminated for a minute or two.

'I'm taking the Duke of Alton's place. Three years. Just while I'm looking round for a place of my own. Your father couldn't sell if he wanted to, I suppose?'

Bundle felt her breath taken away. She had a nightmare vision of England with innumerable Cootes in innumerable counterparts of Chimneys – all, be it understood, with an entirely new system of plumbing installed.

She felt a sudden violent resentment which, she told herself, was absurd. After all, contrasting Lord Caterham with Sir Oswald Coote, there was no doubt as to who would go to the wall. Sir Oswald had one of those powerful personalities which make all those with whom they come in contact appear faded. He was, as Lord Caterham had said, a human steam-roller. And yet, undoubtedly, in many ways, Sir Oswald was a stupid man. Apart from his special line of knowledge and his terrific driving force, he was probably intensely ignorant. A hundred delicate appreciations of life which Lord Caterham could and did enjoy were a sealed book to Sir Oswald.

Whilst indulging in these reflections Bundle continued to chat pleasantly. Herr Eberhard, she heard, had arrived, but was lying down with a nervous headache. This was told her by Mr O'Rourke, who managed to find a place by her side and keep it.

Altogether, Bundle went up to dress in a pleasant mood of expectation, with a slight nervous dread hovering in the background whenever she thought of the imminent arrival of Mrs Macatta. Bundle felt that dalliance with Mrs Macatta was going to prove no primrose path.

Her first shock was when she came down, demurely attired in a black lace frock, and passed along the hall. A footman was standing there – at least a man dressed as a footman. But that square, burly figure lent itself badly to the deception. Bundle stopped and stared.

'Superintendent Battle,' she breathed.

'That's right, Lady Eileen.'

'Oh!' said Bundle uncertainly. 'Are you here to – to –?'

'Keep an eye on things.'

'I see.'

'That warning letter, you know,' said the superintendent, 'fairly put the wind up Mr Lomax. Nothing would do for him but that I should come down myself.'

'But don't you think –' began Bundle, and stopped. She hardly liked to suggest to the superintendent that his disguise was not a particularly efficient one. He seemed to have 'police officer' written all over him, and Bundle could hardly imagine the most unsuspecting criminal failing to be put on his guard.

'You think,' said the superintendent stolidly, 'that I might be Recognized?'

He gave the final word a distinct capital letter.

'I did think so – yes –' admitted Bundle.

Something that might conceivably have been intended for a smile crossed the woodenness of Superintendent Battle's features.

'Put them on their guard, eh? Well, Lady Eileen, why not?'

'Why not?' echoed Bundle – rather stupidly, she felt.

Superintendent Battle was nodding his head slowly.

'We don't want any unpleasantness, do we?' he said. 'Don't want to be too clever – just show any light-fingered gentry that may be about – well, just show them that there's somebody on the spot, so to speak.'

Bundle gazed at him in some admiration. She could imagine that the sudden appearance of so renowned a personage as Superintendent Battle might have a depressing effect on any scheme and the hatchers of it.

'It's a great mistake to be too clever,' Superintendent Battle was repeating. 'The great thing is not to have any unpleasantness this week-end.'

Bundle passed on, wondering how many of her fellow guests had recognized or would recognize the Scotland Yard detective. In the drawing-room George was standing with a puckered brow and an orange envelope in his hand.

'Most vexatious,' he said. 'A telegram from Mrs Macatta to say she will be unable to be with us. Her children are suffering from mumps.'

Bundle's heart gave a throb of relief.

'I especially feel this on your account, Eileen,' said George kindly. 'I know how anxious you were to meet her. The Countess too will be sadly disappointed.'

'Oh, never mind,' said Bundle. 'I should hate it if she'd come and given me mumps.'

'A very distressing complaint,' agreed George. 'But I do not think that infection could be carried that way. Indeed, I am sure that Mrs Macatta would have run no risk of that kind. She is a most highly principled woman, with a very real sense of her responsibilities to the community. In these days of national stress, we must all take into account –'

On the brink of embarking on a speech, George pulled himself up short.

'But it must be for another time,' he said. 'Fortunately there is no hurry in your case. But the Countess, alas, is only a visitor to our shores.'

'She's a Hungarian, isn't she?' said Bundle, who was curious about the Countess.

'Yes. You have heard, no doubt, of the Young Hungarian party. The Countess is a leader of that party. A woman of great wealth, left a widow at an early age, she has devoted her money and her talents to the public service. She has especially devoted herself to the problem of infant mortality – a terrible one under present conditions in Hungary. I – Ah! here is Herr Eberhard.'

The German inventor was younger than Bundle had imagined him. He was probably not more than thirty-three or four. He was boorish and ill at ease. And yet his personality was not an unpleasing one. His blue eyes were more shy than furtive, and his more unpleasant mannerisms, such as the one that Bill had described of gnawing his finger-nails, arose, she thought, more from nervousness than from any other cause. He was thin and weedy in appearance and looked anaemic and delicate.

He conversed rather awkwardly with Bundle in stilted English and they both welcomed the interruption of the joyous Mr O'Rourke. Presently Bill bustled in – there is no other word for it: in the same such way does a favoured Newfoundland make his entrance – and at once came over to Bundle. He was looking perplexed and harassed.

'Hullo, Bundle. Heard you'd got here. Been kept with my nose to the grindstone all the blessed afternoon or I'd have seen you before.'

'Cares of State heavy tonight?' suggested O'Rourke sympathetically.

Bill groaned.

'I don't know what your fellow's like,' he complained. 'Looks a good-natured, tubby little chap. But Codders is absolutely impossible. Drive, drive, drive, from morning to night. Everything you do is wrong, and everything you haven't done you ought to have done.'

'Quite like a quotation from the prayer book,' remarked Jimmy, who had just strolled up.

Bill glanced at him reproachfully.

'Nobody knows,' he said pathetically, 'what I have to put up with.'

'Entertaining the Countess, eh?' suggested Jimmy. 'Poor Bill, that must have been a sad strain to a woman-hater like yourself.'

'What's this?' asked Bundle.

'After tea,' said Jimmy with a grin, 'the Countess asked Bill to show her round the interesting old place.'

'Well, I couldn't refuse, could I?' said Bill, his countenance assuming a brick-red tint.

Bundle felt faintly uneasy. She knew, only too well, the susceptibility of Mr William Eversleigh to female charms. In the hand of a woman like the Countess, Bill would be as wax. She wondered once more whether Jimmy Thesiger had been wise to take Bill into their confidence.

'The Countess,' said Bill, 'is a very charming woman. And no end intelligent. You should have seen her going round the house. All sorts of questions she asked.'

'What kind of questions?' asked Bundle suddenly.

Bill was vague.

'Oh! I don't know. About the history of it. And old furniture. And – oh! all sorts of things.'

At that moment the Countess swept into the room. She seemed a shade breathless. She was looking magnificent in a close-fitting black velvet gown. Bundle noticed how Bill gravitated at once to her immediate neighbourhood. The serious spectacled young man joined him.

'Bill and Pongo have both got it badly,' observed Jimmy Thesiger with a laugh.

Bundle was by no means so sure that it was a laughing matter.

CHAPTER 17

AFTER DINNER

George was not a believer in modern innovations. The Abbey was innocent of anything so up to date as central heating. Consequently, when the ladies entered the drawing-room after dinner, the temperature of the room was woefully inadequate to the needs of modern evening clothes. The fire that burnt in the well-furnished steel grate became as a magnet. The three women huddled round it.

'Brrrrrrrrr!' said the Countess, a fine, exotic foreign sound.

'The days are drawing in,' said Lady Coote, and drew a flowered atrocity of a scarf closer about her ample shoulders.

'Why on earth doesn't George have the house properly heated?' said Bundle.

'You English, you never heat your houses,' said the Countess.

She took out her long cigarette holder and began to smoke.

'That grate is old-fashioned,' said Lady Coote. 'The heat goes up the chimney instead of into the room.'

'Oh!' said the Countess.

There was a pause. The Countess was so plainly bored by her company that conversation became difficult.

'It's funny,' said Lady Coote, breaking the silence, 'that Mrs Macatta's children should have mumps. At least, I don't mean exactly funny –'

'What,' said the Countess, 'are mumps?'

Bundle and Lady Coote started simultaneously to explain. Finally, between them, they managed it.

'I suppose Hungarian children have it?' asked Lady Coote.

'Eh?' said the Countess.

'Hungarian children. They suffer from it?'

'I do not know,' said the Countess. 'How should I?'

Lady Coote looked at her in some surprise.

'But I understood that you worked –'

'Oh, that!' The Countess uncrossed her legs, took her cigarette holder from her mouth and began to talk rapidly.

'I will tell you some horrors,' she said. 'Horrors that I have seen. Incredible! You would not believe!'

And she was as good as her word. She talked fluently and with a graphic power of description. Incredible scenes of starvation and misery were painted by her for the benefit of her audience. She spoke of Buda Pesth shortly after the war and traced its vicissitudes to the present day. She was dramatic, but she was also, to Bundle's mind, a little like a gramophone record. You turned her on, and there you were. Presently, just as suddenly, she would stop.

Lady Coote was thrilled to the marrow – that much was clear. She sat with her mouth slightly open and her large, sad, dark eyes fixed on the Countess. Occasionally, she interpolated a comment of her own.

'One of my cousins had three children burned to death. Awful, wasn't it?'

The Countess paid no attention. She went on and on. And she finally stopped as suddenly as she had begun.

'There!' she said. 'I have told you. We have money – but no organization. It is organization we need.'

Lady Coote sighed.

'I've heard my husband say that nothing can be done without regular methods. He attributes his own success entirely to that. He declares he would never have got on without them.'

She sighed again. A sudden fleeting vision passed before her eyes of a Sir Oswald who had not got on in the world. A Sir Oswald who retained, in all essentials, the attributes of that cheery young man in the bicycle shop. Just for a second it occurred to her how much pleasanter life might have been for her if Sir Oswald had *not* had regular methods.

By a quite understandable association of ideas she turned to Bundle.

'Tell me, Lady Eileen,' she said; 'do you like that head gardener of yours?'

'MacDonald? Well –' Bundle hesitated. 'One couldn't exactly *like* MacDonald,' she explained apologetically. 'But he's a first-class gardener.'

'Oh! I know he is,' said Lady Coote.

'He's all right if he's kept in his place,' said Bundle.

'I suppose so,' said Lady Coote.

She looked enviously at Bundle, who appeared to approach the task of keeping MacDonald in his place so lightheartedly.

'I'd just adore a high-toned garden,' said the Countess dreamily.

Bundle stared, but at that moment a diversion occurred. Jimmy Thesiger entered the room and spoke directly to her in a strange, hurried voice.

'I say, will you come and see those etchings now? They're waiting for you.'

Bundle left the room hurriedly, Jimmy close behind her.

'What etchings?' she asked, as the drawing-room door closed behind her.

'No etchings,' said Jimmy. 'I'd got to say something to get hold of you. Come on, Bill is waiting for us in the library. There's nobody there.'

Bill was striding up and down the library, clearly in a very perturbed state of mind.

'Look here,' he burst out, 'I don't like this.'

'Don't like what?'

'You being mixed up in this. Ten to one there's going to be a rough-house and then –'

He looked at her with a kind of pathetic dismay that gave Bundle a warm and comfortable feeling.

'She ought to be kept out of it, oughtn't she, Jimmy?'

He appealed to the other.

'I've told her so,' said Jimmy.

'Dash it all, Bundle, I mean – someone might get hurt.'

Bundle turned round to Jimmy.

'How much have you told him?'

'Oh! everything.'

'I haven't got the hang of it all yet,' confessed Bill. 'You in that place in Seven Dials and all that.' He looked at her unhappily. 'I say, Bundle, I wish you wouldn't.'

'Wouldn't what?'

'Get mixed up in these sort of things.'

'Why not?' said Bundle. 'They're exciting.'

'Oh, yes – exciting. But they may be damnably dangerous. Look at poor old Ronny.'

'Yes,' said Bundle. 'If it hadn't been for your friend Ronny, I don't suppose I should ever have got what you call "mixed up" in this thing. But I am. And it's no earthly use your bleating about it.'

'I know you're the most frightful sport, Bundle, but –'

'Cut out the compliments. Let's make plans.'

To her relief, Bill reacted favourably to the suggestion.

'You're right about the formula,' he said. 'Eberhard's got some sort of formula with him, or rather Sir Oswald has. The stuff has been tested out at his works – very secretly and all that. Eberhard has been down there with him. They're all in the study now – what you might call coming down to brass tacks.'

'How long is Sir Stanley Digby staying?' asked Jimmy.

'Going back to town tomorrow.'

'H'm,' said Jimmy. 'Then one thing's quite clear. If, as I suppose, Sir Stanley will be taking the formula with him, any funny business there's going to be will be tonight.'

'I suppose it will.'

'Not a doubt of it. That narrows the thing down very comfortably. But the bright lads will have to be their very brightest. We must come down to details. First of all, where will the sacred formula be tonight? Will Eberhard have it, or Sir Oswald Coote?'

'Neither. I understand it's to be handed over to the Air Minister this evening, for him to take to town tomorrow. In that case O'Rourke will have it. Sure to.'

'Well, there's only one thing for it. If we believe someone's going to have a shot at pinching that paper, we've got to keep watch tonight, Bill, my boy.'

Bundle opened her mouth as though to protest, but shut it again without speaking.

'By the way,' continued Jimmy, 'did I recognize the commissionaire from Harrods in the hall this evening, or was it our old friend Lestrade from Scotland Yard?'

'Scintillating, Watson,' said Bill.

'I suppose,' said Jimmy, 'that we are rather butting in on his preserves.'

'Can't be helped,' said Bill. 'Not if we mean to see this thing through.'

'Then it's agreed,' said Jimmy. 'We divide the night into two watches?'

Again Bundle opened her mouth, and again shut it without speaking.

'Right you are,' agreed Bill. 'Who'll take first duty?'

'Shall we spin for it?'

'Might as well.'

'All right. Here goes. Heads you first and I second. Tails, vice versa.'

Bill nodded. The coin spun in the air. Jimmy bent to look at it.

'Tails,' he said.

'Damn,' said Bill. 'You get first half and probably any fun that's going.'

'Oh, you never know,' said Jimmy. 'Criminals are very uncertain. What time shall I wake you? Three?'

'That's about fair, I think.'

And now, at last, Bundle spoke:

'What about *me*?' she asked.

'Nothing doing. You go to bed and sleep.'

'Oh!' said Bundle. 'That's not very exciting.'

'You never know,' said Jimmy kindly. 'You may be murdered in your sleep while Bill and I escape scot-free.'

'Well, there's always that possibility. Do you know, Jimmy, I don't half like the look of that countess. I suspect her.'

'Nonsense,' cried Billy hotly. 'She's absolutely above suspicion.'

'How do you know?' retorted Bundle.

'Because I do. Why, one of the fellows at the Hungarian Embassy vouched for her.'

'Oh!' said Bundle, momentarily taken aback by his fervour.

'You girls are all the same,' grumbled Bill. 'Just because she's a jolly good-looking woman –'

Bundle was only too well acquainted with this unfair masculine line of argument.

'Well, don't you go and pour confidences into her shell-pink ear,' she remarked. 'I'm going to bed. I was bored stiff with that drawing-room and I'm not going back.'

She left the room. Bill looked at Jimmy.

'Good old Bundle,' he said. 'I was afraid we might have trouble with her. You know how keen she is to be in everything. I think the way she took it was just wonderful.'

'So did I,' said Jimmy. 'It staggered me.'

'She's got some sense, Bundle has. She knows when a thing's plumb impossible. I say, oughtn't we to have some lethal weapons? Chaps usually do when they're going on this sort of stunt.'

'I have a blue-nosed automatic,' said Jimmy with gentle pride. 'It weighs several pounds and looks most dangerous. I'll lend it to you when the time comes.'

Bill looked at him with respect and envy.

'What made you think of getting that?' he said.

'I don't know,' said Jimmy carelessly. 'It just came to me.'

'I hope we shan't go and shoot the wrong person,' said Bill with some anxiety.

'That would be unfortunate,' said Mr Thesiger gravely.

CHAPTER 18

JIMMY'S ADVENTURES

Our chronicle must here split into three separate and distinct portions. The night was to prove an eventful one and each of the three persons involved saw it from his or her own individual angle.

We will begin with that pleasant and engaging youth, Mr Jimmy Thesiger, at a moment when he has at last exchanged final good-nights with his fellow conspirator, Bill Eversleigh.

'Don't forget,' said Bill, '3 a.m. If you're still alive, that is,' he added kindly.

'I may be an ass,' said Jimmy, with rancorous remembrance of the remark Bundle had repeated to him, 'but I'm not nearly so much of an ass as I look.'

'That's what you said about Gerry Wade,' said Bill slowly. 'Do you remember? And that very night he –'

'Shut up, you damned fool,' said Jimmy. 'Haven't you got *any* tact?'

'Of course I've got tact,' said Bill. 'I'm a budding diplomatist. All diplomatists have tact.'

'Ah!' said Jimmy. 'You must be still in what they call the larval stage.'

'I can't get over Bundle,' said Bill, reverting abruptly to a former topic. 'I should certainly have said that she'd be – well, difficult. Bundle's improved. She's improved very much.'

'That's what your Chief was saying,' said Jimmy. 'He said he was agreeably surprised.'

'I thought Bundle was laying it on a bit thick myself,' said Bill. 'But Codders is such an ass he'd swallow anything. Well, night-night. I expect you'll have a bit of a job waking me when the times comes – but stick to it.'

'It won't be much good if you've taken a leaf out of Gerry Wade's book,' said Jimmy maliciously.

Bill looked at him reproachfully.

'What the hell do you want to go and make a chap uncomfortable for?' he demanded.

'I'm only getting my own back,' said Jimmy. 'Toddle along.'

But Bill lingered. He stood uncomfortably, first on one foot and then on the other.

'Look here,' he said.

'Yes?'

'What I mean to say is – well, I mean you'll be all right and all that, won't you? It's all very well ragging but when I think of poor Gerry – and then poor old Ronny –'

Jimmy gazed at him in exasperation. Bill was one of those who undoubtedly meant well, but the result of his efforts would not be described as heartening.

'I see,' he remarked, 'that I shall have to show you Leopold.'

He slipped his hand into the pocket of the dark-blue suit into which he had just changed and held out something for Bill's inspection.

'A real, genuine, blue-nosed automatic,' he said with modest pride.

'No. I say,' said Bill, 'is it really?'

He was undoubtedly impressed.

'Stevens, my man, got him for me. Warranted clean and methodical in his habits. You press the button and Leopold does the rest.'

'Oh!' said Bill. 'I say, Jimmy?'

'Yes?'

'Be careful, won't you? I mean, don't go loosing that thing off at anybody. Pretty awkward if you shot old Digby walking in his sleep.'

'That's all right,' said Jimmy. 'Naturally, I want to get value out of old Leopold now I've bought him, but I'll curb my blood-thirsty instincts as far as possible.'

'Well, night-night,' said Bill for the fourteenth time, and this time really did depart.

Jimmy was left alone to take up his vigil.

Sir Stanley Digby occupied a room at the extremity of the west wing. A bathroom adjoined it on one side, and on the other a communicating door led into a smaller room, which was tenanted by Mr Terence O'Rourke. The doors of these three rooms gave on to a short corridor. The watcher had a simple task. A chair placed inconspicuously in the shadow of an oak press just where the corridor ran into the main gallery formed a perfect vantage ground. There was no other way into the west wing, and anyone going to or from it could not fail to be seen. One electric light was still on.

Jimmy ensconced himself comfortably, crossed his legs and waited. Leopold lay in readiness across his knee.

He glanced at his watch. It was twenty minutes to one – just an hour since the household had retired to rest. Not a sound broke the stillness, except for the far-off ticking of a clock somewhere.

Somehow or other, Jimmy did not much care for that sound. It recalled things. Gerald Wade – and those seven ticking clocks on the mantelpiece . . . Whose hand had placed them there, and why? He shivered.

It was a creepy business, this waiting. He didn't wonder that things happened at spiritualistic séances. Sitting in the gloom, one got all worked up – ready to start at the least sound. And unpleasant thoughts came in on a fellow.

Ronny Devereux! Ronny Devereux and Gerry Wade! Both young, both full of life and energy; ordinary, jolly, healthy young men. And now, where were they? Dank earth . . . worms getting them . . . Ugh! Why couldn't he put these horrible thoughts out of his mind?

He looked again at his watch. Twenty minutes past one only. How the time crawled.

Extraordinary girl, Bundle! Fancy having the nerve and daring actually to get into the midst of that Seven Dials place. Why hadn't he had the nerve and initiative to think of that? He supposed because the thing *was* so fantastic.

No. 7. Who the hell could No. 7 be? Was he, perhaps, in the house at this minute? Disguised as a servant. He couldn't, surely, be one of the guests? No, that was impossible. But then, the whole thing was impossible. If he hadn't believed Bundle to be essentially truthful – well, he would have thought she had invented the whole thing.

He yawned. Queer, to feel sleepy, and yet at the same time strung up. He looked again at his watch. Ten minutes to two. Time was getting on.

And then, suddenly, he held his breath and leaned forward, listening. He had heard something.

The minutes went past . . . There it was again. The creak of a board . . . But it came from downstairs somewhere. There it was again! A slight, ominous creak. Somebody was moving stealthily about the house.

Jimmy sprang noiselessly to his feet. He crept silently to the head of the staircase. Everything seemed perfectly quiet. Yet he was quite certain he had really heard that stealthy sound. It was not imagination.

Very quietly and cautiously he crept down the staircase, Leopold clasped tightly in his right hand. Not a sound in the big hall. If he had been correct in assuming that the muffled sound came from directly beneath him, then it must have come from the library.

Jimmy stole to the door of it, listened, but heard nothing; then, suddenly flinging open the door, he switched on the lights.

Nothing! The big room was flooded with light. But it was empty.

Jimmy frowned.

'I could have sworn –' he murmured to himself.

The library was a large room with three windows which opened on to the terrace. Jimmy strode across the room. The middle window was unlatched.

He opened it and stepped out on to the terrace, looking from end to end of it. Nothing!

'Looks all right,' he murmured to himself. 'And yet –'

He remained for a minute lost in thought. Then he stepped back into the library. Crossing to the door, he locked it and put the key in his pocket. Then he switched off the light. He stood for a minute listening, then crossed softly to the open window and stood there, Leopold ready in his hand.

Was there, or was there not, a soft patter of feet along the terrace? No. – his imagination. He grasped Leopold tightly and stood listening . . .

In the distance a stable clock chimed two.

CHAPTER 19

BUNDLE'S ADVENTURES

Bundle Brent was a resourceful girl – she was also a girl of imagination. She had foreseen that Bill, if not Jimmy, would make objections to her participation in the possible dangers of the night. It was not Bundle's idea to waste time in argument. She had laid her own plans and made her own arrangements. A glance from her bedroom window shortly before dinner had been highly satisfactory. She had known that the grey walls of the Abbey were plentifully adorned with ivy, but the ivy outside her window was particularly solid looking and would present no difficulties to one of her athletic propensities.

She had no fault to find with Bill's and Jimmy's arrangements as far as they went. But in her opinion they did not go far enough. She offered no criticism, because she intended to see to that side of things herself. Briefly, while Jimmy and Bill were devoting themselves to the inside of the Abbey, Bundle intended to devote her attentions to the outside.

Her own meek acquiescence in the tame role assigned to her gave her an infinity of pleasure, though she wondered scornfully how either of the two men could be so easily deceived. Bill, of course, had never been famous for scintillating brain power. On the other hand, he knew, or should know, his Bundle. And she considered that Jimmy Thesiger, though only slightly acquainted with her, ought to have known better than to imagine that she could be so easily and summarily disposed of.

Once in the privacy of her own room, Bundle set rapidly to work. First she discarded her evening dress and the negligible trifle which she wore beneath it, and started again, so to speak, from the foundations. Bundle had not brought her maid with her, and she had packed herself. Otherwise, the puzzled Frenchwoman might have wondered why her lady took a pair of riding breeches and no further equine equipment.

Arrayed in riding breeches, rubber-soled shoes, and a dark-coloured pullover, Bundle was ready for the fray. She glanced at the time. As yet, it was only half-past twelve. Too early by far. Whatever was going to happen would not happen for some time yet. The occupants of the house must all be given time to get off to sleep. Half-past one was the time fixed by Bundle for the start of operations.

She switched off her light and sat down by the window to wait. Punctually at the appointed moment, she rose, pushed up the sash and swung her leg over the sill. The night was a fine one, cold and still. There was starlight but no moon.

She found the descent very easy. Bundle and her two sisters had run wild in the park at Chimneys as small children, and they could all climb like cats. Bundle arrived on a flower-bed, rather breathless, but quite unscathed.

She paused a minute to take stock of her plans. She knew that the rooms occupied by the Air Minister and his secretary were in the west wing; that was the opposite side of the house from where Bundle was now standing. A terrace ran along the south and west side of the house, ending abruptly against a walled fruit garden.

Bundle stepped out of her flower-bed and turned the corner of the house to where the terrace began on the south side. She crept very quietly along it, keeping close to the shadow of the house. But, as she reached the second corner, she got a shock, for a man was standing there, with the clear intention of barring her way.

The next instant she had recognized him.

'Superintendent Battle! You did give me a fright!'

'That's what I'm here for,' said the superintendent pleasantly.

Bundle looked at him. It struck her now, as so often before, how remarkably little camouflage there was about him. He was large and solid and noticeable. He was, somehow, very English. But of one thing Bundle was quite sure. Superintendent Battle was no fool.

'What are you really doing here?' she asked, still in a whisper.

'Just seeing,' said Battle, 'that nobody's about who shouldn't be.'

'Oh!' said Bundle, rather taken aback.

'You, for instance, Lady Eileen. I don't suppose you usually take a walk at this time of night.'

'Do you mean,' said Bundle slowly, 'that you want me to go back?'

Superintendent Battle nodded approvingly.

'You're very quick, Lady Eileen. That's just what I do mean. Did you – er – come out of a door, or the window?'

'The window. It's easy as anything climbing down this ivy.'

Supertintendent Battle looked up at it thoughtfully.

'Yes,' he said. 'I should say it would be.'

'And you want me to go back?' said Bundle. 'I'm rather sick about that. I wanted to go round on to the west terrace.'

'Perhaps you won't be the only one who'll want to do that,' said Battle.

'Nobody could miss seeing you,' said Bundle rather spitefully.

The superintendent seemed rather pleased than otherwise.

'I hope they won't,' he said. '*No unpleasantness*. That's my motto. And if you'll excuse me, Lady Eileen, I think it's time you were going back to bed.'

The firmness of his tone admitted no parley. Rather crestfallen, Bundle retraced her steps. She was half-way up the ivy when a sudden idea occurred to her, and she nearly relaxed her grip and fell.

Supposing Superintendent Battle suspected *her*.

There had been something – yes, surely there had been something in his manner that vaguely suggested the idea. She couldn't help laughing as she crawled over the sill into her bedroom. Fancy the solid superintendent suspecting *her*!

Though she had so far obeyed Battle's orders as to returning to her room, Bundle had no intention of going to bed and sleeping. Nor did she think that Battle had really intended her to do so. He was not a man to expect impossibilities. And to remain quiescent when something daring and exciting might be going on was a sheer impossibility to Bundle.

She glanced at her watch. It was ten minutes to two. After a moment or two of irresolution, she cautiously opened her door. Not a sound. Everything was still and peaceful. She stole cautiously along the passage.

Once she halted, thinking she heard a board creak somewhere, but then convinced that she was mistaken, she went on again. She was now in the main corridor, making her way to the west wing. She reached the angle of intersection and peered cautiously round – then she stared in blank surprise.

The watcher's post was empty. Jimmy Thesiger was not there.

Bundle stared in complete amazement. What had happened? Why had Jimmy left his post? What did it mean?

At that moment she heard a clock strike two.

She was still standing there, debating what to do next, when suddenly her heart gave a leap and then seemed to stand still. *The door handle of Terence O'Rourke's room was slowly turning*.

Bundle watched, fascinated. But the door did not open. Instead the knob turned slowly to its original position. What did it mean?

Suddenly Bundle came to a resolution. Jimmy, for some unknown reason, had deserted his post. She must get hold of Bill.

Quickly and noiselessly, Bundle fled along the way she had come. She burst unceremoniously into Bill's room.

'Bill, wake up! Oh, do wake up!'

It was an urgent whisper she sent forth, but there came no response to it.

'Bill,' breathed Bundle.

Impatiently she switched on the lights, and then stood dumbfounded.

The room was empty, and the bed had not even been slept in.

Where then was Bill?

Suddenly she caught her breath. *This was not Bill's room*. The dainty negligé thrown over a chair, the feminine knick-knacks on the dressing-table, the black velvet evening dress thrown carelessly over a chair – Of course, in her haste she had mistaken the doors. This was the Countess Radzky's room.

But where, oh where, was the countess?

And just as Bundle was asking herself this question, the silence of the night was suddenly broken, and in no uncertain manner.

The clamour came from below. In an instant Bundle had sped out of the Countess's room and downstairs. The sounds came from the library – a violent crashing of chairs being overturned.

Bundle rattled vainly at the library door. It was locked. But she could clearly hear the struggle that was going on within – the panting and scuffling, curses in many tones, the occasional crash as some light piece of furniture came into the line of battle.

And then, sinister and distinct, breaking the peace of the night for good and all, two shots in rapid succession.

CHAPTER 20

LORAINE'S ADVENTURES

Loraine Wade sat up in bed and switched on the light. It was exactly ten minutes to one. She had gone to bed early – at half-past nine. She possessed the useful art of being able to wake herself up at the required time, so she had been able to enjoy some hours of refreshing sleep.

Two dogs slept in the room with her, and one of these now raised his head and looked at her inquiringly.

'Quiet, Lurcher,' said Loraine, and the big animal put his head down again obediently, watching her from between his shaggy eyelashes.

It is true that Bundle had once doubted the meekness of Loraine Wade, but that brief moment of suspicion had passed. Loraine had seemed so entirely reasonable, so willing to be kept out of everything.

And yet, if you studied the girl's face, you saw that there was strength of purpose in the small, resolute jaw and the lips that closed together so firmly.

Loraine rose and dressed herself in a tweed coat and skirt. Into one pocket of the coat she dropped an electric torch. Then she opened the drawer of her dressing-table and took out a small ivory-handled pistol – almost a toy in appearance. She had bought it the day before at Harrods and she was very pleased with it.

She gave a final glance round the room to see if she had forgotten anything, and at that moment the big dog rose and came over to her, looking up at her with pleading eyes and wagging its tail.

'No, Lurcher. Can't go. Missus can't take you. Got to stay here and be a good boy.'

She dropped a kiss on the dog's head, made him lie down on his rug again, and then slipped noiselessly out of the room, closing the door behind her.

She let herself out of the house by a side door and made her way round to the garage, where her little two-seater car was in readiness. There was a gentle slope, and she let the car run silently down it, not starting the engine till she was some way from the house. Then she glanced at the watch on her arm and pressed her foot down on the accelerator.

She left the car at a spot she had previously marked down. There was a gap there in the fencing that she could easily get through. A few minutes later, slightly muddy, Loraine stood inside the grounds of Wyvern Abbey.

As noiselessly as possible, she made her way towards the venerable ivy-coloured building. In the distance a stable clock chimed two.

Loraine's heart beat faster as she drew near to the terrace. There was no one about – no sign of life anywhere. Everything seemed peaceful and undisturbed. She reached the terrace and stood there, looking about her.

Suddenly, without the least warning, something from above fell with a flop almost at her feet. Loraine stooped to pick it up. It was a brown paper packet, loosely wrapped. Holding it, Loraine looked up.

There was an open window just above her head, and even as she looked a leg swung over it and a man began to climb down the ivy.

Loraine waited no more. She took to her heels and ran, still clasping the brown paper packet.

Behind her, the noise of a struggle suddenly broke out. A hoarse voice: 'Lemme go'; another that she knew well: 'Not if I know it – ah, you would, would you?'

Still Loraine ran – blindly, as though panic-stricken – right round the corner of the terrace – and slap into the arms of a large, solidly built man.

'There, there,' said Superintendent Battle kindly.

Loraine was struggling to speak.

'Oh, quick! – oh, quick! They're killing each other. Oh, do be quick!'

There was a sharp crack of a revolver shot – and then another.

Superintendent Battle started to run. Loraine followed. Back round the corner of the terrace and along to the library window. The window was open.

Battle stooped and switched on an electric torch. Loraine was close behind him, peering over his shoulder. She gave a little sobbing gasp.

On the threshold of the window lay Jimmy Thesiger in what looked like a pool of blood. His right arm lay dangling in a curious position.

Loraine gave a sharp cry.

'He's dead,' she wailed. 'Oh, Jimmy – Jimmy – he's dead!'

'Now, now,' said Superintendent Battle soothingly. 'Don't you take on so. The young gentleman isn't dead, I'll be bound. See if you can find the lights and turn them on.'

Loraine obeyed. She stumbled across the room, found the switch by the door and pressed it down. The room was flooded with light. Superintendent Battle uttered a sigh of relief.

'It's all right – he's only shot in the right arm. He's fainted through loss of blood. Come and give me a hand with him.'

There was a pounding on the library door. Voices were heard, asking, expostulating, demanding.

Loraine looked doubtfully at it.

'Shall I –?'

'No hurry,' said Battle. 'We'll let them in presently. You come and give me a hand.'

Loraine came obediently. The superintendent had produced a large, clean pocket-handkerchief and was neatly bandaging the wounded man's arm. Loraine helped him.

'He'll be all right,' said the superintendent. 'Don't you worry.

As many lives as cats, these young fellows. It wasn't the loss of blood knocked him out either. He must have caught his head a crack on the floor as he fell.'

Outside, the knocking on the door had become tremendous. The voice of George Lomax, furiously upraised, came loud and distinct:

'Who is in there? Open the door at once.'

Superintendent Battle sighed.

'I suppose we shall have to,' he said. 'A pity.'

His eyes darted round, taking in the scene. An automatic lay by Jimmy's side. The superintendent picked it up gingerly, holding it very delicately, and examined it. He grunted and laid it on the table. Then he stepped across and unlocked the door.

Several people fell into the room. Nearly everybody said something at the same minute. George Lomax, spluttering with obdurate words which refused to come with sufficient fluency, exclaimed:

'The – the – the meaning of this? Ah! It's you, superintendent; what's happened? I say – what has – happened?'

Bill Eversleigh said; 'My God! Old Jimmy!' and stared at the limp figure on the ground.

Lady Coote, clad in a resplendent purple dressing-gown, cried out: 'The poor boy!' and swept past Superintendent Battle to bend over the prostrate Jimmy in a motherly fashion.

Bundle said: 'Loraine!'

Herr Eberhard said: '*Gott im Himmel*!' and other words of that nature.

Sir Stanley Digby said: 'My God, what's all this?'

A housemaid said: 'Look at the blood,' and screamed with pleasurable excitement.

A footman said: 'Lor!'

The butler said, with a good deal more bravery in his manner than had been noticeable a few minutes earlier: 'Now then, this won't do!' and waved away under-servants.

The efficient Mr Rupert Bateman said to George: 'Shall we get rid of some of these people, sir?'

Then they all took fresh breath.

'Incredible!' said George Lomax. 'Battle, what has *happened*?'

Battle gave him a look, and George's discreet habits assumed their usual way.

'Now then,' he said, moving to the door, 'everyone go back to bed, please. There's been a – er –'

'A little accident,' said Superintendent Battle easily.

'A – er – an accident. I shall be much obliged if everyone will go back to bed.'

Everyone was clearly reluctant to do so.

'Lady Coote – please –'

'The poor boy,' said Lady Coote in a motherly fashion.

She rose from a kneeling position with great reluctance. And as she did so, Jimmy stirred and sat up.

'Hallo!' he said thickly. 'What's the matter?'

He looked round him vacantly for a minute or two and then intelligence returned to his eye.

'Have you got him? he demanded eagerly.

'Got who?'

'The man. Climbed down the ivy. I was by the window there. Grabbed him and we had no end of a set-to –'

'One of those nasty, murderous cat burglars,' said Lady Coote. 'Poor boy.'

Jimmy was looking round him.

'I say – I'm afraid we – er – have made rather a mess of things. Fellow was as strong as an ox and we went fairly waltzing round.'

The condition of the room was clear proof of this statement. Everything light and breakable within a range of twelve feet that could be broken *had* been broken.

'And what happened then?'

But Jimmy was looking round for something.

'Where's Leopold? The pride of the blue-nosed automatics?'

Battle indicated the pistol on the table.

'Is this yours, Mr Thesiger?'

'That's right. That's little Leopold. How many shots have been fired?'

'One shot.'

Jimmy looked chagrined.

'I'm disappointed in Leopold,' he murmured. 'I can't have pressed the button properly, or he'd have gone on shooting.'

'Who shot first?'

'I did, I'm afraid,' said Jimmy. 'You see, the man twisted himself out of my grasp suddenly. I saw him making for the window and I closed my finger down on Leopold and let him have it. He turned in the window and fired at me and – well, I suppose after that I took the count.'

He rubbed his head rather ruefully.

But Sir Stanley Digby was suddenly alert.

'Climbing down the ivy, you said? My God, Lomax, you don't think they've got away with it?'

He rushed from the room. For some curious reason nobody spoke during his absence. In a few minutes Sir Stanley returned. His round, chubby face was white as death.

'My God, Battle,' he said, 'they've got it. O'Rourke's fast asleep – drugged, I think. I can't wake him. And the papers have vanished.'

CHAPTER 21

THE RECOVERY OF THE FORMULA

'*Der liebe Gott!*' said Herr Eberhard in a whisper.

His face had gone chalky white.

George turned a face of dignified reproach on Battle.

'Is this true, Battle? I left all arrangements in your hands.'

The rock-like quality of the superintendent showed out well. Not a muscle of his face moved.

'The best of us are defeated sometimes, sir,' he said quietly.

'Then you mean – you really mean – that the document is gone?'

But to everyone's surprise Superintendent Battle shook his head.

'No, no, Mr Lomax, it's not so bad as you think. Everything's all right. But you can't lay the credit for it at my door. You've got to thank this young lady.'

He indicated Loraine, who stared at him in surprise. Battle stepped across to her and gently took the brown paper parcel which she was still clutching mechanically.

'I think, Mr Lomax,' he said, 'that you will find what you want here.'

Sir Stanley Digby, quicker in action than George, snatched at the package and tore it open, investigating its contents eagerly. A sigh of relief escaped him and he mopped his brow. Herr Eberhard fell upon the child of his brain and clasped it to his heart, whilst a torrent of German burst from him.

Sir Stanley turned to Loraine, shaking her warmly by the hand.

'My dear young lady,' he said, 'we are infinitely obliged to you, I am sure.'

'Yes, indeed,' said George. 'Though I – er –'

He paused in some perplexity, staring at a young lady who was a total stranger to him. Loraine looked appealingly at Jimmy, who came to the rescue.

'We – this is Miss Wade.' said Jimmy. 'Gerald Wade's sister.'

'Indeed,' said George, shaking her warmly by the hand. 'My dear Miss Wade, I must express my deep gratitude to you for what you have done. I must confess that I do not quite see –'

He paused delicately and four of the persons present felt that explanations were going to be fraught with much difficulty. Superintendent Battle came to the rescue.

'Perhaps we'd better not go into that just now, sir,' he suggested tactfully.

The efficient Mr Bateman created a further diversion.

'Wouldn't it be wise for someone to see to O'Rourke? Don't you think, sir, that a doctor had better be sent for?'

'Of course,' said George. 'Of course. Most remiss of us not to have thought of it before.' He looked towards Bill. 'Get Dr Cartwright on the telephone. Ask him to come. Just hint, if you can, that – er – discretion should be observed.'

Bill went off on his errand.

'I will come up with you, Digby,' said George. 'Something, possibly, could be done – measures should, perhaps, be taken – whilst awaiting the arrival of the doctor.'

He looked rather helplessly at Rupert Bateman. Efficiency always makes itself felt. It was Pongo who was really in charge of the situation.

'Shall I come up with you, sir?'

George accepted the offer with relief. Here, he felt, was someone on whom he could lean. He experienced that sense of complete trust in Mr Bateman's efficiency which came to all those who encountered that excellent young man.

The three men left the room together. Lady Coote, murmuring in deep rich tones: 'The poor young fellow. Perhaps I could do something –' hurried after them.

'That's a very motherly woman,' observed the superintendent thoughtfully. 'A very motherly woman. I wonder –'

Three pairs of eyes looked at him inquiringly.

'I was wondering,' said Superintendent Battle slowly, 'where Sir Oswald Coote may be.'

'Oh!' gasped Loraine. 'Do you think he's been murdered?'

Battle shook his head at her reproachfully.

'No need for anything so melodramatic,' he said. 'No – I rather think –'

He paused, his head on one side, listening – one large hand raised to enjoin silence.

In another minute they all heard what his sharper ears had been the first to notice. Footsteps coming along the terrace outside. They rang out clearly with no kind of subterfuge about them. In another minute the window was blocked by a bulky figure which stood there regarding them and who conveyed, in an odd way, a sense of dominating the situation.

Sir Oswald, for it was he, looked slowly from one face to another. His keen eyes took in the details of the situation. Jimmy, with his roughly bandaged arm; Bundle, in her somewhat anomalous attire; Loraine, a perfect stranger to him. His eyes came last to Superintendent Battle. He spoke sharply and crisply.

'What's been happening here, officer?'

'Attempted robbery, sir.'

'*Attempted* – eh?'

'Thanks to this young lady, Miss Wade, the thieves failed to get away with it.'

'Ah!' he said again, his scrutiny ended. 'And now, officer, what about *this*?'

He held out a small Mauser pistol which he carried delicately by the butt.

'Where did you find that, Sir Oswald?'

'On the lawn outside. I presume it must have been thrown down by one of the thieves as he took to his heels. I've held it carefully, as I thought you might wish to examine it for fingerprints.'

'You think of everything, Sir Oswald,' said Battle.

He took the pistol from the other, handling it with equal care, and laid it down on the table beside Jimmy's Colt.

'And now, if you please,' said Sir Oswald, 'I should like to hear exactly what occurred.'

Superintendent Battle gave a brief résumé of the events of the night. Sir Oswald frowned thoughtfully.

'I understand,' he said sharply. 'After wounding and disabling Mr Thesiger, the man took to his heels and ran, throwing away the pistol as he did so. What I cannot understand is why no one pursued him.'

'It wasn't till we heard Mr Thesiger's story that we knew there was anyone to pursue,' remarked Superintendent Battle dryly.

'You didn't – er – catch sight of him making off as you turned the corner of the terrace?'

'No, I missed him by just about forty seconds, I should say. There's no moon and he'd be invisible as soon as he'd left the terrace. He must have leapt for it as soon as he'd fired the shot.'

'H'm,' said Sir Oswald. 'I still think that a search should have been organized. Someone else should have been posted –'

'There are three of my men in the grounds,' said the superintendent quietly.

'Oh!' Sir Oswald seemed rather taken aback.

'They were told to hold and detain anyone attempting to leave the grounds.'

'And yet – they haven't done so?'

'And yet they haven't done so,' agreed Battle gravely.

Sir Oswald looked at him as though something in the words puzzled him. He said sharply:

'Are you telling me all that you know, Superintendent Battle?'

'All that I *know* – yes, Sir Oswald. What I think is a different matter. Maybe I think some rather curious things – but until thinking's got you somewhere it's no use talking about it.'

'And yet,' said Sir Oswald slowly, 'I should like to know what you think, Superintendent Battle.'

'For one thing, sir, I think there's a lot too much ivy about this place – excuse me, sir, you've got a bit on your coat – yes, a great deal too much ivy. It complicates things.'

Sir Oswald stared at him, but any reply he might have contemplated making was arrested by the entrance of Rupert Bateman.

'Oh, there you are, Sir Oswald. I'm so glad. Lady Coote has just discovered that you were missing – and she has been insisting upon it that you had been murdered by the thieves. I really, think, Sir Oswald, that you had better come to her at once. She is terribly upset.'

'Maria is an incredibly foolish woman,' said Sir Oswald. 'Why should I be murdered? I'll come with you, Bateman.'

He left the room with his secretary.

'That's a very efficient young man,' said Battle, looking after them. 'What's his name – Bateman?'

Jimmy nodded.

'Bateman – Rupert,' he said. 'Commonly known as Pongo. I was at school with him.'

'Were you? Now, that's interesting, Mr Thesiger. What was your opinion of him in those days?'

'Oh, he was always the same sort of ass.'

'I shouldn't have thought,' said Battle mildly, 'that he was an ass.'

'Oh, you know what I mean. Of course he wasn't really an ass. Tons of brains and always swotting at things. But deadly serious. No sense of humour.'

'Ah!' said Superintendent Battle. 'That's a pity. Gentlemen who have no sense of humour get to taking themselves too seriously – and that leads to mischief.'

'I can't imagine Pongo getting into mischief,' said Jimmy. 'He's done extremely well for himself so far – dug himself in with old Coote and looks like being a permanency in the job.'

'Superintendent Battle,' said Bundle.

'Yes, Lady Eileen?'

'Don't you think it very odd that Sir Oswald didn't say what he was doing wandering about in the garden in the middle of the night?'

'Ah!' said Battle. 'Sir Oswald's a great man – and a great man always knows better than to explain unless an explanation is demanded. To rush into explanations and excuses is always a sign of weakness. Sir Oswald knows that as well as I do. He's not going to come in explaining and apologizing – not he. He just stalks in and hauls *me* over the coals. He's a big man, Sir Oswald.'

Such a warm admiration sounded in the superintendent's tones that Bundle pursued the subject no further.

'And now,' said Superintendent Battle, looking round with a slight twinkle in his eye, 'now that we're together and friendly like – I *should* like to hear just how Miss Wade happened to arrive on the scene so pat.'

'She ought to be ashamed of herself,' said Jimmy. 'Hoodwinking us all as she did.'

'Why should I be kept out of it all?' cried Loraine passionately. 'I never meant to be – no, not the very first day in your rooms when you both explained how the best thing for me to do was to stay quietly at home and keep out of danger. I didn't say anything, but I made up my mind then.'

'I half expected it,' said Bundle. 'You were so surprisingly meek about it. I might have known you were up to something.'

'I thought you were remarkably sensible,' said Jimmy Thesiger.

'You would, Jimmy dear,' said Loraine. 'It was easy enough to deceive you.'

'Thank you for these kind words,' said Jimmy. 'Go on, and don't mind me.'

'When you rang up and said there might be danger, I was more determined than ever,' went on Loraine. 'I went to Harrods and bought a pistol. Here it is.'

She produced the dainty weapon and Superintendent Battle took it from her and examined it.

'Quite a deadly little toy, Miss Wade,' he said. 'Have you had much – er – practice with it?'

'None at all,' said Loraine. 'But I thought if I took it with me – well, that it would give me a comforting feeling.'

'Quite so,' said Battle gravely.

'My idea was to come over here and see what was going on. I left my car in the road and climbed through the hedge and came up to the terrace. I was just looking about me when – plop – something fell right at my feet. I picked it up and then looked to see where it could have come from. And then I saw the man climbing down the ivy and I ran.'

'Just so,' said Battle. 'Now, Miss Wade, can you describe the man at all?'

The girl shook her head.

'It was too dark to see much. I think he was a big man – but that's about all.'

'And now you, Mr Thesiger.' Battle turned to him. 'You struggled with the man – can you tell me anything about him?'

'He was a pretty hefty individual – that's all I can say. He gave a few hoarse whispers – that's when I had him by the throat. He said "Lemme go, guvnor," something like that.'

'An uneducated man, then?'

'Yes, I suppose he was. He spoke like one.'

'I still don't quite understand about the packet,' said Loraine. 'Why should he throw it down as he did? Was it because it hampered him climbing?'

'No,' said Battle. 'I've got an entirely different theory about that. That packet, Miss Wade, was deliberately thrown down to you – or so I believe.'

'To *me*?'

'Shall we say – to the person the thief thought you were.'

'This is getting very involved,' said Jimmy.

'Mr Thesiger, when you came into this room, did you switch on the light at all?'

'Yes.'

'And there was no one in the room?'

'No one at all.'

'But previously you thought you heard someone moving about down here?'

'Yes.'

'And then, after trying the window, you switched off the light again and locked the door?'

Jimmy nodded.

Superintendent Battle looked slowly around him. His glance was arrested by a big screen of Spanish leather which stood near one of the bookcases.

Brusquely he strode across the room and looked behind it.

He uttered a sharp ejaculation, which brought the three young people quickly to his side.

Huddled on the floor, in a dead faint, lay the Countess Radzky.

CHAPTER 22

THE COUNTESS RADZKY'S STORY

The Countess's return to consciousness was very different from that of Jimmy Thesiger. It was more prolonged and infinitely more artistic.

Artistic was Bundle's word. She had been zealous in her ministrations – largely consisting of the application of cold water – and the Countess had instantly responded, passing a white, bewildered hand across her brow and murmuring faintly.

It was at this point that Bill, at last relieved from his duties with telephone and doctors, had come bustling into the room and had instantly proceeded to make (in Bundle's opinion) a most regrettable idiot of himself.

He had hung over the Countess with a concerned and anxious face and had addressed a series of singularly idiotic remarks to her:

'I say, Countess. It's all right. It's really all right. Don't try to talk. It's bad for you. Just lie still. You'll be all right in a minute. It'll all come back to you. Don't say anything till you're quite all right. Take your time. Just lie still and close your eyes. You'll remember everything in a minute. Have another sip of water. Have some brandy. That's the stuff. Don't you think, Bundle, that some brandy . . . ?'

'For God's sake, Bill, leave her alone,' said Bundle crossly. 'She'll be all right.'

And with an expert hand she flipped a good deal of cold water on to the exquisite make-up of the Countess's face.

The Countess flinched and sat up. She looked considerably more wide awake.

'Ah!' she murmured. 'I am here. Yes, I am here.'

'Take your time,' said Bill. 'Don't talk till you feel quite all right again.'

The Countess drew the folds of a very transparent negligé closer around her.

'It is coming back to me,' she murmured. 'Yes, it is coming back.'

She looked at the little crowd grouped around her. Perhaps

something in the attentive faces struck her as unsympathetic. In any case she smiled deliberately up at the one face which clearly displayed a very opposite emotion.

'Ah, my big Englishman,' she said very softly, 'do not distress yourself. All is well with me.'

'Oh! I say, but are you sure?' demanded Bill anxiously.

'Quite sure.' She smiled at him reassuringly. 'We Hungarians, we have nerves of steel.'

A look of intense relief passed over Bill's face. A fatuous look settled down there instead – a look which made Bundle earnestly long to kick him.

'Have some water,' she said coldly.

The Countess refused water. Jimmy, kindlier to beauty in distress, suggested a cocktail. The Countess reacted favourably to this suggestion. When she had swallowed it, she looked round once more, this time with a livelier eye.

'Tell me, what has happened?' she demanded briskly.

'We were hoping you might be able to tell us that,' said Superintendent Battle.

The Countess looked at him sharply. She seemed to become aware of the big, quiet man for the first time.

'I went to your room,' said Bundle. 'The bed hadn't been slept in and you weren't there.'

She paused – looking accusingly at the Countess. The latter closed her eyes and nodded her head slowly.

'Yes, yes, I remember it all now. Oh, it was horrible!' She shuddered. 'Do you want me to tell you?'

Superintendent Battle said, 'If you please' at the same moment that Bill said, 'Not if you don't feel up to it.'

The Countess looked from one to the other, but the quiet, masterful eye of Superintendent Battle won the game.

'I could not sleep,' began the Countess. 'The house – it oppressed me. I was all, as you say, on wires, the cat on the hot bricks. I knew that in the state I was in it was useless to think of going to bed. I walked about my room. I read. But the books placed there did not interest me greatly. I thought I would come down and find something more absorbing.'

'Very natural,' said Bill.

'Very often done, I believe,' said Battle.

'So as soon as the idea occurred to me, I left my room and came down. The house was very still –'

'Excuse me,' interrupted the Superintendent, 'but can you give me an idea of the time when this occurred?'

'I never know the time,' said the Countess superbly, and swept on with her story.

'The house was very quiet. One could even hear the little mouse run, if there had been one. I come down the stairs – very quietly –'

'Very quietly?'

'Naturally I do not want to disturb the household,' said the Countess reproachfully. 'I come in here. I go into this corner and I search the shelves for a suitable book.'

'Having of course switched on the light?'

'No, I did not switch on the light. I had, you see, my little electric torch with me. With that, I scanned the shelves.'

'Ah!' said the Superintendent.

'Suddenly,' continued the Countess dramatically, 'I hear something. A stealthy sound. A muffled footstep. I switch out my torch and listen. The footsteps draw nearer – stealthy, horrible footsteps. I shrink behind the screen. In another minute the door opens and the light is switched on. The man – the burglar is in the room.'

'Yes, but I say –' began Mr Thesiger.

A large-sized foot pressed his, and realizing that Superintendent Battle was giving him a hint, Jimmy shut up.

'I nearly died of fear,' continued the Countess. 'I tried not to breathe. The man waited for a minute, listening. Then, still with that horrible, stealthy tread –'

Again Jimmy opened his mouth in protest, and again shut it.

'– he crossed to the window and peered out. He remained there for a minute or two, then he recrossed the room and turned out the lights again, locking the door. I am terrified. He is in the room, moving stealthily about in the dark. Ah, it is horrible. Suppose he should come upon me in the dark! In another minute I hear him again by the window. Then silence. I hope that perhaps he may have gone out that way. As the minutes pass and I hear no further sound, I am almost sure that he has done so. Indeed I am in the very act of switching on my torch and investigating when – *prestissimo!* – it all begins.'

'Yes?'

'Ah! But it was terrible – never – never shall I forget it! Two men trying to murder each other. Oh, it was horrible! They reeled about the room, and furniture crashed in every direction. I thought, too, that I heard a woman scream – but that was not in the room. It was outside somewhere. The criminal had a hoarse voice. He croaked rather than spoke. He kept saying "Lemme go – lemme go." The other man was a gentleman. He had a cultured English voice.'

Jimmy looked gratified.

'He swore – mostly,' continued the Countess.

'Clearly a gentleman,' said Superintendent Battle.

'And then,' continued the Countess, 'a flash and a shot. The bullet hit the bookcase beside me. I – I suppose I must have fainted.'

She looked up at Bill. He took her hand and patted it.

'You poor dear,' he said. 'How rotten for you.'

'Silly idiot,' thought Bundle.

Superintendent Battle had moved on swift, noiseless feet over to the bookcase a little to the right of the screen. He bent down, searching. Presently he stooped and picked something up.

'It wasn't a bullet, Countess,' he said. 'It's the shell of the cartridge. Where were you standing when you fired, Mr Thesiger.'

Jimmy took up a position by the window.

'As nearly as I can see, about here.'

Superintendent Battle placed himself in the same spot.

'That's right,' he agreed. 'The empty shell would throw right rear. It's a .455. I don't wonder the Countess thought it was a bullet in the dark. It hit the bookcase about a foot from her. The bullet itself grazed the window frame and we'll find it outside tomorrow – unless your assailant happens to be carrying it about in him.'

Jimmy shook his head regretfully.

'Leopold, I fear, did not cover himself with glory,' he remarked sadly.

The Countess was looking at him with most flattering attention.

'Your arm!' she exclaimed. 'It is all tied up! Was it you then –?'

Jimmy made her a mock bow.

'I'm so glad I've got a cultured, English voice,' he said. 'And I can assure you that I wouldn't have dreamed of using the language I did if I had had any suspicion that a lady was present.'

'I did not understand all of it,' the Countess hastened to explain. 'Although I had an English governess when I was young –'

'It isn't the sort of thing she'd be likely to teach you,' agreed Jimmy. 'Kept you busy with your uncle's pen, and the umbrella of the gardener's niece. I know the sort of stuff.'

'But what has happened?' asked the Countess. 'That is what I want to know. I demand to know what has happened.'

There was a moment's silence whilst everybody looked at Superintendent Battle.

'It's very simple,' said Battle mildly. 'Attempted robbery. Some political papers stolen from Sir Stanley Digby. The thieves nearly got away with them, but thanks to this young lady' – he indicated Loraine – 'they didn't.'

The Countess flashed a glance at the girl – rather an odd glance.

'Indeed,' she said coldly.

'A very fortunate coincidence that she happened to be there,' said Superintendent Battle, smiling.

The Countess gave a little sigh and half closed her eyes again.

'It is absurd, but I still feel extremely faint,' she murmured.

'Of course you do,' cried Bill. 'Let me help you up to your room. Bundle will come with you.'

'It is very kind of Lady Eileen,' said the Countess, 'but I should prefer to be alone. I am really quite all right. Perhaps you will just help me up the stairs.'

She rose to her feet, accepted Bill's arm and, leaning heavily on it, went out of the room. Bundle followed as far as the hall, but, the Countess reiterating her assurance – with some tartness – that she was quite all right, she did not accompany them upstairs.

But as she stood watching the Countess's graceful form, supported by Bill, slowly mounting the stairway, she stiffened suddenly to acute attention. The Countess's negligé, as previously mentioned, was thin – a mere veil of orange chiffon. Through it Bundle saw distinctly below the right shoulder-blade *a small black mole.*

With a gasp, Bundle swung impetuously round to where Superintendent Battle was just emerging from the library. Jimmy and Loraine had preceded him.

'There,' said Battle. 'I've fastened the window and there will be a man on duty outside. And I'll lock the door and take the key. In the morning we'll do what the French call reconstruct the crime – Yes, Lady Eileen, what is it?'

'Superintendent Battle, I must speak with you – at once.'

'Why, certainly, I –'

George Lomax suddenly appeared, Dr Cartwright by his side.

'Ah, there you are, Battle. You'll be relieved to hear that there's nothing seriously wrong with O'Rourke.'

'I never thought there would be much wrong with Mr O'Rourke,' said Battle.

'He's had a strong hypodermic administered to him,' said the doctor. 'He'll wake perfectly all right in the morning, perhaps a bit of a head, perhaps not. Now then, young man, let's look at this bullet wound of yours.'

'Come on, nurse,' said Jimmy to Loraine. 'Come and hold the basin or my hand. Witness a strong man's agony. You know the stunt.'

Jimmy, Loraine and the doctor went off together. Bundle continued to throw agonized glances in the direction of Superintendent Battle, who had been buttonholed by George.

The superintendent waited patiently till a pause occurred in George's loquacity. He then swiftly took advantage of it.

'I wonder, sir, if I might have a word privately with Sir Stanley? In the little study at the end there.'

'Certainly,' said George. 'Certainly. I'll go and fetch him at once.'

He hurried off upstairs again. Battle drew Bundle swiftly into the drawing-room and shut the door.

'Now, Lady Eileen, what is it?'

'I'll tell you as quickly as I can – but it's rather long and complicated.'

As concisely as she could, Bundle related her introduction to the Seven Dials Club and her subsequent adventures there. When she had finished, Superintendent Battle drew a long breath. For once, his facial woodenness was laid aside.

'Remarkable,' he said. 'Remarkable. I wouldn't have believed it possible – even for you, Lady Eileen. I ought to have known better.'

'But you did give me a hint, Superintendent Battle. You told me to ask Bill Eversleigh.'

'It's dangerous to give people like you a hint, Lady Eileen. I never dreamt of your going to the lengths you have.'

'Well, it's all right, Superintendent Battle. My death doesn't lie at your door.'

'Not yet, it doesn't,' said Battle grimly.

He stood as though in thought, turning things over in his mind. 'What Mr Thesiger was about, letting you run into danger like that, I can't think,' he said presently.

'He didn't know till afterwards,' said Bundle. 'I'm not a complete mug, Superintendent Battle. And, anyway, he's got his hands full looking after Miss Wade.'

'Is that so?' said the Superintendent. 'Ah!'

He twinkled a little.

'I shall have to detail Mr Eversleigh to look after you, Lady Eileen.'

'Bill!' said Bundle contemptuously. 'But, Superintendent Battle, you haven't heard the end of my story. The woman I saw there – Anna – No. 1. Yes, No. 1 is the Countess Radzky.'

And rapidly she went on to describe her recognition of the mole.

To her surprise the Superintendent hemmed and hawed.

'A mole isn't much to go upon, Lady Eileen. Two women might have an identical mole very easily. You must remember that the Countess Radzky is a very well-known figure in Hungary.'

'Then this isn't the real Countess Radzky. I tell you I'm sure this is the same woman I saw there. And look at her tonight – the way we found her. I don't believe she ever fainted at all.'

'Oh, I shouldn't say that, Lady Eileen. That empty shell striking the bookcase beside her might have frightened any woman half out of her wits.'

'But what was she doing there anyway? One doesn't come down to look for a book with an electric torch.'

Battle scratched his cheek. He seemed unwilling to speak. He began to pace up and down the room, as though making up his mind. At last he turned to the girl.

'See here, Lady Eileen, I'm going to trust you. The Countess's conduct *is* suspicious. I know that as well as you do. It's very suspicious – but we've got to go carefully. There mustn't be any unpleasantness with the Embassies. One has got to be *sure*.'

'I see. If you were *sure* . . .'

'There's something else. During the war, Lady Eileen, there was a great outcry about German spies being left at large. Busybodies wrote letters to the papers about it. We paid no attention. Hard words didn't hurt us. The small fry were left alone. Why? Because through them, sooner or later, *we got the big fellow – the man at the top*.'

'You mean?'

'Don't bother about what I mean, Lady Eileen. But remember this. *I know all about the Countess*. And I want her let alone.

'And now,' added Superintendent Battle ruefully, 'I've got to think of something to say to Sir Stanley Digby!'

CHAPTER 23

SUPERINTENDENT BATTLE IN CHARGE

It was ten o'clock on the following morning. The sun poured in through the windows of the library, where Superintendent Battle had been at work since six. On a summons from him, George Lomax, Sir Oswald Coote and Jimmy Thesiger had just joined him, having repaired the fatigues of the night with a substantial breakfast. Jimmy's arm was in a sling, but he bore little trace of the night's affray.

The superintendent eyed all three of them benevolently, somewhat with the air of a kindly curator explaining a museum to little boys. On the table beside him were various objects, neatly labelled. Amongst them Jimmy recognized Leopold.

'Ah, Superintendent,' said George, 'I have been anxious to know how you have progressed. Have you caught the man?'

'He'll take a lot of catching, he will,' said the superintendent.

His failure in that respect did not appear to rankle with him.

George Lomax did not look particularly well pleased. He detested levity of any kind.

'I've got everything taped out pretty clearly,' went on the detective.

He took up two objects from the table.

'Here we've got the two bullets. The largest is a .455, fired from Mr Thesiger's Colt automatic. Grazed the window sash and I found it embedded in the trunk of that cedar tree. This little fellow was fired from the Mauser .25. After passing through Mr Thesiger's arm, it embedded itself in this armchair here. As for the pistol itself –'

'Well?' said Sir Oswald eagerly. 'Any fingerprints?'

Battle shook his head.

'The man who handled it wore gloves,' he said slowly.

'A pity,' said Sir Oswald.

'A man who knew his business would wear gloves. Am I right in thinking, Sir Oswald, that you found this pistol just about twenty yards from the bottom of the steps leading up to the terrace?'

Sir Oswald stepped to the window.

'Yes, almost exactly, I should say.'

'I don't want to find fault, but it would have been wiser on your part, sir, to leave it exactly as you found it.'

'I am sorry,' said Sir Oswald stiffly.

'Oh, it doesn't matter. I've been able to reconstruct things. There were your footprints, you see, leading up from the bottom of the garden, and a place where you had obviously stopped and stooped down, and a kind of dent in the grass which was highly suggestive. By the way, what was your theory of the pistol being there?'

'I presumed that it had been dropped by the man in his flight.'

Battle shook his head.

'Not dropped. Sir Oswald. There are two points against that. To begin with, there are only one set of footprints crossing the lawn just there – your own.'

'I see,' said Sir Oswald thoughtfully.

'Can you be sure of that, Battle?' put in George.

'Quite sure, sir. There is one other set of tracks crossing the lawn, Miss Wade's, but they are a good deal further to the left.'

He paused, and then went on: 'And there's the dent in the ground. The pistol must have struck the ground with some force. It all points to its having been thrown.'

'Well, why not?' said Sir Oswald. 'Say the man fled down the path to the left. He'd leave no footprints on the path and he'd hurl the pistol away from him into the middle of the lawn, eh, Lomax?'

George agreed by a nod of the head.

'It's true that he'd leave no footprints on the path,' said Battle, 'but from the shape of the dent and the way the turf was cut, I don't think the pistol was thrown from that direction. I think it was thrown from the terrace here.'

'Very likely,' said Sir Oswald. 'Does it matter, Superintendent?'

'Ah, yes, Battle,' broke in George. 'Is it – er – strictly relevant?'

'Perhaps not, Mr Lomax. But we like to get things just so, you know. I wonder now if one of you gentlemen would take this pistol and throw it. Will you, Sir Oswald? That's very kind. Stand just there in the window. Now fling it into the middle of the lawn.'

Sir Oswald complied, sending the pistol flying through the air with a powerful sweep of his arm. Jimmy Thesiger drew near with breathless interest. The superintendent lumbered off after it like a well-trained retriever. He reappeared with a beaming face.

'That's it, sir. Just the same kind of mark. Although, by the way, you sent it a good ten yards farther. But then, you're a very powerfully built man, aren't you, Sir Oswald? Excuse me, I thought I heard someone at the door.'

The superintendent's ears must have been very much sharper than anyone else's. Nobody else had heard a sound, but Battle was proved right, for Lady Coote stood outside, a medicine glass in her hand.

'Your medicine, Oswald,' she said, advancing into the room. 'You forgot it after breakfast.'

'I'm very busy, Maria,' said Sir Oswald. 'I don't want my medicine.'

'You would never take it if it wasn't for me,' said his wife serenely, advancing upon him. 'You're just like a naughty little boy. Drink it up now.'

And meekly, obediently, the great steel magnate drank it up!

Lady Coote smiled sadly and sweetly at everyone.

'Am I interrupting you? Are you very busy? Oh, look at those revolvers. Nasty, noisy, murdering things. To think, Oswald, that you might have been shot by the burglar last night.'

'You must have been alarmed when you found he was missing, Lady Coote,' said Battle.

'I didn't think of it at first,' confessed Lady Coote. 'This poor boy here' – she indicated Jimmy – 'being shot – and everything so dreadful, but so exciting. It wasn't till Mr Bateman asked me where Sir Oswald was that I remembered he'd gone out half an hour before for a stroll.'

'Sleepless, eh, Sir Oswald?' asked Battle.

'I am usually an excellent sleeper,' said Sir Oswald. 'But I must confess that last night I felt unusually restless. I thought the night air would do me good.'

'You came out through this window, I suppose?'

Was it his fancy, or did Sir Oswald hesitate for a moment before replying?

'Yes.'

'In your pumps too,' said Lady Coote, 'instead of putting thick shoes on. What would you do without me to look after you?'

She shook her head sadly.

'I think, Maria, if you don't mind leaving us – we have still a lot to discuss.'

'I know, dear, I'm just going.'

Lady Coote withdrew, carrying the empty medicine glass as though it were a goblet out of which she had just administered a death potion.

'Well, Battle,' said George Lomax, 'it all seems clear enough. Yes, perfectly clear. The man fires a shot, disabling Mr Thesiger, flings away the weapon, runs along the terrace and down the gravel path.'

'Where he ought to have been caught by my men,' put in Battle.

'Your men, if I may say so, Battle, seem to have been singularly remiss. They didn't see Miss Wade come in. If they could miss her coming in, they could easily miss the thief going out.'

Superintendent Battle opened his mouth to speak, then seemed to think better of it. Jimmy Thesiger looked at him curiously. He would have given a lot to know just what was in Superintendent Battle's mind.

'Must have been a champion runner,' was all the Scotland Yard man contented himself with saying.

'How do you mean, Battle?'

'Just what I say, Mr Lomax. I was round the corner of the terrace myself not fifty seconds after the shot was fired. And for a man to run all that distance towards me and get round the corner of the path before I appeared round the side of the house – well, as I say, he must have been a champion runner.'

'I am at a loss to understand you, Battle. You have some idea of your own which I have not yet – er – grasped. You say the man did not go across the lawn, and now you hint – What exactly do you hint? That the man did not go down the path? Then in your opinion – er – where *did* he go?'

For answer, Superintendent Battle jerked an eloquent thumb upwards.

'Eh?' said George.

The superintendent jerked harder than ever. George raised his head and looked at the ceiling.

'Up there,' said Battle. 'Up the ivy again.'

'Nonsense, Superintendent. What you are suggesting is impossible.'

'Not at all impossible, sir. He'd done it once. He could do it twice.'

'I don't mean impossible in that sense. But if the man wanted to escape, he'd never bolt back into the house.'

'Safest place for him, Mr Lomax.'

'But Mr O'Rourke's door was still locked on the inside when we came to him.'

'And how did you get to him? Through Sir Stanley's room. That's the way our man went. Lady Eileen tells me she saw the door knob of Mr O'Rourke's room move. That was when our friend was up there the first time. I suspect the key was under Mr O'Rourke's pillow. But his exit is clear enough the second time – through the communicating door and through Sir Stanley's room, which, of course, was empty. Like everyone else, Sir Stanley is rushing downstairs to the library. Our man's got a clear course.'

'And where did he go then?'

Superintendent Battle shrugged his burly shoulders and became evasive.

'Plenty of ways open. Into an empty room on the other side of the house and down the ivy again – out through a side door – or, just possibly, if it was an inside job, he – well, stayed in the house.'

George looked at him in shocked surprise.

'Really, Battle, I should – I should feel it very deeply if one of my servants – er – I have the most perfect reliance on them – it would distress me very much to have to suspect –'

'Nobody's asking you to suspect anyone, Mr Lomax. I'm just putting all the possibilities before you. The servants may be all right – probably are.'

'You have disturbed me,' said George. 'You have disturbed me greatly.'

His eyes appeared more protuberant than ever.

To distract him, Jimmy poked delicately at a curious blackened object on the table.

'What's this?' he asked.

'That's exhibit Z,' said Battle. 'The last of our little lot. It is, or rather it has been, a glove.'

He picked it up, the charred relic, and manipulated it with pride.

'Where did you find it?' asked Sir Oswald.

Battle jerked his head over his shoulder.

'In the grate – nearly burnt, but not quite. Queer; looks as though it had been chewed by a dog.'

'It might possibly be Miss Wade's,' suggested Jimmy. 'She has several dogs.'

The Superintendent shook his head.

'This isn't a lady's glove – no, not even the large kind of loose glove ladies wear nowadays. Put it on, sir, a moment.'

He adjusted the blackened object over Jimmy's hand.

'You see – it's large even for you.'

'Do you attach importance to this discovery?' inquired Sir Oswald coldly.

'You never know, Sir Oswald, what's going to be important or what isn't.'

There was a sharp tap at the door and Bundle entered.

'I'm so sorry,' she said apologetically. 'But Father has just rung up. He says I must come home because everybody is worrying him.'

She paused.

'Yes, my dear Eileen?' said George encouragingly, perceiving that there was more to come.

'I wouldn't have interrupted you – only that I thought it might perhaps have something to do with all this. You see, what has upset Father is that one of our footmen is missing. He went out last night and hasn't come back.'

'What is the man's name?' It was Sir Oswald who took up the cross-examination.

'John Bauer.'

'An Englishman?'

'I believe he calls himself a Swiss – but I think he's a German. He speaks English perfectly, though.'

'Ah!' Sir Oswald drew in his breath with a long, satisfied hiss. 'And he has been at Chimneys – how long?'

'Just under a month.'

Sir Oswald turned to the other two.

'Here is our missing man. You know, Lomax, as well as I do, that several foreign Governments are after the thing. I remember the man now perfectly – tall, well-drilled fellow. Came about a fortnight before we left. A clever move. Any new servants here would be closely scrutinized, but at Chimneys, five miles away –' He did not finish the sentence.

'You think the plan was laid so long beforehand?'

'Why not? There are millions in that formula, Lomax. Doubtless Bauer hoped to get access to my private papers at Chimneys, and to learn something of forthcoming arrangements from them. It seems likely that he may have had an accomplice in this house – someone who put him wise to the lie of the land and who saw to the doping of O'Rourke. But Bauer was the man Miss Wade saw climbing down the ivy – the big, powerful man.'

He turned to Superintendent Battle.

'Bauer was your man, Superintendent. And, somehow or other, you let him slip through your fingers.'

CHAPTER 24

BUNDLE WONDERS

There was no doubt that Superintendent Battle was taken aback. He fingered his chin thoughtfully.

'Sir Oswald is right, Battle,' said George. 'This is the man. Any hope of catching him?'

'There may be, sir. It certainly looks – well, suspicious. Of course the man may turn up again – at Chimneys, I mean.'

'Do you think it likely?'

'No, it isn't,' confessed Battle. 'Yes, it certainly looks as though Bauer were the man. But I can't quite see how he got in and out of these grounds unobserved.'

'I have already told you my opinion of the men you posted,' said George. 'Hopelessly inefficient – I don't mean to blame you, Superintendent, but –' His pause was eloquent.

'Ah, well,' said Battle lightly, 'my shoulders are broad.'

He shook his head and sighed.

'I must get to the telephone at once. Excuse me, gentlemen. I'm sorry, Mr Lomax – I feel I've rather bungled this business, But it's been puzzling, more puzzling than you know.'

He strode hurriedly from the room.

'Come into the garden,' said Bundle to Jimmy. 'I want to talk to you.'

They went out together through the window. Jimmy stared down at the lawn, frowning.

'What's the matter?' asked Bundle.

Jimmy explained the circumstances of the pistol throwing.

'I'm wondering,' he ended, 'what was in old Battle's mind when he got Coote to throw the pistol. Something, I'll swear. Anyhow, it landed up about ten yards farther than it should have done. You know, Bundle, Battle's a deep one.'

'He's an extraordinary man,' said Bundle. 'I want to tell you about last night.'

She retailed her conversation with the Superintendent. Jimmy listened attentively.

'So the Countess is No. 1,' he said thoughtfully. 'It all hangs together very well. No. 2 – Bauer – comes over from Chimneys.

He climbs up into O'Rourke's room, knowing that O'Rourke has had a sleeping draught administered to him – by the Countess somehow or other. The arrangement is that he is to throw the papers to the Countess, who will be waiting below. Then she'll nip back through the library and up to her room. If Bauer's caught leaving the grounds, they'll find nothing on him. Yes, it was a good plan – but it went wrong. No sooner is the Countess in the library than she hears me coming and has to jump behind the screen. Jolly awkward for her, because she can't warn her accomplice. No. 2 pinches the papers, looks out of the window, sees, as he thinks, the Countess waiting, pitches the papers down to her and proceeds to climb down the ivy, where he finds a nasty surprise in the shape of me waiting for him. Pretty nervy work for the Countess waiting behind her screen. All things considered, she told a pretty good story. Yes, it all hangs together very well.'

'Too well,' said Bundle decidedly.

'Eh?' said Jimmy surprised.

'What about No. 7 – No. 7, who never appears, but lives in the background. The Countess and Bauer? No, it's not so simple as that. Bauer was here last night, yes. But he was only here in case things went wrong – as they have done. His part is the part of scapegoat; to draw all attention from No. 7 – the boss.'

'I say, Bundle,' said Jimmy anxiously, 'you haven't been reading too much sensational literature, have you?'

Bundle threw him a glance of dignified reproach.

'Well,' said Jimmy, 'I'm not yet like the Red Queen. I can't believe six impossible things before breakfast.'

'It's after breakfast,' said Bundle.

'Or even after breakfast. We've got a perfectly good hypothesis which fits the facts – and you won't have it at any price, simply because, like the old riddle, you want to make things more difficult.'

'I'm sorry,' said Bundle, 'but I cling passionately to a mysterious No. 7 being a member of the house party.'

'What does Bill think?'

'Bill,' said Bundle coldly, 'is impossible.'

'Oh!' said Jimmy. 'I suppose you've told him about the Countess? He ought to be warned. Heaven knows what he'll go blabbing about otherwise.'

'He won't hear a word against her,' said Bundle. 'He's – oh, simply idiotic. I wish you'd drive it home to him about that mole.'

'You forget I wasn't in the cupboard,' said Jimmy. 'And anyway I'd rather not argue with Bill about his lady friend's mole. But surely he can't be such an ass as not to see that everything fits in?'

'He's every kind of ass,' said Bundle bitterly. 'You made the greatest mistake, Jimmy, in ever telling him at all.'

'I'm sorry,' said Jimmy. 'I didn't see it at the time – but I do now. I was a fool, but dash it all, old Bill –'

'You know what foreign adventuresses are,' said Bundle. 'How they get hold of one.'

'As a matter of fact, I don't,' said Jimmy. 'One has never tried to get hold of me.' And he sighed.

For a moment or two there was silence. Jimmy was turning things over in his mind. The more he thought about them the more unsatisfactory they seemed.

'You say that Battle wants the Countess left alone,' he said at last.

'Yes.'

'The idea being that through her he will get at someone else?'

Bundle nodded.

Jimmy frowned deeply as he tried to see where this led. Clearly Battle had some very definite idea in his mind.

'Sir Stanley Digby went up to town early this morning, didn't he,' he said.

'Yes.'

'O'Rourke with him?'

'Yes, I think so.'

'You don't think – no, that's impossible.'

'What?'

'That O'Rourke can be mixed up in this in any way.'

'It's possible,' said Bundle thoughtfully. 'He's got what one calls a very vivid personality. No, it wouldn't surprise me if – oh, to tell the truth, nothing would surprise me! In fact, there's only one person I'm really sure isn't No. 7.'

'Who's that?'

'Superintendent Battle.'

'Oh! I thought you were going to say George Lomax.'

'Ssh, here he comes.'

George was, indeed, bearing down upon them in an unmistakable manner. Jimmy made an excuse and slipped away. George sat down by Bundle.

'My dear Eileen, must you really leave us?'

'Well, Father seems to have got the wind up rather badly. I think I'd better go home and hold his hand.'

'This little hand will indeed be comforting,' said George, taking it and pressing it playfully. 'My dear Eileen, I understand your reasons and I honour you for them. In these days of changed and unsettled conditions –'

'He's off,' thought Bundle desperately.

'– when family life is at a premium – all the old standards falling! – It becomes our class to set an example to show that we, at least, are unaffected by modern conditions. They call us the Die Hards – I am proud of the term – I repeat I am proud of the term! There are things that *should* die hard – dignity, beauty, modesty, the sanctity of family life, filial respect – who dies if these shall live? As I was saying, my dear Eileen, I envy you the privileges of your youth. Youth! What a wonderful thing! What a wonderful word! And we do not appreciate it until we grow to – er – maturer years. I confess, my dear child, that I have in the past been disappointed by your levity. I see now that it was but the careless and charming levity of a child. I perceive now the serious and earnest beauty of your mind. You will allow me, I hope, to help you with your reading?'

'Oh, thank you,' said Bundle faintly.

'And you must never be afraid of me again. I was shocked when Lady Caterham told me that you stood in awe of me. I can assure you that I am a very humdrum sort of person.'

The spectacle of George being modest struck Bundle spellbound. George continued:

'Never be shy with me, dear child. And do not be afraid of boring me. It will be a great delight to me to – if I may say so – form your budding mind. I will be your political mentor. We have never needed young women of talent and charm in the Party more than we need them today. You may well be destined to follow in the footsteps of your aunt, Lady Caterham.'

This awful prospect knocked Bundle out completely. She could only stare helplessly at George. This did not discourage him – on the contrary. His main objection to women was that they talked too much. It was seldom that he found what he considered a really good listener. He smiled benignly at Bundle.

'The butterfly emerging from the chrysalis. A wonderful picture. I have a very interesting work on political economy. I will look it out now, and you can take it to Chimneys with you. When you have finished it, I will discuss it with you. Do not hesitate to write to me if any point puzzles you. I have many public duties but by unsparing work I can always make time for the affairs of my friends. I will look for the book.'

He strode away. Bundle gazed after him with a dazed expression. She was roused by the unexpected advent of Bill.

'Look here,' said Bill. 'What the hell was Codders holding your hand for?'

'It wasn't my hand,' said Bundle wildly. 'It was my budding mind.'

'Don't be an ass, Bundle.'

'Sorry, Bill, but I'm a little worried. Do you remember saying that Jimmy ran a grave risk down here?'

'So he does,' said Bill. 'It's frightfully hard to escape from Codders once he's got interested in you. Jimmy will be caught in the toils before he knows where he is.'

'It's not Jimmy who's caught – it's me,' said Bundle wildly. 'I shall have to meet endless Mrs Macattas, and read political economy and discuss it with George, and heaven knows where it will end!'

Bill whistled.

'Poor old Bundle. Been laying it on a bit thick, haven't you?'

'I must have done. Bill, I feel horribly entangled.'

'Never mind,' said Bill consolingly. 'George doesn't really believe in women standing for Parliament, so you won't have to stand up on platforms and talk a lot of junk, or kiss dirty babies in Bermondsey. Come and have a cocktail. It's nearly lunch-time.'

Bundle got up and walked by his side obediently.

'And I do so hate politics,' she murmured piteously.

'Of course you do. So do all sensible people. It's only people like Codders and Pongo who take them seriously and revel in them. But all the same,' said Bill, reverting suddenly to a former point, 'you oughtn't to let Codders hold your hand.'

'Why on earth not?' said Bundle. 'He's known me all my life.'

'Well, I don't like it.'

'Virtuous William – Oh, I say, look at Superintendent Battle.'

They were just passing in through a side door. A cupboard-like room opened out of the little hallway. In it were kept golf clubs, tennis racquets, bowls and other features of country house life. Superintendent Battle was conducting a minute examination of various golf clubs. He looked up a little sheepishly at Bundle's exclamation.

'Going to take up golf, Superintendent Battle?'

'I might do worse, Lady Eileen. They say it's never too late to start. And I've got one good quality that will tell at any game.'

'What's that?' asked Bill.

'I don't know when I'm beaten. If everything goes wrong, I turn to and start again!'

And with a determined look on his face, Superintendent Battle came out and joined them, shutting the door behind him.

CHAPTER 25

JIMMY LAYS HIS PLANS

Jimmy Thesiger was feeling depressed. Avoiding George, whom he suspected of being ready to tackle him on serious subjects, he stole quietly away after lunch. Proficient as he was in details of the Santa Fé boundary dispute, he had no wish to stand an examination on it this minute.

Presently what he hoped would happen came to pass. Loraine Wade, also unaccompanied, strolled down one of the shady garden paths. In a moment Jimmy was by her side. They walked for some minutes in silence and then Jimmy said tentatively:

'Loraine?'

'Yes?'

'Look here, I'm a bad chap at putting things – but what about it? What's wrong with getting a special licence and being married and living together happily ever afterwards?'

Loraine displayed no embarrassment at this surprising proposal. Instead she threw back her head and laughed frankly.

'Don't laugh at a chap,' said Jimmy reproachfully.

'I can't help it. You were so funny.'

'Loraine – you are a little devil.'

'I'm not. I'm what's called a thoroughly nice girl.'

'Only to those who don't know you – who are taken in by your delusive appearance of meekness and decorum.'

'I like your long words.'

'All out of crossword puzzles.'

'So educative.'

'Loraine, dear, don't beat about the bush. Will you or won't you?'

Loraine's face sobered. It took on its characteristic appearance of determination. Her small mouth hardened and her little chin shot out aggressively.

'No, Jimmy. Not while things are as they are at present – all unfinished.'

'I know we haven't done what we set out to do,' agreed Jimmy. 'But all the same – well, it's the end of a chapter. The papers are safe at the Air Ministry. Virtue triumphant. And – for the moment – nothing doing.'

'So – let's get married?' said Loraine with a slight smile.

'You've said it. Precisely the idea.'

But again Loraine shook her head.

'No, Jimmy. Until this thing's wound up – until we're safe –'

'You think we're in danger?'

'Don't you?'

Jimmy's cherubic pink face clouded over.

'You're right,' he said at last. 'If that extraordinary rigmarole of Bundle's is true – and I suppose, incredible as it sounds, it must be true – then we're not safe till we've settled with No. 7!'

'And the others?'

'No. – the others don't count. It's No. 7 with his own ways of working that frightens me. Because I don't know who he is or where to look for him.'

Loraine shivered.

'I've been frightened,' she said in a low voice. 'Ever since Gerry's death . . .'

'You needn't be frightened. There's nothing for you to be frightened about. You leave everything to me. I tell you, Loraine – *I'll get No. 7 yet.* Once we get him – well, I don't think there'll be much trouble with the rest of the gang, whoever they are.'

'*If* you get him – and suppose he gets you?'

'Impossible,' said Jimmy cheerfully. 'I'm much too clever. Always have a good opinion of yourself – that's my motto.'

'When I think of the things that might have happened last night –' Loraine shivered.

'Well, they didn't,' said Jimmy. 'We're both here, safe and sound – though I must admit my arm is confoundedly painful.'

'Poor boy.'

'Oh, one must expect to suffer in a good cause. And what with my wounds and my cheerful conversation, I've made a complete conquest of Lady Coote.'

'Oh! Do you think that important?'

'I've an idea it may come in useful.'

'You've got some plan in your mind, Jimmy. What is it?'

'The young hero never tells his plans,' said Jimmy firmly. 'They mature in the dark.'

'You are an idiot, Jimmy.'

'I know. I know. That's what everyone says. But I can assure you, Loraine, there's a lot of brain-work going on underneath. Now what about your plans? Got any?'

'Bundle has suggested that I should go to Chimneys with her for a bit.'

'Excellent,' said Jimmy approvingly. 'Nothing could be better. I'd like an eye kept on Bundle anyway. You never know what mad thing she won't get up to next. She's so frightfully unexpected. And the worst of it is, she's so astonishingly successful. I tell you, keeping Bundle out of mischief is a whole-time job.'

'Bill ought to look after her,' suggested Loraine.

'Bill's pretty busy elsewhere.'

'Don't you believe it,' said Loraine.

'What? Not the Countess? But the lad's potty about her.' Loraine continued to shake her head.

'There's something there I don't quite understand. But it's not the Countess with Bill – it's Bundle. Why, this morning, Bill was talking to me when Mr Lomax came out and sat down by

Bundle. He took her hand or something, and Bill was off like – like a rocket.'

'What a curious taste some people have,' observed Mr Thesiger. 'Fancy anyone who was talking to you wanting to do anything else. But you surprise me very much, Loraine. I thought our simple Bill was enmeshed in the toils of the beautiful foreign adventuress. Bundle thinks so, I know.'

'Bundle may,' said Loraine. 'But I tell you, Jimmy, it isn't so.'

'Then what's the big idea?'

'Don't you think it possible that Bill is doing a bit of sleuthing on his own?'

'Bill? He hasn't got the brains.'

'I'm not so sure. When a simple, muscular person like Bill does set out to be subtle, no one ever gives him credit for it.'

'And in consequence he can put in some good work. Yes, there's something in that. But all the same I'd never have thought it of Bill. He's doing the Countess's little woolly lamb to perfection. I think you're wrong, you know, Loraine. The Countess is an extraordinarily beautiful woman – not my type of course,' put in Mr Thesiger hastily – 'and old Bill has always had a heart like an hotel.'

Loraine shook her head, unconvinced.

'Well,' said Jimmy, 'have it your own way. We seem to have more or less settled things. You go back with Bundle to Chimneys, and for heaven's sake keep her from poking about in that Seven Dials place again. Heaven knows what will happen if she does.'

Loraine nodded.

'And now,' said Jimmy, 'I think a few words with Lady Coote would be advisable.'

Lady Coote was sitting on a garden seat doing wool-work. The subject was a disconsolate and somewhat misshapen young woman weeping over an urn.

Lady Coote made room for Jimmy by her side, and he promptly, being a tactful young man, admired her work.

'Do you like it?' said Lady Coote, pleased. 'It was begun by my Aunt Selina the week before she died. Cancer of the liver, poor thing.'

'How beastly,' said Jimmy.

'And how is the arm?'

'Oh, it's feeling quite all right. Bit of a nuisance and all that, you know.'

'You'll have to be careful,' said Lady Coote in a warning voice. 'I've known blood-poisoning set in – and in that case you might lose your arm altogether.'

'Oh! I say, I hope not.'

'I'm only warning you,' said Lady Coote.

'Where are you hanging out now?' inquired Mr Thesiger. 'Town – or where?'

Considering that he knew the answer to his query perfectly well, he put the question with a praiseworthy amount of ingenuousness.

Lady Coote sighed heavily.

'Sir Oswald has taken the Duke of Alton's place. Letherbury. You know it, perhaps?'

'Oh, rather. Topping place, isn't it?'

'Oh, I don't know,' said Lady Coote. 'It's a very large place, and gloomy, you know. Rows of picture galleries with such forbidding-looking people. What they call Old Masters are very depressing, I think. You should have seen a little house we had in Yorkshire, Mr Thesiger. When Sir Oswald was plain Mr Coote. Such a nice lounge hall and a cheerful drawing-room with an ingle-nook – a white striped paper with a frieze of wisteria I chose for it, I remember. Satin stripe, you know, not moiré. Much better taste, I always think. The dining-room faced north-east, so we didn't get much sun in it, but with a good bright scarlet paper and a set of those comic hunting prints – why, it was as cheerful as Christmas.'

In the excitement of these reminiscences, Lady Coote dropped several little balls of wool, which Jimmy dutifully retrieved.

'Thank you, my dear,' said Lady Coote. 'Now, what was I saying? Oh – about houses – yes, I do like a cheerful house. And choosing things for it gives you an interest.'

'I suppose Sir Oswald will be buying a place of his own one of these days,' suggested Jimmy. 'And then you can have it just as you like.'

Lady Coote shook her head sadly.

'Sir Oswald talks of a firm doing it – and you know what that means.'

'Oh! But they'd consult you!'

'It would be one of those grand places – all for the antique. They'd look down on the things I call comfortable and homey. Not but that Sir Oswald wasn't very comfortable and satisfied in his home always, and I daresay his tastes are just the same underneath. But nothing will suit him now but the best! He's got on wonderfully, and naturally he wants something to show for it, but many's the time I wonder where it will end.'

Jimmy looked sympathetic.

'It's like a runaway horse,' said Lady Coote. 'Got the bit between its teeth and away it goes. It's the same with Sir Oswald. He's got on, and he's got on, till he can't stop getting on. He's one of the richest men in England – but does that satisfy him? No, he wants still more. He wants to be – I don't know what he wants to be! I can tell you, it frightens me sometimes!'

'Like the Persian Johnny,' said Jimmy, 'who went about wailing for fresh worlds to conquer.'

Lady Coote nodded acquiescence without much knowing what Jimmy was talking about.

'What I wonder is – will his stomach stand it?' she went on tearfully. 'To have him an invalid – with his ideas – oh, it won't bear thinking of.'

'He looks very hearty,' said Jimmy consolingly.

'He's got something on his mind,' said Lady Coote. 'Worried, that's what he is. *I* know.'

'What's he worried about?'

'I don't know. Perhaps something at the works. It's a great comfort for him having Mr Bateman. Such an earnest young man – and so conscientious.'

'Marvellously conscientious,' agreed Jimmy.

'Oswald thinks a lot of Mr Bateman's judgment. He says that Mr Bateman is always right.'

'That was one of his worst characteristics years ago,' said Jimmy feelingly.

Lady Coote looked slightly puzzled.

'That was an awfully jolly week-end I had with you at Chimneys,' said Jimmy. 'I mean it would have been awfully jolly if it hadn't been for poor old Gerry kicking the bucket. Jolly nice girls.'

'I find girls very perplexing,' said Lady Coote. 'Not romantic, you know. Why, I embroidered some handkerchiefs for Sir Oswald with my own hair when we were engaged.'

'Did you?' said Jimmy. 'How marvellous. But I suppose girls haven't got long hair to do that nowadays.'

'That's true,' admitted Lady Coote. 'But, oh, it shows in lots of other ways. I remember when I was a girl, one of my – well, my young men – picked up a handful of gravel, and a girl who was with me said at once that he was treasuring it because my feet had trodden on it. Such a pretty idea, I thought. Though it turned out afterwards that he was taking a course in mineralogy – or do I mean geology? – at a technical school. But I liked the idea – and stealing a girl's handkerchief and treasuring it – all those sort of things.'

'Awkward if the girl wanted to blow her nose,' said the practical Mr Thesiger.

Lady Coote laid down her wool-work and looked searchingly but kindly at him.

'Come now,' she said. 'Isn't there some nice girl that you fancy? That you'd like to work and make a little home for?'

Jimmy blushed and mumbled.

'I thought you got on very well with one of those girls at Chimneys that time – Vera Daventry.'

'Socks?'

'They do call her that,' admitted Lady Coote. 'I can't think why. It isn't pretty.'

'Oh, she's a topper,' said Jimmy. 'I'd like to meet her again.'

'She's coming down to stay with us next week-end.'

'Is she?' said Jimmy, trying to infuse a large amount of wistful longing into the two words.

'Yes. Would – would you like to come?'

'I *would*,' said Jimmy heartily. 'Thanks ever so much, Lady Coote.'

And reiterating fervent thanks, he left her.

Sir Oswald presently joined his wife.

'What has that young jackanapes been boring you about?' he demanded. 'I can't stand that young fellow.'

'He's a dear boy,' said Lady Coote. 'And so brave. Look how he got wounded last night.'

'Yes, messing around where he'd no business to be.'

'I think you're very unfair, Oswald.'

'Never done an honest day's work in his life. A real waster if there ever was one. He'd never get on if he had his way to make in the world.'

'You must have got your feet damp last night,' said Lady Coote. 'I hope you won't get pneumonia. Freddie Richards died of it the other day. Dear me, Oswald, it makes my blood run cold to think of you wandering about with a dangerous burglar loose in the grounds. He might have shot you. I've asked Mr Thesiger down for next week-end, by the way.'

'Nonsense,' said Sir Oswald. 'I won't have that young man in my house, do you hear, Maria?'

'Why not?'

'That's my business.'

'I'm so sorry, dear,' said Lady Coote placidly. 'I've asked him now, so it can't be helped. Pick up that ball of pink wool, will you, Oswald?'

Sir Oswald complied, his face black as thunder. He looked at his wife and hesitated. Lady Coote was placidly threading her wool needle.

'I particularly don't want Thesiger down next week-end,' he said at last. 'I've heard a good deal about him from Bateman. He was at school with him.'

'What did Mr Bateman say?'

'He'd no good to say of him. In fact, he warned me very seriously against him.'

'He did, did he?' said Lady Coote thoughtfully.

'And I have the highest respect for Bateman's judgment. I've never known him wrong.'

'Dear me,' said Lady Coote. 'What a mess I seem to have made of things. Of course, I should never have asked him if I had known. You should have told me all this before, Oswald. It's too late now.'

She began to roll up her work very carefully. Sir Oswald looked at her, made as if to speak, then shrugged his shoulders. He followed her into the house. Lady Coote, walking ahead, wore a very faint smile on her face. She was fond of her husband, but she was also fond – in a quiet, unobtrusive, wholly womanly manner – of getting her own way.

CHAPTER 26

MAINLY ABOUT GOLF

'That friend of yours is a nice girl, Bundle,' said Lord Caterham.

Loraine had been at Chimneys for nearly a week, and had earned the high opinion of her host – mainly because of the charming readiness she had shown to be instructed in the science of the mashie shot.

Bored by his winter abroad, Lord Caterham had taken up golf. He was an execrable player and in consequence was profoundly enthusiastic over the game. He spent most of his mornings lifting mashie shots over various shrubs and bushes – or, rather, essaying to loft them, hacking large bits out of the velvety turf and generally reducing MacDonald to despair.

'We must lay out a little course,' said Lord Caterham, addressing a daisy. 'A sporting little course. Now then, just watch this one, Bundle. Off the right knee, slow back, keep the head still and use the wrists.'

The ball, heavily topped, scudded across the lawn and disappeared into the unfathomed depths of a great bank of rhododendrons.

'Curious,' said Lord Caterham. 'What did I do then, I wonder? As I was saying, Bundle, that friend of yours is a very nice girl. I really think I am inducing her to take quite an interest in the game. She hit some excellent shots this morning – really quite as good as I could do myself.'

Lord Caterham took another careless swing and removed an immense chunk of turf. MacDonald, who was passing, retrieved it and stamped it firmly back. The look he gave Lord Caterham would have caused anyone but an ardent golfer to sink through the earth.

'If MacDonald has been guilty of cruelty to Cootes, which I strongly suspect,' said Bundle, 'he's being punished now.'

'Why shouldn't I do as I like in my own garden?' demanded her father. 'MacDonald ought to be interested in the way my game is coming on – the Scotch are a great golfing nation.'

'You poor old man,' said Bundle. 'You'll never be a golfer – but at any rate it keeps you out of mischief.'

'Not at all,' said Lord Caterham. 'I did the long sixth in five the other day. The pro was very surprised when I told him about it.'

'He would be,' said Bundle.

'Talking of Cootes, Sir Oswald plays a fair game – a very fair game. Not a pretty style – too stiff. But straight down the middle every time. But curious how the cloven hoof shows – won't give you a six-inch putt! Makes you put it in every time. Now I don't like that.'

'I suppose he's a man who likes to be sure,' said Bundle.

'It's contrary to the spirit of the game,' said her father. 'And he's not interested in the theory of the thing either. Now, that secretary chap, Bateman, is quite different. It's the theory interests him. I was slicing badly with my spoon; and he said it all came from too much right arm; and he evolved a very interesting theory. It's all left arm in golf – the left arm is the arm that counts. He says he plays tennis left-handed but golf with ordinary clubs because there his superiority with the left arm tells.'

'And did he play very marvellously?' inquired Bundle.

'No, he didn't,' confessed Lord Caterham. 'But then he may have been off his game. I see the theory all right and I think there's a lot in it. Ah! Did you see that one, Bundle? Right over the rhododendrons. A perfect shot. Ah! If one could be sure of doing that every time – Yes, Tredwell, what is it?'

Tredwell addressed Bundle.

'Mr Thesiger would like to speak to you on the telephone, my lady.'

Bundle set off at full speed for the house, yelling 'Loraine, Loraine,' as she did so. Loraine joined her just as she was lifting the receiver.

'Hallo, is that you, Jimmy?'

'Hallo. How are you?'

'Very fit, but a bit bored.'

'How's Loraine?'

'She's all right. She's here. Do you want to speak to her?'

'In a minute. I've got a lot to say. To begin with, I'm going down to the Cootes for the week-end,' he said significantly. 'Now, look here, Bundle, you don't know how one gets hold of skeleton keys, do you?'

'Haven't the foggiest. Is it really necessary to take skeleton keys to the Cootes?'

'Well, I had a sort of idea they'd come in handy. You don't know the sort of shop one gets them at?'

'What you want is a kindly burglar friend to show you the ropes.'

'I do, Bundle, I do. And unfortunately I haven't got one. I thought perhaps your bright brain might grapple successfully with the problem. But I suppose I shall have to fall back upon Stevens as usual. He'll be getting some funny ideas in his head soon about me – first a blue-nosed automatic – and now skeleton keys. He'll think I've joined the criminal classes.'

'Jimmy?' said Bundle.

'Yes?'

'Look here – be careful, won't you? I mean if Sir Oswald finds you nosing around with skeleton keys – well, I should think he could be very unpleasant when he likes.'

'Young man of pleasing appearance in the dock! All right, I'll be careful. Pongo's the fellow I'm really frightened of. He sneaks around so on those flat feet of his. You never hear him coming. And he always did have a genius for poking his nose in where he wasn't wanted. But trust to the boy hero.'

'Well, I wish Loraine and I were going to be there to look after you.'

'Thank you, nurse. As a matter of fact, though, I have a scheme.'

'Yes?'

'Do you think you and Loraine might have a convenient car breakdown near Letherbury tomorrow morning? It's not so very far from you, is it?'

'Forty miles. That's nothing.'

'I thought it wouldn't be – to you! Don't kill Loraine though. I'm rather fond of Loraine. All right, then – somewhere round about quarter to half-past twelve.'

'So that they invite us to lunch?'

'That's the idea. I say, Bundle, I ran into that girl Socks yesterday, and what do you think – Terence O'Rourke is going to be down there this week-end!'

'Jimmy, do you think he –?'

'Well – suspect everyone, you know. That's what they say. He's a wild lad, and daring as they make them. I wouldn't put it past him to run a secret society. He and the Countess might be in this together. He was out in Hungary last year.'

'But he could pinch the formula any time.'

'That's just what he couldn't. He'd have to do it under circumstances where he couldn't be suspected. But the retreat up the ivy and into his own bed – well, that would be rather neat. Now for instructions. After a few polite nothings to Lady Coote, you and Loraine are to get hold of Pongo and O'Rourke by hook or by crook and keep them occupied till lunch-time. See? It oughtn't to be difficult for a couple of beautiful girls like you.'

'You're using the best butter, I see.'

'A plain statement of fact.'

'Well, at any rate, your instructions are duly noted. Do you want to talk to Loraine now?'

Bundle passed over the receiver and tactfully left the room.

CHAPTER 27

NOCTURNAL ADVENTURE

Jimmy Thesiger arrived at Letherbury on a sunny autumn afternoon and was greeted affectionately by Lady Coote and with cold dislike by Sir Oswald. Aware of the keen matchmaking eye of Lady Coote upon him, Jimmy took pains to make himself extremely agreeable to Socks Daventry.

O'Rourke was there in excellent spirits. He was inclined to be official and secretive about the mysterious events at the Abbey, about which Socks catechized him freely, but his official reticence took a novel form . . . namely that of embroidering the tale of events in such a fantastic manner that nobody could possibly guess what the truth might have been.

'Four masked men with revolvers? Is that really so?' demanded Socks severely.

'Ah! I'm remembering now that there was the round half-dozen of them to hold me down and force the stuff down my throat. Sure, and I thought it was poison, and I done for entirely.'

'And what was stolen, or what did they try and steal?'

'What else but the crown jewels of Russia that were brought to Mr Lomax secretly to deposit in the Bank of England.'

'What a bloody liar you are,' said Socks without emotion.

'A liar, I? And the jewels brought over by aeroplane with my best friend as pilot. This is secret history I'm telling you, Socks. Will you ask Jimmy Thesiger there if you don't believe me. Not that I'd be putting any trust in what he'd say.'

'Is it true,' said Socks, 'that George Lomax came down without his false teeth? That's what I want to know.'

'There were two revolvers,' said Lady Coote. 'Nasty things. I saw them myself. It's a wonder this poor boy wasn't killed.'

'Oh, I was born to be hanged,' said Jimmy.

'I hear that there was a Russian countess there of subtle beauty,' said Socks. 'And that she vamped Bill.'

'Some of the things she said about Buda Pesth were too dreadful,' said Lady Coote. 'I shall never forget them. Oswald, we must send a subscription.'

Sir Oswald grunted.

'I'll make a note of it, Lady Coote,' said Rupert Bateman.

'Thank you, Mr Bateman. I feel one ought to do something as a thank offering. I can't imagine how Sir Oswald escaped being shot – letting alone die of pneumonia.'

'Don't be foolish, Maria,' said Sir Oswald.

'I've always had a horror of cat burglars,' said Lady Coote.

'Think of having the luck to meet one face to face. How thrilling!' murmured Socks.

'Don't you believe it,' said Jimmy. 'It's damned painful.' And he patted his right arm gingerly.

'How is the poor arm?' inquired Lady Coote.

'Oh, pretty well all right now. But it's been the most confounded nuisance having to do everything with the left hand. I'm no good whatever with it.'

'Every child should be brought up to be ambidexterous,' said Sir Oswald.

'Oh!' said Socks, somewhat out of her depth. 'Is that like seals?'

'Not amphibious,' said Mr Bateman. 'Ambidexterous means using either hand equally well.'

'Oh!' said Socks, looking at Sir Oswald with respect. 'Can you?'

'Certainly; I can write with either hand.'

'But not with both at once?'

'That would not be practical,' said Sir Oswald shortly.

'No,' said Socks thoughtfully. 'I suppose that would be a bit too subtle.'

'It would be a grand thing now in a Government department,' observed Mr O'Rourke, 'if one could keep the right hand from knowing what the left hand was doing.'

'Can you use both hands?'

'No, indeed. I'm the most right-handed person that ever was.'

'But you deal cards with your left hand,' said the observant Bateman. 'I noticed the other night.'

'Oh, but that's different entirely,' said Mr O'Rourke easily.

A gong with a sombre note pealed out and everyone went upstairs to dress for dinner.

After dinner Sir Oswald and Lady Coote, Mr Bateman and Mr O'Rourke played bridge and Jimmy passed a flirtatious evening with Socks. The last words Jimmy heard as he retreated up the staircase that night were Sir Oswald saying to his wife:

'You'll never make a bridge player, Maria.'

And her reply:

'I know, dear. So you always say. You owe Mr O'Rourke another pound, Oswald. That's right.'

It was some two hours later that Jimmy crept noiselessly (or so he hoped) down the stairs. He made one brief visit to the dining-room and then found his way to Sir Oswald's study. There, after listening intently for a minute or two, he set to work. Most of the drawers of the desk were locked, but a curiously shaped bit of wire in Jimmy's hand soon saw to that. One by one the drawers yielded to his manipulations.

Drawer by drawer he sorted through methodically, being careful to replace everything in the same order. Once or twice he stopped to listen, fancying he heard some distant sound. But he remained undisturbed.

The last drawer was looked through. Jimmy now knew – or could have known had he been paying attention – many interesting details relating to steel; but he had found nothing of what he wanted – a reference to Herr Eberhard's invention or anything that could give him a clue to the identity of the mysterious No. 7. He had, perhaps, hardly hoped that he would. It was an off-chance and he had taken it – but he had not expected much result – except by sheer luck.

He tested the drawers to make sure that he had relocked them securely. He knew Rupert Bateman's powers of minute observation and glanced round the room to make sure that he had left no incriminating trace of his presence.

'That's that,' he muttered to himself softly. 'Nothing there. Well, perhaps I'll have better luck tomorrow morning – if the girls only play up.'

He came out of the study, closing the door behind him and locking it. For a moment he thought he heard a sound quite near him, but decided he had been mistaken. He felt his way noiselessly along the great hall. Just enough light came from the high vaulted windows to enable him to pick his way without stumbling into anything.

Again he heard a soft sound – he heard it quite certainly this time and without the possibility of making a mistake. He was not alone in the hall. Somebody else was there, moving as stealthily as he was. His heart beat suddenly very fast.

With a sudden spring he jumped to the electric switch and turned on the lights. The sudden glare made him blink – but he saw plainly enough. Not four feet away stood Rupert Bateman.

'My goodness, Pongo,' cried Jimmy, 'you did give me a start. Slinking about like that in the dark.'

'I heard a noise,' explained Mr Bateman severely. 'I thought burglars had got in and I came down to see.'

Jimmy looked thoughtfully at Mr Bateman's rubber-soled feet.

'You think of everything, Pongo,' he said genially. 'Even a lethal weapon.'

His eye rested on the bulge in the other's pocket.

'It's as well to be armed. One never knows whom one may meet.'

'I am glad you didn't shoot,' said Jimmy. 'I'm a bit tired of being shot at.'

'I might easily have done so,' said Mr Bateman.

'It would be dead against the law if you did,' said Jimmy. 'You've got to make quite sure the beggar's house-breaking, you know, before you pot at him. You mustn't jump to conclusions.

Otherwise you'd have to explain why you shot a guest on a perfectly innocent errand like mine.'

'By the way what did you come down for?'

'I was hungry,' said Jimmy. 'I rather fancied a dry biscuit.'

'There are some biscuits in a tin by your bed,' said Rupert Bateman.

He was staring at Jimmy very intently through his horn-rimmed spectacles.

'Ah! That's where the staff work has gone wrong, old boy. There's a tin there with 'Biscuits for Starving Visitors' on it. But when the starving visitor opened it – nothing inside. So I just toddled down to the dining-room.'

And with a sweet, ingenuous smile, Jimmy produced from his dressing-gown pocket a handful of biscuits.

There was a moment's pause.

'And now I think I'll toddle back to bed,' said Jimmy. 'Night-night, Pongo.'

With an affectation of nonchalance, he mounted the staircase. Rupert Bateman followed him. At the doorway of his room, Jimmy paused as if to say good night once more.

'It's an extraordinary thing about these biscuits,' said Mr Bateman. 'Do you mind if I just –?'

'Certainly, laddie, look for yourself.'

Mr Bateman strode across the room, opened the biscuit box and stared at its emptiness.

'Very remiss,' he murmured. 'Well, good night.'

He withdrew. Jimmy sat on the edge of his bed listening for a minute.

'That was a narrow shave,' he murmured to himself. 'Suspicious sort of chap, Pongo. Never seems to sleep. Nasty habit of his, prowling around with a revolver.'

He got up and opened one of the drawers of the dressing-table. Beneath an assortment of ties lay a pile of biscuits.

'There's nothing for it,' said Jimmy. 'I shall have to eat the damned things. Ten to one, Pongo will come prowling round in the morning.'

With a sigh, he settled down to a meal of biscuits for which he had no inclination whatever.

CHAPTER 28

SUSPICIONS

It was just on the appointed hour of twelve o'clock that Bundle and Loraine entered the park gates, having left the Hispano at an adjacent garage.

Lady Coote greeted the two girls with surprise, but distinct pleasure, and immediately pressed them to stay to lunch.

O'Rourke, who had been reclining in an immense armchair, began at once to talk with great animation to Loraine, who was listening with half an ear to Bundle's highly technical explanation of the mechanical trouble which had affected the Hispano.

'And we said,' ended Bundle, 'how marvellous that the brute should have broken down just here! Last time it happened was on a Sunday at a place called Little Speddlington under the Hill. And it lived up to its name, I can tell you.'

'That would be a grand name on the films,' remarked O'Rourke.

'Birth place of the simple country maiden,' suggested Socks.

'I wonder now,' said Lady Coote, 'where Mr Thesiger is?'

'He's in the billiard-room, I think,' said Socks. 'I'll fetch him.'

She went off, but had hardly gone a minute when Rupert Bateman appeared upon the scene, with the harassed and serious air usual to him.

'Yes, Lady Coote? Thesiger said you were asking for me. How do you do, Lady Eileen –'

He broke off to greet the two girls, and Loraine immediately took the field.

'Oh, Mr Bateman! I've been wanting to see you. Wasn't it you who was telling me what to do for a dog when he is continually getting sore paws?'

The secretary shook his head.

'It must have been someone else, Miss Wade. Though, as a matter of fact, I do happen to know –'

'What a wonderful man you are,' interrupted Loraine. 'You know about everything.'

'One should keep abreast of modern knowledge,' said Mr Bateman seriously. 'Now about your dog's paws –'

Terence O'Rourke murmured *sotto voce* to Bundle:

''Tis a man like that writes all those little paragraphs in the weekly papers. "It is not generally known that to keep a brass fender uniformly bright, etc.;" "The dorper beetle is one of the most interesting characters in the insect world;" "The marriage customs of the Fingalese Indian;" and so on.'

'General information, in fact.'

'And what more horrible two words could you have?' said Mr O'Rourke, and added piously: 'Thank the heavens above I'm an educated man and know nothing whatever upon any subject at all.'

'I see you've got clock golf here,' said Bundle to Lady Coote.

'I'll take you on at it, Lady Eileen,' said O'Rourke.

'Let's challenge those two,' said Bundle. 'Loraine, Mr O'Rourke and I want to take you and Mr Bateman on at clock golf.'

'Do play, Mr Bateman,' said Lady Coote, as the secretary showed a momentary hesitation. 'I'm sure Sir Oswald doesn't want you.'

The four went out on the lawn.

'Very cleverly managed, what?' whispered Bundle to Loraine. 'Congratulations on our girlish tact.'

The round ended just before one o'clock, victory going to Bateman and Loraine.

'But I think you'll agree with me, partner,' said Mr O'Rourke, 'that we played a more sporting game.'

He lagged a little behind with Bundle.

'Old Pongo's a cautious player – and takes no risks. Now, with me it's neck or nothing. And a fine motto through life, don't you agree, Lady Eileen?'

'Hasn't it ever landed you in trouble?' asked Bundle laughing.

'To be sure it has. Millions of times. But I'm still going strong. Sure, it'll take the hangman's noose to defeat Terence O'Rourke.'

Just then Jimmy Thesiger strolled round the corner of the house.

'Bundle, by all that's wonderful!' he exclaimed.

'You've missed competing in the Autumn Meeting,' said O'Rourke.

'I'd gone for a stroll,' said Jimmy. 'Where did these girls drop from?'

'We came on our flat feet,' said Bundle. 'The Hispano let us down.'

And she narrated the circumstances of the breakdown.

Jimmy listened with sympathetic attention.

'Hard luck,' he vouchsafed. 'If it's going to take some time, I'll run you back in my car after lunch.'

A gong sounded at that moment and they all went in. Bundle observed Jimmy covertly. She thought she had noticed an unusual note of exultance in his voice. She had the feeling that things had gone well.

After lunch they took a polite leave of Lady Coote, and Jimmy volunteered to run them down to the garage in his car. As soon as they had started the same words burst simultaneously from both girls' lips:

'Well?'

Jimmy chose to be provoking.

'Well?'

'Oh, pretty hearty, thanks. Slight indigestion owing to over-indulgence in dry biscuits.'

'But what has happened?'

'I tell you. Devotion to the cause made me eat too many dry biscuits. But did our hero flinch? No, he did not.'

'Oh, Jimmy,' said Loraine reproachfully, and he softened.

'What do you really want to know?'

'Oh, everything. Didn't we do it well? I mean, the way we kept Pongo and Terence O'Rourke in play.'

'I congratulate you on the handling of Pongo. O'Rourke was probably a sitter – but Pongo is made of other stuff. There's only one word for that lad – it was in the *Sunday Newsbag* crossword last week. Word of ten letters meaning everywhere at once. Ubiquitous. That described Pongo down to the ground. You can't go anywhere without running into him – and the worst of it is you never hear him coming.'

'You think he's dangerous?'

'Dangerous? Of course he's not dangerous. Fancy Pongo being dangerous. He's an ass. But, as I said just now, he's an ubiquitous ass. He doesn't even seem to need sleep like ordinary mortals. In fact, to put it bluntly, the fellow's a damned nuisance.'

And, in a somewhat aggrieved manner, Jimmy described the events of the previous evening.

Bundle was not very sympathetic.

'I don't know what you think you're doing anyway, mooching around here.'

'No. 7,' said Jimmy crisply. 'That's what I'm after. No. 7.'

'And you think you'll find him in this house?'

'I thought I might find a clue.'

'And you didn't?'

'Not last night – no.'

'But this morning,' said Loraine, breaking in suddenly. 'Jimmy, you did find something this morning. I can see it by your face.'

'Well, I don't know if it is anything. But during the course of my stroll –'

'Which stroll didn't take you far from the house, I imagine.'

'Strangely enough, it didn't. Round trip of the interior, we might call it. Well, as I say, I don't know whether there's anything in it or not. But I found this.'

With the celerity of a conjurer he produced a small bottle and tossed it over to the girls. It was half full of a white powder.

'What do you think it is?' asked Bundle.

'A white crystalline powder, that's what it is,' said Jimmy. 'And to any reader of detective fiction those words are both familiar and suggestive. Of course, if it turns out to be a new kind of patent tooth-powder, I shall be chagrined and annoyed.'

'Where did you find it?' asked Bundle sharply.

'Ah!' said Jimmy, 'that's my secret.'

And from that point he would not budge in spite of cajolery and insult.

'Here we are at the garage,' he said. 'Let's hope the high-mettled Hispano has not been subjected to any indignities.'

The gentleman at the garage presented a bill for five shillings and made a few vague remarks about loose nuts. Bundle paid him with a sweet smile.

'It's nice to know we all get money for nothing sometimes,' she murmured to Jimmy.

The three stood together in the road, silent for the moment as they each pondered the situation.

'I know,' said Bundle suddenly.

'Know what?'

'Something I meant to ask you – and nearly forgot. Do you remember that glove Superintendent Battle found – the half-burnt one?'

'Yes.'

'Didn't you say that he tried it on your hand?'

'Yes – it was a shade big. That fits in with the idea of its being a big, hefty man who wore it.'

'That's not at all what I'm bothering about. Never mind the size of it. George and Sir Oswald were both there too, weren't they?'

'Yes.'

'He could have given it to either of them to fit on?'

'Yes, of course –'

'But he didn't. He chose you. Jimmy, don't you see what that means?'

Mr Thesiger stared at her.

'I'm sorry, Bundle. Possibly the jolly old brain isn't functioning as well as usual, but I haven't the faintest idea what you're talking about.'

'Don't you see, Loraine?'

Loraine looked at her curiously, but shook her head.

'Does it mean anything in particular?'

'Of course it does. Don't you see – Jimmy had his right hand in a sling.'

'By Jove, Bundle,' said Jimmy slowly. 'It was rather odd now I come to think of it; it's being a left-hand glove, I mean. Battle never said anything.'

'He wasn't going to draw attention to it. By trying it on you it might pass without notice being drawn to it, and he talked about the size just to put everybody off. But surely it must mean that the man who shot at you held the pistol in his *left* hand.'

'So we've got to look for a left-handed man,' said Loraine thoughtfully.

'Yes, and I'll tell you another thing. That was what Battle was doing looking through the golf clubs. He was looking for a left-handed man's.'

'By Jove,' said Jimmy suddenly.

'What is it?'

'Well, I don't suppose there's anything in it, but it's rather curious.'

He retailed the conversation at tea the day before.

'So Sir Oswald Coote is ambidexterous?' said Bundle.

'Yes. And I remember now on that night at Chimneys – you know, the night Gerry Wade died – I was watching the bridge and thinking idly how awkwardly someone was dealing – and then realizing that it was because they were dealing with the left hand. Of course, it must have been Sir Oswald.'

They all three looked at each other. Loraine shook her head.

'A man like Sir Oswald Coote! It's impossible. What could he have to gain by it?'

'It seems absurd,' said Jimmy. 'And yet –'

'No. 7 has his own ways of working,' quoted Bundle softly. 'Supposing this is the way Sir Oswald has really made his fortune?'

'But why stage all that comedy at the Abbey when he'd had the formula at his own works?'

'There might be ways of explaining that,' said Loraine. 'The same line of argument you used about Mr O'Rourke. Suspicion had to be diverted from him and placed in another quarter.'

Bundle nodded eagerly.

'It all fits in. Suspicion is to fall on Bauer and the Countess. Who on earth would ever dream of suspecting Sir Oswald Coote?'

'I wonder if Battle does,' said Jimmy slowly.

Some chord of memory vibrated in Bundle's mind. *Superintendent Battle plucking an ivy leaf off the millionaire's coat.*

Had Battle suspected all the time?

CHAPTER 29

SINGULAR BEHAVIOUR OF GEORGE LOMAX

'Mr Lomax is here, my lord.'

Lord Caterham started violently, for, absorbed in the intricacies of what not to do with the left wrist, he had not heard the butler approach over the soft turf. He looked at Tredwell more in sorrow than in anger.

'I told you at breakfast, Tredwell, that I should be particularly engaged this morning.'

'Yes, my lord, but –'

'Go and tell Mr Lomax that you have made a mistake, that I am out in the village, that I am laid up with the gout, or, if all else fails, that I am dead.'

'Mr Lomax, my lord, has already caught sight of your lordship when driving up the drive.'

Lord Caterham sighed deeply.

'He would. Very well, Tredwell, I am coming.'

In a manner highly characteristic, Lord Caterham was always most genial when his feelings were in reality the reverse. He greeted George now with a heartiness quite unparalleled.

'My dear fellow, my dear fellow. Delighted to see you. Absolutely delighted. Sit down. Have a drink. Well, well, this is splendid!'

And having pushed George into a large arm-chair, he sat down opposite him and blinked nervously.

'I wanted to see you very particularly,' said George.

'Oh!' said Lord Caterham faintly, and his heart sank, whilst his mind raced actively over all the dread possibilities that might lie behind that simple phrase.

'*Very* particularly,' said George with heavy emphasis.

Lord Caterham's heart sank lower than ever. He felt that something was coming worse than anything he had yet thought of.

'Yes?' he said, with a courageous attempt at nonchalance.

'Is Eileen at home?'

Lord Caterham felt reprieved, but slightly surprised.

'Yes, yes,' he said. 'Bundle's here. Got that friend of hers with her – the little Wade girl. Very nice girl – *very* nice girl. Going to be quite a good golfer one day. Nice easy swing –'

He was chatting garrulously on when George interrupted with ruthlessness:

'I am glad that Eileen is at home. Perhaps I might have an interview with her presently?'

'Certainly, my dear fellow, certainly.' Lord Caterham still felt very surprised, but was still enjoying the sensation of reprieve. 'If it doesn't bore you.'

'Nothing could bore me less,' said George. 'I think, Caterham, if I may say so, that you hardly appreciate the fact that Eileen is grown up. She is no longer a child. She is a woman, and, if I may say so, a very charming and talented woman. The man who succeeds in winning her love will be extremely lucky. I repeat it – extremely lucky.'

'Oh, I daresay,' said Lord Caterham. 'But she's very restless, you know. Never content to be in one place for more than two minutes together. However, I daresay young fellows don't mind that nowadays.'

'You mean that she is not content to stagnate. Eileen has brains, Caterham; she is ambitious. She interests herself in the questions of the day, and brings her fresh and vivid young intellect to bear upon them.'

Lord Caterham stared at him. It occurred to him that what was so often referred to as 'the strain of modern life' had begun to tell upon George. Certainly his description of Bundle seemed to Lord Caterham ludicrously unlike.

'Are you sure you are feeling quite well?' he asked anxiously.

George waved the inquiry aside impatiently.

'Perhaps, Caterham, you begin to have some inkling of my purpose in visiting you this morning. I am not a man to undertake fresh responsibilities lightly. I have a proper sense, I hope, of what is due to the position I hold. I have given this matter my deep and earnest consideration. Marriage, especially at my age, is not to be undertaken without full – er – consideration. Equality of birth, similarity of tastes, general suitability, and the same religious creed – all these things are necessary and the pros and cons have to be weighed and considered. I can, I think, offer my wife a position in society that is not to be despised. Eileen will grace that position admirably. By birth and breeding she is fitted for it, and her brains and her acute political sense cannot but further my career to our mutual advantage. I am aware, Caterham, that there is – er – some disparity in years. But I can assure you that I feel full of vigour – in my prime. The balance of years should be on the husband's side. And Eileen has serious tastes – an older man will suit her better than some young jackanapes without either experience or *savoir-faire*. I can assure you, my dear Caterham, that I will cherish her – er – exquisite youth; I will cherish it – er – it will be appreciated. To watch the exquisite flower of her mind unfolding – what a privilege! And to think that I never realized –'

He shook his head deprecatingly and Lord Caterham, finding his voice with difficulty, said blankly:

'Do I understand you to mean – ah, my dear fellow, you can't want to marry Bundle?'

'You are surprised. I suppose to you it seems sudden. I have your permission, then, to speak to her?'

'Oh, yes,' said Lord Caterham. 'If it's permission you want – of course you can. But you know, Lomax, I really shouldn't if I were you. Just go home and think it over like a good fellow. Count twenty. All that sort of thing. Always a pity to propose and make a fool of yourself.'

'I daresay you mean your advice kindly, Caterham, though I must confess that you put it somewhat strangely. But I have made up my mind to put my fortune to the test. I may see Eileen?'

'Oh, it's nothing to do with me,' said Lord Caterham hastily; 'Eileen settles her own affairs. If she came to me tomorrow and said she was going to marry the chauffeur, I shouldn't make any objections. It's the only way nowadays. Your children can make life damned unpleasant if you don't give in to them in every way. I say to Bundle, "Do as you like, but don't worry me," and really, on the whole, she is amazingly good about it.'

George stood up, intent upon his purpose.

'Where shall I find her?'

'Well, really, I don't know,' said Lord Caterham vaguely. 'She might be anywhere. As I told you just now, she's never in the same place for two minutes together. No repose.'

'And I suppose Miss Wade will be with her? It seems to me, Caterham, that the best plan would be for you to ring the bell and ask your butler to find her, saying that I wish to speak to her for a few minutes.'

Lord Caterham pressed the bell obediently.

'Oh, Tredwell,' he said, when the bell was answered. 'Just find her ladyship, will you. Tell her Mr Lomax is anxious to speak to her in the drawing-room.'

'Yes, my lord.'

Tredwell withdrew. George seized Lord Caterham's hand and wrung it warmly, much to the latter's discomfort.

'A thousand thanks,' he said. 'I hope soon to bring you good news.'

He hastened from the room.

'Well,' said Lord Caterham. 'Well!'

And after a long pause:

'What *has* Bundle been up to?'

The door opened again.

'Mr Eversleigh, my lord.'

As Bill hastened in, Lord Caterham caught his hand and spoke earnestly.

'Hullo, Bill. You're looking for Lomax, I suppose? Look here, if you want to do a good turn, hurry to the drawing-room and tell him the Cabinet have called an immediate meeting, or get him away somehow. It's really not fair to let the poor devil make an ass of himself all for some silly girl's prank.'

'I've not come for Codders,' said Bill. 'Didn't know he was here. It's Bundle I want to see. Is she anywhere about?'

'You can't see her,' said Lord Caterham. 'Not just now, at any rate. George is with her.'

'Well – what does it matter?'

'I think it does rather,' said Lord Caterham. 'He's probably spluttering horribly at this minute, and we mustn't do anything to make it worse for him.'

'But what is he saying?'

'Heaven knows,' said Lord Caterham. 'A lot of damned nonsense, anyway. Never say too much, that was always my motto. Grab the girl's hand and let events take their course.'

Bill stared at him.

'But look here, sir, I'm in a hurry. I must talk to Bundle –'

'Well, I don't suppose you'll have to wait long. I must confess I'm rather glad to have you here with me – I suppose Lomax will insist on coming back and talking to me when it's all over.'

'When what's all over? What is Lomax supposed to be doing?'

'Hush,' said Lord Caterham. 'He's proposing.'

'Proposing? Proposing what?'

'Marriage. To Bundle. Don't ask me why. I suppose he's come to what they call the dangerous age. I can't explain it any other way.'

'Proposing to Bundle? The dirty swine. At his age.'

Bill's face grew crimson.

'He says he's in the prime of life,' said Lord Caterham cautiously.

'He? Why, he's decrepit – senile! I –' Bill positively choked.

'Not at all,' said Lord Caterham coldly. 'He's five years younger than I am.'

'Of all the damned cheek! Codders and Bundle! A girl like Bundle! You oughtn't to have allowed it.'

'I never interfere,' said Lord Caterham.

'You ought to have told him what you thought of him.'

'Unfortunately modern civilization rules that out,' said Lord Caterham regretfully. 'In the Stone Age now – but, dear me, I suppose even then I shouldn't be able to do it – being a small man.'

'Bundle! Bundle! Why, I've never dared to ask Bundle to marry me because I knew she'd only laugh. And George – a disgusting wind-bag, an unscrupulous hypocritical old hot-air merchant – a foul, poisonous self-advertiser –'

'Go on,' said Lord Caterham. 'I am enjoying this.'

'My God!' said Bill simply and with feeling. 'Look here, I must be off.'

'No, no, don't go. I'd much rather you stayed. Besides, you want to see Bundle.'

'Not now. This has driven everything else out of my head. You don't know where Jimmy Thesiger is, by any chance? I believe he was staying with the Cootes. Is he there still?'

'I think he went back to town yesterday. Bundle and Loraine were over there on Saturday. If you'll only wait –'

But Bill shook his head energetically and rushed from the room. Lord Caterham tiptoed out into the hall, seized a hat and made a hurried exit by the side door. In the distance he observed Bill streaking down the drive in his car.

'That young man will have an accident,' he thought.

Bill, however, reached London without any mischance, and proceeded to park his car in St James's Square. Then he sought out Jimmy Thesiger's rooms. Jimmy was at home.

'Hullo, Bill. I say, what's the matter? You don't look your usual bright little self.'

'I'm worried,' said Bill. 'I was worried anyway, and then something else turned up and gave me a jolt.'

'Oh!' said Jimmy. 'How lucid! What's it all about? Can I do anything?'

Bill did not reply. He sat staring at the carpet and looking so puzzled and uncomfortable that Jimmy felt his curiosity aroused.

'Has anything very extraordinary occurred, William?' he asked gently.

'Something damned odd. I can't make head or tail of it.'

'The Seven Dials business?'

'Yes – the Seven Dials business. I got a letter this morning.'

'A letter? What sort of letter?'

'A letter from Ronny Devereux's executors.'

'Good Lord! After all this time!'

'It seems he left instructions. If he was to die suddenly, a certain sealed envelope was to be sent to me exactly a fortnight after his death.'

'And they've sent it to you?'

'Yes.'

'You've opened it?'

'Yes.'

'Well – what did it say?'

Bill turned a glance upon him, such a strange and uncertain one that Jimmy was startled.

'Look here,' he said. 'Pull yourself together, old man. It seems to have knocked the wind out of you, whatever it is. Have a drink.'

He poured out a stiff whisky and soda and brought it over to Bill, who took it obediently. His face still bore the same dazed expression.

'It's what's in the letter,' he said. 'I simply can't believe it, that's all.'

'Oh, nonsense,' said Jimmy. 'You must get into the habit of believing six impossible things before breakfast. I do it regularly. Now then, let's hear all about it. Wait a minute.'

He went outside.

'Stevens!'

'Yes, sir?'

'Just go out and get me some cigarettes, will you? I've run out.'

'Very good, sir.'

Jimmy waited till he heard the front door close. Then he came back into the sitting-room. Bill was just in the act of setting down his empty glass. He looked better, more purposeful and more master of himself.

'Now then,' said Jimmy. 'I've sent Stevens out so that we can't be overheard. Are you going to tell me all about it?'

'It's so incredible.'

'Then it's sure to be true. Come on, out with it.'

Bill drew a deep breath.

'I will. I'll tell you everything.'

CHAPTER 30

AN URGENT SUMMONS

Loraine, playing with a small and delectable puppy, was somewhat surprised when Bundle rejoined her after an absence of twenty minutes, in a breathless state and with an indescribable expression on her face.

'Whoof,' said Bundle, sinking on to a garden seat. 'Whoof.'

'What's the matter?' asked Loraine, looking at her curiously.

'George is the matter – George Lomax.'

'What's he been doing?'

'Proposing to me. It was awful. He spluttered and he stuttered, but he would go through with it – he must have learnt it out of a book, I think. There was no stopping him. Oh, how I hate men who splutter! And, unfortunately, I didn't know the reply.'

'You must have known what you wanted to do.'

'Naturally I'm not going to marry an apologetic idiot like George. What I mean is, I didn't know the correct reply from the book of etiquette. I could only just say flatly: "No, I won't." What I ought to have said was something about being very sensible of the honour he had done me and so on and so on. But I got so rattled that in the end I jumped out of the window and bolted.'

'Really, Bundle, that's not like you.'

'Well, I never dreamt of such a thing happening. George – who I always thought hated me – and he did too. What a fatal thing it is to pretend to take an interest in a man's pet subject. You should have heard the drivel George talked about my girlish mind and the pleasure it would be to form it. My mind! If George knew one quarter of what was going on in my mind, he'd faint with horror!'

Loraine laughed. She couldn't help it.

'Oh, I know it's my own fault. I let myself in for this. There's Father dodging round that rhododendron. Hallo, Father.'

Lord Caterham approached with a hangdog expression.

'Lomax gone, eh?' he remarked with somewhat forced geniality.

'A nice business you let me in for,' said Bundle. 'George told me he had your full approval and sanction.'

'Well,' said Lord Caterham, 'what did you expect me to say? As a matter of fact, I didn't say that at all, or anything like it.'

'I didn't really think so,' said Bundle. 'I assumed that George had talked you into a corner and reduced you to such a state that you could only nod your head feebly.'

'That's very much what happened. How did he take it? Badly?'

'I didn't wait to see,' said Bundle. 'I'm afraid I was rather abrupt.'

'Oh well,' said Lord Caterham. 'Perhaps that was the best way. Thank goodness in the future Lomax won't always be running over as he has been in the habit of doing, worrying me about things. Everything is for the best they say. Have you seen my jigger anywhere?'

'A mashie shot or two would steady my nerves, I think,' said Bundle. 'I'll take you on for sixpence, Loraine.'

An hour passed very peacefully. The three returned to the house in a harmonious spirit. A note lay on the hall table.

'Mr Lomax left that for you, my lord,' explained Tredwell. 'He was much disappointed to find that you had gone out.'

Lord Caterham tore it open. He uttered a pained ejaculation and turned upon his daughter. Tredwell had retired.

'Really, Bundle, you might have made yourself clear, I think.'

'What do you mean?'

'Well, read this.'

Bundle took it and read:

'My dear Caterham, – I am sorry not to have had a word with you. I thought I made it clear that I wanted to see you again after my interview with Eileen. She, dear child, was evidently quite unaware of the feelings I entertained towards her. She was, I am afraid, much startled. I have no wish to hurry her in any way. Her girlish confusion was very charming, and I entertain an even higher regard for her, as I much appreciate her maidenly reserve. I must give her time to become accustomed to the idea. Her very confusion shows that she is not wholly indifferent to me and I have no doubts of my ultimate success.

'Believe me, dear Caterham,
'Your sincere friend,
'George Lomax.'

'Well,' said Bundle. 'Well, I'm damned!'

Words failed her.

'The man must be mad,' said Lord Caterham. 'No one could write those things about you, Bundle, unless they were slightly touched in the head. Poor chap, poor chap. But what persistence! I don't wonder he got into the Cabinet. It would serve him right if you did marry him, Bundle.'

The telephone rang and Bundle moved forward to answer it. In another minute George and his proposal were forgotten, and she was beckoning eagerly to Loraine. Lord Caterham went off to his own sanctum.

'It's Jimmy,' said Bundle. 'And he's tremendously excited about something.'

'Thank goodness I've caught you,' said Jimmy's voice. 'There's no time to be lost. Loraine's there, too?'

'Yes, she's here.'

'Well, look here, I haven't got time to explain everything – in fact, I can't through the telephone. But Bill has been round to see me with the most amazing story you ever heard. If it's true – well, if it's true, it's the biggest scoop of the century. Now, look here, this is what you've got to do. Come up to town at once, both of you. Garage the car somewhere and go straight to the Seven Dials Club. Do you think that when you get there you can get rid of that footman fellow?'

'Alfred? Rather. You leave that to me.'

'Good. Get rid of him and watch out for me and Bill. Don't show yourselves at the windows, but when we drive up, let us in at once. See?'

'Yes.'

'That's all right then. Oh, Bundle, don't let on that you're going up to town. Make some other excuse. Say your taking Loraine home. How would that do?'

'Splendidly. I say, Jimmy, I'm thrilled to the core.'

'And you might as well make your will before starting.'

'Better and better. But I wish I knew what it was all about.'

'You will as soon as we meet. I'll tell you this much. We're going to get ready the hell of a surprise for No. 7!'

Bundle hung up the receiver and turned to Loraine, giving her a rapid résumé of the conversation. Loraine rushed upstairs and hurriedly packed her suitcase, and Bundle put her head round her father's door.

'I'm taking Loraine home, Father.'

'Why? I had no idea she was going today.'

'They want her back,' said Bundle vaguely. 'Just telephoned. Bye-bye.'

'Here, Bundle, wait a minute. When will you be home?'

'Don't know. Expect me when you see me.'

With this unceremonious exit Bundle rushed upstairs, put a hat on, slipped into her fur coat and was ready to start. She had already ordered the Hispano to be brought round.

The journey to London was without adventure, except such as was habitually provided by Bundle's driving. They left the car at a garage and proceeded direct to the Seven Dials Club.

The door was opened to them by Alfred. Bundle pushed her way past him without ceremony and Loraine followed.

'Shut the door, Alfred,' said Bundle. 'Now, I've come here especially to do you a good turn. The police are after you.'

'Oh, my lady!'

Alfred turned chalk white.

'I've come to warn you because you did me a good turn the other night,' went on Bundle rapidly. 'There's a warrant out for Mr Mosgorovsky, and the best thing you can do is to clear out of here as quick as you can. If you're not found here, they won't bother about you. Here's ten pounds to help you get away somewhere.'

In three minutes' time an incoherent and badly scared Alfred had left 14 Hunstanton Street with only one idea in his head – never to return.

'Well, I've managed that all right,' said Bundle with satisfaction.

'Was it necessary to be so – well, drastic?' Loraine demurred.

'It's safer,' said Bundle. 'I don't know what Jimmy and Bill are up to, but we don't want Alfred coming back in the middle of it and wrecking everything. Hallo, here they are. Well, they haven't wasted much time. Probably watching round the corner to see Alfred leave. Go down and open the door to them, Loraine.'

Loraine obeyed. Jimmy Thesiger alighted from the driving seat.

'You stop here for a moment, Bill,' he said. 'Blow the horn if you think anyone's watching the place.'

He ran up the steps and banged the door behind him. He looked pink and elated.

'Hallo, Bundle, there you are. Now then, we've got to get down to it. Where's the key of the room you got into last time?'

'It was one of the downstairs keys. We'd better bring the lot up.'

'Right you are, but be quick. Time's short.'

The key was easily found, the baize-lined door swung back and the three entered. The room was exactly as Bundle had seen it before, with the seven chairs grouped round the table. Jimmy surveyed it for a minute or two in silence. Then his eyes went to the two cupboards.

'Which is the cupboard you hid in, Bundle?'

'This one.'

Jimmy went to it and flung the door open. The same collection of miscellaneous glassware covered the shelves.

'We shall have to shift all this stuff,' he murmured. 'Run down and get Bill, Loraine. There's no need for him to keep watch outside any longer.'

Loraine ran off.

'What are you going to do?' inquired Bundle impatiently.

Jimmy was down on his knees, trying to peer through the crack of the other cupboard door.

'Wait till Bill comes and you shall hear the whole story. This is his staff work – and a jolly creditable bit of work it is. Hallo – what's Loraine flying up the stairs for as though she's got a mad bull after her?'

Loraine was indeed racing up the stairs as fast as she could. She burst in upon them with an ashen face and terror in her eyes.

'Bill – Bill – Oh, Bundle – Bill!'

'What about Bill?'

Jimmy caught her by the shoulder.

'For God's sake, Loraine, what's happened?'

Loraine was still gasping.

'Bill – I think he's dead – he's in the car still – but he doesn't move or speak. I'm sure he's dead.'

Jimmy muttered an oath and sprang for the stairs, Bundle behind him, her heart pounding unevenly and an awful feeling of desolation spreading over her.

Bill – dead? Oh, no! Oh, no! Not that. Please God – not that.

Together she and Jimmy reached the car, Loraine behind them.

Jimmy peered under the hood. Bill was sitting as he had left him, leaning back. But his eyes were closed and Jimmy's pull at his arm brought no response.

'I can't understand it,' muttered Jimmy. 'But he's not dead. Cheer up, Bundle. Look here, we've got to get him into the house. Let's pray to goodness no policeman comes along. If anybody says anything, he's our sick friend we're helping into the house.'

Between the three of them they got Bill into the house without much difficulty, and without attracting much attention, save for an unshaven gentleman, who said sympathetically:

'Genneman's 'ad a couple, I shee,' and nodded his head sapiently.

'Into the little back room downstairs,' said Jimmy. 'There's a sofa there.'

They got him safely on to the sofa and Bundle knelt down beside him and took his limp wrist in her hand.

'His pulse is beating,' she said. 'What *is* the matter with him?'

'He was all right when I left him just now,' said Jimmy. 'I wonder if someone's managed to inject some stuff into him. It would be easily done – just a prick. The man might have been asking him the time. There's only one thing for it. I must get him a doctor at once. You stay here and look after him.'

He hurried to the door, then paused.

'Look here – don't be scared, either of you. But I'd better leave you my revolver. I mean – just in case. I'll be back just as soon as I possibly can.'

He laid the revolver down on the little table by the sofa, then hurried off. They heard the front door bang behind him.

The house seemed very still now. The two girls stayed motionless by Bill. Bundle still kept her finger on his pulse. It seemed to be beating very fast and irregularly.

'I wish we could do something,' she whispered to Loraine. 'This is awful.'

Loraine nodded.

'I know. It seems ages since Jimmy went and yet it's only a minute and a half.'

'I keep hearing things,' said Bundle. 'Footsteps and boards creaking upstairs – and yet I know it's only imagination.'

'I wonder why Jimmy left us the revolver,' said Loraine. 'There can't really be danger.'

'If they could get Bill –' said Bundle and stopped.

Loraine shivered.

'I know – but we're in the house. Nobody can get in without our hearing them. And anyway we've got the revolver.'

Bundle turned her attention back again to Bill.

'I wish I knew what to do. Hot coffee. You give them that sometimes.'

'I've got some smelling-salts in my bag,' said Loraine. 'And some brandy. Where is it? Oh, I must have left it in the room upstairs.'

'I'll get it,' said Bundle. 'They might do some good.'

She sped quickly up the stairs, across the gaming room and through the open door into the meeting place. Loraine's bag was lying on the table.

As Bundle stretched out her hand to take it, she heard a noise from behind her. Hidden behind the door a man stood ready with a sand-bag in his hand. Before Bundle could turn her head, he had struck.

With a faint moan, Bundle slipped down, an unconscious heap upon the floor.

CHAPTER 31

THE SEVEN DIALS

Very slowly Bundle returned to consciousness. She was aware of a dark, spinning blackness, the centre of which was a violent, throbbing ache. Punctuating this were sounds. A voice that she knew very well saying the same thing over and over again.

The blackness span less violently. The ache was now definitely located as being in Bundle's own head. And she was sufficiently herself to take an interest in what the voice was saying.

'Darling, darling Bundle. Oh, darling Bundle. She's dead; I know she's dead. Oh, my darling. Bundle, darling, darling Bundle. I do love you so. Bundle – darling – darling –'

Bundle lay quite still with her eyes shut. But she was now fully conscious. Bill's arms held her closely.

'Bundle darling – Oh, dearest, darling Bundle. Oh, my dear love. Oh, Bundle – Bundle. What shall I do? Oh, darling one – my Bundle – my own dearest, sweetest Bundle. Oh, God, what shall I do? I've killed her. I've killed her.'

Reluctantly – very reluctantly – Bundle spoke.

'No, you haven't, you silly idiot,' she said.

Bill gave a gasp of utter amazement.

'Bundle – you're alive.'

'Of course I'm alive.'

'How long have you been – I mean when did you come to?'

'About five minutes ago.'

'Why didn't you open your eyes – or say something?'

'Didn't want to. I was enjoying myself.'

'Enjoying yourself?'

'Yes. Listening to all the things you were saying. You'll never say them so well again. You'll be too beastly self-conscious.'

Bill had turned a dark brick-red.

'Bundle – you really didn't mind? You know, I *do* love you so. I have for ages. But I never have dared to tell you so.'

'You silly juggins,' said Bundle. 'Why?'

'I thought you'd only laugh at me. I mean – you've got brains and all that – you'll marry some bigwig.'

'Like George Lomax?' suggested Bundle.

'I don't mean a fatuous ass like Codders. But some really fine chap who'll be worthy of you – though I don't think anyone could be that,' ended Bill.

'You're rather a dear, Bill.'

'But, Bundle, seriously, could you ever? I mean, could you ever bring yourself to?'

'Could I ever bring myself to do what?'

'Marry me. I know I'm awfully thick-headed – but I do love you, Bundle. I'd be your dog or your slave or your anything.'

'You're very like a dog,' said Bundle. 'I like dogs. They're so friendly and faithful and warm-hearted. I think that perhaps I could just bring myself to marry you, Bill – with a great effort, you know.'

Bill's response to this was to relinquish his grasp of her and recoil violently. He looked at her with amazement in his eyes.

'Bundle – you don't mean it?'

'There's nothing for it,' said Bundle. 'I see I shall have to relapse into unconsciousness again.'

'Bundle – darling –' Bill caught her to him. He was trembling violently. 'Bundle – do you really mean it – do you? – you don't know how much I love you.'

'Oh, Bill,' said Bundle.

There is no need to describe in detail the conversation of the next ten minutes. It consisted mostly of repetitions.

'And do you really love me?' said Bill, incredulously, for the twentieth time as he at last released her.

'Yes – yes – yes. Now do let's be sensible. I've got a racking head still, and I've been nearly squeezed to death by you. I want to get the hang of things. Where are we and what's happened?'

For the first time, Bundle began to take stock of her surroundings. They were in the secret room, she noted, and the baize door was closed and presumably locked. They were prisoners, then!

Bundle's eyes came back to Bill. Quite oblivious of her question he was watching her with adoring eyes.

'Bill, darling,' said Bundle, 'pull yourself together. We've got to get out of here.'

'Eh?' said Bill. 'What? Oh, yes. That'll be all right. No difficulty about that.'

'It's being in love makes you feel like that,' said Bundle. 'I feel rather the same myself. As though everything's easy and possible.'

'So it is,' said Bill. 'Now that I know you care for me –'

'Stop it,' said Bundle. 'Once we begin again any serious conversation will be hopeless. Unless you pull yourself together and become sensible, I shall very likely change my mind.'

'I shan't let you,' said Bill. 'You don't think that once having got you I'd be such a fool as to let you go, do you?'

'You would not coerce me against my will, I hope,' said Bundle grandiloquently.

'Wouldn't I?' said Bill. 'You just watch me do it, that's all.'

'You really are rather a darling, Bill. I was afraid you might be too meek, but I see there's going to be no danger of that. In another half-hour you'd be ordering me about. Oh, dear, we're getting silly again. Now, look here, Bill. We've got to get out of here.'

'I tell you that'll be quite all right. I shall –'

He broke off, obedient to a pressure from Bundle's hand. She was leaning forward, listening intently. Yes, she had not been mistaken. A step was crossing the outer room. The key was thrust into the lock and turned. Bundle held her breath. Was it Jimmy coming to rescue them – or was it someone else?

The door opened and the black-bearded Mr Mosgorovsky stood on the threshold.

Immediately Bill took a step forward, standing in front of Bundle.

'Look here,' he said, 'I want a word with you privately.'

The Russian did not reply for a minute or two. He stood stroking his long, silky black beard and smiling quietly to himself.

'So,' he said at last, 'it is like that. Very well. The lady will be pleased to come with me.'

'It's all right, Bundle,' said Bill. 'Leave it to me. You go with this chap. Nobody's going to hurt you. I know what I'm doing.'

Bundle rose obediently. That note of authority in Bill's voice was new to her. He seemed absolutely sure of himself and confident of being able to deal with the situation. Bundle wondered vaguely what it was that Bill had – or thought he had – up his sleeve.

She passed out of the room in front of the Russian. He followed her, closing the door behind him and locking it.

'This way, please,' he said.

He indicated the staircase and she mounted obediently to the floor above. Here she was directed to pass into a small frowsy room, which she took to be Alfred's bedroom.

Mosgorovsky said: 'You will wait here quietly, please. There must be no noise.'

Then he went out, closing the door behind him and locking her in.

Bundle sat down on a chair. Her head was aching badly still and she felt incapable of sustained thought. Bill seemed to have the sitaution well in hand. Sooner or later, she supposed, someone would come and let her out.

The minutes passed. Bundle's watch had stopped, but she judged that over an hour had passed since the Russian had brought her here. What was happening? What, indeed, *had* happened?

At last she heard footsteps on the stairs. It was Mosgorovsky once more. He spoke very formally to her.

'Lady Eileen Brent, you are wanted at an emergency meeting of the Seven Dials Society. Please follow me.'

He led the way down the stairs and Bundle followed him. He opened the door of the secret chamber and Bundle passed in, catching her breath in surprise as she did so.

She was seeing for the second time what she had only had a glimpse of the first time through her peep-hole. The masked figures were sitting round the table. As she stood there, taken aback by the suddenness of it, Mosgorovsky slipped into his place, adjusting his clock mask as he did so.

But this time the chair at the head of the table was occupied. No. 7 was in his place.

Bundle's heart beat violently. She was standing at the foot of the table directly facing him and she stared and stared at the mocking piece of hanging stuff, with the clock dial on it, that hid his features.

He sat quite immovable and Bundle got an odd sensation of power radiating from him. His inactivity was not the inactivity of weakness – and she wished violently, almost hysterically, that he would speak – that he would make some sign, some gesture – not just sit there like a gigantic spider in the middle of its web waiting remorselessly for its prey.

She shivered, and as she did so Mosgorovsky rose. His voice, smooth, silky, persuasive, seemed curiously far away.

'Lady Eileen, you have been present unasked at the secret councils of this society. It is therefore necessary that you should identify yourself with our aims and ambitions. The place two o'clock, you may notice, is vacant. It is that place that is offered to you.'

Bundle gasped. The thing was like a fantastic nightmare. Was it possible that she, Bundle Brent, was being asked to join a murderous secret society? Had the same proposition been made to Bill, and had he refused indignantly?

'I can't do that,' she said bluntly.

'Do not answer precipitately.'

She fancied that Mosgorovsky, beneath his clock mask, was smiling significantly into his beard.

'You do not as yet know, Lady Eileen, what it is you are refusing.'

'I can make a pretty good guess,' said Bundle.

'Can you?'

It was the voice of seven o'clock. It awoke some vague chord of memory in Bundle's brain. Surely she knew that voice?

Very slowly No. 7 raised a hand to his head and fumbled with the fastening of the mask.

Bundle held her breath. At last – she was going to *know*.

The mask fell.

Bundle found herself looking into the expressionless, wooden face of Superintendent Battle.

CHAPTER 32

BUNDLE IS DUMBFOUNDED

'That's right,' said Battle, as Mosgorovsky leapt up and came round to Bundle. 'Get a chair for her. It's been a bit of a shock, I can see.'

Bundle sank down on the chair. She felt limp and faint with surprise. Battle went on talking in a quiet, comfortable way wholly characteristic of him.

'You didn't expect to see me, Lady Eileen. No, and no more did some of the others sitting round the table. Mr Mosgorovsky's been my lieutenant in a manner of speaking. He's been in the know all along. But most of the others have taken their orders blindly from him.'

Still Bundle said no word. She was – a most unusual state of affairs for her – simply incapable of speech.

Battle nodded at her comprehendingly, seeming to understand the state of her feelings.

'You'll have to get rid of one or two preconceived ideas of yours, I'm afraid, Lady Eileen. About this society, for instance – I know it's common enough in books – a secret organization of criminals with a mysterious super-criminal at the head of it whom no one ever sees. That sort of thing may exist in real life, but I can only say that I've never come across anything of the sort, and I've had a good deal of experience one way or another.

'But there's a lot of romance in the world, Lady Eileen. People, especially young people, like reading about such things, and they like still better really *doing* them. I'm going to introduce you now to a very creditable band of amateurs that has done remarkably fine work for my Department, work that nobody else could have done. If they've chosen rather melodramatic trappings, well, why shouldn't they? They've been willing to face real danger – danger of the very worst kind – and they've done it for these reasons: love of danger for its own sake – which to my mind is a very healthy sign in these Safety First days – and an honest wish to serve their country.

'And now, Lady Eileen, I'm going to introduce you. First of all, there's Mr Mosgorovsky, whom you already know in a manner of speaking. As you're aware, he runs the club and he runs a host of other things too. He's our most valuable Secret Anti-Bolshevist Agent in England. No. 5 is Count Andras of the Hungarian Embassy, a very near and dear friend of the late Gerald Wade. No. 4 is Mr Hayward Phelps, an American journalist, whose British sympathies are very keen and whose aptitude for scenting "news" is remarkable. No. 3 –'

He stopped, smiling, and Bundle stared dumbfounded into the sheepish, grinning face of Bill Eversleigh.

'No. 2,' went on Battle in a graver voice, 'can only show an empty place. It is the place belonging to Mr Ronald Devereux, a very gallant young gentleman who died for his country if any man ever did. No. 1 – well, No. 1 was Mr Gerald Wade, another very gallant gentleman who died in the same way. His place was taken – not without some grave misgivings on my part – by a lady – a lady who has proved her fitness to have it and who has been a great help to us.'

The last to do so, No. 1, removed her mask, and Bundle looked without surprise into the beautiful, dark face of Countess Radzky.

'I might have known,' said Bundle resentfully, 'that you were too completely the beautiful foreign adventuress to be anything of the kind really.'

'But you don't know the real joke,' said Bill. '*Bundle, this is Babe St Maur* – you remember my telling you about her and what a ripping actress she was – and she's about proved it.'

'That's so,' said Miss Maur in pure transatlantic nasal. 'But it's not a terrible lot of credit to me, because Poppa and Momma came from that part of Yurrup – so I got the patter fairly easy. Gee, but I nearly gave myself away once at the Abbey, talking about gardens.'

She paused and then said abruptly:

'It's – it's not been just fun. You see, I was kinder engaged to Ronny, and when he handed in his checks – well, I had to do something to track down the skunk who murdered him. That's all.'

'I'm completely bewildered,' said Bundle. 'Nothing is what it seems.'

'It's very simple, Lady Eileen,' said Superintendent Battle. 'It began with some of the young people wanting a bit of excitement. It was Mr Wade who first got on to me. He suggested the formation of a band of what you might call amateur workers to do a bit of secret service work. I warned him that it might be dangerous – but he wasn't the kind to weigh that in the balance. I made it plain to him that anyone who came in must do so on that understanding. But, bless you, that wasn't going to stop any of Mr Wade's friends. And so the thing began.'

'But what was the object of it all?' asked Bundle.

'We wanted a certain man – wanted him badly. He wasn't an ordinary crook. He worked in Mr Wade's world, a kind of Raffles, but much more dangerous than any Raffles ever was or could be. He was out for big stuff, international stuff. Twice already valuable secret inventions had been stolen, and clearly stolen by someone who had inside knowledge. The professionals had had a try – and failed. Then the amateurs took on – and succeeded.'

'Succeeded?'

'Yes – but they didn't come out of it unscathed. The man was dangerous. Two lives fell victim to him and he got away with it. But the Seven Dials stuck to it. And as I say they succeeded. Thanks to Mr Eversleigh, the man was caught at last red-handed.'

'Who was he?' asked Bundle. 'Do I know him?'

'You know him very well, Lady Eileen. His name is Mr Jimmy Thesiger, and he was arrested this afternoon.'

CHAPTER 33

BATTLE EXPLAINS

Superintendent Battle settled down to explain. He spoke comfortably and cosily.

'I didn't suspect him myself for a long time. The first hint of it I had was when I heard what Mr Devereux's last words had been. Naturally, you took them to mean that Mr Devereux was trying to send word to Mr Thesiger that the Seven Dials had killed him. That's what the words seemed to mean on their face value. But of course I knew that that couldn't be so. It was the Seven Dials that Mr Devereux wanted told – and what he wanted them told was something about Mr Jimmy Thesiger.

'The thing seemed incredible, because Mr Devereux and Mr Thesiger were close friends. But I remembered something else – that these thefts must have been committed by someone who was absolutely in the know. Someone, who, if not in the Foreign Office himself, was in the way of hearing all its chit-chat. And I found it very hard to find out where Mr Thesiger got his money. The income his father left him was a small one, yet he was able to live at a most expensive rate. Where did the money come from?

'I knew that Mr Wade had been very excited by something that he had found out. He was quite sure that he was on the right track. He didn't confide in anyone about what he thought that track was, but he did say something to Mr Devereux about being on the point of making sure. That was just before they both went down to Chimneys for that week-end. As you know, Mr Wade died there – apparently from an overdose of a sleeping draught. It seemed straightforward enough, but Mr Devereux did not accept that explanation for a minute. He was convinced that Mr Wade had been very cleverly put out of the way and that someone in the house must actually be the criminal we were all after. He came, I think, very near confiding in Mr Thesiger, for he certainly had no suspicions of him at that moment. But something held him back.

'Then he did a rather curious thing. He arranged seven clocks upon the mantelpiece, throwing away the eighth. It was meant as a symbol that the Seven Dials would revenge the death of one of their members – and he watched eagerly to see if anyone betrayed themselves or showed signs of perturbation.'

'And it was Jimmy Thesiger who poisoned Gerry Wade?'

'Yes, he slipped the stuff into a whisky and soda which Mr Wade had downstairs before retiring to bed. That's why he was already feeling sleepy when he wrote that letter to Miss Wade.'

'Then the footman, Bauer, hadn't anything to do with it?' asked Bundle.

'Bauer was one of our people, Lady Eileen. It was thought likely that our crook would go for Herr Eberhard's invention and Bauer was got into the house to watch events on our behalf. But he wasn't able to do much. As I say, Mr Thesiger administered the fatal dose easily enough. Later, when everyone was asleep, a bottle, glass and empty chloral bottle were placed by Mr Wade's bedside by Mr Thesiger. Mr Wade was unconscious then, and his fingers were probably pressed round the glass and the bottle so that they should be found there if any questions should arise. I don't know what effect the seven clocks on the mantelpiece made on Mr Thesiger. He certainly didn't let on anything to Mr Devereux. All the same, I think he had a bad five minutes now and again thinking of them. And I think he kept a pretty wary eye on Mr Devereux after that.

'We don't know exactly what happened next. No one saw much of Mr Devereux after Mr Wade's death. But it is clear that he worked along the same lines that he knew Mr Wade had been working on and reached the same result – namely, that Mr Thesiger was the man. I fancy, too, that he was betrayed in the same way.'

'You mean?'

'Through Miss Loraine Wade. Mr Wade was devoted to her – I believe he hoped to marry her – she wasn't really his sister, of course – and there is no doubt that he told her more than he should have done. But Miss Loraine Wade was devoted body and soul to Mr Thesiger. She would do anything he told her. She passed on the information to him. In the same way, later, Mr Devereux was attracted to her, and probably warned her against Mr Thesiger. So Mr Devereux in turn was silenced – and died trying to send word to the Seven Dials that his murderer was Mr Thesiger.'

'How ghastly,' cried Bundle. 'If I had only known.'

'Well, it didn't seem likely. In fact, I could hardly credit it myself. But then we came to the affair at the Abbey. You will remember how awkward it was – specially awkward for Mr Eversleigh here. You and Mr Thesiger were hand in glove. Mr Eversleigh had already been embarrassed by your insisting on being brought to this place, and when he found that you had actually overheard what went on at a meeting, he was dumbfounded.'

The superintendent paused and a twinkle came into his eye.

'So was I, Lady Eileen. I never dreamed of such a thing being possible. You put one over on me there all right.

'Well, Mr Eversleigh was in a dilemma. He couldn't let you into the secret of the Seven Dials without letting Mr Thesiger in also – and that would never do. It all suited Mr Thesiger very well, of course, for it gave him a *bona fide* reason for getting himself asked to the Abbey, which made things easier for him.

'I may say that the Seven Dials had already sent a warning letter to Mr Lomax. That was to ensure his applying to me for assistance, so that I should be able to be on the spot in a perfectly natural manner. I made no secret of my presence, as you know.'

And again the superintendent's eye twinkled.

'Well, ostensibly, Mr Eversleigh and Mr Thesiger were to divide the night into two watches. Really, Mr Eversleigh and Miss St Maur did so. She was on guard at the library window when she heard Mr Thesiger coming and had to dart behind the screen.

'And now comes the cleverness of Mr Thesiger. Up to a point he told me a perfectly true story, and I must admit that with the fight and everything, I was distinctly shaken – and began to wonder whether he had had anything to do with the theft at all, or whether we were completely on the wrong track. There were one or two suspicious circumstances that pointed in an entirely different direction, and I can tell you I didn't know what to make of things, when something turned up to clinch matters.

'I found the burnt glove in the fire-place with the teeth marks on it – and then – well – I knew that I'd been right after all. But, upon my word, he was a clever one.'

'What actually happened?' said Bundle. 'Who was the other man?'

'There wasn't any other man. Listen, and I'll show you how in the end I reconstructed the whole story. To begin with, Mr Thesiger and Miss Wade were in this together. And they have a rendezvous for an exact time. Miss Wade comes over in her car, climbs through the fence and comes up to the house. She's got a perfectly good story if anyone stops her – the one she told eventually. But she arrived unmolested on the terrace just after the clock had struck two.

'Now, I may say to begin with that she was seen coming in. My men saw her, but they had orders to stop nobody coming in – only going out. I wanted, you see, to find out as much as possible. Miss Wade arrives on the terrace, and at that minute a parcel falls at her feet and she picks it up. A man comes down the ivy and she starts to run. What happens next? The struggle – and presently the revolver shots. What will everyone do? Rush to the scene of the fight. And Miss Loraine Wade could have left the grounds and driven off with the formula safely in her possession.

'But things don't happen quite like that. Miss Wade runs straight into my arms. And at that moment the game changes. It's no longer attack but defence. Miss Wade tells her story. It is perfectly true and perfectly sensible.

'And now we come to Mr Thesiger. One thing struck me at once. The bullet wound alone couldn't have caused him to faint. Either he had fallen and hit his head – or – well he hadn't fainted at all. Later we had Miss St Maur's story. It agreed perfectly with Mr Thesiger's – there was only one suggestive point. Miss St Maur said that after the lights were turned out and Mr Thesiger went over to the window, he was so still that she thought he must have left the room and gone outside. Now, if anyone is in the room, you can hardly help hearing their breathing if you are listening for it. Supposing, then, that Mr Thesiger *had* gone outside. Where next? Up the ivy to Mr O'Rourke's room – Mr O'Rourke's whisky and soda having been doped the night before. He gets the papers, throws them down to the girl, climbs down the ivy again, and – starts the fight. That's easy enough when you come to think of it. Knock the tables down, stagger about, speak in your own voice and then in a hoarse half-whisper. And then, the final touch, the two revolver shots. His own Colt automatic, bought openly the day before, is fired at an imaginary assailant. Then, with his left gloved hand, he takes from his pocket the small Mauser pistol and shoots himself through the fleshy part of the right arm. He flings the pistol through the window, tears off the glove with his teeth, and throws it into the fire. When I arrive he is lying on the floor in a faint.'

Bundle drew a deep breath.

'You didn't realize all this at the time, Superintendent Battle?'

'No, that I didn't. I was taken in as much as anyone could be. It wasn't till long afterwards that I pieced it all together. Finding the glove was the beginning of it. Then I made Sir Oswald throw the pistol through the window. It fell a good way farther on than it should have done. But a man who is right-handed doesn't throw nearly as far with the left hand. Even then it was only suspicion – and a very faint suspicion at that.

'But there was one point struck me. The papers were obviously thrown down for someone to pick up. If Miss Wade was there by accident, who was the real person? Of course, for those who weren't in the know, that question was answered easily enough – the Countess. But there I had the pull over you. *I knew the Countess was all right*. So what follows? Why, the idea that the papers had actually been picked up by the person they were meant for. And the more I thought of it, the more it seemed to me a very remarkable coincidence that Miss Wade should have arrived at the exact moment she did.'

'It must have been very difficult for you when I came to you full of suspicion about the Countess.'

'It was, Lady Eileen. I had to say something to put you off the scent. And it was very difficult for Mr Eversleigh here, with the lady coming out of a dead faint and no knowing what she might say.'

'I understand Bill's anxiety now,' said Bundle. 'And the way he kept urging her to take time and not talk till she felt quite all right.'

'Poor old Bill,' said Miss St Maur. 'That poor baby had to be vamped against his will – getting madder'n a hornet every minute.'

'Well,' said Superintendent Battle, 'there it was. I suspected Mr Thesiger – but I couldn't get definite proof. On the other hand, Mr Thesiger himself was rattled. He realized more or less what he was up against in the Seven Dials – but he wanted badly to know who No. 7 was. He got himself asked to the Cootes under the impression that Sir Oswald Coote was No. 7.'

'I suspected Sir Oswald,' said Bundle, 'especially when he came in from the garden that night.'

'I never suspected him,' said Battle. 'But I don't mind telling you that I *did* have my suspicions of that young chap, his secretary.'

'Pongo?' said Bill. 'Not old Pongo?'

'Yes, Mr Eversleigh, old Pongo as you call him. A very efficient gentleman and one that could have put anything through if he'd a mind to. I suspected him partly because he'd been the one to take the clocks into Mr Wade's room that night. It would have been easy for him to put the bottle and glass by the bedside then. And then, for another thing, he was left-handed. That glove pointed straight to him – if it hadn't been for one thing –'

'What?'

'The teeth marks – only a man whose right hand was incapacitated would have needed to tear off that glove with his teeth.'

'So Pongo was cleared.'

'So Pongo was cleared, as you say. I'm sure it would be a great surprise to Mr Bateman to know he was ever suspected.'

'It would,' agreed Bill. 'A solemn card – a silly ass like Pongo. How could you ever think –'

'Well, as far as that goes, Mr Thesiger was what you might describe as an empty-headed young ass of the most brainless description. One of the two was playing a part. When I decided that it was Mr Thesiger, I was interested to get Mr Bateman's opinion of him. All along, Mr Bateman had the gravest suspicions of Mr Thesiger and frequently said as much to Sir Oswald.'

'It's curious,' said Bill, 'but Pongo always is right. It's maddening.'

'Well, as I say,' went on Superintendent Battle, 'we got Mr Thesiger fairly on the run, badly rattled over this Seven Dials business and uncertain just where the danger lay. That we got him in the end was solely through Mr Eversleigh. He knew what he was up against, and he risked his life cheerfully. But he never dreamt that you would be dragged into it, Lady Eileen.'

'My God, no,' said Bill with feeling.

'He went round to Mr Thesiger's rooms with a cooked-up tale,' continued Battle. 'He was to pretend that certain papers of Mr Devereux's had come into his hands. Those papers were to suggest a suspicion of Mr Thesiger. Naturally, as the honest friend, Mr Eversleigh rushed round, sure that Mr Thesiger would have an explanation. We calculated that if we were right, Mr Thesiger would try and put Mr Eversleigh out of the way, and we were fairly certain as to the way he'd do it. Sure enough, Mr Thesiger gave his guest a whisky and soda. During the minute or two that his host was out of the room. Mr Eversleigh poured that into a jar on the mantelpiece, but he had to pretend, of course, that the drug was taking effect. It would be slow, he knew, not sudden. He began his story, and Mr Thesiger at first denied it all indignantly, but as soon as he saw (or thought he saw) that the drug was taking effect, he admitted everything and told Mr Eversleigh that he was the third victim.

'When Mr Eversleigh was nearly unconscious, Mr Thesiger took him down to the car and helped him in. The hood was up. He must already have telephoned to you unknown to Mr Eversleigh. He made a clever suggestion to you. You were to say that you were taking Miss Wade home.

'You made no mention of a message from him. Later when your body was found here, Miss Wade would swear that you had driven her home and gone up to London with the idea of penetrating into this house by yourself.

'Mr Eversleigh continued to play his part, that of the unconscious man. I may say that as soon as the two young men had left Jermyn Street, one of my men gained admission and found the doctored whisky, which contained enough hydrochloride of morphia to kill two men. Also the car they were in was followed. Mr Thesiger drove out of town to a well-known golf course, where he showed himself for a few minutes, speaking of playing a round. That, of course, was for an alibi, should one be needed. He left the car with Mr Eversleigh in it a little way down the road. Then he drove back to town and to the Seven Dials Club. As soon as he saw Alfred leave, he drove up to the door, spoke to Mr Eversleigh as he got out in case you might be listening and came into the house and played his little comedy.

'When he pretended to go for a doctor, he really only slammed the door and then crept quietly upstairs and hid behind the door of this room, where Miss Wade would presently send you up on some excuse. Mr Eversleigh, of course, was horror-struck when he saw you, but he thought it best to keep up the part he was playing. He knew our people were watching the house, and he imagined that there was no immediate danger intended to you. He could always "come to life" at any moment. When Mr Thesiger threw his revolver on the table and apparently left the house it seemed safer than ever. As for the next bit –' He paused, looking at Bill. 'Perhaps you'd like to tell that, sir.'

'I was still lying on that bally sofa,' said Bill, 'trying to look done in and getting the fidgets worse and worse. Then I heard someone run down the stairs, and Loraine got up and went to the door. I heard Thesiger's voice, but not what he said. I heard Loraine say: "That's all right – it's gone splendidly." Then he said: "Help me carry him up. It will be a bit of a job, but I want them both together there – a nice little surprise for No. 7." I didn't quite understand what they were jawing about, but they hauled me up the stairs somehow or other. It *was* a bit of a job for them. I made myself a dead weight all right. They heaved me in here, and then I heard Loraine say: "You're sure it's all right? She won't come round?" And Jimmy said – the damned blackguard: "No fear. I hit her with all my might."

'They went away and locked the door, and then I opened my eyes and saw you. My God, Bundle, I shall never feel so perfectly awful again. I thought you were dead.'

'I suppose my hat saved me,' said Bundle.

'Partly,' said Superintendent Battle. 'But partly it was Mr Thesiger's wounded arm. He didn't realize it himself – but it had only half its usual strength. Still, that's all no credit to the Department. We didn't take the care of you we ought to have done, Lady Eileen – and it's a black blot on the whole business.'

'I'm very tough,' said Bundle. 'And also rather lucky. What I can't get over is Loraine being in it. She was such a gentle little thing.'

'Ah!' said the Superintendent. 'So was the Pentonville murderess that killed five children. You can't go by that. She's got bad blood in her – her father ought to have seen the inside of a prison more than once.'

'You've got her too?'

Superintendent Battle nodded.

'I daresay they won't hang her – juries are soft-hearted. But young Thesiger will swing all right – and a good thing too – a more utterly depraved and callous criminal I never met.'

'And now,' he added, 'if your head isn't aching too badly, Lady Eileen, what about a little celebration? There's a nice little restaurant round the corner.'

Bundle heartily agreed.

'I'm starving, Superintendent Battle. Besides,' she looked round. 'I've got to get to know all my colleagues.'

'The Seven Dials,' said Bill. 'Hurrah! Some fizz is what we need. Do they run to fizz at this place, Battle?'

'You won't have anything to complain of, sir. You leave it to me.'

'Superintendent Battle,' said Bundle, 'you are a wonderful man. I'm sorry you're married already. As it is, I shall have to put up with Bill.'

CHAPTER 34

LORD CATERHAM APPROVES

'Father,' said Bundle, 'I've got to break a piece of news to you. You're going to lose me.'

'Nonsense,' said Lord Caterham. 'Don't tell me that you're suffering from galloping consumption or a weak heart or anything like that, because I simply don't believe it.'

'It's not death,' said Bundle. 'It's marriage.'

'Very nearly as bad,' said Lord Caterham. 'I suppose I shall have to come to the wedding, all dressed up in tight uncomfortable clothes, and give you away. And Lomax may think it necessary to kiss me in the vestry.'

'Good heavens! You don't think I'm going to marry George, do you?' cried Bundle.

'Well, something like that seemed to be in the wind last time I saw you,' said her father. 'Yesterday morning, you know.'

'I'm going to be married to someone a hundred times nicer than George,' said Bundle.

'I hope so, I'm sure,' said Lord Caterham. 'But one never knows. I don't feel you're really a good judge of character, Bundle. You told me that young Thesiger was a cheerful inefficient, and from all I hear now it seems that he was one of the most efficient criminals of the day. The sad thing is that I never met him. I was thinking of writing my reminiscences soon – with a special chapter on murderers I have met – and by a purely technical oversight, I never met this young man.'

'Don't be silly,' said Bundle. 'You know you haven't got the energy to write reminiscences or anything else.'

'I wasn't actually going to write them myself,' said Lord

Caterham. 'I believe that's never done. But I met a very charming girl the other day and that's her special job. She collects the material and does all the actual writing.'

'And what do you do?'

'Oh, just give her a few facts for half an hour every day. Nothing more than that.' After a slight pause, Lord Catherham said: 'She was a nice-looking girl – very restful and sympathetic.'

'Father,' said Bundle, 'I have a feeling that without me you will run into deadly danger.'

'Different kinds of danger suit different kinds of people,' said Lord Caterham.

He was moving away, when he turned back and said over his shoulder:

'By the way, Bundle, who *are* you marrying?'

'I was wondering,' said Bundle, 'when you were going to ask me that. I'm going to marry Bill Eversleigh.'

The egoist thought it over for a minute. Then he nodded in complete satisfaction.

'Excellent,' he said. 'He's scratch, isn't he? He and I can play together in the foursomes in the Autumn Meeting.'